Praise for Alice Munro's *Family Furnishings*

PENGUIN

Family Furnishings

ALICE MUNRO grew up in Wingham, Ontario, and attended the University of Western Ontario. She has published thirteen collections of stories and a novel. During her distinguished career she has been the recipient of many awards, including two Giller Prizes, three Governor General's Awards, the National Book Critics Circle Award, and the Man Booker International Prize. In 2013 she was awarded the Nobel Prize for Literature. Her stories have appeared in *The New Yorker*, *Atlantic Monthly*, *Harper's Magazine*, *The Paris Review*, *Granta*, and many other publications, and her collections have been translated into thirteen languages.

ALSO BY ALICE MUNRO

Dear Life

Too Much Happiness

Alice Munro's Best

The View from Castle Rock

Runaway

Hateship, Friendship, Courtship, Loveship, Marriage

The Love of a Good Woman

A Wilderness Station: Selected Stories, 1968–1994

Open Secrets

Friend of My Youth

The Progress of Love

The Moons of Jupiter

Who Do You Think You Are?

Something I've Been Meaning to Tell You

Lives of Girls and Women

Dance of the Happy Shades

Family Furnishings

SELECTED STORIES

1995–2014

~

ALICE MUNRO

Foreword by Jane Smiley

PENGUIN

an imprint of Penguin Canada Books Inc., a Penguin Random House Company

Published by the Penguin Group
Penguin Canada Books Inc., 320 Front Street West, Suite 1400,
Toronto, Ontario M5V 3B6, Canada

Penguin Group (USA) LLC, 375 Hudson Street, New York, New York 10014, U.S.A.
Penguin Books Ltd, 80 Strand, London WC2R 0RL, England
Penguin Ireland, 25 St Stephen's Green, Dublin 2, Ireland (a division of Penguin Books Ltd)
Penguin Group (Australia), 707 Collins Street, Melbourne, Victoria 3008, Australia
(a division of Pearson Australia Group Pty Ltd)
Penguin Books India Pvt Ltd, 11 Community Centre, Panchsheel Park,
New Delhi – 110 017, India
Penguin Group (NZ), 67 Apollo Drive, Rosedale, Auckland 0632, New Zealand
(a division of Pearson New Zealand Ltd)
Penguin Books (South Africa) (Pty) Ltd, 24 Sturdee Avenue, Rosebank,
Johannesburg 2196, South Africa

Penguin Books Ltd, Registered Offices: 80 Strand, London WC2R 0RL, England

Published in Penguin paperback by Penguin Canada Books Inc., 2015.
Simultaneously published in the U.S.A. by Vintage Books,
a division of Penguin Random House LLC, New York.

1 2 3 4 5 6 7 8 9 10   (BVG)

All of the stories herein were previously published in the following collections:
Dear Life (Alfred A. Knopf, New York, and Douglas Gibson Books, Toronto, 2012)
Hateship, Friendship, Courtship, Loveship, Marriage (Alfred A. Knopf, New York,
and McClelland & Stewart, Toronto, 2001)
The Love of a Good Woman (Alfred A. Knopf, New York, and
McClelland & Stewart, Toronto, 1998)
Runaway (Alfred A. Knopf, New York, and McClelland & Stewart, Toronto, 2004)
Too Much Happiness (Alfred A. Knopf, New York, and
Douglas Gibson Books, Toronto, 2009)
The View from Castle Rock (Alfred A. Knopf, New York,
and McClelland & Stewart, Toronto, 2006)

Manufactured in the U.S.A.

LIBRARY AND ARCHIVES CANADA CATALOGUING IN PUBLICATION
Munro, Alice, 1931-
[Short stories. Selections]
Family furnishings : selected stories, 1995-2014 / Alice Munro.

Reprint. Originally published: Toronto : McClelland & Stewart, 2014.
ISBN 978-0-14-319424-8 (paperback)

I. Title.

PS8576.U57A6 2015   C813'.54   C2015-903918-5

American Library of Congress Cataloging in Publication data available

Visit the Penguin Canada website at www.penguin.ca

Special and corporate bulk purchase rates available;
please see www.penguin.ca/corporatesales or call 1-800-810-3104.

Contents

~

Foreword

~

IN 1971, ALICE MUNRO PUBLISHED HER SECOND BOOK, *Lives of Girls and Women*. Sometimes I read the title as an assertion of the importance of the lives of girls and women, and sometimes I read the title as a self-effacing acknowledgement, or even a warning—these are only the lives of girls and women; don't bother to read about them if you don't care. And in this paradox resides the literary career of a great writer who is simultaneously strange and down-to-earth, daring and straightforward. I cannot read any Alice Munro story without believing every word, as if Alice herself is inside the head of Sophia Kovalevsky ("Too Much Happiness"), or the head of a woman whose husband has murdered their three children ("Dimensions"), or the head of a man whose wife is institutionalized with dementia ("The Bear Came over the Mountain"). As a reader and as a writer, I embrace every phrase and every observation almost without being able to help myself, because every one seems as true and as involving as can be.

Munro's style has always asked to be taken at face value. "The Love of a Good Woman," the opening story of this collection of stories that Munro has published since the mid-nineties, begins, "For the last couple of decades, there has been a museum in Walley, dedicated to preserving photos and butter churns and horse harnesses and an old dentist's chair and a cumbersome apple peeler and such curiosities as the pretty little porcelain-and-glass insulators that were used on telegraph poles." She is promising no drama, no transcendence, only the peculiarity of objects that contain the history of our world and our ancestors, if not ourselves. The adjectives gather toward the end of the sentence like fireflies—"old," then "cumbersome," then "pretty little," applied to something that almost no one might have noticed. Through these adjectives, Munro's consciousness enters the museum, and the promise is that history will come alive, not the history of great events or famous people but of those who might have made practical use of these objects indoors and outdoors. "The Love of a Good Woman" is full of moral reversals and paradoxes—it is, in fact, a murder mystery transformed into an everyday event, and therefore much more interesting, since the actions and motives of the characters remain unknown to some and consciously hidden by others. What we come to care about is not what happened to the man who is found by some boys, drowned in his car in the middle of a lake, but the emotional life and the thought processes of Enid, a good woman, who makes her living caring for difficult patients, and who has a lingering fondness for Rupert, a boy she and her friends had teased in middle school. Those random objects in the first sentence, attended to by the narrative voice, promise detail, contemplation, care.

In a short interview Munro did with Deborah Treisman, for *The New Yorker* upon the publication of her last book of stories, *Dear Life,* Munro reflects on her choice of form with typical modesty. She says, "For years and years I thought that stories were just practice, till I got time to write a novel. Then I found that they were all I could do, and so I faced that. I suppose that my trying to get so much into stories has been a compensation." Munro, though, has made of the short story something new, using precision of language and complexity of emotion to cut out the relaxed parts of the novel and focus on the essence of transformation. One of my favorite stories in this volume is "Too Much Happiness," which I might have written as a three-hundred-page historical account. Sophia Kovalevsky is that rarest of beings, a female mathematical genius, and Russian, to boot. She wins a prestigious prize but has a hard time finding employment, she marries for escape, not love, and must juggle her talents, her obligations, and her social position every minute of every day. Munro begins in her usual authoritative way, signaling that she understands Sophia's mathematical insights, and she weaves into the narrative Sophia's past and present dilemmas, getting close enough for us to witness Sophia's surprise at the sight of her lover in a crowd, then far enough away for us to survey the landscape Sophia travels through in her attempt to escape a smallpox outbreak. Sophia is convincingly Russian, convincingly a woman of her time, convincingly appealing. The arc of her very dramatic story lasts seventy-five pages, and then is done, reduced, concentrated, left to simmer in the reader's mind with all sorts of thoughts about the history of women, and one's own history of trying to make something of the life one is given, overwhelming and too soon finished, for since Munro's chosen form is the short story, her overriding theme is brevity—look now, act now, contemplate now, because soon, very soon, this thing that involves you will be over.

Perhaps Alice Munro's particular brilliance to a novelist like me is her inventiveness. A novelist may come up with a couple of dozen ideas in a productive lifetime—or many fewer (Jane Austen, six; F. Scott Fitzgerald, five; Harper Lee, one)—but a writer of stories is a receiver of tales, gossip, anecdotes, and incidents, a person so alert, so attentive, so imaginative that any event might be made into a work of art. In the course of her career, Munro has published one novel and 139 stories. She has always been investigative of both her own experience and the experiences of others; in the last six volumes, written since 1996, she has gotten more experimental rather than less. Every story has given us the Alice Munro we thought we knew from "Royal Beatings" and "The Beggar Maid," plus another Alice Munro, familiar in her style and technique but ready to take on new subjects, new settings, new interpretations of old material. A good example of this last is "Working for a Living," in which Munro delves more deeply into her own family life, especially from the perspective of her father—how he got into the fox-fur business just at the wrong time, and what it meant, once that business failed, for him to go to work at a local foundry as a caretaker. Into this story of what might be considered tragedy or failure, Munro inserts not only her customary compassion and complexity, but also an intriguing larger picture—family history set into geography, geology, and ecosystem, moments of memory that explode into both feeling and analysis. A daughter's love drives the story, but so does a man's sense of himself.

Or maybe my favorite story in this volume is "The View from Castle Rock," also a historical narrative, but entirely unlike "Too Much Happiness." It is based on Munro's investigations into her

(Laidlaw) family's background in a peculiar part of a peculiar country, the Ettrick Valley in Scotland, between the English border and Edinburgh, also the home of James Hogg, a Laidlaw cousin who published one of the most interesting and prophetic novels of his day, *The Private Memoirs and Confessions of a Justified Sinner*. "The View from Castle Rock" accompanies the Laidlaw immigrants to America, employing the present tense so evocatively and with such convincing feelings (not only emotions, but also sights, sounds, sensations) that even the author herself must step back and write, "And I am surely one of the liars the old man talks about, in what I have written about the voyage. Except for Walter's journal, and the letters, the story is full of my invention." Like every Munro story, this autobiographical narrative packs an unexpected, hidden punch, reminding us in the twenty-first century that what is gained grows out of what is lost, and our main responsibility is to understand both sides of the equation.

In her Nobel Prize interview, Munro comments on the benefits of growing up and beginning to write in the middle of nowhere. Asked if she was intimidated by the idea of writing, she says, "I don't think I could have been so brave if I had been living in a town, competing with people on what can be called a generally higher cultural level. I didn't have to cope with that. I was the only person I knew who wrote stories, though I didn't tell them to anybody, and as far as I knew, at least for a while, I was the only person who could do this in the world." It is a familiar arc for a writer—like that of Nikolai Gogol, growing up in Ukraine, like that of Jane Austen, slipping her writings under a sheet of blotting paper when other members of her family come into the room, like that of George Eliot, rusticated in Warwickshire, it is the tale of a child who feels a kinship, and even a sense of equality, with unknown authors of books, a child who listens, reads, tells herself stories (and changes the endings—in the same interview Munro recalls listening to "The Little Mermaid," then retelling it to herself so that it ends without suffering), a child who pays attention to the people around her because they are the humans nearby, and their lives have plenty of worth and plenty of suspense, no matter what people from cities might think of them.

I would not call Alice Munro a political writer (though she says in her interview, "I never knew about the word 'feminism,' but of course I was a feminist"). Of her intentions, she says, "What I wanted was every last thing, every layer of speech and thought, stroke of light on bark or walls, every smell, pothole, pain, crack, delusion, held still and held together—radiant, everlasting" (*Lives of Girls and Women*). In avoiding the novel, she also seems to have avoided the pitfalls of political theory, à la Tolstoy or Zola, Vargas Llosa or Virginia Woolf. Even so, underlying all of her work there is a political assertion—that the lives of girls and women, the lives of hired girls and men who work in foundries, the lives of unfaithful wives and faithful wives, the lives of bullies and the bullied are all equally complex and equally worthy of portrayal. About halfway into "Hateship, Friendship, Courtship, Loveship, Marriage," for example, we meet Edith and Sabitha, two girls who are thrown together almost by chance, and who turn out to be steering the progress of the romance that is the subject of the story in an entirely unexpected way, more or less as a joke upon the protagonist, Johanna, whom they disdain. They are not alike—Sabitha possesses a common streak of adolescent cruelty, but Edith, even though she goes along with the tease, does not, and the reader feels both her discomfort and her readiness to see what might happen. In "Dimensions," Munro dares to suggest that a man who kills his children not only has an inner life, but that his inner life ends up being the very thing that gives a bit of comfort to his wife. Is Munro on the man's side simply because she sees him as human? Her thinking is too complex for that—she strives to see him whole, to understand the point of view of someone most people must recoil from, and in doing so, she offers the reader a gift about what it means to be human.

In addition to the Nobel, Munro has won as many prizes as any other living writer—twenty-two in all, including three Governor General's Prizes and two Giller Prizes, in Canada, the National Book Critics' Circle Award and three O. Henry Awards in the United States, and the Man Booker International Prize in the U.K., given for a body of work, like the Nobel, rather than for a single book. What do we make of this? Well, for one thing, her level of accomplishment remains steady—the care and thought she puts into her stories have not tapered off, rather she builds on earlier work without somehow betraying it. This is highly unusual in an author, and shows, I think, an inherently contemplative temperament, an ability to think through her subject, to see it from every angle, and to incorporate her perceptions so that the subject seems to be completely explored. Almost uniquely self-aware, she knows this—in "Home," a story of a middle-aged woman's return to the very place she had always longed so deeply to escape and then remembered obsessively, she writes, "It has changed for me. I have written about it and used it up. Here are more or less the same banks and hardware and grocery stores and the barbershop and the Town Hall tower, but all their secret, plentiful messages for me have drained away." When we finish one of Munro's stories we feel that she has given us all that we need to know—I find it almost impossible to read more than a single story in a day, and some of the long ones, like "The View from Castle Rock," invite me to take my time, to savor each paragraph. If the material is sensational, Munro tempers it with thought and insight, so that I am invited to look deeply at it. And yet her style is always accessible, her characters and her incidents recognizable. Unlike many modernist authors (say, James Joyce), Munro does not assert that subjectivity should be privileged and that the inner lives of others, as depicted in words, are almost incomprehensible—she asserts that the world we all share is continually interesting, continually worthy of investigation, that we can, and should attempt to understand one another, that the payoff for that attempt at understanding might be something utterly unexpected, like the comfort Doree takes, in "Dimensions," in her husband's imagination of the afterlives of their murdered children.

In 1983, Benjamin DeMott wrote in *The New York Times*, "Witty, subtle, passionate, [*The Moons of Jupiter* is] exceptionally knowledgeable about the content and movement—the entanglements and entailments—of individual human feeling. And the knowledge it offers can't be looked up elsewhere." But Munro arouses in her readers more than praise and respect. When she won the Nobel shortly after declaring that she didn't plan to write anymore, the tributes that poured in were those of devotees—Julian Barnes wrote, "I have sometimes tried to work out how she does it but never succeeded, and I am happy in this failure, because no one else can—or should be allowed to—write like the great Alice Munro." Sheila Heti wrote, "You look at her and think, Of course, just put all of your intelligence and sensitivity and vitality into your work in a consistent way. There is nothing else. She lives in a small town, has had the same agent since the seventies, doesn't review books or do many interviews. She seems not to waste her time. She just goes straight to what matters most." Lorrie Moore wrote, "Her genius is in the strange detail that resurfaces, but it is also in the largeness of vision being brought to bear (and press on) a smaller genre or form that has few such wide-seeing practitioners. She is a short-story writer who is looking over and past every ostensible boundary, and has thus reshaped an idea of narrative brevity and reimagined what a story can do." Perhaps my favorite tribute is by Canadian author David Macfarlane: "I asked myself this question while reading 'Cortes Island' the other morning. The sun was just coming up. The coffee was almost gone. And even though I was paying such enjoyably close attention to Alice Munro, I couldn't quite figure out how she does what she does. I'm guessing by magic. And I decided, as I continued reading, to leave it at that."

And so we have these wonderful stories to savor, wise stories by a wise woman who did not start out intending to show us anything, but started out intending to discover everything.

—Jane Smiley

Family Furnishings

The Love of a Good Woman

~

FOR THE LAST COUPLE OF DECADES, there has been a museum in Walley, dedicated to preserving photos and butter churns and horse harnesses and an old dentist's chair and a cumbersome apple peeler and such curiosities as the pretty little porcelain-and-glass insulators that were used on telegraph poles.

Also there is a red box, which has the letters D. M. WILLENS, OPTOMETRIST printed on it, and a note beside it, saying, "This box of optometrist's instruments though not very old has considerable local significance, since it belonged to Mr. D. M. Willens, who drowned in the Peregrine River, 1951. It escaped the catastrophe and was found, presumably by the anonymous donor, who dispatched it to be a feature of our collection."

The ophthalmoscope could make you think of a snowman. The top part, that is—the part that's fastened onto the hollow handle. A large disk, with a smaller disk on top. In the large disk a hole to look through, as the various lenses are moved. The handle is heavy because the batteries are still inside. If you took the batteries out and put in the rod that is provided, with a disk on either end, you could plug in an electric cord. But it might have been necessary to use the instrument in places where there wasn't any electricity.

The retinoscope looks more complicated. Underneath the round forehead clamp is something like an elf's head, with a round flat face and a pointed metal cap. This is tilted at a forty-five-degree angle to a slim column, and out of the top of the column a tiny light is supposed to shine. The flat face is made of glass and is a dark sort of mirror.

Everything is black, but that is only paint. In some places where the optometrist's hand must have rubbed most often, the paint has disappeared and you can see a patch of shiny silver metal.

I. JUTLAND

THIS PLACE was called Jutland. There had been a mill once, and some kind of small settlement, but that had all gone by the end of the last century, and the place had never amounted to much at any time. Many people believed that it had been named in honor of the famous sea battle fought during the First World War, but actually everything had been in ruins years before that battle ever took place.

The three boys who came out here on a Saturday morning early in the spring of 1951 believed, as most children did, that the name came from the old wooden planks that jutted out of the earth of the riverbank and from the other straight thick boards that stood up in the nearby water, making an uneven palisade. (These were in fact the remains of a dam, built before the days of cement.) The planks and a heap of foundation stones and a lilac bush and some huge apple trees deformed by black knot and the shallow ditch of the millrace that filled up with nettles every summer were the only other signs of what had been here before.

There was a road, or a track, coming back from the township road, but it had never been gravelled, and appeared on the maps only as a dotted line, a road allowance. It was used quite a bit in the summer by people driving to the river to swim or at night by couples looking for a place to park. The turnaround spot came before you got to the ditch, but the whole area was so overrun by nettles, and cow parsnip, and woody wild hemlock in a wet year, that cars would sometimes have to back out all the way to the proper road.

The car tracks to the water's edge on that spring morning were easy to spot but were not taken notice of by these boys, who were thinking only about swimming. At least, they would call it swimming; they would go back to town and say that they had been swimming at Jutland before the snow was off the ground.

It was colder here upstream than on the river flats close to the town. There was not a leaf out yet on the riverbank trees—the only green you saw was from patches of leeks on the ground and marsh marigolds fresh as spinach, spread along any little stream that gullied its way down to the river. And on the opposite bank under some cedars they saw what they were especially looking for—a long, low, stubborn snowbank, gray as stones.

Not off the ground.

So they would jump into the water and feel the cold hit them like ice daggers. Ice daggers shooting up behind their eyes and jabbing the tops of their skulls from the inside. Then they would move their arms and legs a few times and haul themselves out, quaking and letting their teeth rattle; they would push their numb limbs into their clothes and feel the painful recapture of their bodies by their startled blood and the relief of making their brag true.

The tracks that they didn't notice came right through the ditch—in which there was nothing growing now, there was only the flat dead straw-colored grass of the year before. Through the ditch and into the river without trying to turn around. The boys tramped over them. But by this time they were close enough to the water to have had their attention caught by something more extraordinary than car tracks.

There was a pale-blue shine to the water that was not a reflection of sky. It was a whole car, down in the pond on a slant, the front wheels and the nose of it poking into the mud on the bottom, and the bump of the trunk nearly breaking the surface. Light blue was in those days an unusual color for a car, and its bulgy shape was unusual, too. They knew it right away. The little English car, the Austin, the only one of its kind surely in the whole county. It belonged to Mr. Willens, the optometrist. He looked like a cartoon character when he drove it, because he was a short but thick man, with heavy shoulders and a large head. He always seemed to be crammed into his little car as if it was a bursting suit of clothes.

The car had a panel in its roof, which Mr. Willens opened in warm weather. It was open now. They could not see very well what was inside. The color of the car made its shape plain in the water, but the water was really not very clear, and it obscured what was not so bright. The boys squatted down on the bank, then lay on their stomachs and pushed their heads out like turtles, trying to see. There was something dark and furry, something like a big animal tail, pushed up through the hole in the roof and moving idly in the water. This was shortly seen to be an arm, covered by the sleeve of a dark jacket of some heavy and hairy material. It seemed that inside the car a man's body—it had to be the body of Mr. Willens—had got into a peculiar position. The force of the water—for even in the millpond there was a good deal of force in the water at this time of year—must have somehow lifted him from the seat and pushed him about, so that one shoulder was up near the car roof and one arm had got free. His head must have been shoved down against the driver's door and window. One front wheel was stuck deeper in the river bottom than the other, which meant that the car was on a slant from side to side as well as back to front. The window in fact must have been open and the head sticking out for the body to be lodged in that position. But they could not get to see that. They could picture Mr. Willens's face as they knew it—a big square face, which often wore a theatrical sort of frown but was never seriously intimidating. His thin crinkly hair was reddish or brassy on top, and combed diagonally over his forehead. His eyebrows were darker than his hair, thick and fuzzy like caterpillars stuck above his eyes. This was a face already grotesque to them, in the way that many adult faces were, and they were not afraid to see it drowned. But all they got to see was that arm and his pale hand. They could see the hand quite plain once they got used to looking through the water. It rode there tremulously and irresolutely, like a feather, though it looked as solid as dough. And as ordinary, once you got used to its being there at all. The fingernails were all like neat little faces, with their intelligent everyday look of greeting, their sensible disowning of their circumstances.

"Son of a gun," these boys said. With gathering energy and a tone of deepening respect, even of gratitude. "*Son of a gun.*"

IT WAS their first time out this year. They had come across the bridge over the Peregrine River, the single-lane double-span bridge known locally as Hell's Gate or the Death Trap—though the danger had really more to do with the sharp turn the road took at the south end of it than with the bridge itself.

There was a regular walkway for pedestrians, but they didn't use it. They never remembered using it. Perhaps years ago, when they were so young as to be held by the hand. But that time had vanished for them; they refused to recognize it even if they were shown the evidence in snapshots or forced to listen to it in family conversation.

They walked now along the iron shelf that ran on the opposite side of the bridge from the walkway. It was about eight inches wide and a foot or so above the bridge floor. The Peregrine River was rushing the winter load of ice and snow, now melted, out into Lake Huron. It was barely back within its banks after the yearly flood that turned the flats into a lake and tore out the young trees and bashed any boat or hut within its reach. With the runoff from the fields muddying the water and the pale sunlight on its surface, the water looked like butterscotch pudding on the boil. But if you fell into it, it would freeze your blood and fling you out into the lake, if it didn't brain you against the buttresses first.

Cars honked at them—a warning or a reproof—but they paid no attention. They proceeded single file, as self-possessed as sleepwalkers. Then, at the north end of the bridge, they cut down to the flats, locating the paths they remembered from the year before. The flood had been so recent that these paths were not easy to follow. You had to kick your way through beaten-down brush and jump from one hummock of mud-plastered grass to another. Sometimes they jumped carelessly and landed in mud or pools of leftover floodwater, and once their feet were wet they gave up caring where they landed. They squelched through the mud and splashed in the pools so that the water came in over the tops of their rubber boots. The wind was warm; it was pulling the clouds apart into threads of old wool, and the gulls and crows were quarrelling and diving over the river. Buzzards were circling over them, on the high lookout; the robins had just returned, and the red-winged blackbirds were darting in pairs, striking bright on your eyes as if they had been dipped in paint.

"Should've brought a twenty-two."

"Should've brought a twelve-gauge."

They were too old to raise sticks and make shooting noises. They spoke with casual regret, as if guns were readily available to them.

They climbed up the north banks to a place where there was bare sand. Turtles were supposed to lay their eggs in this sand. It was too early yet for that to happen, and in fact the story of turtle eggs dated from years back—none of these boys had ever seen any. But they kicked and stomped the sand, just in case. Then they looked around for the place where last year one of them, in company with another boy, had found a cow's hipbone, carried off by the flood from some slaughter pile. The river could be counted on every year to sweep off and deposit elsewhere a good number of surprising or cumbersome or bizarre or homely objects. Rolls of wire, an intact set of steps, a bent shovel, a corn kettle. The hipbone had been found caught on the branch of a sumac—which seemed proper, because all those smooth branches were like cow horns or deer antlers, some with rusty cone tips.

They crashed around for some time—Cece Ferns showed them the exact branch—but they found nothing.

It was Cece Ferns and Ralph Diller who had made that find, and when asked where it was at present Cece Ferns said, "Ralph took it." The two boys who were with him now—Jimmy Box and Bud Salter—knew why that would have to be. Cece could never take anything home unless it was of a size to be easily concealed from his father.

They talked of more useful finds that might be made or had been made in past years. Fence rails could be used to build a raft, pieces of stray lumber could be collected for a planned shack or boat. Real luck would be to get hold of some loose muskrat traps. Then you could go into business. You could pick up enough lumber for stretching boards and steal the knives for skinning. They spoke of taking over an empty shed they knew of, in the blind alley behind what used to be the livery barn. There was a padlock on it, but you could probably get in through the window, taking the boards off it at night and replacing them at daybreak. You could take a flashlight to work by. No—a lantern. You could skin the muskrats and stretch the pelts and sell them for a lot of money.

This project became so real to them that they started to worry about leaving valuable pelts in the shed all day. One of them would have to stand watch while the others went out on the traplines. (Nobody mentioned school.)

This was the way they talked when they got clear of town. They talked as if they were free—or almost free—agents, as if they didn't go to school or live with families or suffer any of the indignities put on them because of their age. Also, as if the countryside and other people's establishments would provide them with all they needed for their undertakings and adventures, with only the smallest risk and effort on their part.

Another change in their conversation out here was that they practically gave up using names. They didn't use each other's real names much anyway—not even family nicknames such as Bud. But at school nearly everyone had another name, some of these having to do with the way people looked or talked, like Goggle or Jabber, and some, like Sore-arse and Chickenfucker, having to do with incidents real or fabulous in the lives of those named, or in the lives—such names were handed down for decades—of their brothers, fathers, or uncles. These were the names they let go of when they were out in the bush or on the river flats. If they had to get one another's attention, all they said was "Hey." Even the use of names that were outrageous and obscene and that grown-ups supposedly never heard would have spoiled a sense they had at these times, of taking each other's looks, habits, family, and personal history entirely for granted.

And yet they hardly thought of each other as friends. They would never have designated someone as a best friend or a next-best friend, or joggled people around in these positions, the way girls did. Any one of at least a dozen boys could have been substituted for any one of these three, and accepted by the others in exactly the same way. Most members of that company were between nine and twelve years old, too old to be bound by yards and neighborhoods but too young to have jobs—even jobs sweeping the sidewalk in front of stores or delivering groceries by bicycle. Most of them lived in the north end of town, which meant that they would be expected to get a job of that sort as soon as they were old enough, and that none of them would ever be sent away to Appleby or to Upper Canada College. And none of them lived in a shack or had a relative in jail. Just the same, there were notable differences as to how they lived at home and what was expected of them in life. But these differences dropped away as soon as they were out of sight of the county jail and the grain elevator and the church steeples and out of range of the chimes of the courthouse clock.

ON THEIR WAY BACK they walked fast. Sometimes they trotted but did not run. Jumping, dallying, splashing, were all abandoned, and the noises they'd made on their way out, the hoots and howls, were put aside as well. Any windfall of the flood was taken note of but passed by. In fact they made their way as adults would do, at a fairly steady speed and by the most reasonable route, with the weight on them of where they had to go and what had to be done next. They had something close in front of them, a picture in front of their eyes that came between them and the world, which was the thing most adults seemed to have. The pond, the car, the arm, the hand. They had some idea that when they got to a certain spot they would start to shout. They would come into town yelling and waving their news around them and everybody would be stock-still, taking it in.

They crossed the bridge the same way as always, on the shelf. But they had no sense of risk or courage or nonchalance. They might as well have taken the walkway.

Instead of following the sharp-turning road from which you could reach both the harbor and the square, they climbed straight up the bank on a path that came out near the railway sheds. The clock played its quarter-after chimes. A quarter after twelve.

THIS WAS the time when people were walking home for dinner. People from offices had the afternoon off. But people who worked in stores were getting only their customary hour—the stores stayed open till ten or eleven o'clock on Saturday night.

Most people were going home to a hot, filling meal. Pork chops, or sausages, or boiled beef, or cottage roll. Potatoes for certain, mashed or fried; winter-stored root vegetables or cabbage or creamed onions. (A few housewives, richer or more feckless, might have opened a tin of peas or butter beans.) Bread, muffins, preserves, pie. Even those people who didn't have a home to go to, or who for some reason didn't want to go there, would be sitting down to much the same sort of food at the Duke of Cumberland, or the Merchants' Hotel, or for less money behind the foggy windows of Shervill's Dairy Bar.

Those walking home were mostly men. The women were already there—they were there all the time. But some women of middle age who worked in stores or offices for a reason that was not their fault—dead husbands or sick husbands or never any husband at all—were friends of the boys' mothers, and they called out greetings even across the street (it was worst for Bud Salter, whom they called Buddy) in a certain amused or sprightly way that brought to mind all they knew of family matters, or distant infancies.

Men didn't bother greeting boys by name, even if they knew them well. They called them "boys" or "young fellows" or, occasionally, "sirs."

"Good day to you, sirs."

"You boys going straight home now?"

"What monkey business you young fellows been up to this morning?"

All these greetings had a degree of jocularity, but there were differences. The men who said "young fellows" were better disposed—or wished to seem better disposed—than the ones who said "boys." "Boys" could be the signal that a telling off was to follow, for offenses that could be either vague or specific. "Young fellows" indicated that the speaker had once been young himself. "Sirs" was outright mockery and disparagement but didn't open the way to any scolding, because the person who said that could not be bothered.

When answering, the boys didn't look up past any lady's purse or any man's Adam's apple. They said "Hullo" clearly, because there might be some kind of trouble if you didn't, and in answer to queries they said "Yessir" and "Nosir" and "Nothing much." Even on this day, such voices speaking to them caused some alarm and confusion, and they replied with the usual reticence.

At a certain corner they had to separate. Cece Ferns, always the most anxious about getting home, pulled away first. He said, "See you after dinner."

Bud Salter said, "Yeah. We got to go downtown then."

This meant, as they all understood, "downtown to the Police Office." It seemed that without needing to consult each other they had taken up a new plan of operation, a soberer way of telling their news. But it wasn't clearly said that they wouldn't be telling anything at home. There wasn't any good reason why Bud Salter or Jimmy Box couldn't have done that.

Cece Ferns never told anything at home.

CECE FERNS was an only child. His parents were older than most boys' parents, or perhaps they only seemed older, because of the disabling life they lived together. When he got away from the other boys, Cece started to trot, as he usually did for the last block home. This was not because he was eager to get there or because he thought he could make anything better when he did. It may have been to make the time pass quickly, because the last block had to be full of apprehension.

His mother was in the kitchen. Good. She was out of bed though still in her wrapper. His father wasn't there, and that was good, too. His father worked at the grain elevator and got Saturday afternoon off, and if he wasn't home by now it was likely that he had gone straight to the Cumberland. That meant it would be late in the day before they had to deal with him.

Cece's father's name was Cece Ferns, too. It was a well-known and generally an affectionately known name in Walley, and somebody telling a story even thirty or forty years later would take it for granted that everybody would know it was the father who was being talked about, not the son. If a person relatively new in town said, "That doesn't sound like Cece," he would be told that nobody meant *that* Cece.

"Not him, we're talking about his old man."

They talked about the time Cece Ferns went to the hospital—or was taken there—with pneumonia, or some other desperate thing, and the nurses wrapped him in wet towels or sheets to get the fever down. The fever sweated out of him, and all the towels and sheets turned brown. It was the nicotine in him. The nurses had never seen anything like it. Cece was delighted. He claimed to have been smoking tobacco and drinking alcohol since he was ten years old.

And the time he went to church. It was hard to imagine why, but it was the Baptist church, and his wife was a Baptist, so perhaps he went to please her, though that was even harder to imagine. They were serving Communion the Sunday he went, and in the Baptist church the bread is bread but the wine is grape juice. "What's this?" cried Cece Ferns aloud. "If this is the blood of the Lamb then he must've been pretty damn anemic."

Preparations for the noon meal were under way in the Fernses' kitchen. A loaf of sliced bread was sitting on the table and a can of diced beets had been opened. A few slices of bologna had been fried—before the eggs, though they should have been done after—and were being kept slightly warm on top of the stove. And now Cece's mother had started the eggs. She was bending over the stove with the egg lifter in one hand and the other hand pressed to her stomach, cradling a pain.

Cece took the egg lifter out of her hand and turned down the electric heat, which was way too high. He had to hold the pan off the burner while the burner cooled down, in order to keep the egg whites from getting too tough or burning at the edges. He hadn't been in time to wipe out the old grease and plop a bit of fresh lard in the pan. His mother never wiped out the old grease, just let it sit from one meal to the next and put in a bit of lard when she had to.

When the heat was more to his liking, he put the pan down and coaxed the lacy edges of the eggs into tidy circles. He found a clean spoon and dribbled a little hot fat over the yokes to set them. He and his mother liked their eggs cooked this way, but his mother often couldn't manage it right. His father liked his eggs turned over and flattened out like pancakes, cooked hard as shoe leather and blackened with pepper. Cece could cook them the way he wanted, too.

None of the other boys knew how practiced he was in the kitchen—just as none of them knew about the hiding place he had made outside the house in the blind corner past the dining-room window, behind the Japanese barberry.

His mother sat in the chair by the window while he was finishing up the eggs. She kept an eye on the street. There was still a chance that his father would come home for something to eat. He might not be drunk yet. But the way he behaved didn't always depend on how drunk he was. If he came into the kitchen now he might tell Cece to make him some eggs, too. Then he might ask him where his apron was and say that he would make some fellow a dandy wife. That would be how he'd behave if he was in a good mood. In another sort of mood he would start off by staring at Cece in a certain way—that is, with an exaggerated, absurdly threatening expression—and telling him he better watch out.

"Smart bugger, aren't you? Well, all I got to say to you is better watch out."

Then if Cece looked back at him, or maybe if he didn't look back, or if he dropped the egg lifter or set it down with a clatter—or even if he was sliding around being extra cautious about not dropping anything and not making a noise—his father was apt to start showing his teeth and snarling like a dog. It would have been ridiculous—it was ridiculous—except that he meant business. A minute later the food and the dishes might be on the floor, and the chairs or the table overturned, and he might be chasing Cece around the room yelling how he was going to get him this time, flatten his face on the hot burner, how would he like that? You would be certain he'd gone crazy. But if at this moment a knock came at the door—if a friend of his arrived, say, to pick him up—his face would reassemble itself in no time and he would open the door and call out the friend's name in a loud bantering voice.

"I'll be with you in two shakes. I'd ask you in, but the wife's been pitching the dishes around again."

He didn't intend this to be believed. He said such things in order to turn whatever happened in his house into a joke.

Cece's mother asked him if the weather was warming up and where he had been that morning.

"Yeah," he said, and, "Out on the flats."

She said that she'd thought she could smell the wind on him.

"You know what I'm going to do right after we eat?" she said. "I'm going to take a hot-water bottle and go right back to bed and maybe I'll get my strength back and feel like doing something."

That was what she nearly always said she was going to do, but she always announced it as if it was an idea that had just occurred to her, a hopeful decision.

BUD SALTER had two older sisters who never did anything useful unless his mother made them. And they never confined their hair arranging, nail polishing, shoe cleaning, making up, or even dressing activities to their bedrooms or the bathroom. They spread their combs and curlers and face powder and nail polish and shoe polish all over the house. Also they loaded every chair back with their newly ironed dresses and blouses and spread out their drying sweaters on towels on every clear space of floor. (Then they screamed at you if you walked near them.) They stationed themselves in front of various mirrors—the mirror in the hall coat stand, the mirror in the dining-room buffet, and the mirror beside the kitchen door with the shelf underneath always loaded with safety pins, bobby pins, pennies, buttons, bits of pencils..Sometimes one of them would stand in front of a mirror for twenty minutes or so, checking herself from various angles, inspecting her teeth and pulling her hair back then shaking it forward. Then she would walk away apparently satisfied or at least finished—but only as far as the next room, the next mirror, where she would begin all over again just as if she had been delivered a new head.

Right now his older sister, the one who was supposed to be good-looking, was taking the pins out of her hair in front of the kitchen mirror. Her head was covered with shiny curls like snails. His other sister, on orders from his mother, was mashing the potatoes. His five-year-old brother was sitting in place at the table, banging his knife and fork up and down and yelling, "Want some service. Want some service."

He got that from their father, who did it for a joke.

Bud passed by his brother's chair and said quietly, "Look. She's putting lumps in the mashed potatoes again."

He had his brother convinced that lumps were something you added, like raisins to rice pudding, from a supply in the cupboard.

His brother stopped chanting and began complaining.

"I won't eat none if she puts in lumps. Mama, I won't eat none if she puts lumps."

"Oh, don't be silly," Bud's mother said. She was frying apple slices and onion rings with the pork chops. "Quit whining like a baby."

"It was Bud got him started," the older sister said. "Bud went and told him she was putting lumps in. Bud always tells him that and he doesn't know any better."

"Bud ought to get his face smashed," said Doris, the sister who was mashing the potatoes. She didn't always say such things idly—she had once left a claw scar down the side of Bud's cheek.

Bud went over to the dresser, where there was a rhubarb pie cooling. He took a fork and began carefully, secretly prying at it, letting out delicious steam, a delicate smell of cinnamon. He was trying to open one of the vents in the top of it so that he could get a taste of the filling. His brother saw what he was doing but was too scared to say anything. His brother was spoiled and was defended by his sisters all the time—Bud was the only person in the house he respected.

"Want some service," he repeated, speaking now in a thoughtful undertone.

Doris came over to the dresser to get the bowl for the mashed potatoes. Bud made an incautious movement, and part of the top crust caved in.

"So now he's wrecking the pie," Doris said. "Mama—he's wrecking your pie."

"Shut your damn mouth," Bud said.

"Leave that pie alone," said Bud's mother with a practiced, almost serene severity. "Stop swearing. Stop tattle-telling. Grow up."

JIMMY BOX sat down to dinner at a crowded table. He and his father and his mother and his four-year-old and six-year-old sisters lived in his grandmother's house with his grandmother and his great-aunt Mary and his bachelor uncle. His father had a bicycle-repair shop in the shed behind the house, and his mother worked in Honeker's Department Store.

Jimmy's father was crippled—the result of a polio attack when he was twenty-two years old. He walked bent forward from the hips, using a cane. This didn't show so much when he was working in the shop, because such work often means being bent over anyway. When he walked along the street he did look very strange, but nobody called him names or did an imitation of him. He had once been a notable hockey player and baseball player for the town, and some of the grace and valor of the past still hung around him, putting his present state into perspective, so that it could be seen as a phase (though a final one). He helped this perception along by cracking silly jokes and taking an optimistic tone, denying the pain that showed in his sunken eyes and kept him awake many nights. And, unlike Cece Ferns's father, he didn't change his tune when he came into his own house.

But, of course, it wasn't his own house. His wife had married him after he was crippled, though she had got engaged to him before, and it seemed the natural thing to do to move in with her mother, so that the mother could look after any children who came along while the wife went on working at her job. It seemed the natural thing to the wife's mother as well, to take on another family—just as it seemed natural that her sister Mary should move in with the rest of them when her eyesight failed, and that her son Fred, who was extraordinarily shy, should continue to live at home unless he found some place he liked better. This was a family who accepted burdens of one kind or another with even less fuss than they accepted the weather. In fact, nobody in that house would have spoken of Jimmy's father's condition or Aunt Mary's eyesight as burdens or problems, any more than they would of Fred's shyness. Drawbacks and adversity were not to be noticed, not to be distinguished from their opposites.

There was a traditional belief in the family that Jimmy's grandmother was an excellent cook, and this might have been true at one time, but in recent years there had been a falling off. Economies were practiced beyond what there was any need for now. Jimmy's mother and his uncle made decent wages and his aunt Mary got a pension and the bicycle shop was fairly busy, but one egg was used instead of three and the meat loaf got an extra cup of oatmeal. There was an attempt to compensate by overdoing the Worcestershire sauce or sprinkling too much nutmeg on the custard. But nobody complained. Everybody praised. Complaints were as rare as lightning balls in that house. And everybody said "Excuse me," even the little girls said "Excuse me," when they bumped into each other. Everybody passed and pleased and thank-you'd at the table as if there was company every day. This was the way they managed, all of them crammed so tight in the house, with clothes piled on every hook, coats hung over the banister, and cots set up permanently in the dining room for Jimmy and his uncle Fred, and the buffet hidden under a load of clothing waiting to be ironed or mended. Nobody pounded on the stairsteps or shut doors hard or turned the radio up loud or said anything disagreeable.

Did this explain why Jimmy kept his mouth shut that Saturday at dinnertime? They all kept their mouths shut, all three of them. In Cece's case it was easy to understand. His father would never have stood for Cece's claiming so important a discovery. He would have called him a liar as a matter of course. And Cece's mother, judging everything by the effect it would have on his father, would have understood—correctly—that even his going to the Police

Office with his story would cause disruption at home, so she would have told him to please just keep quiet. But the two other boys lived in quite reasonable homes and they could have spoken. In Jimmy's house there would have been consternation and some disapproval, but soon enough they would have admitted that it was not Jimmy's fault.

Bud's sisters would have asked if he was crazy. They might even have twisted things around to imply that it was just like him, with his unpleasant habits, to come upon a dead body. His father, however, was a sensible, patient man, used to listening to many strange rigmaroles in his job as a freight agent at the railway station. He would have made Bud's sisters shut up, and after some serious talk to make sure Bud was telling the truth and not exaggerating he would have phoned the Police Office.

It was just that their houses seemed too full. Too much was going on already. This was true in Cece's house just as much as in the others, because even in his father's absence there was the threat and memory all the time of his haywire presence.

"DID you tell?"

"Did you?"

"Me neither."

They walked downtown, not thinking about the way they were going. They turned onto Shipka Street and found themselves going past the stucco bungalow where Mr. and Mrs. Willens lived. They were right in front of it before they recognized it. It had a small bay window on either side of the front door and a top step wide enough for two chairs, not there at present but occupied on summer evenings by Mr. Willens and his wife. There was a flat-roofed addition to one side of the house, with another door opening toward the street and a separate walk leading up to it. A sign beside that door said D. M. WILLENS, OPTOMETRIST. None of the boys themselves had visited that office, but Jimmy's aunt Mary went there regularly for her eyedrops, and his grandmother got her glasses there. So did Bud Salter's mother.

The stucco was a muddy pink color and the doors and window frames were painted brown. The storm windows had not been taken off yet, as they hadn't from most of the houses in town. There was nothing special at all about the house, but the front yard was famous for its flowers. Mrs. Willens was a renowned gardener who didn't grow her flowers in long rows beside the vegetable garden, as Jimmy's grandmother and Bud's mother grew theirs. She had them in round beds and crescent beds and all over, and in circles under the trees. In a couple of weeks daffodils would fill this lawn. But at present the only thing in bloom was a forsythia bush at the corner of the house. It was nearly as high as the eaves and it sprayed yellow into the air the way a fountain shoots water.

The forsythia shook, not with the wind, and out came a stooped brown figure. It was Mrs. Willens in her old gardening clothes, a lumpy little woman in baggy slacks and a ripped jacket and a peaked cap that might have been her husband's—it slipped down too low and almost hid her eyes. She was carrying a pair of shears.

They slowed right down—it was either that or run. Maybe they thought that she wouldn't notice them, that they could turn themselves into posts. But she had seen them already; that was why she came hastening through.

"I see you're gawking at my forsythia," said Mrs. Willens. "Would you like some to take home?"

What they had been gawking at was not the forsythia but the whole scene—the house looking just as usual, the sign by the office door, the curtains letting light in. Nothing hollow or ominous, nothing that said that Mr. Willens was not inside and that his car was not in the garage behind his office but in Jutland Pond. And Mrs. Willens out working in her yard, where anybody would expect her to be—everybody in town said so—the minute the snow was melted. And calling out in her familiar tobacco-roughened voice, abrupt and challenging but not unfriendly—a voice identifiable half a block away or coming from the back of any store.

"Wait," she said. "Wait, now, I'll get you some."

She began smartly, selectively snapping off the bright-yellow branches, and when she had all she wanted she came towards them behind a screen of flowers.

"Here you are," she said. "Take these home to your mothers. It's always good to see the forsythia, it's the very first thing in the

spring." She was dividing the branches among them. "Like all
Gaul," she said. "All Gaul is divided into three parts. You must
know about that if you take Latin."

"We aren't in high school yet," said Jimmy, whose life at home
had readied him, better than the others, for talking to ladies.

"Aren't you?" she said. "Well, you've got all sorts of things to
look forward to. Tell your mothers to put them in lukewarm water.
Oh, I'm sure they already know that. I've given you branches that
aren't all the way out yet, so they should last and last."

They said thank you—Jimmy first and the others picking it
up from him. They walked towards downtown with their arms
loaded. They had no intention of turning back and taking the flowers home, and they counted on her not having any good idea of
where their homes were. Half a block on, they sneaked looks back
to see if she was watching.

She wasn't. The big house near the sidewalk blocked the view
in any case.

The forsythia gave them something to think about. The embarrassment of carrying it, the problem of getting rid of it. Otherwise,
they would have to think about Mr. Willens and Mrs. Willens.
How she could be busy in her yard and he could be drowned in
his car. Did she know where he was or did she not? It seemed that
she couldn't. Did she even know that he was gone? She had acted
as if there was nothing wrong, nothing at all, and when they were
standing in front of her this had seemed to be the truth. What they
knew, what they had seen, seemed actually to be pushed back, to be
defeated, by her not knowing it.

Two girls on bicycles came wheeling around the corner. One
was Bud's sister Doris. At once these girls began to hoot and yell.

"Oh, look at the flowers," they shouted. "Where's the wedding?
Look at the beautiful bridesmaids."

Bud yelled back the worst thing he could think of.

"You got blood all over your arse."

Of course she didn't, but there had been an occasion when this
had really been so—she had come home from school with blood
on her skirt. Everybody had seen it, and it would never be forgotten.

He was sure she would tell on him at home, but she never did.

Her shame about that other time was so great that she could not refer to it even to get him in trouble.

THEY REALIZED then that they had to dump the flowers at once, so they simply threw the branches under a parked car. They brushed a few stray petals off their clothes as they turned onto the square.

Saturdays were still important then; they brought the country people into town. Cars were already parked around the square and on the side streets. Big country boys and girls and smaller children from the town and the country were heading for the movie matinee.

It was necessary to pass Honeker's in the first block. And there, in full view in one of the windows, Jimmy saw his mother. Back at work already, she was putting the hat straight on a female dummy, adjusting the veil, then fiddling with the shoulders of the dress. She was a short woman and she had to stand on tiptoe to do this properly. She had taken off her shoes to walk on the window carpet. You could see the rosy plump cushions of her heels through her stockings, and when she stretched you saw the back of her knee through the slit in her skirt. Above that was a wide but shapely behind and the line of her panties or girdle. Jimmy could hear in his mind the little grunts she would be making; also he could smell the stockings that she sometimes took off as soon as she got home, to save them from runs. Stockings and underwear, even clean female underwear, had a faint, private smell that was both appealing and disgusting.

He hoped two things. That the others hadn't noticed her (they had, but the idea of a mother dressed up every day and out in the public world of town was so strange to them that they couldn't comment, could only dismiss it) and that she would not, please not, turn around and spot him. She was capable, if she did that, of rapping on the glass and mouthing hello. At work she lost the hushed discretion, the studied gentleness, of home. Her obligingness turned from meek to pert. He used to be delighted by this other side of her, this friskiness, just as he was by Honeker's, with its extensive counters of glass and varnished wood, its big mirrors at the top of the staircase, in which he could see himself climbing up to Ladies' Wear, on the second floor.

"Here's my young mischief," his mother would say, and sometimes slip him a dime. He could never stay more than a minute;
Mr. or Mrs. Honeker might be watching.

Young mischief.

Words that were once as pleasant to hear as the tinkle of dimes
and nickels had now turned slyly shaming.

They were safely past.

In the next block they had to pass the Duke of Cumberland,
but Cece had no worries. If his father had not come home at dinnertime, it meant he would be in there for hours yet. But the word
"Cumberland" always fell across his mind heavily. From the days
when he hadn't even known what it meant, he got a sense of sorrowful plummeting. A weight hitting dark water, far down.

Between the Cumberland and the Town Hall was an unpaved
alley, and at the back of the Town Hall was the Police Office. They
turned into this alley and soon a lot of new noise reached them,
opposing the street noise. It was not from the Cumberland—the
noise in there was all muffled up, the beer parlor having only
small, high windows like a public toilet. It was coming from the
Police Office. The door to that office was open on account of the
mild weather, and even out in the alley you could smell the pipe
tobacco and cigars. It wasn't just the policemen who sat in there,
especially on Saturday afternoons, with the stove going in winter
and the fan in summer and the door open to let in the pleasant air on an in-between day like today. Colonel Box would be
there—in fact, they could already hear the wheeze he made, the
long-drawn-out aftereffects of his asthmatic laughter. He was a
relative of Jimmy's, but there was a coolness in the family because
he did not approve of Jimmy's father's marriage. He spoke to
Jimmy, when he recognized him, in a surprised, ironic tone of
voice. "If he ever offers you a quarter or anything, you say you
don't need it," Jimmy's mother had told him. But Colonel Box
had never made such an offer.

Also, Mr. Pollock would be there, who had retired from the
drugstore, and Fergus Solley, who was not a half-wit but looked
like one, because he had been gassed in the First World War. All
day these men and others played cards, smoked, told stories, and
drank coffee at the town's expense (as Bud's father said). Anybody

wanting to make a complaint or a report had to do it within sight of them and probably within earshot.

Run the gauntlet.

They came almost to a stop outside the open door. Nobody had noticed them. Colonel Box said, "I'm not dead yet," repeating the final line of some story. They began to walk past slowly with their heads down, kicking at the gravel. Round the corner of the building they picked up speed. By the entry to the men's public toilet there was a recent streak of lumpy vomit on the wall and a couple of empty bottles on the gravel. They had to walk between the refuse bins and the high watchful windows of the town clerk's office, and then they were off the gravel, back on the square.

"I got money," Cece said. This matter-of-fact announcement brought them all relief. Cece jingled change in his pocket. It was the money his mother had given him after he washed up the dishes, when he went into the front bedroom to tell her he was going out. "Help yourself to fifty cents off the dresser," she had said. Sometimes she had money, though he never saw his father give her any. And whenever she said "Help yourself" or gave him a few coins, Cece understood that she was ashamed of their life, ashamed for him and in front of him, and these were the times when he hated the sight of her (though he was glad of the money). Especially if she said that he was a good boy and he was not to think she wasn't grateful for all he did.

They took the street that led down to the harbor. At the side of Paquette's Service Station there was a booth from which Mrs. Paquette sold hot dogs, ice cream, candy, and cigarettes. She had refused to sell them cigarettes even when Jimmy said they were for his uncle Fred. But she didn't hold it against them that they'd tried. She was a fat, pretty woman, a French Canadian.

They bought some licorice whips, black and red. They meant to buy some ice cream later when they weren't so full from dinner. They went over to where there were two old car seats set up by the fence under a tree that gave shade in summer. They shared out the licorice whips.

Captain Tervitt was sitting on the other seat.

Captain Tervitt had been a real captain, for many years, on the lake boats. Now he had a job as a special constable. He stopped

the cars to let the children cross the street in front of the school
and kept them from sledding down the side street in winter. He
blew his whistle and held up one big hand, which looked like a
clown's hand, in a white glove. He was still tall and straight and
broad-shouldered, though old and white-haired. Cars would do
what he said, and children, too.

At night he went around checking the doors of all the stores
to see that they were locked and to make sure that there was
nobody inside committing a burglary. During the day he often
slept in public. When the weather was bad he slept in the library
and when it was good he chose some seat out-of-doors. He didn't
spend much time in the Police Office, probably because he was
too deaf to follow the conversation without his hearing aid in,
and like many deaf people he hated his hearing aid. And he was
used to being solitary, surely, staring out over the bow of the lake
boats.

His eyes were closed and his head tilted back so that he could
get the sun in his face. When they went over to talk to him (and
the decision to do this was made without any consultation,
beyond one resigned and dubious look) they had to wake him
from his doze. His face took a moment to register—where and
when and who. Then he took a large old-fashioned watch out of
his pocket, as if he counted on children always wanting to be told
the time. But they went on talking to him, with their expressions
agitated and slightly shamed. They were saying, "Mr. Willens is
out in Jutland Pond," and "We seen the car," and "Drownded."
He had to hold up his hand and make shushing motions while the
other hand went rooting around in his pants pocket and came up
with his hearing aid. He nodded his head seriously, encouragingly, as if to say, Patience, patience, while he got the device settled in his ear. Then both hands up—Be still, be still—while he
was testing. Finally another nod, of a brisker sort, and in a stern
voice—but making a joke to some extent of his sternness—he
said, "Proceed."

Cece, who was the quietest of the three—as Jimmy was the
politest and Bud the mouthiest—was the one who turned everything around.

"Your fly's undone," he said.

Then they all whooped and ran away.

THEIR ELATION did not vanish right away. But it was not something that could be shared or spoken about: they had to pull apart. Cece went home to work on his hideaway. The cardboard floor, which had been frozen through the winter, was sodden now and needed to be replaced. Jimmy climbed into the loft of the garage, where he had recently discovered a box of old Doc Savage magazines that had once belonged to his uncle Fred. Bud went home and found nobody there but his mother, who was waxing the dining-room floor. He looked at comic books for an hour or so and then he told her. He believed that his mother had no experience or authority outside their house and that she would not make up her mind about what to do until she had phoned his father. To his surprise, she immediately phoned the police. Then she phoned his father. And somebody went to round up Cece and Jimmy.

A police car drove into Jutland from the township road, and all was confirmed. A policeman and the Anglican minister went to see Mrs. Willens.

"I didn't want to bother you," Mrs. Willens was reported to have said. "I was going to give him till dark."

She told them that Mr. Willens had driven out to the country yesterday afternoon to take some drops to an old blind man. Sometimes he got held up, she said. He visited people, or the car got stuck.

Was he downhearted or anything like that? the policeman asked her.

"Oh, surely not," the minister said. "He was the bulwark of the choir."

"The word was not in his vocabulary," said Mrs. Willens.

Something was made of the boys' sitting down and eating their dinners and never saying a word. And then buying a bunch of licorice whips. A new nickname—Deadman—was found and settled on each of them. Jimmy and Bud bore it till they left town, and Cece—who married young and went to work in the elevator—saw it passed on to his two sons. By that time nobody thought of what it referred to.

The insult to Captain Tervitt remained a secret.

Each of them expected some reminder, some lofty look of injury or judgment, the next time they had to pass under his uplifted arm, crossing the street to the school. But he held up his gloved hand, his noble and clownish white hand, with his usual benevolent composure. He gave consent.

Proceed.

II. HEART FAILURE

"GLOMERULONEPHRITIS," Enid wrote in her notebook. It was the first case that she had ever seen. The fact was that Mrs. Quinn's kidneys were failing, and nothing could be done about it. Her kidneys were drying up and turning into hard and useless granular lumps. Her urine at present was scanty and had a smoky look, and the smell that came out on her breath and through her skin was acrid and ominous. And there was another, fainter smell, like rotted fruit, that seemed to Enid related to the pale-lavender-brown stains appearing on her body. Her legs twitched in spasms of sudden pain and her skin was subject to a violent itching, so that Enid had to rub her with ice. She wrapped the ice in towels and pressed the packs to the spots in torment.

"How do you contract that kind of a disease anyhow?" said Mrs. Quinn's sister-in-law. Her name was Mrs. Green. Olive Green. (It had never occurred to her how that would sound, she said, until she got married and all of a sudden everybody was laughing at it.) She lived on a farm a few miles away, out on the highway, and every few days she came and took the sheets and towels and nightdresses home to wash. She did the children's washing as well, brought everything back freshly ironed and folded. She even ironed the ribbons on the nightdresses. Enid was grateful to her—she had been on jobs where she had to do the laundry herself, or, worse still, load it onto her mother, who would pay to have it done in town. Not wanting to offend but seeing which way the questions were tending, she said, "It's hard to tell."

"Because you hear one thing and another," Mrs. Green said. "You hear that sometimes a woman might take some pills. They get these pills to take for when their period is late and if they take them just like the doctor says and for a good purpose that's fine, but if they take too many and for a bad purpose their kidneys are wrecked. Am I right?"

"I've never come in contact with a case like that," Enid said.

Mrs. Green was a tall, stout woman. Like her brother Rupert, who was Mrs. Quinn's husband, she had a round, snub-nosed, agreeably wrinkled face—the kind that Enid's mother called "potato Irish." But behind Rupert's good-humored expression there was wariness and withholding. And behind Mrs. Green's there was yearning. Enid did not know for what. To the simplest conversation Mrs. Green brought a huge demand. Maybe it was just a yearning for news. News of something momentous. An event.

Of course, an event was coming, something momentous at least in this family. Mrs. Quinn was going to die, at the age of twenty-seven. (That was the age she gave herself—Enid would have put some years on it, but once an illness had progressed this far age was hard to guess.) When her kidneys stopped working altogether, her heart would give out and she would die. The doctor had said to Enid, "This'll take you into the summer, but the chances are you'll get some kind of a holiday before the hot weather's over."

"Rupert met her when he went up north," Mrs. Green said. "He went off by himself, he worked in the bush up there. She had some kind of a job in a hotel. I'm not sure what. Chambermaid job. She wasn't raised up there, though—she says she was raised in an orphanage in Montreal. She can't help that. You'd expect her to speak French, but if she does she don't let on."

Enid said, "An interesting life."

"You can say that again."

"An interesting life," said Enid. Sometimes she couldn't help it—she tried a joke where it had hardly a hope of working. She raised her eyebrows encouragingly, and Mrs. Green did smile.

But was she hurt? That was just the way Rupert would smile, in high school, warding off some possible mockery.

"He never had any kind of a girlfriend before that," said Mrs. Green.

Enid had been in the same class as Rupert, though she did not mention that to Mrs. Green. She felt some embarrassment now because he was one of the boys—in fact, the main one—that she and her girlfriends had teased and tormented. "Picked on," as they used to say. They had picked on Rupert, following him up the street calling out, "Hello, Rupert. Hello, Ru-pert," putting him into a state of agony, watching his neck go red. "Rupert's got scarlet fever," they would say. "Rupert, you should be quarantined." And they would pretend that one of them—Enid, Joan McAuliffe, Marian Denny—had a case on him. "She wants to speak to you, Rupert. Why don't you ever ask her out? You could phone her up at least. She's dying to talk to you."

They did not really expect him to respond to these pleading overtures. But what joy if he had. He would have been rejected in short order and the story broadcast all over the school. Why? Why did they treat him this way, long to humiliate him? Simply because they could.

Impossible that he would have forgotten. But he treated Enid as if she was a new acquaintance, his wife's nurse, come into his house from anywhere at all. And Enid took her cue from him.

Things had been unusually well arranged here, to spare her extra work. Rupert slept at Mrs. Green's house, and ate his meals there. The two little girls could have been there as well, but it would have meant putting them into another school—there was nearly a month to go before school was out for the summer.

Rupert came into the house in the evenings and spoke to his children.

"Are you being good girls?" he said.

"Show Daddy what you made with your blocks," said Enid. "Show Daddy your pictures in the coloring book."

The blocks, the crayons, the coloring books, were all provided by Enid. She had phoned her mother and asked her to see what things she could find in the old trunks. Her mother had done that, and brought along as well an old book of cutout dolls which she had collected from someone—Princesses Elizabeth and Margaret Rose and their many outfits. Enid hadn't been able to get the little girls to say thank you until she put all these things on a high shelf and announced that they would stay there till thank you was said.

Lois and Sylvie were seven and six years old, and as wild as little barn cats.

Rupert didn't ask where the playthings came from. He told his daughters to be good girls and asked Enid if there was anything she needed from town. Once she told him that she had replaced the lightbulb in the cellarway and that he could get her some spare bulbs.

"I could have done that," he said.

"I don't have any trouble with lightbulbs," said Enid. "Or fuses or knocking in nails. My mother and I have done without a man around the house for a long time now." She meant to tease a little, to be friendly, but it didn't work.

Finally Rupert would ask about his wife, and Enid would say that her blood pressure was down slightly, or that she had eaten and kept down part of an omelette for supper, or that the ice packs seemed to ease her itchy skin and she was sleeping better. And Rupert would say that if she was sleeping he'd better not go in.

Enid said, "Nonsense." To see her husband would do a woman more good than to have a little doze. She took the children up to bed then, to give man and wife a time of privacy. But Rupert never stayed more than a few minutes. And when Enid came back downstairs and went into the front room—now the sickroom—to ready the patient for the night, Mrs. Quinn would be lying back against the pillows, looking agitated but not dissatisfied.

"Doesn't hang around here very long, does he?" Mrs. Quinn would say. "Makes me laugh. Ha-ha-ha, how-are-you? Ha-ha-ha, off-we-go. Why don't we take her out and throw her on the manure pile? Why don't we just dump her out like a dead cat? That's what he's thinking. Isn't he?"

"I doubt it," said Enid, bringing the basin and towels, the rubbing alcohol and the baby powder.

"I doubt it," said Mrs. Quinn quite viciously, but she submitted readily enough to having her nightgown removed, her hair smoothed back from her face, a towel slid under her hips. Enid was used to people making a fuss about being naked, even when they were very old or very ill. Sometimes she would have to tease or badger them into common sense. "Do you think I haven't seen any bottom parts before?" she would say. "Bottom parts, top parts, it's pretty boring after a while. You know, there's just the two ways we're made." But Mrs. Quinn was without shame, opening her legs and raising herself a bit to make the job easier. She was a little bird-boned woman, queerly shaped now, with her swollen abdomen and limbs and her breasts shrunk to tiny pouches with dried-currant nipples.

"Swole up like some kind of pig," Mrs. Quinn said. "Except for my tits, and they always were kind of useless. I never had no big udders on me, like you. Don't you get sick of the sight of me? Won't you be glad when I'm dead?"

"If I felt like that I wouldn't be here," said Enid.

"Good riddance to bad rubbish," said Mrs. Quinn. "That's what you'll all say. Good riddance to bad rubbish. I'm no use to him anymore, am I? I'm no use to any man. He goes out of here every night and he goes to pick up women, doesn't he?"

"As far as I know, he goes to his sister's house."

"As far as you know. But you don't know much."

Enid thought she knew what this meant, this spite and venom, the energy saved for ranting. Mrs. Quinn was flailing about for an enemy. Sick people grew to resent well people, and sometimes that was true of husbands and wives, or even of mothers and their children. Both husband and children in Mrs. Quinn's case. On a Saturday morning, Enid called Lois and Sylvie from their games under the porch, to come and see their mother looking pretty. Mrs. Quinn had just had her morning wash, and was in a clean night-gown, with her fine, sparse, fair hair brushed and held back by a blue ribbon. (Enid took a supply of these ribbons with her when she went to nurse a female patient—also a bottle of cologne and a cake of scented soap.) She did look pretty—or you could see at least that she had once been pretty, with her wide forehead and cheekbones (they almost punched the skin now, like china door-knobs) and her large greenish eyes and childish translucent teeth and small stubborn chin.

The children came into the room obediently if unenthusiastically.

Mrs. Quinn said, "Keep them off of my bed, they're filthy."

"They just want to see you," said Enid.

"Well, now they've seen me," said Mrs. Quinn. "Now they can go."

This behavior didn't seem to surprise or disappoint the children. They looked at Enid, and Enid said, "All right, now, your mother better have a rest," and they ran out and slammed the kitchen door.

"Can't you get them to quit doing that?" Mrs. Quinn said. "Every time they do it, it's like a brick hits me in my chest."

You would think these two daughters of hers were a pair of rowdy orphans, wished on her for an indefinite visit. But that was the way some people were, before they settled down to their dying and sometimes even up to the event itself. People of a gentler nature—it would seem—than Mrs. Quinn might say that they knew how much their brothers, sisters, husbands, wives, and children had always hated them, how much of a disappointment they had been to others and others had been to them, and how glad they knew everybody would be to see them gone. They might say this at the end of peaceful, useful lives in the midst of loving families, where there was no explanation at all for such fits. And usually the fits passed. But often, too, in the last weeks or even days of life there was mulling over of old feuds and slights or whimpering about some unjust punishment suffered seventy years earlier. Once a woman had asked Enid to bring her a willow platter from the cupboard and Enid had thought that she wanted the comfort of looking at this one pretty possession for the last time. But it turned out that she wanted to use her last, surprising strength to smash it against the bedpost.

"Now I know my sister's never going to get her hands on that," she said.

And often people remarked that their visitors were only coming to gloat and that the doctor was responsible for their sufferings. They detested the sight of Enid herself, for her sleepless strength and patient hands and the way the juices of life were so admirably balanced and flowing in her. Enid was used to that, and she was able to understand the trouble they were in, the trouble of dying and also the trouble of their lives that sometimes overshadowed that.

But with Mrs. Quinn she was at a loss.

It was not just that she couldn't supply comfort here. It was that she couldn't want to. She could not conquer her dislike of this doomed, miserable young woman. She disliked this body that she had to wash and powder and placate with ice and alcohol rubs. She understood now what people meant when they said that they hated sickness and sick bodies; she understood the women who had said to her, I don't know how you do it, I could never be a nurse, that's the one thing I could never be. She disliked this particular body, all the particular signs of its disease. The smell of it and the discoloration, the malignant-looking little nipples and the pathetic ferretlike teeth. She saw all this as the sign of a willed corruption. She was as bad as Mrs. Green, sniffing out rampant impurity. In spite of being a nurse who knew better, and in spite of its being her job—and surely her nature—to be compassionate. She didn't know why this was happening. Mrs. Quinn reminded her somewhat of girls she had known in high school—cheaply dressed, sickly-looking girls with dreary futures, who still displayed a hardfaced satisfaction with themselves. They lasted only a year or two—they got pregnant, most of them got married. Enid had nursed some of them in later years, in home childbirth, and found their confidence exhausted and their bold streak turned into meekness, or even piety. She was sorry for them, even when she remembered how determined they had been to get what they had got.

Mrs. Quinn was a harder case. Mrs. Quinn might crack and crack, but there would be nothing but sullen mischief, nothing but rot inside her.

Worse even than the fact that Enid should feel this revulsion was the fact that Mrs. Quinn knew it. No patience or gentleness or cheerfulness that Enid could summon would keep Mrs. Quinn from knowing. And Mrs. Quinn made knowing it her triumph.

Good riddance to bad rubbish.

WHEN ENID WAS twenty years old, and had almost finished her nurse's training, her father was dying in the Walley hospital. That was when he said to her, "I don't know as I care for this career of yours. I don't want you working in a place like this."

Enid bent over him and asked what sort of place he thought he was in. "It's only the Walley hospital," she said.

"I know that," said her father, sounding as calm and reasonable as he had always done (he was an insurance and real-estate agent). "I know what I'm talking about. Promise me you won't."

"Promise you what?" said Enid.

"You won't do this kind of work," her father said. She could not get any further explanation out of him. He tightened up his mouth as if her questioning disgusted him. All he would say was "Promise."

"What is all this about?" Enid asked her mother, and her mother said, "Oh, go ahead. Go ahead and promise him. What difference is it going to make?"

Enid thought this a shocking thing to say, but made no comment. It was consistent with her mother's way of looking at a lot of things.

"I'm not going to promise anything I don't understand," she said. "I'm probably not going to promise anything anyway. But if you know what he's talking about you ought to tell me."

"It's just this idea he's got now," her mother said. "He's got an idea that nursing makes a woman coarse."

Enid said, "Coarse."

Her mother said that the part of nursing her father objected to was the familiarity nurses had with men's bodies. Her father thought—he had decided—that such familiarity would change a girl, and furthermore that it would change the way men thought about that girl. It would spoil her good chances and give her a lot of other chances that were not so good. Some men would lose interest and others would become interested in the wrong way.

"I suppose it's all mixed up with wanting you to get married," her mother said.

"Too bad if it is," said Enid.

But she ended up promising. And her mother said, "Well, I hope that makes you happy." Not "makes him happy." "Makes *you*." It seemed that her mother had known before Enid did just how tempting this promise would be. The deathbed promise, the self-denial, the wholesale sacrifice. And the more absurd the better. This was what she had given in to. And not for love of her father, either (her mother implied), but for the thrill of it. Sheer noble perversity.

"If he'd asked you to give up something you didn't care one way or the other about, you'd probably have told him nothing doing," her mother said. "If for instance he'd asked you to give up wearing lipstick. You'd still be wearing it."

Enid listened to this with a patient expression.

"Did you pray about it?" said her mother sharply.

Enid said yes.

She withdrew from nursing school; she stayed at home and kept busy. There was enough money that she did not have to work. In fact, her mother had not wanted Enid to go into nursing in the first place, claiming that it was something poor girls did, it was a way out for girls whose parents couldn't keep them or send them to college. Enid did not remind her of this inconsistency. She painted a fence, she tied up the rosebushes for winter. She learned to bake and she learned to play bridge, taking her father's place in the weekly games her mother played with Mr. and Mrs. Willens from next door. In no time at all she became—as Mr. Willens said—a scandalously good player. He took to turning up with chocolates or a pink rose for her, to make up for his own inadequacies as a partner.

She went skating in the winter evenings. She played badminton. She had never lacked friends, and she didn't now. Most of the people who had been in the last year of high school with her were finishing college now, or were already working at a distance, as teachers or nurses or chartered accountants. But she made friends with others who had dropped out before senior year to work in banks or stores or offices, to become plumbers or milliners. The girls in this group were dropping like flies, as they said of each other—they were dropping into matrimony. Enid was an organizer of bridal showers and a help at trousseau teas. In a couple of years would come the christenings, where she could expect to be a favorite godmother. Children not related to her would grow up calling her Aunt. And she was already a sort of honorary daughter to women of her mother's age and older, the only young woman who had time for the Book Club and the Horticultural Society. So, quickly and easily, still in her youth, she was slipping into this essential, central, yet isolated role.

But in fact it had been her role all along. In high school she was always the class secretary or class social convener. She was well liked and high-spirited and well dressed and good-looking, but she was slightly set apart. She had friends who were boys but never a boyfriend. She did not seem to have made a choice this way, but she was not worried about it, either. She had been preoccupied with her ambition—to be a missionary, at one embarrassing stage, and then to be a nurse. She had never thought of nursing as just something to do until she got married. Her hope was to be good, and do good, and not necessarily in the orderly, customary, wifely way.

AT NEW YEAR'S she went to the dance in the Town Hall. The man who danced with her most often, and escorted her home, and pressed her hand good night, was the manager of the creamery—a man in his forties, never married, an excellent dancer, an avuncular friend to girls unlikely to find partners. No woman ever took him seriously.

"Maybe you should take a business course," her mother said. "Or why shouldn't you go to college?"

Where the men might be more appreciative, she was surely thinking.

"I'm too old," said Enid.

Her mother laughed. "That only shows how young you are," she said. She seemed relieved to discover that her daughter had a touch of folly natural to her age—that she could think twenty-one was at a vast distance from eighteen.

"I'm not going to troop in with kids out of high school," Enid said. "I mean it. What do you want to get rid of me for anyway? I'm fine here." This sulkiness or sharpness also seemed to please and reassure her mother. But after a moment she sighed, and said, "You'll be surprised how fast the years go by."

That August there were a lot of cases of measles and a few of polio at the same time. The doctor who had looked after Enid's father, and had observed her competence around the hospital, asked her if she would be willing to help out for a while, nursing people at home. She said that she would think about it.

"You mean pray?" her mother said, and Enid's face took on a stubborn, secretive expression that in another girl's case might have had to do with meeting her boyfriend.

"That promise," she said to her mother the next day. "That was about working in a hospital, wasn't it?"

Her mother said that she had understood it that way, yes.

"And with graduating and being a registered nurse?"

Yes, yes.

So if there were people who needed nursing at home, who couldn't afford to go to the hospital or did not want to go, and if Enid went into their houses to nurse them, not as a registered nurse but as what they called a practical nurse, she would hardly be breaking her promise, would she? And since most of those needing her care would be children or women having babies, or old people dying, there would not be much danger of the coarsening effect, would there?

"If the only men you get to see are men who are never going to get out of bed again, you have a point," said her mother.

But she could not keep from adding that what all this meant was that Enid had decided to give up the possibility of a decent job in a hospital in order to do miserable backbreaking work in miserable primitive houses for next to no money. Enid would find herself pumping water from contaminated wells and breaking ice in winter washbasins and battling flies in summer and using an outdoor toilet. Scrub boards and coal-oil lamps instead of washing machines and electricity. Trying to look after sick people in those conditions and cope with housework and poor weaselly children as well.

"But if that is your object in life," she said, "I can see that the worse I make it sound the more determined you get to do it. The only thing is, I'm going to ask for a couple of promises myself. Promise me you'll boil the water you drink. And you won't marry a farmer."

Enid said, "Of all the crazy ideas."

That was sixteen years ago. During the first of those years people got poorer and poorer. There were more and more of them who could not afford to go to the hospital, and the houses where Enid worked had often deteriorated almost to the state that her mother had described. Sheets and diapers had to be washed by hand in houses where the washing machine had broken down and could not be repaired, or the electricity had been turned off, or where there had never been any electricity in the first place. Enid did not work without pay, because that would not have been fair to the other women who did the same kind of nursing, and who did not have the same options as she did. But she gave most of the money back, in the form of children's shoes and winter coats and trips to the dentist and Christmas toys.

Her mother went around canvassing her friends for old baby cots, and high chairs and blankets, and worn-out sheets, which she herself ripped up and hemmed to make diapers. Everybody said how proud she must be of Enid, and she said yes, she surely was.

"But sometimes it's a devil of a lot of work," she said. "This being the mother of a saint."

THEN CAME the war, and the great shortage of doctors and nurses, and Enid was more welcome than ever. As she was for a while after the war, with so many babies being born. It was only now, with the hospitals being enlarged and many farms getting prosperous, that it looked as if her responsibilities might dwindle away to the care of those who had bizarre and hopeless afflictions, or were so irredeemably cranky that hospitals had thrown them out.

THIS SUMMER there was a great downpour of rain every few days, and then the sun came out very hot, glittering off the drenched leaves and grass. Early mornings were full of mist—they were so close, here, to the river—and even when the mist cleared off you could not see very far in any direction, because of the overflow and density of summer. The heavy trees, the bushes all bound up with wild grapevines and Virginia creeper, the crops of corn and barley and wheat and hay. Everything was ahead of itself, as people said. The hay was ready to cut in June, and Rupert had to rush to get it into the barn before a rain spoiled it.

He came into the house later and later in the evenings, having worked as long as the light lasted. One night when he came the house was in darkness, except for a candle burning on the kitchen table.

Enid hurried to unhook the screen door.

"Power out?" said Rupert.

Enid said, "Shhh." She whispered to him that she was letting the children sleep downstairs, because the upstairs rooms were so hot. She had pushed the chairs together and made beds on them with quilts and pillows. And of course she had had to turn the lights out so that they could get to sleep. She had found a candle in one of the drawers, and that was all she needed, to see to write by, in her notebook.

"They'll always remember sleeping here," she said. "You always remember the times when you were a child and you slept some-where different."

He set down a box that contained a ceiling fan for the sickroom. He had been into Walley to buy it. He had also bought a newspaper, which he handed to Enid.

"Thought you might like to know what's going on in the world," he said.

She spread the paper out beside her notebook, on the table. There was a picture of a couple of dogs playing in a fountain.

"It says there's a heat wave," she said. "Isn't it nice to find out about it?"

Rupert was carefully lifting the fan out of its box.

"That'll be wonderful," she said. "It's cooled off in there now, but it'll be such a comfort to her tomorrow."

"I'll be over early to put it up," he said. Then he asked how his wife had been that day.

Enid said that the pains in her legs had been easing off, and the new pills the doctor had her on seemed to be letting her get some rest.

"The only thing is, she goes to sleep so soon," she said. "It makes it hard for you to get a visit."

"Better she gets the rest," Rupert said.

This whispered conversation reminded Enid of conversations in high school, when they were both in their senior year and that earlier teasing, or cruel flirtation, or whatever it was, had long been abandoned. All that last year Rupert had sat in the seat behind hers, and they had often spoken to each other briefly, always to some immediate purpose. Have you got an ink eraser? How do you spell "incriminate"? Where is the Tyrrhenian Sea? Usually it was Enid, half turning in her seat and able only to sense, not see, how close Rupert was, who started these conversations. She did want to borrow an eraser, she was in need of information, but also she wanted to be sociable. And she wanted to make amends—she felt ashamed of the way she and her friends had treated him. It would do no good to apologize—that would just embarrass him all over again. He was only at ease when he sat behind her, and knew that she could not look him in the face. If they met on the street he would look away until the last minute, then mutter the faintest greeting while she sang out "Hello, Rupert," and heard an echo of the old tormenting tones she wanted to banish.

But when he actually laid a finger on her shoulder, tapping for attention, when he bent forward, almost touching or maybe really touching—she could not tell for sure—her thick hair that was wild even in a bob, then she felt forgiven. In a way, she felt honored. Restored to seriousness and to respect.

Where, where exactly, is the Tyrrhenian Sea?

She wondered if he remembered anything at all of that now.

She separated the back and front parts of the paper. Margaret Truman was visiting England, and had curtsied to the royal family. The King's doctors were trying to cure his Buerger's disease with vitamin E.

She offered the front part to Rupert. "I'm going to look at the crossword," she said. "I like to do the crossword—it relaxes me at the end of the day."

Rupert sat down and began to read the paper, and she asked him if he would like a cup of tea. Of course he said not to bother, and she went ahead and made it anyway, understanding that this reply might as well be yes in country speech.

"It's a South American theme," she said, looking at the crossword. "Latin American theme. First across is a musical . . . *garment*. A musical garment? Garment. A lot of letters. Oh. Oh. I'm lucky tonight. Cape Horn!

"You see how silly they are, these things," she said, and rose and poured the tea.

If he did remember, did he hold anything against her? Maybe her blithe friendliness in their senior year had been as unwelcome, as superior-seeming to him, as that early taunting?

When she first saw him in this house, she thought that he had not changed much. He had been a tall, solid, round-faced boy, and he was a tall, heavy, round-faced man. He had worn his hair cut so short, always, that it didn't make much difference that there was less of it now and that it had turned from light brown to gray-brown. A permanent sunburn had taken the place of his blushes. And whatever troubled him and showed in his face might have been just the same old trouble—the problem of occupying space in the world and having a name that people could call you by, being somebody they thought they could know.

She thought of them sitting in the senior class. A small class, by that time—in five years the unstudious, the carefree, and the indifferent had been weeded out, leaving these overgrown, grave, and docile children learning trigonometry, learning Latin. What kind of life did they think they were preparing for? What kind of people did they think they were going to be?

She could see the dark-green, softened cover of a book called *History of the Renaissance and Reformation*. It was secondhand, or tenthhand—nobody ever bought a new textbook. Inside were written all the names of the previous owners, some of whom were middle-aged housewives or merchants around the town. You could not imagine them learning these things, or underlining "Edict of Nantes" with red ink and writing "N.B." in the margin.

Edict of Nantes. The very uselessness, the exotic nature, of the things in those books and in those students' heads, in her own head then and Rupert's, made Enid feel a tenderness and wonder. It wasn't that they had meant to be something that they hadn't become. Nothing like that. Rupert couldn't have imagined anything but farming this farm. It was a good farm, and he was an only son. And she herself had ended up doing exactly what she must have wanted to do. You couldn't say that they had chosen the wrong lives or chosen against their will or not understood their choices. Just that they had not understood how time would pass and leave them not more but maybe a little less than what they used to be.

" 'Bread of the Amazon,' " she said. " 'Bread of the Amazon'?"

Rupert said, "Manioc?"

Enid counted. "Seven letters," she said. "Seven."

He said, "Cassava?"

"Cassava? That's a double *s*? Cassava."

MRS. QUINN became more capricious daily about her food. Sometimes she said she wanted toast, or bananas with milk on them. One day she said peanut-butter cookies. Enid prepared all these things—the children could eat them anyway—and when they were ready Mrs. Quinn could not stand the look or the smell of them. Even Jell-O had a smell she could not stand.

Some days she hated all noise; she would not even have the fan going. Other days she wanted the radio on, she wanted the station that played requests for birthdays and anniversaries and called people up to ask them questions. If you got the answer right you won a trip to Niagara Falls, a tankful of gas, or a load of groceries or tickets to a movie.

"It's all fixed," Mrs. Quinn said. "They just pretend to call somebody up—they're in the next room and already got the answer told to them. I used to know somebody that worked for a radio, that's the truth."

On these days her pulse was rapid. She talked very fast in a light, breathless voice. "What kind of car is that your mother's got?" she said.

"It's a maroon-colored car," said Enid.

"What *make*?" said Mrs. Quinn.

Enid said she did not know, which was the truth. She had known, but she had forgotten.

"Was it new when she got it?"

"Yes," said Enid. "Yes. But that was three or four years ago."

"She lives in that big rock house next door to Willenses?"

Yes, said Enid.

"How many rooms it got? Sixteen?"

"Too many."

"Did you go to Mr. Willens's funeral when he got drownded?"

Enid said no. "I'm not much for funerals."

"I was supposed to go. I wasn't awfully sick then, I was going with Herveys up the highway, they said I could get a ride with them and then her mother and her sister wanted to go and there wasn't enough room in back. Then Clive and Olive went in the truck and I could've scrunched up in their front seat but they never thought to ask me. Do you think he drownded himself?"

Enid thought of Mr. Willens handing her a rose. His jokey gallantry that made the nerves of her teeth ache, as from too much sugar.

"I don't know. I wouldn't think so."

"Did him and Mrs. Willens get along all right?"

"As far as I know, they got along beautifully."

"Oh, is that so?" said Mrs. Quinn, trying to imitate Enid's reserved tone. "Bee-you-tif-ley."

ENID SLEPT on the couch in Mrs. Quinn's room. Mrs. Quinn's devastating itch had almost disappeared, as had her need to urinate. She slept through most of the night, though she would have spells of harsh and angry breathing. What woke Enid up and kept her awake was a trouble of her own. She had begun to have ugly dreams. These were unlike any dreams she had ever had before. She used to think that a bad dream was one of finding herself in an unfamiliar house where the rooms kept changing and there was always more work to do than she could handle, work undone that she thought she had done, innumerable distractions. And then, of course, she had what she thought of as romantic dreams, in which some man would have his arm around her or even be embracing her. It might be a stranger or a man she knew—sometimes a man whom it was quite a joke to think of in that way. These dreams made her thoughtful or a little sad but relieved in some way to know that such feelings were possible for her. They could be embarrassing, but were nothing, nothing at all compared with the dreams that she was having now. In the dreams that came to her now she would be copulating or trying to copulate (sometimes she was prevented by intruders or shifts of circumstances) with utterly forbidden and unthinkable partners. With fat squirmy babies or patients in bandages or her own mother. She would be slick with lust, hollow and groaning with it, and she would set to work with roughness and an attitude of evil pragmatism. "Yes, this will have to do," she would say to herself. "This will do if nothing better comes along." And this coldness of heart, this matter-of-fact depravity, simply drove her lust along. She woke up unrepentant, sweaty and exhausted, and lay like a carcass until her own self, her shame and disbelief, came pouring back into her. The sweat went cold on her skin. She lay there shivering in the warm night, with disgust and humiliation. She did not dare go back to sleep. She got used to the dark and the long rectangles of the net-curtained windows filled with a faint light. And the sick woman's breath grating and scolding and then almost disappearing.

If she was a Catholic, she thought, was this the sort of thing that could come out at confession? It didn't seem like the sort of thing she could even bring out in a private prayer. She didn't pray much anymore, except formally, and to bring the experiences she had just been through to the attention of God seemed absolutely useless, disrespectful. He would be insulted. She was insulted, by her own mind. Her religion was hopeful and sensible and there was no room in it for any sort of rubbishy drama, such as the invasion of the devil into her sleep. The filth in her mind was in her, and there was no point in dramatizing it and making it seem important. Surely not. It was nothing, just the mind's garbage.

In the little meadow between the house and the riverbank there were cows. She could hear them munching and jostling, feeding at night. She thought of their large gentle shapes in there with the money musk and chicory, the flowering grasses, and she thought, They have a lovely life, cows.

It ends, of course, in the slaughterhouse. The end is disaster.

For everybody, though, the same thing. Evil grabs us when we are sleeping; pain and disintegration lie in wait. Animal horrors, all worse than you can imagine beforehand. The comforts of bed and the cows' breath, the pattern of the stars at night—all that can get turned on its head in an instant. And here she was, here was Enid, working her life away pretending it wasn't so. Trying to ease people. Trying to be good. An angel of mercy, as her mother had said, with less and less irony as time went on. Patients and doctors, too, had said it.

And all the time how many thought that she was a fool? The people she spent her labors on might secretly despise her. Thinking they'd never do the same in her place. Never be fool enough. No. *Miserable offenders,* came into her head. *Miserable offenders. Restore them that are penitent.*

So she got up and went to work; as far as she was concerned, that was the best way to be penitent. She worked very quietly but steadily through the night, washing the cloudy glasses and sticky plates that were in the cupboards and establishing order where there was none before. None. Teacups had sat between the ketchup and the mustard and toilet paper on top of a pail of honey. There was no waxed paper or even newspaper laid out on the shelves.

Brown sugar in the bag was as hard as rock. It was understandable that things should have gone downhill in the last few months, but it looked as if there had been no care, no organization here, ever. All the net curtains were gray with smoke and the windowpanes were greasy. The last bit of jam had been left to grow fuzz in the jar, and vile-smelling water that had held some ancient bouquet had never been dumped out of its jug. But this was a good house still, that scrubbing and painting could restore.

Though what could you do about the ugly brown paint that had been recently and sloppily applied to the front-room floor?

When she had a moment later in the day she pulled the weeds out of Rupert's mother's flower beds, dug up the burdocks and twitch grass that were smothering the valiant perennials.

She taught the children to hold their spoons properly and to say grace.

> *Thank you for the world so*
> *sweet,*
> *Thank you for the food we eat . . .*

She taught them to brush their teeth and after that to say their prayers.

"God bless Mama and Daddy and Enid and Aunt Olive and Uncle Clive and Princess Elizabeth and Margaret Rose." After that each added the name of the other. They had been doing it for quite a while when Sylvie said, "What does it mean?"

Enid said, "What does what mean?"

"What does it mean 'God bless'?"

ENID MADE EGGNOGS, not flavoring them even with vanilla, and fed them to Mrs. Quinn from a spoon. She fed her a little of the rich liquid at a time, and Mrs. Quinn was able to hold down what was given to her in small amounts. If she could not do that, Enid spooned out flat, lukewarm ginger ale.

The sunlight, or any light, was as hateful as noise to Mrs. Quinn by now. Enid had to hang thick quilts over the windows, even when the blinds were pulled down. With the fan shut off, as Mrs. Quinn demanded, the room became very hot, and sweat dripped from Enid's forehead as she bent over the bed attending to the patient. Mrs. Quinn went into fits of shivering; she could never be warm enough.

"This is dragging out," the doctor said. "It must be those milkshakes you're giving her, keeping her going."

"Eggnogs," said Enid, as if it mattered.

Mrs. Quinn was often now too tired or weak to talk. Sometimes she lay in a stupor, with her breathing so faint and her pulse so lost and wandering that a person less experienced than Enid would have taken her for dead. But at other times she rallied, wanted the radio on, then wanted it off. She knew perfectly well who she was still, and who Enid was, and she sometimes seemed to be watching Enid with a speculative or inquiring look in her eyes. Color was long gone from her face and even from her lips, but her eyes looked greener than they had in the past—a milky, cloudy green. Enid tried to answer the look that was bent on her.

"Would you like me to get a priest to talk to you?"

Mrs. Quinn looked as if she wanted to spit.

"Do I look like a Mick?" she said.

"A minister?" said Enid. She knew this was the right thing to ask, but the spirit in which she asked it was not right—it was cold and faintly malicious.

No. This was not what Mrs. Quinn wanted. She grunted with displeasure. There was some energy in her still, and Enid had the feeling that she was building it up for a purpose. "Do you want to talk to your children?" she said, making herself speak compassionately and encouragingly. "Is that what you want?"

No.

"Your husband? Your husband will be here in a little while."

Enid didn't know that for sure. Rupert arrived so late some nights, after Mrs. Quinn had taken the final pills and gone to sleep. Then he sat with Enid. He always brought her the newspaper. He asked what she wrote in her notebooks—he noticed that there were two—and she told him. One for the doctor, with a record of blood pressure and pulse and temperature, a record of what was eaten, vomited, excreted, medicines taken, some general summing up of the patient's condition. In the other notebook, for herself, she wrote many of the same things, though perhaps not so exactly, but she added details about the weather and what was happening all around. And things to remember.

"For instance, I wrote something down the other day," she said. "Something that Lois said. Lois and Sylvie came in when Mrs. Green was here and Mrs. Green was mentioning how the berry bushes were growing along the lane and stretching across the road, and Lois said, 'It's like in "Sleeping Beauty."' Because I'd read them the story. I made a note of that."

Rupert said, "I'll have to get after those berry canes and cut them back."

Enid got the impression that he was pleased by what Lois had said and by the fact that she had written it down, but it wasn't possible for him to say so.

One night he told her that he would be away for a couple of days, at a stock auction. He had asked the doctor if it was all right, and the doctor had said to go ahead.

That night he had come before the last pills were given, and Enid supposed that he was making a point of seeing his wife awake before that little time away. She told him to go right into Mrs. Quinn's room, and he did, and shut the door after him. Enid picked up the paper and thought of going upstairs to read it, but the children probably weren't asleep yet; they would find excuses for calling her in. She could go out on the porch, but there were mosquitoes at this time of day, especially after a rain like the afternoon's.

She was afraid of overhearing some intimacy or perhaps the suggestion of a fight, then having to face him when he came out. Mrs. Quinn was building up to a display—of that Enid felt sure. And before she made up her mind where to go she did overhear something. Not the recriminations or (if it was possible) the endearments, or perhaps even weeping, that she had been half expecting, but a laugh. She heard Mrs. Quinn weakly laughing, and the laughter had the mockery and satisfaction in it that Enid had heard before but also something she hadn't heard before, not in her life—something deliberately vile. She didn't move, though she should have, and she was at the table still, she was still there staring at the door of the room, when he came out a moment later. He didn't avoid her eyes—or she his. She couldn't. Yet she couldn't have said for sure that he saw her. He just looked at her and went on outside. He looked as if he had caught hold of an electric wire and begged pardon—who of?—that his body was given over to this stupid catastrophe.

The next day Mrs. Quinn's strength came flooding back, in that unnatural and deceptive way that Enid had seen once or twice in others. Mrs. Quinn wanted to sit up against the pillows. She wanted the fan turned on.

Enid said, "What a good idea."

"I could tell you something you wouldn't believe," Mrs. Quinn said.

"People tell me lots of things," said Enid.

"Sure. Lies," Mrs. Quinn said. "I bet it's all lies. You know Mr. Willens was right here in this room?"

III. MISTAKE

MRS. QUINN had been sitting in the rocker getting her eyes examined and Mr. Willens had been close up in front of her with the thing up to her eyes, and neither one of them heard Rupert come in, because he was supposed to be cutting wood down by the river. But he had sneaked back. He sneaked back through the kitchen not making any noise—he must have seen Mr. Willens's car outside before he did that—then he opened the door to this room just easy, till he saw Mr. Willens there on his knees holding the thing up to her eye and he had the other hand on her leg to keep his balance. He had grabbed her leg to keep his balance and her skirt got scrunched up and her leg showed bare, but that was all there was to it and she couldn't do a thing about it, she had to concentrate on keeping still.

So Rupert got in the room without either of them hearing him come in and then he just gave one jump and landed on Mr. Willens like a bolt of lightning and Mr. Willens couldn't get up or turn around, he was down before he knew it. Rupert banged his head up and down on the floor, Rupert banged the life out of him, and she jumped up so fast the chair went over and Mr. Willens's box where he kept his eye things got knocked over and all the things flew out of it. Rupert just walloped him, and maybe he hit the leg of the stove, she didn't know what. She thought, It's me next. But she couldn't get round them to run out of the room. And then she saw Rupert wasn't going to go for her after all. He was out of wind and he just set the chair up and sat down in it. She went to Mr. Willens then and hauled him around, as heavy as he was, to get him right side up. His eyes were not quite open, not shut either, and there was dribble coming out of his mouth. But no skin broke on his face or bruise you could see—maybe it wouldn't have come up yet. The stuff coming out of his mouth didn't even look like blood. It was pink stuff, and if you wanted to know what it looked like it looked exactly like when the froth comes up when you're boiling the strawberries to make jam. Bright pink. It was smeared over his face from when Rupert had him facedown. He made a sound, too, when she was turning him over. *Glug-glug.* That was all there was to it. *Glug-glug* and he was laid out like a stone.

Rupert jumped out of the chair so it was still rocking, and he started picking up all the things and putting each one back where it went in Mr. Willens's box. Getting everything fitted in the way it should go. Wasting the time that way. It was a special box lined with red plush and a place in it for each one of his things that he used and you had to get everything in right or the top wouldn't go down. Rupert got it so the top went on and then he just sat down in the chair again and started pounding on his knees.

On the table there was one of those good-for-nothing cloths, it was a souvenir of when Rupert's mother and father went up north to see the Dionne Quintuplets. She took it off the table and wrapped it around Mr. Willens's head to soak up the pink stuff and so they wouldn't have to keep on looking at him.

Rupert kept banging his big flat hands. She said, Rupert, we got to bury him somewhere.

Rupert just looked at her, like to say, Why?

She said they could bury him down in the cellar, which had a dirt floor.

"That's right," said Rupert. "Where are we going to bury his car?"

She said they could put it in the barn and cover it up with hay.

He said too many people came poking around the barn.

Then she thought, Put him in the river. She thought of him sitting in his car right under the water. It came to her like a picture. Rupert didn't say anything at first, so she went into the kitchen and got some water and cleaned Mr. Willens up so he wouldn't dribble on anything. The goo was not coming up in his mouth anymore. She got his keys, which were in his pocket. She could feel, through the cloth of his pants, the fat of his leg still warm.

She said to Rupert, Get moving.

He took the keys.

They hoisted Mr. Willens up, she by the feet and Rupert by the head, and he weighed a ton. He was like lead. But as she carried him one of his shoes kind of kicked her between the legs, and she thought, There you are, you're still at it, you horny old devil. Even his dead old foot giving her the nudge. Not that she ever let him do anything, but he was always ready to get a grab if he could. Like grabbing her leg up under her skirt when he had the thing to her eye and she couldn't stop him and Rupert had to come sneaking in and get the wrong idea.

Over the doorsill and through the kitchen and across the porch and down the porch steps. All clear. But it was a windy day, and, first thing, the wind blew away the cloth she had wrapped over Mr. Willens's face.

Their yard couldn't be seen from the road, that was lucky. Just the peak of the roof and the upstairs window. Mr. Willens's car couldn't be seen.

Rupert had thought up the rest of what to do. Take him to Jutland, where it was deep water and the track going all the way back and it could look like he just drove in from the road and mistook his way. Like he turned off on the Jutland road, maybe it was dark and he just drove into the water before he knew where he was at. Like he just made a mistake.

He did. Mr. Willens certainly did make a mistake.

The trouble was it meant driving out their lane and along the road to the Jutland turn. But nobody lived down there and it was a dead end after the Jutland turn, so just the half mile or so to pray you never met anybody. Then Rupert would get Mr. Willens over in the driver's seat and push the car right off down the bank into the water. Push the whole works down into the pond. It was going to be a job to do that, but Rupert at least was a strong bugger. If he hadn't been so strong they wouldn't have been in this mess in the first place.

Rupert had a little trouble getting the car started because he had never driven one like that, but he did, and got turned around and drove off down the lane with Mr. Willens kind of bumping over against him. He had put Mr. Willens's hat on his head—the hat that had been sitting on the seat of the car.

Why take his hat off before he came into the house? Not just to be polite but so he could easier get a clutch on her and kiss her. If you could call that kissing, all that pushing up against her with the box still in one hand and the other grabbing on, and sucking away at her with his dribbly old mouth. Sucking and chewing away at her lips and her tongue and pushing himself up at her and the corner of the box sticking into her and digging her behind. She was so surprised and he got such a hold she didn't know how to get out of it. Pushing and sucking and dribbling and digging into her and hurting her all at the same time. He was a dirty old brute.

She went and got the Quintuplets cloth where it had blown onto the fence. She looked hard for blood on the steps or any mess on the porch or through the kitchen, but all she found was in the front room, also some on her shoes. She scrubbed up what was on the floor and scrubbed her shoes, which she took off, and not till she had all that done did she see a smear right down her front. How did she come by that? And the same time she saw it she heard a noise that turned her to stone. She heard a car and it was a car she didn't know and it was coming down the lane.

She looked through the net curtain and sure enough. A new-looking car and dark green. Her smeared-down front and shoes off and the floor wet. She moved back where she couldn't be seen, but she couldn't think of where to hide. The car stopped and a car door opened, but the engine didn't cut off. She heard the door shut and then the car turned around and she heard the sound of it driving back up the lane. And she heard Lois and Sylvie on the porch.

It was the teacher's boyfriend's car. He picked up the teacher

every Friday afternoon, and this was a Friday. So the teacher said
to him, Why don't we give these ones a lift home, they're the littlest
and they got the farthest to go and it looks like it's going to rain.

It did rain, too. It had started by the time Rupert got back, walking home along the riverbank. She said, A good thing, it'll muddy
up your tracks where you went to push it over. He said he'd took
his shoes off and worked in his sock feet. So you must have got
your brains going again, she said.

Instead of trying to soak the stuff out of that souvenir cloth or
the blouse she had on, she decided to burn the both of them in the
stove. They made a horrible smell and the smell made her sick.
That was the whole beginning of her being sick. That and the paint.
After she cleaned up the floor, she could still see where she thought
there was a stain, so she got the brown paint left over from when
Rupert painted the steps and she painted over the whole floor. That
started her throwing up, leaning over and breathing in that paint.
And the pains in her back—that was the start of them, too.

After she got the floor painted she just about quit going into the
front room. But one day she thought she had better put some other
cloth on that table. It would make things look more normal. If she
didn't, then her sister-in-law was sure to come nosing around and
say, Where's that cloth Mom and Dad brought back the time they
went to see the Quints? If she had a different cloth on she could say,
Oh, I just felt like a change. But no cloth would look funny.

So she got a cloth Rupert's mother had embroidered with flower
baskets and took it in there and she could still smell the smell. And
there on the table was sitting the dark-red box with Mr. Willens's
things in it and his name on it and it had been sitting there all the
time. She didn't even remember putting it there or seeing Rupert
put it there. She had forgot all about it.

She took that box and hid it in one place and then she hid it in
another. She never told where she hid it and she wasn't going to.
She would have smashed it up, but how do you smash all those
things in it? Examining things. Oh, Missus, would you like me to
examine your eyes for you, just sit down here and just you relax
and you just shut the one eye and keep the other one wide open.
Wide open, now. It was like the same game every time, and she
wasn't supposed to suspect what was going on, and when he had

the thing out looking in her eye he wanted her to keep her panties on, him the dirty old cuss puffing away getting his fingers slicked in and puffing away. Her not supposed to say anything till he stops and gets the looker thing packed up in his box and all and then she's supposed to say, "Oh, Mr. Willens, now, how much do I owe you for today?"

And that was the signal for him to get her down and thump her like an old billy goat. Right on the bare floor to knock her up and down and try to bash her into pieces. Dingey on him like a blowtorch.

How'd you've liked that?

Then it was in the papers. Mr. Willens found drowned.

They said his head got bunged up knocking against the steering wheel. They said he was alive when he went in the water. What a laugh.

IV. LIES

ENID STAYED AWAKE all night—she didn't even try to sleep. She could not lie down in Mrs. Quinn's room. She sat in the kitchen for hours. It was an effort for her to move, even to make a cup of tea or go to the bathroom. Moving her body shook up the information that she was trying to arrange in her head and get used to. She had not undressed, or unrolled her hair, and when she brushed her teeth she seemed to be doing something laborious and unfamiliar. The moonlight came through the kitchen window—she was sitting in the dark—and she watched a patch of light shift through the night, on the linoleum, and disappear. She was surprised by its disappearance and then by the birds waking up, the new day starting. The night had seemed so long and then too short, because nothing had been decided.

She got up stiffly and unlocked the door and sat on the porch in the beginning light. Even that move jammed her thoughts together. She had to sort through them again and set them on two sides. What had happened—or what she had been told had happened—on one side. What to do about it on the other. What to do about it—that was what would not come clear to her.

The cows had been moved out of the little meadow between the house and the riverbank. She could open the gate if she wanted to and go in that direction. She knew that she should go back, instead, and check on Mrs. Quinn. But she found herself pulling open the gate bolt.

The cows hadn't cropped all the weeds. Sopping wet, they brushed against her stockings. The path was clear, though, under the riverbank trees, those big willows with the wild grape hanging on to them like monkeys' shaggy arms. Mist was rising so that you could hardly see the river. You had to fix your eyes, concentrate, and then a spot of water would show through, quiet as water in a pot. There must be a moving current, but she could not find it.

Then she saw a movement, and it wasn't in the water. There was a boat moving. Tied to a branch, a plain old rowboat was being lifted very slightly, lifted and let fall. Now that she had found it, she kept watching it, as if it could say something to her. And it did. It said something gentle and final.

You know. You know.

WHEN THE CHILDREN woke up they found her in bountiful good spirits, freshly washed and dressed and with her hair loose. She had already made the Jell-O crammed with fruit that would be ready for them to eat at noon. And she was mixing batter for cookies that could be baked before it got too hot to use the oven.

"Is that your father's boat?" she said. "Down on the river?"

Lois said yes. "But we're not supposed to play in it." Then she said, "If you went down with us we could." They had caught on at once to the day's air of privilege, its holiday possibilities, Enid's unusual mix of languor and excitement.

"We'll see," said Enid. She wanted to make the day a special one for them, special aside from the fact—which she was already almost certain of—that it would be the day of their mother's death. She wanted them to hold something in their minds that could throw a redeeming light on whatever came later. On herself, that is, and whatever way she would affect their lives later.

That morning Mrs. Quinn's pulse had been hard to find and she had not been able, apparently, to raise her head or open her eyes. A great change from yesterday, but Enid was not surprised. She had thought that great spurt of energy, that wicked outpouring talk, would be the last. She held a spoon with water in it to Mrs. Quinn's lips, and Mrs. Quinn drew a little of the water in. She made a mewing sound—the last trace, surely, of all her complaints. Enid did not call the doctor, because he was due to visit anyway later that day, probably early in the afternoon.

She shook up soapsuds in a jar and bent a piece of wire, and then another piece, to make bubble wands. She showed the children how to make bubbles, blowing steadily and carefully until as large a shining bladder as possible trembled on the wire, then shaking it delicately free. They chased the bubbles around the yard and kept them afloat till breezes caught them and hung them in the trees or on the eaves of the porch. What kept them alive then seemed to be the cries of admiration, screams of joy, rising up from below. Enid put no restriction on the noise they could make, and when the soapsud mixture was all used up she made more.

The doctor phoned when she was giving the children their lunch—Jell-O and a plate of cookies sprinkled with colored sugar and glasses of milk into which she had stirred chocolate syrup. He said he had been held up by a child's falling out of a tree and he would probably not be out before suppertime. Enid said softly, "I think she may be going."

"Well, keep her comfortable if you can," the doctor said. "You know how as well as I do."

Enid didn't phone Mrs. Green. She knew that Rupert would not be back yet from the auction and she didn't think that Mrs. Quinn, if she ever had another moment of consciousness, would want to see or hear her sister-in-law in the room. Nor did it seem likely that she would want to see her children. And there would be nothing good about seeing her for them to remember.

She didn't bother trying to take Mrs. Quinn's blood pressure anymore, or her temperature—just sponged off her face and arms and offered the water, which was no longer noticed. She turned on the fan, whose noise Mrs. Quinn had so often objected to. The smell rising from the body seemed to be changing, losing its ammoniac sharpness. Changing into the common odor of death.

She went out and sat on the steps. She took off her shoes and stockings and stretched out her legs in the sun. The children began cautiously to pester her, asking if she would take them down to the river, if they could sit in the boat, or if they found the oars could she take them rowing. She knew enough not to go that far in the way of desertion, but she asked them, Would they like to have a swimming pool? Two swimming pools? And she brought out the two laundry tubs, set them on the grass, and filled them with water from the cistern pump. They stripped to their underpants and lolled in the water, becoming Princess Elizabeth and Princess Margaret Rose.

"What do you think," said Enid, sitting on the grass with her head back and her eyes shut, "what do you think, if a person does something very bad, do they have to be punished?"

"Yes," said Lois immediately. "They have to get a licking."

"Who did it?" said Sylvie.

"Just thinking of anybody," said Enid. "Now, what if it was a very bad thing but nobody knew they did it? Should they tell that they did and be punished?"

Sylvie said, "I would know they did it."

"You would not," said Lois. "How would you know?"

"I would've seed them."

"You would not."

"You know the reason I think they should be punished?" Enid said. "It's because of how bad they are going to feel, in themselves. Even if nobody did see them and nobody ever knew. If you do something very bad and you are not punished you feel worse, and feel far worse, than if you are."

"Lois stold a green comb," Sylvie said.

"I did not," said Lois.

"I want you to remember that," Enid said.

Lois said, "It was just laying the side the road."

Enid went into the sickroom every half hour or so to wipe Mrs. Quinn's face and hands with a damp cloth. She never spoke to her and never touched her hand, except with the cloth. She had never absented herself like this before with anybody who was dying. When she opened the door at around half past five she knew there was nobody alive in the room. The sheet was pulled out and Mrs. Quinn's head was hanging over the side of the bed, a fact that Enid did not record or mention to anybody. She had the body straightened out and cleaned and the bed put to rights before the doctor came. The children were still playing in the yard.

"JULY 5. Rain early a.m. L. and S. playing under porch. Fan off and on, complains noise. Half cup eggnog spoon at a time. B.P. up, pulse rapid, no complaints pain. Rain didn't cool off much. R.Q. in evening. Hay finished.

"July 6. Hot day, vy. close. Try fan but no. Sponge often. R.Q. in evening. Start to cut wheat tomorrow. Everything 1 or 2 wks ahead due to heat, rain.

"July 7. Cont'd heat. Won't take eggnog. Ginger ale from spoon. Vy. weak. Heavy rain last night, wind. R.Q. not able to cut, grain lodged some places.

"July 8. No eggnog. Ginger ale. Vomiting a.m. More alert. R.Q. to go to calf auction, gone 2 days. Dr. says go ahead.

"July 9. Vy. agitated. Terrible talk.

"July 10. Patient Mrs. Rupert (Jeanette) Quinn died today approx. 5 p.m. Heart failure due to uremia. (Glomerulonephritis.)"

ENID NEVER made a practice of waiting around for the funerals of people she had nursed. It seemed to her a good idea to get out of the house as soon as she decently could. Her presence could not help being a reminder of the time just before the death, which might have been dreary and full of physical disaster, and was now going to be glossed over with ceremony and hospitality and flowers and cakes.

Also, there was usually some female relative who would be in place to take over the household completely, putting Enid suddenly in the position of unwanted guest.

Mrs. Green, in fact, arrived at the Quinns' house before the undertaker did. Rupert was not back yet. The doctor was in the kitchen drinking a cup of tea and talking to Enid about another case that she could take up now that this was finished. Enid was hedging, saying that she had thought of taking some time off. The children were upstairs. They had been told that their mother had gone to heaven, which for them had put the cap on this rare and eventful day.

Mrs. Green was shy until the doctor left. She stood at the window to see him turn his car around and drive away. Then she said, "Maybe I shouldn't say it right now, but I will. I'm glad it happened now and not later when the summer was over and they were started back to school. Now I'll have time to get them used to living at our place and used to the idea of the new school they'll be going to. Rupert, he'll have to get used to it, too."

This was the first time that Enid had realized that Mrs. Green meant to take the children to live with her, not just to stay for a while. Mrs. Green was eager to manage the move, had been looking forward to it, probably, for some time. Very likely she had the children's rooms ready and material bought to make them new clothes. She had a large house and no children of her own.

"You must be wanting to get off home yourself," she said to Enid. As long as there was another woman in the house it might look like a rival home, and it might be harder for her brother to see the necessity of moving the children out for good. "Rupert can run you in when he gets here."

Enid said that it was all right, her mother was coming out to pick her up.

"Oh, I forgot your mother," said Mrs. Green. "Her and her snappy little car."

She brightened up and began to open the cupboard doors, checking on the glasses and the teacups—were they clean for the funeral?

"Somebody's been busy," she said, quite relieved about Enid now and ready to be complimentary.

Mr. Green was waiting outside, in the truck, with the Greens' dog, General. Mrs. Green called upstairs for Lois and Sylvie, and they came running down with some clothes in brown paper bags. They ran through the kitchen and slammed the door, without taking any notice of Enid.

"That's something that's going to have to change," said Mrs. Green, meaning the door slamming. Enid could hear the children shouting their greetings to General and General barking excitedly in return.

TWO DAYS LATER Enid was back, driving her mother's car herself. She came late in the afternoon, when the funeral would have been well over. There were no extra cars parked outside, which meant that the women who had helped in the kitchen had all gone home, taking with them the extra chairs and teacups and the large coffeepot that belonged to their church. The grass was marked with car tracks and some dropped crushed flowers.

She had to knock on the door now. She had to wait to be asked in.

She heard Rupert's heavy, steady footsteps. She spoke some greeting to him when he stood in front of her on the other side of the screen door, but she didn't look into his face. He was in his shirtsleeves, but was wearing his suit trousers. He undid the hook of the door.

"I wasn't sure anybody would be here," Enid said. "I thought you might still be at the barn."

Rupert said, "They all pitched in with the chores."

She could smell whiskey when he spoke, but he didn't sound drunk.

"I thought you were one of the women come back to collect something you forgot," he said.

Enid said, "I didn't forget anything. I was just wondering, how are the children?"

"They're fine. They're at Olive's."

It seemed uncertain whether he was going to ask her in. It was bewilderment that stopped him, not hostility. She had not prepared herself for this first awkward part of the conversation. So that she wouldn't have to look at him, she looked around at the sky.

"You can feel the evenings getting shorter," she said. "Even if it isn't a month since the longest day."

"That's true," said Rupert. Now he opened the door and stood aside and she went in. On the table was a cup without a saucer. She sat down at the opposite side of the table from where he had been sitting. She was wearing a dark-green silk-crepe dress and suede shoes to match. When she put these things on she had thought how this might be the last time that she would dress herself and the last clothes she would ever wear. She had done her hair up in a French braid and powdered her face. Her care, her vanity, seemed foolish but were necessary to her. She had been awake now three nights in a row, awake every minute, and she had not been able to eat, even to fool her mother.

"Was it specially difficult this time?" her mother had said. She hated discussion of illness or deathbeds, and the fact that she had brought herself to ask this meant that Enid's upset was obvious.

"Was it the children you'd got fond of?" she said. "The poor little monkeys."

Enid said it was just the problem of settling down after a long case, and a hopeless case of course had its own strain. She did not go out of her mother's house in the daytime, but she did go for walks at night, when she could be sure of not meeting anybody and having to talk. She had found herself walking past the walls of the county jail. She knew there was a prison yard behind those walls where hangings had once taken place. But not for years and years. They must do it in some large central prison now, when they had to do it. And it was a long time since anybody from this community had committed a sufficiently serious crime.

SITTING ACROSS THE TABLE from Rupert, facing the door of Mrs. Quinn's room, she had almost forgotten her excuse, lost track of the way things were to go. She felt her purse in her lap, the weight of her camera in it—that reminded her.

"There is one thing I'd like to ask you," she said. "I thought I might as well now, because I wouldn't get another chance."

Rupert said, "What's that?"

"I know you've got a rowboat. So I wanted to ask you to row me out to the middle of the river. And I could get a picture. I'd like to get a picture of the riverbank. It's beautiful there, the willow trees along the bank."

"All right," said Rupert, with the careful lack of surprise that country people will show, regarding the frivolity—the rudeness, even—of visitors.

That was what she was now—a visitor.

Her plan was to wait until they got out to the middle of the river, then to tell him that she could not swim. First ask him how deep he thought the water would be there—and he would surely say, after all the rain they had been having, that it might be seven or eight, or even ten, feet. Then tell him that she could not swim. And that would not be a lie. She had grown up in Walley, on the lake, she had played on the beach every summer of her childhood, she was a strong girl and good at games, but she was frightened of the water, and no coaxing or demonstrating or shaming had ever worked with her—she had not learned to swim.

He would only have to give her a shove with one of the oars and topple her into the water and let her sink. Then leave the boat out on the water and swim to shore, change his clothes, and say that he had come in from the barn or from a walk and found the car there, and where was she? Even the camera if found would make it more plausible. She had taken the boat out to get a picture, then somehow fallen into the river.

Once he understood his advantage, she would tell him. She would ask, Is it true?

If it was not true, he would hate her for asking. If it was true—and didn't she believe all the time that it was true?—he would hate her in another, more dangerous way. Even if she said at once—and meant it, she would mean it—that she was never going to tell.

She would speak very quietly all the time, remembering how voices carry out on the water on a summer evening.

I am not going to tell, but you are. You can't live on with that kind of secret.

You cannot live in the world with such a burden. You will not be able to stand your life.

If she had got so far, and he had neither denied what she said nor pushed her into the river, Enid would know that she had won the gamble. It would take some more talking, more absolutely firm but quiet persuasion, to bring him to the point where he would start to row back to shore.

Or, lost, he would say, What will I do? and she would take him one step at a time, saying first, Row back.

The first step in a long, dreadful journey. She would tell him every step and she would stay with him for as many of them as she could. Tie up the boat now. Walk up the bank. Walk through the meadow. Open the gate. She would walk behind him or in front, whichever seemed better to him. Across the yard and up the porch and into the kitchen.

They will say goodbye and get into their separate cars and then it will be his business where he goes. And she will not phone the Police Office the next day. She will wait and they will phone her and she will go to see him in jail. Every day, or as often as they will let her, she will sit and talk to him in jail, and she will write him letters as well. If they take him to another jail she will go there; even if she is allowed to see him only once a month she will be close by. And in court—yes, every day in court, she will be sitting where he can see her.

She does not think anyone would get a death sentence for this sort of murder, which was in a way accidental, and was surely a crime of passion, but the shadow is there, to sober her when she feels that these pictures of devotion, of a bond that is like love but beyond love, are becoming indecent.

Now it has started. With her asking to be taken on the river, her excuse of the picture. Both she and Rupert are standing up, and she is facing the door of the sickroom—now again the front room—which is shut.

She says a foolish thing.

"Are the quilts taken down off the windows?"

He doesn't seem to know for a minute what she is talking about. Then he says, "The quilts. Yes. I think it was Olive took them down. In there was where we had the funeral."

"I was only thinking. The sun would fade them."

He opens the door and she comes around the table and they stand looking into the room. He says, "You can go in if you like. It's all right. Come in."

The bed is gone, of course. The furniture is pushed back against the walls. The middle of the room, where they would have set up the chairs for the funeral, is bare. So is the space in between the north windows—that must have been where they put the coffin. The table where Enid was used to setting the basin, and laying out cloths, cotton wool, spoons, medicine, is jammed into a corner and has a bouquet of delphiniums sitting on it. The tall windows still hold plenty of daylight.

"Lies" is the word that Enid can hear now, out of all the words that Mrs. Quinn said in that room. *Lies. I bet it's all lies.*

COULD A PERSON make up something so detailed and diabolical? The answer is yes. A sick person's mind, a dying person's mind, could fill up with all kinds of trash and organize that trash in a most convincing way. Enid's own mind, when she was asleep in this room, had filled up with the most disgusting inventions, with filth. Lies of that nature could be waiting around in the corners of a person's mind, hanging like bats in the corners, waiting to take advantage of any kind of darkness. You can never say, Nobody could make that up. Look how elaborate dreams are, layer over layer in them, so that the part you can remember and put into words is just the bit you can scratch off the top.

When Enid was four or five years old she had told her mother that she had gone into her father's office and that she had seen him sitting behind his desk with a woman on his knee. All she could remember about this woman, then and now, was that she wore a hat with a great many flowers on it and a veil (a hat quite out of fashion even at that time), and that her blouse or dress was unbuttoned and there was one bare breast sticking out, the tip of it disappearing into Enid's father's mouth. She had told her mother about this in perfect certainty that she had seen it. She said, "One of her fronts was stuck in Daddy's mouth." She did not know the word for breasts, though she did know they came in pairs.

Her mother said, "Now, Enid. What are you talking about? What on earth is a front?"

"Like an ice-cream cone," Enid said.

And she saw it that way, exactly. She could see it that way still. The biscuit-colored cone with its mound of vanilla ice cream squashed against the woman's chest and the wrong end sticking into her father's mouth.

Her mother then did a very unexpected thing. She undid her own dress and took out a dull-skinned object that flopped over her hand. "Like this?" she said.

Enid said no. "An ice-cream cone," she said.

"Then that was a dream," her mother said. "Dreams are sometimes downright silly. Don't tell Daddy about it. It's too silly."

Enid did not believe her mother right away, but in a year or so she saw that such an explanation had to be right, because ice-cream cones did not ever arrange themselves in that way on ladies' chests and they were never so big. When she was older still she realized that the hat must have come from some picture.

Lies.

· · ·

SHE HADN'T ASKED HIM yet, she hadn't spoken. Nothing yet committed her to asking. It was still *before*. Mr. Willens had still driven himself into Jutland Pond, on purpose or by accident. Everybody still believed that, and as far as Rupert was concerned Enid believed it, too. And as long as that was so, this room and this house and her life held a different possibility, an entirely different possibility from the one she had been living with (or glorying in—however you wanted to put it) for the last few days. The different possibility was coming closer to her, and all she needed to do was to keep quiet and let it come. Through her silence, her collaboration in a silence, what benefits could bloom. For others, and for herself.

This was what most people knew. A simple thing that it had taken her so long to understand. This was how to keep the world habitable.

She had started to weep. Not with grief but with an onslaught of relief that she had not known she was looking for. Now she looked into Rupert's face and saw that his eyes were bloodshot and the skin around them puckered and dried out, as if he had been weeping, too.

He said, "She wasn't lucky in her life."

Enid excused herself and went to get her handkerchief, which was in her purse on the table. She was embarrassed now that she had dressed herself up in readiness for such a melodramatic fate.

"I don't know what I was thinking of," she said. "I can't walk down to the river in these shoes."

Rupert shut the door of the front room.

"If you want to go we can still go," he said. "There ought to be a pair of rubber boots would fit you somewhere."

Not hers, Enid hoped. No. Hers would be too small.

Rupert opened a bin in the woodshed, just outside the kitchen door. Enid had never looked into that bin. She had thought it contained firewood, which she had certainly had no need of that summer. Rupert lifted out several single rubber boots and even snow boots, trying to find a pair.

"These look like they might do," he said. "They maybe were Mother's. Or even mine before my feet got full size."

He pulled out something that looked like a piece of a tent, then, by a broken strap, an old school satchel.

"Forgot all the stuff that was in here," he said, letting these things fall back and throwing the unusable boots on top of them. He dropped the lid and gave a private, grieved, and formal-sounding sigh.

A house like this, lived in by one family for so long a time, and neglected for the past several years, would have plenty of bins, drawers, shelves, suitcases, trunks, crawl spaces full of things that it would be up to Enid to sort out, saving and labelling some, restoring some to use, sending others by the boxload to the dump. When she got that chance she wouldn't balk at it. She would make this house into a place that had no secrets from her and where all order was as she had decreed.

He set the boots down in front of her while she was bent over unbuckling her shoes. She smelled under the whiskey the bitter breath that came after a sleepless night and a long harsh day; she smelled the deeply sweat-soaked skin of a hardworked man that no washing—at least the washing he did—could get quite fresh. No bodily smell—even the smell of semen—was unfamiliar to her, but there was something new and invasive about the smell of a body so distinctly not in her power or under her care.

That was welcome.

"See can you walk," he said.

She could walk. She walked in front of him to the gate. He bent over her shoulder to swing it open for her. She waited while he bolted it, then stood aside to let him walk ahead, because he had brought a little hatchet from the woodshed, to clear their path.

"The cows were supposed to keep the growth down," he said. "But there's things cows won't eat."

She said, "I was only down here once. Early in the morning."

The desperation of her frame of mind then had to seem childish to her now.

Rupert went along chopping at the big fleshy thistles. The sun cast a level, dusty light on the bulk of the trees ahead. The air was clear in some places, then suddenly you would enter a cloud of tiny bugs. Bugs no bigger than specks of dust that were constantly in motion yet kept themselves together in the shape of a pillar or a cloud. How did they manage to do that? And how did they choose one spot over another to do it in? It must have something to do with feeding. But they never seemed to be still enough to feed.

When she and Rupert went underneath the roof of summer leaves it was dusk, it was almost night. You had to watch that you didn't trip over roots that swelled up out of the path, or hit your head on the dangling, surprisingly tough-stemmed vines. Then a flash of water came through the black branches. The lit-up water near the opposite bank of the river, the trees over there still decked out in light. On this side—they were going down the bank now, through the willows—the water was tea-colored but clear.

And the boat waiting, riding in the shadows, just the same.

"The oars are hid," said Rupert. He went into the willows to locate them. In a moment she lost sight of him. She went closer to the water's edge, where her boots sank into the mud a little and held her. If she tried to, she could still hear Rupert's movements in the bushes. But if she concentrated on the motion of the boat, a slight and secretive motion, she could feel as if everything for a long way around had gone quiet.

Jakarta

~

KATH AND SONJE HAVE A PLACE of their own on the beach, behind some large logs. They have chosen this not only for shelter from the occasional sharp wind—they've got Kath's baby with them—but because they want to be out of sight of a group of women who use the beach every day. They call these women the Monicas.

The Monicas have two or three or four children apiece. They are all under the leadership of the real Monica, who walked down the beach and introduced herself when she first spotted Kath and Sonje and the baby. She invited them to join the gang.

They followed her, lugging the carry-cot between them. What else could they do? But since then they lurk behind the logs.

The Monicas' encampment is made up of beach umbrellas, towels, diaper bags, picnic hampers, inflatable rafts and whales, toys, lotions, extra clothing, sun hats, thermos bottles of coffee, paper cups and plates, and thermos tubs in which they carry homemade fruit-juice Popsicles.

They are either frankly pregnant or look as if they might be pregnant, because they have lost their figures. They trudge down to the water's edge, hollering out the names of their children who are riding and falling off logs or the inflatable whales.

"Where's your hat? Where's your ball? You've been on that thing long enough now, let Sandy have a turn."

Even when they talk to each other their voices have to be raised high, over the shouts and squalls of their children.

"You can get ground round as cheap as hamburger if you go to Woodward's."

"I tried zinc ointment but it didn't work."

"Now he's got an abscess in the groin."

"You can't use baking powder, you have to use soda."

These women aren't so much older than Kath and Sonje. But they've reached a stage in life that Kath and Sonje dread. They turn the whole beach into a platform. Their burdens, their strung-out progeny and maternal poundage, their authority, can annihilate the bright water, the perfect small cove with the red-limbed arbutus trees, the cedars, growing crookedly out of the high rocks. Kath feels their threat particularly, since she's a mother now herself. When she nurses her baby she often reads a book, sometimes smokes a cigarette, so as not to sink into a sludge of animal function. And she's nursing so that she can shrink her uterus and flatten her stomach, not just provide the baby—Noelle—with precious maternal antibodies.

Kath and Sonje have their own thermos of coffee and their extra towels, with which they've rigged up a shelter for Noelle. They have their cigarettes and their books. Sonje has a book by Howard Fast. Her husband has told her that if she has to read fiction that's who she should be reading. Kath is reading the short stories of Katherine Mansfield and the short stories of D. H. Lawrence. Sonje has got into the habit of putting down her own book and picking up whichever book of Kath's that Kath is not reading at the moment. She limits herself to one story and then goes back to Howard Fast.

When they get hungry one of them makes the trek up a long flight of wooden steps. Houses ring this cove, up on the rocks under the pine and cedar trees. They are all former summer cottages, from the days before the Lions Gate Bridge was built, when people from Vancouver would come across the water for their vacations. Some cottages—like Kath's and Sonje's—are still quite primitive and cheap to rent. Others, like the real Monica's, are much improved. But nobody intends to stay here; everybody's planning to move on to a proper house. Except for Sonje and her husband, whose plans seem more mysterious than anybody else's.

There is an unpaved crescent road serving the houses, and joined at either end to Marine Drive. The enclosed semicircle is full of tall trees and an undergrowth of ferns and salmonberry bushes, and various intersecting paths, by which you can take a short-cut out to the store on Marine Drive. At the store Kath and Sonje will buy takeout French fries for lunch. More often it's Kath who makes this expedition, because it's a treat for her to walk under the trees—something she can't do anymore with the baby carriage.

When she first came here to live, before Noelle was born, she would cut through the trees nearly every day, never thinking of her freedom. One day she met Sonje. They had both worked at the Vancouver Public Library a little while before this, though they had not been in the same department and had never talked to each other. Kath had quit in the sixth month of pregnancy as you were required to do, lest the sight of you should disturb the patrons, and Sonje had quit because of a scandal.

Or, at least, because of a story that had got into the newspapers. Her husband, Cottar, who was a journalist working for a magazine that Kath had never heard of, had made a trip to Red China. He was referred to in the paper as a left-wing writer. Sonje's picture appeared beside his, along with the information that she worked in the library. There was concern that in her job she might be promoting Communist books and influencing children who used the library, so that they might become Communists. Nobody said that she had done this—just that it was a danger. Nor was it against the law for somebody from Canada to visit China. But it turned out that Cottar and Sonje were both Americans, which made their behavior more alarming, perhaps more purposeful.

"I know that girl," Kath had said to her husband, Kent, when she saw Sonje's picture. "At least I know her to see her. She always seems kind of shy. She'll be embarrassed about this."

"No she won't," said Kent. "Those types love to feel persecuted, it's what they live for."

The head librarian was reported as saying that Sonje had nothing to do with choosing books or influencing young people—she spent most of her time typing out lists.

"Which was funny," Sonje said to Kath, after they had recognized each other, and spoken and spent about half an hour talking on the path. The funny thing was that she did not know how to type.

She wasn't fired, but she had quit anyway. She thought she might as well, because she and Cottar had some changes coming up in their future.

Kath wondered if one change might be a baby. It seemed to her that life went on, after you finished school, as a series of further examinations to be passed. The first one was getting married. If you hadn't done that by the time you were twenty-five, that examination had to all intents and purposes been failed. (She always signed her name "Mrs. Kent Mayberry" with a sense of relief and mild elation.) Then you thought about having the first baby. Waiting a year before you got pregnant was a good idea. Waiting two years was a little more prudent than necessary. And three years started people wondering. Then down the road somewhere was the second baby. After that the progression got dimmer and it was hard to be sure just when you had arrived at wherever it was you were going.

Sonje was not the sort of friend who would tell you that she was trying to have a baby and how long she'd been trying and what techniques she was using. She never talked about sex in that way, or about her periods or any behavior of her body—though she soon told Kath things that most people would consider much more shocking. She had a graceful dignity—she had wanted to be a ballet dancer until she got too tall, and she didn't stop regretting that until she met Cottar, who said, "Oh, another little bourgeois girl hoping she'll turn into a dying swan." Her face was broad, calm, pink skinned—she never wore any makeup, Cottar was against makeup—and her thick fair hair was pinned up in a bushy chignon. Kath thought she was wonderful looking—both seraphic and intelligent.

Eating their French fries on the beach, Kath and Sonje discuss characters in the stories they've been reading. How is it that no woman could love Stanley Burnell? What is it about Stanley? He is such a boy, with his pushy love, his greed at the table, his self-satisfaction. Whereas Jonathan Trout—oh, Stanley's wife, Linda, should have married Jonathan Trout, Jonathan who glided through the water while Stanley splashed and snorted. "Greetings, my celestial peach blossom," says Jonathan in his velvety bass voice. He is full of irony, he is subtle and weary. "The shortness of life, the shortness of life," he says. And Stanley's brash world crumbles, discredited.

Something bothers Kath. She can't mention it or think about it. Is Kent something like Stanley?

One day they have an argument. Kath and Sonje have an unexpected and disturbing argument about a story by D. H. Lawrence. The story is called "The Fox."

At the end of that story the lovers—a soldier and a woman named March—are sitting on the sea cliffs looking out on the Atlantic, towards their future home in Canada. They are going to leave England, to start a new life. They are committed to each other, but they are not truly happy. Not yet.

The soldier knows that they will not be truly happy until the woman gives her life over to him, in a way that she has not done so far. March is still struggling against him, to hold herself separate from him, she is making them both obscurely miserable by her efforts to hang on to her woman's soul, her woman's mind. She must stop this—she must stop thinking and stop wanting and let her consciousness go under, until it is submerged in his. Like the reeds that wave below the surface of the water. Look down, look down—see how the reeds wave in the water, they are alive but they never break the surface. And that is how her female nature must live within his male nature. Then she will be happy and he will be strong and content. Then they will have achieved a true marriage.

Kath says that she thinks this is stupid.

She begins to make her case. "He's talking about sex, right?"

"Not just," says Sonje. "About their whole life."

"Yes, but sex. Sex leads to getting pregnant. I mean in the normal course of events. So March has a baby. She probably has more than one. And she has to look after them. How can you do that if your mind is waving around under the surface of the sea?"

"That's taking it very literally," says Sonje in a slightly superior tone.

"You can either have thoughts and make decisions or you can't," says Kath. "For instance—the baby is going to pick up a razor blade. What do you do? Do you just say, Oh, I think I'll just float around here till my husband comes home and he can make up his mind, that is our mind, about whether this is a good idea?"

Sonje said, "That's taking it to extremes."

Each of their voices has hardened. Kath is brisk and scornful, Sonje grave and stubborn.

"Lawrence didn't want to have children," Kath says. "He was jealous of the ones Frieda had from being married before."

Sonje is looking down between her knees, letting sand fall through her fingers.

"I just think it would be beautiful," she says. "I think it would be beautiful, if a woman could."

Kath knows that something has gone wrong. Something is wrong with her own argument. Why is she so angry and excited? And why did she shift over to talking about babies, about children? Because she has a baby and Sonje doesn't? Did she say that about Lawrence and Frieda because she suspects that it is partly the same story with Cottar and Sonje?

When you make the argument on the basis of the children, about the woman having to look after the children, you're in the clear. You can't be blamed. But when Kath does that she is covering up. She can't stand that part about the reeds and the water, she feels bloated and suffocated with incoherent protest. So it is herself she is thinking of, not of any children. She herself is the very woman that Lawrence is railing about. And she can't reveal that straight out because it might make Sonje suspect—it might make Kath herself suspect—an impoverishment in Kath's life.

Sonje who has said, during another alarming conversation, "My happiness depends on Cottar."

My happiness depends on Cottar.

That statement shook Kath. She would never have said it about Kent. She didn't want it to be true of herself.

But she didn't want Sonje to think that she was a woman who had missed out on love. Who had not considered, who had not been offered, the prostration of love.

II

KENT REMEMBERED the name of the town in Oregon to which Cottar and Sonje had moved. Or to which Sonje had moved, at the end of the summer. She had gone there to look after Cottar's mother while Cottar took off on another journalistic junket to the Far East. There was some problem real or imagined about Cottar's getting back into the United States after his trip to China. When he came back the next time he and Sonje planned to meet in Canada, maybe move the mother up there too.

There wasn't much chance that Sonje would be living in the town now. There was just a slight chance that the mother might be. Kent said that it wasn't worth stopping for, but Deborah said, Why not, wouldn't it be interesting to find out? And an inquiry at the Post Office brought directions.

Kent and Deborah drove out of town through the sand dunes—Deborah doing the driving as she had done for most of this long leisurely trip. They had visited Kent's daughter Noelle, who was living in Toronto, and his two sons by his second wife, Pat—one of them in Montreal and the other in Maryland. They had stayed with some old friends of Kent's and Pat's who now lived in a gated community in Arizona, and with Deborah's parents—who were around Kent's age—in Santa Barbara. Now they were headed up the West Coast, home to Vancouver, but taking it easy every day, so as not to tire Kent out.

The dunes were covered with grass. They looked like ordinary hills, except where a naked sandy shoulder was revealed, to make the landscape look playful. A child's construction, swollen out of scale.

The road ended at the house they'd been told to look for. It couldn't be mistaken. There was the sign—PACIFIC SCHOOL OF DANCE. And Sonje's name, and a FOR SALE sign underneath. There was an old woman using shears on one of the bushes in the garden.

So Cottar's mother was still alive. But Kent remembered now that Cottar's mother was blind. That was why somebody had to go and live with her, after Cottar's father died.

What was she doing hacking away with those shears if she was blind?

He had made the usual mistake, of not realizing how many years—decades—had gone by. And how truly ancient the mother would have to be by now. How old Sonje would be, how old he was himself. For it was Sonje, and at first she did not know him either. She bent over to stick the shears into the ground, she wiped her hands on her jeans. He felt the stiffness of her movements in his own joints. Her hair was white and skimpy, blowing in the light ocean breeze that had found its way in here among the dunes. Some firm covering of flesh had gone from her bones. She had always been rather flat chested but not so thin in the waist. A broad-backed, broad-faced, Nordic sort of girl. Though her name didn't come from that ancestry—he remembered a story of her being named Sonje because her mother loved Sonja Henie's movies. She changed the spelling herself and scorned her mother's frivolity. They all scorned their parents then, for something.

He couldn't see her face very well in the bright sun. But he saw a couple of shining silver-white spots where skin cancers, probably, had been cut away.

"Well Kent," she said. "How ridiculous. I thought you were somebody come to buy my house. And is this Noelle?"

So she had made her mistake too.

Deborah was in fact a year younger than Noelle. But there was nothing of the toy wife about her. Kent had met her after his first operation. She was a physiotherapist, never married, and he a widower. A serene, steady woman who distrusted fashion and irony—she wore her hair in a braid down her back. She had introduced him to yoga, as well as the prescribed exercises, and now she had him taking vitamins and ginseng as well. She was tactful and incurious almost to the point of indifference. Perhaps a woman of her generation took it for granted that everybody had a well-peopled and untranslatable past.

Sonje invited them into the house. Deborah said that she would leave them to have their visit—she wanted to find a health-food store (Sonje told her where one was) and to take a walk on the beach.

The first thing Kent noticed about the house was that it was chilly. On a bright summer day. But houses in the Pacific Northwest are seldom as warm as they look—move out of the sun and you feel at once a clammy breath. Fogs and rainy winter cold must have entered this house for a long time almost without opposition. It was a large wooden bungalow, ramshackle though not austere, with its verandah and dormers. There used to be a lot of houses like this in West Vancouver, where Kent still lived. But most of them had been sold as teardowns.

The two large connected front rooms were bare, except for an upright piano. The floor was scuffed gray in the middle, darkly waxed at the corners. There was a railing along one wall and opposite that a dusty mirror in which he saw two lean white-haired figures pass. Sonje said that she was trying to sell the place—well, he could see that by the sign—and that since this part was set up as a dance studio she thought she might as well leave it that way.

"Somebody could still make an okay thing out of it," she said. She said that they had started the school around 1960, soon after they heard that Cottar was dead. Cottar's mother—Delia—played the piano. She played it until she was nearly ninety years old and lost her marbles. ("Excuse me," said Sonje, "but you do get rather nonchalant about things.") Sonje had to put her in a nursing home where she went every day to feed her, though Delia didn't know her anymore. And she hired new people to play the piano, but things didn't work out. Also she was getting so that she couldn't show the pupils anything, just tell them. So she saw that it was time to give up.

She used to be such a stately girl, not very forthcoming. In fact not very friendly, or so he had thought. And now she was scurrying and chattering in the way of people who were too much alone.

"It did well when we started, little girls were all excited then about ballet, and then all that sort of thing went out, you know, it was too formal. But never completely, and then in the eighties people came moving in here with young families and it seemed they had lots of money, how did they get so much money? And it could have been successful again but I couldn't quite manage it."

She said that perhaps the spirit went out of it or the need went out of it when her mother-in-law died.

"We were the best of friends," she said. "Always."

The kitchen was another big room, which the cupboards and appliances didn't properly fill. The floor was gray and black tiles—or perhaps black and white tiles, the white made gray by dirty scrub water. They passed along a hallway lined with shelves, shelves right up to the ceiling crammed with books and tattered magazines, possibly even newspapers. A smell of the brittle old paper. Here the floor had a covering of sisal matting, and that continued into a side porch, where at last he had a chance to sit down. Rattan chairs and settee, the genuine article, that might be worth some money if they hadn't been falling apart. Bamboo blinds also not in the best condition, rolled up or half lowered, and outside some overgrown bushes pressing against the windows. Kent didn't know many names of plants, but he recognized these bushes as the sort that grow where the soil is sandy. Their leaves were tough and shiny—the greens looking as if dipped in oil.

As they passed through the kitchen Sonje had put the kettle on for tea. Now she sank down in one of the chairs as if she too was glad to settle. She held up her grubby big-knuckled hands.

"I'll clean up in a minute," she said. "I didn't ask you if you wanted tea. I could make coffee. Or if you like I could skip them both and make us a gin and tonic. Why don't I do that? It sounds like a good idea to me."

The telephone was ringing. A disturbing, loud, old-fashioned ring. It sounded as if it was just outside in the hall, but Sonje hurried back to the kitchen.

She talked for some time, stopping to take the kettle off when it whistled. He heard her say "visitor right now" and hoped she wasn't putting off someone who wanted to look at the house. Her nervy tone made him think this wasn't just a social call, and that it perhaps had something to do with money. He made an effort not to hear any more.

The books and papers stacked in the hall had reminded him of the house that Sonje and Cottar lived in above the beach. In fact the whole sense of discomfort, of disregard, reminded him. That living room had been heated by a stone fireplace at one end, and though a fire was going—the only time he had been there—old ashes were spilling out of it and bits of charred orange peel, bits of garbage. And there were books, pamphlets, everywhere. Instead of a sofa there was a cot—you had to sit with your feet on the floor and nothing at your back, or else crawl back and lean against the wall with your feet drawn up under you. That was how Kath and Sonje sat. They pretty well stayed out of the conversation. Kent sat in a chair, from which he had removed a dull-covered book with the title *The Civil War in France*. Is that what they're calling the French Revolution now? he thought. Then he saw the author's name, Karl Marx. And even before that he felt the hostility, the judgment, in the room. Just as you'd feel in a room full of gospel tracts and pictures of Jesus on a donkey, Jesus on the Sea of Galilee, a judgment passed down on you. Not just from the books and papers—it was in the fireplace mess and the rug with its pattern worn away and the burlap curtains. Kent's shirt and tie were wrong. He had suspected that by the way Kath looked at them, but once he put them on he was going to wear them anyway. She was wearing one of his old shirts over jeans fastened with a string of safety pins. He had thought that a sloppy outfit to go out to dinner in, but concluded that maybe it was all she could get into.

That was right before Noelle was born.

Cottar was cooking the meal. It was a curry, and turned out to be very good. They drank beer. Cottar was in his thirties, older than Sonje and Kath and Kent. Tall, narrow shouldered, with a high bald forehead and wispy sideburns. A rushed, hushed, confidential way of talking.

There was also an older couple, a woman with low-slung breasts and graying hair rolled up at the back of her neck and a short straight man rather scruffy in his clothes but with something dapper about his manner, his precise and edgy voice and habit of making tidy box shapes with his hands. And there was a young man, a redhead, with puffy watery eyes and speckled skin. He was a part-time student who supported himself by driving the truck that dropped off newspapers for the delivery boys to pick up. Evidently he had just started this job, and the older man, who knew him, began to tease him about the shame of delivering such a paper. Tool of the capitalist classes, mouthpiece of the elite.

Even though this was said in a partly joking way, Kent couldn't let it pass. He thought he might as well jump in then as later. He said he didn't see much wrong with that paper.

They were just waiting for something like that. The older man had already drawn out the information that Kent was a pharmacist and worked for one of the chain drugstores. And the young man had already said, "Are you on the management track?" in a way that suggested the others would see this as a joke but Kent wouldn't. Kent had said he hoped so.

The curry was served, and they ate it, and drank more beer, and the fire was replenished and the spring sky went dark and the lights of Point Grey showed up across Burrard Inlet, and Kent took it upon himself to defend capitalism, the Korean War, nuclear weapons,

John Foster Dulles, the execution of the Rosenbergs—whatever the others threw at him. He scoffed at the idea that American companies were persuading African mothers to buy formula and not to nurse their babies, and that the Royal Canadian Mounted Police were behaving brutally to Indians, and above all at the notion that Cottar's phone might be tapped. He quoted *Time* magazine and announced that he was doing so.

The younger man clapped his knees and wagged his head from side to side and manufactured an incredulous laugh.

"I can't believe this guy. Can you believe this guy? I can't."

Cottar kept mobilizing arguments and tried to keep a rein on exasperation, because he saw himself as a reasoning man. The older man went off on professorial tangents and the low-slung woman made interjections in a tone of poisonous civility.

"Why are you in such a hurry to defend authority wherever it rears its delightful head?"

Kent didn't know. He didn't know what propelled him. He didn't even take these people seriously, as the enemy. They hung around on the fringes of real life, haranguing and thinking themselves important, the way fanatics of any sort did. They had no solidity, when you compared them with the men Kent worked with. In the work Kent did, mistakes mattered, responsibility was constant, you did not have time to fool around with ideas about whether chain drugstores were a bad idea or indulge in some paranoia about drug companies. That was the real world and he went out into it every day with the weight of his future and Kath's on his shoulders. He accepted that, he was even proud of it, he was not going to apologize to a roomful of groaners.

"Life is getting better in spite of what you say," he had told them. "All you have to do is look around you."

He did not disagree with his younger self now. He thought he had been brash maybe, but not wrong. But he wondered about the anger in that room, all the bruising energy, what had become of it.

Sonje was off the phone. She called to him from the kitchen, "I am definitely going to skip the tea and get to that gin and tonic."

When she brought the drinks he asked her how long Cottar had been dead, and she told him more than thirty years. He drew his breath in, and shook his head. That long?

"He died very quickly of some tropical bug," Sonje said. "It happened in Jakarta. He was buried before I even knew he was sick. Jakarta used to be called Batavia, did you know that?"

Kent said, "Vaguely."

"I remember your house," she said. "The living room was really a porch, it was all the way across the front, like ours. There were blinds made of awning material, green and brown stripes. Kath liked the light coming through them, she said it was jungly light. You called it a glorified shack. Every time you mentioned it. The Glorified Shack."

"It was on posts stuck in cement," Kent said. "They were rotting. It was a wonder it didn't fall down."

"You and Kath used to go out looking at houses," said Sonje. "On your day off you'd walk around some subdivision or other with Noelle in the baby carriage. You'd look at all the new houses. You know what those subdivisions were like then. There were never any sidewalks because people weren't supposed to walk anymore and they'd taken down all the trees and the houses were just stuck together staring at each other through the picture windows."

Kent said, "What else could anybody afford, for a start?"

"I know, I know. But you'd say, 'Which one do you like?' and Kath would never answer. So finally you got exasperated and said, well, what sort of house did she like, anywhere, and she said, 'The Glorified Shack.'"

Kent could not remember that happening. But he supposed it had. Anyway it was what Kath had told Sonje.

III

COTTAR AND SONJE were having a farewell party, before Cottar went off to the Philippines or Indonesia or wherever he was going, and Sonje went to Oregon to stay with his mother. Everybody who lived along the beach was asked—since the party was going to be held out-of-doors, that was the only sensible policy. And some people Sonje and Cottar had lived with in a communal house, before they moved to the beach, were asked, and journalists Cottar knew, and people Sonje had worked with in the library.

"Just everybody," Kath said, and Kent said cheerfully, "More pinkos?" She said she didn't know, just everybody.

The real Monica had hired her regular babysitter, and all the children were to be brought to her house, the parents chipping in on the cost. Kath brought Noelle along in her carry-cot just as it was beginning to get dark. She told the sitter that she'd come back before midnight, when Noelle would probably wake up for a feed. She could have brought the supplemental bottle which was made up at home, but she hadn't. She was uncertain about the party and thought she might welcome a chance to get away.

She and Sonje had never talked about the dinner at Sonje's house when Kent got into the fight with everybody. It was the first time Sonje had met Kent and all she said afterwards was that he was really quite good-looking. Kath felt as if the good looks were being thought of as a banal consolation prize.

She had sat that evening with her back against the wall and a cushion hugged against her stomach. She had got into the habit of holding a cushion against the spot where the baby kicked. The cushion was faded and dusty, like everything in Sonje's house (she and Cottar had rented it ready-furnished). Its pattern of blue flowers and leaves had gone silvery. Kath fastened her eyes on these, while they tied Kent up in knots and he didn't even realize it. The young man talked to him with the theatrical rage of a son talking to his father, and Cottar spoke with the worn patience of a teacher to a pupil. The older man was bitterly amused, and the woman was full of moral repugnance, as if she held Kent personally responsible for Hiroshima, Asian girls burned to death in locked factories, for all foul lies and trumpeted hypocrisy. And Kent was asking for most of this, as far as Kath could see. She had dreaded something of the sort, when she saw his shirt and tie and decided to put on jeans instead of her decent maternity skirt. And once she was there she had to sit through it, twisting the cushion this way and that to catch the silver gleam.

Everybody in the room was so certain of everything. When they paused for breath it was just to draw on an everlasting stream of pure virtue, pure certainty.

Except perhaps for Sonje. Sonje didn't say anything. But Sonje drew on Cottar; he was her certainty. She got up to offer more curry, she spoke into one of the brief angry silences.

"It looks as if nobody wanted any coconut."

"Oh, Sonje, are you going to be the tactful hostess?" the older woman said. "Like somebody in Virginia Woolf?"

So it seemed Virginia Woolf was at a discount too. There was so much Kath didn't understand. But at least she knew it was there; she wasn't prepared to say it was nonsense.

Nevertheless she wished her water would break. Anything to deliver her. If she scrambled up and puddled the floor in front of them, they would have to stop.

Afterwards Kent did not seem perturbed about the way the evening had gone. For one thing, he thought he had won. "They're all pinkos, they have to talk that way," he said. "It's the only thing they can do."

Kath was anxious not to talk anymore about politics so she changed the subject, telling him that the older couple had lived with Sonje and Cottar in the communal house. There was also another couple who had since moved away. And there had been an orderly exchange of sexual partners. The older man had an outside mistress and she was in on the exchange part of the time.

Kent said, "You mean young guys would go to bed with that old woman? She's got to be fifty."

Kath said, "Cottar's thirty-eight."

"Even so," said Kent. "It's disgusting."

But Kath found the idea of those stipulated and obligatory copulations exciting as well as disgusting. To pass yourself around obediently and blamelessly, to whoever came up on the list—it was like temple prostitution. Lust served as your duty. It gave her a deep obscene thrill, to think of that.

It hadn't thrilled Sonje. She had not experienced sexual release. Cottar would ask her if she had, when she came back to him, and she had to say no. He was disappointed and she was disappointed for his sake. He explained to her that she was too exclusive and too much tied up in the idea of sexual property and she knew he was right.

"I know he thinks that if I loved him enough I'd be better at it," she said. "But I do love him, agonizingly."

For all the tempting thoughts that came into her mind, Kath believed that she could only, ever, sleep with Kent. Sex was like something they had invented between them. Trying it with some-body else would mean a change of circuits—all of her life would blow up in her face. Yet she could not say she loved Kent agoniz-ingly.

AS SHE WALKED along the beach from Monica's house to Son-je's, she saw people waiting for the party. They stood around in small groups or sat on logs watching the last of the sunset. They drank beer. Cottar and another man were washing out a gar-bage tin in which they would make the punch. Miss Campo, the head librarian, was sitting alone on a log. Kath waved to her viva-ciously but didn't go over to join her. If you joined somebody at this stage, you were caught. Then there were two of you alone. The thing to do was to join a group of three or four, even if you found the conversation—that had looked lively from a distance—to be quite desperate. But she could hardly do that, after waving at Miss Campo. She had to be on her way somewhere. So she went on, past Kent talking to Monica's husband about how long it took to saw up one of the logs on the beach, she went up the steps to Sonje's house and into the kitchen.

Sonje was stirring a big pot of chili, and the older woman from the communal house was setting out slices of rye bread and salami and cheese on a platter. She was dressed just as she had been for the curry dinner—in a baggy skirt and a drab but clinging sweater, the breasts it clung to sloping down to her waist. This had some-thing to do with Marxism, Kath thought—Cottar liked Sonje to go without a brassiere, as well as without stockings or lipstick. Also it had to do with unfettered unjealous sex, the generous uncorrupted appetite that did not balk at a woman of fifty.

A girl from the library was there too, cutting up green peppers and tomatoes. And a woman Kath didn't know was sitting on the kitchen stool, smoking a cigarette.

"Have we ever got a bone to pick with you," the girl from the library said to Kath. "All of us at work. We hear you've got the darlingest baby and you haven't brought her in to show us. Where is she now?"

Kath said, "Asleep I hope."

This girl's name was Lorraine, but Sonje and Kath, recalling their days at the library, had given her the name Debbie Reynolds. She was full of bounce.

"Aww," she said.

The low-slung woman gave her, and Kath, a look of thoughtful distaste.

Kath opened a bottle of beer and handed it to Sonje, who said, "Oh, thanks, I was so concentrated on the chili I forgot I could have a drink." She worried because her cooking wasn't as good as Cottar's.

"Good thing you weren't going to drink that yourself," the girl from the library said to Kath. "It's a no-no if you're nursing."

"I guzzled beer all the time when I was nursing," the woman on the stool said. "I think it was recommended. You piss most of it away anyhow."

This woman's eyes were lined with black pencil, extended at the corners, and her eyelids were painted a purplish blue right up to her sleek black brows. The rest of her face was very pale, or made up to look so, and her lips were so pale a pink that they seemed almost white. Kath had seen faces like this before, but only in magazines.

"This is Amy," said Sonje. "Amy, this is Kath. I'm sorry, I didn't introduce you."

"Sonje, you're always sorry," the older woman said.

Amy took up a piece of cheese that had just been cut, and ate it.

Amy was the name of the mistress. The older woman's husband's mistress. She was a person Kath suddenly wanted to know, to be friends with, just as she had once longed to be friends with Sonje.

THE EVENING had changed into night, and the knots of people on the beach had become less distinct; they showed more disposition to flow together. Down at the edge of the water women had taken off their shoes, reached up and pulled off their stockings if they were wearing any, touched their toes to the water. Most people had given up drinking beer and were drinking punch, and the punch had already begun to change its character. At first it had been mostly rum and pineapple juice, but by now other kinds of fruit juice, and soda water, and vodka and wine had been added.

Those who were taking off their shoes were being encouraged to take off more. Some ran into the water with most of their clothes on, then stripped and tossed the clothes to catchers on shore. Others stripped where they were, encouraging each other by saying it was too dark to see anything. But actually you could see bare bodies splashing and running and falling into the dark water. Monica had brought a great pile of towels down from her house, and was calling out to everyone to wrap themselves up when they came out, so they wouldn't catch their death of cold.

The moon came up through the black trees on top of the rocks, and looked so huge, so solemn and thrilling, that there were cries of amazement. What's that? And even when it had climbed higher in the sky and shrunk to a more normal size people acknowledged it from time to time, saying "The harvest moon" or "Did you see it when it first came up?"

"I actually thought it was a great big balloon."

"I couldn't imagine what it was. I didn't think the moon could be that size, ever."

Kath was down by the water, talking to the man whose wife and mistress she had seen in Sonje's kitchen earlier. His wife was swimming now, a little apart from the shriekers and splashers. In another life, the man said, he had been a minister.

"'The sea of faith was once too at the full,'" he said humorously. "'And round earth's shore, lay like the folds of a bright girdle furled'—I was married to a completely different woman then."

He sighed, and Kath thought he was searching for the rest of the verse.

"'But now I only hear,'" she said, "'its melancholy long withdrawing roar, down the vast edges drear and naked shingles of the world.'" Then she stopped, because it seemed too much to go on with "Oh love let us be true—"

His wife swam towards them, and heaved herself up where the water was only as deep as her knees. Her breasts swung sideways and flung drops of water round her as she waded in.

Her husband opened his arms. He called, "Europa," in a voice of comradely welcome.

"That makes you Zeus," said Kath boldly. She wanted right then to have a man like this kiss her. A man she hardly knew, and cared nothing about. And he did kiss her, he waggled his cool tongue inside her mouth.

"Imagine a continent named after a cow," he said. His wife stood close in front of them, breathing gratefully after the exertion of her swim. She was so close that Kath was afraid of being grazed by her long dark nipples or her mop of black pubic hair.

Somebody had got a fire going, and those who had been in the water were out now, wrapped up in blankets or towels, or crouched behind logs struggling into their clothes.

And there was music playing. The people who lived next door to Monica had a dock and a boathouse. A record player had been brought down, and people were starting to dance. On the dock and with more difficulty on the sand. Even along the top of a log somebody would do a dance step or two, before stumbling and falling or jumping off. Women who had got dressed again, or never got undressed, women who were feeling too restless to stay in one place—as Kath was—went walking along the edge of the water (nobody was swimming anymore, swimming was utterly past and forgotten) and they walked in a different way because of the music. Swaying rather self-consciously, jokingly, then more insolently, like beautiful women in a movie.

Miss Campo was still sitting in the same place, smiling.

The girl Kath and Sonje called Debbie Reynolds was sitting in the sand with her back against a log, crying. She smiled at Kath, she said, "Don't think I'm sad."

Her husband was a college football player who now ran a body-repair shop. When he came into the library to pick up his wife he always looked like a proper football player, faintly disgusted with the rest of the world. But now he knelt beside her and played with her hair.

"It's okay," he said. "It's the way it always takes her. Isn't it, honey?"

"Yes it is," she said.

Kath found Sonje wandering around the fire circle, doling out marshmallows. Some people were able to fit them on sticks and toast them; others tossed them back and forth and lost them in the sand.

"Debbie Reynolds is crying," Kath said. "But it's all right. She's happy."

They began to laugh, and hugged each other, squashing the bag of marshmallows between them.

"Oh I will miss you," Sonje said. "Oh, I will miss our friendship."

"Yes. Yes," Kath said. Each of them took a cold marshmallow and ate it, laughing and looking at each other, full of sweet and forlorn feeling.

"This do in remembrance of me," Kath said. "You are my realest truest friend."

"You are mine," said Sonje. "Realest truest. Cottar says he wants to sleep with Amy tonight."

"Don't let him," said Kath. "Don't let him if it makes you feel awful."

"Oh, it isn't a question of let," Sonje said valiantly. She called out, "Who wants some chili? Cottar's dishing out the chili over there. Chili? Chili?"

Cottar had brought the kettle of chili down the steps and set it in the sand.

"Mind the kettle," he kept saying in a fatherly voice. "Mind the kettle, it's hot."

He squatted to serve people, clad only in a towel that was flapping open. Amy was beside him, giving out bowls.

Kath cupped her hands in front of Cottar.

"Please Your Grace," she said. "I am not worthy of a bowl."

Cottar sprang up, letting go of the ladle, and placed his hands on her head.

"Bless you, my child, the last shall be first." He kissed her bent neck.

"Ahh," said Amy, as if she was getting or giving this kiss herself.

Kath raised her head and looked past Cottar.

"I'd love to wear that kind of lipstick," she said.

Amy said, "Come along." She set down the bowls and took Kath lightly by the waist and propelled her to the steps.

"Up here," she said. "We'll do the whole job on you."

In the tiny bathroom behind Cottar and Sonje's bedroom Amy

spread out little jars and tubes and pencils. She had nowhere to spread them but on the toilet seat. Kath had to sit on the rim of the bathtub, her face almost brushing Amy's stomach. Amy smoothed a liquid over her cheeks and rubbed a paste into her eyelids. Then she brushed on a powder. She brushed and glossed Kath's eyebrows and put three separate coats of mascara on her lashes. She outlined and painted her lips and blotted them and painted them again. She held Kath's face up in her hands and tilted it towards the light.

Someone knocked on the door and then shook it.

"Hang on," Amy called out. Then, "What's the matter with you, can't you go and take a leak behind a log?"

She wouldn't let Kath look in the mirror until it was all done.

"And don't smile," she said. "It spoils the effect."

Kath let her mouth droop, stared sullenly at her reflection. Her lips were like fleshy petals, lily petals. Amy pulled her away. "I didn't mean like that," she said. "Better not look at yourself at all, don't try to look any way, you'll look fine.

"Hold on to your precious bladder, we're getting out," she shouted at the new person or maybe the same person pounding on the door. She scooped her supplies into their bag and shoved it under the bathtub. She said to Kath, "Come on, beautiful."

ON THE DOCK Amy and Kath danced, laughing and challenging each other. Men tried to get in between them, but for a while they managed not to let this happen. Then they gave up, they were separated, making faces of dismay and flapping their arms like grounded birds as they found themselves blocked off, each of them pulled away into the orbit of a partner.

Kath danced with a man she did not remember seeing before during the whole evening. He seemed to be around Cottar's age. He was tall, with a thickened, softened waistline, a mat of dull curly hair, and a spoiled, bruised look around the eyes.

"I may fall off," Kath said. "I'm dizzy. I may fall overboard."

He said, "I'll catch you."

"I'm dizzy but I'm not drunk," she said.

He smiled, and she thought, That's what drunk people always say.

"Really," she said, and it was true because she had not finished even one bottle of beer, or touched the punch.

"Unless I got it through my skin," she said. "Osmosis."

He didn't answer, but pulled her close then released her, holding her eyes.

The sex Kath had with Kent was eager and strenuous, but at the same time reticent. They had not seduced each other but more or less stumbled into intimacy, or what they believed to be intimacy, and stayed there. If there is only to be the one partner in your life nothing has to be made special—it already is so. They had looked at each other naked, but at those times they had not except by chance looked into each other's eyes.

That was what Kath was doing now, all the time, with her unknown partner. They advanced and retreated and circled and dodged, putting on a show for each other, and looking into each other's eyes. Their eyes declared that this show was nothing, nothing compared to the raw tussle they could manage when they chose.

Yet it was all a joke. As soon as they touched they let go again. Close up, they opened their mouths and teased their tongues across their lips and at once drew back, pretending languor.

Kath was wearing a short-sleeved brushed-wool sweater, convenient for nursing because it had a low V neck and was buttoned down the front.

The next time they came close her partner raised his arm as if to protect himself and moved the back of his hand, his bare wrist and forearm across her stiff breasts under their electric wool. That made them stagger, they almost broke their dance. But continued—Kath weak and faltering.

She heard her name being called.

Mrs. Mayberry. Mrs. Mayberry.

It was the babysitter, calling from halfway down Monica's steps. "Your baby. Your baby's awake. Can you come and feed her?"

Kath stopped. She worked her way shakily through the other dancers. Out of the light, she jumped down, and stumbled in the sand. She knew her partner was behind her, she heard him jump behind her. She was ready to offer her mouth or her throat to him. But he caught her hips, turned her around, dropped to his knees, and kissed her crotch through her cotton pants. Then he rose up lightly for such a large man, they turned away from each other at the same moment. Kath hurried into the light and climbed the steps to Monica's house. Panting, and pulling herself up by the railing, like an old woman.

The babysitter was in the kitchen.

"Oh, your husband," she said. "Your husband just came in with the bottle. I didn't know what the arrangement was or I could have saved myself yelling."

Kath went on into Monica's living room. The only light there came from the hall and the kitchen, but she could see that it was a real living room, not a modified porch like hers and Sonje's. There was a Danish modern coffee table and upholstered furniture and draw drapes.

Kent was sitting in an armchair, feeding Noelle from her supplemental bottle.

"Hi," he said, speaking quietly though Noelle was sucking too vigorously to be even half asleep.

"Hi," said Kath, and sat down on the sofa.

"I just thought this would be a good idea," he said. "In case you'd been drinking."

Kath said, "I haven't. Been drinking." She raised a hand to her breasts to test their fullness, but the stir of the wool gave her such a shock of desire that she couldn't press further.

"Well now you can, if you want to," Kent said.

She sat just on the edge of the sofa, leaning forward, longing to ask him, did he come here by the front or the back way? That is, along the road or along the beach? If he had come along the beach he was almost bound to have seen the dancing. But there were quite a lot of people dancing on the dock now, so perhaps he would not have noticed individual dancers.

Nevertheless, the babysitter had spotted her. And he would have heard the babysitter calling her, calling her name. Then he would have looked to see where the babysitter was directing her call.

That is, if he came by the beach. If he came by the road and entered the house by the hall not the kitchen he wouldn't have seen the dancers at all.

"Did you hear her calling me?" Kath said. "Is that why you went home and got the bottle?"

"I'd already thought about it," he said. "I thought it was time." He held up the bottle to see how much Noelle had taken.

"Hungry," he said.

She said, "Yes."

"So now's your opportunity. If you want to get sloshed."

"Is that what you are? Sloshed?"

"I've taken on my fair share," he said. "Go on if you want to. Have yourself a time."

She thought his cockiness sounded sad and faked. He must have seen her dancing. Or else he would have said, "What have you done to your face?"

"I'd sooner wait for you," she said.

He frowned at the baby, tipping up the bottle.

"Nearly finished," he said. "Okay if you want."

"I just have to go to the bathroom," Kath said. And in the bathroom, as she had expected in Monica's house, there was a good supply of Kleenex. She ran the water hot, and soaked and scrubbed, soaked and scrubbed, from time to time flushing a wad of black and purple tissues down the toilet.

IV

IN THE MIDDLE of the second drink, when Kent was talking about the astounding, really obscene prices of real estate these days in West Vancouver, Sonje said, "You know, I have a theory."

"Those places we used to live in," he said. "They went long ago. For a song, compared to now. Now I don't know what you'd get for them. Just for the property. Just for a teardown."

What was her theory? About the price of real estate?

No. It was about Cottar. She did not believe that he was dead.

"Oh, I did at first," she said. "It never occurred to me to doubt it. And then suddenly I just woke up and saw it didn't necessarily have to be true. It didn't have to be true at all."

Think of the circumstances, she said. A doctor had written to her. From Jakarta. That is, the person writing to her said that he was a doctor. He said that Cottar had died and he said what he had died of, he used the medical term which she forgot now. Anyway it was an infectious disease. But how did she know that this person really was a doctor? Or even, granted that he might be a doctor, how did she know that he was telling the truth? It would not be difficult for Cottar to have made the acquaintance of a doctor. To have become friends. Cottar had all sorts of friends.

"Or even to have paid him," she said. "That isn't outside the range of possibility either."

Kent said, "Why would he do that?"

"He wouldn't be the first doctor to do something like that. Maybe he needed the money to keep a clinic going for poor people, how do we know? Maybe he just wanted it for himself. Doctors aren't saints."

"No," said Kent. "I meant Cottar. Why would Cottar do it? And did he have any money?"

"No. He didn't have any himself but—I don't know. It's only one hypothesis anyway. The money. And I was here, you know. I was here to take care of his mother. He really cared about his mother. He knew I'd never desert her. So that was all right.

"It really was all right," she said. "I was very fond of Delia. I didn't find it a burden. I might really have been better suited to taking care of her than to being married to Cottar. And you know, something strange. Delia thought the same as I did. About Cottar. She had the same suspicions. And she never mentioned them to me. I never mentioned mine to her. Each of us thought it would break the other's heart. Then one evening not that long before she—had to go, I was reading her a mystery story that was set in Hong Kong, and she said, 'Maybe that's where Cottar is. Hong Kong.'

"She said she hoped she hadn't upset me. Then I told her what I'd been thinking, and she laughed. We both laughed. You would expect an old mother would be grief-stricken talking about how her only child had run off and left her, but no. Maybe old people aren't like that. Really old people. They don't get grief-stricken anymore. They must figure it's not worth it.

"He knew I'd take care of her, though he probably didn't know how long that would last," she said. "I wish I could show you the doctor's letter, but I threw it out. That was very stupid, but I was distraught at the time. I didn't see how I was going to get through the rest of my life. I didn't think how I should follow up and find out what his credentials were or ask about a death certificate or anything. I thought of all that later and by then I didn't have an address. I couldn't write to the American embassy because they were the last people Cottar would have had anything to do with. And he wasn't a Canadian citizen. Maybe he even had another name. False identity he could slip into. False papers. He used to hint about things like that. That was part of the glamour about him, for me."

"Some of that could have been along the lines of self-dramatizing," Kent said. "Don't you think?"

Sonje said, "Of course I think."

"There wasn't any insurance?"

"Don't be silly."

"If there'd been insurance, they'd have found out the truth."

"Yes but there wasn't," Sonje said. "So. That's what I intend to do."

She said that this was one thing she had never mentioned to her mother-in-law. That after she was on her own, she was going to go looking. She was going to find Cottar, or find the truth.

"I suppose you think that's some wild kind of fantasy?" she said.

Off her rocker, thought Kent with an unpleasant jolt. With every visit he had made on this trip, there had come a moment of severe disappointment. The moment when he realized that the person he was talking to, the person he had made a point of seeking out, was not going to give him whatever it was he had come for. The old friend he had visited in Arizona was obsessed with the dangers of life, in spite of his expensive residence in a protected community. His old friend's wife, who was over seventy, wanted to show him pictures of herself and some other old woman dressed up as Klondike dance-hall girls, for a musical show they had put on. And his grown-up children were caught up in their own lives. That was only natural and not a surprise to him. The surprise was that these lives, the lives his sons and daughter were living, seemed closed in now, somewhat predictable. Even the changes in them that he could foresee or was told were coming—Noelle was on the verge of leaving her second husband—were not very interesting. He had not made any admission of this to Deborah—hardly even to himself—but it was so. And now Sonje. Sonje whom he hadn't particularly liked, whom he'd been wary of in some way, but whom he'd respected, as a bit of a mystery—Sonje had turned into a talkative old woman with a secret screw loose.

And he'd had a reason for coming to see her that they were not getting any closer to, with this rant about Cottar.

"Well to be frank," he said. "It doesn't sound like such a sensible thing to do, to be frank about it."

"A wild-goose chase," said Sonje cheerfully.

"There's a probability he might be dead now anyway."

"True."

"And he could have gone anywhere and lived anywhere. That is if your theory is correct."

"True."

"So the only hope is if he really died then and your theory isn't correct, then you might find out about it and you wouldn't be any further ahead than you are now anyway."

"Oh, I think I would."

"You could do just as well then to stay here and write some letters."

Sonje said she disagreed. She said you couldn't go through official channels regarding this sort of thing.

"You have to make yourself known in the streets."

In the streets of Jakarta—that was where she meant to start. In places like Jakarta people don't shut themselves up. People live in the streets and things are known about them. Shopkeepers know, there's always somebody who knows somebody else and so forth. She would ask questions and word would get around that she was there. A man like Cottar could not have just slipped by. Even after all this time there'd be some memory. Information of one sort or another. Some of it expensive, not all of it truthful. Nevertheless.

Kent thought of asking her what she planned to use for money. Could she have inherited something from her parents? He seemed to remember that they'd cut her off at the time of her marriage. Perhaps she thought she could get a fat price for this property. A long shot, but maybe she was right.

Even so, she could fling it all away in a couple of months. Word would get around that she was there, all right.

"Those cities have changed a lot" was all he said.

"Not that I'd neglect the usual channels," she said. "I'd go after everybody I could. The embassy, the burial records, the medical registry if there is such a thing. In fact I've written letters already.

But all you get is the runaround. You have to confront them in the flesh. You have to be there. Be there. Keep coming around and making a nuisance of yourself and finding out where their soft spots are and be prepared to pass something under the table if you have to. I don't have any illusions about its being easy.

"For instance I expect there'll be devastating heat. It doesn't sound as if it has a good location at all—Jakarta. There are swamps and lowlands all around. I'm not stupid. I'll get my shots and take all the precautions. I'll take my vitamins, and Jakarta being started by the Dutch there shouldn't be any shortage of gin. The Dutch East Indies. It's not a very old city, you know. It was built I think sometime in the 1600s. Just a minute. I have all sorts of—I'll show you—I have—"

She set down her glass which had been empty for some time, got up quickly, and after a couple of steps caught her foot in the torn sisal and lurched forward, but steadied herself by holding on to the door frame and didn't fall. "Got to get rid of this old matting," she said, and hurried into the house.

He heard a struggle with stiff drawers, then a sound as of a pile of papers falling, and all through this she kept talking to him, in that half-frantic reassuring way of people desperate not to lose your attention. He could not make out what she was saying, or didn't try to. He was taking the opportunity to swallow a pill—something he'd been thinking about doing for the last half hour. It was a small pill that didn't require him to take a drink—his glass was empty too—and he could probably have got it to his mouth without Sonje's noticing what he was doing. But something like shyness or superstition prevented him from trying. He did not mind Deborah's constant awareness of his condition, and his children of course had to know, but there seemed to be some sort of ban against revealing it to his contemporaries.

The pill was just in time. A tide of faintness, unfriendly heat, threatened disintegration, came crawling upwards and broke out in sweat drops on his temples. For a few minutes he felt this presence making headway, but by a controlled calm breathing and a casual rearrangement of his limbs he held his own against it. During this time Sonje reappeared with a batch of papers—maps and printed sheets that she must have copied from library books.

Some of them slipped from her hands as she sat down. They lay scattered around on the sisal.

"Now, what they call old Batavia," she said. "That's very geometrically laid out. Very Dutch. There's a suburb called Weltevreden. It means 'well contented.' So wouldn't it be a joke if I found him living there? There's the Old Portuguese Church. Built in the late 1600s. It's a Muslim country of course. They have the biggest mosque there in Southeast Asia. Captain Cook put in to have his ships repaired, he was very complimentary about the shipyards. But he said the ditches out in the bogs were foul. They probably still are. Cottar never looked very strong, but he took better care of himself than you'd think. He wouldn't just go wandering round malarial bogs or buying drinks from a street vendor. Well of course now, if he's there, I expect he'll be completely acclimatized. I don't know what to expect. I can see him gone completely native or I can see him nicely set up with his little brown woman waiting on him. Eating fruit beside a pool. Or he could be going around begging for the poor."

As a matter of fact there was one thing Kent remembered. The night of the party on the beach, Cottar wearing nothing but an insufficient towel had come up to him and asked him what he knew, as a pharmacist, about tropical diseases.

But that had not seemed out of line. Anybody going where he was going might have done the same.

"You're thinking of India," he said to Sonje.

He was stabilized now, the pill giving him back some reliability of his inner workings, halting what had felt like the runoff of bone marrow.

"You know one reason I know he's not dead?" said Sonje. "I don't dream about him. I dream about dead people. I dream all the time about my mother-in-law."

"I don't dream," Kent said.

"Everybody dreams," said Sonje. "You just don't remember."

He shook his head.

Kath was not dead. She lived in Ontario. In the Haliburton district, not so far from Toronto.

"Does your mother know I'm here?" he'd said to Noelle. And she'd said, "Oh, I think so. Sure."

But there came no knock on the door. When Deborah asked him if he wanted to make a detour he had said, "Let's not go out of our way. It wouldn't be worth it."

Kath lived alone beside a small lake. The man she had lived with for a long time, and built the house with, was dead. But she had friends, said Noelle, she was all right.

When Sonje had mentioned Kath's name, earlier in the conversation, he had the warm and dangerous sense of these two women still being in touch with each other. There was the risk then of hearing something he didn't want to know but also the silly hope that Sonje might report to Kath how well he was looking (and he was, he believed so, with his weight fairly steady and the tan he'd picked up in the Southwest) and how satisfactorily he was married. Noelle might have said something of the kind, but somehow Sonje's word would count for more than Noelle's. He waited for Sonje to speak of Kath again.

But Sonje had not taken that tack. Instead it was all Cottar, and stupidity, and Jakarta.

THE DISTURBANCE was outside now—not in him but outside the windows, where the wind that had been stirring the bushes, all this time, had risen to push hard at them. And these were not the sort of bushes that stream their long loose branches before such a wind. Their branches were tough and their leaves had enough weight so that each bush had to be rocked from its roots. Sunlight flashed off the oily greens. For the sun still shone, no clouds had arrived with the wind, it didn't mean rain.

"Another drink?" said Sonje. "Easier on the gin?"

No. After the pill, he couldn't.

Everything was in a hurry. Except when everything was desperately slow. When they drove, he waited and waited, just for Deborah to get to the next town. And then what? Nothing. But once in a while came a moment when everything seemed to have something to say to you. The rocking bushes, the bleaching light. All in a flash, in a rush, when you couldn't concentrate. Just when you wanted summing up, you got a speedy, goofy view, as from a fun-ride. So you picked up the wrong idea, surely the wrong idea. That somebody dead might be alive and in Jakarta.

But when you knew somebody was alive, when you could drive to the very door, you let the opportunity pass.

What wouldn't be worth it? To see her a stranger that he couldn't believe he'd ever been married to, or to see that she could never be a stranger yet was unaccountably removed?

"They got away," he said. "Both of them."

Sonje let the papers on her lap slide to the floor to lie with the others.

"Cottar and Kath," he said.

"This happens almost every day," she said. "Almost every day this time of year, this wind in the late afternoon."

The coin spots on her face picked up the light as she talked, like signals from a mirror.

"Your wife's been gone a long time," she said. "It's absurd, but young people seem unimportant to me. As if they could vanish off the earth and it wouldn't really matter."

"Just the opposite," Kent said. "That's us you're talking about. That's us."

Because of the pill his thoughts stretch out long and gauzy and lit up like vapor trails. He travels a thought that has to do with staying here, with listening to Sonje talk about Jakarta while the wind blows sand off the dunes.

A thought that has to do with not having to go on, to go home.

The Children Stay

~

THIRTY YEARS AGO, a family was spending a holiday together on the east coast of Vancouver Island. A young father and mother, their two small daughters, and an older couple, the husband's parents.

What perfect weather. Every morning, every morning it's like this, the first pure sunlight falling through the high branches, burning away the mist over the still water of Georgia Strait. The tide out, a great empty stretch of sand still damp but easy to walk on, like cement in its very last stage of drying. The tide is actually less far out; every morning, the pavilion of sand is shrinking, but it still seems ample enough. The changes in the tide are a matter of great interest to the grandfather, not so much to anyone else.

Pauline, the young mother, doesn't really like the beach as well as she likes the road that runs behind the cottages for a mile or so north till it stops at the bank of the little river that runs into the sea.

If it wasn't for the tide, it would be hard to remember that this is the sea. You look across the water to the mountains on the mainland, the ranges that are the western wall of the continent of North America. These humps and peaks coming clear now through the mist and glimpsed here and there through the trees, by Pauline as she pushes her daughter's stroller along the road, are also of interest to the grandfather. And to his son Brian, who is Pauline's husband. The two men are continually trying to decide which is what. Which of these shapes are actual continental mountains and which are improbable heights of the islands that ride in front of the shore? It's hard to sort things out when the array is so complicated and parts of it shift their distance in the day's changing light.

But there is a map, set up under glass, between the cottages and the beach. You can stand there looking at the map, then looking at what's in front of you, looking back at the map again, until you get things sorted out. The grandfather and Brian do this every day, usually getting into an argument—though you'd think there would not be much room for disagreement with the map right there. Brian chooses to see the map as inexact. But his father will not hear a word of criticism about any aspect of this place, which was his choice for the holiday. The map, like the accommodation and the weather, is perfect.

Brian's mother won't look at the map. She says it boggles her mind. The men laugh at her, they accept that her mind is boggled. Her husband believes that this is because she is a female. Brian believes that it's because she's his mother. Her concern is always about whether anybody is hungry yet, or thirsty, whether the children have their sun hats on and have been rubbed with protective lotion. And what is the strange bite on Caitlin's arm that doesn't look like the bite of a mosquito? She makes her husband wear a floppy cotton hat and thinks that Brian should wear one too—she reminds him of how sick he got from the sun, that summer they went to the Okanagan, when he was a child. Sometimes Brian says to her, "Oh, dry up, Mother." His tone is mostly affectionate, but his father may ask him if that's the way he thinks he can talk to his mother nowadays.

"She doesn't mind," says Brian.

"How do you know?" says his father.

"Oh for Pete's sake," says his mother.

PAULINE SLIDES OUT OF BED as soon as she's awake every morning, slides out of reach of Brian's long, sleepily searching arms and legs. What wakes her are the first squeaks and mutters of the baby, Mara, in the children's room, then the creak of the crib as Mara—sixteen months old now, getting to the end of babyhood—pulls herself up to stand hanging on to the railing. She continues her soft amiable talk as Pauline lifts her out—Caitlin, nearly five, shifting about but not waking, in her nearby bed—and as she is carried into the kitchen to be changed, on the floor. Then she is settled into her stroller, with a biscuit and a bottle of apple juice, while Pauline gets into her sundress and sandals, goes to the bathroom, combs out her hair—all as quickly and quietly as possible. They leave the cottage; they head past some other cottages for the bumpy unpaved road that is still mostly in deep morning shadow, the floor of a tunnel under fir and cedar trees.

The grandfather, also an early riser, sees them from the porch of his cottage, and Pauline sees him. But all that is necessary is a wave. He and Pauline never have much to say to each other (though sometimes there's an affinity they feel, in the midst of some long-drawn-out antics of Brian's or some apologetic but insistent fuss made by the grandmother; there's an awareness of not looking at each other, lest their look should reveal a bleakness that would discredit others).

On this holiday Pauline steals time to be by herself—being with Mara is still almost the same thing as being by herself. Early-morning walks, the late-morning hour when she washes and hangs out the diapers. She could have had another hour or so in the afternoons, while Mara is napping. But Brian has fixed up a shelter on the beach, and he carries the playpen down every day, so that Mara can nap there and Pauline won't have to absent herself. He says his parents may be offended if she's always sneaking off. He agrees though that she does need some time to go over her lines for the play she's going to be in, back in Victoria, this September.

Pauline is not an actress. This is an amateur production, but she is not even an amateur actress. She didn't try out for the role, though it happened that she had already read the play. *Eurydice* by Jean Anouilh. But then, Pauline has read all sorts of things.

She was asked if she would like to be in this play by a man she met at a barbecue, in June. The people at the barbecue were mostly teachers and their wives or husbands—it was held at the house of the principal of the high school where Brian teaches. The woman who taught French was a widow—she had brought her grown son who was staying for the summer with her and working as a night clerk in a downtown hotel. She told everybody that he had got a job teaching at a college in western Washington State and would be going there in the fall.

Jeffrey Toom was his name. "Without the *b*," he said, as if the staleness of the joke wounded him. It was a different name from his mother's, because she had been widowed twice, and he was the son of her first husband. About the job he said, "No guarantee it'll last, it's a one-year appointment."

What was he going to teach?

"Dram-ah," he said, drawing the word out in a mocking way. He spoke of his present job disparagingly, as well.

"It's a pretty sordid place," he said. "Maybe you heard—a hooker was killed there last winter. And then we get the usual losers checking in to OD or bump themselves off."

People did not quite know what to make of this way of talking and drifted away from him. Except for Pauline.

"I'm thinking about putting on a play," he said. "Would you like to be in it?" He asked her if she had ever heard of a play called *Eurydice*.

Pauline said, "You mean Anouilh's?" and he was unflatteringly surprised. He immediately said he didn't know if it would ever work out. "I just thought it might be interesting to see if you could do something different here in the land of Noël Coward."

Pauline did not remember when there had been a play by Noël Coward put on in Victoria, though she supposed there had been several. She said, "We saw *The Duchess of Malfi* last winter at the college. And the little theater did *A Resounding Tinkle*, but we didn't see it."

"Yeah. Well," he said, flushing. She had thought he was older than she was, at least as old as Brian (who was thirty, though people were apt to say he didn't act it), but as soon as he started talking to her, in this offhand, dismissive way, never quite meeting her eyes, she suspected that he was younger than he'd like to appear. Now with that flush she was sure of it.

As it turned out, he was a year younger than she was. Twenty-five.

She said that she couldn't be Eurydice; she couldn't act. But Brian came over to see what the conversation was about and said at once that she must try it.

"She just needs a kick in the behind," Brian said to Jeffrey. "She's like a little mule, it's hard to get her started. No, seriously, she's too self-effacing, I tell her that all the time. She's very smart. She's actually a lot smarter than I am."

At that Jeffrey did look directly into Pauline's eyes—impertinently and searchingly—and she was the one who was flushing.

He had chosen her immediately as his Eurydice because of the way she looked. But it was not because she was beautiful. "I'd never put a beautiful girl in that part," he said. "I don't know if I'd ever put a beautiful girl on stage in anything. It's too much. It's distracting."

So what did he mean about the way she looked? He said it was her hair, which was long and dark and rather bushy (not in style at that time), and her pale skin ("Stay out of the sun this summer") and most of all her eyebrows.

"I never liked them," said Pauline, not quite sincerely. Her eyebrows were level, dark, luxuriant. They dominated her face. Like her hair, they were not in style. But if she had really disliked them, wouldn't she have plucked them?

Jeffrey seemed not to have heard her. "They give you a sulky look and that's disturbing," he said. "Also your jaw's a little heavy and that's sort of Greek. It would be better in a movie where I could get you close up. The routine thing for Eurydice would be a girl who looked ethereal. I don't want ethereal."

As she walked Mara along the road, Pauline did work at the lines. There was a speech at the end that was giving her trouble. She bumped the stroller along and repeated to herself, " 'You are terrible, you know, you are terrible like the angels. You think everybody's going forward, as brave and bright as you are—oh, don't look at me, please, darling, don't look at me—perhaps I'm not what you wish I was, but I'm here, and I'm warm, I'm kind, and I love you. I'll give you all the happiness I can. Don't look at me. Don't look. Let me live.' "

She had left something out. " 'Perhaps I'm not what you wish I was, but you feel me here, don't you? I'm warm and I'm kind—' "

She had told Jeffrey that she thought the play was beautiful.

He said, "Really?" What she'd said didn't please or surprise him—he seemed to feel it was predictable, superfluous. He would never describe a play in that way. He spoke of it more as a hurdle to be got over. Also a challenge to be flung at various enemies. At the academic snots—as he called them—who had done *The Duchess of Malfi*. And at the social twits—as he called them—in the little theater. He saw himself as an outsider heaving his weight against these people, putting on his play—he called it his—in the teeth of their contempt and opposition. In the beginning Pauline thought that this must be all in his imagination and that it was more likely these people knew nothing about him. Then something would happen that could be, but might not be, a coincidence. Repairs had to be done on the church hall where the play was to be performed, making it unobtainable. There was an unexpected increase in the cost of printing advertising posters. She found herself seeing it his way. If you were going to be around him much, you almost had to see it his way—arguing was dangerous and exhausting.

"Sons of bitches," said Jeffrey between his teeth, but with some satisfaction. "I'm not surprised."

The rehearsals were held upstairs in an old building on Fisgard Street. Sunday afternoon was the only time that everybody could get there, though there were fragmentary rehearsals during the week. The retired harbor pilot who played Monsieur Henri was able to attend every rehearsal, and got to have an irritating familiarity with everybody else's lines. But the hairdresser—who had experience only with Gilbert and Sullivan but now found herself playing Eurydice's mother—could not leave her shop for long at any other time. The bus driver who played her lover had his daily employment as well, and so had the waiter who played Orphée (he was the only one of them who hoped to be a real actor). Pauline had to depend on sometimes undependable high-school babysitters—for the first six weeks of the summer Brian was busy teaching summer school—and Jeffrey himself had to be at his hotel job by eight o'clock in the evenings. But on Sunday afternoons they were all there. While other people swam at Thetis Lake, or thronged Beacon Hill Park to walk under the trees and feed the ducks, or drove far out of town to the Pacific beaches, Jeffrey and his crew labored in the dusty high-ceilinged room on Fisgard Street. The windows were rounded at the top as in some plain and dignified church, and propped open in the heat with whatever objects could be found—ledger books from the 1920s belonging to the hat shop that had once operated downstairs, or pieces of wood left over from the picture frames made by the artist whose canvases were now stacked against one wall and apparently abandoned. The glass was grimy, but outside the sunlight bounced off the sidewalks, the empty gravelled parking lots, the low stuccoed buildings, with what seemed a special Sunday brightness. Hardly anybody moved through these downtown streets. Nothing was open except the occasional hole-in-the-wall coffee shop or fly-specked convenience store.

Pauline was the one who went out at the break to get soft drinks and coffee. She was the one who had the least to say about the play and the way it was going—even though she was the only one who had read it before—because she alone had never done any acting. So it seemed proper for her to volunteer. She enjoyed her short walk in the empty streets—she felt as if she had become an urban person, someone detached and solitary, who lived in the glare of an important dream. Sometimes she thought of Brian at home, working in the garden and keeping an eye on the children. Or perhaps he had taken them to Dallas Road—she recalled a promise—to sail boats on the pond. That life seemed ragged and tedious compared to what went on in the rehearsal room—the hours of effort, the concentration, the sharp exchanges, the sweating and tension. Even the taste of the coffee, its scalding bitterness, and the fact that it was chosen by nearly everybody in preference to a fresher-tasting and maybe more healthful drink out of the cooler seemed satisfying to her. And she liked the look of the shop-windows. This was not one of the dolled-up streets near the harbor—it was a street of shoe- and bicycle-repair shops, discount linen and fabric stores, of clothes and furniture that had been so long in the windows that they looked secondhand even if they weren't. On some windows sheets of golden plastic as frail and crinkled as old cellophane were stretched inside the glass to protect the merchandise from the sun. All these enterprises had been left behind just for this one day, but they had a look of being fixed in time as much as cave paintings or relics under sand.

WHEN SHE SAID that she had to go away for the two-week holiday Jeffrey looked thunderstruck, as if he had never imagined that things like holidays could come into her life. Then he turned grim and slightly satirical, as if this was just another blow that he might have expected. Pauline explained that she would miss only the one Sunday—the one in the middle of the two weeks—because she and Brian were driving up the island on a Monday and coming back on a Sunday morning. She promised to get back in time for rehearsal. Privately she wondered how she would do this—it always took so much longer than you expected to pack up and get away. She wondered if she could possibly come back by herself, on the morning bus. That would probably be too much to ask for. She didn't mention it.

She couldn't ask him if it was only the play he was thinking about, only her absence from a rehearsal that caused the thundercloud. At the moment, it very likely was. When he spoke to her at rehearsals there was never any suggestion that he ever spoke to her in any other way. The only difference in his treatment of her was that perhaps he expected less of her, of her acting, than he did of the others. And that would be understandable to anybody. She was the only one chosen out of the blue, for the way she looked—the others had all shown up at the audition he had advertised on the signs put up in cafés and bookstores around town. From her he appeared to want an immobility or awkwardness that he didn't want from the rest of them. Perhaps it was because, in the latter part of the play, she was supposed to be a person who had already died.

Yet she thought they all knew, the rest of the cast all knew, what was going on, in spite of Jeffrey's offhand and abrupt and none too civil ways. They knew that after every one of them had straggled off home, he would walk across the room and bolt the staircase door. (At first Pauline had pretended to leave with the rest and had even got into her car and circled the block, but later such a trick had come to seem insulting, not just to herself and Jeffrey, but to the others who she was sure would never betray her, bound as they all were under the temporary but potent spell of the play.)

Jeffrey crossed the room and bolted the door. Every time, this was like a new decision, which he had to make. Until it was done, she wouldn't look at him. The sound of the bolt being pushed into place, the ominous or fatalistic sound of the metal hitting metal, gave her a localized shock of capitulation. But she didn't make a move, she waited for him to come back to her with the whole story of the afternoon's labor draining out of his face, the expression of matter-of-fact and customary disappointment cleared away, replaced by the live energy she always found surprising.

. . .

"so. tell us what this play of yours is about," Brian's father said. "Is it one of those ones where they take their clothes off on the stage?"

"Now don't tease her," said Brian's mother.

Brian and Pauline had put the children to bed and walked over to his parents' cottage for an evening drink. The sunset was behind them, behind the forests of Vancouver Island, but the mountains in front of them, all clear now and hard-cut against the sky, shone in its pink light. Some high inland mountains were capped with pink summer snow.

"Nobody takes their clothes off, Dad," said Brian in his booming schoolroom voice. "You know why? Because they haven't got any clothes on in the first place. It's the latest style. They're going to put on a bare-naked *Hamlet* next. Bare-naked *Romeo and Juliet*. Boy, that balcony scene where Romeo is climbing up the trellis and he gets stuck in the rosebushes—"

"Oh, Brian," said his mother.

"The story of Orpheus and Eurydice is that Eurydice died," Pauline said. "And Orpheus goes down to the underworld to try to get her back. And his wish is granted, but only if he promises not to look at her. Not to look back at her. She's walking behind him—"

"Twelve paces," said Brian. "As is only right."

"It's a Greek story, but it's set in modern times," said Pauline. "At least this version is. More or less modern. Orpheus is a musician travelling around with his father—they're both musicians—and Eurydice is an actress. This is in France."

"Translated?" Brian's father said.

"No," said Brian. "But don't worry, it's not in French. It was written in Transylvanian."

"It's so hard to make sense of anything," Brian's mother said with a worried laugh. "It's so hard, with Brian around."

"It's in English," Pauline said.

"And you're what's-her-name?"

She said, "I'm Eurydice."

"He get you back okay?"

"No," she said. "He looks back at me, and then I have to stay dead."

"Oh, an unhappy ending," Brian's mother said.

"You're so gorgeous?" said Brian's father skeptically. "He can't stop himself from looking back?"

"It's not that," said Pauline. But at this point she felt that something had been achieved by her father-in-law, he had done what he meant to do, which was the same thing that he nearly always meant to do, in any conversation she had with him. And that was to break through the structure of some explanation he had asked her for, and she had unwillingly but patiently given, and, with a seemingly negligent kick, knock it into rubble. He had been dangerous to her for a long time in this way, but he wasn't particularly so tonight.

But Brian did not know that. Brian was still figuring out how to come to her rescue.

"Pauline is gorgeous," Brian said.

"Yes indeed," said his mother.

"Maybe if she'd go to the hairdresser," his father said. But Pauline's long hair was such an old objection of his that it had become a family joke. Even Pauline laughed. She said, "I can't afford to till we get the verandah roof fixed." And Brian laughed boisterously, full of relief that she was able to take all this as a joke. It was what he had always told her to do.

"Just kid him back," he said. "It's the only way to handle him."

"Yeah, well, if you'd got yourselves a decent house," said his father. But this like Pauline's hair was such a familiar sore point that it couldn't rouse anybody. Brian and Pauline had bought a handsome house in bad repair on a street in Victoria where old mansions were being turned into ill-used apartment buildings. The house, the street, the messy old Garry oaks, the fact that no basement had been blasted out under the house, were all a horror to Brian's father. Brian usually agreed with him and tried to go him one further. If his father pointed at the house next door all crisscrossed with black fire escapes, and asked what kind of neighbors they had, Brian said, "Really poor people, Dad. Drug addicts." And when his father wanted to know how it was heated, he'd said, "Coal furnace. Hardly any of them left these days, you can get coal really cheap. Of course it's dirty and it kind of stinks."

So what his father said now about a decent house might be some kind of peace signal. Or could be taken so.

Brian was an only son. He was a math teacher. His father was a civil engineer and part owner of a contracting company. If he had hoped that he would have a son who was an engineer and might come into the company, there was never any mention of it. Pauline had asked Brian whether he thought the carping about their house and her hair and the books she read might be a cover for this larger disappointment, but Brian had said, "Nope. In our family we complain about just whatever we want to complain about. We ain't subtle, ma'am."

Pauline still wondered, when she heard his mother talking about how teachers ought to be the most honored people in the world and they did not get half the credit they deserved and that she didn't know how Brian managed it, day after day. Then his father might say, "That's right," or, "I sure wouldn't want to do it, I can tell you that. They couldn't pay me to do it."

"Don't worry, Dad," Brian would say. "They wouldn't pay you much."

Brian in his everyday life was a much more dramatic person than Jeffrey. He dominated his classes by keeping up a parade of jokes and antics, extending the role that he had always played, Pauline believed, with his mother and father. He acted dumb, he bounced back from pretended humiliations, he traded insults. He was a bully in a good cause—a chivvying cheerful indestructible bully.

"Your boy has certainly made his mark with us," the principal said to Pauline. "He has not just survived, which is something in itself. He has made his mark."

Your boy.

Brian called his students boneheads. His tone was affectionate, fatalistic. He said that his father was the King of the Philistines, a pure and natural barbarian. And that his mother was a dishrag, good-natured and worn out. But however he dismissed such people, he could not be long without them. He took his students on camping trips. And he could not imagine a summer without this shared holiday. He was mortally afraid, every year, that Pauline would refuse to go along. Or that, having agreed to go, she was going to be miserable, take offense at something his father said, complain about how much time she had to spend with his mother, sulk because there was no way they could do anything by themselves. She might decide to spend all day in their own cottage, reading and pretending to have a sunburn.

All those things had happened, on previous holidays. But this year she was easing up. He told her he could see that, and he was grateful to her.

"I know it's an effort," he said. "It's different for me. They're my parents and I'm used to not taking them seriously."

Pauline came from a family that took things so seriously that her parents had got a divorce. Her mother was now dead. She had a distant, though cordial, relationship with her father and her two much older sisters. She said that they had nothing in common. She knew Brian could not understand how that could be a reason. She saw what comfort it gave him, this year, to see things going so well. She had thought it was laziness or cowardice that kept him from breaking the arrangement, but now she saw that it was something far more positive. He needed to have his wife and his parents and his children bound together like this, he needed to involve Pauline in his life with his parents and to bring his parents to some recognition of her—though the recognition, from his father, would always be muffled and contrary, and from his mother too profuse, too easily come by, to mean much. Also he wanted Pauline to be connected, he wanted the children to be connected, to his own childhood—he wanted these holidays to be linked to holidays of his childhood with their lucky or unlucky weather, car troubles or driving records, boating scares, bee stings, marathon Monopoly games, to all the things that he told his mother he was bored to death hearing about. He wanted pictures from this summer to be taken, and fitted into his mother's album, a continuation of all the other pictures that he groaned at the mention of.

The only time they could talk to each other was in bed, late at night. But they did talk then, more than was usual with them at home, where Brian was so tired that often he fell immediately asleep. And in ordinary daylight it was often hard to talk to him because of his jokes. She could see the joke brightening his eyes (his coloring was very like hers—dark hair and pale skin and gray eyes, but her eyes were cloudy and his were light, like clear water over stones). She could see it pulling at the corners of his mouth, as he foraged among your words to catch a pun or the start of a rhyme—anything that could take the conversation away, into absurdity. His whole body, tall and loosely joined together and still almost as skinny as a teenager's, twitched with comic propensity. Before she married him, Pauline had a friend named Gracie, a rather grumpy-looking girl, subversive about men. Brian had thought her a girl whose spirits needed a boost, and so he made even more than the usual effort. And Gracie said to Pauline, "How can you stand the nonstop show?"

"That's not the real Brian," Pauline had said. "He's different when we're alone." But looking back, she wondered how true that had ever been. Had she said it simply to defend her choice, as you did when you had made up your mind to get married?

So talking in the dark had something to do with the fact that she could not see his face. And that he knew she couldn't see his face.

But even with the window open on the unfamiliar darkness and stillness of the night, he teased a little. He had to speak of Jeffrey as Monsieur le Directeur, which made the play or the fact that it was a French play slightly ridiculous. Or perhaps it was Jeffrey himself, Jeffrey's seriousness about the play, that had to be called in question.

Pauline didn't care. It was such a pleasure and a relief to her to mention Jeffrey's name.

Most of the time she didn't mention him; she circled around that pleasure. She described all the others, instead. The hairdresser and the harbor pilot and the waiter and the old man who claimed to have once acted on the radio. He played Orphée's father and gave Jeffrey the most trouble, because he had the stubbornest notions of his own, about acting.

The middle-aged impresario Monsieur Dulac was played by a twenty-four-year-old travel agent. And Mathias, who was Eurydice's former boyfriend, presumably around her own age, was played by the manager of a shoe store, who was married and a father of children.

Brian wanted to know why Monsieur le Directeur hadn't cast these two the other way round.

"That's the way he does things," Pauline said. "What he sees in us is something only he can see."

For instance, she said, the waiter was a clumsy Orphée.

"He's only nineteen, he's so shy Jeffrey has to keep at him. He tells him not to act like he's making love to his grandmother. He has to tell him what to do. *Keep your arms around her a little longer, stroke her here a little.* I don't know how it's going to work—I just have to trust Jeffrey, that he knows what he's doing."

"'Stroke her here a little'?" said Brian. "Maybe I should come around and keep an eye on these rehearsals."

When she had started to quote Jeffrey Pauline had felt a giving-way in her womb or the bottom of her stomach, a shock that had travelled oddly upwards and hit her vocal cords. She had to cover up this quaking by growling in a way that was supposed to be an imitation (though Jeffrey never growled or ranted or carried on in any theatrical way at all).

"But there's a point about him being so innocent," she said hurriedly. "Being not so physical. Being awkward." And she began to talk about Orphée in the play, not the waiter. Orphée has a problem with love or reality. Orphée will not put up with anything less than perfection. He wants a love that is outside of ordinary life. He wants a perfect Eurydice.

"Eurydice is more realistic. She's carried on with Mathias and with Monsieur Dulac. She's been around her mother and her mother's lover. She knows what people are like. But she loves Orphée. She loves him better in a way than he loves her. She loves him better because she's not such a fool. She loves him like a human person."

"But she's slept with those other guys," Brian said.

"Well with Mr. Dulac she had to, she couldn't get out of it. She didn't want to, but probably after a while she enjoyed it, because after a certain point she couldn't help enjoying it."

So Orphée is at fault, Pauline said decidedly. He looks at Eurydice on purpose, to kill her and get rid of her because she is not perfect. Because of him she has to die a second time.

Brian, on his back and with his eyes wide open (she knew that because of the tone of his voice) said, "But doesn't he die too?"

"Yes. He chooses to."

"So then they're together?"

"Yes. Like Romeo and Juliet. *Orphée is with Eurydice at last.* That's what Monsieur Henri says. That's the last line of the play. That's the end." Pauline rolled over onto her side and touched her cheek to Brian's shoulder—not to start anything but to emphasize what she said next. "It's a beautiful play in one way, but in another it's so silly. And it isn't really like *Romeo and Juliet* because it isn't bad luck or circumstances. It's on purpose. So they don't have to go on with life and get married and have kids and buy an old house and fix it up and—"

"And have affairs," said Brian. "After all, they're French."

Then he said, "Be like my parents."

Pauline laughed. "Do they have affairs? I can imagine."

"Oh sure," said Brian. "I meant their life.

"Logically I can see killing yourself so you won't turn into your parents," Brian said. "I just don't believe anybody would do it."

"Everybody has choices," Pauline said dreamily. "Her mother and his father are both despicable in a way, but Orphée and Eurydice don't have to be like them. They're not corrupt. Just because she's slept with those men doesn't mean she's corrupt. She wasn't in love then. She hadn't met Orphée. There's one speech where he tells her that everything she's done is sticking to her, and it's disgusting. Lies she's told him. The other men. It's all sticking to her forever. And then of course Monsieur Henri plays up to that. He tells Orphée that he'll be just as bad and that one day he'll walk down the street with Eurydice and he'll look like a man with a dog he's trying to lose."

To her surprise, Brian laughed.

"No," she said. "That's what's stupid. It's not inevitable. It's not inevitable at all."

They went on speculating, and comfortably arguing, in a way that was not usual, but not altogether unfamiliar to them. They had done this before, at long intervals in their married life—talked half the night about God or fear of death or how children should be educated or whether money was important. At last they admitted to being too tired to make sense any longer, and arranged themselves in a comradely position and went to sleep.

FINALLY A RAINY DAY. Brian and his parents were driving into Campbell River to get groceries, and gin, and to take Brian's father's car to a garage, to see about a problem that had developed on the drive up from Nanaimo. This was a very slight problem, but there was the matter of the new-car warranty's being in effect at present, so Brian's father wanted to get it seen to as soon as possible. Brian had to go along, with his car, just in case his father's car had to be left in the garage. Pauline said that she had to stay home because of Mara's nap.

She persuaded Caitlin to lie down too—allowing her to take her music box to bed with her if she played it very softly. Then Pauline spread the script on the kitchen table and drank coffee and went over the scene in which Orphée says that it's intolerable, at last, to stay in two skins, two envelopes with their own blood and oxygen sealed up in their solitude, and Eurydice tells him to be quiet.

"Don't talk. Don't think. Just let your hand wander, let it be happy on its own."

Your hand is my happiness, says Eurydice. Accept that. Accept your happiness.

Of course he says he cannot.

Caitlin called out frequently to ask what time it was. She turned up the sound of the music box. Pauline hurried to the bedroom door and hissed at her to turn it down, not to wake Mara.

"If you play it like that again I'll take it away from you. Okay?"

But Mara was already rustling around in her crib, and in the next few minutes there were sounds of soft, encouraging conversation from Caitlin, designed to get her sister wide awake. Also of the music being quickly turned up and then down. Then of Mara rattling the crib railing, pulling herself up, throwing her bottle out onto the floor, and starting the bird cries that would grow more and more desolate until they brought her mother.

"I didn't wake her," Caitlin said. "She was awake all by herself. It's not raining anymore. Can we go down to the beach?"

She was right. It wasn't raining. Pauline changed Mara, told Caitlin to get her bathing suit on and find her sand pail. She got into her own bathing suit and put her shorts over it, in case the rest of the family arrived home while she was down there. ("Dad doesn't like the way some women just go right out of their cottages in their bathing suits," Brian's mother had said to her. "I guess he and I just grew up in other times.") She picked up the script to take it along, then laid it down. She was afraid that she would get too absorbed in it and take her eyes off the children for a moment too long.

The thoughts that came to her, of Jeffrey, were not really thoughts at all—they were more like alterations in her body. This could happen when she was sitting on the beach (trying to stay in the half shade of a bush and so preserve her pallor, as Jeffrey had ordered) or when she was wringing out diapers or when she and Brian were visiting his parents. In the middle of Monopoly games, Scrabble games, card games. She went right on talking, listening, working, keeping track of the children, while some memory of her secret life disturbed her like a radiant explosion. Then a warm weight settled, reassurance filling up all her hollows. But it didn't last, this comfort leaked away, and she was like a miser whose windfall has vanished and who is convinced such luck can never strike again. Longing buckled her up and drove her to the discipline of counting days. Sometimes she even cut the days into fractions to figure out more exactly how much time had gone.

She thought of going into Campbell River, making some excuse, so that she could get to a phone booth and call him. The cottages had no phones—the only public phone was in the hall of the lodge. But she did not have the number of the hotel where Jeffrey worked. And besides that, she could never get away to Campbell River in the evening. She was afraid that if she called him at home in the daytime his mother the French teacher might answer. He said his mother hardly ever left the house in the summer. Just once, she had taken the ferry to Vancouver for the day. Jeffrey had phoned Pauline to ask her to come over. Brian was teaching, and Caitlin was at her play group.

Pauline said, "I can't. I have Mara."

Jeffrey said, "Who? Oh. Sorry." Then "Couldn't you bring her along?"

She said no.

"Why not? Couldn't you bring some things for her to play with?"

No, said Pauline. "I couldn't," she said. "I just couldn't." It seemed too dangerous to her, to trundle her baby along on such a guilty expedition. To a house where cleaning fluids would not be stowed on high shelves, and all pills and cough syrups and cigarettes and buttons put safely out of reach. And even if she escaped poisoning or choking, Mara might be storing up time bombs—memories of a strange house where she was strangely disregarded, of a closed door, noises on the other side of it.

"I just wanted you," Jeffrey said. "I just wanted you in my bed."

She said again, weakly, "No."

Those words of his kept coming back to her. *I wanted you in my bed.* A half-joking urgency in his voice but also a determination, a practicality, as if "in my bed" meant something more, the bed he spoke of taking on larger, less material dimensions.

Had she made a great mistake with that refusal? With that reminder of how fenced in she was, in what anybody would call her real life?

THE BEACH WAS NEARLY EMPTY—people had got used to its being a rainy day. The sand was too heavy for Caitlin to make a castle or dig an irrigation system—projects she would only undertake with her father, anyway, because she sensed that his interest in them was wholehearted, and Pauline's was not. She wandered a bit forlornly at the edge of the water. She probably missed the presence of other children, the nameless instant friends and occasional stone-throwing water-kicking enemies, the shrieking and splashing and falling about. A boy a little bigger than she was and apparently all by himself stood knee-deep in the water farther down the beach. If these two could get together it might be all right; the whole beach experience might be retrieved. Pauline couldn't tell whether Caitlin was now making little splashy runs into the water for his benefit or whether he was watching her with interest or scorn.

Mara didn't need company, at least for now. She stumbled towards the water, felt it touch her feet and changed her mind, stopped, looked around, and spotted Pauline. "Paw. Paw," she said, in happy recognition. "Paw" was what she said for "Pauline," instead of "Mother" or "Mommy." Looking around overbalanced her—she sat down half on the sand and half in the water, made a squawk of surprise that turned to an announcement, then by some determined ungraceful maneuvers that involved putting her weight on her hands, she rose to her feet, wavering and triumphant. She had been walking for half a year, but getting around on the sand was still a challenge. Now she came back towards Pauline, making some reasonable, casual remarks in her own language.

"Sand," said Pauline, holding up a clot of it. "Look. Mara. Sand."

Mara corrected her, calling it something else—it sounded like "whap." Her thick diaper under her plastic pants and her terry-cloth playsuit gave her a fat bottom, and that, along with her plump cheeks and shoulders and her sidelong important expression, made her look like a roguish matron.

Pauline became aware of someone calling her name. It had been called two or three times, but because the voice was unfamiliar she had not recognized it. She stood up and waved. It was the woman who worked in the store at the lodge. She was leaning over the balcony and calling, "Mrs. Keating. Mrs. Keating? Telephone, Mrs. Keating."

Pauline hoisted Mara onto her hip and summoned Caitlin. She and the little boy were aware of each other now—they were both picking up stones from the bottom and flinging them out into the water. At first she didn't hear Pauline, or pretended not to.

"Store," called Pauline. "Caitlin. Store." When she was sure Caitlin would follow—it was the word "store" that had done it, the reminder of the tiny store in the lodge where you could buy ice cream and candy and cigarettes and mixer—she began the trek across the sand and up the flight of wooden steps above the sand and the salal bushes. Halfway up she stopped, said, "Mara, you weigh a ton," and shifted the baby to her other hip. Caitlin banged a stick against the railing.

"Can I have a Fudgsicle? Mother? Can I?"

"We'll see."

"Can I please have a Fudgsicle?"

"Wait."

The public phone was beside a bulletin board on the other side of the main hall and across from the door to the dining room. A bingo game had been set up in there, because of the rain.

"Hope he's still hanging on," the woman who worked in the store called out. She was unseen now behind her counter.

Pauline, still holding Mara, picked up the dangling receiver and said breathlessly, "Hello?" She was expecting to hear Brian telling her about some delay in Campbell River or asking her what it was she had wanted him to get at the drugstore. It was just the one thing—calamine lotion—so he had not written it down.

"Pauline," said Jeffrey. "It's me."

Mara was bumping and scrambling against Pauline's side, anxious to get down. Caitlin came along the hall and went into the store, leaving wet sandy footprints. Pauline said, "Just a minute, just a minute." She let Mara slide down and hurried to close the door that led to the steps. She did not remember telling Jeffrey the name of this place, though she had told him roughly where it was. She heard the woman in the store speaking to Caitlin in a sharper voice than she would use to children whose parents were beside them.

"Did you forget to put your feet under the tap?"

"I'm here," said Jeffrey. "I didn't get along well without you. I didn't get along at all."

Mara made for the dining room, as if the male voice calling out "Under the *N*—" was a direct invitation to her.

"Here. Where?" said Pauline.

She read the signs that were tacked up on the bulletin board beside the phone.

NO PERSON UNDER FOURTEEN YEARS OF AGE NOT ACCOMPANIED BY ADULT ALLOWED IN BOATS OR CANOES.

FISHING DERBY.

BAKE AND CRAFT SALE, ST. BARTHOLOMEW'S CHURCH.

YOUR LIFE IS IN YOUR HANDS. PALMS AND CARDS READ. REASONABLE AND ACCURATE. CALL CLAIRE.

"In a motel. In Campbell River."

PAULINE KNEW WHERE SHE WAS before she opened her eyes. Nothing surprised her. She had slept but not deeply enough to let go of anything.

She had waited for Brian in the parking area of the lodge, with the children, and had asked him for the keys. She had told him in front of his parents that there was something else she needed, from Campbell River. He asked, What was it? And did she have any money?

"Just something," she said, so he would think that it was tampons or birth control supplies, that she didn't want to mention. "Sure."

"Okay but you'll have to put some gas in," he said.

Later she had to speak to him on the phone. Jeffrey said she had to do it.

"Because he won't take it from me. He'll think I kidnapped you or something. He won't believe it."

But the strangest thing of all the things that day was that Brian did seem, immediately, to believe it. Standing where she had stood not so long before, in the public hallway of the lodge—the bingo game over now but people going past, she could hear them, people on their way out of the dining room after dinner—he said, "Oh. Oh. Oh. Okay" in a voice that would have to be quickly controlled, but that seemed to draw on a supply of fatalism or foreknowledge that went far beyond that necessity.

As if he had known all along, all along, what could happen with her.

"Okay," he said. "What about the car?"

He said something else, something impossible, and hung up, and she came out of the phone booth beside some gas pumps in Campbell River.

"That was quick," Jeffrey said. "Easier than you expected."

Pauline said, "I don't know."

"He may have known it subconsciously. People do know."

She shook her head, to tell him not to say any more, and he said, "Sorry." They walked along the street not touching or talking.

THEY'D HAD TO GO OUT to find a phone booth because there was no phone in the motel room. Now in the early morning looking around at leisure—the first real leisure or freedom she'd had since she came into that room—Pauline saw that there wasn't much of anything in it. Just a junk dresser, the bed without a headboard, an armless upholstered chair, on the window a venetian blind with a broken slat and curtain of orange plastic that was supposed to look like net and that didn't have to be hemmed, just sliced off at the bottom. There was a noisy air conditioner—Jeffrey had turned it off in the night and left the door open on the chain, since the window was sealed. The door was shut now. He must have got up in the night and shut it.

This was all she had. Her connection with the cottage where Brian lay asleep or not asleep was broken, also her connection with the house that had been an expression of her life with Brian, of the way they wanted to live. She had no furniture anymore. She had cut herself off from all the large solid acquisitions like the washer and dryer and the oak table and the refinished wardrobe and the chandelier that was a copy of the one in a painting by Vermeer. And just as much from those things that were particularly hers—the pressed-glass tumblers that she had been collecting and the prayer rug which was of course not authentic, but beautiful. Especially from those things. Even her books, she might have lost. Even her clothes. The skirt and blouse and sandals she had put on for the trip to Campbell River might well be all she had now to her name. She would never go back to lay claim to anything. If Brian got in touch with her to ask what was to be done with things, she would tell him to do what he liked—throw everything into garbage bags and take it to the dump, if that was what he liked. (In fact she knew that he would probably pack up a trunk, which he did, sending on, scrupulously, not only her winter coat and boots but things like the waist cincher she had worn at her wedding and never since, with the prayer rug draped over the top of everything like a final statement of his generosity, either natural or calculated.)

She believed that she would never again care about what sort of rooms she lived in or what sort of clothes she put on. She would not be looking for that sort of help to give anybody an idea of who she was, what she was like. Not even to give herself an idea. What she had done would be enough, it would be the whole thing.

What she was doing would be what she had heard about and read about. It was what Anna Karenina had done and what Madame Bovary had wanted to do. It was what a teacher at Brian's school had done, with the school secretary. He had run off with her. That was what it was called. Running off with. Taking off with. It was spoken of disparagingly, humorously, enviously. It was adultery taken one step further. The people who did it had almost certainly been having an affair already, committing adultery for quite some time before they became desperate or courageous enough to take this step. Once in a long while a couple might claim their love was unconsummated and technically pure, but these people would be thought of—if anybody believed them—as being not only very serious and high-minded but almost devastatingly foolhardy, almost in a class with those who took a chance and gave up everything to go and work in some poor and dangerous country.

The others, the adulterers, were seen as irresponsible, immature, selfish, or even cruel. Also lucky. They were lucky because the sex they had been having in parked cars or the long grass or in each other's sullied marriage beds or most likely in motels like this one must surely have been splendid. Otherwise they would never have got such a yearning for each other's company at all costs or such a faith that their shared future would be altogether better and different in kind from what they had in the past.

Different in kind. That was what Pauline must believe now—that there was this major difference in lives or in marriages or unions between people. That some of them had a necessity, a fatefulness, about them that others did not have. Of course she would have said the same thing a year ago. People did say that, they seemed to believe that, and to believe that their own cases were all of the first, the special kind, even when anybody could see that they were not and that these people did not know what they were talking about. Pauline would not have known what she was talking about.

IT WAS TOO WARM in the room. Jeffrey's body was too warm. Conviction and contentiousness seemed to radiate from it, even in sleep. His torso was thicker than Brian's; he was pudgier around the waist. More flesh on the bones, yet not so slack to the touch. Not so good-looking in general—she was sure most people would say that. And not so fastidious. Brian in bed smelled of nothing. Jeffrey's skin, every time she'd been with him, had had a baked-in, slightly oily or nutty smell. He didn't wash last night—but then, neither did she. There wasn't time. Did he even have a toothbrush with him? She didn't. But she had not known she was staying.

When she met Jeffrey here it was still in the back of her mind that she had to concoct some colossal lie to serve her when she got home. And she—they—had to hurry. When Jeffrey said to her that he had decided that they must stay together, that she would come with him to Washington State, that they would have to drop the play because things would be too difficult for them in Victoria, she had looked at him just in the blank way you'd look at somebody the moment that an earthquake started. She was ready to tell him all the reasons why this was not possible, she still thought she was going to tell him that, but her life was coming adrift in that moment. To go back would be like tying a sack over her head.

All she said was "Are you sure?"

He said, "Sure." He said sincerely, "I'll never leave you."

That did not seem the sort of thing that he would say. Then she realized he was quoting—maybe ironically—from the play. It was what Orphée says to Eurydice within a few moments of their first meeting in the station buffet.

So her life was falling forwards; she was becoming one of those people who ran away. A woman who shockingly and incomprehensibly gave everything up. For love, observers would say wryly. Meaning, for sex. None of this would happen if it wasn't for sex.

And yet what's the great difference there? It's not such a variable procedure, in spite of what you're told. Skins, motions, contact, results. Pauline isn't a woman from whom it's difficult to get results. Brian got them. Probably anybody would, who wasn't wildly inept or morally disgusting.

But nothing's the same, really. With Brian—especially with Brian, to whom she has dedicated a selfish sort of goodwill, with whom she's lived in married complicity—there can never be this stripping away, the inevitable flight, the feelings she doesn't have to strive for but only to give in to like breathing or dying. That she believes can only come when the skin is on Jeffrey, the motions made by Jeffrey, and the weight that bears down on her has Jeffrey's heart in it, also his habits, thoughts, peculiarities, his ambition and loneliness (that for all she knows may have mostly to do with his youth).

For all she knows. There's a lot she doesn't know. She hardly knows anything about what he likes to eat or what music he likes to listen to or what role his mother plays in his life (no doubt a mysterious but important one, like the role of Brian's parents). One thing she's pretty sure of—whatever preferences or prohibitions he has will be definite.

She slides out from under Jeffrey's hand and from under the top sheet which has a harsh smell of bleach, she slips down to the floor where the bedspread is lying and wraps herself quickly in that rag of greenish-yellow chenille. She doesn't want him to open his eyes and see her from behind and note the droop of her buttocks. He's seen her naked before, but generally in a more forgiving moment.

She rinses her mouth and washes herself, using the bar of soap that is about the size of two thin squares of chocolate and firm as stone. She's hard-used between the legs, swollen and stinking. Urinating takes an effort, and it seems she's constipated. Last night when they went out and got hamburgers she found she could not eat. Presumably she'll learn to do all these things again, they'll resume their natural importance in her life. At the moment it's as if she can't quite spare the attention.

She has some money in her purse. She has to go out and buy a toothbrush, toothpaste, deodorant, shampoo. Also vaginal jelly. Last night they used condoms the first two times but nothing the third time.

She didn't bring her watch and Jeffrey doesn't wear one. There's no clock in the room, of course. She thinks it's early—there's still an early look to the light in spite of the heat. The stores probably won't be open, but there'll be someplace where she can get coffee.

Jeffrey has turned onto his other side. She must have wakened him, just for a moment.

They'll have a bedroom. A kitchen, an address. He'll go to work. She'll go to the Laundromat. Maybe she'll go to work too. Selling things, waiting on tables, tutoring students. She knows French and Latin—do they teach French and Latin in American high schools? Can you get a job if you're not an American? Jeffrey isn't.

She leaves him the key. She'll have to wake him to get back in. There's nothing to write a note with, or on.

It is early. The motel is on the highway at the north end of town, beside the bridge. There's no traffic yet. She scuffs along under the cottonwood trees for quite a while before a vehicle of any kind rumbles over the bridge—though the traffic on it shook their bed regularly late into the night.

Something is coming now. A truck. But not just a truck—there's a large bleak fact coming at her. And it has not arrived out of nowhere—it's been waiting, cruelly nudging at her ever since she woke up, or even all night.

Caitlin and Mara.

Last night on the phone, after speaking in such a flat and controlled and almost agreeable voice—as if he prided himself on not being shocked, not objecting or pleading—Brian cracked open. He said with contempt and fury and no concern for whoever might hear him, "Well then—what about the kids?"

The receiver began to shake against Pauline's ear.

She said, "We'll talk—" but he did not seem to hear her.

"The children," he said, in this same shivering and vindictive voice. Changing the word "kids" to "children" was like slamming a board down on her—a heavy, formal, righteous threat.

"The children stay," Brian said. "Pauline. Did you hear me?"

"No," said Pauline. "Yes. I heard you but—"

"All right. You heard me. Remember. The children stay."

It was all he could do. To make her see what she was doing, what she was ending, and to punish her if she did so. Nobody would blame him. There might be finagling, there might be bargaining, there would certainly be humbling of herself, but there it was like a round cold stone in her gullet, like a cannonball. And it would remain there unless she changed her mind entirely. The children stay.

Their car—hers and Brian's—was still sitting in the motel parking lot. Brian would have to ask his father or his mother to drive him up here today to get it. She had the keys in her purse. There were spare keys—he would surely bring them. She unlocked the car door and threw her keys on the seat and locked the door on the inside and shut it.

Now she couldn't go back. She couldn't get into the car and drive back and say that she'd been insane. If she did that he would forgive her, but he'd never get over it and neither would she. They'd go on, though, as people did.

She walked out of the parking lot, she walked along the sidewalk, into town.

The weight of Mara on her hip, yesterday. The sight of Caitlin's footprints on the floor.

Paw. Paw.

She doesn't need the keys to get back to them, she doesn't need the car. She could beg a ride on the highway. Give in, give in, get back to them any way at all, how can she not do that?

A sack over her head.

A fluid choice, the choice of fantasy, is poured out on the ground and instantly hardens; it has taken its undeniable shape.

THIS IS ACUTE PAIN. It will become chronic. Chronic means that it will be permanent but perhaps not constant. It may also mean that you won't die of it. You won't get free of it, but you won't die of it. You won't feel it every minute, but you won't spend many days without it. And you'll learn some tricks to dull it or banish it, trying not to end up destroying what you incurred this pain to get. It isn't his fault. He's still an innocent or a savage, who doesn't know there's a pain so durable in the world. Say to yourself, You lose them anyway. They grow up. For a mother there's always waiting this private slightly ridiculous desolation. They'll forget this time, in one way or another they'll disown you. Or hang around till you don't know what to do about them, the way Brian has.

And still, what pain. To carry along and get used to until it's only the past she's grieving for and not any possible present.

HER CHILDREN HAVE GROWN UP. They don't hate her. For going away or staying away. They don't forgive her, either. Perhaps they wouldn't have forgiven her anyway, but it would have been for something different.

Caitlin remembers a little about the summer at the lodge, Mara nothing. One day Caitlin mentions it to Pauline, calling it "that place Grandma and Grandpa stayed at.

"The place we were at when you went away," she says. "Only we didn't know till later you went away with Orphée."

Pauline says, "It wasn't Orphée."

"It wasn't Orphée? Dad used to say it was. He'd say, 'And then your mother ran away with Orphée.'"

"Then he was joking," says Pauline.

"I always thought it was Orphée. It was somebody else then."

"It was somebody else connected with the play. That I lived with for a while."

"Not Orphée."

"No. Never him."

My Mother's Dream

~

DURING THE NIGHT—or during the time she had been asleep—
there had been a heavy fall of snow.

My mother looked out from a big arched window such as you
find in a mansion or an old-fashioned public building. She looked
down on lawns and shrubs, hedges, flower gardens, trees, all covered by snow that lay in heaps and cushions, not levelled or disturbed by wind. The white of it did not hurt your eyes as it does
in sunlight. The white was the white of snow under a clear sky just
before dawn. Everything was still; it was like "O Little Town of
Bethlehem" except that the stars had gone out.

Yet something was wrong. There was a mistake in this scene. All
the trees, all the shrubs and plants, were out in full summer leaf.
The grass that showed underneath them, in spots sheltered from
the snow, was fresh and green. Snow had settled overnight on the
luxury of summer. A change of season unexplainable, unexpected.
Also, everybody had gone away—though she couldn't think who
"everybody" was—and my mother was alone in the high spacious
house amongst its rather formal trees and gardens.

She thought that whatever had happened would soon be made
known to her. Nobody came, however. The telephone did not ring;
the latch of the garden gate was not lifted. She could not hear any
traffic, and she did not even know which way the street was—or
the road, if she was out in the country. She had to get out of the
house, where the air was so heavy and settled.

When she got outside she remembered. She remembered that
she had left a baby out there somewhere, before the snow had
fallen. Quite a while before the snow had fallen. This memory, this
certainty, came over her with horror. It was as if she was awakening
from a dream. Within her dream she awakened from a dream, to a
knowledge of her responsibility and mistake. She had left her baby

out overnight, she had forgotten about it. Left it exposed somewhere as if it was a doll she tired of. And perhaps it was not last
night but a week or a month ago that she had done this. For a whole
season or for many seasons she had left her baby out. She had been
occupied in other ways. She might even have travelled away from
here and just returned, forgetting what she was returning to.

She went around looking under hedges and broad-leaved plants.
She foresaw how the baby would be shrivelled up. It would be dead,
shrivelled and brown, its head like a nut, and on its tiny shut-up
face there would be an expression not of distress but of bereave-
ment, an old patient grief. There would not be any accusation of
her, its mother—just the look of patience and helplessness with
which it waited for its rescue or its fate.

The sorrow that came to my mother was the sorrow of the baby's
waiting and not knowing it waited for her, its only hope, when she
had forgotten all about it. So small and new a baby that could not
even turn away from the snow. She could hardly breathe for her
sorrow. There would never be any room in her for anything else.
No room for anything but the realization of what she had done.

What a reprieve, then, to find her baby lying in its crib. Lying
on its stomach, its head turned to one side, its skin pale and sweet
as snowdrops and the down on its head reddish like the dawn. Red
hair like her own, on her perfectly safe and unmistakable baby.
The joy to find herself forgiven.

The snow and the leafy gardens and the strange house had all
withdrawn. The only remnant of the whiteness was the blanket
in the crib. A baby blanket of light white wool, crumpled halfway
down the baby's back. In the heat, the real summer heat, the baby
was wearing only a diaper and a pair of plastic pants to keep the
sheet dry. The plastic pants had a pattern of butterflies.

My mother, still thinking no doubt about the snow and the cold
that usually accompanies snow, pulled the blanket up to cover the
baby's bare back and shoulders, its red-downed head.

IT IS EARLY MORNING when this happens in the real world.
The world of July 1945. At a time when, on any other morning, it
would be demanding its first feeding of the day, the baby sleeps
on. The mother, though standing on her feet and with her eyes

open, is still too far deep in sleep in her head to wonder about this. Baby and mother are worn out by a long battle, and the mother has forgotten even that at the moment. Some circuits are closed down; the most unrelenting quiet has settled on her brain and her baby's. The mother—my mother—makes no sense of the daylight which is increasing every moment. She doesn't understand that the sun is coming up as she stands there. No memory of the day before, or of what happened around midnight, comes up to jolt her. She pulls the blanket up over her baby's head, over its mild, satisfied, sleeping profile. She pads back to her own room and falls down on the bed and is again, at once, unconscious.

The house in which this happens is nothing like the house in the dream. It is a one-and-a-half-story white wooden house, cramped but respectable, with a porch that comes to within a few feet of the sidewalk, and a bay window in the dining room looking out on a small hedged yard. It is on a backstreet in a small town that is indistinguishable—to an outsider—from a lot of other small towns to be found ten or fifteen miles apart in the once thickly populated farmland near Lake Huron. My father and his sisters grew up in this house, and the sisters and mother were still living here when my mother joined them—and I joined them too, being large and lively inside her—after my father was killed in the final weeks of the war in Europe.

MY MOTHER—Jill—is standing beside the dining-room table in the bright late afternoon. The house is full of people who have been invited back there after the memorial service in the church. They are drinking tea or coffee and managing to hold in their fingers the dinky sandwiches, or slices of banana bread, nut loaf, pound cake. The custard tarts or raisin tarts with their crumbly pastry are supposed to be eaten with a dessert fork off one of the small china plates that were painted with violets by Jill's mother-in-law when she was a bride. Jill picks everything up with her fingers. Pastry crumbs have fallen, a raisin has fallen, and been smeared into the green velvet of her dress. It's too hot a dress for the day, and it's not a maternity dress at all but a loose sort of robe made for recitals, occasions when she plays her violin in public. The hem rides up in front, due to me. But it's the only thing she owns that is large enough and good enough for her to wear at her husband's memorial service.

What is this eating all about? People can't help but notice. "Eating for two," Ailsa says to a group of her guests, so that they won't get the better of her by anything they say or don't say about her sister-in-law.

Jill has been queasy all day, until suddenly in the church, when she was thinking how bad the organ was, she realized that she was, all of a sudden, as hungry as a wolf. All through "O Valiant Hearts" she was thinking of a fat hamburger dripping with meat juice and melted mayonnaise, and now she is trying to find what concoction of walnuts and raisins and brown sugar, what tooth-jabbing sweetness of coconut icing or soothing mouthful of banana bread or dollop of custard, will do as a substitute. Nothing will, of course, but she keeps on going. When her real hunger is satisfied her imaginary hunger is still working, and even more an irritability amounting almost to panic that makes her stuff into her mouth what she can hardly taste any longer. She couldn't describe this irritability except to say it has something to do with furriness and tightness. The barberry hedge outside the window, thick and bristling in the sunlight, the feel of the velvet dress clinging to her damp armpits, the nosegays of curls—the same color as the raisins in the tarts—bunched on her sister-in-law Ailsa's head, even the painted violets that look like scabs you could pick off the plate, all these things seem particularly horrid and oppressive to her though she knows they are quite ordinary. They seem to carry some message about her new and unexpected life.

Why unexpected? She has known for some time about me and she also knew that George Kirkham might be killed. He was in the air force, after all. (And around her in the Kirkhams' house this afternoon people are saying—though not to her, his widow, or to his sisters—that he was just the sort you always knew would be killed. They mean because he was good-looking and high-spirited and the pride of his family, the one on whom all the hopes had been pinned.) She knew this, but she went ahead with her ordinary life, lugging her violin onto the streetcar on dark winter mornings, riding to the Conservatory where she practiced hour after hour within sound of others but alone in a dingy room with the radiator racket for company, the skin of her hands blotchy at first with the cold, then parched in the dry indoor heat. She went on living in a rented room with an ill-fitting window that let in flies in summer and a windowsill sprinkle of snow in winter, and dreaming—when she wasn't sick—of sausages and meat pies and dark chunks of chocolate. At the Conservatory people treated her pregnancy tactfully, as if it was a tumor. It didn't show for a long time anyway, as first pregnancies generally don't on a big girl with a broad pelvis. Even with me turning somersaults she played in public. Majestically thickened, with her long red hair lying in a bush around her shoulders, her face broad and glowing, her expression full of somber concentration, she played a solo in her most important recital so far. The Mendelssohn Violin Concerto.

She paid some attention to the world—she knew the war was ending. She thought that George might be back soon after I was born. She knew that she wouldn't be able to go on living in her room then—she'd have to live somewhere with him. And she knew that I'd be there, but she thought of my birth as bringing something to an end rather than starting something. It would bring an end to the kicking in the permanent sore spot on one side of her belly and the ache in her genitals when she stands up and the blood rushes into them (as if she'd had a burning poultice laid there). Her nipples will no longer be large and dark and nubbly, and she won't have to wind bandages around her legs with their swollen veins before she gets out of bed every morning. She won't have to urinate every half hour or so, and her feet will shrink back into their ordinary shoes. She thinks that once I'm out I won't give her so much trouble.

After she knew that George would not be coming back she thought about keeping me for a while in that same room. She got a book about babies. She bought the basic things that I would need. There was an old woman in the building who could look after me while she practiced. She would get a war widow's pension and in six more months she would graduate from the Conservatory.

Then Ailsa came down on the train and collected her. Ailsa said, "We couldn't leave you stuck down here all by yourself. Everybody wonders why you didn't come up when George went overseas. It's time you came now."

* * *

"MY FAMILY'S CRACKERS," George had told Jill. "Iona's a nervous wreck and Ailsa should have been a sergeant major. And my mother's senile."

He also said, "Ailsa got the brains, but she had to quit school and go and work in the Post Office when my dad died. I got the looks and there wasn't anything left for poor old Iona but the bad skin and the bad nerves."

Jill met his sisters for the first time when they came to Toronto to see George off. They hadn't been at the wedding, which had taken place two weeks before. Nobody was there but George and Jill and the minister and the minister's wife and a neighbor called in to be the second witness. I was there as well, already tucked up inside Jill, but I was not the reason for the wedding and at the time nobody knew of my existence. Afterwards George insisted that he and Jill take some poker-faced wedding pictures of themselves in one of those do-it-yourself picture booths. He was in relentless high spirits. "That'll fix them," he said, when he looked at the pictures. Jill wondered if there was anybody special he meant to fix. Ailsa? Or the pretty girls, the cute and perky girls, who had 'run after him, writing him sentimental letters and knitting him argyle socks? He wore the socks when he could, he pocketed the presents, and he read the letters out in bars for a joke.

Jill had not had any breakfast before the wedding, and in the midst of it she was thinking of pancakes and bacon.

THE TWO SISTERS were more normal-looking than she had expected. Though it was true about George getting the looks. He had a silky wave to his dark-blond hair and a hard gleeful glint in his eyes and a clean-cut enviable set of features. His only drawback was that he was not very tall. Just tall enough to look Jill in the eye. And to be an air force pilot.

"They don't want tall guys for pilots," he said. "I beat them out there. The beanpole bastards. Lots of guys in the movies are short. They stand on boxes for the kissing."

(At the movies, George could be boisterous. He might hiss the kissing. He didn't go in for it much in real life either. Let's get to the action, he said.)

The sisters were short, too. They were named after places in Scotland, where their parents had gone on their honeymoon before the family lost its money. Ailsa was twelve years older than George, and Iona was nine years older. In the crowd at Union Station they looked dumpy and bewildered. Both of them wore new hats and suits, as if they were the ones who had recently been married. And both were upset because Iona had left her good gloves on the train. It was true that Iona had bad skin, though it wasn't broken out at present and perhaps her acne days were over. It was lumpy with old scars and dingy under the pink powder. Her hair slipped out in droopy tendrils from under her hat and her eyes were teary, either because of Ailsa's scolding or because her brother was going away to war. Ailsa's hair was arranged in bunches of tight permanented curls, with her hat riding on top. She had shrewd pale eyes behind sparkle-rimmed glasses, and round pink cheeks, and a dimpled chin. Both she and Iona had tidy figures—high breasts and small waists and flaring hips—but on Iona this figure looked like something she had picked up by mistake and was trying to hide by stooping her shoulders and crossing her arms. Ailsa managed her curves assertively not provocatively, as if she was made of some sturdy ceramic. And both of them had George's dark-blond coloring, but without his gleam. They didn't seem to share his sense of humor either.

"Well I'm off," George said. "I'm off to die a hero on the field at Passchendaele." And Iona said, "Oh don't say that. Don't talk like that." Ailsa twitched her raspberry mouth.

"I can see the lost-and-found sign from here," she said. "But I don't know if that's just for things you lose in the station or is it for things that they find in the trains? Passchendaele was in the First World War."

"Was it? You sure? I'm too late?" said George, beating his hand on his chest.

And he was burned up a few months later in a training flight over the Irish Sea.

·   ·   ·

AILSA SMILES all the time. She says, "Well of course I am proud. I am. But I'm not the only one to lose somebody. He did what he had to do." Some people find her briskness a bit shocking. But others say, "Poor Ailsa." All that concentrating on George, and saving to send him to law school, and then he flouted her—he signed up; he went off and got himself killed. He couldn't wait.

His sisters sacrificed their own schooling. Even getting their teeth straightened—they sacrificed that. Iona did go to nursing school, but as it turned out getting her teeth fixed would have served her better. Now she and Ailsa have ended up with a hero. Everybody grants it—a hero. The younger people present think it's something to have a hero in the family. They think the importance of this moment will last, that it will stay with Ailsa and Iona forever. "O Valiant Hearts" will soar around them forever. Older people, those who remember the previous war, know that all they've ended up with is a name on the cenotaph. Because the widow, the girl feeding her face, will get the pension.

Ailsa is in a hectic mood partly because she has been up two nights in a row, cleaning. Not that the house wasn't decently clean before. Nevertheless she felt the need to wash every dish, pot, and ornament, polish the glass on every picture, pull out the fridge and scrub behind it, wash the cellar steps off, and pour bleach in the garbage can. The very lighting fixture overhead, over the dining-room table, had to be taken apart, and every piece on it dunked in soapy water, rinsed, and rubbed dry and reassembled. And because of her work at the Post Office Ailsa couldn't start this till after supper. She is the postmistress now, she could have given herself a day off, but being Ailsa she would never do that.

Now she's hot under her rouge, twitchy in her dark-blue lace-collared crepe dress. She can't stay still. She refills the serving plates and passes them around, deplores the fact that people's tea may have got cold, hurries to make a fresh pot. Mindful of her guests' comfort, asking after their rheumatism or minor ailments, smiling in the face of her tragedy, repeating over and over again that hers is a common loss, that she must not complain when so many others are in the same boat, that George would not want his friends to grieve but to be thankful that all together we have ended the war. All in a high and emphatic voice of cheerful reproof that people are used to from the Post Office. So that they are left with an uncertain feeling of perhaps having said the wrong thing, just as in the Post Office they may be made to understand that their handwriting cannot help but be a trial or their packages are done up sloppily.

Ailsa is aware that her voice is too high and that she is smiling too much and that she has poured out tea for people who said they didn't want any more. In the kitchen, while warming the teapot, she says, "I don't know what's the matter with me. I'm all wound up."

The person she says this to is Dr. Shantz, her neighbor across the backyard.

"It'll soon be over," he says. "Would you like a bromide?"

His voice undergoes a change as the door from the dining room opens. The word "bromide" comes out firm and professional.

Ailsa's voice changes too, from forlorn to valiant. She says, "Oh, no thank you. I'll just try and keep going on my own."

IONA'S JOB is supposed to be to watch over their mother, to see that she doesn't spill her tea—which she may do not out of clumsiness but forgetfulness—and that she is taken away if she starts to sniffle and cry. But in fact Mrs. Kirkham's manners are gracious most of the time and she puts people at ease more readily than Ailsa does. For a quarter of an hour at a time she understands the situation—or she seems to—and she speaks bravely and cogently about how she will always miss her son but is grateful she still has her daughters: Ailsa so efficient and reliable, a wonder as she's always been, and Iona the soul of kindness. She even remembers to speak of her new daughter-in-law but perhaps gives a hint of being out of line when she mentions what most women of her age don't mention at a social gathering, and with men listening. Looking at Jill and me, she says, "And we all have a comfort to come."

Then passing from room to room or guest to guest, she forgets entirely, she looks around her own house and says, "Why are we here? What a lot of people—what are we celebrating?" And catching on to the fact that it all has something to do with George, she says, "Is it George's wedding?" Along with her up-to-date information she has lost some of her mild discretion. "It's not your wedding, is it?" she says to Iona. "No. I didn't think so. You never had a boyfriend, did you?" A let's-face-facts, devil-take-the-hindmost note has come into her voice. When she spots Jill she laughs. "That's not the bride, is it? Oh-oh. Now we understand."

But the truth comes back to her as suddenly as it went away.

"Is there news?" she says. "News about George?" And it's then that the weeping starts that Ailsa was afraid of.

"Get her out of the way if she starts making a spectacle," Ailsa had said.

Iona isn't able to get her mother out of the way—she has never been able to exert authority over anybody in her life—but Dr. Shantz's wife catches the old woman's arm.

"George is dead?" says Mrs. Kirkham fearfully, and Mrs. Shantz says, "Yes he is. But you know his wife is having a baby."

Mrs. Kirkham leans against her; she crumples and says softly, "Could I have my tea?"

EVERYWHERE my mother turns in that house, it seems she sees a picture of my father. The last and official one, of him in his uniform, sits on an embroidered runner on the closed sewing machine in the bay of the dining-room window. Iona puts flowers around it, but Ailsa took them away. She said it made him look too much like a Catholic saint. Hanging above the stairs there is one of him at six years old, out on the sidewalk, with his knee in his wagon, and in the room where Jill sleeps there's one of him beside his bicycle, with his *Free Press* newspaper sack. Mrs. Kirkham's room has the one of him dressed for the grade-eight operetta, with a gold cardboard crown on his head. Being unable to carry a tune, he couldn't have a leading role, but he was of course picked for the best background role, that of the king.

The hand-tinted studio photo over the buffet shows him at the age of three, a blurred blond tot dragging a rag doll by one leg. Ailsa thought of taking that down because it might seem tearjerking, but she left it up rather than show a bright patch on the wallpaper. And no one said anything about it but Mrs. Shantz, who paused and said what she had said sometimes before, and not tearfully but with a faintly amused appreciation.

"Ah—Christopher Robin."

People were used to not paying much attention to what Mrs. Shantz said.

In all of his pictures George looks bright as a dollar. There's always a sunny dip of hair over his brow, unless he's wearing his officer's hat or his crown. And even when he was little more than an infant he looked as if he knew himself to be a capering, calculating, charming sort of fellow. The sort who never let people alone, who whipped them up to laugh. At his own expense occasionally, but usually at other people's. Jill recalls when she looks at him how he drank but never seemed drunk and how he occupied himself getting other drunk people to confess to him their fears, prevarications, virginity, or two-timing, which he would then turn into jokes or humiliating nicknames that his victims pretended to enjoy. For he had legions of followers and friends, who maybe latched on to him out of fear—or maybe just because, as was always said of him, he livened things up. Wherever he was was the center of the room, and the air around him crackled with risk and merriment.

What was Jill to make of such a lover? She was nineteen when she met him, and nobody had ever claimed her before. She couldn't understand what attracted him, and she could see that nobody else could understand it, either. She was a puzzle to most people of her own age, but a dull puzzle. A girl whose life was given over to the study of the violin and who had no other interests.

That was not quite true. She would snuggle under her shabby quilts and imagine a lover. But he was never a shining cutup like George. She thought of some warm and bearlike fellow, or of a musician a decade older than herself and already legendary, with a fierce potency. Her notions of love were operatic, though that was not the sort of music she most admired. But George made jokes when he made love; he pranced around her room when he had finished; he made rude and infantile noises. His brisk performances brought her little of the pleasure she knew from her assaults on herself, but she was not exactly disappointed.

Dazed at the speed of things was more like it. And expecting to be happy—grateful and happy—when her mind caught up with physical and social reality. George's attentions, and her marriage—those were all like a brilliant extension of her life. Lighted rooms showing up full of a bewildering sort of splendor.

Then came the bomb or the hurricane, the not unlikely stroke of disaster, and the whole extension was gone. Blown up and vanished, leaving her with the same space and options she'd had before. She had lost something, certainly. But not something she had really got hold of, or understood as more than a hypothetical layout of the future.

She has had enough to eat, now. Her legs ache from standing so long. Mrs. Shantz is beside her, saying, "Have you had a chance to meet any of George's local friends?"

She means the young people keeping to themselves in the hall doorway. A couple of nice-looking girls, a young man still wearing a naval uniform, others. Looking at them, Jill thinks clearly that no one is really sorry. Ailsa perhaps, but Ailsa has her own reasons. No one is really sorry George is dead. Not even the girl who was crying in church and looks as if she will cry some more. Now that girl can remember that she was in love with George and think that he was in love with her—in spite of all—and never be afraid of what he may do or say to prove her wrong. And none of them will have to wonder, when a group of people clustered around George have started laughing, whom they are laughing at or what George is telling them. Nobody will have to strain to keep up with him or figure out how to stay in his good graces anymore.

It doesn't occur to her that if he had lived George might have become a different person, because she doesn't think of becoming a different person herself.

She says, "No," with a lack of enthusiasm that causes Mrs. Shantz to say, "I know. It's hard meeting new people. Particularly—if I was you I would rather go and lie down."

Jill was almost sure she was going to say "go and have a drink." But there's nothing being offered here, only tea and coffee. Jill hardly drinks anyway. She can recognize the smell on someone's breath, though, and she thought she smelled it on Mrs. Shantz.

"Why don't you?" says Mrs. Shantz. "These things are a great strain. I'll tell Ailsa. Go on now."

MRS. SHANTZ is a small woman with fine gray hair, bright eyes, and a wrinkled, pointed face. Every winter she spends a month by herself in Florida. She has money. The house that she and her husband built for themselves, behind the Kirkhams' house, is long and low and blindingly white, with curved corners and expanses of glass bricks. Dr. Shantz is twenty or twenty-five years younger than she is—a thickset, fresh, and amiable-looking man with a high smooth forehead and fair curly hair. They have no children. It is believed that she has some, from a first marriage, but they don't come to visit her. In fact the story is that Dr. Shantz was her son's friend, brought home from college, and that he fell in love with his friend's mother, she fell in love with her son's friend, there was a divorce, and here they are married, living in luxurious, close-mouthed exile.

Jill did smell whiskey. Mrs. Shantz carries a flask whenever she goes to a gathering of which—as she says—she can have no reasonable hopes. Drink does not make her fall about or garble her words or pick fights or throw her arms about people. The truth may be that she's always a little bit drunk but never really drunk. She is used to letting the alcohol enter her body in a reasonable, reassuring way, so that her brain cells never get soaked or quite dried out. The only giveaway is the smell (which many people in this dry town attribute to some medicine she has to take or even to an ointment that she has to rub on her chest). That, and perhaps a deliberateness about her speech, the way she seems to clear a space around each word. She says things of course which a woman brought up around here would not say. She tells things on herself. She tells about being mistaken every once in a while for her husband's mother. She says most people go into a tailspin when they discover their mistake, they're so embarrassed. But some women—a waitress, maybe—will fasten on Mrs. Shantz quite a dirty look, as if to say, What's he doing wasted on you?

And Mrs. Shantz just says to them, "I know. It isn't fair. But life isn't fair and you might as well get used to it."

There isn't any way this afternoon that she can space her sips properly. The kitchen and even the poky pantry behind it are places where women can be coming and going at any time. She has to go upstairs to the bathroom, and that not too often. When she does that late in the afternoon, a little while after Jill has disappeared, she finds the bathroom door locked. She thinks of nipping into one of the bedrooms and is wondering which one is empty, which occupied by Jill. Then she hears Jill's voice coming from the bath-room, saying, "Just a minute," or something like that. Something quite ordinary, but the tone of voice is strained and frightened.

Mrs. Shantz takes a quick swallow right there in the hall, seizing the excuse of emergency.

"Jill? Are you all right? Can you let me in?"

Jill is on her hands and knees, trying to mop up the puddle on the bathroom floor. She has read about the water breaking—just as she has read about contractions, show, transition stage, placenta—but just the same the escape of warm fluid surprised her. She has to use toilet paper, because Ailsa took all the regular towels away and put out the smooth scraps of embroidered linen called guest towels.

She holds on to the rim of the tub to pull herself up. She unbolts the door and that's when the first pain astonishes her. She is not to have a single mild pain, or any harbingers or orchestrated first stage of labor; it's all to be an unsparing onslaught and ripping headlong delivery.

"Easy," says Mrs. Shantz, supporting her as well as she can. "Just tell me which room is yours, we'll get you lying down."

Before they even reach the bed Jill's fingers dig into Mrs. Shantz's thin arm to leave it black and blue.

"Oh, this is fast," Mrs. Shantz says. "This is a real mover and shaker for a first baby. I'm going to get my husband."

In that way I was born right in the house, about ten days early if Jill's calculations were to be relied on. Ailsa had barely time to get the company cleared out before the place was filled with Jill's noise, her disbelieving cries and the great shameless grunts that followed.

Even if a mother had been taken by surprise and had given birth at home, it was usual by that time to move her and the baby into the hospital afterwards. But there was some sort of summer flu in town, and the hospital had filled up with the worst cases, so Dr. Shantz decided that Jill and I would be better off at home. Iona after all had finished part of her nurse's training, and she could take her two-week holiday now, to look after us.

JILL REALLY KNEW NOTHING about living in a family. She had grown up in an orphanage. From the age of six to sixteen she had slept in a dormitory. Lights turned on and off at a specified time, furnace never operating before or beyond a specified date. A long oilcloth-covered table where they ate and did their homework, a factory across the street. George had liked the sound of that. It would make a girl tough, he said. It would make her self-possessed, hard and solitary. It would make her the sort who would not expect any romantic nonsense. But the place had not been run in such a heartless way as perhaps he thought, and the people who ran it had not been ungenerous. Jill was taken to a concert, with some others, when she was twelve years old, and there she decided that she must learn to play the violin. She had already fooled around with the piano at the orphanage. Somebody took enough interest to get her a secondhand, very second-rate violin, and a few lessons, and this led, finally, to a scholarship at the Conservatory. There was a recital for patrons and directors, a party with best dresses, fruit punch, speeches, and cakes. Jill had to make a little speech herself, expressing gratitude, but the truth was that she took all this pretty much for granted. She was sure that she and some violin were naturally, fatefully connected, and would have come together without human help.

In the dormitory she had friends, but they went off early to factories and offices and she forgot about them. At the high school that the orphans were sent to, a teacher had a talk with her. The words "normal" and "well rounded" came up in the talk. The teacher seemed to think that music was an escape from something or a substitute for something. For sisters and brothers and friends and dates. She suggested that Jill spread her energy around instead of concentrating on one thing. Loosen up, play volleyball, join the school orchestra if music was what she wanted.

Jill started to avoid that particular teacher, climbing the stairs or going round the block so as not to have to speak to her. Just as she stopped reading any page from which the words "well rounded" or the word "popular" leapt out at her.

At the Conservatory it was easier. There she met people quite as un–well rounded, as hard driven, as herself. She formed a few rather absentminded and competitive friendships. One of her friends had an older brother who was in the air force, and this brother happened to be a victim and worshipper of George Kirkham's. He and George dropped in on a family Sunday-night supper, at which Jill was a guest. They were on their way to get drunk somewhere else. And that was how George met Jill. My father met my mother.

THERE HAD TO BE SOMEBODY at home all the time, to watch Mrs. Kirkham. So Iona worked the night shift at the bakery. She decorated cakes—even the fanciest wedding cakes—and she got the first round of bread loaves in the oven at five o'clock. Her hands, which shook so badly that she could not serve anybody a teacup, were strong and clever and patient, even inspired, at any solitary job.

One morning after Ailsa had gone off to work—this was during the short time that Jill was in the house before I was born—Iona hissed from the bedroom as Jill was going by. As if there was a secret. But who was there now in the house to keep a secret from? It couldn't be Mrs. Kirkham.

Iona had to struggle to get a stuck drawer of her bureau open. "Darn," she said, and giggled. "Darn it. There."

The drawer was full of baby clothes—not plain necessary shirts and nightgowns such as Jill had bought at a shop that sold seconds, factory rejects, in Toronto, but knitted bonnets, sweaters and bootees and soakers, handmade tiny gowns. All possible pastel colors or combinations of colors—no blue or pink prejudice—with crocheted trimming and minute embroidered flowers and birds and lambs. The sort of stuff that Jill had barely known existed. She would have known, if she had done any thorough research in baby departments or peering into baby carriages, but she hadn't.

"Of course I don't know what you've got," Iona said. "You may have got so many things already, or maybe you don't like home-made, I don't know—" Her giggling was a kind of punctuation of speech and it was also an extension of her tone of apology. Everything she said, every look and gesture, seemed to be clogged up, overlaid with a sticky honey or snuffled mucus of apology, and Jill did not know how to deal with this.

"It's really nice," she said flatly.

"Oh no, I didn't know if you'd even want it. I didn't know if you'd like it at all."

"It's lovely."

"I didn't do it all, I bought some of it. I went to the church bazaar and the Hospital Auxiliary, their bazaar, I just thought it would be nice, but if you don't like it or maybe you don't need it I can just put it in the Missionary Bale."

"I do need it," Jill said. "I haven't got anything like this at all."

"Haven't you really? What I did isn't so good, but maybe what the church ladies did or the Auxiliary, maybe you'd think that was all right."

Was this what George had meant about Iona's being a nervous wreck? (According to Ailsa, her breakdown at the nursing school had been caused by her being a bit too thin-skinned and the supervisor's being a bit too hard on her.) You might think she was clamoring for reassurance, but whatever reassurance you tried seemed to be not enough, or not to get through to her. Jill felt as if Iona's words and giggles and sniffles and damp looks (no doubt she had damp hands as well) were things crawling on her—on Jill—mites trying to get under her skin.

But this was something she got used to, in time. Or Iona toned it down. Both she and Iona felt relief—it was as if a teacher had gone out of the room—when the door closed behind Ailsa in the morning. They took to having a second cup of coffee, while Mrs. Kirkham washed the dishes. She did this job very slowly—looking around for the drawer or shelf where each item should go—and with some lapses. But with rituals, too, which she never omitted, such as scattering the coffee grounds on a bush by the kitchen door.

"She thinks the coffee makes it grow," Iona whispered. "Even if she puts it on the leaves not the ground. Every day we have to take the hose and rinse it off."

Jill thought that Iona sounded like the girls who were most picked on at the orphanage. They were always eager to pick on somebody else. But once you got Iona past her strung-out apologies or barricades of humble accusations ("Of course I'm the last person they'd consult about anything down at the shop," "Of course Ailsa wouldn't listen to my opinion," "Of course George never made any secret about how he despised me") you might get her to talk about fairly interesting things. She told Jill about the house that had been their grandfather's and was now the center wing of the hospital, about the specific shady deals that had lost their father his job, and about a romance that was going on between two married people at the bakery. She also mentioned the supposed previous history of the Shantzes, and even the fact that Ailsa was soft on Dr. Shantz. The shock treatment Iona had had after her nervous breakdown seemed perhaps to have blown a hole in her discretion, and the voice that came through this hole—once the disguising rubbish had been cleared away—was baleful and sly.

And Jill might as well spend her time chatting—her fingers had got too puffy now to try to play the violin.

AND THEN I WAS BORN and everything changed, especially for Iona.

Jill had to stay in bed for a week, and even after she got up she moved like a stiff old woman and breathed warily each time she lowered herself into a chair. She was all painfully stitched together, and her stomach and breasts were bound tight as a mummy's—that was the custom then. Her milk came in plentifully; it was leaking through the binding and onto the sheets. Iona loosened the binding and tried to connect the nipple to my mouth. But I would not take it. I refused to take my mother's breast. I screamed blue murder. The big stiff breast might just as well have been a snouted beast rummaging in my face. Iona held me, she gave me a little warm boiled water, and I quieted down. I was losing weight, though. I couldn't live on water. So Iona mixed up a formula and took me out of Jill's arms where I stiffened and wailed. Iona rocked and soothed me and touched my cheek with the rubber nipple and that turned out to be what I preferred. I drank the formula greedily and kept it down. Iona's arms and the nipple that she was in charge of became my chosen home. Jill's breasts had to be bound even tighter, and she had to forgo liquids (remember, this was in the hot weather) and endure the ache until her milk dried up.

"What a monkey, what a monkey," crooned Iona. "You are a monkey, you don't want your mommy's good milk."

I soon got fatter and stronger. I could cry louder. I cried if anybody but Iona tried to hold me. I rejected Ailsa and Dr. Shantz with his thoughtfully warmed hands, but of course it was my aversion to Jill that got the most attention.

Once Jill was out of bed Iona got her sitting in the chair where she herself usually sat to feed me; she put her own blouse around Jill's shoulders and the bottle in Jill's hand.

No use, I was not fooled. I batted my cheek against the bottle and straightened my legs and hardened my abdomen into a ball. I would not accept the substitution. I cried. I would not give in.

My cries were still thin new-baby cries, but they were a disturbance in the house, and Iona was the only person who had the power to stop them. Touched or spoken to by a non-Iona, I cried. Put down to sleep, not rocked by Iona, I cried myself into exhaustion and slept for ten minutes and woke ready to go at it again. I had no good times or fussy times. I had the Iona-times and the Iona-desertion-times, which might become—oh, worse and worse—the other-people-times, mostly Jill-times.

How could Iona go back to work, then, once her two weeks were up? She couldn't. There wasn't any question of it. The bakery had to get someone else. Iona had gone from being the most negligible to being the most important person in the house; she was the one who stood between those who lived there and constant discordance, unanswerable complaint. She had to be up at all hours to keep the household in any sort of ease. Dr. Shantz was concerned; even Ailsa was concerned.

"Iona, don't wear yourself out."

And yet a wonderful change had taken place. Iona was pale but her skin glowed, as if she had finally passed out of adolescence. She could look anybody in the eye. And there was no more trembling, hardly any giggling, no sly cringing in her voice, which had grown as bossy as Ailsa's and more joyful. (Never more joyful than when she was scolding me for my attitude to Jill.)

"Iona's in seventh heaven—she just adores that baby," Ailsa told people. But in fact Iona's behavior seemed too brisk for adoration. She did not care how much noise she made, quelling mine. She tore up the stairs calling breathlessly, "I'm coming, I'm coming, hold your horses." She would walk around with me carelessly plastered to her shoulder, held with one hand, while the other hand accomplished some task connected with my maintenance. She ruled in the kitchen, commandeering the stove for the sterilizer, the table for the mixing of the formula, the sink for the baby wash. She swore cheerfully, even in Ailsa's presence, when she had misplaced or spilled something.

She knew herself to be the only person who didn't wince, who didn't feel the distant threat of annihilation, when I sent up my first signal wail. Instead, she was the one whose heart jumped into double time, who felt like dancing, just from the sense of power she had, and gratitude.

Once her bindings were off and she'd seen the flatness of her stomach, Jill took a look at her hands. The puffiness seemed to be all gone. She went downstairs and got her violin out of the closet and took off its cover. She was ready to try some scales.

This was on a Sunday afternoon. Iona had lain down for a nap, one ear always open to hear my cry. Mrs. Kirkham too was lying down. Ailsa was painting her fingernails in the kitchen. Jill began to tune the violin.

My father and my father's family had no real interest in music. They didn't quite know this. They thought that the intolerance or even hostility they felt towards a certain type of music (this showed even in the way they pronounced the word "classical") was based on a simple strength of character, an integrity and a determination not to be fooled. As if music that departed from a simple tune was trying to put something over on you, and everybody knew this, deep down, but some people—out of pretentiousness, from want of simplicity and honesty—would never admit that it was so. And out of this artificiality and spineless tolerance came the whole world of symphony orchestras, opera, and ballet, concerts that put people to sleep.

Most of the people in this town felt the same way. But because she hadn't grown up here Jill did not understand the depth of this feeling, the taken-for-granted extent of it. My father had never made a parade of it, or a virtue of it, because he didn't go in for virtues. He had liked the idea of Jill's being a musician—not because of the music but because it made her an odd choice, as did her clothes and her way of living and her wild hair. Choosing her, he showed people what he thought of them. Showed those girls who had hoped to get their hooks in him. Showed Ailsa.

Jill had closed the curtained glass doors of the living room and she tuned up quite softly. Perhaps no sound escaped. Or if Ailsa heard something in the kitchen, she might have thought it was a sound from outdoors, a radio in the neighborhood.

Now Jill began to play her scales. It was true that her fingers were no longer puffy, but they felt stiff. Her whole body felt stiff, her stance was not quite natural, she felt the instrument clamped onto her in a distrustful way. But no matter, she would get into her scales. She was sure that she had felt this way before, after she'd had flu, or when she was very tired, having overstrained herself practicing, or even for no reason at all.

I woke without a whimper of discontent. No warning, no buildup. Just a shriek, a waterfall of shrieks descended on the house, a cry unlike any cry I'd managed before. The letting loose of a new flood of unsuspected anguish, a grief that punished the world with its waves full of stones, the volley of woe sent down from the windows of the torture chamber.

Iona was up at once, alarmed for the first time at any noise made by me, crying, "What is it, what is it?"

And Ailsa, rushing around to shut the windows, was calling out, "It's the fiddle, it's the fiddle." She threw open the doors of the living room.

"Jill. Jill. This is awful. This is just awful. Don't you hear your baby?"

She had to wrench out the screen under the living-room window, so that she could get it down. She had been sitting in her kimono to do her nails, and now a boy going by on a bicycle looked in and saw her kimono open over her slip.

"My God," she said. She hardly ever lost control of herself to this extent. "Will you put that thing away."

Jill set her violin down.

Ailsa ran out into the hall and called up to Iona.

"It's Sunday. Can't you get it to stop?"

Jill walked speechlessly and deliberately out to the kitchen, and there was Mrs. Kirkham in her stocking feet, clinging to the counter.

"What's the matter with Ailsa?" she said. "What did Iona do?"

Jill went out and sat down on the back step. She looked across at the glaring, sunlit back wall of the Shantzes' white house. All around were other hot backyards and hot walls of other houses.

Inside them people well known to each other by sight and by name and by history. And if you walked three blocks east from here or five blocks west, six blocks south or ten blocks north, you would come to walls of summer crops already sprung high out of the earth, fenced fields of hay and wheat and corn. The fullness of the country. Nowhere to breathe for the reek of thrusting crops and barnyards and jostling munching animals. Woodlots at a distance beckoning like pools of shade, of peace and shelter, but in reality they were boiling up with bugs.

How can I describe what music is to Jill? Forget about landscapes and visions and dialogues. It is more of a problem, I would say, that she has to work out strictly and daringly, and that she has taken on as her responsibility in life. Suppose then that the tools that serve her for working on this problem are taken away. The problem is still there in its grandeur and other people sustain it, but it is removed from her. For her, just the back step and the glaring wall and my crying. My crying is a knife to cut out of her life all that isn't useful. To me.

"Come in," says Ailsa through the screen door. "Come on in. I shouldn't have yelled at you. Come in, people will see."

By evening the whole episode could be passed off lightly. "You must've heard the caterwauling over here today," said Ailsa to the Shantzes. They had asked her over to sit on their patio, while Iona settled me to sleep.

"Baby isn't a fan of the fiddle apparently. Doesn't take after Mommy."

Even Mrs. Shantz laughed.

"An acquired taste."

Jill heard them. At least she heard the laughing, and guessed what it was about. She was lying on her bed reading *The Bridge of San Luis Rey*, which she had helped herself to from the bookcase, without understanding that she should ask Ailsa's permission. Every so often the story blanked out on her and she heard those laughing voices over in the Shantzes' yard, then the next-door patter of Iona's adoration, and she broke out in a sullen sweat. In a fairy tale she would have risen off the bed with the strength of a young giantess and gone through the house breaking furniture and necks.

WHEN I WAS almost six weeks old, Ailsa and Iona were supposed to take their mother on an annual overnight visit to Guelph, to stay with some cousins. Iona wanted to take me along. But Ailsa brought in Dr. Shantz to convince her that it was not a good idea to take a small baby on such a trip in hot weather. Then Iona wanted to stay at home.

"I can't drive and look after Mother both," said Ailsa.

She said that Iona was getting too wrapped up in me, and that a day and a half looking after her own baby was not going to be too much for Jill.

"Is it, Jill?"

Jill said no.

Iona tried to pretend it wasn't that she wanted to stay with me. She said that driving on a hot day made her carsick.

"You don't drive, you just have to sit there," Ailsa said. "What about me? I'm not doing it for fun. I'm doing it because they expect us."

Iona had to sit in the back, which she said made her carsickness worse. Ailsa said it wouldn't look right to put their mother there. Mrs. Kirkham said she didn't mind. Ailsa said no. Iona rolled down the window as Ailsa started the car. She fixed her eyes on the window of the upstairs room where she had put me down to sleep after my morning bath and bottle. Ailsa waved to Jill, who stood at the front door.

"Goodbye little mother," she called, in a cheerful, challenging voice that reminded Jill somehow of George. The prospect of getting away from the house and the new threat of disruption that was lodged in it seemed to have lifted Ailsa's spirits. And perhaps it also felt good to her—felt reassuring—to have Iona back in her proper place.

IT WAS ABOUT TEN O'CLOCK in the morning when they left, and the day ahead was to be the longest and the worst in Jill's experience. Not even the day of my birth, her nightmare labor, could compare to it. Before the car could have reached the next town, I woke in distress, as if I could feel Iona's being removed from me.

Iona had fed me such a short time before that Jill did not think I could possibly be hungry. But she discovered that I was wet, and though she had read that babies did not need to be changed every time they were found wet and that wasn't usually what made them cry, she decided to change me. It wasn't the first time she had done this, but she had never done it easily, and in fact Iona had taken over more often than not and got the job finished. I made it as hard as I could—I flailed my arms and legs, arched my back, tried my best to turn over, and of course kept up my noise. Jill's hands shook, she had trouble driving the pins through the cloth. She pretended to be calm, she tried talking to me, trying to imitate Iona's baby talk and fond cajoling, but it was no use, such stumbling insincerity enraged me further. She picked me up once she had my diaper pinned, she tried to mold me to her chest and shoulder, but I stiffened as if her body was made of red-hot needles. She sat down, she rocked me. She stood up, she bounced me. She sang to me the sweet words of a lullaby that were filled and trembling with her exasperation, her anger, and something that could readily define itself as loathing.

We were monsters to each other. Jill and I.

At last she put me down, more gently than she would have liked to do, and I quieted, in my relief it seemed at getting away from her. She tiptoed from the room. And it wasn't long before I started up again.

So it continued. I didn't cry nonstop. I would take breaks of two or five or ten or twenty minutes. When the time came for her to offer me the bottle I accepted it, I lay in her arm stiffly and snuffled warningly as I drank. Once half the milk was down I returned to the assault. I finished the bottle eventually, almost absentmindedly, between wails. I dropped off to sleep and she put me down. She crept down the stairs; she stood in the hall as if she had to judge a safe way to go. She was sweating from her ordeal and from the heat of the day. She moved through the precious brittle silence into the kitchen and dared to put the coffeepot on the stove.

Before the coffee was perked I sent a meat cleaver cry down on her head.

She realized that she had forgotten something. She hadn't burped me after the bottle. She went determinedly upstairs and picked me up and walked with me patting and rubbing my angry back, and in a while I burped, but I didn't stop crying and she gave up; she laid me down.

What is it about an infant's crying that makes it so powerful, able to break down the order you depend on, inside and outside of yourself? It is like a storm—insistent, theatrical, yet in a way pure and uncontrived. It is reproachful rather than supplicating—it comes out of a rage that can't be dealt with, a birthright rage free of love and pity, ready to crush your brains inside your skull.

All Jill can do is walk around. Up and down the living-room rug, round and round the dining-room table, out to the kitchen where the clock tells her how slowly, slowly time is passing. She can't stay still to take more than a sip of her coffee. When she gets hungry she can't stop to make a sandwich but eats cornflakes out of her hands, leaving a trail all over the house. Eating and drinking, doing any ordinary thing at all, seem as risky as doing such things in a little boat out in the middle of a tempest or in a house whose beams are buckling in an awful wind. You can't take your attention from the tempest or it will rip open your last defenses. You try for sanity's sake to fix on some calm detail of your surroundings, but the wind's cries—my cries—are able to inhabit a cushion or a figure in the rug or a tiny whirlpool in the window glass. I don't allow escape.

The house is shut up like a box. Some of Ailsa's sense of shame has rubbed off on Jill, or else she's been able to manufacture some shame of her own. A mother who can't appease her own baby—what is more shameful? She keeps the doors and windows shut. And she doesn't turn the portable floor fan on because in fact she's forgotten about it. She doesn't think anymore in terms of practical relief. She doesn't think that this Sunday is one of the hottest days of the summer and maybe that is what is the matter with me. An experienced or instinctive mother would surely have given me an airing instead of granting me the powers of a demon. Prickly heat would have been what came to her mind, instead of rank despair.

Sometime in the afternoon, Jill makes a stupid or just desperate decision. She doesn't walk out of the house and leave me. Stuck in the prison of my making, she thinks of a space of her own, an escape within. She gets out her violin, which she has not touched since the day of the scales, the attempt that Ailsa and Iona have turned into a family joke. Her playing can't wake me up, because I'm wide awake already, and how can it make me any angrier than I am?

In a way she does me honor. No more counterfeit soothing, no more pretend lullabies or concern for tummy-ache, no petsy-wetsy whatsamatter. Instead she will play Mendelssohn's Violin Concerto, the piece she played at her recital and must play again at her examination to get her graduating diploma.

The Mendelssohn is her choice—rather than the Beethoven Violin Concerto which she more passionately admires—because she believes the Mendelssohn will get her higher marks. She thinks she can master—has mastered—it more fully; she is confident that she can show off and impress the examiners without the least fear of catastrophe. This is not a work that will trouble her all her life, she has decided; it is not something she will struggle with and try to prove herself at forever.

She will just play it.

She tunes up, she does a few scales, she attempts to banish me from her hearing. She knows she's stiff, but this time she's prepared for that. She expects her problems to lessen as she gets into the music.

She starts to play it, she goes on playing, she goes on and on, she plays right through to the end. And her playing is terrible. It's a torment. She hangs on, she thinks this must change, she can change it, but she can't. Everything is off, she plays as badly as Jack Benny does in one of his resolute parodies. The violin is bewitched, it hates her. It gives her back a stubborn distortion of everything she intends. Nothing could be worse than this—it's worse than if she looked in the mirror and saw her reliable face caved in, sick and leering. A trick played on her that she couldn't believe, and would try to disprove by looking away and looking back, away and back, over and over again. That is how she goes on playing, trying to undo the trick. But not succeeding. She gets worse, if anything; sweat pours down her face and arms and the sides of her body, and her hand slips—there is simply no bottom to how badly she can play.

Finished. She is finished altogether. The piece that she mastered months ago and perfected since, so that nothing in it remained formidable or even tricky, has completely defeated her. It has shown her to herself as somebody emptied out, vandalized. Robbed overnight.

She doesn't give up. She does the worst thing. In this state of desperation she starts in again; she will try the Beethoven. And of course it's no good, it's worse and worse, and she seems to be howling, heaving inside. She sets the bow and the violin down on the living-room sofa, then picks them up and shoves them underneath it, getting them out of sight because she has a picture of herself smashing and wrecking them against a chair back, in a sickening dramatic display.

I haven't given up in all this time. Naturally I wouldn't, against such competition.

Jill lies down on the hard sky-blue brocade sofa where nobody ever lies or even sits, unless there's company, and she actually falls asleep. She wakes up after who knows how long with her hot face pushed down into the brocade, its pattern marked on her cheek, her mouth drooling a little and staining the sky-blue material. My racket still or again going on rising and falling like a hammering headache. And she has got a headache, too. She gets up and pushes her way—that's what it feels like—through the hot air to the kitchen cupboard where Ailsa keeps the 222's. The thick air makes her think of sewage. And why not? While she slept I dirtied my diaper, and its ripe smell has had time to fill the house.

222's. Warm another bottle. Climb the stairs. She changes the diaper without lifting me from the crib. The sheet as well as the diaper is a mess. The 222's are not working yet and her headache increases in fierceness as she bends over. Haul the mess out, wash off my scalded parts, pin on a clean diaper, and take the dirty diaper and sheet into the bathroom to be scrubbed off in the toilet. Put them in the pail of disinfectant which is already full to the brim because the usual baby wash has not been done today. Then get to me with the bottle. I quiet again enough to suck. It's a wonder I have the energy left to do that, but I do. The feeding is more than an hour late, and I have real hunger to add to—but maybe also subvert—my store of grievance. I suck away, I finish the bottle, and then worn out I go to sleep, and this time actually stay asleep.

Jill's headache dulls. Groggily she washes out my diapers and shirts and gowns and sheets. Scrubs them and rinses them and even boils the diapers to defeat the diaper rash to which I am prone. She wrings them all out by hand. She hangs them up indoors because the next day is Sunday, and Ailsa, when she returns, will not want to see anything hanging outdoors on Sunday. Jill would just as soon not have to appear outside, anyway, especially now with evening thickening and people sitting out, taking advantage of the cool. She dreads being seen by the neighbors—even being greeted by the friendly Shantzes—after what they must have listened to today.

And such a long time it takes for today to be over. For the long reach of sunlight and stretched shadows to give out and the monumental heat to stir a little, opening sweet cool cracks. Then all of a sudden the stars are out in clusters and the trees are enlarging themselves like clouds, shaking down peace. But not for long and not for Jill. Well before midnight comes a thin cry—you could not call it tentative, but thin at least, experimental, as if in spite of the day's practice I have lost the knack. Or as if I actually wonder if it's worth it. A little rest then, a false respite or giving up. But after that a thoroughgoing, an anguished, unforgiving resumption. Just when Jill had started to make more coffee, to deal with the remnants of her headache. Thinking that this time she might sit by the table and drink it.

Now she turns the burner off.

It's almost time for the last bottle of the day. If the feeding before had not been delayed, I'd be ready now. Perhaps I am ready? While it's warming, Jill thinks she'll dose herself with a couple more 222's. Then she thinks maybe that won't do; she needs something stronger. In the bathroom cupboard she finds only Pepto-Bismol, laxatives, foot powder, prescriptions she wouldn't touch. But she knows that Ailsa takes something strong for her menstrual cramps, and she goes into Ailsa's room and looks through her bureau drawers until she finds a bottle of pain pills lying, logically, on top of a pile of sanitary pads. These are prescription pills, too, but the label says clearly what they're for. She removes two of them and goes back to the kitchen and finds the water in the pan around the milk boiling, the milk too hot.

She holds the bottle under the tap to cool it—my cries coming down at her like the clamor of birds of prey over a gurgling river—and she looks at the pills waiting on the counter and she thinks, *Yes.* She gets out a knife and shaves a few grains off one of the pills, takes the nipple off the bottle, picks up the shaved grains on the blade of the knife, and sprinkles them—just a sprinkle of white dust—over the milk. Then she swallows one and seven-eighths or maybe one and eleven-twelfths or even one and fifteen-sixteenths of a pill herself, and takes the bottle upstairs. She lifts up my immediately rigid body and gets the nipple into my accusing mouth. The milk is still a little too warm for my liking and at first I spit it back at her. Then in a while I decide that it will do, and I swallow it all down.

IONA IS SCREAMING. Jill wakes up to a house full of hurtful sunlight and Iona's screaming.

The plan was that Ailsa and Iona and their mother would visit with their relatives in Guelph until the late afternoon, avoiding driving during the hot part of the day. But after breakfast Iona began to make a fuss. She wanted to get home to the baby, she said she had hardly slept all night for worrying. It was embarrassing to keep on arguing with her in front of the relatives, so Ailsa gave in and they arrived home late in the morning and opened the door of the still house.

Ailsa said, "Phew. Is this what it always smells like in here, only we're so used to it we don't notice?"

Iona ducked past her and ran up the stairs.

Now she's screaming.

Dead. Dead. Murderer.

She knows nothing about the pills. So why does she scream "Murderer"? It's the blanket. She sees the blanket pulled up right over my head. Suffocation. Not poison. It has not taken her any time, not half a second, to get from "dead" to "murderer." It's an immediate flying leap. She grabs me from the crib, with the death blanket twisted round me, and holding the blanketed bundle squeezed against her body she runs screaming out of the room and into Jill's room.

Jill is struggling up, dopily, after twelve or thirteen hours of sleep.

"You've killed my baby," Iona is screaming at her.

Jill doesn't correct her—she doesn't say, *Mine.* Iona holds me out accusingly to show me to Jill, but before Jill can get any kind of a look at me I have been snatched back. Iona groans and doubles up as if she's been shot in the stomach. Still holding on to me she stumbles down the stairs, bumping into Ailsa who is on her way up. Ailsa is almost knocked off her feet; she hangs on to the banister and Iona takes no notice; she seems to be trying to squeeze the bundle of me into a new terrifying hole in the middle of her body. Words come out of her between fresh groans of recognition.

Baby. Love my. Darling. Ooh. Oh. Get the. Suffocated. Blanket. Baby. Police.

Jill has slept with no covers over her and without changing into a nightdress. She is still in yesterday's shorts and halter, and she's not sure if she's waking from a night's sleep or a nap. She isn't sure where she is or what day it is. And what did Iona say? Groping her way up out of a vat of warm wool, Jill sees rather than hears Iona's cries, and they're like red flashes, hot veins in the inside of her eyelids. She clings to the luxury of not having to understand, but then she knows she has understood. She knows it's about me.

But Jill thinks that Iona has made a mistake. Iona has got into the wrong part of the dream. That part is all over.

The baby is all right. Jill took care of the baby. She went out and found the baby and covered it up. All right.

In the downstairs hall, Iona makes an effort and shouts some words all together. "She pulled the blanket all the way over its head, she smothered it."

Ailsa comes downstairs hanging on to the banister.

"Put it down," she says. "Put it down."

Iona squeezes me and groans. Then she holds me out to Ailsa and says, "Look. Look."

Ailsa whips her head aside. "I won't," she says. "I won't look." Iona comes close to push me into her face—I am still all wrapped up in my blanket, but Ailsa doesn't know that and Iona doesn't notice or doesn't care.

Now it's Ailsa screaming. She runs to the other side of the dining-room table screaming, "Put it down. Put it down. I'm not going to look at a corpse."

Mrs. Kirkham comes in from the kitchen, saying, "Girls. Oh, girls. What's the trouble between you? I can't have this, you know."

"Look," says Iona, forgetting Ailsa and coming around the table to show me to her mother.

Ailsa gets to the hall phone and gives the operator Dr. Shantz's number.

"Oh, a baby," says Mrs. Kirkham, twitching the blanket aside.

"She smothered it," Iona says.

"Oh, no," says Mrs. Kirkham.

Ailsa is talking to Dr. Shantz on the phone, telling him in a shaky voice to get over here at once. She turns from the phone and looks at Iona, gulps to steady herself, and says, "Now you. You pipe down."

Iona gives a high-pitched defiant yelp and runs away from her, across the hall into the living room. She is still hanging on to me.

Jill has come to the top of the stairs. Ailsa spots her.

She says, "Come on down here."

She has no idea what she's going to do to Jill, or say to her, once she gets her down. She looks as if she wants to slap her. "It's no good now getting hysterical," she says.

Jill's halter is twisted partway round so that most of one breast has got loose.

"Fix yourself up," says Ailsa. "Did you sleep in your clothes? You look drunk."

Jill seems to herself to be walking still in the snowy light of her dream. But the dream has been invaded by these frantic people.

Ailsa is able to think now about some things that have to be done. Whatever has happened, there has got to be no question of such a thing as a murder. Babies do die, for no reason, in their sleep. She has heard of that. No question of the police. No autopsy—a sad quiet little funeral. The obstacle to this is Iona. Dr. Shantz can give Iona a needle now; the needle will put her to sleep. But he can't go on giving her a needle every day.

The thing is to get Iona into Morrisville. This is the Hospital for the Insane, which used to be called the Asylum and in the future will be called the Psychiatric Hospital, then the Mental Health Unit. But most people just call it Morrisville, after the village nearby.

Going to Morrisville, they say. They took her off to Morrisville. Carry on like that and you're going to end up in Morrisville.

Iona has been there before and she can go there again. Dr. Shantz can get her in and keep her in until it's judged she's ready to come out. Affected by the baby's death. Delusions. Once that is established she won't pose a threat. Nobody will pay any attention to what she says. She will have had a breakdown. In fact it looks as if that may be the truth—it looks as if she might be halfway to a breakdown already, with that yelping and running around. It might be permanent. But probably not. There's all kinds of treatment nowadays. Drugs to calm her down, and shock if it's better to blot out some memories, and an operation they do, if they have to, on people who are obstinately confused and miserable. They don't do that at Morrisville—they have to send you to the city.

For all this—which has gone through her mind in an instant—Ailsa will have to count on Dr. Shantz. Some obliging lack of curiosity on his part and a willingness to see things her way. But that should not be hard for anybody who knows what she has been through. The investment she has made in this family's respectability and the blows she's had to take, from her father's shabby career and her mother's mixed-up wits to Iona's collapse at nursing school and George's going off to get killed. Does Ailsa deserve a public scandal on top of this—a story in the papers, a trial, maybe even a sister-in-law in jail?

Dr. Shantz would not think so. And not just because he can tote up these reasons from what he has observed as a friendly neighbor. Not just because he can appreciate that people who have to do without respectability must sooner or later feel the cold.

The reasons he has for helping Ailsa are all in his voice as he comes running in the back door now, through the kitchen, calling her name.

Jill at the bottom of the stairs has just said, "The baby's all right."

And Ailsa has said, "You keep quiet until I tell you what to say."

Mrs. Kirkham stands in the doorway between the kitchen and the hall, square in Dr. Shantz's path.

"Oh, I'm glad to see you," she says. "Ailsa and Iona are all upset with each other. Iona found a baby at the door and now she says it's dead."

Dr. Shantz picks Mrs. Kirkham up and puts her aside. He says again, "Ailsa?" and reaches out his arms, but ends up just setting his hands down hard on her shoulders.

Iona comes out of the living room empty-handed.

Jill says, "What did you do with the baby?"

"Hid it," Iona says saucily, and makes a face at her—the kind of face a terminally frightened person can make, pretending to be vicious.

"Dr. Shantz is going to give you a needle," Ailsa says. "That'll put paid to you."

Now there is an absurd scene of Iona running around, throwing herself at the front door—Ailsa jumps to block her—and then at the stairs, which is where Dr. Shantz gets hold of her and straddles her, pinning her arms and saying, "Now, now, now, Iona. Take it easy. You'll be okay in a little while." And Iona yells and whimpers and subsides. The noises she makes, and her darting about, her efforts at escape, all seem like playacting. As if—in spite of being quite literally at her wit's end—she finds the effort of standing up to Ailsa and Dr. Shantz so nearly impossible that she can only try to manage it by this sort of parody. Which makes it clear—and maybe this is what she really intends—that she is not standing up to them at all but falling apart. Falling apart as embarrassingly and inconveniently as possible with Ailsa shouting at her, "You ought to be disgusted with yourself."

Administering the needle, Dr. Shantz says, "That-a-girl Iona. There now."

Over his shoulder he says to Ailsa, "Look after your mother. Get her to sit down."

Mrs. Kirkham is wiping tears with her fingers. "I'm all right dear," she says to Ailsa. "I just wish you girls wouldn't fight. You should have told me Iona had a baby. You should have let her keep it."

Mrs. Shantz, wearing a Japanese kimono over her summer pajamas, comes into the house by the kitchen door.

"Is everybody all right?" she calls.

She sees the knife lying on the kitchen counter and thinks it prudent to pick it up and put it in a drawer. When people are making a scene the last thing you want is a knife ready to hand.

In the midst of this Jill thinks she has heard a faint cry. She has climbed clumsily over the banister to get around Iona and Dr. Shantz—she ran partway up the stairs again when Iona came running in that direction—and has lowered herself to the floor. She goes through the double doors into the living room where at first she sees no sign of me. But the faint cry comes again and she follows the sound to the sofa and looks underneath it.

That's where I am, pushed in beside the violin.

During that short trip from the hall to the living room, Jill has remembered everything, and it seems as if her breath stops and horror crowds in at her mouth, then a flash of joy sets her life going again, when just as in the dream she comes upon a live baby, not a little desiccated nutmeg-headed corpse. She holds me. I don't stiffen or kick or arch my back. I am still pretty sleepy from the sedative in my milk which knocked me out for the night and half a day and which, in a larger quantity—maybe not so much larger, at that—would have really finished me off.

IT WASN'T THE BLANKET AT ALL. Anybody who took a serious look at that blanket could see that it was so light and loosely woven that it could not prevent my getting all the air I needed. You could breathe through it just as easily as through a fishnet.

Exhaustion might have played a part. A whole day's howling, such a furious feat of self-expression, might have worn me out. That, and the white dust that fell on my milk, had knocked me into a deep and steadfast sleep with breathing so slight that Iona had not been able to detect it. You would think she would notice that I was not cold and you would think that all that moaning and crying out and running around would have brought me up to consciousness in a hurry. I don't know why that didn't happen. I think she didn't notice because of her panic and the state she was in even before she found me, but I don't know why I didn't cry sooner. Or maybe I did cry and in the commotion nobody heard me. Or maybe Iona did hear me and took a look at me and stuffed me under the sofa because by that time everything had been spoiled.

Then Jill heard. Jill was the one.

Iona was carried to that same sofa. Ailsa slipped off her shoes to save the brocade, and Mrs. Shantz went upstairs to get a light quilt to put over her.

"I know she doesn't need it for warmth," she said. "But I think when she wakes up she'll feel better to have a quilt over her."

Before this, of course, everybody had gathered round to take note of my being alive. Ailsa was blaming herself for not having discovered that right away. She hated to admit that she had been afraid to look at a dead baby.

"Iona's nerves must be contagious," she said. "I absolutely should have known."

She looked at Jill as if she was going to tell her to go and put a blouse on over her halter. Then she recalled how roughly she had spoken to her, and for no reason as it turned out, so she didn't say anything. She did not even try to convince her mother that Iona had not had a baby, though she said in an undertone, to Mrs. Shantz, "Well, that could start the rumor of the century."

"I'm so glad nothing terrible happened," Mrs. Kirkham said. "I thought for a minute Iona had done away with it. Ailsa, you must try not to blame your sister."

"No Momma," said Ailsa. "Let's go sit down in the kitchen."

There was one bottle of formula made up that by rights I should have demanded and drunk earlier that morning. Jill put it on to warm, holding me in the crook of her arm all the time.

She had looked at once for the knife, when she came into the kitchen, and seen in wonderment that it wasn't there. But she could make out the faintest dust on the counter—or she thought she could. She wiped it with her free hand before she turned the tap on to get the water to heat the bottle.

Mrs. Shantz busied herself making coffee. While it was perking she put the sterilizer on the stove and washed out yesterday's bottles. She was being tactful and competent, just managing to hide the fact that there was something about this whole debacle and disarray of feelings that buoyed her up.

"I guess Iona did have an obsession about the baby," she said. "Something like this was bound to happen."

Turning from the stove to address the last of these words to her husband and Ailsa, she saw that Dr. Shantz was pulling Ailsa's hands down from where she held them, on either side of her head.

Too speedily and guiltily he took his own hands away. If he had not done that, it would have looked like ordinary comfort he was administering. As a doctor is certainly entitled to do.

"You know Ailsa, I think your mother ought to lie down too," said Mrs. Shantz thoughtfully and without a break. "I think I'll go and persuade her. If she can get to sleep this may all pass right out of her head. Out of Iona's too, if we're lucky."

Mrs. Kirkham had wandered out of the kitchen almost as soon as she got there. Mrs. Shantz found her in the living room looking at Iona, and fiddling with the quilt to make sure she was well covered. Mrs. Kirkham did not really want to lie down. She wanted to have things explained to her—she knew that her own explanations were somehow out of kilter. And she wanted to have people talk to her as they used to do, not in the peculiarly gentle and self-satisfied way they did now. But because of her customary politeness and her knowledge that the power she had in the household was negligible, she allowed Mrs. Shantz to take her upstairs.

Jill was reading the instructions for making baby formula. They were printed on the side of the corn syrup tin. When she heard the footsteps going up the stairs she thought that there was something she had better do while she had the chance. She carried me into the living room and laid me down on a chair.

"There now," she whispered confidentially. "You stay still."

She knelt down and nudged and gently tugged the violin out of its hiding place. She found its cover and case and got it properly stowed away. I stayed still—not yet being quite able to turn over—and I stayed quiet.

Left alone by themselves, alone in the kitchen, Dr. Shantz and Ailsa probably did not seize this chance to embrace, but only looked at each other. With their knowledge, and without promises or despair.

IONA ADMITTED that she hadn't felt for a pulse. And she never claimed that I was cold. She said I felt stiff. Then she said not stiff but heavy. So heavy, she said, she instantly thought I could not be alive. A lump, a dead weight.

I think there is something to this. I don't believe that I was dead, or that I came back from the dead, but I do think that I was at a distance, from which I might or might not have come back. I think that the outcome was not certain and that will was involved. It was up to me, I mean, to go one way or the other.

And Iona's love, which was certainly the most wholehearted love I will ever receive, didn't decide me. Her cries and her crushing me into her body didn't work, were not finally persuasive. Because it wasn't Iona I had to settle for. (Could I have known that—could I even have known that it wasn't Iona, in the end, who would do me the most good?) It was Jill. I had to settle for Jill and for what I could get from her, even if it might look like half a loaf.

To me it seems that it was only then that I became female. I know that the matter was decided long before I was born and was plain to everybody else since the beginning of my life, but I believe that it was only at the moment when I decided to come back, when I gave up the fight against my mother (which must have been a fight for something like her total surrender) and when in fact I chose survival over victory (death would have been victory), that I took on my female nature.

And to some extent Jill took on hers. Sobered and grateful, not even able to risk thinking about what she'd just escaped, she took on loving me, because the alternative to loving was disaster.

DR. SHANTZ suspected something, but he let it go. He asked Jill how I had been the day before. Fussy? She said yes, very fussy. He said that premature babies, even slightly premature babies, were susceptible to shocks and you had to be careful with them. He recommended that I always be put to sleep on my back.

Iona did not have to have shock treatment. Dr. Shantz gave her pills. He said that she had overstrained herself looking after me. The woman who had taken over her job at the bakery wanted to give it up—she did not like working nights. So Iona went back there.

THAT'S WHAT I REMEMBER BEST about my summer visits to my aunts, when I was six or seven years old. Being taken down to the bakery at the strange, usually forbidden hour of midnight and watching Iona put on her white hat and apron, watching her knead the great white mass of dough that shifted and bubbled like something alive. Then cutting out cookies and feeding me the leftover bits and on special occasions sculpting a wedding cake. How bright and white that big kitchen was, with night filling every window. I scraped the wedding icing from the bowl—the melting stabbing irresistible sugar.

Ailsa thought I should not be up so late, or eat so much sweet stuff. But she didn't do anything about it. She said she wondered what my mother would say—as if Jill was the person who swung the weight, not herself. Ailsa had some rules that I didn't have to observe at home—hang up that jacket, rinse that glass before you dry it, else it'll have spots—but I never saw the harsh, hounding person Jill remembered.

Nothing slighting was ever said then, about Jill's music. After all, she made our living at it. She had not been finally defeated by the Mendelssohn. She got her diploma; she graduated from the Conservatory. She cut her hair and got thin. She was able to rent a duplex near High Park in Toronto, and hire a woman to look after me part of the time, because she had her war widow's pension. And then she found a job with a radio orchestra. She was to be proud that all her working life she was employed as a musician and never had to fall back on teaching. She said that she knew that she was not a great violinist, she had no marvellous gift or destiny, but at least she could make her living doing what she wanted to do. Even after she married my stepfather, after we moved with him to Edmonton (he was a geologist), she went on playing in the symphony orchestra there. She played up until a week before each of my half sisters was born. She was lucky, she said—her husband never objected.

Iona did have a couple of further setbacks, the more serious one when I was about twelve. She was taken to Morrisville for several weeks. I think she was given insulin there—she returned fat and loquacious. I came back to visit while she was away, and Jill came with me, bringing my first little sister who had been born shortly before. I understood from the talk between my mother and Ailsa that it would not have been advisable to bring a baby into the house if Iona was there; it might have "set her off." I don't know if the episode that sent her to Morrisville had anything to do with a baby.

I felt left out of things on that visit. Both Jill and Ailsa had taken up smoking, and they would sit up late at night, drinking coffee and smoking cigarettes at the kitchen table, while they waited for the baby's one o'clock feeding. (My mother fed this baby from her breasts—I was glad to hear that no such intimate body-heated meals had been served to me.) I remember coming downstairs sulkily because I couldn't sleep, then turning talkative, full of giddy bravado, trying to break into their conversation. I understood that they were talking over things they didn't want me to hear about. They had become, unaccountably, good friends.

I grabbed for a cigarette, and my mother said, "Go on now, leave those alone. We're talking." Ailsa told me to get something to drink out of the fridge, a Coke or a ginger ale. So I did, and instead of taking it upstairs I went outside.

I sat on the back step, but the women's voices immediately went too low for me to make out any of their soft regretting or reassuring. So I went prowling around the backyard, beyond the patch of light thrown through the screen door.

The long white house with the glass-brick corners was occupied by new people now. The Shantzes had moved away, to live year-round in Florida. They sent my aunts oranges, which Ailsa said would make you forever disgusted with the kind of oranges you could buy in Canada. The new people had put in a swimming pool, which was used mostly by the two pretty teenage daughters—girls who would look right through me when they met me on the street—and by the daughters' boyfriends. Some bushes had grown up fairly high between my aunts' yard and theirs, but it was still possible for me to watch them running around the pool and pushing each other in, with great shrieks and splashes. I despised their antics because I took life seriously and had a much more lofty and tender notion of romance. But I would have liked to get their attention just the same. I would have liked for one of them to see my pale pajamas moving in the dark, and to scream out in earnest, thinking that I was a ghost.

Hateship, Friendship, Courtship, Loveship, Marriage

~

YEARS AGO, before the trains stopped running on so many of the branch lines, a woman with a high, freckled forehead and a frizz of reddish hair came into the railway station and inquired about shipping furniture.

The station agent often tried a little teasing with women, especially the plain ones who seemed to appreciate it.

"Furniture?" he said, as if nobody had ever had such an idea before. "Well. Now. What kind of furniture are we talking about?"

A dining-room table and six chairs. A full bedroom suite, a sofa, a coffee table, end tables, a floor lamp. Also a china cabinet and a buffet.

"Whoa there. You mean a houseful."

"It shouldn't count as that much," she said. "There's no kitchen things and only enough for one bedroom."

Her teeth were crowded to the front of her mouth as if they were ready for an argument.

"You'll be needing the truck," he said.

"No. I want to send it on the train. It's going out west, to Saskatchewan."

She spoke to him in a loud voice as if he was deaf or stupid, and there was something wrong with the way she pronounced her words. An accent. He thought of Dutch—the Dutch were moving in around here—but she didn't have the heft of the Dutch women or the nice pink skin or the fair hair. She might have been under forty, but what did it matter? No beauty queen, ever.

He turned all business.

"First you'll need the truck to get it to here from wherever you got it. And we better see if it's a place in Saskatchewan where the train goes through. Otherways you'd have to arrange to get it picked up, say, in Regina."

"It's Gdynia," she said. "The train goes through."

He took down a greasy-covered directory that was hanging from a nail and asked how she would spell that. She helped herself to the pencil that was also on a string and wrote on a piece of paper from her purse: *G D Y N I A.*

"What kind of nationality would that be?"

She said she didn't know.

He took back the pencil to follow from line to line.

"A lot of places out there it's all Czechs or Hungarians or Ukrainians," he said. It came to him as he said this that she might be one of those. But so what, he was only stating a fact.

"Here it is, all right, it's on the line."

"Yes," she said. "I want to ship it Friday—can you do that?"

"We can ship it, but I can't promise what day it'll get there," he said. "It all depends on the priorities. Somebody going to be on the lookout for it when it comes in?"

"Yes."

"It's a mixed train Friday, two-eighteen p.m. Truck picks it up Friday morning. You live here in town?"

She nodded, writing down the address. 106 Exhibition Road.

It was only recently that the houses in town had been numbered, and he couldn't picture the place, though he knew where Exhibition Road was. If she'd said the name McCauley at that time he might have taken more of an interest, and things might have turned out differently. There were new houses out there, built since the war, though they were called "wartime houses." He supposed it must be one of those.

"Pay when you ship," he told her.

"Also, I want a ticket for myself on the same train. Friday afternoon."

"Going same place?"

"Yes."

"You can travel on the same train to Toronto, but then you have to wait for the Transcontinental, goes out ten-thirty at night. You want sleeper or coach? Sleeper you get a berth, coach you sit up in the day car."

She said she would sit up.

"Wait in Sudbury for the Montreal train, but you won't get off there, they'll just shunt you around and hitch on the Montreal cars. Then on to Port Arthur and then to Kenora. You don't get off till Regina, and there you have to get off and catch the branch-line train."

She nodded as if he should just get on and give her the ticket.

Slowing down, he said, "But I won't promise your furniture'll arrive when you do, I wouldn't think it would get in till a day or two after. It's all the priorities. Somebody coming to meet you?"

"Yes."

"Good. Because it won't likely be much of a station. Towns out there, they're not like here. They're mostly pretty rudimentary affairs."

She paid for the passenger ticket now, from a roll of bills in a cloth bag in her purse. Like an old lady. She counted her change, too. But not the way an old lady would count it—she held it in her hand and flicked her eyes over it, but you could tell she didn't miss a penny. Then she turned away rudely, without a good-bye.

"See you Friday," he called out.

She wore a long, drab coat on this warm September day, also a pair of clunky laced-up shoes, and ankle socks.

He was getting a coffee out of his thermos when she came back and rapped on the wicket.

"The furniture I'm sending," she said. "It's all good furniture, it's like new. I wouldn't want it to get scratched or banged up or in any way damaged. I don't want it to smell like livestock, either."

"Oh, well," he said. "The railway's pretty used to shipping things. And they don't use the same cars for shipping furniture they use for shipping pigs."

"I'm concerned that it gets there in just as good a shape as it leaves here."

"Well, you know, when you buy your furniture, it's in the store, right? But did you ever think how it got there? It wasn't made in the store, was it? No. It was made in some factory someplace, and it got shipped to the store, and that was done quite possibly by train. So that being the case, doesn't it stand to reason the railway knows how to look after it?"

She continued to look at him without a smile or any admission of her female foolishness.

"I hope so," she said. "I hope they do."

THE STATION AGENT would have said, without thinking about it, that he knew everybody in town. Which meant that he knew about half of them. And most of those he knew were the core people, the ones who really were "in town" in the sense that they had not arrived yesterday and had no plans to move on. He did not know the woman who was going to Saskatchewan because she did not go to his church or teach his children in school or work in any store or restaurant or office that he went into. Nor was she married to any of the men he knew in the Elks or the Oddfellows or the Lions Club or the Legion. A look at her left hand while she was getting the money out had told him—and he was not surprised—that she was not married to anybody. With those shoes, and ankle socks instead of stockings, and no hat or gloves in the afternoon, she might have been a farm woman. But she didn't have the hesitation they generally had, the embarrassment. She didn't have country manners—in fact, she had no manners at all. She had treated him as if he was an information machine. Besides, she had written a town address—Exhibition Road. The person she really reminded him of was a plainclothes nun he had seen on television, talking about the missionary work she did somewhere in the jungle—probably they had got out of their nuns' clothes there because it made it easier for them to clamber around. This nun had smiled once in a while to show that her religion was supposed to make people happy, but most of the time she looked out at her audience as if she believed that other people were mainly in the world for her to boss around.

ONE MORE THING Johanna meant to do she had been putting off doing. She had to go into the dress shop called Milady's and buy herself an outfit. She had never been inside that shop—when she had to buy anything, like socks, she went to Callaghans Mens Ladies and Childrens Wear. She had lots of clothes inherited from Mrs. Willets, things like this coat that would never wear out. And Sabitha—the girl she looked after, in Mr. McCauley's house—was showered with costly hand-me-downs from her cousins.

In Milady's window there were two mannequins wearing suits with quite short skirts and boxy jackets. One suit was a rusty-gold color and the other a soft deep green. Big gaudy paper maple leaves were scattered round the mannequins' feet and pasted here and there on the window. At the time of year when most people's concern was to rake up leaves and burn them, here they were the chosen thing. A sign written in flowing black script was stuck diagonally across the glass. It said: *Simple Elegance, the Mode for Fall.*

She opened the door and went inside.

Right ahead of her, a full-length mirror showed her in Mrs. Willets's high-quality but shapeless long coat, with a few inches of lumpy bare legs above the ankle socks.

They did that on purpose, of course. They set the mirror there so you could get a proper notion of your deficiencies, right away, and then—they hoped—you would jump to the conclusion that you had to buy something to alter the picture. Such a transparent trick that it would have made her walk out, if she had not come in determined, knowing what she had to get.

Along one wall was a rack of evening dresses, all fit for belles of the ball with their net and taffeta, their dreamy colors. And beyond them, in a glass case so no profane fingers could get at them, half a dozen wedding gowns, pure white froth or vanilla satin or ivory lace, embroidered in silver beads or seed pearls. Tiny bodices, scalloped necklines, lavish skirts. Even when she was younger she could never have contemplated such extravagance, not just in the matter of money but in expectations, in the preposterous hope of transformation, and bliss.

It was two or three minutes before anybody came. Maybe they had a peephole and were eyeing her, thinking she wasn't their kind of customer and hoping she would go away.

She would not. She moved beyond the mirror's reflection—stepping from the linoleum by the door to a plushy rug—and at long last the curtain at the back of the store opened and out stepped Milady herself, dressed in a black suit with glittery buttons. High heels, thin ankles, girdle so tight her nylons rasped, gold hair skinned back from her made-up face.

"I thought I could try on the suit in the window," Johanna said in a rehearsed voice. "The green one."

"Oh, that's a lovely suit," the woman said. "The one in the window happens to be a size ten. Now you look to be—maybe a fourteen?"

She rasped ahead of Johanna back to the part of the store where the ordinary clothes, the suits and daytime dresses, were hung.

"You're in luck. Fourteen coming up."

The first thing Johanna did was look at the price tag. Easily twice what she'd expected, and she was not going to pretend otherwise.

"It's expensive enough."

"It's very fine wool." The woman monkeyed around till she found the label, then read off a description of the material that Johanna wasn't really listening to because she had caught at the hem to examine the workmanship.

"It feels as light as silk, but it wears like iron. You can see it's lined throughout, lovely silk-and-rayon lining. You won't find it bagging in the seat and going out of shape the way the cheap suits do. Look at the velvet cuffs and collar and the little velvet buttons on the sleeve."

"I see them."

"That's the kind of detail you pay for, you just do not get it otherwise. I love the velvet touch. It's only on the green one, you know—the apricot one doesn't have it, even though they're exactly the same price."

Indeed it was the velvet collar and cuffs that gave the suit, in Johanna's eyes, its subtle look of luxury and made her long to buy it. But she was not going to say so.

"I might as well go ahead and try it on."

This was what she'd come prepared for, after all. Clean underwear and fresh talcum powder under her arms.

The woman had enough sense to leave her alone in the bright cubicle. Johanna avoided the glass like poison till she'd got the skirt straight and the jacket done up.

At first she just looked at the suit. It was all right. The fit was all right—the skirt shorter than what she was used to, but then what she was used to was not the style. There was no problem with the suit. The problem was with what stuck out of it. Her neck and her face and her hair and her big hands and thick legs.

"How are you getting on? Mind if I take a peek?"

Peek all you want to, Johanna thought, it's a case of a sow's ear, as you'll soon see.

The woman tried looking from one side, then the other.

"Of course, you'll need your nylons on and your heels. How does it feel? Comfortable?"

"The suit feels fine," Johanna said. "There's nothing the matter with the suit."

The woman's face changed in the mirror. She stopped smiling. She looked disappointed and tired, but kinder.

"Sometimes that's just the way it is. You never really know until you try something on. The thing is," she said, with a new, more moderate conviction growing in her voice, "the thing is you have a fine figure, but it's a strong figure. You have large bones and what's the matter with that? Dinky little velvet-covered buttons are not for you. Don't bother with it anymore. Just take it off."

Then when Johanna had got down to her underwear there was a tap and a hand through the curtain.

"Just slip this on, for the heck of it."

A brown wool dress, lined, with a full skirt gracefully gathered, three-quarter sleeves and a plain round neckline. About as plain as you could get, except for a narrow gold belt. Not as expensive as the suit, but still the price seemed like a lot, when you considered all there was to it.

At least the skirt was a more decent length and the fabric made a noble swirl around her legs. She steeled herself and looked in the glass.

This time she didn't look as if she'd been stuck into the garment for a joke.

The woman came and stood beside her, and laughed, but with relief.

"It's the color of your eyes. You don't need to wear velvet. You've got velvet eyes."

That was the kind of soft-soaping Johanna would have felt bound to scoff at, except that at the moment it seemed to be true. Her eyes were not large, and if asked to describe their color she would have said, "I guess they're a kind of a brown." But now they looked to be a really deep brown, soft and shining.

It wasn't that she had suddenly started thinking she was pretty or anything. Just that her eyes were a nice color, if they had been a piece of cloth.

"Now, I bet you don't wear dress shoes very often," the woman said. "But if you had nylons on and just a minimum kind of pump— And I bet you don't wear jewelry, and you're quite right, you don't need to, with that belt."

To cut off the sales spiel Johanna said, "Well, I better take it off so you can wrap it up." She was sorry to lose the soft weight of the skirt and the discreet ribbon of gold around her waist. She had never in her life had this silly feeling of being enhanced by what she had put on herself.

"I just hope it's for a special occasion," the woman called out as Johanna was hastening into her now dingy-looking regular clothes.

"It'll likely be what I get married in," said Johanna.

She was surprised at that coming out of her mouth. It wasn't a major error—the woman didn't know who she was and would probably not be talking to anybody who did know. Still, she had meant to keep absolutely quiet. She must have felt she owed this person something—that they'd been through the disaster of the green suit and the discovery of the brown dress together and that was a bond. Which was nonsense. The woman was in the business of selling clothes, and she'd just succeeded in doing that.

"Oh!" the woman cried out. "Oh, that's wonderful."

Well, it might be, Johanna thought, and then again it might not. She might be marrying anybody. Some miserable farmer who wanted a workhorse around the place, or some wheezy old half-cripple looking for a nurse. This woman had no idea what kind of man she had lined up, and it wasn't any of her business anyway.

"I can tell it's a love match," the woman said, just as if she had read these disgruntled thoughts. "That's why your eyes were shining in the mirror. I've wrapped it all in tissue paper, all you have to do is take it out and hang it up and the material will fall out beautifully. Just give it a light press if you want, but you probably won't even need to do that."

Then there was the business of handing over the money. They both pretended not to look, but both did.

"It's worth it," the woman said. "You only get married the once. Well, that's not always strictly true—"

"In my case it'll be true," Johanna said. Her face was hotly flushed because marriage had not, in fact, been mentioned. Not even in the last letter. She had revealed to this woman what she was counting on, and that had perhaps been an unlucky thing to do.

"Where did you meet him?" said the woman, still in that tone of wistful gaiety. "What was your first date?"

"Through family," Johanna said truthfully. She wasn't meaning to say any more but heard herself go on. "The Western Fair. In London."

"The Western Fair," the woman said. "In London." She could have been saying "the Castle Ball."

"We had his daughter and her friend with us," said Johanna, thinking that in a way it would have been more accurate to say that he and Sabitha and Edith had her, Johanna, with them.

"Well, I can say my day has not been wasted. I've provided the dress for somebody to be a happy bride in. That's enough to justify my existence." The woman tied a narrow pink ribbon around the dress box, making a big, unnecessary bow, then gave it a wicked snip with the scissors.

"I'm here all day," she said. "And sometimes I just wonder what I think I'm doing. I ask myself, What do you think you're doing here? I put up a new display in the window and I do this and that to entice the people in, but there are days—there are *days*—when I do not see one soul come in that door. I know—people think these clothes are too expensive—but they're *good*. They're good clothes. If you want the quality you have to pay the price."

"They must come in when they want something like those," said Johanna, looking towards the evening dresses. "Where else could they go?"

"That's just it. They don't. They go to the city—that's where they go. They'll drive fifty miles, a hundred miles, never mind the gas, and tell themselves that way they get something better than I've got here. And they haven't. Not better quality, not better selection. Nothing. Just that they'd be ashamed to say they bought their wedding outfits in town. Or they'll come in and try something on and say they have to think about it. I'll be back, they say. And I think, Oh, yes, I know what that means. It means they'll try to find the same thing cheaper in London or Kitchener, and even if it isn't cheaper, they'll buy it there once they've driven all that way and got sick of looking.

"I don't know," she said. "Maybe if I was a local person it would make a difference. It's very clique-y here, I find. You're not local, are you?"

Johanna said, "No."

"Don't you find it clique-y?"

Cleeky.

"Hard for an outsider to break in, is what I mean."

"I'm used to being on my own," Johanna said.

"But you found somebody. You won't be on your own anymore and isn't that lovely? Some days I think how grand it would be, to be married and stay at home. Of course, I used to be married, and I worked anyway. Ah, well. Maybe the man in the moon will walk in here and fall in love with me and then I'll be all set!"

JOHANNA HAD TO HURRY—that woman's need for conversation had delayed her. She was hurrying to be back at the house, her purchase stowed away, before Sabitha got home from school.

Then she remembered that Sabitha wasn't there, having been carried off on the weekend by her mother's cousin, her Aunt Roxanne, to live like a proper rich girl in Toronto and go to a rich girl's school. But she continued to walk fast—so fast some smart aleck holding up the wall of the drugstore called out to her, "Where's the fire?" and she slowed down a bit, not to attract attention.

The dress box was awkward—how could she have known the store would have its own pink cardboard boxes, with *Milady's* written across them in purple handwriting? A dead giveaway.

She felt a fool for mentioning a wedding, when he hadn't mentioned it and she ought to remember that. So much else had been said—or written—such fondness and yearning expressed, that the actual marrying seemed just to have been overlooked. The way you might speak about getting up in the morning and not about having breakfast, though you certainly intended to have it.

Nevertheless she should have kept her mouth shut.

She saw Mr. McCauley walking in the opposite direction up the other side of the street. That was all right—even if he had met her head-on he would never have noticed the box she carried. He would have raised a finger to his hat and passed her by, presumably notic-ing that she was his housekeeper but possibly not. He had other things on his mind, and for all anybody knew might be looking at some town other than the one they saw. Every working day—and sometimes, forgetfully, on holidays or Sundays—he got dressed in one of his three-piece suits and his light overcoat or his heavy over-coat, and his gray fedora and his well-polished shoes, and walked from Exhibition Road uptown to the office he still maintained over what had been the harness and luggage store. It was spoken of as an Insurance Office, though it was quite a long time since he had actively sold insurance. Sometimes people climbed the stairs to see him, maybe to ask some question about their policies or more likely about lot boundaries, the history of some piece of real estate in town or farm out in the country. His office was full of maps old and new, and he liked nothing better than to lay them out and get into a discussion that expanded far beyond the question asked. Three or four times a day he emerged and walked the street, as now. During the war he had put the McLaughlin-Buick up on blocks in the barn, and walked everywhere to set an example. He still seemed to be setting an example, fifteen years later. Hands clasped behind his back, he was like a kind landlord inspecting his property or a preacher happy to observe his flock. Of course, half the people that he met had no idea who he was.

The town had changed, even in the time Johanna had been here. Trade was moving out to the highway, where there was a new dis-count store and a Canadian Tire and a motel with a lounge and topless dancers. Some downtown shops had tried to spruce them-selves up with pink or mauve or olive paint, but already that paint was curling on the old brick and some of the interiors were empty. Milady's was almost certain to follow suit.

If Johanna was the woman in there, what would she have done? She'd never have got in so many elaborate evening dresses, for a start. What instead? If you made the switch to cheaper clothes you'd only be putting yourself in competition with Callaghans and the discount place, and there probably wasn't trade enough to go around. So what about going into fancy baby clothes, children's clothes, trying to pull in the grandmothers and aunts who had the money and would spend it for that kind of thing? Forget about the mothers, who would go to Callaghans, having less money and more sense.

But if it was her in charge—Johanna—she would never be able to pull in anybody. She could see what needed to be done, and how, and she could round up and supervise people to do it, but she could never charm or entice. Take it or leave it, would be her attitude. No doubt they would leave it.

It was the rare person who took to her, and she'd been aware of that for a long time. Sabitha certainly hadn't shed any tears when she said good-bye—though you could say Johanna was the nearest thing Sabitha had to a mother, since her own mother had died. Mr. McCauley would be upset when she left because she'd given good service and it would be hard to replace her, but that would be all he thought about. Both he and his granddaughter were spoiled and self-centered. As for the neighbors, they would no doubt rejoice. Johanna had had problems on both sides of the property. On one side it was the neighbors' dog digging in her garden, burying and retrieving his supply of bones, which he could better have done at home. And on the other it was the black cherry tree, which was on the McCauleys' property but bore most of its cherries on the branches hanging over into the next yard. In both cases she had raised a fuss, and won. The dog was tied up and the other neighbors left the cherries alone. If she got up on the stepladder she could reach well over into their yard, but they no longer chased the birds out of the branches and it made a difference to the crop.

Mr. McCauley would have let them pick. He would have let the dog dig. He would let himself be taken advantage of. Part of the reason was that these were new people and lived in new houses and so he preferred not to pay attention to them. At one time there had been just three or four large houses on Exhibition Road. Across from them were the fairgrounds, where the fall fair was held (officially called the Agricultural Exhibition, hence the name), and in between were orchard trees, small meadows. A dozen years ago or so that land had been sold off in regular lot sizes and houses had been put up—small houses in alternating styles, one kind with an upstairs and the other kind without. Some were already getting to look pretty shabby.

There were only a couple of houses whose occupants Mr.

McCauley knew and was friendly with—the schoolteacher, Miss Hood, and her mother, and the Shultzes, who ran the Shoe Repair shop. The Shultzes' daughter, Edith, was or had been Sabitha's great friend. It was natural, with their being in the same grade at school—at least last year, once Sabitha had been held back—and living near each other. Mr. McCauley hadn't minded—maybe he had some idea that Sabitha would be removed before long to live a different sort of life in Toronto. Johanna would not have chosen Edith, though the girl was never rude, never troublesome when she came to the house. And she was not stupid. That might have been the problem—she was smart and Sabitha was not so smart. She had made Sabitha sly.

That was all over now. Now that the cousin, Roxanne—Mrs. Huber—had shown up, the Schultz girl was all part of Sabitha's childish past.

> *I am going to arrange to get all your furniture out to you on*
> *the train as soon as they can take it and prepaid as soon as*
> *they tell me what it will cost. I have been thinking you will*
> *need it now. I guess it will not be that much of a surprise that*
> *I thought you would not mind it if I went along to be of help to*
> *you as I hope I can be.*

This was the letter she had taken to the Post Office, before she went to make arrangements at the railway station. It was the first letter she had ever sent to him directly. The others had been slipped in with the letters she made Sabitha write. And his to her had come in the same way, tidily folded and with her name, Johanna, typed on the back of the page so there would be no mistaking. That kept the people in the Post Office from catching on, and it never hurt to save a stamp. Of course, Sabitha could have reported to her grandfather, or even read what was written to Johanna, but Sabitha was no more interested in communicating with the old man than she was in letters—the writing or the receiving of them.

The furniture was stored back in the barn, which was just a town barn, not a real barn with animals and a granary. When Johanna got her first look at everything a year or so ago, she found it grimy with dust and splattered with pigeon droppings. The pieces had been piled in carelessly without anything to cover them. She had hauled what she could carry out into the yard, leaving space in the barn to get at the big pieces she couldn't carry—the sofa and buffet and china cabinet and dining table. The bedstead she could take apart. She went at the wood with soft dustrags, then lemon oil, and when she was finished it shone like candy. Maple candy—it was bird's-eye maple wood. It looked glamorous to her, like satin bedspreads and blond hair. Glamorous and modern, a total contrast to all the dark wood and irksome carving of the furniture she cared for in the house. She thought of it as *his* furniture then, and still did when she got it out this Wednesday. She had put old quilts over the bottom layer to protect everything there from what was piled on top, and sheets over what was on top to protect that from the birds, and as a result there was only a light dust. But she wiped everything and lemon-oiled it before she put it back, protected in the same way, to wait for the truck on Friday.

Dear Mr. McCauley,

I am leaving on the train this afternoon (Friday). I realize this is without giving my notice to you, but I will waive my last pay, which would be three weeks owing this coming Monday. There is a beef stew on the stove in the double boiler that just needs warming up. Enough there for three meals or maybe could be stretched to a fourth. As soon as it is hot and you have got all you want, put the lid on and put it away in the fridge. Remember, put the lid on at once not to take chances with it getting spoiled. Regards to you and to Sabitha and will probably be in touch when I am settled.

Johanna Parry.

P.S. I have shipped his furniture to Mr. Boudreau as he may need it. Remember to make sure when you reheat there is enough water in bottom part of the double boiler.

Mr. McCauley had no trouble finding out that the ticket Johanna had bought was to Gdynia, Saskatchewan. He phoned the station agent and asked. He could not think how to describe Johanna—was she old or young-looking, thin or moderately heavy, what was the color of her coat?—but that was not necessary when he mentioned the furniture.

When this call came through there were a couple of people in the station waiting for the evening train. The agent tried to keep his voice down at first, but he became excited when he heard about the stolen furniture (what Mr. McCauley actually said was "and I believe she took some furniture with her"). He swore that if he had known who she was and what she was up to he would never have let her set foot on the train. This assertion was heard and repeated and believed, nobody asking how he could have stopped a grown woman who had paid for her ticket, unless he had some proof right away that she was a thief. Most people who repeated his words believed that he could and would have stopped her—they believed in the authority of station agents and of upright-walking fine old men in three-piece suits like Mr. McCauley.

The beef stew was excellent, as Johanna's cooking always was, but Mr. McCauley found he could not swallow it. He disregarded the instruction about the lid and left the pot sitting open on the stove and did not even turn off the burner until the water in the bottom pot boiled away and he was alerted by a smell of smoking metal.

This was the smell of treachery.

He told himself to be thankful at least that Sabitha was taken care of and he did not have that to worry about. His niece—his wife's cousin, actually, Roxanne—had written to tell him that from what she had seen of Sabitha on her summer visit to Lake Simcoe the girl was going to take some handling.

"Frankly I don't think you and that woman you've hired are going to be up to it when the boys come swarming around."

She did not go so far as to ask him whether he wanted another Marcelle on his hands, but that was what she meant. She said she would get Sabitha into a good school where she could be taught manners at least.

He turned on the television for a distraction, but it was no use. It was the furniture that galled him. It was Ken Boudreau. The fact was that three days before—on the very day that

Johanna had bought her ticket, as the station agent had now told him—Mr. McCauley had received a letter from Ken Boudreau asking him to (a) advance some money against the furniture belonging to him (Ken Boudreau) and his dead wife, Marcelle, which was stored in Mr. McCauley's barn, or (b) if he could not see his way to doing that, to sell the furniture for as much as he could get and send the money as quickly as he could to Saskatchewan. There was no mention of the loans that had already been made by father-in-law to son-in-law, all against the value of this furniture and amounting to more than it could ever be sold for. Could Ken Boudreau have forgotten all about that? Or did he simply hope—and this was more probable—that his father-in-law would have forgotten?

He was now, it seemed, the owner of a hotel. But his letter was full of diatribes against the fellow who had formerly owned it and who had misled him as to various particulars.

"If I can just get over this hurdle," he said, "then I am convinced I can still make a go of it." But what was the hurdle? A need for immediate money, but he did not say whether it was owing to the former owner, or to the bank, or to a private mortgage holder, or what. It was the same old story—a desperate, wheedling tone mixed in with some arrogance, some sense of its being what was owed him, because of the wounds inflicted on him, the shame suffered, on account of Marcelle.

With many misgivings but remembering that Ken Boudreau was after all his son-in-law and had fought in the war and been through God-knows-what trouble in his marriage, Mr. McCauley had sat down and written a letter saying that he did not have any idea how to go about getting the best price for the furniture and it would be very difficult for him to find out and that he was enclosing a check, which he would count as an outright personal loan. He wished his son-in-law to acknowledge it as such and to remember the number of similar loans made in the past—already, he believed, exceeding any value of the furniture. He was enclosing a list of dates and amounts. Apart from fifty dollars paid nearly two years ago (with a promise of regular payments to follow), he had received nothing. His son-in-law must surely understand that as a result of these unpaid and interest-free loans Mr. McCauley's income had declined, since he would otherwise have invested the money.

He had thought of adding, "I am not such a fool as you seem to think," but decided not to, since that would reveal his irritation and perhaps his weakness.

And now look. The man had jumped the gun and enlisted Johanna in his scheme—he would always be able to get around women—and got hold of the furniture as well as the check. She had paid for the shipping herself, the station agent had said. The flashy-looking modern maple stuff had been overvalued in the deals already made and they would not get much for it, especially when you counted what the railway had charged. If they had been cleverer they would simply have taken something from the house, one of the old cabinets or parlor settees too uncomfortable to sit on, made and bought in the last century. That, of course, would have been plain stealing. But what they had done was not far off.

He went to bed with his mind made up to prosecute.

He woke in the house alone, with no smell of coffee or breakfast coming from the kitchen—instead, there was a whiff of the burned pot still in the air. An autumn chill had settled in all the high-ceilinged, forlorn rooms. It had been warm last evening and on preceding evenings—the furnace had not been turned on yet, and when Mr. McCauley did turn it on the warm air was accompanied by a blast of cellar damp, of mold and earth and decay. He washed and dressed slowly, with forgetful pauses, and spread some peanut butter on a piece of bread for his breakfast. He belonged to a generation in which there were men who were said not to be able even to boil water, and he was one of them. He looked out the front windows and saw the trees on the other side of the racetrack swallowed up in the morning fog, which seemed to be advancing, not retreating as it should at this hour, across the track itself. He seemed to see in the fog the looming buildings of the old Exhibition Grounds—homely, spacious buildings, like enormous barns. They had stood for years and years unused—all through the war—and he forgot what happened to them in the end. Were they torn down, or did they fall down? He abhorred the races that took place now, the crowds and the loudspeaker and the illegal drinking and the ruinous uproar of the summer Sundays. When he thought of that he thought of his poor girl Marcelle, sitting on the verandah steps and calling out to grown schoolmates who had got out of their parked cars and were hurrying to see the races. The fuss she made, the joy she expressed at being back in town, the hugging and holding people up, talking a mile a minute, rattling on about childhood days and how she'd missed everybody. She had said that the only thing not perfect about life was missing her husband, Ken, left out west because of his work.

She went out there in her silk pajamas, with straggly, uncombed, dyed-blond hair. Her arms and legs were thin, but her face was somewhat bloated, and what she claimed was her tan seemed a sickly brown color not from the sun. Maybe jaundice.

The child had stayed inside and watched television—Sunday cartoons that she was surely too old for.

He couldn't tell what was wrong, or be sure that anything was. Marcelle went away to London to have some female thing done and died in the hospital. When he phoned her husband to tell him, Ken Boudreau said, "What did she take?"

If Marcelle's mother had been alive still, would things have been any different? The fact was that her mother, when she was alive, had been as bewildered as he was. She had sat in the kitchen crying while their teenage daughter, locked into her room, had climbed out the window and slid down the verandah roof to be welcomed by carloads of boys.

The house was full of a feeling of callous desertion, of deceit. He and his wife had surely been kind parents, driven to the wall by Marcelle. When she had eloped with an airman, they had hoped that she would be all right, at last. They had been generous to the two of them as to the most proper young couple. But it all fell apart. To Johanna Parry he had likewise been generous, and look how she too had gone against him.

He walked to town and went into the hotel for his breakfast. The waitress said, "You're bright and early this morning."

And while she was still pouring out his coffee he began to tell her about how his housekeeper had walked out on him without any warning or provocation, not only left her job with no notice but taken a load of furniture that had belonged to his daughter, that now was supposed to belong to his son-in-law but didn't really, having been bought with his daughter's wedding money. He told her how his daughter had married an airman, a good-looking, plausible fellow who wasn't to be trusted around the corner.

"Excuse me," the waitress said. "I'd love to chat, but I got people waiting on their breakfast. Excuse me—"

He climbed the stairs to his office, and there, spread out on his desk, were the old maps he had been studying yesterday in an effort to locate exactly the very first burying ground in the county (abandoned, he believed, in 1839). He turned on the light and sat down, but he found he could not concentrate. After the waitress's reproof—or what he took for a reproof—he hadn't been able to eat his breakfast or enjoy his coffee. He decided to go out for a walk to calm himself down.

But instead of walking along in his usual way, greeting people and passing a few words with them, he found himself bursting into speech. The minute anybody asked him how he was this morning he began in a most uncharacteristic, even shameful way to blurt out his woes, and like the waitress, these people had business to attend to and they nodded and shuffled and made excuses to get away. The morning didn't seem to be warming up in the way foggy fall mornings usually did; his jacket wasn't warm enough, so he sought the comfort of the shops.

People who had known him the longest were the most dismayed. He had never been anything but reticent—the well-mannered gentleman, his mind on other times, his courtesy a deft apology for privilege (which was a bit of a joke, because the privilege was mostly in his recollections and not apparent to others). He should have been the last person to air wrongs or ask for sympathy—he hadn't when his wife died, or even when his daughter died—yet here he was, pulling out some letter, asking if it wasn't a shame the way this fellow had taken him for money over and over again, and even now when he'd taken pity on him once more the fellow had connived with his housekeeper to steal the furniture. Some thought it was his own furniture he was talking about—they believed the old man had been left without a bed or a chair in his house. They advised him to go to the police.

"That's no good, that's no good," he said. "How can you get blood from a stone?"

He went into the Shoe Repair shop and greeted Herman Shultz.

"Do you remember those boots you resoled for me, the ones I got in England? You resoled them four or five years ago."

The shop was like a cave, with shaded bulbs hanging down over various workplaces. It was abominably ventilated, but its manly smells—of glue and leather and shoe-blacking and fresh-cut felt soles and rotted old ones—were comfortable to Mr. McCauley. Here his neighbor Herman Shultz, a sallow, expert, spectacled workman, bent-shouldered, was occupied in all seasons—driving in iron nails and clinch nails and, with a wicked hooked knife, cutting the desired shapes out of leather. The felt was cut by something like a miniature circular saw. The buffers made a scuffing noise and the sandpaper wheel made a rasp and the emery stone on a tool's edge sang high like a mechanical insect and the sewing machine punched the leather in an earnest industrial rhythm. All the sounds and smells and precise activities of the place had been familiar to Mr. McCauley for years but never identified or reflected upon before. Now Herman, in his blackened leather apron with a boot on one hand, straightened up, smiled, nodded, and Mr. McCauley saw the man's whole life in this cave. He wished to express sympathy or admiration or something more that he didn't understand.

"Yes, I do," Herman said. "They were nice boots."

"Fine boots. You know I got them on my wedding trip. I got them in England. I can't remember now where, but it wasn't in London."

"I remember you telling me."

"You did a fine job on them. They're still doing well. Fine job, Herman. You do a good job here. You do honest work."

"That's good." Herman took a quick look at the boot on his hand. Mr. McCauley knew that the man wanted to get back to his work, but he couldn't let him.

"I've just had an eye-opener. A shock."

"Have you?"

The old man pulled out the letter and began to read bits of it aloud, with interjections of dismal laughter.

"Bronchitis. He says he's sick with bronchitis. He doesn't know where to turn. *I don't know who to turn to.* Well he always knows who to turn to. When he's run through everything else, turn to me. *A few hundred just till I get on my feet.* Begging and pleading with me and all the time he's conniving with my housekeeper. Did you know that? She stole a load of furniture and went off out west with it. They were hand in glove. This is a man I've saved the skin of, time and time again. And never a penny back. No, no, I have to be honest and say fifty dollars. Fifty out of hundreds and hundreds. Thousands. He was in the Air Force in the war, you know. Those shortish fellows, they were often in the Air Force. Strutting around thinking they were war heroes. Well, I guess I shouldn't say that, but I think the war spoiled some of those fellows, they never could adjust to life afterwards. But that's not enough of an excuse. Is it? I can't excuse him forever because of the war."

"No you can't."

"I knew he wasn't to be trusted the first time I met him. That's the extraordinary thing. I knew it and I let him rook me all the same. There are people like that. You take pity on them just for being the crooks they are. I got him his insurance job out there, I had some connections. Of course he mucked it up. A bad egg. Some just are."

"You're right about that."

Mrs. Shultz was not in the store that day. Usually she was the one at the counter, taking in the shoes and showing them to her husband and reporting back what he said, making out the slips, and taking the payment when the restored shoes were handed back. Mr. McCauley remembered that she had had some kind of operation during the summer.

"Your wife isn't in today? Is she well?"

"She thought she'd better take it easy today. I've got my girl in."

Herman Shultz nodded towards the shelves to the right of the counter, where the finished shoes were displayed. Mr. McCauley turned his head and saw Edith, the daughter, whom he hadn't noticed when he came in. A childishly thin girl with straight black hair, who kept her back to him, rearranging the shoes. That was just the way she had seemed to slide in and out of sight when she came to his house as Sabitha's friend. You never got a good look at her face.

"You're going to help your father out now?" Mr. McCauley said. "You're through with school?"

"It's Saturday," said Edith, half turning, faintly smiling.

"So it is. Well, it's a good thing to help your father, anyway. You must take care of your parents. They've worked hard and they're good people." With a slight air of apology, as if he knew he was being sententious, Mr. McCauley said, "Honor thy father and thy mother, that thy days may be long in the—"

Edith said something not for him to hear. She said, "Shoe Repair shop."

"I'm taking up your time, I'm imposing on you," said Mr. McCauley sadly. "You have work to do."

"There's no need for you to be sarcastic," said Edith's father when the old man had gone.

HE TOLD EDITH'S MOTHER all about Mr. McCauley at supper.

"He's not himself," he said. "Something's come over him."

"Maybe a little stroke," she said. Since her own operation—for gallstones—she spoke knowledgeably and with a placid satisfaction about the afflictions of other people.

Now that Sabitha had gone, vanished into another sort of life that had, it seemed, always been waiting for her, Edith had reverted to being the person she had been before Sabitha came here. "Old for her age," diligent, critical. After three weeks at high school she knew that she was going to be very good at all the new subjects—Latin, Algebra, English Literature. She believed that her cleverness was going to be recognized and acclaimed and an important future would open out for her. The past year's silliness with Sabitha was slipping out of sight.

Yet when she thought about Johanna's going off out west she felt a chill from her past, an invasive alarm. She tried to bang a lid down on that, but it wouldn't stay.

As soon as she had finished washing the dishes she went off to her room with the book they had been assigned for literature class. *David Copperfield.*

She was a child who had never received more than tepid reproofs from her parents—old parents to have a child of her age, which was said to account for her being the way she was—but she felt in perfect accord with David in his unhappy situation. She felt that she was one like him, one who might as well have been an orphan, because she would probably have to run away, go into hiding, fend for herself, when the truth became known and her past shut off her future.

IT HAD ALL BEGUN with Sabitha saying, on the way to school, "We have to go by the Post Office. I have to send a letter to my dad."

They walked to and from school together every day. Sometimes they walked with their eyes closed, or backwards. Sometimes when they met people they gabbled away softly in a nonsense language, to cause confusion. Most of their good ideas were Edith's. The only idea Sabitha introduced was the writing down of a boy's name and your own, and the stroking out of all letters that were duplicated and the counting of the remainder. Then you ticked off the counted number on your fingers, saying, *Hateship, friendship, courtship, loveship, marriage,* till you got the verdict on what could happen between you and that boy.

"That's a fat letter," said Edith. She noticed everything, and she remembered everything, quickly memorizing whole pages of the textbooks in a way the other children found sinister. "Did you have a lot of things to write to your dad?" she said, surprised, because she could not credit this—or at least could not credit that Sabitha would get them on paper.

"I only wrote on one page," Sabitha said, feeling the letter.

"A-ha," said Edith. "Ah. Ha."

"Aha what?"

"I bet she put something else in. Johanna did."

The upshot of this was that they did not take the letter directly to the Post Office, but saved it and steamed it open at Edith's house after school. They could do such things at Edith's house because her mother worked all day at the Shoe Repair shop.

Dear Mr. Ken Boudreau,

I just thought I would write and send my thanks to you for the nice things you said about me in your letter to your daughter. You do not need to worry about me leaving. You say that I am a person you can trust. That is the meaning I take and as far as I know it is true. I am grateful to you for saying that, since some people feel that a person like me that they do not know the background of is Beyond the Pale. So I thought I would tell you something about myself. I was born in Glasgow, but my mother had to give me up when she got married. I was taken to the Home at the age of five. I looked for her to come back, but she didn't and I got used to it there and they weren't Bad. At the age of eleven I was brought to Canada on a Plan and lived with the Dixons, working on their Market Gardens. School was in the Plan, but I didn't see much of it. In winter I worked in the house for the Mrs. but circumstances made me think of leaving, and being big and strong for my age got taken on at a Nursing Home looking after the old people. I did not mind the work, but for better money went and worked in a Broom Factory. Mr. Willets that owned it had an old mother that came in to see how things were going, and she and I took to each other some way. The atmosphere was giving me breathing troubles so she said I should come and work for her and I did. I lived with her 12 yrs. on a lake called Mourning Dove Lake up north. There was only the two of us, but I could take care of everything outside and in, even running the motorboat and driving the car. I learned to read properly because her eyes were going bad and she liked me to read to her. She died at the age of 96. You might say what a life for a young person, but I was happy. We ate together every meal and I slept in her room the last year and a half. But after she died the family gave me one wk. to pack up. She had left me some money and I guess they did not like that. She wanted me to use it for Education but I would have to go in with kids. So when I saw the ad Mr. McCauley put in the Globe and Mail I came to see about it. I needed work to get over missing Mrs. Willets. So I guess I have bored you long enough with my History and you'll be relieved I have got up to the Present. Thank you for your good opinion and for taking me along to the Fair. I am not one for the rides or for eating the stuff but it was still certainly a pleasure to be included.

Your friend, Johanna Parry.

Edith read Johanna's words aloud, in an imploring voice and with a woebegone expression.

"I was born in Glasgow, but my mother had to give me up when she took one look at me—"

"Stop," said Sabitha. "I'm laughing so hard I'll be sick."

"How did she get her letter in with yours without you knowing?"

"She just takes it from me and puts it in an envelope and writes on the outside because she doesn't think my writing is good enough."

Edith had to put Scotch tape on the flap of the envelope to make it stick, since there wasn't enough sticky stuff left. "She's in love with him," she said.

"Oh, puke-puke," said Sabitha, holding her stomach. "She can't be. Old Johanna."

"What did he say about her, anyway?"

"Just about how I was supposed to respect her and it would be too bad if she left because we were lucky to have her and he didn't have a home for me and Grandpa couldn't raise a girl by himself and blah-blah. He said she was a lady. He said he could tell."

"So then she falls in lo-ove."

The letter remained with Edith overnight, lest Johanna discover that it hadn't been posted and was sealed with Scotch tape. They took it to the Post Office the next morning.

"Now we'll see what he writes back. Watch out," said Edith.

NO LETTER CAME for a long time. And when it did, it was a disappointment. They steamed it open at Edith's house, but found nothing inside for Johanna.

Dear Sabitha,

Christmas finds me a bit short this year, sorry I don't have more than a two-dollar bill to send you. But I hope you are in good health and have a Merry Christmas and keep up your schoolwork. I have not been feeling so well myself, having got Bronchitis, which I seem to do every winter, but this is the first time it landed me in bed before Christmas. As you see by the address I am in a new place. The apartment was in a very noisy location and too many people dropping in hoping for a party. This is a boardinghouse, which suits me fine as I was never good at the shopping and the cooking.

> *Merry Christmas and love, Dad.*

"Poor Johanna," said Edith. "Her heart will be bwoken."
Sabitha said, "Who cares?"
"Unless we do it," Edith said.
"What?"
"*Answer* her."

They would have to type their letter, because Johanna would notice that it was not in Sabitha's father's handwriting. But the typing was not difficult. There was a typewriter in Edith's house, on a card table in the front room. Her mother had worked in an office before she was married and she sometimes earned a little money still by writing the sort of letters that people wanted to look official. She had taught Edith the basics of typing, in the hope that Edith too might get an office job someday.

"Dear Johanna," said Sabitha, "I am sorry I cannot be in love with you because you have got those ugly spots all over your face."

"I'm going to be serious," said Edith. "So shut up."

She typed, "I was so glad to get the letter—" speaking the words of her composition aloud, pausing while she thought up more, her voice becoming increasingly solemn and tender. Sabitha sprawled on the couch, giggling. At one point she turned on the television, but Edith said, "Pul-eeze. How can I concentrate on my e-motions with all that shit going on?"

Edith and Sabitha used the words "shit" and "bitch" and "Jesus Christ" when they were alone together.

Dear Johanna,

I was so glad to get the letter you put in with Sabitha's and to find out about your life. It must often have been a sad and lonely one though Mrs. Willets sounds like a lucky person for you to find. You have remained industrious and uncomplaining and I must say that I admire you very much.

*My own life has been a checkered one and I have never exactly
settled down. I do not know why I have this inner restlessness
and loneliness, it just seems to be my fate. I am always meeting
people and talking to people but sometimes I ask myself, Who
is my friend? Then comes your letter and you write at the
end of it, Your friend. So I think, Does she really mean that?
And what a very nice Christmas present it would be for me if
Johanna would tell me that she is my friend. Maybe you just
thought it was a nice way to end a letter and you don't really
know me well enough. Merry Christmas anyway.*

Your friend, Ken Boudreau.

The letter went home to Johanna. The one to Sabitha had ended
up being typed as well because why would one be typed and not
the other? They had been sparing with the steam this time and
opened the envelope very carefully so there would be no telltale
Scotch tape.

"Why couldn't we type a new envelope? Wouldn't he do that if
he typed the letter?" said Sabitha, thinking she was being clever.

"Because a new *envelope* wouldn't have a *postmark* on it.
Dumb-dumb."

"What if she answers it?"

"We'll read it."

"Yah, what if she answers it and sends it direct to *him?*"

Edith didn't like to show she had not thought of that.

"She won't. She's sly. Anyway, you write him back right away to
give her the idea she can slip it in with yours."

"I hate writing stupid letters."

"Go on. It won't kill you. Don't you want to see what she says?"

Dear Friend,

*You ask me do I know you well enough to be your friend and
my answer is that I think I do. I have only had one Friend in
my life, Mrs. Willets who I loved and she was so good to me
but she is dead. She was a lot older than me and the trouble
with Older Friends is they die and leave you. She was so old*

*she would call me sometimes by another person's name. I did
not mind it though.*

*I will tell you a strange thing. That picture that you got the
photographer at the Fair to take, of you and Sabitha and her
friend Edith and me, I had it enlarged and framed and set in
the living room. It is not a very good picture and he certainly
charged you enough for what it is, but it is better than nothing.
So the day before yesterday I was dusting around it and I
imagined I could hear you say Hello to me. Hello, you said, and
I looked at your face as well as you can see it in the picture and I
thought, Well, I must be losing my mind. Or else it is a sign of a
letter coming. I am just fooling, I don't really believe in anything
like that. But yesterday there was a letter. So you see it is not
asking too much of me to be your friend. I can always find a way
to keep busy but a true Friend is something else again.*

Your Friend, Johanna Parry.

Of course, that could not be replaced in the envelope. Sabitha's
father would spot something fishy in the references to a letter he
had never written. Johanna's words had to be torn into tiny pieces
and flushed down the toilet at Edith's house.

WHEN THE LETTER CAME telling about the hotel it was months
and months later. It was summer. And it was just by luck that
Sabitha had picked that letter up, since she had been away for three
weeks, staying at the cottage on Lake Simcoe that belonged to her
Aunt Roxanne and her Uncle Clark.

Almost the first thing Sabitha said, coming into Edith's house,
was, "Ugga-ugga. This place stinks."

"Ugga-ugga" was an expression she had picked up from her
cousins.

Edith sniffed the air. "I don't smell anything."

"It's like your dad's shop, only not so bad. They must bring it
home on their clothes and stuff."

Edith attended to the steaming and opening. On her way from
the Post Office, Sabitha had bought two chocolate eclairs at the
bakeshop. She was lying on the couch eating hers.

"Just one letter. For you," said Edith. "Pore old Johanna. Of course he never actually *got* hers."

"Read it to me," said Sabitha resignedly. "I've got sticky guck all over my hands."

Edith read it with businesslike speed, hardly pausing for the periods.

Well, Sabitha, my fortunes have taken a different turn, as you can see I am not in Brandon anymore but in a place called Gdynia. And not in the employ of my former bosses. I have had an exceptionally hard winter with my chest troubles and they, that is my bosses, thought I should be out on the road even if I was in danger of developing pneumonia so this developed into quite an argument so we all decided to say farewell. But luck is a strange thing and just about that time I came into possession of a Hotel. It is too complicated to explain the ins and outs but if your grandfather wants to know about it just tell him a man who owed me money which he could not pay let me have this hotel instead. So here I am moved from one room in a boardinghouse to a twelve-bedroom building and from not even owning the bed I slept in to owning several. It's a wonderful thing to wake up in the morning and know you are your own boss. I have some fixing up to do, actually plenty, and will get to it as soon as the weather warms up. I will need to hire somebody to help and later on I will hire a good cook to have a restaurant as well as the beverage room. That ought to go like hotcakes as there is none in this town. Hope you are well and doing your schoolwork and developing good habits.

Love, Your Dad.

Sabitha said, "Have you got some coffee?"

"Instant," said Edith. "Why?"

Sabitha said that iced coffee was what everybody had been drinking at the cottage and they were all crazy about it. She was crazy about it too. She got up and messed around in the kitchen, boiling the water and stirring up the coffee with milk and ice cubes. "What we really ought to have is vanilla ice cream," she said. "Oh, my Gad, is it ever wonderful. Don't you want your eclair?"

Oh, my Gad.

"Yes. All of it," said Edith meanly.

All these changes in Sabitha in just three weeks—during the time Edith had been working in the shop and her mother recovering at home from her operation. Sabitha's skin was an appetizing golden-brown color, and her hair was cut shorter and fluffed out around her face. Her cousins had cut it and given her a permanent. She wore a sort of playsuit, with shorts cut like a skirt and buttons down the front and frills over the shoulders in a becoming blue color. She had got plumper, and when she leaned over to pick up her glass of iced coffee, which was on the floor, she displayed a smooth, glowing cleavage.

Breasts. They must have started growing before she went away, but Edith had not noticed. Maybe they were just something you woke up with one morning. Or did not.

However they came, they seemed to indicate a completely unearned and unfair advantage.

Sabitha was full of talk about her cousins and life at the cottage. She would say, "Listen, I've got to tell you about this, it's a scream—" and then ramble on about what Aunt Roxanne said to Uncle Clark when they had the fight, how Mary Jo drove with the top down and without a license in Stan's car (who was Stan?) and took them all to a drive-in—and what was the scream or the point of the story somehow never became clear.

But after a while other things did. The real adventures of the summer. The older girls—that included Sabitha—slept in the upstairs of the boathouse. Sometimes they had tickling fights—they would all gang up on someone and tickle her till she shrieked for mercy and agreed to pull her pajama pants down to show if she had hair. They told stories about girls at boarding school who did things with hairbrush handles, toothbrush handles. *Ugga-ugga.* Once a couple of cousins put on a show—one girl got on top of the other and pretended to be the boy and they wound their legs around each other and groaned and panted and carried on.

Uncle Clark's sister and her husband came to visit on their honeymoon, and he was seen to put his hand inside her swimsuit.

"They really loved each other, they were at it day and night," said Sabitha. She hugged a cushion to her chest. "People can't help it when they're in love like that."

One of the cousins had already done it with a boy. He was one of the summer help in the gardens of the resort down the road. He took her out in a boat and threatened to push her out until she agreed to let him do it. So it wasn't her fault.

"Couldn't she swim?" said Edith.

Sabitha pushed the cushion between her legs. "Oooh," she said. "Feels so nice."

Edith knew all about the pleasurable agonies Sabitha was feeling, but she was appalled that anybody would make them public. She herself was frightened of them. Years ago, before she knew what she was doing, she had gone to sleep with the blanket between her legs and her mother had discovered her and told her about a girl she had known who did things like that all the time and had eventually been operated on for the problem.

"They used to throw cold water on her, but it didn't cure her," her mother had said. "So she had to be cut."

Otherwise her organs would get congested and she might die.

"Stop," she said to Sabitha, but Sabitha moaned defiantly and said, "It's nothing. We all did it like this. Haven't you got a cushion?"

Edith got up and went to the kitchen and filled her empty iced-coffee glass with cold water. When she got back Sabitha was lying limp on the couch, laughing, the cushion flung on the floor.

"What did you think I was doing?" she said. "Didn't you know I was kidding?"

"I was thirsty," Edith said.

"You just drank a whole glass of iced coffee."

"I was thirsty for water."

"Can't have any fun with you." Sabitha sat up. "If you're so thirsty why don't you drink it?"

They sat in a moody silence until Sabitha said, in a conciliatory but disappointed tone, "Aren't we going to write Johanna another letter? Let's write her a lovey-dovey letter."

Edith had lost a good deal of her interest in the letters, but she was gratified to see that Sabitha had not. Some sense of having power over Sabitha returned, in spite of Lake Simcoe and the breasts. Sighing, as if reluctantly, she got up and took the cover off the typewriter.

"My darlingest Johanna—" said Sabitha.

"No. That's too sickening."

"She won't think so."

"She will so," said Edith.

She wondered whether she should tell Sabitha about the danger of congested organs. She decided not to. For one thing, that information fell into a category of warnings she had received from her mother and never known whether to wholly trust or distrust. It had not fallen as low, in credibility, as the belief that wearing foot-rubbers in the house would ruin your eyesight, but there was no telling—someday it might.

And for another thing—Sabitha would just laugh. She laughed at warnings—she would laugh even if you told her that chocolate eclairs would make her fat.

"Your last letter made me so happy—"

"Your last letter filled me with rap-ture—" said Sabitha.

"—made me so happy to think I did have a true friend in the world, which is you—"

"I could not sleep all night because I was longing to crush you in my arms—" Sabitha wrapped her arms around herself and rocked back and forth.

"*No.* Often I have felt so lonely in spite of a gregarious life and not known where to turn—"

"What does that mean—'gregarious'? She won't know what it means."

"*She* will."

That shut Sabitha up and perhaps hurt her feelings. So at the end Edith read out, "I must say good-bye and the only way I can do it is to imagine you reading this and blushing—" "Is that more what you want?"

"Reading it in bed with your nightgown on," said Sabitha, always quickly restored, "and thinking how I would crush you in my arms and I would suck your titties—"

My Dear Johanna,

Your last letter made me so happy to think I have a true friend in the world, which is you. Often I have felt so lonely in spite of a gregarious life and not known where to turn.

Well, I have told Sabitha in my letter about my good fortune and how I am going into the hotel business. I did not tell her actually how sick I was last winter because I did not want to worry her. I do not want to worry you, either, dear Johanna, only to tell you that I thought of you so often and longed to see your dear sweet face. When I was feverish I thought that I really did see it bending over me and I heard your voice telling me I would soon be better and I felt the ministrations of your kind hands. I was in the boardinghouse and when I came to out of my fever there was a lot of teasing going on as to, who is this Johanna? But I was sad as could be to wake and find you were not there. I really wondered if you could have flown through the air and been with me, even though I knew that could not have happened. Believe me, believe me, the most beautiful movie star could not have been as welcome to me as you. I don't know if I should tell you the other things you were saying to me because they were very sweet and intimate but they might embarrass you. I hate to end this letter because it feels now as if I have my arms around you and I am talking to you quietly in the dark privacy of our room, but I must say good-bye and the only way I can do it is to imagine you reading this and blushing. It would be wonderful if you were reading it in bed with your nightgown on and thinking how I would like to crush you in my arms.

L-v-, Ken Boudreau.

Somewhat surprisingly, there was no reply to this letter. When Sabitha had written her half-page, Johanna put it in the envelope and addressed it and that was that.

· · ·

WHEN JOHANNA GOT OFF THE TRAIN there was nobody to
meet her. She did not let herself worry about that—she had been
thinking that her letter might not, after all, have got here before she
did. (In fact it had, and was lying in the Post Office, uncollected,
because Ken Boudreau, who had not been seriously sick last winter,
really did have bronchitis now and for several days had not come
in for his mail. On this day it had been joined by another envelope,
containing the check from Mr. McCauley. But payment on that
had already been stopped.)

What was of more concern to her was that there did not appear
to be a town. The station was an enclosed shelter with benches
along the walls and a wooden shutter pulled down over the window
of the ticket office. There was also a freight shed—she supposed it
was a freight shed—but the sliding door to it would not budge.
She peered through a crack between the planks until her eyes got
used to the dark in there, and she saw that it was empty, with a dirt
floor. No crates of furniture there. She called out, "Anybody here?
Anybody here?" several times, but she did not expect a reply.

She stood on the platform and tried to get her bearings.

About half a mile away there was a slight hill, noticeable at once
because it had a crown of trees. And the sandy-looking track that
she had taken, when she saw it from the train, for a back lane into a
farmer's field—that must be the road. Now she saw the low shapes
of buildings here and there in the trees—and a water tower, which
looked from this distance like a toy, a tin soldier on long legs.

She picked up her suitcase—this would not be too difficult; she
had carried it, after all, from Exhibition Road to the other railway
station—and set out.

There was a wind blowing, but this was a hot day—hotter than
the weather she had left in Ontario—and the wind seemed hot
as well. Over her new dress she was wearing her same old coat,
which would have taken up too much room in the suitcase. She
looked with longing to the shade of the town ahead, but when she
got there she found that the trees were either spruce, which were
too tight and narrow to give much shade, or raggedy thin-leaved
cottonwoods, which blew about and let the sun through anyway.

There was a discouraging lack of formality, or any sort of organization, to this place. No sidewalks, or paved streets, no imposing buildings except a big church like a brick barn. A painting over its door, showing the Holy Family with clay-colored faces and staring blue eyes. It was named for an unheard-of saint—Saint Voytech.

The houses did not show much forethought in their situation or planning. They were set at different angles to the road, or street, and most of them had mean-looking little windows stuck here and there, with snow porches like boxes round the doors. Nobody was out in the yards, and why should they be? There was nothing to tend, only clumps of brown grass and once a big burst of rhubarb, gone to seed.

The main street, if that's what it was, had a raised wooden walk on one side only, and some unconsolidated buildings, of which a grocery store (containing the Post Office) and a garage seemed to be the only ones functioning. There was one two-story building that she thought might be the hotel, but it was a bank and it was closed.

The first human being she saw—though two dogs had barked at her—was a man in front of the garage, busy loading chains into the back of his truck.

"Hotel?" he said. "You come too far."

He told her that it was down by the station, on the other side of the tracks and along a bit, it was painted blue and you couldn't miss it.

She set the suitcase down, not from discouragement but because she had to have a moment's rest.

He said he would ride her down there if she wanted to wait a minute. And though it was a new kind of thing for her to accept such an offer, she soon found herself riding in the hot, greasy cab of his truck, rocking down the dirt road that she had just walked up, with the chains making a desperate racket in the back.

"So—where'd you bring this heat wave from?" he said.

She said Ontario, in a tone that promised nothing further.

"Ontario," he said regretfully. "Well. There 'tis. Your hotel." He took one hand off the wheel. The truck gave an accompanying lurch as he waved to a two-story flat-roofed building that she hadn't missed but had seen from the train, as they came in. She had taken it then for a large and fairly derelict, perhaps abandoned, family home. Now that she had seen the houses in town, she knew that she should not have dismissed it so readily. It was covered with sheets of tin stamped to look like bricks and painted a light blue. There was the one word HOTEL, in neon tubing, no longer lit, over the doorway.

"I am a dunce," she said, and offered the man a dollar for the ride.

He laughed. "Hang on to your money. You never know when you'll need it."

Quite a decent-looking car, a Plymouth, was parked outside this hotel. It was very dirty, but how could you help that, with these roads?

There were signs on the door advertising a brand of cigarettes, and of beer. She waited till the truck had turned before she knocked—knocked because it didn't look as if the place could in any way be open for business. Then she tried the door to see if it was open, and walked into a little dusty room with a staircase, and then into a large dark room in which there was a billiard table and a bad smell of beer and an unswept floor. Off in a side room she could see the glimmer of a mirror, empty shelves, a counter. These rooms had the blinds pulled tightly down. The only light she saw was coming through two small round windows, which turned out to be set in double swinging doors. She went on through these into a kitchen. It was lighter, because of a row of high—and dirty—windows, uncovered, in the opposite wall. And here were the first signs of life—somebody had been eating at the table and had left a plate smeared with dried ketchup and a cup half full of cold black coffee.

One of the doors off the kitchen led outside—this one was locked—and one to a pantry in which there were several cans of food, one to a broom closet, and one to an enclosed stairway. She climbed the steps, bumping her suitcase along in front of her because the space was narrow. Straight ahead of her on the second floor she saw a toilet with the seat up.

The door of the bedroom at the end of the hall was open, and in there she found Ken Boudreau.

She saw his clothes before she saw him. His jacket hanging

up on a corner of the door and his trousers on the doorknob, so that they trailed on the floor. She thought at once that this was no way to treat good clothes, so she went boldly into the room—leaving her suitcase in the hall—with the idea of hanging them up properly.

He was in bed, with only a sheet over him. The blanket and his shirt were lying on the floor. He was breathing restlessly as if about to wake up, so she said, "Good morning. Afternoon."

The bright sunlight was coming in the window, hitting him almost in the face. The window was closed and the air horribly stale—smelling, for one thing, of the full ashtray on the chair he used as a bed table.

He had bad habits—he smoked in bed.

He did not wake up at her voice—or he woke only partway. He began to cough.

She recognized this as a serious cough, a sick man's cough. He struggled to lift himself up, still with his eyes closed, and she went over to the bed and hoisted him. She looked for a handkerchief or a box of tissues, but she saw nothing so she reached for his shirt on the floor, which she could wash later. She wanted to get a good look at what he spat up.

When he had hacked up enough, he muttered and sank down into the bed, gasping, the charming cocky-looking face she remembered crumpled up in disgust. She knew from the feel of him that he had a fever.

The stuff that he had coughed out was greenish-yellow—no rusty streaks. She carried the shirt to the toilet sink, where rather to her surprise she found a bar of soap, and washed it out and hung it on the door hook, then thoroughly washed her hands. She had to dry them on the skirt of her new brown dress. She had put that on in another little toilet—the *Ladies* on the train—not more than a couple of hours ago. She had been wondering then if she should have got some makeup.

In a hall closet she found a roll of toilet paper and took it into his room for the next time he had to cough. She picked up the blanket and covered him well, pulled the blind down to the sill and raised the stiff window an inch or two, propping it open with the ashtray she had emptied. Then she changed, out in the hall, from the brown dress into old clothes from her suitcase. A lot of use a nice dress or any makeup in the world would be now.

She was not sure how sick he was, but she had nursed Mrs. Willets—also a heavy smoker—through several bouts of bronchitis, and she thought she could manage for a while without having to think about getting a doctor. In the same hall closet was a pile of clean, though worn and faded, towels, and she wet one of these and wiped his arms and legs, to try to get his fever down. He came half awake at this and began to cough again. She held him up and made him spit into the toilet paper, examined it once more and threw it down the toilet and washed her hands. She had a towel now to dry them on. She went downstairs and found a glass in the kitchen, also an empty, large ginger-ale bottle, which she filled with water. This she attempted to make him drink. He took a little, protested, and she let him lie down. In five minutes or so she tried again. She kept doing this until she believed he had swallowed as much as he could hold without throwing up.

Time and again he coughed and she lifted him up, held him with one arm while the other hand pounded on his back to help loosen the load in his chest. He opened his eyes several times and seemed to take in her presence without alarm or surprise—or gratitude, for that matter. She sponged him once more, being careful to cover immediately with the blanket the part that had just been cooled.

She noticed that it had begun to get dark, and she went down into the kitchen, found the light switch. The lights and the old electric stove were working. She opened and heated a can of chicken-with-rice soup, carried it upstairs and roused him. He swallowed a little from the spoon. She took advantage of his momentary wakefulness to ask if he had a bottle of aspirin. He nodded yes, then became very confused when trying to tell her where. "In the wastebasket," he said.

"No, no," she said. "You don't mean wastebasket."

"In the—in the—"

He tried to shape something with his hands. Tears came into his eyes.

"Never mind," Johanna said. "Never mind."

His fever went down anyway. He slept for an hour or more without coughing. Then he grew hot again. By that time she had found the aspirin—they were in a kitchen drawer with such things as a screwdriver and some lightbulbs and a ball of twine—and she got a couple into him. Soon he had a violent coughing fit, but she didn't think he threw them up. When he lay down she put her ear to his chest and listened to the wheezing. She had already looked for mustard to make a plaster with, but apparently there wasn't any. She went downstairs again and heated some water and brought it in a basin. She tried to make him lean over it, tenting him with towels, so that he could breathe the steam. He would cooperate only for a moment or so, but perhaps it helped—he hacked up quantities of phlegm.

His fever went down again and he slept more calmly. She dragged in an armchair she had found in one of the other rooms and she slept too, in snatches, waking and wondering where she was, then remembering and getting up and touching him—his fever seemed to be staying down—and tucking in the blanket. For her own cover she used the everlasting old tweed coat that she had Mrs. Willets to thank for.

He woke. It was full morning. "What are you doing here?" he said, in a hoarse, weak voice.

"I came yesterday," she said. "I brought your furniture. It isn't here yet, but it's on its way. You were sick when I got here and you were sick most of the night. How do you feel now?"

He said, "Better," and began to cough. She didn't have to lift him, he sat up on his own, but she went to the bed and pounded his back. When he finished, he said, "Thank you."

His skin now felt as cool as her own. And smooth—no rough moles, no fat on him. She could feel his ribs. He was like a delicate, stricken boy. He smelled like corn.

"You swallowed the phlegm," she said. "Don't do that, it's not good for you. Here's the toilet paper, you have to spit it out. You could get trouble with your kidneys, swallowing it."

"I never knew that," he said. "Could you find the coffee?"

The percolator was black on the inside. She washed it as well as she could and put the coffee on. Then she washed and tidied herself, wondering what kind of food she should give him. In the pantry there was a box of biscuit mix. At first she thought she would have to mix it with water, but she found a can of milk powder as well. When the coffee was ready she had a pan of biscuits in the oven.

AS SOON AS HE HEARD HER busy in the kitchen, he got up to go to the toilet. He was weaker than he'd thought—he had to lean over and put one hand on the tank. Then he found some under-wear on the floor of the hall closet where he kept clean clothes. He had figured out by now who this woman was. She had said she came to bring him his furniture, though he hadn't asked her or anybody to do that—hadn't asked for the furniture at all, just the money. He should know her name, but he couldn't remember it. That was why he opened her purse, which was on the floor of the hall beside her suitcase. There was a name tag sewn to the lining.

Johanna Parry, and the address of his father-in-law, on Exhibition Road.

Some other things. A cloth bag with a few bills in it. Twenty-seven dollars. Another bag with change, which he didn't bother to count. A bright blue bankbook. He opened it up automatically, without expectations of anything unusual.

A couple of weeks ago Johanna had been able to transfer the whole of her inheritance from Mrs. Willets into her bank account, adding it to the amount of money she had saved. She had explained to the bank manager that she did not know when she might need it.

The sum was not dazzling, but it was impressive. It gave her substance. In Ken Boudreau's mind, it added a sleek upholstery to the name Johanna Parry.

"Were you wearing a brown dress?" he said, when she came up with the coffee.

"Yes, I was. When I first got here."

"I thought it was a dream. It was you."

"Like in your other dream," Johanna said, her speckled fore-head turning fiery. He didn't know what that was all about and hadn't the energy to inquire. Possibly a dream he'd wakened from when she was here in the night—one he couldn't now remember. He coughed again in a more reasonable way, with her handing him some toilet paper.

"Now," she said, "where are you going to set your coffee?" She pushed up the wooden chair that she had moved to get at him more easily. "There," she said. She lifted him under the arms and wedged the pillow in behind him. A dirty pillow, without a case, but she had covered it last night with a towel.

"Could you see if there's any cigarettes downstairs?"

She shook her head, but said, "I'll look. I've got biscuits in the oven."

KEN BOUDREAU was in the habit of lending money, as well as borrowing it. Much of the trouble that had come upon him—or that he had got into, to put it another way—had to do with not being able to say no to a friend. Loyalty. He had not been drummed out of the peacetime Air Force, but had resigned out of loyalty to the friend who had been hauled up for offering insults to the C.O. at a mess party. At a mess party, where everything was supposed to be a joke and no offense taken—it was not fair. And he had lost the job with the fertilizer company because he took a company truck across the American border without permission, on a Sunday, to pick up a buddy who had got into a fight and was afraid of being caught and charged.

Part and parcel of the loyalty to friends was the difficulty with bosses. He would confess that he found it hard to knuckle under. "Yes, sir" and "no, sir" were not ready words in his vocabulary. He had not been fired from the insurance company, but he had been passed over so many times that it seemed they were daring him to quit, and eventually he did.

Drink had played a part, you had to admit that. And the idea that life should be a more heroic enterprise than it ever seemed to be nowadays.

He liked to tell people he'd won the hotel in a poker game. He was not really much of a gambler, but women liked the sound of that. He didn't want to admit that he'd taken it sight unseen in payment of a debt. And even after he saw it, he told himself it could be salvaged. The idea of being his own boss did appeal to him. He did not see it as a place where people would stay—except perhaps hunters, in the fall. He saw it as a drinking establishment and a restaurant. If he could get a good cook. But before anything much could happen money would have to be spent. Work had to be done—more than he could possibly do himself though he was not unhandy. If he could live through the winter doing what he could by himself, proving his good intentions, he thought maybe he could get a loan from the bank. But he needed a smaller loan just to get through the winter, and that was where his father-in-law came into the picture. He would rather have tried somebody else, but nobody else could so easily spare it.

He had thought it a good idea to put the request in the form of a proposal to sell the furniture, which he knew the old man would never bestir himself enough to do. He was aware, not very specifically, of loans still outstanding from the past—but he was able to think of those as sums he'd been entitled to, for supporting Marcelle during a period of bad behavior (hers, at a time when his own hadn't started) and for accepting Sabitha as his child when he had his doubts. Also, the McCauleys were the only people he knew who had money that nobody now alive had earned.

I brought your furniture.

He was unable to figure out what that could mean for him, at present. He was too tired. He wanted to sleep more than he wanted to eat when she came with the biscuits (and no cigarettes). To satisfy her he ate half of one. Then he fell dead asleep. He came only half awake when she rolled him on one side, then the other, getting the dirty sheet out from under him, then spreading the clean one and rolling him onto that, all without making him get out of bed or really wake up.

"I found a clean sheet, but it's thin as a rag," she said. "It didn't smell too good, so I hung it on the line awhile."

Later he realized that a sound he'd been hearing for a long time in a dream was really the sound of the washing machine. He wondered how that could be—the hot-water tank was defunct. She must have heated tubs of water on the stove. Later still, he heard the unmistakable sound of his own car starting up and driving away. She would have got the keys from his pants pocket.

She might be driving away in his only worthwhile possession, deserting him, and he could not even phone the police to nab her. The phone was cut off, even if he'd been able to get to it.

That was always a possibility—theft and desertion—yet he turned over on the fresh sheet, which smelled of prairie wind and grass, and went back to sleep, knowing for certain that she had only gone to buy milk and eggs and butter and bread and other supplies—even cigarettes—that were necessary for a decent life, and that she would come back and be busy downstairs and that the sound of her activity would be like a net beneath him, heaven-sent, a bounty not to be questioned.

There was a woman problem in his life right now. Two women, actually, a young one and an older one (that is, one of about his own age) who knew about each other and were ready to tear each other's hair out. All he had got from them recently was howling and complaining, punctuated with their angry assertions that they loved him.

Perhaps a solution had arrived for that, as well.

WHEN SHE WAS BUYING GROCERIES in the store, Johanna heard a train, and driving back to the hotel, she saw a car parked at the railway station. Before she had even stopped Ken Boudreau's car she saw the furniture crates piled up on the platform. She talked to the agent—it was his car there—and he was very surprised and irritated by the arrival of all these big crates. When she had got out of him the name of a man with a truck—a clean truck, she insisted—who lived twenty miles away and sometimes did hauling, she used the station phone to call the man and half bribed, half ordered him to come right away. Then she impressed upon the agent that he must stay with the crates till the truck arrived. By suppertime the truck had come, and the man and his son had unloaded all the furniture and carried it into the main room of the hotel.

The next day she took a good look around. She was making up her mind.

The day after that she judged Ken Boudreau to be able to sit up and listen to her, and she said, "This place is a sinkhole for money. The town is on its last legs. What should be done is to take out everything that can bring in any cash and sell it. I don't mean the furniture that was shipped in, I mean things like the pool table and the kitchen range. Then we ought to sell the building to somebody who'll strip the tin off it for junk. There's always a bit to be made off stuff you'd never think had any value. Then— What was it you had in mind to do before you got hold of the hotel?"

He said that he had had some idea of going to British Columbia, to Salmon Arm, where he had a friend who had told him one time he could have a job managing orchards. But he couldn't go because the car needed new tires and work done on it before he could undertake a long trip, and he was spending all he had just to live. Then the hotel had fallen into his lap.

"Like a ton of bricks," she said. "Tires and fixing the car would be a better investment than sinking anything into this place. It would be a good idea to get out there before the snow comes. And ship the furniture by rail again, to make use of it when we get there. We have got all we need to furnish a home."

"It's maybe not all that firm of an offer."

She said, "I know. But it'll be all right."

He understood that she did know, and that it was, it would be, all right. You could say that a case like his was right up her alley.

Not that he wouldn't be grateful. He'd got to a point where gratitude wasn't a burden, where it was natural—especially when it wasn't demanded.

Thoughts of regeneration were starting. *This is the change I need.* He had said that before, but surely there was one time when it would be true. The mild winters, the smell of the evergreen forests and the ripe apples. *All we need to make a home.*

HE HAS HIS PRIDE, she thought. That would have to be taken account of. It might be better never to mention the letters in which he had laid himself open to her. Before she came away, she had destroyed them. In fact she had destroyed each one as soon as she'd read it over well enough to know it by heart, and that didn't take long. One thing she surely didn't want was for them ever to fall into the hands of young Sabitha and her shifty friend. Especially the part in the last letter, about her nightgown, and being in bed. It wasn't that such things wouldn't go on, but it might be thought vulgar or sappy or asking for ridicule, to put them on paper.

She doubted they'd see much of Sabitha. But she would never thwart him, if that was what he wanted.

This wasn't really a new experience, this brisk sense of expansion and responsibility. She'd felt something the same for Mrs. Willets—another fine-looking, flighty person in need of care and management. Ken Boudreau had turned out to be a bit more that way than she was prepared for, and there were the differences you had to expect with a man, but surely there was nothing in him that she couldn't handle.

After Mrs. Willets her heart had been dry, and she had considered it might always be so. And now such a warm commotion, such busy love.

MR. MCCAULEY died about two years after Johanna's departure. His funeral was the last one held in the Anglican church. There was a good turnout for it. Sabitha—who came with her mother's cousin, the Toronto woman—was now self-contained and pretty and remarkably, unexpectedly slim. She wore a sophisticated black hat and did not speak to anybody unless they spoke to her first. Even then, she did not seem to remember them.

The death notice in the paper said that Mr. McCauley was survived by his granddaughter Sabitha Boudreau and his son-in-law Ken Boudreau, and Mr. Boudreau's wife Johanna, and their infant son Omar, of Salmon Arm, B.C.

Edith's mother read this out—Edith herself never looked at the local paper. Of course, the marriage was not news to either of them—or to Edith's father, who was around the corner in the front room, watching television. Word had got back. The only news was Omar.

"Her with a *baby*," Edith's mother said.

Edith was doing her Latin translation at the kitchen table. *Tu ne quaesieris, scire nefas, quem mihi, quem tibi—*

In the church she had taken the precaution of not speaking to Sabitha first, before Sabitha could not speak to her.

She was not really afraid, anymore, of being found out—though she still could not understand why they hadn't been. And in a way, it seemed only proper that the antics of her former self should not be connected with her present self—let alone with the real self that she expected would take over once she got out of this town and away from all the people who thought they knew her. It was the whole twist of consequence that dismayed her—it seemed fantastical, but dull. Also insulting, like some sort of joke or inept warning, trying to get its hooks into her. For where, on the list of things she planned to achieve in her life, was there any mention of her being responsible for the existence on earth of a person named Omar?

Ignoring her mother, she wrote, "You must not ask, it is forbidden for us to know—"

She paused, chewing her pencil, then finished off with a chill of satisfaction, "—what fate has in store for me, or for you—"

Family Furnishings

~

ALFRIDA. My father called her Freddie. The two of them were first cousins and lived on adjoining farms and then for a while in the same house. One day they were out in the fields of stubble playing with my father's dog, whose name was Mack. That day the sun shone, but did not melt the ice in the furrows. They stomped on the ice and enjoyed its crackle underfoot.

How could she remember a thing like that? my father said. She made it up, he said.

"I did not," she said.

"You did so."

"I did not."

All of a sudden they heard bells pealing, whistles blowing. The town bell and the church bells were ringing. The factory whistles were blowing in the town three miles away. The world had burst its seams for joy, and Mack tore out to the road, because he was sure a parade was coming. It was the end of the First World War.

THREE TIMES A WEEK, we could read Alfrida's name in the paper. Just her first name—Alfrida. It was printed as if written by hand, a flowing, fountain-pen signature. Round and About the Town, with Alfrida. The town mentioned was not the one close by, but the city to the south, where Alfrida lived, and which my family visited perhaps once every two or three years.

Now is the time for all you future June brides to start registering your preferences at the China Cabinet, and I must tell you that if I were a bride-to-be—which alas I am not—I might resist all the patterned dinner sets, exquisite as they are, and go for the pearly-white, the ultra-modern Rosenthal . . .

Beauty treatments may come and beauty treatments may go, but the masques they slather on you at Fantine's Salon are guaranteed—speaking of brides—to make your skin bloom like orange blossoms. And to make the bride's mom—and the bride's aunts and for all I know her grandmom—feel as if they'd just taken a dip in the Fountain of Youth . . .

You would never expect Alfrida to write in this style, from the way she talked.

She was also one of the people who wrote under the name of Flora Simpson, on the Flora Simpson Housewives' Page. Women from all over the countryside believed that they were writing their letters to the plump woman with the crimped gray hair and the forgiving smile who was pictured at the top of the page. But the truth—which I was not to tell—was that the notes that appeared at the bottom of each of their letters were produced by Alfrida and a man she called Horse Henry, who otherwise did the obituaries. The women gave themselves such names as Morning Star and Lily-of-the-Valley and Green Thumb and Little Annie Rooney and Dishmop Queen. Some names were so popular that numbers had to be assigned to them—Goldilocks 1, Goldilocks 2, Goldilocks 3.

Dear Morning Star, Alfrida or Horse Henry would write,

Eczema is a dreadful pest, especially in this hot weather we're having, and I hope the baking soda does some good. Home treatments certainly ought to be respected, but it never hurts to seek out your doctor's advice. It's splendid news to hear your hubby is up and about again. It can't have been any fun with both of you under the weather . . .

In all the small towns of that part of Ontario, housewives who belonged to the Flora Simpson Club would hold an annual summer picnic. Flora Simpson always sent her special greetings but explained that there were just too many events for her to show up at all of them and she did not like to make distinctions. Alfrida said that there had been talk of sending Horse Henry done up in a wig and pillow bosoms, or perhaps herself leering like the Witch of Babylon (not even she, at my parents' table, could quote the Bible accurately and say "Whore") with a ciggie-boo stuck to her lipstick. But, oh, she said, the paper would kill us. And anyway, it would be too mean.

She always called her cigarettes ciggie-boos. When I was fifteen or sixteen she leaned across the table and asked me, "How would you like a ciggie-boo, too?" The meal was finished, and my younger brother and sister had left the table. My father was shaking his head. He had started to roll his own.

I said thank you and let Alfrida light it and smoked for the first time in front of my parents.

They pretended that it was a great joke.

"Ah, will you look at your daughter?" said my mother to my father. She rolled her eyes and clapped her hands to her chest and spoke in an artificial, languishing voice. "I'm like to faint."

"Have to get the horsewhip out," my father said, half rising in his chair.

This moment was amazing, as if Alfrida had transformed us into new people. Ordinarily, my mother would say that she did not like to see a woman smoke. She did not say that it was indecent, or unladylike—just that she did not like it. And when she said in a certain tone that she did not like something it seemed that she was not making a confession of irrationality but drawing on a private source of wisdom, which was unassailable and almost sacred. It was when she reached for this tone, with its accompanying expression of listening to inner voices, that I particularly hated her.

As for my father, he had beaten me, in this very room, not with a horsewhip but his belt, for running afoul of my mother's rules and wounding my mother's feelings, and for answering back. Now it seemed that such beatings could occur only in another universe.

My parents had been put in a corner by Alfrida—and also by me—but they had responded so gamely and gracefully that it was really as if all three of us—my mother and my father and myself—had been lifted to a new level of ease and aplomb. In that instant I could see them—particularly my mother—as being capable of a kind of lightheartedness that was scarcely ever on view.

All due to Alfrida.

Alfrida was always referred to as a career girl. This made her seem to be younger than my parents, though she was known to be about the same age. It was also said that she was a city person. And the city, when it was spoken of in this way, meant the one she lived and worked in. But it meant something else as well—not just a distinct configuration of buildings and sidewalks and streetcar lines or even a crowding together of individual people. It meant something more abstract that could be repeated over and over, something like a hive of bees, stormy but organized, not useless or deluded exactly, but disturbing and sometimes dangerous. People went into such a place when they had to and were glad when they got out. Some, however, were attracted to it—as Alfrida must have been, long ago, and as I was now, puffing on my cigarette and trying to hold it in a nonchalant way, though it seemed to have grown to the size of a baseball bat between my fingers.

MY FAMILY did not have a regular social life—people did not come to the house for dinner, let alone to parties. It was a matter of class, maybe. The parents of the boy I married, about five years after this scene at the dinner table, invited people who were not related to them to dinner, and they went to afternoon parties that they spoke of, unself-consciously, as cocktail parties. It was a life such as I had read of in magazine stories, and it seemed to me to place my in-laws in a world of storybook privilege.

What our family did was put boards in the dining-room table two or three times a year to entertain my grandmother and my aunts—my father's older sisters—and their husbands. We did this at Christmas or Thanksgiving, when it was our turn, and perhaps also when a relative from another part of the province showed up on a visit. This visitor would always be a person rather like the aunts and their husbands and never the least bit like Alfrida.

My mother and I would start preparing for such dinners a couple of days ahead. We ironed the good tablecloth, which was as heavy as a bed quilt, and washed the good dishes, which had been sitting in the china cabinet collecting dust, and wiped the legs of the dining-room chairs, as well as making the jellied salads, the pies and cakes, that had to accompany the central roast turkey or baked ham and bowls of vegetables. There had to be far too much to eat, and most of the conversation at the table had to do with the food, with the company saying how good it was and being urged to have more, and saying that they couldn't, they were stuffed, and then the aunts' husbands relenting, taking more, and the aunts taking just a little more and saying that they shouldn't, they were ready to bust.

And dessert still to come.

There was hardly any idea of a general conversation, and in fact there was a feeling that conversation that passed beyond certain understood limits might be a disruption, a showing-off. My mother's understanding of the limits was not reliable, and she sometimes could not wait out the pauses or honor the aversion to follow-up. So when somebody said, "Seen Harley upstreet yesterday," she was liable to say, perhaps, "Do you think a man like Harley is a confirmed bachelor? Or he just hasn't met the right person?"

As if, when you mentioned seeing a person you were bound to have something further to say, something *interesting*.

Then there might be a silence, not because the people at the table meant to be rude but because they were flummoxed. Till my father would say with embarrassment, and oblique reproach, "He seems to get on all right by hisself."

If his relatives had not been present, he would more likely have said "himself."

And everybody went on cutting, spooning, swallowing, in the glare of the fresh tablecloth, with the bright light pouring in through the newly washed windows. These dinners were always in the middle of the day.

The people at that table were quite capable of talk. Washing and drying the dishes, in the kitchen, the aunts would talk about who had a tumor, a septic throat, a bad mess of boils. They would tell about how their own digestions, kidneys, nerves were functioning. Mention of intimate bodily matters seemed never to be so out of place, or suspect, as the mention of something read in a magazine, or an item in the news—it was improper somehow to pay attention to anything that was not close at hand. Meanwhile, resting on the porch, or during a brief walk out to look at the crops, the aunts' husbands might pass on the information that somebody was in a tight spot with the bank, or still owed money on an expensive piece of machinery, or had invested in a bull that was a disappointment on the job.

It could have been that they felt clamped down by the formality of the dining room, the presence of bread-and-butter plates and dessert spoons, when it was the custom, at other times, to put a piece of pie right onto a dinner plate that had been cleaned up with bread. (It would have been an offense, however, not to set things out in this proper way. In their own houses, on like occasions, they would put their guests through the same paces.) It may have been just that eating was one thing, and talking was something else.

When Alfrida came it was altogether another story. The good cloth would be spread and the good dishes would be out. My mother would have gone to a lot of trouble with the food and she would be nervous about the results—probably she would have abandoned the usual turkey-and-stuffing-and-mashed-potatoes menu and made something like chicken salad surrounded by mounds of molded rice with cut-up pimientos, and this would be followed by a dessert involving gelatin and egg white and whipped cream, taking a long, nerve-racking time to set because we had no refrigerator and it had to be chilled on the cellar floor. But the constraint, the pall over the table, was quite absent. Alfrida not only accepted second helpings, she asked for them. And she did this almost absentmindedly, and tossed off her compliments in the same way, as if the food, the eating of the food, was a secondary though agreeable thing, and she was really there to talk, and make other people talk, and anything you wanted to talk about—almost anything—would be fine.

She always visited in summer, and usually she wore some sort of striped, silky sundress, with a halter top that left her back bare. Her back was not pretty, being sprinkled with little dark moles, and her shoulders were bony and her chest nearly flat. My father would always remark on how much she could eat and remain thin. Or he turned truth on its head by noting that her appetite was as picky as ever, but she still hadn't been prevented from larding on the fat. (It was not considered out of place in our family to comment about fatness or skinniness or pallor or ruddiness or baldness.)

Her dark hair was done up in rolls above her face and at the sides, in the style of the time. Her skin was brownish-looking, netted with fine wrinkles, and her mouth wide, the lower lip rather thick, almost drooping, painted with a hearty lipstick that left a smear on the teacup and water tumbler. When her mouth was opened wide—as it nearly always was, talking or laughing—you could see that some of her teeth had been pulled at the back. Nobody could say that she was good-looking—any woman over twenty-five seemed to me to have pretty well passed beyond the possibility of being good-looking, anyway, to have lost the right to be so, and perhaps even the desire—but she was fervent and dashing. My father said thoughtfully that she had zing.

Alfrida talked to my father about things that were happening in the world, about politics. My father read the paper, he listened to the radio, he had opinions about these things but rarely got a chance to talk about them. The aunts' husbands had opinions too, but theirs were brief and unvaried and expressed an everlasting distrust of all public figures and particularly all foreigners, so that most of the time all that could be got out of them were grunts of dismissal. My grandmother was deaf—nobody could tell how much she knew or what she thought about anything, and the aunts themselves seemed fairly proud of how much they didn't know or didn't have to pay attention to. My mother had been a school-teacher, and she could readily have pointed out all the countries of Europe on the map, but she saw everything through a personal haze, with the British Empire and the royal family looming large and everything else diminished, thrown into a jumble-heap that it was easy for her to disregard.

Alfrida's views were not really so far away from those of the uncles. Or so it appeared. But instead of grunting and letting the subject go, she gave her hooting laugh, and told stories about prime ministers and the American president and John L. Lewis and the mayor of Montreal—stories in which they all came out badly. She told stories about the royal family too, but there she made a dis-tinction between the good ones like the king and queen and the beautiful Duchess of Kent and the dreadful ones like the Windsors and old King Eddy, who—she said—had a certain disease and had marked his wife's neck by trying to strangle her, which was why she always had to wear her pearls. This distinction coincided pretty well with one my mother made but seldom spoke about, so she did not object—though the reference to syphilis made her wince.

I smiled at it, knowingly, with a foolhardy composure.

Alfrida called the Russians funny names. Mikoyan-sky. Uncle Joe-sky. She believed that they were pulling the wool over everybody's eyes, and that the United Nations was a farce that would never work and that Japan would rise again and should have been finished off when there was the chance. She didn't trust Quebec either. Or the pope. There was a problem for her with Senator McCarthy—she would have liked to be on his side, but his being a Catholic was a stumbling block. She called the pope the poop. She relished the thought of all the crooks and scoundrels to be found in the world.

Sometimes it seemed as if she was putting on a show—a display, maybe to tease my father. To rile him up, as he himself would have said, to get his goat. But not because she disliked him or even wanted to make him uncomfortable. Quite the opposite. She might have been tormenting him as young girls torment boys at school, when arguments are a peculiar delight to both sides and insults are taken as flattery. My father argued with her, always in a mild steady voice, and yet it was clear that he had the intention of goading her on. Sometimes he would do a turnaround, and say that maybe she was right—that with her work on the newspaper, she must have sources of information that he couldn't have. You've put me straight, he would say, if I had any sense I'd be obliged to you. And she would say, Don't give me that load of baloney.

"You two," said my mother, in mock despair and perhaps in real exhaustion, and Alfrida told her to go and have a lie-down, she deserved it after this splendiferous dinner, she and I would manage the dishes. My mother was subject to a tremor in her right arm, a stiffness in her fingers, that she believed came when she got overtired.

While we worked in the kitchen Alfrida talked to me about celebrities—actors, even minor movie stars, who had made stage appearances in the city where she lived. In a lowered voice still broken by wildly disrespectful laughter she told me stories of their bad behavior, the rumors of private scandals that had never made it into the magazines. She mentioned queers, man-made bosoms, household triangles—all things that I had found hints of in my reading but felt giddy to hear about, even at third or fourth hand, in real life.

Alfrida's teeth always got my attention, so that even in these confidential recitals I sometimes lost track of what was being said.

Those teeth that were left, across the front, were each of a slightly different color, no two alike. Some with a fairly strong enamel tended towards shades of dark ivory, others were opalescent, shadowed with lilac, and giving out fish-flashes of silver rims, occasionally a gleam of gold. People's teeth in those days seldom made such a solid, handsome show as they do now, unless they were false. But these teeth of Alfrida's were unusual in their individuality, clear separation, and large size. When Alfrida let out some jibe that was especially, knowingly outrageous, they seemed to leap to the fore like a palace guard, like jolly spear-fighters.

"She always did have trouble with her teeth," the aunts said. "She had that abscess, remember, the poison went all through her system."

How like them, I thought, to toss aside Alfrida's wit and style and turn her teeth into a sorry problem.

"Why doesn't she just have them all out and be done with it?" they said.

"Likely she couldn't afford it," said my grandmother, surprising everybody as she sometimes did, by showing that she had been keeping up with the conversation all along.

And surprising me with the new, everyday sort of light this shed on Alfrida's life. I had believed that Alfrida was rich—rich at least in comparison with the rest of the family. She lived in an apartment—I had never seen it, but to me that fact conveyed at least the idea of a very civilized life—and she wore clothes that were not homemade, and her shoes were not Oxfords like the shoes of practically all the other grown-up women I knew—they were sandals made of bright strips of the new plastic. It was hard to know whether my grandmother was simply living in the past, when getting your false teeth was the solemn, crowning expense of a lifetime, or whether she really knew things about Alfrida's life that I never would have guessed.

The rest of the family was never present when Alfrida had dinner at our house. She did go to see my grandmother, who was her aunt, her mother's sister. My grandmother no longer lived at her own house but lived alternately with one or the other of the aunts, and Alfrida went to whichever house she was living in at the time, but not to the other house, to see the other aunt who was as much her cousin as my father was. And the meal she took was never with any of them. Usually she came to our house first and visited awhile, and then gathered herself up, as if reluctantly, to make the other visit. When she came back later and we sat down to eat, nothing derogatory was said outright against the aunts and their husbands, and certainly nothing disrespectful about my grandmother. In fact, it was the way that my grandmother would be spoken of by Alfrida—a sudden sobriety and concern in her voice, even a touch of fear (what about her blood pressure, had she been to the doctor lately, what did he have to say?)—that made me aware of the difference, the coolness or possibly unfriendly restraint, with which she asked after the others. Then there would be a similar restraint in my mother's reply, and an extra gravity in my father's—a caricature of gravity, you might say—that showed how they all agreed about something they could not say.

On the day when I smoked the cigarette Alfrida decided to take this a bit further, and she said solemnly, "How about Asa, then? Is he still as much of a conversation grabber as ever?"

My father shook his head sadly, as if the thought of this uncle's garrulousness must weigh us all down.

"Indeed," he said. "He is indeed."

Then I took my chance.

"Looks like the roundworms have got into the hogs," I said. "Yup."

Except for the "yup," this was just what my uncle had said, and he had said it at this very table, being overcome by an uncharacteristic need to break the silence or to pass on something important that had just come to mind. And I said it with just his stately grunts, his innocent solemnity.

Alfrida gave a great, approving laugh, showing her festive teeth. "That's it, she's got him to a *T*."

My father bent over his plate, as if to hide how he was laughing too, but of course not really hiding it, and my mother shook her head, biting her lips, smiling. I felt a keen triumph. Nothing was said to put me in my place, no reproof for what was sometimes called my sarcasm, my being smart. The word "smart" when it was used about me, in the family, might mean intelligent, and then it was used rather grudgingly—"oh, she's smart enough some ways"—or it might be used to mean pushy, attention-seeking, obnoxious. *Don't be so smart.*

Sometimes my mother said sadly, "You have a cruel tongue."

Sometimes—and this was a great deal worse—my father was disgusted with me.

"What makes you think you have the right to run down decent people?"

This day nothing like that happened—I seemed to be as free as a visitor at the table, almost as free as Alfrida, and flourishing under the banner of my own personality.

BUT THERE WAS A GAP about to open, and perhaps that was the last time, the very last time, that Alfrida sat at our table. Christmas cards continued to be exchanged, possibly even letters—as long as my mother could manage a pen—and we still read Alfrida's name in the paper, but I cannot recall any visits during the last couple of years I lived at home.

It may have been that Alfrida asked if she could bring her friend and had been told that she could not. If she was already living with him, that would have been one reason, and if he was the same man she had later, the fact that he was married would have been another. My parents would have been united in this. My mother had a horror of irregular sex or flaunted sex—of any sex, you might say, for the proper married kind was not acknowledged at all—and my father too judged these matters strictly at that time in his life. He might have had a special objection, also, to a man who could get a hold over Alfrida.

She would have made herself cheap in their eyes. I can imagine either one of them saying it. *She didn't need to go and make herself cheap.*

But she may not have asked at all, she may have known enough not to. During the time of those earlier, lively visits there may have been no man in her life, and then when there was one, her attention may have shifted entirely. She may have become a different person then, as she certainly was later on.

Or she may have been wary of the special atmosphere of a household where there is a sick person who will go on getting sicker and never get better. Which was the case with my mother, whose symptoms joined together, and turned a corner, and instead of a worry and an inconvenience became her whole destiny.

"The poor thing," the aunts said.

And as my mother was changed from a mother into a stricken presence around the house, these other, formerly so restricted females in the family seemed to gain some little liveliness and increased competence in the world. My grandmother got herself a hearing aid—something nobody would have suggested to her. One of the aunts' husbands—not Asa, but the one called Irvine—died, and the aunt who had been married to him learned to drive the car and got a job doing alterations in a clothing store and no longer wore a hairnet.

They called to see my mother, and saw always the same thing—that the one who had been better-looking, who had never quite let them forget she was a schoolteacher, was growing month by month more slow and stiff in the movements of her limbs and more thick and importunate in her speech, and that nothing was going to help her.

They told me to take good care of her.

"She's your mother," they reminded me.

"The poor thing."

Alfrida would not have been able to say those things, and she might not have been able to find anything to say in their place.

Her not coming to see us was all right with me. I didn't want people coming. I had no time for them, I had become a furious housekeeper—waxing the floors and ironing even the dish towels, and this was all done to keep some sort of disgrace (my mother's deterioration seemed to be a unique disgrace that infected us all) at bay. It was done to make it seem as if I lived with my parents and my brother and my sister in a normal family in an ordinary house, but the moment somebody stepped in our door and saw my mother they saw that this was not so and they pitied us. A thing I could not stand.

I WON A SCHOLARSHIP. I didn't stay home to take care of my mother or of anything else. I went off to college. The college was in the city where Alfrida lived. After a few months she asked me to come for supper, but I could not go, because I worked every evening of the week except on Sundays. I worked in the city library, down-town, and in the college library, both of which stayed open until nine o'clock. Some time later, during the winter, Alfrida asked me again, and this time the invitation was for a Sunday. I told her that I could not come because I was going to a concert.

"Oh—a date?" she said, and I said yes, but at the time it was not true. I would go to the free Sunday concerts in the college audito-rium with another girl, or two or three other girls, for something to do and in the faint hope of meeting some boys there.

"Well you'll have to bring him around sometime," Alfrida said. "I'm dying to meet him."

Towards the end of the year I did have someone to bring, and I had actually met him at a concert. At least, he had seen me at a concert and had phoned me up and asked me to go out with him. But I would never have brought him to meet Alfrida. I would never have brought any of my new friends to meet her. My new friends were people who said, "Have you read *Look Homeward Angel*? Oh, you have to read that. Have you read *Buddenbrooks*?" They were people with whom I went to see *Forbidden Games* and *Les Enfants du Paradis* when the Film Society brought them in. The boy I went out with, and later became engaged to, had taken me to the Music Building, where you could listen to records at lunch hour. He introduced me to Gounod and because of Gounod I loved opera, and because of opera I loved Mozart.

When Alfrida left a message at my rooming house, asking me to call back, I never did. After that she didn't call again.

SHE STILL WROTE FOR THE PAPER—occasionally I glanced at one of her rhapsodies about Royal Doulton figurines or imported ginger biscuits or honeymoon negligees. Very likely she was still answering the letters from the Flora Simpson housewives, and still laughing at them. Now that I was living in that city I seldom looked at the paper that had once seemed to me the center of city life—and even, in a way, the center of our life at home, sixty miles away. The jokes, the compulsive insincerity, of people like Alfrida and Horse Henry now struck me as tawdry and boring.

I did not worry about running into her, even in this city that was not, after all, so very large. I never went into the shops that she mentioned in her column. I had no reason ever to walk past the newspaper building, and she lived far away from my rooming house, somewhere on the south side of town.

Nor did I think that Alfrida was the kind of person to show up at the library. The very word, "library," would probably make her turn down her big mouth in a parody of consternation, as she used to do at the books in the bookcase in our house—those books not bought in my time, some of them won as school prizes by my teen-aged parents (there was my mother's maiden name, in her beautiful lost handwriting), books that seemed to me not like things bought in a store at all, but like presences in the house just as the trees outside the window were not plants but presences rooted in the ground. *The Mill on the Floss, The Call of the Wild, The Heart of Midlothian.* "Lot of hotshot reading in there," Alfrida had said. "Bet you don't crack those very often." And my father had said no, he didn't, falling in with her comradely tone of dismissal or even contempt and to some extent telling a lie, because he did look into them, once in a long while, when he had the time.

That was the kind of lie that I hoped never to have to tell again, the contempt I hoped never to have to show, about the things that really mattered to me. And in order not to have to do that, I would pretty well have to stay clear of the people I used to know.

AT THE END of my second year I was leaving college—my scholarship had covered only two years there. It didn't matter—I was planning to be a writer anyway. And I was getting married.

Alfrida had heard about this, and she got in touch with me again.

"I guess you must've been too busy to call me, or maybe nobody ever gave you my messages," she said.

I said that maybe I had been, or maybe they hadn't.

This time I agreed to visit. A visit would not commit me to anything, since I was not going to be living in this city in the future. I picked a Sunday, just after my final exams were over, when my fiancé was going to be in Ottawa for a job interview. The day was bright and sunny—it was around the beginning of May. I decided to walk. I had hardly ever been south of Dundas Street or east of Adelaide, so there were parts of the city that were entirely strange to me. The shade trees along the northern streets had just come out in leaf, and the lilacs, the ornamental crab apple trees, the beds of tulips were all in flower, the lawns like fresh carpets. But after a while I found myself walking along streets where there were no shade trees, streets where the houses were hardly an arm's reach from the sidewalk, and where such lilacs as there were—lilacs will grow anywhere—were pale, as if sun-bleached, and their fragrance did not carry. On these streets, as well as houses there were narrow apartment buildings, only two or three stories high—some with the utilitarian decoration of a rim of bricks around their doors, and some with raised windows and limp curtains falling out over their sills.

Alfrida lived in a house, not in an apartment building. She had the whole upstairs of a house. The downstairs, at least the front part of the downstairs, had been turned into a shop, which was closed, because of Sunday. It was a secondhand shop—I could see through the dirty front windows a lot of nondescript furniture with stacks of old dishes and utensils set everywhere. The only thing that caught my eye was a honey pail, exactly like the honey pail with a blue sky and a golden beehive in which I had carried my lunch to school when I was six or seven years old. I could remember reading over and over the words on its side.

All pure honey will granulate.

I had no idea then what "granulate" meant, but I liked the sound of it. It seemed ornate and delicious.

I had taken longer to get there than I had expected and I was very hot. I had not thought that Alfrida, inviting me to lunch, would present me with a meal like the Sunday dinners at home, but it was cooked meat and vegetables I smelled as I climbed the outdoor stairway.

"I thought you'd got lost," Alfrida called out above me. "I was about to get up a rescue party."

Instead of a sundress she was wearing a pink blouse with a floppy bow at the neck, tucked into a pleated brown skirt. Her hair was no longer done up in smooth rolls but cut short and frizzed around her face, its dark brown color now harshly touched with red. And her face, which I remembered as lean and summer-tanned, had got fuller and somewhat pouchy. Her makeup stood out on her skin like orange-pink paint in the noon light.

But the biggest difference was that she had got false teeth, of a uniform color, slightly overfilling her mouth and giving an anxious edge to her old expression of slapdash eagerness.

"Well—haven't you plumped out," she said. "You used to be so skinny."

This was true, but I did not like to hear it. Along with all the girls at the rooming house, I ate cheap food—copious meals of Kraft dinners and packages of jam-filled cookies. My fiancé, so sturdily and possessively in favor of everything about me, said that he liked full-bodied women and that I reminded him of Jane Russell. I did not mind his saying that, but usually I was affronted when people had anything to say about my appearance. Particularly when it was somebody like Alfrida—somebody who had lost all importance in my life. I believed that such people had no right to be looking at me, or forming any opinions about me, let alone stating them.

This house was narrow across the front, but long from front to back. There was a living room whose ceiling sloped at the sides and whose windows overlooked the street, a hall-like dining room with no windows at all because side bedrooms with dormers opened off it, a kitchen, a bathroom also without windows that got its daylight through a pebbled-glass pane in its door, and across the back of the house a glassed-in sunporch.

The sloping ceilings made the rooms look makeshift, as if they were only pretending to be anything but bedrooms. But they were crowded with serious furniture—dining-room table and chairs, kitchen table and chairs, living-room sofa and recliner—all meant 'for larger, proper rooms. Doilies on the tables, squares of embroidered white cloth protecting the backs and arms of sofa and chairs, sheer curtains across the windows and heavy flowered drapes at the sides—it was all more like the aunts' houses than I would have thought possible. And on the dining-room wall—not in the bathroom or bedroom but in the dining room—there hung a picture that was the silhouette of a girl in a hoopskirt, all constructed of pink satin ribbon.

A strip of tough linoleum was laid down on the dining-room floor, on the path from the kitchen to the living room.

Alfrida seemed to guess something of what I was thinking.

"I know I've got far too much stuff in here," she said. "But it's my parents' stuff. It's family furnishings, and I couldn't let them go."

I had never thought of her as having parents. Her mother had died long ago, and she had been brought up by my grandmother, who was her aunt.

"My dad and mother's," Alfrida said. "When Dad went off, your grandma kept it because she said it ought to be mine when I grew up, and so here it is. I couldn't turn it down, when she went to that trouble."

Now it came back to me—the part of Alfrida's life that I had forgotten about. Her father had married again. He had left the farm and got a job working for the railway. He had some other children, the family moved from one town to another, and sometimes Alfrida used to mention them, in a joking way that had something to do with how many children there had been and how close they came together and how much the family had to move around.

"Come and meet Bill," Alfrida said.

Bill was out on the sunporch. He sat, as if waiting to be summoned, on a low couch or daybed that was covered with a brown plaid blanket. The blanket was rumpled—he must have been lying on it recently—and the blinds on the windows were all pulled down to their sills. The light in the room—the hot sunlight coming through the rain-marked yellow blinds—and the rumpled rough blanket and faded, dented cushion, even the smell of the blanket, and of the masculine slippers, old scuffed slippers that had lost their shape and pattern, reminded me—just as much as the doilies and the heavy polished furniture in the inner rooms had done, and the ribbon-girl on the wall—of my aunts' houses. There, too, you could come upon a shabby male hideaway with its furtive yet insistent odors, its shamefaced but stubborn look of contradicting the female domain.

Bill stood up and shook my hand, however, as the uncles would never have done with a strange girl. Or with any girl. No specific rudeness would have held them back, just a dread of appearing ceremonious.

He was a tall man with wavy, glistening gray hair and a smooth but not young-looking face. A handsome man, with the force of his good looks somehow drained away—by indifferent health, or some bad luck, or lack of gumption. But he had still a worn courtesy, a way of bending towards a woman, that suggested the meeting would be a pleasure, for her and for himself.

Alfrida directed us into the windowless dining room where the lights were on in the middle of this bright day. I got the impression that the meal had been ready some time ago, and that my late arrival had delayed their usual schedule. Bill served the roast chicken and dressing, Alfrida the vegetables. Alfrida said to Bill, "Honey, what do you think that is beside your plate?" and then he remembered to pick up his napkin.

He had not much to say. He offered the gravy, he inquired as to whether I wanted mustard relish or salt and pepper, he followed the conversation by turning his head towards Alfrida or towards me. Every so often he made a little whistling sound between his teeth, a shivery sound that seemed meant to be genial and appreciative and that I thought at first might be a prelude to some remark. But it never was, and Alfrida never paused for it. I have since seen reformed drinkers who behaved somewhat as he did—chiming in agreeably but unable to carry things beyond that, helplessly preoccupied. I never knew whether that was true of Bill, but he did seem to carry around a history of defeat, of troubles borne and lessons learned. He had an air too of gallant accommodation towards whatever choices had gone wrong or chances hadn't panned out.

These were frozen peas and carrots, Alfrida said. Frozen vegetables were fairly new at the time.

"They beat the canned," she said. "They're practically as good as fresh."

Then Bill made a whole statement. He said they were better than fresh. The color, the flavor, everything was better than fresh. He said it was remarkable what they could do now and what would be done by way of freezing things in the future.

Alfrida leaned forward, smiling. She seemed almost to hold her breath, as if he was her child taking unsupported steps, or a first lone wobble on a bicycle.

There was a way they could inject something into a chicken, he told us, there was a new process that would have every chicken coming out the same, plump and tasty. No such thing as taking a risk on getting an inferior chicken anymore.

"Bill's field is chemistry," Alfrida said.

When I had nothing to say to this she added, "He worked for Gooderhams."

Still nothing.

"The distillers," she said. "Gooderhams Whisky."

The reason that I had nothing to say was not that I was rude or bored (or any more rude than I was naturally at that time, or more bored than I had expected to be) but that I did not understand that I should ask questions—almost any questions at all, to draw a shy male into conversation, to shake him out of his abstraction and set him up as a man of a certain authority, therefore the man of the house. I did not understand why Alfrida looked at him with such a fiercely encouraging smile. All of my experience of a woman with men, of a woman listening to her man, hoping and hoping that he will establish himself as somebody she can reasonably be proud of, was in the future. The only observation I had made of couples was of my aunts and uncles and of my mother and father, and those husbands and wives seemed to have remote and formalized connections and no obvious dependence on each other.

Bill continued eating as if he had not heard this mention of his profession and his employer, and Alfrida began to question me about my courses. She was still smiling, but her smile had changed. There was a little twitch of impatience and unpleasantness in it, as if she was just waiting for me to get to the end of my explanations so that she could say—as she did say—"You couldn't get me to read that stuff for a million dollars."

"Life's too short," she said. "You know, down at the paper we sometimes get somebody that's been through all that. Honors English. Honors Philosophy. You don't know what to do with them. They can't write worth a nickel. I've told you that, haven't I?" she said to Bill, and Bill looked up and gave her his dutiful smile.

She let this settle.

"So what do you do for fun?" she said.

A Streetcar Named Desire was being done in a theater in Toronto at that time, and I told her that I had gone down on the train with a couple of friends to see it.

Alfrida let the knife and fork clatter onto her plate.

"That filth," she cried. Her face leapt out at me, carved with disgust. Then she spoke more calmly but still with a virulent displeasure.

"You went *all the way to Toronto* to see that filth."

We had finished the dessert, and Bill picked that moment to ask if he might be excused. He asked Alfrida, then with the slightest bow he asked me. He went back to the sunporch and in a little while we could smell his pipe. Alfrida, watching him go, seemed to forget about me and the play. There was a look of such stricken tenderness on her face that when she stood up I thought she was going to follow him. But she was only going to get her cigarettes.

She held them out to me, and when I took one she said, with a deliberate effort at jollity, "I see you kept up the bad habit I got you started on." She might have remembered that I was not a child anymore and I did not have to be in her house and that there was no point in making an enemy of me. And I wasn't going to argue—I did not care what Alfrida thought about Tennessee Williams. Or what she thought about anything else.

"I guess it's your own business," Alfrida said. "You can go where you want to go." And she added, "After all—you'll pretty soon be a married woman."

By her tone, this could mean either "I have to allow that you're grown up now" or "Pretty soon you'll have to toe the line."

We got up and started to collect the dishes. Working close to each other in the small space between the kitchen table and counter and the refrigerator, we soon developed without speaking about it a certain order and harmony of scraping and stacking and putting the leftover food into smaller containers for storage and filling the sink with hot, soapy water and pouncing on any piece of cutlery that hadn't been touched and slipping it into the baize-lined drawer in the dining-room buffet. We brought the ashtray out to the kitchen and stopped every now and then to take a restorative, businesslike drag on our cigarettes. There are things women agree on or don't agree on when they work together in this way—whether it is all right to smoke, for instance, or preferable not to smoke because some migratory ash might find its way onto a clean dish, or whether every single thing that has been on the table has to be washed even if it has not been used—and it turned out that Alfrida and I agreed. Also, the thought that I could get away, once the dishes were done, made me feel more relaxed and generous. I had already said that I had to meet a friend that afternoon.

"These are pretty dishes," I said. They were creamy-colored, slightly yellowish, with a rim of blue flowers.

"Well—they were my mother's wedding dishes," Alfrida said. "That was one other good thing your grandma did for me. She packed up all my mother's dishes and put them away until the time came when I could use them. Jeanie never knew they existed. They wouldn't have lasted long, with that bunch."

Jeanie. That bunch. Her stepmother and the half brothers and sisters.

"You know about that, don't you?" Alfrida said. "You know what happened to my mother?"

Of course I knew. Alfrida's mother had died when a lamp exploded in her hands—that is, she died of burns she got when a lamp exploded in her hands—and my aunts and my mother had spoken of this regularly. Nothing could be said about Alfrida's mother or about Alfrida's father, and very little about Alfrida herself—without that death being dragged in and tacked onto it. It was the reason that Alfrida's father left the farm (always somewhat of a downward step morally if not financially). It was a reason to be desperately careful with coal oil, and a reason to be grateful for electricity, whatever the cost. And it was a dreadful thing for a child of Alfrida's age, whatever. (That is—whatever she had done with herself since.)

If it hadn't've been for the thunderstorm she wouldn't ever have been lighting a lamp in the middle of the afternoon.

She lived all that night and the next day and the next night and it would have been the best thing in the world for her if she hadn't've.

And just the year after that the Hydro came down their road, and they didn't have need of the lamps anymore.

The aunts and my mother seldom felt the same way about anything, but they shared a feeling about this story. The feeling was in their voices whenever they said Alfrida's mother's name. The story seemed to be a horrible treasure to them, something our family could claim that nobody else could, a distinction that would never be let go. To listen to them had always made me feel as if there was some obscene connivance going on, a fond fingering of whatever was grisly or disastrous. Their voices were like worms slithering around in my insides.

Men were not like this, in my experience. Men looked away from frightful happenings as soon as they could and behaved as if there was no use, once things were over with, in mentioning them or thinking about them ever again. They didn't want to stir themselves up, or stir other people up.

So if Alfrida was going to talk about it, I thought, it was a good thing that my fiancé had not come. A good thing that he didn't have to hear about Alfrida's mother, on top of finding out about my mother and my family's relative or maybe considerable poverty. He admired opera and Laurence Olivier's *Hamlet*, but he had no time for tragedy—for the squalor of tragedy—in ordinary life. His parents were healthy and good-looking and prosperous (though he said of course that they were dull), and it seemed he had not had to know anybody who did not live in fairly sunny circumstances. Failures in life—failures of luck, of health, of finances—all struck him as lapses, and his resolute approval of me did not extend to my ramshackle background.

"They wouldn't let me in to see her, at the hospital," Alfrida said, and at least she was saying this in her normal voice, not preparing the way with any special piety, or greasy excitement. "Well, I probably wouldn't have let me in either, if I'd been in their shoes. I've no idea what she looked like. Probably all bound up like a mummy. Or if she wasn't she should have been. I wasn't there when it happened, I was at school. It got very dark and the teacher turned the lights on—we had the lights, at school—and we all had to stay till the thunderstorm was over. Then my Aunt Lily—well, your grandmother—she came to meet me and took me to her place. And I never got to see my mother again."

I thought that was all she was going to say but in a moment she continued, in a voice that had actually brightened up a bit, as if she was preparing for a laugh.

"I yelled and yelled my fool head off that I wanted to see her. I carried on and carried on, and finally when they couldn't shut me up your grandmother said to me, 'You're just better off not to see her. You would not want to see her, if you knew what she looks like now. You wouldn't want to remember her this way.'

"But you know what I said? I remember saying it. I said, But she would want to see me. *She would want to see me.*"

·Then she really did laugh, or make a snorting sound that was evasive and scornful.

"I must've thought I was a pretty big cheese, mustn't I? *She would want to see me.*"

This was a part of the story I had never heard.

And the minute that I heard it, something happened. It was as if a trap had snapped shut, to hold these words in my head. I did not exactly understand what use I would have for them. I only knew how they jolted me and released me, right away, to breathe a different kind of air, available only to myself.

She would want to see me.

The story I wrote, with this in it, would not be written till years later, not until it had become quite unimportant to think about who had put the idea into my head in the first place.

I thanked Alfrida and said that I had to go. Alfrida went to call Bill to say good-bye to me, but came back to report that he had fallen asleep.

"He'll be kicking himself when he wakes up," she said. "He enjoyed meeting you."

She took off her apron and accompanied me all the way down the outside steps. At the bottom of the steps was a gravel path leading around to the sidewalk. The gravel crunched under our feet and she stumbled in her thin-soled house shoes.

She said, "Ouch! Goldarn it," and caught hold of my shoulder.

"How's your dad?" she said.

"He's all right."

"He works too hard."

I said, "He has to."

"Oh, I know. And how's your mother?"

"She's about the same."

She turned aside towards the shop window.

"Who do they think is ever going to buy this junk? Look at that honey pail. Your dad and I used to take our lunch to school in pails just like that."

"So did I," I said.

"Did you?" She squeezed me. "You tell your folks I'm thinking about them, will you do that?"

ALFRIDA DID NOT COME to my father's funeral. I wondered if that was because she did not want to meet me. As far as I knew she had never made public what she held against me; nobody else would know about it. But my father had known. When I was home visiting him and learned that Alfrida was living not far away—in my grandmother's house, in fact, which she had finally inherited—I had suggested that we go to see her. This was in the flurry between my two marriages, when I was in an expansive mood, newly released and able to make contact with anyone I chose.

My father said, "Well, you know, Alfrida was a bit upset."

He was calling her Alfrida now. When had that started?

I could not even think, at first, what Alfrida might be upset about. My father had to remind me of the story, published several years ago, and I was surprised, even impatient and a little angry, to think of Alfrida's objecting to something that seemed now to have so little to do with her.

"It wasn't Alfrida at all," I said to my father. "I changed it, I wasn't even thinking about her. It was a character. Anybody could see that."

But as a matter of fact there was still the exploding lamp, the mother in her charnel wrappings, the staunch, bereft child.

"Well," my father said. He was in general quite pleased that I had become a writer, but there were reservations he had about what might be called my character. About the fact that I had ended my marriage for personal—that is, wanton—reasons, and the way I went around justifying myself—or perhaps, as he would have said, weaseling out of things. He would not say so—it was not his business anymore.

I asked him how he knew that Alfrida felt this way.

He said, "A letter."

A letter, though they lived not far apart. I did feel sorry to think that he had had to bear the brunt of what could be taken as my thoughtlessness, or even my wrongdoing. Also that he and Alfrida seemed now to be on such formal terms. I wondered what he was leaving out. Had he felt compelled to defend me to Alfrida, as he had to defend my writing to other people? He would do that now, though it was never easy for him. In his uneasy defense he might have said something harsh.

Through me, peculiar difficulties had developed for him.

There was a danger whenever I was on home ground. It was the danger of seeing my life through other eyes than my own. See- ing it as an ever-increasing roll of words like barbed wire, intricate, bewildering, uncomforting—set against the rich productions, the food, flowers, and knitted garments, of other women's domestic- ity. It became harder to say that it was worth the trouble.

Worth my trouble, maybe, but what about anyone else's?

My father had said that Alfrida was living alone now. I asked him what had become of Bill. He said that all of that was outside of his jurisdiction. But he believed there had been a bit of a rescue operation.

"Of Bill? How come? Who by?"

"Well, I believe there was a wife."

"I met him at Alfrida's once. I liked him."

"People did. Women."

I HAD TO CONSIDER that the rupture might have had nothing to do with me. My stepmother had urged my father into a new sort of life. They went bowling and curling and regularly joined other couples for coffee and doughnuts at Tim Horton's. She had been a widow for a long time before she married him, and she had many friends from those days who became new friends for him. What had happened with him and Alfrida might have been simply one of the changes, the wearing-out of old attachments, that I under- stood so well in my own life but did not expect to happen in the lives of older people—particularly, as I would have said, in the lives of people at home.

My stepmother died just a little while before my father. After their short, happy marriage they were sent to separate cemeteries to lie beside their first, more troublesome, partners. Before either of those deaths Alfrida had moved back to the city. She didn't sell the house, she just went away and left it. My father wrote to me, "That's a pretty funny way of doing things."

THERE WERE A LOT OF PEOPLE at my father's funeral, a lot of people I didn't know. A woman came across the grass in the cemetery to speak to me—I thought at first she must be a friend of my stepmother's. Then I saw that the woman was only a few years past my own age. The stocky figure and crown of gray-blond curls and floral-patterned jacket made her look older.

"I recognized you by your picture," she said. "Alfrida used to always be bragging about you."

I said, "Alfrida's not dead?"

"Oh, no," the woman said, and went on to tell me that Alfrida was in a nursing home in a town just north of Toronto.

"I moved her down there so's I could keep an eye on her."

Now it was easy to tell—even by her voice—that she was somebody of my own generation, and it came to me that she must be one of the other family, a half sister of Alfrida's, born when Alfrida was almost grown up.

She told me her name, and it was of course not the same as Alfrida's—she must have married. And I couldn't recall Alfrida's ever mentioning any of her half family by their first names.

I asked how Alfrida was, and the woman said her eyesight was so bad that she was legally blind. And she had a serious kidney problem, which meant that she had to be on dialysis twice a week.

"Other than that—?" she said, and laughed. I thought, yes, a sister, because I could hear something of Alfrida in that reckless, tossed laugh.

"So she doesn't travel too good," she said. "Or else I would've brought her. She still gets the paper from here and I read it to her sometimes. That's where I saw about your dad."

I wondered out loud, impulsively, if I should go to visit, at the nursing home. The emotions of the funeral—all the warm and relieved and reconciled feelings opened up in me by the death of my father at a reasonable age—prompted this suggestion. It would have been hard to carry out. My husband—my second husband—and I had only two days here before we were flying to Europe on an already delayed holiday.

"I don't know if you'd get so much out of it," the woman said.

"She has her good days. Then she has her bad days. You never know. Sometimes I think she's putting it on. Like, she'll sit there all day and whatever anybody says to her, she'll just say the same thing. *Fit as a fiddle and ready for love.* That's what she'll say all day long. *Fit-as-a-fiddle-and-ready-for-love.* She'll drive you crazy. Then other days she can answer all right."

Again, her voice and laugh—this time half submerged—reminded me of Alfrida, and I said, "You know I must have met you, I remember once when Alfrida's stepmother and her father dropped in, or maybe it was only her father and some of the children—"

"Oh, that's not who I am," the woman said. "You thought I was Alfrida's sister? Glory. I must be looking my age."

I started to say that I could not see her very well, and it was true. In October the afternoon sun was low, and it was coming straight into my eyes. The woman was standing against the light, so that it was hard to make out her features or her expression.

She twitched her shoulders nervously and importantly. She said, "Alfrida was my birth mom."

Mawm. Mother.

Then she told me, at not too great length, the story that she must have told often, because it was about an emphatic event in her life and an adventure she had embarked on alone. She had been adopted by a family in eastern Ontario; they were the only family she had ever known ("and I love them dearly"), and she had married and had her children, who were grown up before she got the urge to find out who her own mother was. It wasn't too easy, because of the way records used to be kept, and the secrecy ("It was kept one hundred percent secret that she had me"), but a few years ago she had tracked down Alfrida.

"Just in time too," she said. "I mean, it was time somebody came along to look after her. As much as I can."

I said, "I never knew."

"No. Those days, I don't suppose too many did. They warn you, when you start out to do this, it could be a shock when you show up. Older people, it's still heavy-duty. However, I don't think she minded. Earlier on, maybe she would have."

There was some sense of triumph about her, which wasn't hard to understand. If you have something to tell that will stagger someone, and you've told it, and it has done so, there has to be a balmy moment of power. In this case it was so complete that she felt a need to apologize.

"Excuse me talking all about myself and not saying how sorry I am about your dad."

I thanked her.

"You know Alfrida told me that your dad and her were walking home from school one day, this was in high school. They couldn't walk all the way together because, you know, in those days, a boy and a girl, they would just get teased something terrible. So if he got out first he'd wait just where their road went off the main road, outside of town, and if she got out first she would do the same, wait for him. And one day they were walking together and they heard all the bells starting to ring and you know what that was? It was the end of the First World War."

I said that I had heard that story too.

"Only I thought they were just children."

"Then how could they be coming home from high school, if they were just children?"

I said that I had thought they were out playing in the fields.

"They had my father's dog with them. He was called Mack."

"Maybe they had the dog all right. Maybe he came to meet them. I wouldn't think she'd get mixed up on what she was telling me. She was pretty good on remembering anything involved your dad."

Now I was aware of two things. First, that my father was born in 1902, and that Alfrida was close to the same age. So it was much more likely that they were walking home from high school than that they were playing in the fields, and it was odd that I had never thought of that before. Maybe they had said they were in the fields, that is, walking home across the fields. Maybe they had never said "playing."

Also, that the feeling of apology or friendliness, the harmlessness that I had felt in this woman a little while before, was not there now.

I said, "Things get changed around."

"That's right," the woman said. "People change things around. You want to know what Alfrida said about you?"

Now. I knew it was coming now.

"What?"

"She said you were smart, but you weren't ever quite as smart as you thought you were."

I made myself keep looking into the dark face against the light. Smart, too smart, not smart enough.

I said, "Is that all?"

"She said you were kind of a cold fish. That's her talking, not me. I haven't got anything against you."

THAT SUNDAY, after the noon dinner at Alfrida's, I set out to walk all the way back to my rooming house. If I walked both ways, I reckoned that I would have covered about ten miles, which ought to offset the effects of the meal I had eaten. I felt overfull, not just of food but of everything that I had seen and sensed in the apartment. The crowded, old-fashioned furnishings. Bill's silences. Alfrida's love, stubborn as sludge, and inappropriate, and hopeless—as far as I could see—on the grounds of age alone.

After I had walked for a while, my stomach did not feel so heavy. I made a vow not to eat anything for the next twenty-four hours. I walked north and west, north and west, on the streets of the tidily rectangular small city. On a Sunday afternoon there was hardly any traffic, except on the main thoroughfares. Sometimes my route coincided with a bus route for a few blocks. A bus might go by with only two or three people in it. People I did not know and who did not know me. What a blessing.

I had lied, I was not meeting any friends. My friends had mostly all gone home to wherever they lived. My fiancé would be away until the next day—he was visiting his parents, in Cobourg, on the way home from Ottawa. There would be nobody in the rooming house when I got there—nobody I had to bother talking to or listening to. I had nothing to do.

When I had walked for over an hour, I saw a drugstore that was open. I went in and had a cup of coffee. The coffee was reheated, black and bitter—its taste was medicinal, exactly what I needed. I was already feeling relieved, and now I began to feel happy. Such happiness, to be alone. To see the hot late-afternoon light on the sidewalk outside, the branches of a tree just out in leaf, throwing their skimpy shadows. To hear from the back of the shop the sounds of the ball game that the man who had served me was listening to on the radio. I did not think of the story I would make about Alfrida—not of that in particular—but of the work I wanted to do, which seemed more like grabbing something out of the air than constructing stories. The cries of the crowd came to me like big heartbeats, full of sorrows. Lovely formal-sounding waves, with their distant, almost inhuman assent and lamentation.

This was what I wanted, this was what I thought I had to pay attention to, this was how I wanted my life to be.

Nettles

~

IN THE SUMMER of 1979, I walked into the kitchen of my friend Sunny's house near Uxbridge, Ontario, and saw a man standing at the counter, making himself a ketchup sandwich.

I have driven around in the hills northeast of Toronto, with my husband—my second husband, not the one I had left behind that summer—and I have looked for the house, in an idly persistent way, I have tried to locate the road it was on, but I have never succeeded. It has probably been torn down. Sunny and her husband sold it a few years after I visited them. It was too far from Ottawa, where they lived, to serve as a convenient summer place. Their children, as they became teenagers, balked at going there. And there was too much upkeep work for Johnston—Sunny's husband—who liked to spend his weekends golfing.

I have found the golf course—I think it the right one, though the ragged verges have been cleaned up and there is a fancier clubhouse.

IN THE COUNTRYSIDE where I lived as a child, wells would go dry in the summer. This happened once in about every five or six years, when there was not enough rain. These wells were holes dug in the ground. Our well was a deeper hole than most, but we needed a good supply of water for our penned animals—my father raised silver foxes and mink—so one day the well driller arrived with impressive equipment, and the hole was extended down, down, deep into the earth until it found the water in the rock. From that time on we could pump out pure, cold water no matter what the time of year and no matter how dry the weather. That was something to be proud of. There was a tin mug hanging on the pump, and when I drank from it on a burning day, I thought of black rocks where the water ran sparkling like diamonds.

The well driller—he was sometimes called the well digger, as if nobody could be bothered to be precise about what he did and the older description was the more comfortable—was a man named Mike McCallum. He lived in the town close by our farm but he did not have a house there. He lived in the Clark Hotel—he had come there in the spring, and he would stay until he finished up whatever work he found to do in this part of the country. Then he would move on.

Mike McCallum was a younger man than my father, but he had a son who was a year and two months older than I was. This boy lived with his father in hotel rooms or boardinghouses, wherever his father was working, and he went to whatever school was at hand. His name was Mike McCallum too.

I know exactly how old he was because that is something children establish immediately, it is one of the essential matters on which they negotiate whether to be friends or not. He was nine and I was eight. His birthday was in April, mine in June. The summer holidays were well under way when he arrived at our house with his father.

His father drove a dark-red truck that was always muddy or dusty. Mike and I climbed into the cab when it rained. I don't remember whether his father went into our kitchen then, for a smoke and a cup of tea, or stood under a tree, or went right on working. Rain washed down the windows of the cab and made a racket like stones on the roof. The smell was of men—their work clothes and tools and tobacco and mucky boots and sour-cheese socks. Also of damp long-haired dog, because we had taken Ranger in with us. I took Ranger for granted, I was used to having him follow me around and sometimes for no good reason I would order him to stay home, go off to the barn, leave me alone. But Mike was fond of him and always addressed him kindly and by name, telling him our plans and waiting for him when he took off on one of his dog-projects, chasing a groundhog or a rabbit. Living as he did with his father, Mike could never have a dog of his own.

One day when Ranger was with us he chased a skunk, and the skunk turned and sprayed him. Mike and I were held to be somewhat to blame. My mother had to stop whatever she was doing and drive into town and get several large tins of tomato juice. Mike persuaded Ranger to get into a tub and we poured the tomato juice over him and brushed it into his hair. It looked as if we were washing him in blood. How many people would it take to supply that much blood? we wondered. How many horses? Elephants?

I had more acquaintance with blood and animal-killing than Mike did. I took him to see the spot in the corner of the pasture near the barnyard gate where my father shot and butchered the horses that were fed to the foxes and mink. The ground was trodden bare and appeared to have a deep blood-stain, an iron-red cast to it. Then I took him to the meat-house in the barnyard where the horse carcasses were hung before being ground up for feed. The meat-house was just a shed with wire walls and the walls were black with flies, drunk on the smell of carrion. We got shingles and smashed them dead.

Our farm was small—nine acres. It was small enough for me to have explored every part of it, and every part had a particular look and character, which I could not have put into words. It is easy to see what would be special about the wire shed with the long, pale horse carcasses hung from brutal hooks, or about the trodden blood-soaked ground where they had changed from live horses into those supplies of meat. But there were other things, such as the stones on either side of the barn gangway, that had just as much to say to me, though nothing memorable had ever occurred there. On one side there was a big smooth whitish stone that bulged out and dominated all the others, and so that side had to me an expansive and public air, and I would always choose to climb that way rather than on the other side, where the stones were darker and clung together in a more mean-spirited way. Each of the trees on the place had likewise an attitude and a presence—the elm looked serene and the oak threatening, the maples friendly and workaday, the hawthorn old and crabby. Even the pits on the river flats— where my father had sold off gravel years ago—had their distinct character, perhaps easiest to spot if you saw them full of water at the receding of the spring floods. There was the one that was small and round and deep and perfect; the one that was spread out like a tail; and the one that was wide and irresolute in shape and always with a chop on it because the water was so shallow.

Mike saw all these things from a different angle. And so did I, now that I was with him. I saw them his way and mine, and my way was by its very nature incommunicable, so that it had to stay secret. His had to do with immediate advantage. The large pale stone in the gangway was for jumping off, taking a short hard run and then launching yourself out into the air, to clear the smaller stones in the slope beneath and land on the packed earth by the stable door. All the trees were for climbing, but particularly the maple next to the house, with the branch that you could crawl out on, so as to drop yourself onto the verandah roof. And the gravel pits were simply for leaping into, with the shouts of animals leaping on their prey, after a furious run through the long grass. If it had been earlier in the year, Mike said, when these held more water, we could have built a raft.

That project was considered, with regard to the river. But the river in August was almost as much a stony road as it was a watercourse, and instead of trying to float down it or swim in it we took off our shoes and waded—jumping from one bare bone-white rock to another and slipping on the scummy rocks below the surface, plowing through mats of flat-leafed water lilies and other water plants whose names I can't recall or never knew (wild parsnip, water hemlock?). These grew so thick they looked as if they must be rooted on islands, on dry land, but they were actually growing out of river muck, and trapped our legs in their snaky roots.

This river was the same one that ran publicly through the town, and walking upstream, we came in sight of the double-span highway bridge. When I was by myself or just with Ranger I had never gone as far as the bridge, because there were usually town people there. They came to fish over the side, and when the water was high enough boys jumped from the railing. They wouldn't be doing that now, but it was more than likely some of them would be splashing around down below—loudmouthed and hostile as town children always were.

Tramps were another possibility. But I said nothing of this to Mike, who went ahead of me as if the bridge was an ordinary destination and there was nothing unpleasant or forbidden about it. Voices reached us, and as I expected they were the voices of boys yelling—you would think the bridge belonged to them. Ranger had followed us this far, unenthusiastically, but now he veered off towards the bank. He was an old dog by this time, and he had never been indiscriminately fond of children.

There was a man fishing, not off the bridge but from the bank, and he swore at the commotion Ranger made getting out of the water. He asked us whether we couldn't keep our arse of a dog at home. Mike went straight on as if this man had only whistled at us, and then we passed into the shadow of the bridge itself, where I had never been in my life.

The floor of the bridge was our roof, with streaks of sunlight showing between the planks. And now a car passed over, with a sound of thunder and a blotting out of the light. We stood still for this event, looking up. Under-the-bridge was a place on its own, not just a short stretch of the river. When the car had passed and the sun shone through the cracks again, its reflection on the water cast waves of light, queer bubbles of light, high on the cement pilings. Mike yelled to test the echo, and I did the same, but faintly, because the boys on the shore, the strangers, on the other side of the bridge scared me more than tramps would have done.

I went to the country school beyond our farm. Enrollment there had dwindled to the point where I was the only child in my class. But Mike had been going to the town school since spring and these boys were not strangers to him. He would probably have been playing with them, and not with me, if his father had not had the idea of taking him along on his jobs, so that he could—now and then— keep an eye on him.

There must have been some words of greeting passed, between these town boys and Mike.

Hey. What do you think you're doing here?

Nothing. What do you think you're doing?

Nothing. Who's that you got with you?

Nobody. Just her.

Nnya-nnya. Just her.

There was in fact a game going on, which was taking up everybody's attention. And everybody included girls—there were girls farther up on the bank, intent on their own business—though we were all past the age at which groups of boys and girls played together as a customary thing. They might have followed the boys out from town—pretending not to follow—or the boys might have come along after them, intending some harassment, but somehow when they all got together this game had taken shape and had needed everybody in it, so the usual restrictions had broken down. And the more people who were in it, the better the game was, so it was easy for Mike to become involved, and bring me in after him.

It was a game of war. The boys had divided themselves into two armies who fought each other from behind barricades roughly made of tree branches, and also from the shelter of the coarse, sharp grass, and of the bulrushes and water weeds that were higher than our heads. The chief weapons were balls of clay, mud balls, about the size of baseballs. There happened to be a special source of clay, a gray pit hollowed out, half hidden by weeds, partway up the bank (discovery of this might have been what suggested the game), and it was there that the girls were working, preparing the ammunition. You squeezed and patted the sticky clay into as hard a ball as you could make—there could be some gravel in it and binding material of grass, leaves, bits of twigs gathered at the spot, but no stones added on purpose—and there had to be a great many of these balls, because they were good for only one throw. There was no possibility of picking up the balls that had missed and packing them together and throwing them over again.

The rules of the war were simple. If you were hit by a ball—the official name for them was cannonballs—in the face, head, or body, you had to fall down dead. If you were hit in the arms or legs you had to fall down, but you were only wounded. Then another thing that girls had to do was crawl out and drag the wounded soldiers back to a trampled place that was the hospital. Leaves were plastered on their wounds and they were supposed to lie still till they counted to one hundred. When they'd done that they could get up and fight again. The dead soldiers were not supposed to get up until the war was over, and the war was not over till everybody on one side was dead.

The girls as well as the boys were divided into two sides, but since there were not nearly as many girls as boys we could not serve as munitions makers and nurses for just one soldier. There were alliances, just the same. Each girl had her own pile of balls and was working for particular soldiers, and when a soldier fell wounded he would call out a girl's name, so that she could drag him away and dress his wounds as soon as possible. I made weapons for Mike and mine was the name Mike called. There was so much noise going on—constant cries of "You're dead," either triumphant or outraged (outraged because of course people who were supposed to be dead were always trying to sneak back into the fighting) and the barking of a dog, not Ranger, who had somehow got mixed up in the battle—so much noise that you had to be always alert for the boy's voice that called your own name. There was a keen alarm when the cry came, a wire zinging through your whole body, a fanatic feeling of devotion. (At least it was so for me who, unlike the other girls, owed my services to only one warrior.)

I don't suppose, either, that I had ever played in a group, like this, before. It was such a joy to be part of a large and desperate enterprise, and to be singled out, within it, to be essentially pledged to the service of a fighter. When Mike was wounded he never opened his eyes, he lay limp and still while I pressed the slimy large leaves to his forehead and throat and—pulling out his shirt—to his pale, tender stomach, with its sweet and vulnerable belly button.

Nobody won. The game disintegrated, after a long while, in arguments and mass resurrections. We tried to get some of the clay off us, on the way home, by lying down flat in the river water. Our shorts and shirts were filthy and dripping.

It was late in the afternoon. Mike's father was getting ready to leave.

"For Christ's sake," he said.

We had a part-time hired man who came to help my father when there was a butchering or some extra job to be done. He had an elderly, boyish look and a wheezing asthmatic way of breathing. He liked to grab me and tickle me until I thought I would suffocate. Nobody interfered with this. My mother didn't like it, but my father told her it was only a joke.

He was there in the yard, helping Mike's father.

"You two been rolling in the mud," he said. "First thing you know you gonna have to get married."

From behind the screen door my mother heard that. (If the men had known she was there, neither one of them would have spoken as he had.) She came out and said something to the hired man, in a low, reproving voice, before she said anything about the way we looked.

I heard part of what she said.

Like brother and sister.

The hired man looked at his boots, grinning helplessly.

She was wrong. The hired man was closer to the truth than she was. We were not like brother and sister, or not like any brother and sister I had ever seen. My one brother was hardly more than a baby, so I had no experience of that on my own. And we were not like the wives and husbands I knew, who were old, for one thing, and who lived in such separate worlds that they seemed barely to recognize one another. We were like sturdy and accustomed sweethearts, whose bond needs not much outward expression. And for me at least that was solemn and thrilling.

I knew that the hired man was talking about sex, though I don't think I knew the word "sex." And I hated him for that even more than I usually hated him. Specifically, he was wrong. We did not go in for any showings and rubbings and guilty intimacies—there was none of that bothered search for hiding places, none of the twiddling pleasure and frustration and immediate, raw shame. Such scenes had taken place for me with a boy cousin and with a couple of slightly older girls, sisters, who went to my school. I disliked these partners before and after the event and would angrily deny, even in my own mind, that any of these things had happened. Such escapades could never have been considered, with anybody for whom I felt any fondness or respect—only with people who disgusted me, as those randy abhorrent itches disgusted me with myself.

In my feelings for Mike the localized demon was transformed into a diffuse excitement and tenderness spread everywhere under the skin, a pleasure of the eyes and ears and a tingling contentment, in the presence of the other person. I woke up every morning hungry for the sight of him, for the sound of the well driller's truck as it came bumping and rattling down the lane. I worshipped, without any show of it, the back of his neck and the shape of his head, the frown of his eyebrows, his long, bare toes and his dirty elbows, his loud and confident voice, his smell. I accepted readily, even devoutly, the roles that did not have to be explained or worked out between us—that I would aid and admire him, he would direct and stand ready to protect me.

AND ONE MORNING the truck did not come. One morning, of course, the job was all finished, the well capped, the pump reinstated, the fresh water marvelled at. There were two chairs fewer at the table for the noon meal. Both the older and the younger Mike had always eaten that meal with us. The younger Mike and I never talked and barely looked at each other. He liked to put ketchup on his bread. His father talked to my father, and the talk was mostly about wells, accidents, water tables. A serious man. All work, my father said. Yet he—Mike's father—ended nearly every speech with a laugh. The laugh had a lonely boom in it, as if he was still down the well.

They did not come. The work was finished, there was no reason for them ever to come again. And it turned out that this job was the last one that the well driller had to do in our part of the country. He had other jobs lined up elsewhere, and he wanted to get to them as soon as he could, while the good weather lasted. Living as he did, in the hotel, he could just pack up and be gone. And that was what he had done.

Why did I not understand what was happening? Was there no good-bye, no awareness that when Mike climbed into the truck on that last afternoon, he was going for good? No wave, no head turned towards me—or not turned towards me—when the truck, heavy now with all the equipment, lurched down our lane for the last time? When the water gushed out—I remember it gushing out, and everybody gathering round to have a drink—why did I not understand how much had come to an end, for me? I wonder now if there was a deliberate plan not to make too much of the occasion, to eliminate farewells, so that I—or we—should not become too unhappy and troublesome.

It doesn't seem likely that such account would be taken of children's feelings, in those days. They were our business, to suffer or suppress.

I did not become troublesome. After the first shock I did not let anybody see a thing. The hired man teased me whenever he caught sight of me ("Did your boyfriend run away on you?"), but I never looked his way.

I must have known that Mike would be leaving. Just as I knew that Ranger was old and that he would soon die. Future absence I accepted—it was just that I had no idea, till Mike disappeared, of what absence could be like. How all my own territory would be altered, as if a landslide had gone through it and skimmed off all meaning except loss of Mike. I could never again look at the white stone in the gangway without thinking of him, and so I got a feeling of aversion towards it. I had that feeling also about the limb of the maple tree, and when my father cut it off because it was too near the house, I had it about the scar that was left.

One day weeks afterwards, when I was wearing my fall coat, I was standing by the door of the shoe store while my mother tried on shoes, and I heard a woman call, "Mike." She ran past the store, calling, "Mike." I was suddenly convinced that this woman whom I did not know must be Mike's mother—I knew, though not from him, that she was separated from his father, not dead—and that they had come back to town for some reason. I did not consider whether this return might be temporary or permanent, only—I was now running out of the store—that in another minute I would see Mike.

The woman had caught up with a boy about five years old, who had just helped himself to an apple out of a bushel of apples that was standing on the sidewalk in front of the grocery shop next door.

I stopped and stared at this child in disbelief, as if an outrageous, an unfair enchantment had taken place before my eyes.

A common name. A stupid flat-faced child with dirty blond hair.

My heart was beating in big thumps, like howls happening in my chest.

SUNNY MET MY BUS in Uxbridge. She was a large-boned, bright-faced woman, with silvery-brown, curly hair caught back by unmatched combs on either side of her face. Even when she put on weight—which she had done—she did not look matronly, but majestically girlish.

She swept me into her life as she had always done, telling me that she had thought she was going to be late because Claire had got a bug in her ear that morning and had to be taken to the hospital to have it flushed out, then the dog threw up on the kitchen step, probably because it hated the trip and the house and the country, and when she—Sunny—had left to get me Johnston was making the boys clean it up because they had wanted a dog, and Claire was complaining that she could still hear something going *bzz-bzz* in her ear.

"So suppose we go someplace nice and quiet and get drunk and never go back there?" she said. "We have to, though. Johnston invited a friend whose wife and kids are away in Ireland, and they want to go and play golf."

Sunny and I had been friends in Vancouver. Our pregnancies had dovetailed nicely, so that we could manage with one set of maternity clothes. In my kitchen or in hers, once a week or so, distracted by our children and sometimes reeling for lack of sleep, we stoked ourselves up on strong coffee and cigarettes and launched out on a rampage of talk—about our marriages, our fights, our personal deficiencies, our interesting and discreditable motives, our foregone ambitions. We read Jung at the same time and tried to keep track of our dreams. During that time of life that is supposed to be a reproductive daze, with the woman's mind all swamped by maternal juices, we were still compelled to discuss Simone de Beauvoir and Arthur Koestler and *The Cocktail Party*.

Our husbands were not in this frame of mind at all. When we tried to talk about such things with them they would say, "Oh, that's just literature" or "You sound like Philosophy 101."

NOW WE HAD BOTH moved away from Vancouver. But Sunny had moved with her husband and her children and her furniture, in the normal way and for the usual reason—her husband had got another job. And I had moved for the newfangled reason that was approved of mightily but fleetingly and only in some special circles—leaving husband and house and all the things acquired during the marriage (except of course the children, who were to be parcelled about) in the hope of making a life that could be lived without hypocrisy or deprivation or shame.

I lived now on the second floor of a house in Toronto. The people downstairs—the people who owned the house—had come from Trinidad a dozen years before. All up and down the street, the old brick houses with their verandahs and high, narrow windows, the former homes of Methodists and Presbyterians who had names like Henderson and Grisham and McAllister, were full up with olive- or brownish-skinned people who spoke English in a way unfamiliar to me if they spoke it at all, and who filled the air at all hours with the smell of their spicy-sweet cooking. I was happy with all this—it made me feel as if I had made a true change, a long necessary voyage from the house of marriage. But it was too much to expect of my daughters, who were ten and twelve years old, that they should feel the same way. I had left Vancouver in the spring and they had come to me at the beginning of the summer holidays, supposedly to stay for the whole two months. They found the smells of the street sickening and the noise frightening. It was hot, and they could not sleep even with the fan I bought. We had to keep the windows open, and the backyard parties lasted sometimes till four o'clock.

Expeditions to the Science Centre and the C.N. Tower, to the Museum and the Zoo, treats in the cooled restaurants of department stores, a boat trip to Toronto Island, could not make up to them the absence of their friends or reconcile them to the travesty of a home that I provided. They missed their cats. They wanted their own rooms, the freedom of the neighborhood, the dawdling stay-at-home days.

For a while they did not complain. I heard the older one say to the younger one, "Let Mom think we're happy. Or she'll feel bad."

At last a blowup. Accusations, confessions of misery (even exaggerations of misery, as I thought, developed for my benefit). The younger wailing, "Why can't you just live at home?" and the older telling her bitterly, "Because she hates Dad."

I phoned my husband—who asked me nearly the same question and provided, on his own, nearly the same answer. I changed the tickets and helped my children pack and took them to the airport. All the way we played a silly game introduced by the older girl. You had to pick a number—27, 42—and then look out of the window and count the men you saw, and the 27th or 42nd man, or whatever, would be the one you had to marry. When I came back, alone, I gathered up all reminders of them—a cartoon the younger one had drawn, a *Glamour* magazine that the older one had bought, various bits of jewelry and clothing they could wear in Toronto but not at home—and stuffed them into a garbage bag. And I did more or less the same thing every time I thought of them—I snapped my mind shut. There were miseries that I could bear—those connected with men. And other miseries—those connected with children—that I could not.

I went back to living as I had lived before they came. I stopped cooking breakfast and went out every morning to get coffee and fresh rolls at the Italian deli. The idea of being so far freed from domesticity enchanted me. But I noticed now, as I hadn't done before, the look on some of the faces of the people who sat every morning on the stools behind the window or at the sidewalk tables—people for whom this was in no way a fine and amazing thing to be doing but the stale habit of a lonely life.

Back home, then, I would sit and write for hours at a wooden table under the windows of a former sunporch now become a makeshift kitchen. I was hoping to make my living as a writer. The sun soon heated up the little room, and the backs of my legs—I would be wearing shorts—stuck to the chair. I could smell the peculiar sweetish chemical odor of my plastic sandals absorbing the sweat of my feet. I liked that—it was the smell of my industry, and, I hoped, of my accomplishment. What I wrote wasn't any better than what I'd managed to write back in the old life while the potatoes cooked or the laundry thumped around in its automatic cycle. There was just more of it, and it wasn't any worse—that was all.

Later in the day I would have a bath and probably go to meet one or another of my women friends. We drank wine at the sidewalk tables in front of little restaurants on Queen Street or Baldwin Street or Brunswick Street and talked about our lives—chiefly about our lovers, but we felt queasy saying "lover," so we called them "the men we were involved with." And sometimes I met the man I was involved with. He had been banished when the children were with me, though I had broken this rule twice, leaving my daughters in a frigid movie-house.

I had known this man before I left my marriage and he was the immediate reason I had left it, though I pretended to him—and to everyone else—that this was not so. When I met him I tried to be carefree and to show an independent spirit. We exchanged news—I made sure I had news—and we laughed, and went for walks in the ravine, but all I really wanted was to entice him to have sex with me, because I thought the high enthusiasm of sex fused people's best selves. I was stupid about these matters, in a way that was very risky, particularly for a woman of my age. There were times when I would be so happy, after our encounters—dazzled and secure—and there were other times when I would lie stone-heavy with misgiving. After he had taken himself off, I would feel tears running out of my eyes before I knew that I was weeping. And this was because of some shadow I had glimpsed in him or some offhandedness, or an oblique warning he'd given me. Outside the windows, as it got dark, the backyard parties would begin, with music and shouting and provocations that later might develop into fights, and I would be frightened, not of any hostility but of a kind of nonexistence.

In one of these moods I phoned Sunny, and got the invitation to spend the weekend in the country.

"IT'S BEAUTIFUL HERE," I said.

But the country we were driving through meant nothing to me. The hills were a series of green bumps, some with cows. There were low concrete bridges over weed-choked streams. Hay was harvested in a new way, rolled up and left in the fields.

"Wait till you see the house," Sunny said. "It's squalid. There was a mouse in the plumbing. Dead. We kept getting these little hairs in the bathwater. That's all dealt with now, but you never know what will be next."

She did not ask me—was it delicacy or disapproval?—about my new life. Maybe she just did not know how to begin, could not imagine it. I would have told her lies, anyway, or half-lies. *It was hard to make the break but it had to be done. I miss the children terribly but there is always a price to be paid. I am learning to leave a man free and to be free myself. I am learning to take sex lightly, which is hard for me because that's not the way I started out and I'm not young but I am learning.*

A weekend, I thought. It seemed a very long time.

The bricks of the house showed a scar where a verandah had been torn away. Sunny's boys were tromping around in the yard.

"Mark lost the ball," the older one—Gregory—shouted.

Sunny told him to say hello to me.

"Hello. Mark threw the ball over the shed and now we can't find it."

The three-year-old girl, born since I'd last seen Sunny, came running out of the kitchen door and then halted, surprised at the sight of a stranger. But she recovered herself and told me, "There was a bug thing flew in my head."

Sunny picked her up and I took up my overnight bag and we walked into the kitchen, where Mike McCallum was spreading ketchup on a piece of bread.

"IT'S YOU," WE SAID, almost on the same breath. We laughed, I rushed towards him and he moved towards me. We shook hands.

"I thought it was your father," I said.

I don't know if I'd got as far as thinking of the well driller. I had thought, Who is that familiar-looking man? A man who carried his body lightly, as if he would think nothing of climbing in and out of wells. Short-cropped hair, going gray, deep-set light-colored eyes. A lean face, good-humored yet austere. A customary, not disagreeable, reserve.

"Couldn't be," he said. "Dad's dead."

Johnston came into the kitchen with the golf bags, and greeted me, and told Mike to hurry up, and Sunny said, "They know each other, honey. They knew each other. Of all things."

"When we were kids," Mike said.

Johnston said, "Really? That's remarkable." And we all said together what we saw he was about to say.

"Small world."

Mike and I were still looking at each other and laughing—we seemed to be making it clear to each other that this discovery which Sunny and Johnston might think remarkable was to us a comically dazzling flare-up of good fortune.

All afternoon while the men were gone I was full of happy energy. I made a peach pie for our supper and read to Claire so that she would settle for her nap, while Sunny took the boys fishing, unsuccessfully, in the scummy creek. Then she and I sat on the floor of the front room with a bottle of wine and became friends again, talking about books instead of life.

THE THINGS MIKE REMEMBERED were different from the things I remembered. He remembered walking around on the narrow top of some old cement foundation and pretending it was as high as the tallest building and that if we stumbled we would fall to our deaths. I said that must have been somewhere else, then I remembered the foundations for a garage that had been poured, and the garage never built, where our lane met the road. Did we walk on that?

We did.

I remembered wanting to holler loudly under the bridge but being afraid of the town kids. He did not remember any bridge.

We both remembered the clay cannonballs, and the war.

We were washing the dishes together, so that we could talk all we wanted without being rude.

He told me how his father had died. He had been killed in a road accident, coming back from a job near Bancroft.

"Are your folks still alive?"

I said that my mother was dead and that my father had married again.

At some point I told him that I had separated from my husband, I was living in Toronto. I said that my children had been with me for a while but were now on a holiday with their father.

He told me that he lived in Kingston, but had not been there very long. He had met Johnston recently, through his work. He was, like Johnston, a civil engineer. His wife was an Irish girl, born in Ireland but working in Canada when he met her. She was a nurse. Right now she was back in Ireland, in County Clare, visiting her family. She had the kids with her.

"How many kids?"

"Three."

When the dishes were finished we went into the front room and offered to play Scrabble with the boys, so that Sunny and Johnston could go for a walk. One game—then it was supposed to be bedtime. But they persuaded us to start another round, and we were still playing when their parents came back.

"What did I tell you?" said Johnston.

"It's the same game," Gregory said. "You said we could finish the game and it's the same game."

"I bet," said Sunny.

She said it was a lovely night, and she and Johnston were getting spoiled, having live-in baby-sitters.

"Last night we actually went to the movie and Mike stayed with the kids. An old movie. *Bridge over the River Kwai.*"

"*On,*" Johnston said. "*On the River Kwai.*"

Mike said, "I'd seen it anyway. Years ago."

"It was pretty good," said Sunny. "Except I didn't agree with the ending. I thought the ending was wrong. You know when Alec Guinness sees the wire in the water, in the morning, and he realizes somebody's going to blow up the bridge? And he goes berserk and then it gets so complicated and everybody has to get killed and everything? Well, I think he just should have seen the wire and known what was going to happen and stayed on the bridge and got blown up with it. I think that's what his character would have done and it would have been more dramatically effective."

"No, it wouldn't," Johnston said, in the tone of somebody who had been through this argument before. "Where's the suspense?"

"I agree with Sunny," I said. "I remember thinking the ending was too complicated."

"Mike?" said Johnston.

"I thought it was pretty good," Mike said. "Pretty good the way it was."

"Guys against the women," Johnston said. "Guys win."

Then he told the boys to pack up the Scrabble game and they obeyed. But Gregory thought of asking to see the stars. "This is the only place we can ever see them," he said. "At home it's all the lights and crap."

"Watch it," his father said. But he said, Okay then, five minutes, and we all went outside and looked at the sky. We looked for the Pilot Star, close beside the second star in the handle of the Big Dipper. If you could see that one, Johnston said, then your eyesight was good enough to get you into the Air Force, at least that was the way it was during the Second World War.

Sunny said, "Well, I can see it, but then I knew beforehand that it's there."

Mike said, the same with him.

"I could see it," said Gregory scornfully. "I could see it whether I knew it was there or not."

"I could see it too," Mark said.

Mike was standing a little ahead of me and to one side. He was actually closer to Sunny than he was to me. Nobody was behind us, and I wanted to brush against him—just lightly and accidentally against his arm or shoulder. Then if he didn't stir away—out of courtesy, taking my touch for a genuine accident?—I wanted to lay a finger against his bare neck. Was that what he would have done, if he had been standing behind me? Was that what he would have been concentrating on, instead of the stars?

I had the feeling, however, that he was a scrupulous man, he would refrain.

And for that reason, certainly, he would not come to my bed that night. It was so risky as to be impossible, in any case. There were three bedrooms upstairs—the guest room and the parents' room both opening off the larger room where the children slept. Anybody approaching either of the smaller bedrooms had to do so through the children's room. Mike, who had slept in the guest room last night, had been moved downstairs, to the foldout sofa in the front room. Sunny had given him fresh sheets rather than unmaking and making up again the bed he had left for me.

"He's pretty clean," she said. "And after all, he's an old friend."

Lying in those same sheets did not make for a peaceful night. In my dreams, though not in reality, they smelled of water-weeds, river mud, and reeds in the hot sun.

I knew that he wouldn't come to me no matter how small the risk was. It would be a sleazy thing to do, in the house of his friends, who would be—if they were not already—the friends of his wife as well. And how could he be sure that it was what I wanted? Or that it was what he really wanted? Even I was not sure of it. Up till now, I had always been able to think of myself as a woman who was faithful to the person she was sleeping with at any given time.

My sleep was shallow, my dreams monotonously lustful, with irritating and unpleasant subplots. Sometimes Mike was ready to cooperate, but we met with obstacles. Sometimes he got side-tracked, as when he said that he had brought me a present, but he had mislaid it, and it was of great importance to him to find it. I told him not to mind, that I was not interested in the present, for he himself was my present, the person I loved and always had loved, I said that. But he was preoccupied. And sometimes he reproached me.

All night—or at least whenever I woke up, and I woke often—the crickets were singing outside my window. At first I thought it was birds, a chorus of indefatigable night-birds. I had lived in cities long enough to have forgotten how crickets can make a perfect waterfall of noise.

It has to be said, too, that sometimes when I woke I found myself stranded on a dry patch. Unwelcome lucidity. What do you really know of this man? Or he of you? What music does he like, what are his politics? What are his expectations of women?

"DID YOU TWO SLEEP WELL?" Sunny said.

Mike said, "Out like a light."

I said, "Okay. Fine."

Everybody was invited to brunch that morning at the house of some neighbors who had a swimming pool. Mike said that he thought he would rather just go round the golf course, if that would be okay.

Sunny said, "Sure," and looked at me. I said, "Well, I don't know if I—" and Mike said, "You don't play golf, do you?"

"No."

"Still. You could come and caddy for me."

"I'll come and caddy," Gregory said. He was ready to attach himself to any expedition of ours, sure that we would be more liberal and entertaining than his parents.

Sunny said no. "You're coming with us. Don't you want to go in the pool?"

"All the kids pee in that pool. I hope you know that."

JOHNSTON HAD WARNED US before we left that there was a prediction of rain. Mike had said that we'd take our chances. I liked his saying "we" and I liked riding beside him, in the wife's seat. I felt a pleasure in the idea of us as a couple—a pleasure that I knew was light-headed as an adolescent girl's. The notion of being a wife beguiled me, just as if I had never been one. This had never happened with the man who was now my actual lover. Could I really have settled in, with a true love, and somehow just got rid of the parts of me that did not fit, and been happy?

But now that we were alone, there was some constraint.

"Isn't the country here beautiful?" I said. And today I meant it. The hills looked softer, under this cloudy white sky, than they had looked yesterday in the brazen sunlight. The trees, at the end of summer, had a raggedy foliage, many of their leaves beginning to rust around the edges, and some had actually turned brown or red. I recognized different leaves now. I said, "Oak trees."

"This is sandy soil," Mike said. "All through here—they call it Oak Ridges."

I said I supposed that Ireland was beautiful.

"Parts of it are really bare. Bare rock."

"Did your wife grow up there? Does she have that lovely accent?"

"You'd think she did, if you heard her. But when she goes back there, they tell her she's lost it. They tell her she sounds just like an American. American's what they always say—they don't bother with Canadian."

"And your kids—I guess they don't sound Irish at all?"

"Nope."

"What are they anyway—boys or girls?"

"Two boys and a girl."

I had an urge now to tell him about the contradictions, the griefs and necessities of my life. I said, "I miss my kids."

But he said nothing. No sympathetic word, no encouragement. It might be that he thought it unseemly to talk of our partners or our children, under the circumstances.

Soon after that we pulled into the parking lot beside the clubhouse, and he said, rather boisterously, as if to make up for his stiffness, "Looks like the rain scare's kept the Sunday golfers home." There was only one car in the lot.

He got out and went into the office to pay the visitor's fee.

I had never been on a golf course. I had seen the game being played on television, once or twice and never by choice, and I had an idea that some of the clubs were called irons, or some of the irons clubs, and that there was one of them called a niblick, and that the course itself was called the links. When I told him this Mike said, "Maybe you're going to be awfully bored."

"If I am I'll go for a walk."

That seemed to please him. He laid the weight of his warm hand on my shoulder and said, "You would, too."

My ignorance did not matter—of course I did not really have to caddy—and I was not bored. All there was for me to do was to follow him around, and watch him. I didn't even have to watch him. I could have watched the trees at the edges of the course—they were tall trees with feathery tops and slender trunks, whose name I was not sure of—acacia?—and they were ruffled by occasional winds that we could not feel at all, here below. Also there were flocks of birds, blackbirds or starlings, flying about with a communal sense of urgency, but only from one treetop to another. I remembered now that birds did that; in August or even late July they began to have noisy mass meetings, preparing for the trip south.

Mike talked now and then, but it was hardly to me. There was no need for me to reply, and in fact I couldn't have done so. I thought he talked more, though, than a man would have done if he'd been playing here by himself. His disconnected words were reproaches or cautious congratulations or warnings to himself, or they were hardly words at all—just the kind of noises that are meant to convey meaning, and that do convey meaning, in the long intimacy of lives lived in willing proximity.

This was what I was supposed to do, then—to give him an amplified, an extended notion of himself. A more comfortable notion, you might say, a reassuring sense of human padding around his solitude. He wouldn't have expected this in quite the same way, or asked it quite so naturally and easily, if I had been another man. Or if I had been a woman with whom he did not feel some established connection.

I didn't think this out. It was all there in the pleasure I felt come over me as we made our way around the links. Lust that had given me shooting pains in the night was all chastened and trimmed back now into a tidy pilot flame, attentive, wifely. I followed his setting up and choosing and pondering and squinting and swinging, and watched the course of the ball, which always seemed to me triumphant but to him usually problematic, to the site of our next challenge, our immediate future.

Walking there, we hardly talked at all. Will it rain? we said. Did you feel a drop? I thought I felt a drop. Maybe not. This was not dutiful weather talk—it was all in the context of the game. Would we finish the round or not?

As it turned out, we would not. There was a drop of rain, definitely a drop of rain, then another, then a splatter. Mike looked along the length of the course, to where the clouds had changed color, becoming dark blue instead of white, and he said without particular alarm or disappointment, "Here comes our weather." He began methodically to pack up and fasten his bag.

We were then about as far away as we could be from the clubhouse. The birds had increased their commotion, and were wheeling about overhead in an agitated, indecisive way. The tops of the trees were swaying, and there was a sound—it seemed to be above us—like the sound of a wave full of stones crashing on the beach. Mike said, "Okay, then. We better get in here," and he took my hand and hurried us across the mown grass into bushes and the tall weeds that grew between the course and the river.

The bushes right at the edge of the grass had dark leaves and an almost formal look, as if they had been a hedge, set out there. But they were in a clump, growing wild. They also looked impenetrable, but close up there were little openings, the narrow paths that animals or people looking for golf balls had made. The ground sloped slightly downward, and once you were through the irregular wall of bushes you could see a bit of the river—the river that was in fact the reason for the sign at the gate, the name on the clubhouse. Riverside Golf Club. The water was steel gray, and looked to be rolling, not breaking in a chop the way pond water would do, in this rush of weather. Between it and us there was a meadow of weeds, all of it seemed in bloom. Goldenrod, jewelweed with its red and yellow bells, and what I thought were flowering nettles with pinkish-purple clusters, and wild asters. Grapevine, too, grabbing and wrapping whatever it could find, and tangling underfoot. The soil was soft, not quite gummy. Even the most frail-stemmed, delicate-looking plants had grown up almost as high as, or higher

than, our heads. When we stopped and looked up through them
we could see trees at a little distance tossing around like bouquets. And something coming, from the direction of the midnight
clouds. It was the real rain, coming at us behind this splatter we
were getting, but it appeared to be so much more than rain. It was
as if a large portion of the sky had detached itself and was bearing
down, bustling and resolute, taking a not quite recognizable but
animate shape. Curtains of rain—not veils but really thick and
wildly slapping curtains—were driven ahead of it. We could see
them distinctly, when all we were feeling, still, were these light,
lazy drops. It was almost as if we were looking through a window,
and not quite believing that the window would shatter, until it did,
and rain and wind hit us, all together, and my hair was lifted and
fanned out above my head. I felt as if my skin might do that next.

I tried to turn around then—I had an urge, that I had not felt
before, to run out of the bushes and head for the clubhouse. But I
could not move. It was hard enough to stand up—out in the open
the wind would have knocked you down at once.

Stooping, butting his head through the weeds and against the
wind, Mike got around in front of me, all the time holding on to
my arm. Then he faced me, with his body between me and the
storm. That made as much difference as a toothpick might have
done. He said something, right into my face, but I could not hear
him. He was shouting, but not a sound from him could reach me.
He had hold of both my arms now, he worked his hands down to
my wrists and held them tight. He pulled me down—both of us
staggering, the moment we tried to make any change of position—
so that we were crouched close to the ground. So close together
that we could not look at each other—we could only look down, at
the miniature rivers already breaking up the earth around our feet,
and the crushed plants and our soaked shoes. And even this had
to be seen through the waterfall that was running down our faces.

Mike released my wrists and clamped his hands on my shoulders. His touch was still one of restraint, more than comfort.

We remained like this till the wind passed over. That could not
have been more than five minutes, perhaps only two or three. Rain
still fell, but now it was ordinary heavy rain. He took his hands

away, and we stood up shakily. Our shirts and slacks were stuck
fast to our bodies. My hair fell down over my face in long witch's
tendrils and his hair was flattened in short dark tails to his forehead. We tried to smile, but had hardly the strength for it. Then
we kissed and pressed together briefly. This was more of a ritual, a
recognition of survival rather than of our bodies' inclinations. Our
lips slid against each other, slick and cool, and the pressure of the
embrace made us slightly chilly, as fresh water was squished out of
our clothing.

Every minute, the rain grew lighter. We made our way, slightly
staggering, through the half-flattened weeds, then between the
thick and drenching bushes. Big tree branches had been hurled all
over the golf course. I did not think until later that any one of them
could have killed us.

We walked in the open, detouring around the fallen limbs. The
rain had almost stopped, and the air brightened. I was walking
with my head bent—so that the water from my hair fell to the
ground and not down my face—and I felt the heat of the sun strike
my shoulders before I looked up into its festival light.

I stood still, took a deep breath, and swung my hair out of my
face. Now was the time, when we were drenched and safe and con-
fronted with radiance. Now something had to be said.

"There's something I didn't mention to you."

His voice surprised me, like the sun. But in the opposite way. It
had a weight to it, a warning—determination edged with apology.

"About our youngest boy," he said. "Our youngest boy was
killed last summer."

Oh.

"He was run over," he said. "I was the one ran over him. Backing
out of our driveway."

I stopped again. He stopped with me. Both of us stared ahead.

"His name was Brian. He was three.

"The thing was, I thought he was upstairs in bed. The others
were still up, but he'd been put to bed. Then he'd got up again.

"I should have looked, though. I should have looked more carefully."

I thought of the moment when he got out of the car. The noise he must have made. The moment when the child's mother came running out of the house. *This isn't him, he isn't here, it didn't happen.*

Upstairs in bed.

He started walking again, entering the parking lot. I walked a little behind him. And I did not say anything—not one kind, common, helpless word. We had passed right by that.

He didn't say, It was my fault and I'll never get over it. I'll never forgive myself. But I do as well as I can.

Or, my wife forgives me but she'll never get over it either.

I knew all that. I knew now that he was a person who had hit rock bottom. A person who knew—as I did not know, did not come near knowing—exactly what rock bottom was like. He and his wife knew that together and it bound them, as something like that would either break you apart or bind you, for life. Not that they would live at rock bottom. But they would share a knowledge of it—that cool, empty, locked, and central space.

It could happen to anybody.

Yes. But it doesn't seem that way. It seems as if it happens to this one, that one, picked out specially here and there, one at a time.

I said, "It isn't fair." I was talking about the dealing out of these idle punishments, these wicked and ruinous swipes. Worse like this, perhaps, than when they happen in the midst of plentiful distress, in wars or the earth's disasters. Worst of all when there is the one whose act, probably an uncharacteristic act, is singly and permanently responsible.

That's what I was talking about. But meaning also, *It is not fair. What has this got to do with us?*

A protest so brutal that it seems almost innocent, coming out of such a raw core of self. Innocent, that is, if you are the one it's coming from, and if it has not been made public.

"Well," he said, quite gently. Fairness being neither here nor there.

"Sunny and Johnston don't know about it," he said. "None of the people know, that we met since we moved. It seemed as if it might work better that way. Even the other kids—they don't hardly ever mention him. Never mention his name."

I was not one of the people they had met since they moved. Not one of the people amongst whom they would make their new, hard, normal life. I was a person who knew—that was all. A person he had, on his own, who knew.

"That's strange," he said, looking around before he opened the trunk of the car to stow away the golf case.

"What happened to the guy who was parked here before? Didn't you see another car parked here when we came in? But I never saw one other person on the course. Now that I think of it. Did you?"

I said no.

"Mystery," he said. And again, "Well."

That was a word that I used to hear fairly often, said in that same tone of voice, when I was a child. A bridge between one thing and another, or a conclusion, or a way of saying something that couldn't be any more fully said, or thought.

"A well is a hole in the ground." That was the joking answer.

THE STORM HAD BROUGHT an end to the swimming-pool party. Too many people had been there for everybody to crowd into the house, and those with children had mostly chosen to go home.

While we were driving back, Mike and I had both noticed, and spoken about, a prickling, an itch or burning, on our bare forearms, the backs of our hands, and around our ankles. Places that had not been protected by our clothing when we crouched in the weeds. I remembered the nettles.

Sitting in Sunny's farmhouse kitchen, wearing dry clothes, we told about our adventure and revealed our rashes.

Sunny knew what to do for us. Yesterday's trip with Claire, to the emergency room of the local hospital, had not been this family's first visit. On an earlier weekend the boys had gone down into the weedy mud-bottomed field behind the barn and come back covered with welts and blotches. The doctor said they must have got into some nettles. Must have been rolling in them, was what he said. Cold compresses were prescribed, an antihistamine lotion, and pills. There was still part of a bottle of lotion unused, and there were some pills too, because Mark and Gregory had recovered quickly.

We said no to the pills—our case seemed not serious enough.

Sunny said that she had talked to the woman out on the highway, who put gas in her car, and this woman had said there was a plant whose leaves made the best poultice you could have, for nettle rash. You don't need all them pills and junk, the woman said. The name of the plant was something like calf's foot. Coldfoot? The woman had told her she could find it in a certain road cut, by a bridge.

She was eager to do that, she liked the idea of a folklore remedy. We had to point out that the lotion was already there, and paid for.

Sunny enjoyed ministering to us. In fact, our plight put the whole family into a good humor, brought them out of the doldrums of the drenched day and cancelled plans. The fact that we had chosen to go off together and that we had this adventure—an adventure that left its evidence on our bodies—seemed to rouse in Sunny and Johnston a teasing excitement. Droll looks from him, a bright solicitousness from her. If we had brought back evidence of real misdoing—welts on the buttocks, red splashes on the thighs and belly—they would not of course have been so charmed and forgiving.

The children thought it was funny to see us sitting there with our feet in basins, our arms and hands clumsy with their wrappings of thick cloths. Claire especially was delighted with the sight of our naked, foolish, adult feet. Mike wriggled his long toes for her, and she broke into fits of alarmed giggles.

Well. It would be the same old thing, if we ever met again. Or if we didn't. Love that was not usable, that knew its place. (Some would say not real, because it would never risk getting its neck wrung, or turning into a bad joke, or sadly wearing out.) Not risking a thing yet staying alive as a sweet trickle, an underground resource. With the weight of this new stillness on it, this seal.

I never asked Sunny for news of him, or got any, during all the years of our dwindling friendship.

THOSE PLANTS WITH THE BIG pinkish-purple flowers are not nettles. I have discovered that they are called joe-pye weed. The stinging nettles that we must have got into are more insignificant plants, with a paler purple flower, and stalks wickedly outfitted with fine, fierce, skin-piercing and inflaming spines. Those would be present too, unnoticed, in all the flourishing of the waste meadow.

The Bear Came Over the Mountain

~

FIONA LIVED IN HER PARENTS' HOUSE, in the town where she and Grant went to university. It was a big, bay-windowed house that seemed to Grant both luxurious and disorderly, with rugs crooked on the floors and cup rings bitten into the table varnish. Her mother was Icelandic—a powerful woman with a froth of white hair and indignant far-left politics. The father was an important cardiologist, revered around the hospital but happily subservient at home, where he would listen to strange tirades with an absentminded smile. All kinds of people, rich or shabby-looking, delivered these tirades, and kept coming and going and arguing and conferring, sometimes in foreign accents. Fiona had her own little car and a pile of cashmere sweaters, but she wasn't in a sorority, and this activity in her house was probably the reason.

Not that she cared. Sororities were a joke to her, and so was politics, though she liked to play "The Four Insurgent Generals" on the phonograph, and sometimes also she played the "Internationale," very loud, if there was a guest she thought she could make nervous. A curly-haired, gloomy-looking foreigner was courting her—she said he was a Visigoth—and so were two or three quite respectable and uneasy young interns. She made fun of them all and of Grant as well. She would drolly repeat some of his small-town phrases. He thought maybe she was joking when she proposed to him, on a cold bright day on the beach at Port Stanley. Sand was stinging their faces and the waves delivered crashing loads of gravel at their feet.

"Do you think it would be fun—" Fiona shouted. "Do you think it would be fun if we got married?"

He took her up on it, he shouted yes. He wanted never to be away from her. She had the spark of life.

. . .

JUST BEFORE THEY LEFT their house Fiona noticed a mark on the kitchen floor. It came from the cheap black house shoes she had been wearing earlier in the day.

"I thought they'd quit doing that," she said in a tone of ordinary annoyance and perplexity, rubbing at the gray smear that looked as if it had been made by a greasy crayon.

She remarked that she would never have to do this again, since she wasn't taking those shoes with her.

"I guess I'll be dressed up all the time," she said. "Or semi dressed up. It'll be sort of like in a hotel."

She rinsed out the rag she'd been using and hung it on the rack inside the door under the sink. Then she put on her golden-brown fur-collared ski jacket over a white turtle-necked sweater and tailored fawn slacks. She was a tall, narrow-shouldered woman, seventy years old but still upright and trim, with long legs and long feet, delicate wrists and ankles and tiny, almost comical-looking ears. Her hair, which was light as milkweed fluff, had gone from pale blond to white somehow without Grant's noticing exactly when, and she still wore it down to her shoulders, as her mother had done. (That was the thing that had alarmed Grant's own mother, a small-town widow who worked as a doctor's receptionist. The long white hair on Fiona's mother, even more than the state of the house, had told her all she needed to know about attitudes and politics.)

Otherwise Fiona with her fine bones and small sapphire eyes was nothing like her mother. She had a slightly crooked mouth which she emphasized now with red lipstick—usually the last thing she did before she left the house. She looked just like herself on this day—direct and vague as in fact she was, sweet and ironic.

OVER A YEAR AGO Grant had started noticing so many little yellow notes stuck up all over the house. That was not entirely new. She'd always written things down—the title of a book she'd heard mentioned on the radio or the jobs she wanted to make sure she did that day. Even her morning schedule was written down—he found it mystifying and touching in its precision.

7 a.m. Yoga. 7:30–7:45 teeth face hair. 7:45–8:15 walk. 8:15 Grant and Breakfast.

The new notes were different. Taped onto the kitchen drawers—Cutlery, Dishtowels, Knives. Couldn't she have just opened the drawers and seen what was inside? He remembered a story about the German soldiers on border patrol in Czechoslovakia during the war. Some Czech had told him that each of the patrol dogs wore a sign that said *Hund*. Why? said the Czechs, and the Germans said, Because that is a *hund*.

He was going to tell Fiona that, then thought he'd better not. They always laughed at the same things, but suppose this time she didn't laugh?

Worse things were coming. She went to town and phoned him from a booth to ask him how to drive home. She went for her walk across the field into the woods and came home by the fence line—a very long way round. She said that she'd counted on fences always taking you somewhere.

It was hard to figure out. She said that about fences as if it was a joke, and she had remembered the phone number without any trouble.

"I don't think it's anything to worry about," she said. "I expect I'm just losing my mind."

He asked if she had been taking sleeping pills.

"If I have I don't remember," she said. Then she said she was sorry to sound so flippant.

"I'm sure I haven't been taking anything. Maybe I should be. Maybe vitamins."

Vitamins didn't help. She would stand in doorways trying to figure out where she was going. She forgot to turn on the burner under the vegetables or put water in the coffeemaker. She asked Grant when they'd moved to this house.

"Was it last year or the year before?"

He said that it was twelve years ago.

She said, "That's shocking."

"She's always been a bit like this," Grant said to the doctor. "Once she left her fur coat in storage and just forgot about it. That was when we were always going somewhere warm in the winters. Then she said it was unintentionally on purpose, she said it was like a sin she was leaving behind. The way some people made her feel about fur coats."

He tried without success to explain something more—to explain how Fiona's surprise and apologies about all this seemed somehow like routine courtesy, not quite concealing a private amusement. As if she'd stumbled on some adventure that she had not been expecting. Or was playing a game that she hoped he would catch on to. They had always had their games—nonsense dialects, characters they invented. Some of Fiona's made-up voices, chirping or wheedling (he couldn't tell the doctor this), had mimicked uncannily the voices of women of his that she had never met or known about.

"Yes, well," the doctor said. "It might be selective at first. We don't know, do we? Till we see the pattern of the deterioration, we really can't say."

In a while it hardly mattered what label was put on it. Fiona, who no longer went shopping alone, disappeared from the supermarket while Grant had his back turned. A policeman picked her up as she walked down the middle of the road, blocks away. He asked her name and she answered readily. Then he asked her the name of the prime minister of the country.

"If you don't know that, young man, you really shouldn't be in such a responsible job."

He laughed. But then she made the mistake of asking if he'd seen Boris and Natasha.

These were the Russian wolfhounds she had adopted some years ago as a favor to a friend, then devoted herself to for the rest of their lives. Her taking them over might have coincided with the discovery that she was not likely to have children. Something about her tubes being blocked, or twisted—Grant could not remember now. He had always avoided thinking about all that female apparatus. Or it might have been after her mother died. The dogs' long legs and silky hair, their narrow, gentle, intransigent faces made a fine match for her when she took them out for walks. And Grant himself, in those days, landing his first job at the university (his father-in-law's money welcome in spite of the political taint), might have seemed to some people to have been picked up on another of Fiona's eccentric whims, and groomed and tended and favored. Though he never understood this, fortunately, until much later.

SHE SAID TO HIM, at suppertime on the day of the wandering-off at the supermarket, "You know what you're going to have to do with me, don't you? You're going to have to put me in that place. Shallowlake?"

Grant said, "Meadowlake. We're not at that stage yet."

"Shallowlake, Shillylake," she said, as if they were engaged in a playful competition. "Sillylake. Sillylake it is."

He held his head in his hands, his elbows on the table. He said that if they did think of it, it must be as something that need not be permanent. A kind of experimental treatment. A rest cure.

THERE WAS A RULE that nobody could be admitted during the month of December. The holiday season had so many emotional pitfalls. So they made the twenty-minute drive in January. Before they reached the highway the country road dipped through a swampy hollow now completely frozen over. The swamp-oaks and maples threw their shadows like bars across the bright snow.

Fiona said, "Oh, remember."

Grant said, "I was thinking about that too."

"Only it was in the moonlight," she said.

She was talking about the time that they had gone out skiing at night under the full moon and over the black-striped snow, in this place that you could get into only in the depths of winter. They had heard the branches cracking in the cold.

So if she could remember that so vividly and correctly, could there really be so much the matter with her?

It was all he could do not to turn around and drive home.

THERE WAS ANOTHER RULE which the supervisor explained to him. New residents were not to be visited during the first thirty days. Most people needed that time to get settled in. Before the rule had been put in place, there had been pleas and tears and tantrums, even from those who had come in willingly. Around the third or fourth day they would start lamenting and begging to be taken home. And some relatives could be susceptible to that, so you would have people being carted home who would not get on there any better than they had before. Six months later or sometimes only a few weeks later, the whole upsetting hassle would have to be gone through again.

"Whereas we find," the supervisor said, "we find that if they're left on their own they usually end up happy as clams. You have to practically lure them into a bus to take a trip to town. The same with a visit home. It's perfectly okay to take them home then, visit for an hour or two—they're the ones that'll worry about getting back in time for supper. Meadowlake's their home then. Of course, that doesn't apply to the ones on the second floor, we can't let them go. It's too difficult, and they don't know where they are anyway."

"My wife isn't going to be on the second floor," Grant said.

"No," said the supervisor thoughtfully. "I just like to make everything clear at the outset."

THEY HAD GONE OVER TO MEADOWLAKE a few times several years ago, to visit Mr. Farquar, the old bachelor farmer who had been their neighbor. He had lived by himself in a drafty brick house unaltered since the early years of the century, except for the addition of a refrigerator and a television set. He had paid Grant and Fiona unannounced but well-spaced visits and, as well as local matters, he liked to discuss books he had been reading—about the Crimean War or Polar explorations or the history of firearms. But after he went to Meadowlake he would talk only about the routines of the place, and they got the idea that their visits, though gratifying, were a social burden for him. And Fiona in particular hated the smell of urine and bleach that hung about, hated the perfunctory bouquets of plastic flowers in niches in the dim, low-ceilinged corridors.

Now that building was gone, though it had dated only from the fifties. Just as Mr. Farquar's house was gone, replaced by a gimcrack sort of castle that was the weekend home of some people from Toronto. The new Meadowlake was an airy, vaulted building whose air was faintly pleasantly pine-scented. Profuse and genuine greenery sprouted out of giant crocks.

Nevertheless, it was the old building that Grant would find himself picturing Fiona in during the long month he had to get through without seeing her. It was the longest month of his life, he thought—longer than the month he had spent with his mother visiting relatives in Lanark County, when he was thirteen, and longer than the month that Jacqui Adams spent on holiday with her family, near the beginning of their affair. He phoned Meadowlake every day and hoped that he would get the nurse whose name was Kristy. She seemed a little amused at his constancy, but she would give him a fuller report than any other nurse he got stuck with.

Fiona had caught a cold, but that was not unusual for newcomers.

"Like when your kids start school," Kristy said. "There's a whole bunch of new germs they're exposed to, and for a while they just catch everything."

Then the cold got better. She was off the antibiotics, and she didn't seem as confused as she had been when she came in. (This was the first time Grant had heard about either the antibiotics or the confusion.) Her appetite was pretty good, and she seemed to enjoy sitting in the sunroom. She seemed to enjoy watching television.

One of the things that had been so intolerable about the old Meadowlake had been the way the television was on everywhere, overwhelming your thoughts or conversation wherever you chose to sit down. Some of the inmates (that was what he and Fiona called them then, not residents) would raise their eyes to it, some talked back to it, but most just sat and meekly endured its assault. In the new building, as far as he could recall, the television was in a separate sitting room, or in the bedrooms. You could make a choice to watch it.

So Fiona must have made a choice. To watch what?

During the years that they had lived in this house, he and Fiona had watched quite a bit of television together. They had spied on the lives of every beast or reptile or insect or sea creature that a camera was able to reach, and they had followed the plots of what seemed like dozens of rather similar fine nineteenth-century novels. They had slid into an infatuation with an English comedy about life in a department store and had watched so many reruns that they knew the dialogue by heart. They mourned the disappearance of actors who died in real life or went off to other jobs, then welcomed those same actors back as the characters were born again. They watched the floorwalker's hair going from black to gray and finally back to black, the cheap sets never changing. But these, too, faded; eventually the sets and the blackest hair faded as if dust from the London streets was getting in under the elevator doors, and there was a sadness about this that seemed to affect Grant and Fiona more than any of the tragedies on *Masterpiece Theatre,* so they gave up watching before the final end.

Fiona was making some friends, Kristy said. She was definitely coming out of her shell.

What shell was that? Grant wanted to ask, but checked himself, to remain in Kristy's good graces.

IF ANYBODY PHONED, he let the message go onto the machine. The people they saw socially, occasionally, were not close neighbors but people who lived around the countryside, who were retired, as they were, and who often went away without notice. The first years that they had lived here Grant and Fiona had stayed through the winter. A country winter was a new experience, and they had plenty to do, fixing up the house. Then they had got the idea that they too should travel while they could, and they had gone to Greece, to Australia, to Costa Rica. People would think that they were away on some such trip at present.

He skied for exercise but never went as far as the swamp. He skied around and around in the field behind the house as the sun went down and left the sky pink over a countryside that seemed to be bound by waves of blue-edged ice. He counted off the times he went round the field, and then he came back to the darkening house, turning the television news on while he got his supper. They had usually prepared supper together. One of them made the drinks and the other the fire, and they talked about his work (he was writing a study of legendary Norse wolves and particularly of the great Fenris wolf who swallows up Odin at the end of the world) and about whatever Fiona was reading and what they had been thinking during their close but separate day. This was their time of liveliest intimacy, though there was also, of course, the five or ten minutes of physical sweetness just after they got into bed—something that did not often end up in sex but reassured them that sex was not over yet.

IN A DREAM Grant showed a letter to one of his colleagues whom he had thought of as a friend. The letter was from the roommate of a girl he had not thought of for a while. Its style was sanctimonious and hostile, threatening in a whining way—he put the writer down as a latent lesbian. The girl herself was someone he had parted from decently, and it seemed unlikely that she would want to make a fuss, let alone try to kill herself, which was what the letter was apparently, elaborately, trying to tell him.

The colleague was one of those husbands and fathers who had been among the first to throw away their neckties and leave home to spend every night on a floor mattress with a bewitching young mistress, coming to their offices, their classes, bedraggled and smelling of dope and incense. But now he took a dim view of such shenanigans, and Grant recollected that he had in fact married one of those girls, and that she had taken to giving dinner parties and having babies, just as wives used to do.

"I wouldn't laugh," he said to Grant, who did not think he had been laughing. "And if I were you I'd try to prepare Fiona."

So Grant went off to find Fiona in Meadowlake—the old Meadowlake—and got into a lecture theater instead. Everybody was waiting there for him to teach his class. And sitting in the last, highest row was a flock of cold-eyed young women all in black robes, all in mourning, who never took their bitter stares off him and conspicuously did not write down, or care about, anything he was saying.

Fiona was in the first row, untroubled. She had transformed the lecture room into the sort of corner she was always finding at a party—some high-and-dry spot where she drank wine with mineral water, and smoked ordinary cigarettes and told funny stories about her dogs. Holding out there against the tide, with some people who were like herself, as if the dramas that were being played out in other corners, in bedrooms and on the dark verandah, were nothing but childish comedy. As if chastity was chic, and reticence a blessing.

"Oh, phooey," Fiona said. "Girls that age are always going around talking about how they'll kill themselves."

But it wasn't enough for her to say that—in fact, it rather chilled him. He was afraid that she was wrong, that something terrible had happened, and he saw what she could not—that the black ring was thickening, drawing in, all around his windpipe, all around the top of the room.

HE HAULED HIMSELF out of the dream and set about separating what was real from what was not.

There had been a letter, and the word "RAT" had appeared in black paint on his office door, and Fiona, on being told that a girl had suffered from a bad crush on him, had said pretty much what she said in the dream. The colleague hadn't come into it, the black-robed women had never appeared in his classroom, and nobody had committed suicide. Grant hadn't been disgraced, in fact he had got off easily when you thought of what might have happened just a couple of years later. But word got around. Cold shoulders became conspicuous. They had few Christmas invitations and spent New Year's Eve alone. Grant got drunk, and without its being required of him—also, thank God, without making the error of a confession—he promised Fiona a new life.

The shame he felt then was the shame of being duped, of not having noticed the change that was going on. And not one woman had made him aware of it. There had been the change in the past when so many women so suddenly became available—or it seemed that way to him—and now this new change, when they were saying that what had happened was not what they had had in mind at all. They had collaborated because they were helpless and bewildered, and they had been injured by the whole thing, rather than delighted. Even when they had taken the initiative they had done so only because the cards were stacked against them.

Nowhere was there any acknowledgment that the life of a phi-landerer (if that was what Grant had to call himself—he who had not had half as many conquests or complications as the man who had reproached him in his dream) involved acts of kindness and generosity and even sacrifice. Not in the beginning, perhaps, but at least as things went on. Many times he had catered to a woman's pride, to her fragility, by offering more affection—or a rougher passion—than anything he really felt. All so that he could now find himself accused of wounding and exploiting and destroying self-esteem. And of deceiving Fiona—as of course he had deceived her—but would it have been better if he had done as others had done with their wives and left her?

He had never thought of such a thing. He had never stopped making love to Fiona in spite of disturbing demands elsewhere. He had not stayed away from her for a single night. No making up elaborate stories in order to spend a weekend in San Francisco or in a tent on Manitoulin Island. He had gone easy on the dope and the drink and he had continued to publish papers, serve on committees, make progress in his career. He had never had any intention of throwing up work and marriage and taking to the country to practice carpentry or keep bees.

But something like that had happened after all. He took an early retirement with a reduced pension. The cardiologist had died, after some bewildered and stoical time alone in the big house, and Fiona had inherited both that property and the farmhouse where her father had grown up, in the country near Georgian Bay. She gave up her job, as a hospital coordinator of volunteer services (in that everyday world, as she said, where people actually had troubles that were not related to drugs or sex or intellectual squabbles). A new life was a new life.

Boris and Natasha had died by this time. One of them got sick and died first—Grant forgot which one—and then the other died, more or less out of sympathy.

He and Fiona worked on the house. They got cross-country skis. They were not very sociable, but they gradually made some friends. There were no more hectic flirtations. No bare female toes creeping up under a man's pants leg at a dinner party. No more loose wives.

Just in time, Grant was able to think, when the sense of injustice wore down. The feminists and perhaps the sad silly girl herself and his cowardly so-called friends had pushed him out just in time. Out of a life that was in fact getting to be more trouble than it was worth. And that might eventually have cost him Fiona.

ON THE MORNING OF THE DAY when he was to go back to Meadowlake for the first visit, Grant woke early. He was full of a solemn tingling, as in the old days on the morning of his first planned meeting with a new woman. The feeling was not precisely sexual. (Later, when the meetings had become routine, that was all it was.) There was an expectation of discovery, almost a spiritual expansion. Also timidity, humility, alarm.

He left home too early. Visitors were not allowed before two o'clock. He did not want to sit out in the parking lot, waiting, so he made himself turn the car in a wrong direction.

There had been a thaw. Plenty of snow was left, but the dazzling hard landscape of earlier winter had crumbled. These pocked heaps under a gray sky looked like refuse in the fields.

In the town near Meadowlake he found a florist's shop and bought a large bouquet. He had never presented flowers to Fiona before. Or to anyone else. He entered the building feeling like a hopeless lover or a guilty husband in a cartoon.

"Wow. Narcissus this early," Kristy said. "You must've spent a fortune." She went along the hall ahead of him and snapped on the light in a closet, or sort of kitchen, where she searched for a vase. She was a heavy young woman who looked as if she had given up in every department except her hair. That was blond and voluminous. All the puffed-up luxury of a cocktail waitress's style, or a stripper's, on top of such a workaday face and body.

"There, now," she said, and nodded him down the hall. "Name's right on the door."

So it was, on a nameplate decorated with bluebirds. He wondered whether to knock, and did, then opened the door and called her name.

She wasn't there. The closet door was closed, the bed smoothed. Nothing on the bedside table, except a box of Kleenex and a glass of water. Not a single photograph or picture of any kind, not a book or a magazine. Perhaps you had to keep those in a cupboard.

He went back to the nurses' station, or reception desk, or whatever it was. Kristy said "No?" with a surprise that he thought perfunctory.

He hesitated, holding the flowers. She said, "Okay, okay—let's set the bouquet down here." Sighing, as if he was a backward child on his first day at school, she led him along a hall, into the light of the huge sky windows in the large central space, with its cathedral ceiling. Some people were sitting along the walls, in easy chairs, others at tables in the middle of the carpeted floor. None of them looked too bad. Old—some of them incapacitated enough to need wheelchairs—but decent. There used to be some unnerving sights when he and Fiona went to visit Mr. Farquar. Whiskers on old women's chins, somebody with a bulged-out eye like a rotted plum. Dribblers, head wagglers, mad chatterers. Now it looked as if there'd been some weeding out of the worst cases. Or perhaps drugs, surgery had come into use, perhaps there were ways of treating disfigurement, as well as verbal and other kinds of incontinence—ways that hadn't existed even those few years ago.

There was, however, a very disconsolate woman sitting at the piano, picking away with one finger and never achieving a tune. Another woman, staring out from behind a coffee urn and a stack of plastic cups, looked bored to stone. But she had to be an employee—she wore a pale-green pants outfit like Kristy's.

"See?" said Kristy in a softer voice. "You just go up and say hello and try not to startle her. Remember she may not— Well. Just go ahead."

He saw Fiona in profile, sitting close up to one of the card tables, but not playing. She looked a little puffy in the face, the flab on one cheek hiding the corner of her mouth, in a way it hadn't done before. She was watching the play of the man she sat closest to. He held his cards tilted so that she could see them. When Grant got near the table she looked up. They all looked up—all the players at the table looked up, with displeasure. Then they immediately looked down at their cards, as if to ward off any intrusion.

But Fiona smiled her lopsided, abashed, sly, and charming smile and pushed back her chair and came round to him, putting her fingers to her mouth.

"Bridge," she whispered. "Deadly serious. They're quite rabid about it." She drew him towards the coffee table, chatting. "I can remember being like that for a while at college. My friends and I would cut class and sit in the common room and smoke and play like cutthroats. One's name was Phoebe, I don't remember the others."

"Phoebe Hart," Grant said. He pictured the little hollow-chested, black-eyed girl, who was probably dead by now. Wreathed in smoke, Fiona and Phoebe and those others, rapt as witches.

"You knew her too?" said Fiona, directing her smile now towards the stone-faced woman. "Can I get you anything? A cup of tea? I'm afraid the coffee isn't up to much here."

Grant never drank tea.

He could not throw his arms around her. Something about her voice and smile, familiar as they were, something about the way she seemed to be guarding the players and even the coffee woman from him—as well as him from their displeasure—made that not possible.

"I brought you some flowers," he said. "I thought they'd do to brighten up your room. I went to your room, but you weren't there."

"Well, no," she said. "I'm here."

Grant said, "You've made a new friend." He nodded towards the man she'd been sitting next to. At this moment that man looked up at Fiona and she turned, either because of what Grant had said or because she felt the look at her back.

"It's just Aubrey," she said. "The funny thing is I knew him years and years ago. He worked in the store. The hardware store where my grandpa used to shop. He and I were always kidding around and he could not get up the nerve to ask me out. Till the very last weekend and he took me to a ball game. But when it was over my grandpa showed up to drive me home. I was up visiting for the summer. Visiting my grandparents—they lived on a farm."

"Fiona. I know where your grandparents lived. It's where we live. Lived."

"Really?" she said, not paying full attention because the cardplayer was sending her his look, which was not one of supplication but command. He was a man of about Grant's age, or a little older. Thick coarse white hair fell over his forehead, and his skin was leathery but pale, yellowish-white like an old wrinkled-up kid glove. His long face was dignified and melancholy, and he had something of the beauty of a powerful, discouraged, elderly horse. But where Fiona was concerned he was not discouraged.

"I better go back," Fiona said, a blush spotting her newly fattened face. "He thinks he can't play without me sitting there. It's silly, I hardly know the game anymore. I'm afraid you'll have to excuse me."

"Will you be through soon?"

"Oh, we should be. It depends. If you go and ask that grim-looking lady nicely she'll get you some tea."

"I'm fine," Grant said.

"So I'll leave you then, you can entertain yourself? It must all seem strange to you, but you'll be surprised how soon you get used to it. You'll get to know who everybody is. Except that some of them are pretty well off in the clouds, you know—you can't expect them all to get to know who *you* are."

She slipped back into her chair and said something into Aubrey's ear. She tapped her fingers across the back of his hand.

Grant went in search of Kristy and met her in the hall. She was pushing a cart on which there were pitchers of apple juice and grape juice.

"Just one sec," she said to him, as she stuck her head through a doorway. "Apple juice in here? Grape juice? Cookies?"

He waited while she filled two plastic glasses and took them into the room. Then she came back and put two arrowroot cookies on paper plates.

"Well?" she said. "Aren't you glad to see her participating and everything?"

Grant said, "Does she even know who I am?"

HE COULD NOT DECIDE. She could have been playing a joke. It would not be unlike her. She had given herself away by that little pretense at the end, talking to him as if she thought perhaps he was a new resident.

If that was what she was pretending. If it was a pretense.

But would she not have run after him and laughed at him then, once the joke was over? She would not have just gone back to the game, surely, and pretended to forget about him. That would have been too cruel.

Kristy said, "You just caught her at sort of a bad moment. Involved in the game."

"She's not even playing," he said.

"Well, but her friend's playing. Aubrey."

"So who is Aubrey?"

"That's who he is. Aubrey. Her friend. Would you like a juice?"

Grant shook his head.

"Oh, look," said Kristy. "They get these attachments. That takes over for a while. Best buddy sort of thing. It's kind of a phase."

"You mean she really might not know who I am?"

"She might not. Not today. Then tomorrow—you never know, do you? Things change back and forth all the time and there's nothing you can do about it. You'll see the way it is once you've been coming here for a while. You'll learn not to take it all so serious. Learn to take it day by day."

DAY BY DAY. But things really didn't change back and forth, and he didn't get used to the way they were. Fiona was the one who seemed to get used to him, but only as some persistent visitor who took a special interest in her. Or perhaps even as a nuisance who must be prevented, according to her old rules of courtesy, from realizing that he was one. She treated him with a distracted, social sort of kindness that was successful in holding him back from the most obvious, the most necessary question. He could not demand of her whether she did or did not remember him as her husband of nearly fifty years. He got the impression that she would be embarrassed by such a question—embarrassed not for herself but for him. She would have laughed in a fluttery way and mortified him with her politeness and bewilderment, and somehow she would have ended up not saying either yes or no. Or she would have said either one in a way that gave not the least satisfaction.

Kristy was the only nurse he could talk to. Some of the others treated the whole thing as a joke. One tough old stick laughed in his face. "That Aubrey and that Fiona? They've really got it bad, haven't they?"

Kristy told him that Aubrey had been the local representative of a company that sold weed killer—"and all that kind of stuff"—to farmers.

"He was a fine person," she said, and Grant did not know whether this meant that Aubrey was honest and openhanded and kind to people, or that he was well spoken and well dressed and drove a good car. Probably both.

And then when he was not very old or even retired—she said—he had suffered some unusual kind of damage.

"His wife is the one takes care of him usually. She takes care of him at home. She just put him in here on temporary care so she could get a break. Her sister wanted her to go to Florida. See, she's had a hard time, you wouldn't ever have expected a man like him— They just went on a holiday somewhere and he got something, like some bug, that gave him a terrible high fever? And it put him in a coma and left him like he is now."

He asked her about these affections between residents. Did they ever go too far? He was able now to take a tone of indulgence that he hoped would save him from any lectures.

"Depends what you mean," she said. She kept writing in her record book while deciding how to answer him. When she finished what she was writing she looked up at him with a frank smile.

"The trouble we have in here, it's funny, it's often with some of the ones that haven't been friendly with each other at all. They maybe won't even know each other, beyond knowing, like, is it a man or a woman? You'd think it'd be the old guys trying to crawl in bed with the old women, but you know half the time it's the other way round. Old women going after the old men. Could be they're not so wore out, I guess."

Then she stopped smiling, as if she was afraid she had said too much, or spoken callously.

"Don't take me wrong," she said. "I don't mean Fiona. Fiona is a lady."

Well, what about Aubrey? Grant felt like saying. But he remembered that Aubrey was in a wheelchair.

"She's a real lady," Kristy said, in a tone so decisive and reassuring that Grant was not reassured. He had in his mind a picture of Fiona, in one of her long eyelet-trimmed blue-ribboned nightgowns, teasingly lifting the covers of an old man's bed.

"Well, I sometimes wonder—" he said.

Kristy said sharply, "You wonder what?"

"I wonder whether she isn't putting on some kind of a charade."

"A what?" said Kristy.

MOST AFTERNOONS the pair could be found at the card table. Aubrey had large, thick-fingered hands. It was difficult for him to manage his cards. Fiona shuffled and dealt for him and sometimes moved quickly to straighten a card that seemed to be slipping from his grasp. Grant would watch from across the room her darting move and quick, laughing apology. He could see Aubrey's husbandly frown as a wisp of her hair touched his cheek. Aubrey preferred to ignore her as long as she stayed close.

But let her smile her greeting at Grant, let her push back her chair and get up to offer him tea—showing that she had accepted his right to be there and possibly felt a slight responsibility for him—and Aubrey's face took on its look of sombre consternation. He would let the cards slide from his fingers and fall on the floor, to spoil the game.

So that Fiona had to get busy and put things right.

If they weren't at the bridge table they might be walking along the halls, Aubrey hanging on to the railing with one hand and clutching Fiona's arm or shoulder with the other. The nurses thought that it was a marvel, the way she had got him out of his wheelchair. Though for longer trips—to the conservatory at one end of the building or the television room at the other—the wheelchair was called for.

The television seemed to be always turned to the sports channel and Aubrey would watch any sport, but his favorite appeared to be golf. Grant didn't mind watching that with them. He sat down a few chairs away. On the large screen a small group of spectators and commentators followed the players around the peaceful green, and at appropriate moments broke into a formal sort of applause. But there was silence everywhere as the player made his swing and the ball took its lonely, appointed journey across the sky. Aubrey and Fiona and Grant and possibly others sat and held their breaths, and then Aubrey's breath broke out first, expressing satisfaction or disappointment. Fiona's chimed in on the same note a moment later.

In the conservatory there was no such silence. The pair found themselves a seat among the most lush and thick and tropical-looking plants—a bower, if you like—which Grant had just enough self-control to keep from penetrating. Mixed in with the rustle of the leaves and the sound of splashing water was Fiona's soft talk and her laughter.

Then some sort of chortle. Which of them could it be?

Perhaps neither—perhaps it came from one of the impudent flashy-looking birds who inhabited the corner cages.

Aubrey could talk, though his voice probably didn't sound the way it used to. He seemed to say something now—a couple of thick syllables. *Take care. He's here. My love.*

On the blue bottom of the fountain's pool lay some wishing coins. Grant had never seen anybody actually throwing money in. He stared at these nickels and dimes and quarters, wondering if they had been glued to the tiles—another feature of the building's encouraging decoration.

TEENAGERS AT THE BASEBALL GAME, sitting at the top of the bleachers out of the way of the boy's friends. A couple of inches of bare wood between them, darkness falling, quick chill of the evening late in the summer. The skittering of their hands, the shift of haunches, eyes never lifted from the field. He'll take off his jacket, if he's wearing one, to lay it around her narrow shoulders. Underneath it he can pull her closer to him, press his spread fingers into her soft arm.

Not like today when any kid would probably be into her pants on the first date.

Fiona's skinny soft arm. Teenage lust astonishing her and flashing along all the nerves of her tender new body, as the night thickens beyond the lighted dust of the game.

MEADOWLAKE WAS SHORT ON MIRRORS, so he did not have to catch sight of himself stalking and prowling. But every once in a while it came to him how foolish and pathetic and perhaps unhinged he must look, trailing around after Fiona and Aubrey. And having no luck in confronting her, or him. Less and less sure of what right he had to be on the scene but unable to withdraw. Even at home, while he worked at his desk or cleaned up the house or shovelled snow when necessary, some ticking metronome in his mind was fixed on Meadowlake, on his next visit. Sometimes he seemed to himself like a mulish boy conducting a hopeless courtship, sometimes like one of those wretches who follow celebrated women through the streets, convinced that one day these women will turn around and recognize their love.

He made a great effort, and cut his visits down to Wednesdays and Saturdays. Also he set himself to observing other things about the place, as if he was a sort of visitor at large, a person doing an inspection or a social study.

Saturdays had a holiday bustle and tension. Families arrived in clusters. Mothers were usually in charge, they were like cheerful but insistent sheepdogs herding the men and children. Only the smallest children were without apprehension. They noticed right away the green and white squares on the hall floors and picked one color to walk on, the other to jump over. The bolder ones might try to hitch rides on the back of wheelchairs. Some persisted in these tricks in spite of scolding, and had to be removed to the car. And how happily, then, how readily, some older child or father volunteered to do the removing, and thus opt out of the visit.

It was the women who kept the conversation afloat. Men seemed cowed by the situation, teenagers affronted. Those being visited rode in a wheelchair or stumped along with a cane, or walked stiffly, unaided, at the procession's head, proud of the turnout but somewhat blank-eyed, or desperately babbling, under the stress of it. And now surrounded by a variety of outsiders these insiders did not look like such regular people after all. Female chins might have had their bristles shaved to the roots and bad eyes might be hidden by patches or dark lenses, inappropriate utterances might be controlled by medication, but some glaze remained, a haunted rigidity—as if people were content to become memories of themselves, final photographs.

Grant understood better now how Mr. Farquar must have felt. People here—even the ones who did not participate in any activities but sat around watching the doors or looking out the windows—were living a busy life in their heads (not to mention the life of their bodies, the portentous shifts in their bowels, the stabs and twinges everywhere along the line), and that was a life that in most cases could not very well be described or alluded to in front of visitors. All they could do was wheel or somehow propel themselves about and hope to come up with something that could be displayed or talked about.

There was the conservatory to be shown off, and the big television screen. Fathers thought that was really something. Mothers said the ferns were gorgeous. Soon everybody sat down around the little tables and ate ice cream—refused only by the teenagers, who were dying of disgust. Women wiped away the dribble from shivery old chins and men looked the other way.

There must be some satisfaction in this ritual, and perhaps even the teenagers would be glad, one day, that they had come. Grant was no expert on families.

No children or grandchildren appeared to visit Aubrey, and since they could not play cards—the tables being taken over for the ice cream parties—he and Fiona stayed clear of the Saturday parade. The conservatory was far too popular then for any of their intimate conversations.

Those might be going on, of course, behind Fiona's closed door. Grant could not manage to knock, though he stood there for some time staring at the Disney birds with an intense, a truly malignant dislike.

Or they might be in Aubrey's room. But he did not know where that was. The more he explored this place, the more corridors and seating spaces and ramps he discovered, and in his wanderings he was still apt to get lost. He would take a certain picture or chair as a landmark, and the next week whatever he had chosen seemed to have been placed somewhere else. He didn't like to mention this to Kristy, lest she think he was suffering some mental dislocations of his own. He supposed this constant change and rearranging might be for the sake of the residents—to make their daily exercise more interesting.

He did not mention either that he sometimes saw a woman at a distance that he thought was Fiona, but then thought it couldn't be, because of the clothes the woman was wearing. When had Fiona ever gone in for bright flowered blouses and electric blue slacks? One Saturday he looked out a window and saw Fiona—it must be her—wheeling Aubrey along one of the paved paths now cleared of snow and ice, and she was wearing a silly woolly hat and a jacket with swirls of blue and purple, the sort of thing he had seen on local women at the supermarket.

The fact must be that they didn't bother to sort out the wardrobes of the women who were roughly the same size. And counted on the women not recognizing their own clothes anyway.

They had cut her hair, too. They had cut away her angelic halo. On a Wednesday, when everything was more normal and card games were going on again, and the women in the Crafts Room were making silk flowers or costumed dolls without anybody hanging around to pester or admire them, and when Aubrey and Fiona were again in evidence so that it was possible for Grant to have one of his brief and friendly and maddening conversations with his wife, he said to her, "Why did they chop off your hair?"

Fiona put her hands up to her head, to check.

"Why—I never missed it," she said.

HE THOUGHT HE SHOULD FIND OUT what went on on the second floor, where they kept the people who, as Kristy said, had really lost it. Those who walked around down here holding conversations with themselves or throwing out odd questions at a passerby ("Did I leave my sweater in the church?") had apparently lost only some of it.

Not enough to qualify.

There were stairs, but the doors at the top were locked and only the staff had the keys. You could not get into the elevator unless somebody buzzed for it to open, from behind the desk.

What did they do, after they lost it?

"Some just sit," said Kristy. "Some sit and cry. Some try to holler the house down. You don't really want to know."

Sometimes they got it back.

"You go in their rooms for a year and they don't know you from Adam. Then one day, it's oh, hi, when are we going home. All of a sudden they're absolutely back to normal again."

But not for long.

"You think, wow, back to normal. And then they're gone again." She snapped her fingers. "Like so."

IN THE TOWN where he used to work there was a bookstore that he and Fiona had visited once or twice a year. He went back there by himself. He didn't feel like buying anything, but he had made a list and picked out a couple of the books on it, and then bought another book that he noticed by chance. It was about Iceland. A book of nineteenth-century watercolors made by a lady traveller to Iceland.

Fiona had never learned her mother's language and she had never shown much respect for the stories that it preserved—the stories that Grant had taught and written about, and still did write about, in his working life. She referred to their heroes as "old Njal" or "old Snorri." But in the last few years she had developed an interest in the country itself and looked at travel guides. She read about William Morris's trip, and Auden's. She didn't really plan to travel there. She said the weather was too dreadful. Also—she said—there ought to be one place you thought about and knew about and maybe longed for—but never did get to see.

WHEN GRANT FIRST STARTED TEACHING Anglo-Saxon and Nordic Literature he got the regular sort of students in his classes. But after a few years he noticed a change. Married women started going back to school. Not with the idea of qualifying for a better job or for any job but simply to give themselves something more interesting to think about than their usual housework and hobbies. To enrich their lives. And perhaps it followed naturally that the men who taught them these things would become part of the enrichment, that these men would seem to these women more mysterious and desirable than the men they still cooked for and slept with.

The studies chosen were usually Psychology or Cultural History or English Literature. Archaeology or Linguistics was picked sometimes but dropped when it turned out to be heavy going. Those who signed up for Grant's courses might have a Scandinavian background, like Fiona, or they might have learned something about Norse mythology from Wagner or historical novels. There were also a few who thought he was teaching a Celtic language and for whom everything Celtic had a mystic allure.

He spoke to such aspirants fairly roughly from his side of the desk.

"If you want to learn a pretty language, go and learn Spanish. Then you can use it if you go to Mexico."

Some took his warning and drifted away. Others seemed to be moved in a personal way by his demanding tone. They worked with a will and brought into his office, into his regulated, satisfactory life, the great surprising bloom of their mature female compliance, their tremulous hope of approval.

He chose the woman named Jacqui Adams. She was the opposite of Fiona—short, cushiony, dark-eyed, effusive. A stranger to irony. The affair lasted for a year, until her husband was transferred. When they were saying good-bye, in her car, she began to shake uncontrollably. It was as if she had hypothermia. She wrote to him a few times, but he found the tone of her letters overwrought and could not decide how to answer. He let the time for answering slip away while he became magically and unexpectedly involved with a girl who was young enough to be her daughter.

For another and more dizzying development had taken place while he was busy with Jacqui. Young girls with long hair and sandalled feet were coming into his office and all but declaring themselves ready for sex. The cautious approaches, the tender intimations of feeling required with Jacqui were out the window. A whirlwind hit him, as it did many others, wish becoming action in a way that made him wonder if there wasn't something missed. But who had time for regrets? He heard of simultaneous liaisons, savage and risky encounters. Scandals burst wide open, with high and painful drama all round but a feeling that somehow it was better so. There were reprisals—there were firings. But those fired went off to teach at smaller, more tolerant colleges or Open Learning Centers, and many wives left behind got over the shock and took up the costumes, the sexual nonchalance of the girls who had tempted their men. Academic parties, which used to be so predictable, became a minefield. An epidemic had broken out, it was spreading like the Spanish flu. Only this time people ran after contagion, and few between sixteen and sixty seemed willing to be left out.

Fiona appeared to be quite willing, however. Her mother was dying, and her experience in the hospital led her from her routine work in the registrar's office into her new job. Grant himself did not go overboard, at least in comparison with some people around him. He never let another woman get as close to him as Jacqui had been. What he felt was mainly a gigantic increase in well-being. A tendency to pudginess that he had had since he was twelve years old disappeared. He ran up steps two at a time. He appreciated as never before a pageant of torn clouds and winter sunset seen from his office window, the charm of antique lamps glowing between his neighbors' living-room curtains, the cries of children in the park at dusk, unwilling to leave the hill where they'd been tobogganing. Come summer, he learned the names of flowers. In his classroom, after coaching by his nearly voiceless mother-in-law (her affliction was cancer of the throat), he risked reciting and then translating the majestic and gory ode, the head-ransom, the Hofuolausn, composed to honor King Eric Blood-axe by the skald whom that king had condemned to death. (And who was then, by the same king—and by the power of poetry—set free.) All applauded—even the peaceniks in the class whom he'd cheerfully taunted earlier, asking if they would like to wait in the hall. Driving home that day or maybe another he found an absurd and blasphemous quotation running around in his head.

And so he increased in wisdom and stature—
And in favor with God and man.

That embarrassed him at the time and gave him a superstitious chill. As it did yet. But so long as nobody knew, it seemed not unnatural.

HE TOOK THE BOOK WITH HIM, the next time he went to Meadowlake. It was a Wednesday. He went looking for Fiona at the card tables and did not see her.

A woman called out to him, "She's not here. She's sick." Her voice sounded self-important and excited—pleased with herself for having recognized him when he knew nothing about her. Perhaps also pleased with all she knew about Fiona, about Fiona's life here, thinking it was maybe more than he knew.

"He's not here either," she said.

Grant went to find Kristy.

"Nothing, really," she said, when he asked what was the matter with Fiona. "She's just having a day in bed today, just a bit of an upset."

Fiona was sitting straight up in the bed. He hadn't noticed, the few times that he had been in this room, that this was a hospital bed and could be cranked up in such a way. She was wearing one of her high-necked maidenly gowns, and her face had a pallor that was not like cherry blossoms but like flour paste.

Aubrey was beside her in his wheelchair, pushed as close to the bed as it could get. Instead of the nondescript open-necked shirts he usually wore, he was wearing a jacket and a tie. His natty-looking tweed hat was resting on the bed. He looked as if he had been out on important business.

To see his lawyer? His banker? To make arrangements with the funeral director?

Whatever he'd been doing, he looked worn out by it. He too was gray in the face.

They both looked up at Grant with a stony, grief-ridden apprehension that turned to relief, if not to welcome, when they saw who he was.

Not who they thought he'd be.

They were hanging on to each other's hands and they did not let go.

The hat on the bed. The jacket and tie.

It wasn't that Aubrey had been out. It wasn't a question of where he'd been or whom he'd been to see. It was where he was going.

Grant set the book down on the bed beside Fiona's free hand.

"It's about Iceland," he said. "I thought maybe you'd like to look at it."

"Why, thank you," said Fiona. She didn't look at the book. He put her hand on it.

"Iceland," he said.

She said, "Ice-land." The first syllable managed to hold a tinkle of interest, but the second fell flat. Anyway, it was necessary for her to turn her attention back to Aubrey, who was pulling his great thick hand out of hers.

"What is it?" she said. "What is it, dear heart?"

Grant had never heard her use this flowery expression before.

"Oh, all right," she said. "Oh, here." And she pulled a handful of tissues from the box beside her bed.

Aubrey's problem was that he had begun to weep. His nose had started to run, and he was anxious not to turn into a sorry spectacle, especially in front of Grant.

"Here. Here," said Fiona. She would have tended to his nose her-self and wiped his tears—and perhaps if they had been alone he would have let her do it. But with Grant there Aubrey would not permit it. He got hold of the Kleenex as well as he could and made a few awkward but lucky swipes at his face.

While he was occupied, Fiona turned to Grant.

"Do you by any chance have any influence around here?" she said in a whisper. "I've seen you talking to them—"

Aubrey made a noise of protest or weariness or disgust. Then his upper body pitched forward as if he wanted to throw himself against her. She scrambled half out of bed and caught him and held on to him. It seemed improper for Grant to help her, though of course he would have done so if he'd thought Aubrey was about to tumble to the floor.

"Hush," Fiona was saying. "Oh, honey. Hush. We'll get to see each other. We'll have to. I'll go and see you. You'll come and see me."

Aubrey made the same sound again with his face in her chest, and there was nothing Grant could decently do but get out of the room.

"I just wish his wife would hurry up and get here," Kristy said. "I wish she'd get him out of here and cut the agony short. We've got to start serving supper before long and how are we supposed to get her to swallow anything with him still hanging around?"

Grant said, "Should I stay?"

"What for? She's not sick, you know."

"To keep her company," he said.

Kristy shook her head.

"They have to get over these things on their own. They've got short memories usually. That's not always so bad."

Kristy was not hard-hearted. During the time he had known her Grant had found out some things about her life. She had four children. She did not know where her husband was but thought he might be in Alberta. Her younger boy's asthma was so bad that he would have died one night in January if she had not got him to the emergency ward in time. He was not on any illegal drugs, but she was not so sure about his brother.

To her, Grant and Fiona and Aubrey too must seem lucky. They had got through life without too much going wrong. What they had to suffer now that they were old hardly counted.

Grant left without going back to Fiona's room. He noticed that the wind was actually warm that day and the crows were making an uproar. In the parking lot a woman wearing a tartan pants suit was getting a folded-up wheelchair out of the trunk of her car.

THE STREET HE WAS DRIVING DOWN was called Black Hawks Lane. All the streets around were named for teams in the old National Hockey League. This was in an outlying section of the town near Meadowlake. He and Fiona had shopped in the town regularly but had not become familiar with any part of it except the main street.

The houses looked to have been built all around the same time, perhaps thirty or forty years ago. The streets were wide and curving and there were no sidewalks—recalling the time when it was thought unlikely that anybody would do much walking ever again. Friends of Grant's and Fiona's had moved to places something like this when they began to have their children. They were apologetic about the move at first. They called it "going out to Barbecue Acres."

Young families still lived here. There were basketball hoops over garage doors and tricycles in the driveways. But some of the houses had gone downhill from the sort of family homes they were surely meant to be. The yards were marked by car tracks, the windows were plastered with tinfoil or hung with faded flags.

Rental housing. Young male tenants—single still, or single again.

A few properties seemed to have been kept up as well as possible by the people who had moved into them when they were new—people who hadn't had the money or perhaps hadn't felt the need to move on to someplace better. Shrubs had grown to maturity, pastel vinyl siding had done away with the problem of repainting. Neat fences or hedges gave the sign that the children in the houses had all grown up and gone away, and that their parents no longer saw the point of letting the yard be a common run-through for whatever new children were loose in the neighborhood.

The house that was listed in the phone book as belonging to Aubrey and his wife was one of these. The front walk was paved with flagstones and bordered by hyacinths that stood as stiff as china flowers, alternately pink and blue.

FIONA HAD NOT GOT OVER HER SORROW. She did not eat at mealtimes, though she pretended to, hiding food in her napkin. She was being given a supplementary drink twice a day—someone stayed and watched while she swallowed it down. She got out of bed and dressed herself, but all she wanted to do then was sit in her room. She wouldn't have taken any exercise at all if Kristy or one of the other nurses, and Grant during visiting hours, had not walked her up and down in the corridors or taken her outside.

In the spring sunshine she sat, weeping weakly, on a bench by the wall. She was still polite—she apologized for her tears, and never argued with a suggestion or refused to answer a question. But she wept. Weeping had left her eyes raw-edged and dim. Her cardigan—if it was hers—would be buttoned crookedly. She had not got to the stage of leaving her hair unbrushed or her nails uncleaned, but that might come soon.

Kristy said that her muscles were deteriorating, and that if she didn't improve soon they would put her on a walker.

"But you know once they get a walker they start to depend on it and they never walk much anymore, just get wherever it is they have to go.

"You'll have to work at her harder," she said to Grant. "Try and encourage her."

But Grant had no luck at that. Fiona seemed to have taken a dislike to him, though she tried to cover it up. Perhaps she was reminded, every time she saw him, of her last minutes with Aubrey, when she had asked him for help and he hadn't helped her.

He didn't see much point in mentioning their marriage, now.

She wouldn't go down the hall to where most of the same people were still playing cards. And she wouldn't go into the television room or visit the conservatory.

She said that she didn't like the big screen, it hurt her eyes. And the birds' noise was irritating and she wished they would turn the fountain off once in a while.

So far as Grant knew, she never looked at the book about Iceland, or at any of the other—surprisingly few—books that she had brought from home. There was a reading room where she would sit down to rest, choosing it probably because there was seldom anybody there, and if he took a book off the shelves she would allow him to read to her. He suspected that she did that because it made his company easier for her—she was able to shut her eyes and sink back into her own grief. Because if she let go of her grief even for a minute it would only hit her harder when she bumped into it again. And sometimes he thought she closed her eyes to hide a look of informed despair that it would not be good for him to see.

So he sat and read to her out of one of these old novels about chaste love, and lost-and-regained fortunes, that could have been the discards of some long-ago village or Sunday school library. There had been no attempt, apparently, to keep the contents of the reading room as up-to-date as most things in the rest of the building.

The covers of the books were soft, almost velvety, with designs of leaves and flowers pressed into them, so that they resembled jewelry boxes or chocolate boxes. That women—he supposed it would be women—could carry home like treasure.

THE SUPERVISOR called him into her office. She said that Fiona was not thriving as they had hoped.

"Her weight is going down even with the supplement. We're doing all we can for her."

Grant said that he realized they were.

"The thing is, I'm sure you know, we don't do any prolonged bed care on the first floor. We do it temporarily if someone isn't feeling well, but if they get too weak to move around and be responsible we have to consider upstairs."

He said he didn't think that Fiona had been in bed that often.

"No. But if she can't keep up her strength, she will be. Right now she's borderline."

He said that he had thought the second floor was for people whose minds were disturbed.

"That too," she said.

.   .   .

HE HADN'T REMEMBERED ANYTHING about Aubrey's wife except the tartan suit he had seen her wearing in the parking lot. The tails of the jacket had flared open as she bent into the trunk of the car. He had got the impression of a trim waist and wide buttocks.

She was not wearing the tartan suit today. Brown belted slacks and a pink sweater. He was right about the waist—the tight belt showed she made a point of it. It might have been better if she hadn't, since she bulged out considerably above and below.

She could be ten or twelve years younger than her husband. Her hair was short, curly, artificially reddened. She had blue eyes—a lighter blue than Fiona's, a flat robin's-egg or turquoise blue—slanted by a slight puffiness. And a good many wrinkles made more noticeable by a walnut-stain makeup. Or perhaps that was her Florida tan.

He said that he didn't quite know how to introduce himself.

"I used to see your husband at Meadowlake. I'm a regular visitor there myself."

"Yes," said Aubrey's wife, with an aggressive movement of her chin.

"How is your husband doing?"

The "doing" was added on at the last moment. Normally he would have said, "How is your husband?"

"He's okay," she said.

"My wife and he struck up quite a close friendship."

"I heard about that."

"So. I wanted to talk to you about something if you had a minute."

"My husband did not try to start anything with your wife, if that's what you're getting at," she said. "He did not molest her in any way. He isn't capable of it and he wouldn't anyway. From what I heard it was the other way round."

Grant said, "No. That isn't it at all. I didn't come here with any complaints about anything."

"Oh," she said. "Well, I'm sorry. I thought you did."

That was all she was going to give by way of apology. And she didn't sound sorry. She sounded disappointed and confused.

"You better come in, then," she said. "It's blowing cold in through the door. It's not as warm out today as it looks."

So it was something of a victory for him even to get inside. He hadn't realized it would be as hard as this. He had expected a different sort of wife. A flustered homebody, pleased by an unexpected visit and flattered by a confidential tone.

She took him past the entrance to the living room, saying, "We'll have to sit in the kitchen where I can hear Aubrey." Grant caught sight of two layers of front-window curtains, both blue, one sheer and one silky, a matching blue sofa and a daunting pale carpet, various bright mirrors and ornaments.

Fiona had a word for those sort of swooping curtains—she said it like a joke, though the women she'd picked it up from used it seriously. Any room that Fiona fixed up was bare and bright—she would have been astonished to see so much fancy stuff crowded into such a small space. He could not think what that word was.

From a room off the kitchen—a sort of sunroom, though the blinds were drawn against the afternoon brightness—he could hear the sounds of television.

Aubrey. The answer to Fiona's prayers sat a few feet away, watching what sounded like a ball game. His wife looked in at him. She said, "You okay?" and partly closed the door.

"You might as well have a cup of coffee," she said to Grant.

He said, "Thanks."

"My son got him on the sports channel a year ago Christmas, I don't know what we'd do without it."

On the kitchen counters there were all sorts of contrivances and appliances—coffeemaker, food processor, knife sharpener, and some things Grant didn't know the names or uses of. All looked new and expensive, as if they had just been taken out of their wrappings, or were polished daily.

He thought it might be a good idea to admire things. He admired the coffeemaker she was using and said that he and Fiona had always meant to get one. This was absolutely untrue—Fiona had been devoted to a European contraption that made only two cups at a time.

"They gave us that," she said. "Our son and his wife. They live in Kamloops. B.C. They send us more stuff than we can handle. It wouldn't hurt if they would spend the money to come and see us instead."

Grant said philosophically, "I suppose they're busy with their own lives."

"They weren't too busy to go to Hawaii last winter. You could understand it if we had somebody else in the family, closer at hand. But he's the only one."

The coffee being ready, she poured it into two brown-and-green ceramic mugs that she took from the amputated branches of a ceramic tree trunk that sat on the table.

"People do get lonely," Grant said. He thought he saw his chance now. "If they're deprived of seeing somebody they care about, they do feel sad. Fiona, for instance. My wife."

"I thought you said you went and visited her."

"I do," he said. "That's not it."

Then he took the plunge, going on to make the request he'd come to make. Could she consider taking Aubrey back to Meadowlake maybe just one day a week, for a visit? It was only a drive of a few miles, surely it wouldn't prove too difficult. Or if she'd like to take the time off—Grant hadn't thought of this before and was rather dismayed to hear himself suggest it—then he himself could take Aubrey out there, he wouldn't mind at all. He was sure he could manage it. And she could use a break.

While he talked she moved her closed lips and her hidden tongue as if she was trying to identify some dubious flavor. She brought milk for his coffee, and a plate of ginger cookies.

"Homemade," she said as she set the plate down. There was challenge rather than hospitality in her tone. She said nothing more until she had sat down, poured milk into her coffee and stirred it.

Then she said no.

"No. I can't do that. And the reason is, I'm not going to upset him."

"Would it upset him?" Grant said earnestly.

"Yes, it would. It would. That's no way to do. Bringing him home and taking him back. Bringing him home and taking him back, that's just confusing him."

"But wouldn't he understand that it was just a visit? Wouldn't he get into the pattern of it?"

"He understands everything all right." She said this as if he had offered an insult to Aubrey. "But it's still an interruption. And then

I've got to get him all ready and get him into the car, and he's a big man, he's not so easy to manage as you might think. I've got to maneuver him into the car and pack his chair along and all that and what for? If I go to all that trouble I'd prefer to take him someplace that was more fun."

"But even if I agreed to do it?" Grant said, keeping his tone hopeful and reasonable. "It's true, you shouldn't have the trouble."

"You couldn't," she said flatly. "You don't know him. You couldn't handle him. He wouldn't stand for you doing for him. All that bother and what would he get out of it?"

Grant didn't think he should mention Fiona again.

"It'd make more sense to take him to the mall," she said. "Where he could see kids and whatnot. If it didn't make him sore about his own two grandsons he never gets to see. Or now the lake boats are starting to run again, he might get a charge out of going and watching that."

She got up and fetched her cigarettes and lighter from the window above the sink.

"You smoke?" she said.

He said no thanks, though he didn't know if a cigarette was being offered.

"Did you never? Or did you quit?"

"Quit," he said.

"How long ago was that?"

He thought about it.

"Thirty years. No—more."

He had decided to quit around the time he started up with Jacqui. But he couldn't remember whether he quit first, and thought a big reward was coming to him for quitting, or thought that the time had come to quit, now that he had such a powerful diversion.

"I've quit quitting," she said, lighting up. "Just made a resolution to quit quitting, that's all."

Maybe that was the reason for the wrinkles. Somebody—a woman—had told him that women who smoked developed a special set of fine facial wrinkles. But it could have been from the sun, or just the nature of her skin—her neck was noticeably wrinkled as well. Wrinkled neck, youthfully full and up-tilted breasts. Women of her age usually had these contradictions. The bad and good points, the genetic luck or lack of it, all mixed up together. Very few kept their beauty whole, though shadowy, as Fiona had done.

And perhaps that wasn't even true. Perhaps he only thought that because he'd known Fiona when she was young. Perhaps to get that impression you had to have known a woman when she was young.

So when Aubrey looked at his wife did he see a high-school girl full of scorn and sass, with an intriguing tilt to her robin's-egg blue eyes, pursing her fruity lips around a forbidden cigarette?

"So your wife's depressed?" Aubrey's wife said. "What's your wife's name? I forget."

"It's Fiona."

"Fiona. And what's yours? I don't think I ever was told that."

Grant said, "It's Grant."

She stuck her hand out unexpectedly across the table.

"Hello, Grant. I'm Marian.

"So now we know each other's name," she said, "there's no point in not telling you straight out what I think. I don't know if he's still so stuck on seeing your—on seeing Fiona. Or not. I don't ask him and he's not telling me. Maybe just a passing fancy. But I don't feel like taking him back there in case it turns out to be more than that. I can't afford to risk it. I don't want him getting hard to handle. I don't want him upset and carrying on. I've got my hands full with him as it is. I don't have any help. It's just me here. I'm it."

"Did you ever consider—it *is* very hard for you—" Grant said, "did you ever consider his going in there for good?"

He had lowered his voice almost to a whisper, but she did not seem to feel a need to lower hers.

"No," she said. "I'm keeping him right here."

Grant said, "Well. That's very good and noble of you."

He hoped the word "noble" had not sounded sarcastic. He had not meant it to be.

"You think so?" she said. "Noble is not what I'm thinking about."

"Still. It's not easy."

"No, it isn't. But the way I am, I don't have much choice. If I put him in there I don't have the money to pay for him unless I sell the house. The house is what we own outright. Otherwise I don't have anything in the way of resources. I get the pension next year, and

I'll have his pension and my pension, but even so I could not afford to keep him there and hang on to the house. And it means a lot to me, my house does."

"It's very nice," said Grant.

"Well, it's all right. I put a lot into it. Fixing it up and keeping it up."

"I'm sure you did. You do."

"I don't want to lose it."

"No."

"I'm not *going* to lose it."

"I see your point."

"The company left us high and dry," she said. "I don't know all the ins and outs of it, but basically he got shoved out. It ended up with them saying he owed them money and when I tried to find out what was what he just went on saying it's none of my business. What I think is he did something pretty stupid. But I'm not supposed to ask, so I shut up. You've been married. You are married. You know how it is. And in the middle of me finding out about this we're supposed to go on this trip with these people and can't get out of it. And on the trip he takes sick from this virus you never heard of and goes into a coma. So that pretty well gets *him* off the hook."

Grant said, "Bad luck."

"I don't mean exactly that he got sick on purpose. It just happened. He's not mad at me anymore and I'm not mad at him. It's just life."

"That's true."

"You can't beat life."

She flicked her tongue in a cat's businesslike way across her top lip, getting the cookie crumbs. "I sound like I'm quite the philosopher, don't I? They told me out there you used to be a university professor."

"Quite a while ago," Grant said.

"I'm not much of an intellectual," she said.

"I don't know how much I am, either."

"But I know when my mind's made up. And it's made up. I'm not going to let go of the house. Which means I'm keeping him here and I don't want him getting it in his head he wants to move anyplace else. It was probably a mistake putting him in there so I could get away, but I wasn't going to get another chance, so I took it. So. Now I know better."

She shook out another cigarette.

"I bet I know what you're thinking," she said. "You're thinking there's a mercenary type of a person."

"I'm not making judgments of that sort. It's your life."

"You bet it is."

He thought they should end on a more neutral note. So he asked her if her husband had worked in a hardware store in the summers, when he was going to school.

"I never heard about it," she said. "I wasn't raised here."

DRIVING HOME, he noticed that the swamp hollow that had been filled with snow and the formal shadows of tree trunks was now lighted up with skunk lilies. Their fresh, edible-looking leaves were the size of platters. The flowers sprang straight up like candle flames, and there were so many of them, so pure a yellow, that they set a light shooting up from the earth on this cloudy day. Fiona had told him that they generated a heat of their own as well. Rummaging around in one of her concealed pockets of information, she said that you were supposed to be able to put your hand inside the curled petal and feel the heat. She said that she had tried it, but she couldn't be sure if what she felt was heat or her imagination. The heat attracted bugs.

"Nature doesn't fool around just being decorative."

He had failed with Aubrey's wife. Marian. He had foreseen that he might fail, but he had not in the least foreseen why. He had thought that all he'd have to contend with would be a woman's natural sexual jealousy—or her resentment, the stubborn remains of sexual jealousy.

He had not had any idea of the way she might be looking at things. And yet in some depressing way the conversation had not been unfamiliar to him. That was because it reminded him of conversations he'd had with people in his own family. His uncles, his relatives, probably even his mother, had thought the way Marian thought. They had believed that when other people did not think that way it was because they were kidding themselves—they had got too airy-fairy, or stupid, on account of their easy and protected lives or their education. They had lost touch with reality. Educated people, literary people, some rich people like Grant's socialist in-laws had lost touch with reality. Due to an unmerited good fortune or an innate silliness. In Grant's case, he suspected, they pretty well believed it was both.

That was how Marian would see him, certainly. A silly person, full of boring knowledge and protected by some fluke from the truth about life. A person who didn't have to worry about holding on to his house and could go around thinking his complicated thoughts. Free to dream up the fine, generous schemes that he believed would make another person happy.

What a jerk, she would be thinking now.

Being up against a person like that made him feel hopeless, exasperated, finally almost desolate. Why? Because he couldn't be sure of holding on to himself against that person? Because he was afraid that in the end they'd be right? Fiona wouldn't feel any of that misgiving. Nobody had beat her down, narrowed her in, when she was young. She'd been amused by his upbringing, able to think its harsh notions quaint.

Just the same, they have their points, those people. (He could hear himself now arguing with somebody. Fiona?) There's some advantage to the narrow focus. Marian would probably be good in a crisis. Good at survival, able to scrounge for food and able to take the shoes off a dead body in the street.

Trying to figure out Fiona had always been frustrating. It could be like following a mirage. No—like living in a mirage. Getting close to Marian would present a different problem. It would be like biting into a litchi nut. The flesh with its oddly artificial allure, its chemical taste and perfume, shallow over the extensive seed, the stone.

HE MIGHT HAVE MARRIED HER. Think of it. He might have married some girl like that. If he'd stayed back where he belonged. She'd have been appetizing enough, with her choice breasts. Probably a flirt. The fussy way she had of shifting her buttocks on the kitchen chair, her pursed mouth, a slightly contrived air of menace—that was what was left of the more or less innocent vulgarity of a small-town flirt.

She must have had some hopes, when she picked Aubrey. His good looks, his salesman's job, his white-collar expectations. She must have believed that she would end up better off than she was now. And so it often happened with those practical people. In spite of their calculations, their survival instincts, they might not get as far as they had quite reasonably expected. No doubt it seemed unfair.

In the kitchen the first thing he saw was the light blinking on his answering machine. He thought the same thing he always thought now. Fiona.

He pressed the button before he got his coat off.

"Hello, Grant. I hope I got the right person. I just thought of something. There is a dance here in town at the Legion supposed to be for singles on Saturday night, and I am on the supper committee, which means I can bring a free guest. So I wondered whether you would happen to be interested in that? Call me back when you get a chance."

A woman's voice gave a local number. Then there was a beep, and the same voice started talking again.

"I just realized I'd forgot to say who it was. Well you probably recognized the voice. It's Marian. I'm still not so used to these machines. And I wanted to say I realize you're not a single and I don't mean it that way. I'm not either, but it doesn't hurt to get out once in a while. Anyway, now I've said all this I really hope it's you I'm talking to. It did sound like your voice. If you are interested you can call me and if you are not you don't need to bother. I just thought you might like the chance to get out. It's Marian speaking. I guess I already said that. Okay, then. Good-bye."

Her voice on the machine was different from the voice he'd heard a short time ago in her house. Just a little different in the first message, more so in the second. A tremor of nerves there, an affected nonchalance, a hurry to get through and a reluctance to let go.

Something had happened to her. But when had it happened? If it had been immediate, she had concealed it very successfully all the time he was with her. More likely it came on her gradually, maybe after he'd gone away. Not necessarily as a blow of attraction. Just the realization that he was a possibility, a man on his own. More or less on his own. A possibility that she might as well try to follow up.

But she'd had the jitters when she made the first move. She had put herself at risk. How much of herself, he could not yet tell. Generally a woman's vulnerability increased as time went on, as things progressed. All you could tell at the start was that if there was an edge of it now, there'd be more later.

It gave him a satisfaction—why deny it?—to have brought that out in her. To have roused something like a shimmer, a blurring, on the surface of her personality. To have heard in her testy, broad vowels this faint plea.

He set out the eggs and mushrooms to make himself an omelette. Then he thought he might as well pour a drink.

Anything was possible. Was that true—was anything possible? For instance, if he wanted to, would he be able to break her down, get her to the point where she might listen to him about taking Aubrey back to Fiona? And not just for visits, but for the rest of Aubrey's life. Where could that tremor lead them? To an upset, to the end of her self-preservation? To Fiona's happiness?

It would be a challenge. A challenge and a creditable feat. Also a joke that could never be confided to anybody—to think that by his bad behavior he'd be doing good for Fiona.

But he was not really capable of thinking about it. If he did think about it, he'd have to figure out what would become of him and Marian, after he'd delivered Aubrey to Fiona. It would not work—unless he could get more satisfaction than he foresaw, finding the stone of blameless self-interest inside her robust pulp.

You never quite knew how such things would turn out. You almost knew, but you could never be sure.

She would be sitting in her house now, waiting for him to call. Or probably not sitting. Doing things to keep herself busy. She seemed to be a woman who would keep busy. Her house had certainly shown the benefits of nonstop attention. And there was Aubrey—care of him had to continue as usual. She might have given him an early supper—fitting his meals to a Meadowlake timetable in order to get him settled for the night earlier and free herself of his routine for the day. (What would she do about him when she went to the dance? Could he be left alone or would she get a sitter? Would she tell him where she was going, introduce her escort? Would her escort pay the sitter?)

She might have fed Aubrey while Grant was buying the mushrooms and driving home. She might now be preparing him for bed. But all the time she would be conscious of the phone, of the silence of the phone. Maybe she would have calculated how long it would take Grant to drive home. His address in the phone book would have given her a rough idea of where he lived. She would calculate how long, then add to that time for possible shopping for supper (figuring that a man alone would shop every day). Then a certain amount of time for him to get around to listening to his messages. And as the silence persisted she would think of other things. Other errands he might have had to do before he got home. Or perhaps a dinner out, a meeting that meant he would not get home at suppertime at all.

She would stay up late, cleaning her kitchen cupboards, watching television, arguing with herself about whether there was still a chance.

What conceit on his part. She was above all things a sensible woman. She would go to bed at her regular time thinking that he didn't look as if he'd be a decent dancer anyway. Too stiff, too professorial.

He stayed near the phone, looking at magazines, but he didn't pick it up when it rang again.

"Grant. This is Marian. I was down in the basement putting the wash in the dryer and I heard the phone and when I got upstairs whoever it was had hung up. So I just thought I ought to say I was here. If it was you and if you are even home. Because I don't have a machine obviously, so you couldn't leave a message. So I just wanted. To let you know.

"Bye."

The time was now twenty-five after ten.

Bye.

He would say that he'd just got home. There was no point in bringing to her mind the picture of his sitting here, weighing the pros and cons.

Drapes. That would be her word for the blue curtains—drapes. And why not? He thought of the ginger cookies so perfectly round that she'd had to announce they were homemade, the ceramic coffee mugs on their ceramic tree. A plastic runner, he was sure, protecting the hall carpet. A high-gloss exactness and practicality that his mother had never achieved but would have admired—was that why he could feel this twinge of bizarre and unreliable affection? Or was it because he'd had two more drinks after the first?

The walnut-stain tan—he believed now that it was a tan—of her face and neck would most likely continue into her cleavage, which would be deep, crepey-skinned, odorous and hot. He had that to think of, as he dialled the number that he had already written down. That and the practical sensuality of her cat's tongue. Her gemstone eyes.

FIONA WAS IN HER ROOM but not in bed. She was sitting by the open window, wearing a seasonable but oddly short and bright dress. Through the window came a heady, warm blast of lilacs in bloom and the spring manure spread over the fields.

She had a book open in her lap.

She said, "Look at this beautiful book I found, it's about Iceland. You wouldn't think they'd leave valuable books lying around in the rooms. The people staying here are not necessarily honest. And I think they've got the clothes mixed up. I never wear yellow."

"Fiona . . . ," he said.

"You've been gone a long time. Are we all checked out now?"

"Fiona, I've brought a surprise for you. Do you remember Aubrey?"

She stared at him for a moment, as if waves of wind had come beating into her face. Into her face, into her head, pulling everything to rags.

"Names elude me," she said harshly.

Then the look passed away as she retrieved, with an effort, some bantering grace. She set the book down carefully and stood up and lifted her arms to put them around him. Her skin or her breath gave off a faint new smell, a smell that seemed to him like that of the stems of cut flowers left too long in their water.

"I'm happy to see you," she said, and pulled his earlobes.

"You could have just driven away," she said. "Just driven away without a care in the world and forsook me. Forsooken me. Forsaken."

He kept his face against her white hair, her pink scalp, her sweetly shaped skull. He said, Not a chance.

Runaway

~

CARLA HEARD THE CAR coming before it topped the little rise in the road that around here they called a hill. It's her, she thought. Mrs. Jamieson—Sylvia—home from her holiday in Greece. From the barn door—but far enough inside that she could not readily be seen—she watched the road Mrs. Jamieson would have to drive by on, her place being half a mile farther along the road than Clark and Carla's.

If it was somebody getting ready to turn in at their gate it would be slowing down by now. But still Carla hoped. *Let it not be her.*

It was. Mrs. Jamieson turned her head once, quickly—she had all she could do maneuvering her car through the ruts and puddles the rain had made in the gravel—but she didn't lift a hand off the wheel to wave, she didn't spot Carla. Carla got a glimpse of a tanned arm bare to the shoulder, hair bleached a lighter color than it had been before, more white now than silver-blond, and an expression that was determined and exasperated and amused at her own exasperation—just the way Mrs. Jamieson would look negotiating such a road. When she turned her head there was something like a bright flash—of inquiry, of hopefulness—that made Carla shrink back.

So.

Maybe Clark didn't know yet. If he was sitting at the computer he would have his back to the window and the road.

But Mrs. Jamieson might have to make another trip. Driving home from the airport, she might not have stopped for groceries—not until she'd been home and figured out what she needed. Clark might see her then. And after dark, the lights of her house would show. But this was July, and it didn't get dark till late. She might be so tired that she wouldn't bother with the lights, she might go to bed early.

On the other hand, she might telephone. Any time now.

THIS WAS THE SUMMER of rain and more rain. You heard it first thing in the morning, loud on the roof of the mobile home. The trails were deep in mud, the long grass soaking, leaves overhead sending down random showers even in those moments when there was no actual downpour from the sky and the clouds looked like clearing. Carla wore a high, wide-brimmed old Australian felt hat every time she went outside, and tucked her long thick braid down her shirt.

Nobody showed up for trail rides, even though Clark and Carla had gone around posting signs in all the camping sites, in the cafes, and on the tourist office billboard and anywhere else they could think of. Only a few pupils were coming for lessons and those were regulars, not the batches of schoolchildren on vacation, the busloads from summer camps, that had kept them going through last summer. And even the regulars that they counted on were taking time off for holiday trips, or simply cancelling their lessons because of the weather being so discouraging. If they called too late, Clark charged them for the time anyway. A couple of them had complained, and quit for good.

There was still some income from the three horses that were boarded. Those three, and the four of their own, were out in the field now, poking around in the grass under the trees. They looked as if they couldn't be bothered to notice that the rain was holding off for the moment, the way it often did for a while in the afternoon. Just enough to get your hopes up—the clouds whitening and thinning and letting through a diffuse brightness that never got around to being real sunshine, and was usually gone before supper.

Carla had finished mucking out in the barn. She had taken her time—she liked the rhythm of her regular chores, the high space under the barn roof, the smells. Now she went over to the exercise ring to see how dry the ground was, in case the five o'clock pupil did show up.

Most of the steady showers had not been particularly heavy, or borne on any wind, but last week there had come a sudden stirring and then a blast through the treetops and a nearly horizontal blinding rain. In a quarter of an hour the storm had passed over. But branches lay across the road, hydro lines were down, and a large chunk of the plastic roofing over the ring had been torn loose. There was a puddle like a lake at that end of the track, and Clark had worked until after dark, digging a channel to drain it away.

The roof had not yet been repaired. Clark had strung fence wire across to keep the horses from getting into the mud, and Carla had marked out a shorter track.

On the Web, right now, Clark was hunting for someplace to buy roofing. Some salvage outlet, with prices that they could afford, or somebody trying to get rid of such material secondhand. He would not go to Hy and Robert Buckley's Building Supply in town, which he called Highway Robbers Buggery Supply, because he owed them too much money and had had a fight with them.

Clark had fights not just with the people he owed money to. His friendliness, compelling at first, could suddenly turn sour. There were places he would not go into, where he always made Carla go, because of some row. The drugstore was one such place. An old woman had pushed in front of him—that is, she had gone to get something she'd forgotten and come back and pushed in front, rather than going to the end of the line, and he had complained, and the cashier had said to him, "She has emphysema," and Clark had said, "Is that so? I have piles, myself," and the manager had been summoned, to say that was uncalled-for. And in the coffee shop out on the highway the advertised breakfast discount had not been allowed, because it was past eleven o'clock in the morning, and Clark had argued and then dropped his takeout cup of coffee on the floor—just missing, so they said, a child in its stroller. He said the child was half a mile away and he dropped the cup because no cuff had been provided. They said he had not asked for a cuff. He said he shouldn't have had to ask.

"You flare up," said Carla.

"That's what men do."

She had not said anything to him about his row with Joy Tucker.

Joy Tucker was the librarian from town who boarded her horse with them. The horse was a quick-tempered little chestnut mare named Lizzie—Joy Tucker, when she was in a jokey mood, called her Lizzie Borden. Yesterday she had driven out, not in a jokey mood at all, and complained about the roof's not being fixed yet, and Lizzie looking miserable, as if she might have caught a chill.

There was nothing the matter with Lizzie, actually. Clark had tried—for him—to be placating. But then it was Joy Tucker who flared up and said that their place was a dump, and Lizzie deserved better, and Clark said, "Suit yourself." Joy had not—or not yet—removed Lizzie, as Carla had expected. But Clark, who had formerly made the little mare his pet, had refused to have anything more to do with her. Lizzie's feelings were hurt, in consequence—she was balky when exercised and kicked up a fuss when her hoofs had to be picked out, as they did every day, lest they develop a fungus. Carla had to watch out for nips.

But the worst thing as far as Carla was concerned was the absence of Flora, the little white goat who kept the horses company in the barn and in the fields. There had not been any sign of her for two days. Carla was afraid that wild dogs or coyotes had got her, or even a bear.

She had dreamt of Flora last night and the night before. In the first dream Flora had walked right up to the bed with a red apple in her mouth, but in the second dream—last night—she had run away when she saw Carla coming. Her leg seemed to be hurt but she ran anyway. She led Carla to a barbed-wire barricade of the kind that might belong on some battlefield, and then she—Flora—slipped through it, hurt leg and all, just slithered through like a white eel and disappeared.

The horses had seen Carla go across to the ring and they had all moved up to the fence—looking bedraggled in spite of their New Zealand blankets—so that she would take notice of them on her way back. She talked quietly to them, apologizing for coming empty-handed. She stroked their necks and rubbed their noses and asked whether they knew anything about Flora.

Grace and Juniper snorted and nuzzled up, as if they recognized the name and shared her concern, but then Lizzie butted in between them and knocked Grace's head away from Carla's petting hand. She gave the hand a nip for good measure, and Carla had to spend some time scolding her.

UP UNTIL THREE YEARS AGO Carla never really looked at mobile homes. She didn't call them that, either. Like her parents, she would have thought "mobile home" pretentious. Some people lived in trailers, and that was all there was to it. One trailer was no different from another. When Carla moved in here, when she chose this life with Clark, she began to see things in a new way. After that she started saying "mobile home" and she looked to see how people had fixed them up. The kind of curtains they had hung, the way they had painted the trim, the ambitious decks or patios or extra rooms that had been built on. She could hardly wait to get at such improvements herself.

Clark had gone along with her ideas, for a while. He had built new steps, and spent a lot of time looking for an old wrought-iron railing for them. He didn't make any complaint about the money spent on paint for the kitchen and bathroom or the material for curtains. Her paint job was hasty—she didn't know, at that time, that you should take the hinges off the cupboard doors. Or that you should line the curtains, which had since faded.

What Clark balked at was tearing up the carpet, which was the same in every room and the thing that she had most counted on replacing. It was divided into small brown squares, each with a pattern of darker brown and rust and tan squiggles and shapes. For a long time she had thought these were the same squiggles and shapes, arranged in the same way, in each square. Then when she had had more time, a lot of time, to examine them, she decided that there were four patterns joined together to make identical larger squares. Sometimes she could pick out the arrangement easily and sometimes she had to work to see it.

She did this when it was raining outside and Clark's mood weighted down all their inside space, and he did not want to pay attention to anything but the computer screen. But the best thing to do then was to invent or remember some job to do in the barn. The horses would not look at her when she was unhappy, but Flora, who was never tied up, would come and rub against her, and look up with an expression that was not quite sympathy—it was more like comradely mockery—in her shimmering yellow-green eyes.

Flora had been a half-grown kid when Clark brought her home from a farm where he had gone to bargain for some horse tackle. The people there were giving up on the country life, or at least on the raising of animals—they had sold their horses but failed to get rid of their goats. He had heard about how a goat was able to bring a sense of ease and comfort into a horse stable and he wanted to try it. They had meant to breed her someday but there had never been any signs of her coming into heat.

At first she had been Clark's pet entirely, following him everywhere, dancing for his attention. She was quick and graceful and provocative as a kitten, and her resemblance to a guileless girl in love had made them both laugh. But as she grew older she seemed to attach herself to Carla, and in this attachment she was suddenly much wiser, less skittish—she seemed capable, instead, of a subdued and ironic sort of humor. Carla's behavior with the horses was tender and strict and rather maternal, but the comradeship with Flora was quite different, Flora allowing her no sense of superiority.

"Still no sign of Flora?" she said, as she pulled off her barn boots. Clark had posted a Lost Goat notice on the Web.

"Not so far," he said, in a preoccupied but not unfriendly voice. He suggested, not for the first time, that Flora might have just gone off to find herself a billy.

No word about Mrs. Jamieson. Carla put the kettle on. Clark was humming to himself as he often did when he sat in front of the computer.

Sometimes he talked back to it. *Bullshit,* he would say, replying to some challenge. Or he would laugh—but could not remember what the joke was, when she asked him afterwards.

Carla called, "Do you want tea?" and to her surprise he got up and came into the kitchen.

"So," he said. "So, Carla."

"What?"

"So she phoned."

"Who?"

"Her Majesty. Queen Sylvia. She just got back."

"I didn't hear the car."

"I didn't ask you if you did."

"So what did she phone for?"

"She wants you to go and help her straighten up the house. That's what she said. Tomorrow."

"What did you tell her?"

"I told her sure. But you better phone up and confirm."

Carla said, "I don't see why I have to, if you told her." She poured out their mugs of tea. "I cleaned up her house before she left. I don't see what there could be to do so soon."

"Maybe some coons got in and made a mess of it while she was gone. You never know."

"I don't have to phone her right this minute," she said. "I want to drink my tea and I want to have a shower."

"The sooner the better."

Carla took her tea into the bathroom, calling back, "We have to go to the laundromat. Even when the towels dry out they smell moldy."

"We're not changing the subject, Carla."

Even after she'd got in the shower he stood outside the door and called to her.

"I am not going to let you off the hook, Carla."

She thought he might still be standing there when she came out, but he was back at the computer. She dressed as if she was going to town—she hoped that if they could get out of here, go to the laundromat, get a takeout at the cappuccino place, they might be able to talk in a different way, some release might be possible. She went into the living room with a brisk step and put her arms around him from behind. But as soon as she did that a wave of grief swallowed her up—it must have been the heat of the shower, loosening her tears—and she bent over him, all crumbling and crying.

He took his hands off the keyboard but sat still.

"Just don't be mad at me," she said.

"I'm not mad. I hate when you're like this, that's all."

"I'm like this because you're mad."

"Don't tell me what I am. You're choking me. Start supper."

That was what she did. It was obvious by now that the five o'clock person wasn't coming. She got out the potatoes and began to peel them, but her tears would not stop and she could not see what she was doing. She wiped her face with a paper towel and tore off a fresh one to take with her and went out into the rain. She didn't go into the barn because it was too miserable in there without Flora. She walked along the lane back to the woods. The horses were in the other field. They came over to the fence to watch her. All of them except Lizzie, who capered and snorted a bit, had the sense to understand that her attention was elsewhere.

IT HAD STARTED when they read the obituary, Mr. Jamieson's obituary. That was in the city paper, and his face had been on the evening news. Up until the year before, they had known the Jamiesons only as neighbors who kept to themselves. She taught botany at the college forty miles away, so she had to spend a good deal of her time on the road. He was a poet.

Everybody knew that much. But he seemed to be occupied with other things. For a poet, and for an old man—perhaps twenty years older than Mrs. Jamieson—he was rugged and active. He improved the drainage system on his place, cleaning out the culvert and lining it with rocks. He dug and planted and fenced a vegetable garden, cut paths through the woods, looked after repairs on the house.

The house itself was an odd-looking triangular affair that he had built years ago, with some friends, on the foundation of an old wrecked farmhouse. Those people were spoken of as hippies—though Mr. Jamieson must have been a bit old for that, even then, before Mrs. Jamieson's time. There was a story that they grew marijuana in the woods, sold it, and stored the money in sealed glass jars, which were buried around the property. Clark had heard this from the people he got to know in town. He said it was bullshit.

"Else somebody would have got in and dug it up, before now. Somebody would have found a way to make him tell where it was."

When they read the obituary Carla and Clark learned for the first time that Leon Jamieson had been the recipient of a large prize, five years before his death. A prize for poetry. Nobody had ever mentioned this. It seemed that people could believe in dope money buried in glass jars, but not in money won for writing poetry.

Shortly after this Clark said, "We could've made him pay."

Carla knew at once what he was talking about, but she took it as a joke.

"Too late now," she said. "You can't pay once you're dead."

"He can't. She could."

"She's gone to Greece."

"She's not going to stay in Greece."

"She didn't know," said Carla more soberly.

"I didn't say she did."

"She doesn't have a clue about it."

"We could fix that."

Carla said, "No. No."

Clark went on as if she had not spoken.

"We could say we're going to sue. People get money for stuff like that all the time."

"How could you do that? You can't sue a dead person."

"Threaten to go to the papers. Big-time poet. The papers would eat it up. All we have to do is threaten and she'd cave in."

"You're just fantasizing," Carla said. "You're joking."

"No," said Clark. "Actually, I'm not."

Carla said she did not want to talk about it anymore and he said okay.

But they talked about it the next day, and the next and the next. He sometimes got notions like this that were not practicable, which might even be illegal. He talked about them with growing excitement and then—she wasn't sure why—he dropped them. If the rain had stopped, if this had turned into something like a normal summer, he might have let this idea go the way of the others. But that had not happened, and during the last month he had harped on the scheme as if it was perfectly feasible and serious. The question was how much money to ask for. Too little, and the woman might not take them seriously, she might be inclined to see if they were bluffing. Too much might get her back up and she might become stubborn.

Carla had stopped saying that it was a joke. Instead she told him that it wouldn't work. She said that for one thing, people expected poets to be that way. So it wouldn't be worth paying out money to cover it up.

He said that it would work if it was done right. Carla was to break down and tell Mrs. Jamieson the whole story. Then Clark would move in, as if it had all been a surprise to him, he had just found out. He would be outraged, he would talk about telling the world. He would let Mrs. Jamieson be the one who first mentioned money.

"You were injured. You were molested and humiliated and I was injured and humiliated because you are my wife. It's a question of respect."

Over and over again he talked to her in this way and she tried to deflect him but he insisted.

"Promise," he said. "Promise."

THIS WAS BECAUSE of what she had told him, things she could not now retract or deny.

Sometimes he gets interested in me?

The old guy?

Sometimes he calls me into the room when she's not there?

Yes.

When she has to go out shopping and the nurse isn't there either.

A lucky inspiration of hers, one that instantly pleased him.

So what do you do then? Do you go in?

She played shy.

Sometimes.

He calls you into his room. So? Carla? So, then?

I go in to see what he wants.

So what does he want?

This was asked and told in whispers, even if there was nobody to hear, even when they were in the neverland of their bed. A bedtime story, in which the details were important and had to be added to every time, and this with convincing reluctance, shyness, giggles, *dirty, dirty.* And it was not only he who was eager and grateful. She was too. Eager to please and excite him, to excite herself. Grateful every time it still worked.

And in one part of her mind it *was* true, she saw the randy old man, the bump he made in the sheet, bedridden indeed, almost beyond speech but proficient in sign language, indicating his desire, trying to nudge and finger her into complicity, into obliging stunts and intimacies. (Her refusal a necessity, but also perhaps strangely, slightly disappointing, to Clark.)

Now and then came an image that she had to hammer down,

lest it spoil everything. She would think of the real dim and sheeted body, drugged and shrinking every day in its rented hospital bed, glimpsed only a few times when Mrs. Jamieson or the visiting nurse had neglected to close the door. She herself never actually coming closer to him than that.

In fact she had dreaded going to the Jamiesons', but she needed the money, and she felt sorry for Mrs. Jamieson, who seemed so haunted and bewildered, as if she was walking in her sleep. Once or twice Carla had burst out and done something really silly just to loosen up the atmosphere. The kind of thing she did when clumsy and terrified first-time horseback riders were feeling humiliated. She used to try that too when Clark was stuck in his moods. It didn't work with him anymore. But the story about Mr. Jamieson had worked, decisively.

THERE WAS NO WAY to avoid the puddles in the path or the tall soaked grass alongside it, or the wild carrot which had recently come into flower. But the air was warm enough so that she didn't get chilly. Her clothes were soaked through as if by her own sweat or the tears that ran down her face with the drizzle of rain. Her weeping petered out in time. She had nothing to wipe her nose on—the paper towel now soggy—but she leaned over and blew it hard into a puddle.

She lifted her head and managed the long-drawn-out, vibrating whistle that was her signal—Clark's too—for Flora. She waited a couple of minutes and then called Flora's name. Over and over again, whistle and name, whistle and name.

Flora did not respond.

It was almost a relief, though, to feel the single pain of missing Flora, of missing Flora perhaps forever, compared to the mess she had got into concerning Mrs. Jamieson, and her seesaw misery with Clark. At least Flora's leaving was not on account of anything that she—Carla—had done wrong.

AT THE HOUSE, there was nothing for Sylvia to do except to open the windows. And to think—with an eagerness that dismayed without really surprising her—of how soon she could see Carla.

All the paraphernalia of illness had been removed. The room

that had been Sylvia and her husband's bedroom and then his death chamber had been cleaned out and tidied up to look as if nothing had ever happened in it. Carla had helped with all that during the few frenzied days between the crematorium and the departure for Greece. Every piece of clothing Leon had ever worn and some things he hadn't, including gifts from his sisters that had never been taken out of their packages, had been piled in the backseat of the car and delivered to the Thrift Shop. His pills, his shaving things, unopened cans of the fortified drink that had sustained him as long as anything could, cartons of the sesame seed snaps that at one time he had eaten by the dozens, the plastic bottles full of the lotion that had eased his back, the sheepskins on which he had lain—all of that was dumped into plastic bags to be hauled away as garbage, and Carla didn't question a thing. She never said, "Maybe somebody could use that," or pointed out that whole cartons of cans were unopened. When Sylvia said, "I wish I hadn't taken the clothes to town. I wish I'd burned them all up in the incinerator," Carla had shown no surprise.

They cleaned the oven, scrubbed out the cupboards, wiped down the walls and the windows. One day Sylvia sat in the living room going through all the condolence letters she had received. (There was no accumulation of papers and notebooks to be attended to, as you might have expected with a writer, no unfinished work or scribbled drafts. He had told her, months before, that he had pitched everything. *And no regrets.*)

The south-sloping wall of the house was made up of big windows. Sylvia looked up, surprised by the watery sunlight that had come out—or possibly surprised by the shadow of Carla, bare-legged, bare-armed, on top of a ladder, her resolute face crowned with a frizz of dandelion hair that was too short for the braid. She was vigorously spraying and scrubbing the glass. When she saw Sylvia looking at her she stopped and flung out her arms as if she was splayed there, making a silly gargoyle-like face. They both began to laugh. Sylvia felt this laughter running all through her like a playful stream. She went back to her letters as Carla resumed the cleaning. She decided that all of these kind words—genuine or perfunctory, the tributes and regrets—could go the way of the sheepskins and the crackers.

When she heard Carla taking the ladder down, heard boots on the deck, she was suddenly shy. She sat where she was with her head bowed as Carla came into the room and passed behind her on her way to the kitchen to put the pail and the cloths back under the sink. Carla hardly halted, she was quick as a bird, but she managed to drop a kiss on Sylvia's bent head. Then she went on whistling something to herself.

That kiss had been in Sylvia's mind ever since. It meant nothing in particular. It meant *Cheer up.* Or *Almost done.* It meant that they were good friends who had got through a lot of depressing work together. Or maybe just that the sun had come out. That Carla was thinking of getting home to her horses. Nevertheless, Sylvia saw it as a bright blossom, its petals spreading inside her with tumultuous heat, like a menopausal flash.

Every so often there had been a special girl student in one of her botany classes—one whose cleverness and dedication and awkward egotism, or even genuine passion for the natural world, reminded her of her young self. Such girls hung around her worshipfully, hoped for some sort of intimacy they could not—in most cases—imagine, and they soon got on her nerves.

Carla was nothing like them. If she resembled anybody in Sylvia's life, it would have to be certain girls she had known in high school—those who were bright but never too bright, easy athletes but not strenuously competitive, buoyant but not rambunctious. Naturally happy.

"WHERE I WAS, this little village, this little tiny village with my two old friends, well, it was the sort of place where the very occasional tourist bus would stop, just as if it had got lost, and the tourists would get off and look around and they were absolutely bewildered because they weren't anywhere. There was nothing to buy."

Sylvia was speaking about Greece. Carla was sitting a few feet away from her. The large-limbed, uncomfortable, dazzling girl was sitting there at last, in the room that had been filled with thoughts of her. She was faintly smiling, belatedly nodding.

"And at first," Sylvia said, "at first I was bewildered too. It was so hot. But it's true about the light. It's wonderful. And then I figured out what there was to do, and there were just these few simple things but they could fill the day. You walk half a mile down the road to buy some oil and half a mile in the other direction to buy your bread or your wine, and that's the morning, and you eat some lunch under the trees and after lunch it's too hot to do anything but close the shutters and lie on your bed and maybe read. At first you read. And then it gets so you don't even do that. Why read? Later on you notice the shadows are longer and you get up and go for a swim.

"Oh," she interrupted herself. "Oh, I forgot."

She jumped up and went to get the present she had brought, which in fact she had not forgotten about at all. She had not wanted to hand it to Carla right away, she had wanted the moment to come more naturally, and while she was speaking she had thought ahead to the moment when she could mention the sea, going swimming. And say, as she now said, "Swimming reminded me of this because it's a little replica, you know, it's a little replica of the horse they found under the sea. Cast in bronze. They dredged it up, after all this time. It's supposed to be from the second century b.c."

When Carla had come in and looked around for work to do, Sylvia had said, "Oh, just sit down a minute, I haven't had anybody to talk to since I got back. Please." Carla had sat down on the edge of a chair, legs apart, hands between her knees, looking somehow desolate. As if reaching for some distant politeness she had said, "How was Greece?"

Now she was standing, with the tissue paper crumpled around the horse, which she had not fully unwrapped.

"It's said to represent a racehorse," Sylvia said. "Making that final spurt, the last effort in a race. The rider, too, the boy, you can see he's urging the horse on to the limit of its strength."

She did not mention that the boy had made her think of Carla, and she could not now have said why. He was only about ten or eleven years old. Maybe the strength and grace of the arm that must have held the reins, or the wrinkles in his childish forehead, the absorption and the pure effort there was in some way like Carla cleaning the big windows last spring. Her strong legs in her shorts, her broad shoulders, her big swipes at the glass, and then the way she had splayed herself out as a joke, inviting or even commanding Sylvia to laugh.

"You can see that," Carla said, now conscientiously examining the little bronzy-green statue. "Thank you very much."

"You are welcome. Let's have coffee, shall we? I've just made some. The coffee in Greece was quite strong, a little stronger than I liked, but the bread was heavenly. And the ripe figs, they were astounding. Sit down another moment, please do. You should stop me going on and on this way. What about here? How has life been here?"

"It's been raining most of the time."

"I can see that. I can see it has," Sylvia called from the kitchen end of the big room. Pouring the coffee, she decided that she would keep quiet about the other gift she had brought. It hadn't cost her anything (the horse had cost more than the girl could probably guess), it was only a beautiful small pinkish-white stone she had picked up along the road.

"This is for Carla," she had said to her friend Maggie, who was walking beside her. "I know it's silly. I just want her to have a tiny piece of this land."

She had already mentioned Carla to Maggie, and to Soraya, her other friend there, telling them how the girl's presence had come to mean more and more to her, how an indescribable bond had seemed to grow up between them, and had consoled her in the awful months of last spring.

"It was just to see somebody—somebody so fresh and full of health coming into the house."

Maggie and Soraya had laughed in a kindly but annoying way.

"There's always a girl," Soraya said, with an indolent stretch of her heavy brown arms, and Maggie said, "We all come to it sometime. A crush on a girl."

Sylvia was obscurely angered by that dated word—*crush*.

"Maybe it's because Leon and I never had children," she said. "It's stupid. Displaced maternal love."

Her friends spoke at the same time, saying in slightly different ways something to the effect that it might be stupid but it was, after all, love.

BUT THE GIRL WAS NOT, today, anything like the Carla Sylvia had been remembering, not at all the calm bright spirit, the carefree and generous young creature who had kept her company in Greece.

She had been hardly interested in her gift. Almost sullen as she reached out for her mug of coffee.

"There was one thing I thought you would have liked a lot," said Sylvia energetically. "The goats. They were quite small even when they were full-grown. Some spotty and some white, and they were leaping around up on the rocks just like—like the spirits of the place." She laughed in an artificial way, she couldn't stop herself. "I wouldn't be surprised if they'd had wreaths on their horns. How is your little goat? I forget her name."

Carla said, "Flora."

"Flora."

"She's gone."

"Gone? Did you sell her?"

"She disappeared. We don't know where."

"Oh, I'm sorry. I'm sorry. But isn't there a chance she'll turn up again?"

No answer. Sylvia looked directly at the girl, something that up to now she had not quite been able to do, and saw that her eyes were full of tears, her face blotchy—in fact it looked grubby—and that she seemed bloated with distress.

She didn't do anything to avoid Sylvia's look. She drew her lips tight over her teeth and shut her eyes and rocked back and forth as if in a soundless howl, and then, shockingly, she did howl. She howled and wept and gulped for air and tears ran down her cheeks and snot out of her nostrils and she began to look around wildly for something to wipe with. Sylvia ran and got handfuls of Kleenex.

"Don't worry, here you are, here, you're all right," she said, thinking that maybe the thing to do would be to take the girl in her arms. But she had not the least wish to do that, and it might make things worse. The girl might feel how little Sylvia wanted to do such a thing, how appalled she was in fact by this noisy fit.

Carla said something, said the same thing again.

"Awful," she said. "Awful."

"No it's not. We all have to cry sometimes. It's all right, don't worry."

"It's awful."

And Sylvia could not help feeling how, with every moment of this show of misery, the girl made herself more ordinary, more like one of those soggy students in her—Sylvia's—office. Some of them cried about their marks, but that was often tactical, a brief unconvincing bit of whimpering. The more infrequent, real waterworks would turn out to have something to do with a love affair, or their parents, or a pregnancy.

"It's not about your goat, is it?"

"No. No."

"You better have a glass of water," said Sylvia.

She took time to run it cold, trying to think what else she should do or say, and when she returned with it Carla was already calming down.

"Now. Now," Sylvia said as the water was being swallowed. "Isn't that better?"

"Yes."

"It's not the goat. What is it?"

Carla said, "I can't stand it anymore."

What could she not stand?

It turned out to be the husband.

He was mad at her all the time. He acted as if he hated her. There was nothing she could do right, there was nothing she could say. Living with him was driving her crazy. Sometimes she thought she already was crazy. Sometimes she thought he was.

"Has he hurt you, Carla?"

No. He hadn't hurt her physically. But he hated her. He despised her. He could not stand it when she cried and she could not help crying because he was so mad.

She did not know what to do.

"Perhaps you do know what to do," said Sylvia.

"Get away? I would if I could." Carla began to wail again. "I'd give anything to get away. I can't. I haven't any money. I haven't anywhere in this world to go."

"Well. Think. Is that altogether true?" said Sylvia in her best counselling manner. "Don't you have parents? Didn't you tell me you grew up in Kingston? Don't you have a family there?"

Her parents had moved to British Columbia. They hated Clark. They didn't care if she lived or died.

Brothers or sisters?

One brother nine years older. He was married and in Toronto. He didn't care either. He didn't like Clark. His wife was a snob.

"Have you ever thought of the Women's Shelter?"

"They don't want you there unless you've been beaten up. And everybody would find out and it would be bad for our business."

Sylvia gently smiled.

"Is this a time to think about that?"

Then Carla actually laughed. "I know," she said, "I'm insane."

"Listen," said Sylvia. "Listen to me. If you had the money to go, would you go? Where would you go? What would you do?"

"I would go to Toronto," Carla said readily enough. "But I wouldn't go near my brother. I'd stay in a motel or something and I'd get a job at a riding stable."

"You think you could do that?"

"I was working at a riding stable the summer I met Clark. I'm more experienced now than I was then. A lot more."

"You sound as if you've figured this out," said Sylvia thoughtfully.

Carla said, "I have now."

"So when would you go, if you could go?"

"Now. Today. This minute."

"All that's stopping you is lack of money?"

Carla took a deep breath. "All that's stopping me," she said.

"All right," said Sylvia. "Now listen to what I propose. I don't think you should go to a motel. I think you should take the bus to Toronto and go to stay with a friend of mine. Her name is Ruth Stiles. She has a big house and she lives alone and she won't mind having somebody to stay. You can stay there till you find a job. I'll help you with some money. There must be lots and lots of riding stables around Toronto."

"There are."

"So what do you think? Do you want me to phone and find out what time the bus goes?"

Carla said yes. She was shivering. She ran her hands up and down her thighs and shook her head roughly from side to side.

"I can't believe it," she said. "I'll pay you back. I mean, thank you. I'll pay you back. I don't know what to say."

Sylvia was already at the phone, dialling the bus depot.

"Shh, I'm getting the times," she said. She listened, and hung up. "I know you will. You agree about Ruth's? I'll let her know. There's one problem, though." She looked critically at Carla's shorts and T-shirt. "You can't very well go in those clothes."

"I can't go home to get anything," said Carla in a panic. "I'll be all right."

"The bus will be air-conditioned. You'll freeze. There must be something of mine you could wear. Aren't we about the same height?"

"You're ten times skinnier."

"I didn't use to be."

In the end they decided on a brown linen jacket, hardly worn—Sylvia had considered it to be a mistake for herself, the style too brusque—and a pair of tailored tan pants and a cream-colored silk shirt. Carla's sneakers would have to do with this outfit, because her feet were two sizes larger than Sylvia's.

Carla went to take a shower—something she had not bothered with in her state of mind that morning—and Sylvia phoned Ruth. Ruth was going to be out at a meeting that evening, but she would leave the key with her upstairs tenants and all Carla would have to do was ring their bell.

"She'll have to take a cab from the bus depot, though. I assume she's okay to manage that?" Ruth said.

Sylvia laughed. "She's not a lame duck, don't worry. She is just a person in a bad situation, the way it happens."

"Well good. I mean good she's getting out."

"Not a lame duck at all," said Sylvia, thinking of Carla trying on the tailored pants and linen jacket. How quickly the young recover from a fit of despair and how handsome the girl had looked in the fresh clothes.

The bus would stop in town at twenty past two. Sylvia decided to make omelettes for lunch, to set the table with the dark-blue cloth, and to get down the crystal glasses and open a bottle of wine.

"I hope you're hungry enough to eat something," she said, when Carla came out clean and shining in her borrowed clothes. Her softly freckled skin was flushed from the shower, and her hair was damp and darkened, out of its braid, the sweet frizz now flat against her head. She said she was hungry, but when she tried to get a forkful of the omelette to her mouth her trembling hands made it impossible.

"I don't know why I'm shaking like this," she said. "I must be excited. I never knew it would be this easy."

"It's very sudden," said Sylvia. "Probably it doesn't seem quite real."

"It does, though. Everything now seems really real. Like the time before now, that's when I was in a daze."

"Maybe when you make up your mind to something, when you really make up your mind, that's how it is. Or that's how it should be."

"If you've got a friend," said Carla with a self-conscious smile and a flush spreading over her forehead. "If you've got a true friend. I mean like you." She laid down the knife and fork and raised her wineglass awkwardly with both hands. "Drinking to a true friend," she said, uncomfortably. "I probably shouldn't even take a sip, but I will."

"Me too," said Sylvia with a pretense of gaiety. She drank, but spoiled the moment by saying, "Are you going to phone him? Or what? He'll have to know. At least he'll have to know where you are by the time he'd be expecting you home."

"Not the phone," said Carla, alarmed. "I can't do it. Maybe if you—"

"No," said Sylvia. "No."

"No, that's stupid. I shouldn't have said that. It's just hard to think straight. What I maybe should do, I should put a note in the mailbox. But I don't want him to get it too soon. I don't want us to even drive past there when we're going into town. I want to go the back way. So if I write it—if I write it, could you, could you maybe slip it in the box when you come back?"

Sylvia agreed to this, seeing no good alternative.

She brought pen and paper. She poured a little more wine. Carla sat thinking, then wrote a few words.

I have gone away. I will be all write.

These were the words that Sylvia read when she unfolded the paper, on her way back from the bus depot. She was sure Carla knew *right* from *write*. It was just that she had been talking about *writing* a note, and she was in a state of exalted confusion. More confusion perhaps than Sylvia had realized. The wine had brought out a stream of talk, but it had not seemed to be accompanied by any particular grief or upset. She had talked about the horse barn where she had worked and met Clark when she was eighteen and just out of high school. Her parents wanted her to go to college, and she had agreed as long as she could choose to be a veterinarian. All she really wanted, and had wanted all her life, was to work with animals and live in the country. She had been one of those dorky girls in high school, one of those girls they made rotten jokes about, but she didn't care.

Clark was the best riding teacher they had. Scads of women were after him, they would take up riding just to get him as their teacher. Carla teased him about his women and at first he seemed to like it, then he got annoyed. She apologized and tried to make up for it by getting him talking about his dream—his plan, really—to have a riding school, a horse stable, someplace out in the country. One day she came into the stable and saw him hanging up his saddle and realized she had fallen in love with him.

Now she considered it was sex. It was probably just sex.

WHEN FALL CAME and she was supposed to quit working and leave for college in Guelph, she refused to go, she said she needed a year off.

Clark was very smart but he hadn't waited even to finish high school. He had altogether lost touch with his family. He thought families were like a poison in your blood. He had been an attendant in a mental hospital, a disc jockey on a radio station in Lethbridge, Alberta, a member of a road crew on the highways near Thunder Bay, an apprentice barber, a salesman in an Army Surplus store. And those were only the jobs he told her about.

She had nicknamed him Gypsy Rover, because of the song, an old song her mother used to sing. Now she took to singing it around the house all the time and her mother knew something was up.

> *"Last night she slept in a feather bed*
> *With a silken quilt for cover*

Tonight she'll sleep on the cold hard
    ground—
Beside her gypsy lo-ov-ver."

Her mother said, "He'll break your heart, that's a sure thing." Her stepfather, who was an engineer, did not even grant Clark that much power. "A loser," he called him. "One of those drifters." As if Clark was a bug he could just whisk off his clothes.

So Carla said, "Does a drifter save up enough money to buy a farm? Which, by the way, he has done?" and he only said, "I'm not about to argue with you." She was not his daughter anyway, he added, as if that was the clincher.

So, naturally, Carla had to run away with Clark. The way her parents behaved, they were practically guaranteeing it.

"Will you get in touch with your parents after you're settled?" Sylvia said. "In Toronto?"

Carla lifted her eyebrows, pulled in her cheeks and made a saucy O of her mouth. She said, "Nope."

Definitely a little drunk.

BACK HOME, having left the note in the mailbox, Sylvia cleaned up the dishes that were still on the table, washed and polished the omelette pan, threw the blue napkins and tablecloth in the laundry basket, and opened the windows. She did this with a confusing sense of regret and irritation. She had put out a fresh cake of apple-scented soap for the girl's shower and the smell of it lingered in the house, as it had in the air of the car.

The rain was holding off. She could not stay still, so she went for a walk along the path that Leon had cleared. The gravel he had dumped in the boggy places had mostly washed away. They used to go walking every spring, to look for wild orchids. She taught him the name of every wildflower—all of which, except for trillium, he forgot. He used to call her his Dorothy Wordsworth.

Last spring she went out once and picked him a small bunch of dog's-tooth violets, but he looked at them—as he sometimes looked at her—with mere exhaustion, disavowal.

She kept seeing Carla, Carla stepping onto the bus. Her thanks had been sincere but already almost casual, her wave jaunty. She had got used to her salvation.

Back in the house, at around six o'clock, Sylvia put in a call to Toronto, to Ruth, knowing that Carla would not have arrived yet. She got the answering machine.

"Ruth," said Sylvia. "Sylvia. It's about this girl I sent you. I hope she doesn't turn out to be a bother to you. I hope it'll be all right. You may find her a little full of herself. Maybe it's just youth. Let me know. Okay?"

She phoned again before she went to bed but got the machine, so she said, "Sylvia again. Just checking," and hung up. It was between nine and ten o'clock, not even really dark. Ruth must still be out and the girl would not want to pick up the phone in a strange house. She tried to think of the name of Ruth's upstairs tenants. They surely wouldn't have gone to bed yet. But she could not remember. And just as well. Phoning them would have meant making too much of a fuss, being too anxious, going too far.

She got into the bed but it was impossible to stay there, so she took a light quilt and went out to the living room and lay down on the sofa, where she had slept for the last three months of Leon's life. She did not think it likely that she would get to sleep there either—there were no curtains on the bank of windows and she could tell by the look of the sky that the moon had risen, though she could not see it.

The next thing she knew she was on a bus somewhere—in Greece?—with a lot of people she did not know, and the engine of the bus was making an alarming knocking sound. She woke to find the knocking was at her front door.

Carla?

CARLA HAD KEPT HER HEAD DOWN until the bus was clear of town. The windows were tinted, nobody could see in, but she had to guard herself against seeing out. Lest Clark appear. Coming out of a store or waiting to cross the street, all ignorant of her abandoning him, thinking this an ordinary afternoon. No, thinking it the afternoon when their scheme—his scheme—was put in motion, eager to know how far she had got with it.

Once they were out in the country she looked up, breathed

deeply, took account of the fields, which were slightly violet-tinted through the glass. Mrs. Jamieson's presence had surrounded her with some kind of remarkable safety and sanity and had made her escape seem the most rational thing you could imagine, in fact the only self-respecting thing that a person in Carla's shoes could do. Carla had felt herself capable of an unaccustomed confidence, even of a mature sense of humor, revealing her life to Mrs. Jamieson in a way that seemed bound to gain sympathy and yet to be ironic and truthful. And adapted to live up to what, as far as she could see, were Mrs. Jamieson's—Sylvia's—expectations. She did have a feeling that it would be possible to disappoint Mrs. Jamieson, who struck her as a most sensitive and rigorous person, but she thought that she was in no danger of doing that.

If she didn't have to be around her for too long.

The sun was shining, as it had been for some time. When they sat at lunch it had made the wineglasses sparkle. No rain had fallen since early morning. There was enough of a wind blowing to lift the roadside grass, the flowering weeds, out of their drenched clumps. Summer clouds, not rain clouds, were scudding across the sky. The whole countryside was changing, shaking itself loose, into the true brightness of a July day. And as they sped along she was able to see not much trace at all of the recent past—no big puddles in the fields, showing where the seed had washed out, no miserable spindly cornstalks or lodged grain.

It occurred to her that she must tell Clark about this—that perhaps they had chosen what was for some freakish reason a very wet and dreary corner of the country, and there were other places where they could have been successful.

Or could be yet?

Then it came to her of course that she would not be telling Clark anything. Never again. She would not be concerned about what happened to him, or to Grace or Mike or Juniper or Blackberry or Lizzie Borden. If by any chance Flora came back, she would not hear of it.

This was her second time to leave everything behind. The first time was just like the old Beatles song—her putting the note on the table and slipping out of the house at five o'clock in the morning, meeting Clark in the church parking lot down the street. She was actually humming that song as they rattled away. *She's leaving home, bye-bye.* She recalled now how the sun was coming up behind them, how she looked at Clark's hands on the wheel, the dark hairs on his competent forearms, and breathed in the smell of the inside of the truck, a smell of oil and metal, tools and horse barns. The cold air of the fall morning blew in through the truck's rusted seams. It was the sort of vehicle that nobody in her family ever rode in, that scarcely ever appeared on the streets where they lived.

Clark's preoccupation on that morning with the traffic (they had reached Highway 401), his concern about the truck's behavior, his curt answers, his narrowed eyes, even his slight irritation at her giddy delight—all of that thrilled her. As did the disorder of his past life, his avowed loneliness, the tender way he could have with a horse, and with her. She saw him as the architect of the life ahead of them, herself as captive, her submission both proper and exquisite.

"You don't know what you're leaving behind," her mother wrote to her, in that one letter that she received, and never answered. But in those shivering moments of early-morning flight she certainly did know what she was leaving behind, even if she had rather a hazy idea of what she was going to. She despised her parents, their house, their backyard, their photo albums, their vacations, their Cuisinart, their *powder room,* their walk-in closets, their underground lawn-sprinkling system. In the brief note she had written she had used the word *authentic.*

I have always felt the need of a more authentic kind of life. I know I cannot expect you to understand this.

The bus had stopped now at the first town on the way. The depot was a gas station. It was the very station she and Clark used to drive to, in their early days, to buy cheap gas. In those days their world had included several towns in the surrounding countryside and they had sometimes behaved like tourists, sampling the specialties in grimy hotel bars. Pigs' feet, sauerkraut, potato pancakes, beer. And they would sing all the way home like crazy hillbillies.

But after a while all outings came to be seen as a waste of time and money. They were what people did before they understood the realities of their lives.

She was crying now, her eyes had filled up without her realizing it. She set herself to thinking about Toronto, the first steps ahead. The taxi, the house she had never seen, the strange bed she would sleep in alone. Looking in the phone book tomorrow for the addresses of riding stables, then getting to wherever they were, asking for a job.

She could not picture it. Herself riding on the subway or street-car, caring for new horses, talking to new people, living among hordes of people every day who were not Clark.

A life, a place, chosen for that specific reason—that it would not contain Clark.

The strange and terrible thing coming clear to her about that world of the future, as she now pictured it, was that she would not exist there. She would only walk around, and open her mouth and speak, and do this and do that. She would not really be there. And what was strange about it was that she was doing all this, she was riding on this bus in the hope of recovering herself. As Mrs. Jamieson might say—and as she herself might with satisfaction have said—*taking charge of her own life.* With nobody glowering over her, nobody's mood infecting her with misery.

But what would she care about? How would she know that she was alive?

While she was running away from him—now—Clark still kept his place in her life. But when she was finished running away, when she just went on, what would she put in his place? What else—who else—could ever be so vivid a challenge?

She had managed to stop crying, but she had started to shake. She was in a bad way and would have to take hold, get a grip on herself. "Get a grip on yourself," Clark had sometimes told her, passing through a room where she was scrunched up, trying not to weep, and that indeed was what she must do.

They had stopped in another town. This was the third town away from the one where she had got on the bus, which meant that they had passed through the second town without her even noticing. The bus must have stopped, the driver must have called out the name, and she had not heard or seen anything in her fog of fright. Soon enough they would reach the major highway, they would be tearing along towards Toronto.

And she would be lost.

She would be lost. What would be the point of getting into a taxi and giving the new address, of getting up in the morning and brushing her teeth and going into the world? Why should she get a job, put food in her mouth, be carried by public transportation from place to place?

Her feet seemed now to be at some enormous distance from her body. Her knees, in the unfamiliar crisp pants, were weighted with irons. She was sinking to the ground like a stricken horse who will never get up.

Already the bus had loaded on the few passengers and the parcels that had been waiting in this town. A woman and a baby in its stroller were waving somebody good-bye. The building behind them, the cafe that served as a bus stop, was also in motion. A lique-fying wave passed through the bricks and windows as if they were about to dissolve. In peril of her life, Carla pulled her huge body, her iron limbs, forward. She stumbled, she cried out, "Let me off."

The driver braked, he called out irritably, "I thought you were going to Toronto?" People gave her casually curious looks, nobody seemed to understand that she was in anguish.

"I have to get off here."

"There's a washroom in the back."

"No. No. I have to get off."

"I'm not waiting. You understand that? You got luggage under-neath?"

"No. Yes. No."

"No luggage?"

A voice in the bus said, "Claustrophobia. That's what's the mat-ter with her."

"You sick?" said the driver.

"No. No. I just want off."

"Okay. Okay. Fine by me."

"Come and get me. Please. Come and get me."
"I will."

SYLVIA HAD FORGOTTEN to lock her door. She realized that she should be locking it now, not opening it, but it was too late, she had it open.

And nobody there.

Yet she was sure, sure, the knocking had been real.

She closed the door and this time she locked it.

There was a playful sound, a tinkling tapping sound, coming from the wall of windows. She switched the light on, but saw nothing there, and switched it off again. Some animal—maybe a squirrel? The French doors that opened between windows, leading to the patio, had not been locked either. Not even really closed, having been left open an inch or so from her airing of the house. She started to close them and somebody laughed, nearby, near enough to be in the room with her.

"It's me," a man said. "Did I scare you?"

He was pressed against the glass, he was right beside her.

"It's Clark," he said. "Clark from down the road."

She was not going to ask him in, but she was afraid to shut the door in his face. He could grab it before she could manage that. She didn't want to turn on the light, either. She slept in a long T-shirt. She should have pulled the quilt from the sofa and wrapped it around herself, but it was too late now.

"Did you want to get dressed?" he said. "What I got in here, it could be the very things you need."

He had a shopping bag in his hand. He thrust it at her, but did not try to come with it.

"What?" she said in a choppy voice.

"Look and see. It's not a bomb. There, take it."

She felt inside the bag, not looking. Something soft. And then she recognized the buttons of the jacket, the silk of the shirt, the belt on the pants.

"Just thought you'd better have them back," he said. "They're yours, aren't they?"

She tightened her jaws so that her teeth wouldn't chatter. A fearful dryness had attacked her mouth and throat.

"I understood they were yours," he said softly.

Her tongue moved like a wad of wool. She forced herself to say, "Where's Carla?"

"You mean my wife Carla?"

Now she could see his face more clearly. She could see how he was enjoying himself.

"My wife Carla is home in bed. Asleep in bed. Where she belongs."

He was both a handsome man and a silly-looking man. Tall, lean, well built, but with a slouch that seemed artificial. A contrived, self-conscious air of menace. A lock of dark hair falling over his forehead, a vain little moustache, eyes that appeared both hopeful and mocking, a boyish smile perpetually on the verge of a sulk.

She had always disliked the sight of him—she had mentioned her dislike to Leon, who said that the man was just unsure of himself, just a bit too friendly.

The fact that he was unsure of himself would not make her any safer now.

"Pretty worn out," he said. "After her little adventure. You should've seen your face—you should've seen the look on you when you recognized those clothes. What did you think? Did you think I'd murdered her?"

"I was surprised," said Sylvia.

"I bet you were. After you were such a big help to her running away."

"I helped her—," Sylvia said with considerable effort, "I helped her because she seemed to be in distress."

"Distress," he said, as if examining the word. "I guess she was. She was in very big distress when she jumped off that bus and got on the phone to me to come and get her. She was crying so hard I could hardly make out what it was she was saying."

"She wanted to come back?"

"Oh yeah. You bet she wanted to come back. She was in real hysterics to come back. She is a girl who is very up and down in her emotions. But I guess you don't know her as well as I do."

"She seemed quite happy to be going."

"Did she really? Well, I have to take your word for it. I didn't come here to argue with you."

Sylvia said nothing.

"I came here to tell you I don't appreciate you interfering in my life with my wife."

"She is a human being," said Sylvia, though she knew it would be better if she could keep quiet. "Besides being your wife."

"My goodness, is that so? My wife is a human being? Really? Thank you for the information. But don't try getting smart with me. *Sylvia.*"

"I wasn't trying to get smart."

"Good. I'm glad you weren't. I don't want to get mad. I just have a couple of important things to say to you. One thing, that I don't want you sticking your nose in anywhere, anytime, in my and my wife's life. Another, that I'm not going to want her coming around here anymore. Not that she is going to particularly want to come, I'm pretty sure of that. She doesn't have too good an opinion of you at the moment. And it's time you learned how to clean your own house.

"Now," he said. "Now. Has that sunk in?"

"Quite sufficiently."

"Oh, I really hope it has. I hope so."

Sylvia said, "Yes."

"And you know what else I think?"

"What?"

"I think you owe me something."

"What?"

"I think you owe me—maybe—you owe me an apology."

Sylvia said, "All right. If you think so. I'm sorry."

He shifted, perhaps just to put out his hand, and with the movement of his body she shrieked.

He laughed. He put his hand on the doorframe to make sure she didn't close it.

"What's that?"

"What's what?" he said, as if she was trying out a trick and it would not work. But then he caught sight of something reflected in the window, and he snapped around to look.

Not far from the house was a wide shallow patch of land that often filled up with night fog at this time of year. The fog was there tonight, had been there all this while. But now at one point there was a change. The fog had thickened, taken on a separate shape, transformed itself into something spiky and radiant. First a live dandelion ball, tumbling forward, then condensing itself into an unearthly sort of animal, pure white, hell-bent, something like a giant unicorn, rushing at them.

"Jesus Christ," Clark said softly and devoutly. And grabbed hold of Sylvia's shoulder. This touch did not alarm her at all—she accepted it with the knowledge that he did it either to protect her or to reassure himself.

Then the vision exploded. Out of the fog, and out of the magnifying light—now seen to be that of a car travelling along this back road, probably in search of a place to park—out of this appeared a white goat. A little dancing white goat, hardly bigger than a sheepdog.

Clark let go. He said, "Where the Christ did you come from?"

"It's your goat," said Sylvia. "Isn't it your goat?"

"Flora," he said. "Flora."

The goat had stopped a yard or so away from them, had turned shy and hung her head.

"Flora," Clark said. "Where the hell did you come from? You scared the shit out of us."

Us.

Flora came closer but still did not look up. She butted against Clark's legs.

"Goddamn stupid animal," he said shakily. "Where'd you come from?"

"She was lost," said Sylvia.

"Yeah. She was. Never thought we'd see her again, actually."

Flora looked up. The moonlight caught a glitter in her eyes.

"Scared the shit out of us," Clark said to her. "Were you off looking for a boyfriend? Scared the shit. Didn't you? We thought you were a ghost."

"It was the effect of the fog," Sylvia said. She stepped out of the door now, onto the patio. Quite safe.

"Yeah."

"Then the lights of that car."

"Like an apparition," he said, recovering. And pleased that he had thought of this description.

"Yes."

"The goat from outer space. That's what you are. You are a goddamn goat from outer space," he said, patting Flora. But when Sylvia put out her free hand to do the same—her other hand still held the bag of clothes that Carla had worn—Flora immediately lowered her head as if to prepare for some serious butting.

"Goats are unpredictable," Clark said. "They can seem tame but they're not really. Not after they grow up."

"Is she grown-up? She looks so small."

"She's big as she's ever going to get."

They stood looking down at the goat, as if expecting she would provide them with more conversation. But this was apparently not going to happen. From this moment they could go neither forward nor back. Sylvia believed that she might have seen a shadow of regret cross his face that this was so.

But he acknowledged it. He said, "It's late."

"I guess it is," said Sylvia, just as if this had been an ordinary visit.

"Okay, Flora. Time for us to go home."

"I'll make other arrangements for help if I need it," she said. "I probably won't need it now, anyway." She added almost laughingly, "I'll stay out of your hair."

"Sure," he said. "You better get inside. You'll get cold."

"People used to think night fogs were dangerous."

"That's a new one on me."

"So good night," she said. "Good night, Flora."

The phone rang then.

"Excuse me."

He raised a hand and turned away. "Good night."

It was Ruth on the phone.

"Ah," Sylvia said. "A change in plans."

SHE DID NOT SLEEP, thinking of the little goat, whose appearance out of the fog seemed to her more and more magical. She even wondered if, possibly, Leon could have had something to do with it. If she was a poet she would write a poem about something like this. But in her experience the subjects that she thought a poet could write about did not appeal to Leon.

CARLA HAD NOT HEARD CLARK go out but she woke when he came in. He told her that he had just been out checking around the barn.

"A car went along the road a while ago and I wondered what

they were doing here. I couldn't get back to sleep till I went out and checked whether everything was okay."

"So was it?"

"Far as I could see."

"And then while I was up," he said, "I thought I might as well pay a visit up the road. I took the clothes back."

Carla sat up in bed.

"You didn't wake her up?"

"She woke up. It was okay. We had a little talk."

"Oh."

"It was okay."

"You didn't mention any of that stuff, did you?"

"I didn't mention it."

"It really was all made-up. It really was. You have to believe me. It was all a lie."

"Okay."

"You have to believe me."

"Then I believe you."

"I made it all up."

"Okay."

He got into bed.

"Your feet are cold," she said. "Like they got wet."

"Heavy dew.

"Come here," he said. "When I read your note, it was just like I went hollow inside. It's true. If you ever went away, I'd feel like I didn't have anything left in me."

THE BRIGHT WEATHER HAD CONTINUED. On the streets, in the stores, in the Post Office, people greeted each other by saying that summer had finally arrived. The pasture grass and even the poor beaten crops lifted up their heads. The puddles dried up, the mud turned to dust. A light warm wind blew and everybody felt like doing things again. The phone rang. Inquiries about trail rides, about riding lessons. Summer camps were interested now, having cancelled their trips to museums. Minivans drew up, with their loads of restless children. The horses pranced along the fences, freed from their blankets.

Clark had managed to get hold of a large enough piece of roofing at a good price. He had spent the whole first day after Runaway Day (that was how they referred to Carla's bus trip) fixing the roof of the exercise ring.

For a couple of days, as they went about their chores, he and Carla would wave at each other. If she happened to pass close to him, and there was nobody else around, Carla might kiss his shoulder through the light material of his summer shirt.

"If you ever try to run away on me again I'll tan your hide," he said to her, and she said, "*Would* you?"

"What?"

"Tan my hide?"

"Damn right." He was high-spirited now, irresistible as when she had first known him.

Birds were everywhere. Red-winged blackbirds, robins, a pair of doves that sang at daybreak. Lots of crows, and gulls on reconnoitering missions from the lake, and big turkey buzzards that sat in the branches of a dead oak about half a mile away, at the edge of the woods. At first they just sat there, drying out their voluminous wings, lifting themselves occasionally for a trial flight, flapping around a bit, then composing themselves to let the sun and the warm air do their work. In a day or so they were restored, flying high, circling and dropping to earth, disappearing over the woods, coming back to rest in the familiar bare tree.

Lizzie's owner—Joy Tucker—showed up again, tanned and friendly. She had just got sick of the rain and gone off on her holidays to hike in the Rocky Mountains. Now she was back.

"Perfect timing weatherwise," Clark said. He and Joy Tucker were soon joking as if nothing had happened.

"Lizzie looks to be in good shape," she said. "But where's her little friend? What's her name—Flora?"

"Gone," said Clark. "Maybe she took off to the Rocky Mountains."

"Lots of wild goats out there. With fantastic horns."

"So I hear."

FOR THREE OR FOUR DAYS they had been just too busy to go down and look in the mailbox. When Carla opened it she found the phone bill, some promise that if they subscribed to a certain magazine they could win a million dollars, and Mrs. Jamieson's letter.

My Dear Carla,

I have been thinking about the (rather dramatic) events of the last few days and I find myself talking to myself but really to you, so often that I thought I must speak to you, even if—the best way I can do now—only in a letter. And don't worry— you do not have to answer me.

Mrs. Jamieson went on to say that she was afraid that she had involved herself too closely in Carla's life and had made the mistake of thinking somehow that Carla's happiness and freedom were the same thing. All she cared for was Carla's happiness and she saw now that she—Carla—must find that in her marriage. All she could hope was that perhaps Carla's flight and turbulent emotions had brought her true feelings to the surface and perhaps a recognition in her husband of his true feelings as well.

She said that she would perfectly understand if Carla had a wish to avoid her in the future and that she would always be grateful for Carla's presence in her life during such a difficult time.

The strangest and most wonderful thing in this whole string of events seems to me the reappearance of Flora. In fact it seems rather like a miracle. Where had she been all the time and why did she choose just that moment for her reappearance? I am sure your husband has described it to you. We were talking at the patio door and I—facing out—was the first to see this white something—descending on us out of the night. Of course it was the effect of the ground fog. But truly terrifying. I think I shrieked out loud. I had never in my life felt such bewitchment, in the true sense. I suppose I should be honest and say fear. There we were, two adults, frozen, and then out of the fog comes little lost Flora.

There has to be something special about this. I know of course that Flora is an ordinary little animal and that she

probably spent her time away in getting herself pregnant. In
a sense her return has no connection at all with our human
lives. Yet her appearance at that moment did have a profound
effect on your husband and me. When two human beings
divided by hostility are both, at the same time, mystified—no,
frightened—by the same apparition, there is a bond that
springs up between them, and they find themselves united in
the most unexpected way. United in their humanity—that is
the only way I can describe it. We parted almost as friends. So
Flora has her place as a good angel in my life and perhaps also
in your husband's life and yours.

With all my good wishes, Sylvia Jamieson

As soon as Carla had read this letter she crumpled it up. Then
she burned it in the sink. The flames leapt up alarmingly and she
turned on the tap, then scooped up the soft disgusting black stuff
and put it down the toilet as she should have done in the first place.

She was busy for the rest of that day, and the next, and the next.
During that time she had to take two parties out on the trails,
she had to give lessons to children, individually and in groups. At
night when Clark put his arms around her—busy as he was now,
he was never too tired, never cross—she did not find it hard to be
cooperative.

It was as if she had a murderous needle somewhere in her lungs,
and by breathing carefully, she could avoid feeling it. But every
once in a while she had to take a deep breath, and it was still there.

SYLVIA HAD TAKEN AN APARTMENT in the college town
where she taught. The house was not up for sale—or at least there
wasn't a sign out in front of it. Leon Jamieson had got some kind of
posthumous award—news of this was in the papers. There was no
mention this time of any money.

AS THE DRY GOLDEN DAYS of fall came on—an encouraging and profitable season—Carla found that she had got used
to the sharp thought that had lodged in her. It wasn't so sharp
anymore—in fact, it no longer surprised her. And she was inhab-

ited now by an almost seductive notion, a constant low-lying temptation.

She had only to raise her eyes, she had only to look in one direction, to know where she might go. An evening walk, once her chores for the day were finished. To the edge of the woods, and the bare tree where the buzzards had held their party.

And then the little dirty bones in the grass. The skull with perhaps some shreds of bloodied skin clinging to it. A skull that she could hold like a teacup in one hand. Knowledge in one hand.

Or perhaps not. Nothing there.

Other things could have happened. He could have chased Flora away. Or tied her in the back of the truck and driven some distance and set her loose. Taken her back to the place they'd got her from. Not to have her around, reminding them.

She might be free.

The days passed and Carla didn't go near that place. She held out against the temptation.

Soon

~

TWO PROFILES FACE EACH OTHER. One the profile of a pure white heifer, with a particularly mild and tender expression, the other that of a green-faced man who is neither young nor old. He seems to be a minor official, maybe a postman—he wears that sort of cap. His lips are pale, the whites of his eyes shining. A hand that is probably his offers up, from the lower margin of the painting, a little tree or an exuberant branch, fruited with jewels.

At the upper margin of the painting are dark clouds, and underneath them some small tottery houses and a toy church with its toy cross, perched on the curved surface of the earth. Within this curve a small man (drawn to a larger scale, however, than the buildings) walks along purposefully with a scythe on his shoulder, and a woman, drawn to the same scale, seems to wait for him. But she is hanging upside down.

There are other things as well. For instance, a girl milking a cow, within the heifer's cheek.

Juliet decided at once to buy this print for her parents' Christmas present.

"Because it reminds me of them," she said to Christa, her friend who had come down with her from Whale Bay to do some shopping. They were in the gift shop of the Vancouver Art Gallery.

Christa laughed. "The green man and the cow? They'll be flattered."

Christa never took anything seriously at first, she had to make some joke about it. Juliet wasn't bothered. Three months pregnant with the baby that would turn out to be Penelope, she was suddenly free of nausea, and for that reason, or some other, she was subject to fits of euphoria. She thought of food all the time, and hadn't even wanted to come into the gift shop, because she had spotted a lunchroom.

She loved everything in the picture, but particularly the little figures and rickety buildings at the top of it. The man with the scythe and the woman hanging upside down.

She looked for the title. *I and the Village.*

It made exquisite sense.

"Chagall. I like Chagall," said Christa. "Picasso was a bastard."

Juliet was so happy with what she had found that she could hardly pay attention.

"You know what he is supposed to have said? *Chagall is for shop-girls,*" Christa told her. "So what's wrong with shopgirls? Chagall should have said, Picasso is for people with funny faces."

"I mean, it makes me think of their life," Juliet said. "I don't know why, but it does."

She had already told Christa some things about her parents—how they lived in a curious but not unhappy isolation, though her father was a popular schoolteacher. Partly they were cut off by Sara's heart trouble, but also by their subscribing to magazines nobody around them read, listening to programs on the national radio network, which nobody around them listened to. By Sara's making her own clothes—sometimes ineptly—from *Vogue* patterns, instead of Butterick. Even by the way they preserved some impression of youth instead of thickening and slouching like the parents of Juliet's schoolfellows. Juliet had described Sam as looking like her—long neck, a slight bump to the chin, light-brown floppy hair—and Sara as a frail pale blonde, a wispy untidy beauty.

WHEN PENELOPE was thirteen months old, Juliet flew with her to Toronto, then caught the train. This was in 1969. She got off in a town twenty miles or so away from the town where she had grown up, and where Sam and Sara still lived. Apparently the train did not stop there anymore.

She was disappointed to get off at this unfamiliar station and not to see reappear, at once, the trees and sidewalks and houses she remembered—then, very soon, her own house, Sam and Sara's house, spacious but plain, no doubt with its same blistered and shabby white paint, behind its bountiful soft maple tree.

Sam and Sara, here in this town where she'd never seen them before, were smiling but anxious, diminished.

Sara gave a curious little cry, as if something had pecked her. A couple of people on the platform turned to look.

Apparently it was only excitement.

"We're long and short, but still we match," she said.

At first Juliet did not understand what was meant. Then she figured it out—Sara was wearing a black linen skirt down to her calves and a matching jacket. The jacket's collar and cuffs were of a shiny lime-green cloth with black polka dots. A turban of the same green material covered her hair. She must have made the outfit herself, or got some dressmaker to make it for her. Its colors were unkind to her skin, which looked as if fine chalk dust had settled over it.

Juliet was wearing a black minidress.

"I was wondering what you'd think of me, black in the summertime, like I'm all in mourning," Sara said. "And here you're dressed to match. You look so smart, I'm all in favor of these short dresses."

"And long hair," said Sam. "An absolute hippy." He bent to look into the baby's face. "Hello, Penelope."

Sara said, "What a dolly."

She reached out for Penelope—though the arms that slid out of her sleeves were sticks too frail to hold any such burden. And they did not have to, because Penelope, who had tensed at the first sound of her grandmother's voice, now yelped and turned away, and hid her face in Juliet's neck.

Sara laughed. "Am I such a scarecrow?" Again her voice was ill controlled, rising to shrill peaks and falling away, drawing stares. This was new—though maybe not entirely. Juliet had an idea that people might always have looked her mother's way when she laughed or talked, but in the old days it would have been a spurt of merriment they noticed, something girlish and attractive (though not everybody would have liked that either, they would have said she was always trying to get attention).

Juliet said, "She's so tired."

Sam introduced the young woman who was standing behind them, keeping her distance as if she was taking care not to be identified as part of their group. And in fact it had not occurred to Juliet that she was.

"Juliet, this is Irene. Irene Avery."

Juliet stuck out her hand as well as she could while holding Penelope and the diaper bag, and when it became evident that Irene was not going to shake hands—or perhaps did not notice the intention—she smiled. Irene did not smile back. She stood quite still but gave the impression of wanting to bolt.

"Hello," said Juliet.

Irene said, "Pleased to meet you," in a sufficiently audible voice, but without expression.

"Irene is our good fairy," Sara said, and then Irene's face did change. She scowled a little, with sensible embarrassment.

She was not as tall as Juliet—who was tall—but she was broader in the shoulders and hips, with strong arms and a stubborn chin. She had thick, springy black hair, pulled back from her face into a stubby ponytail, thick and rather hostile black eyebrows, and the sort of skin that browns easily. Her eyes were green or blue, a light surprising color against this skin, and hard to look into, being deep set. Also because she held her head slightly lowered and twisted her face to the side. This wariness seemed hardened and deliberate.

"She does one heck of a lot of work for a fairy," Sam said, with his large strategic grin. "I'll tell the world she does."

And now of course Juliet recalled the mention in letters of some woman who had come in to help, because of Sara's strength having gone so drastically downhill. But she had thought of somebody much older. Irene was surely no older than she was herself.

The car was the same Pontiac that Sam had got secondhand maybe ten years ago. The original blue paint showed in streaks here and there but was mostly faded to gray, and the effects of winter road salt could be seen in its petticoat fringe of rust.

"The old gray mare," said Sara, almost out of breath after the short walk from the railway platform.

"She hasn't given up," said Juliet. She spoke admiringly, as seemed to be expected. She had forgotten that this was what they called the car, though it was the name she had thought up herself.

"Oh, she never gives up," said Sara, once she was settled with Irene's help in the backseat. "And we'd never give up on her."

Juliet got into the front seat, juggling Penelope, who was beginning again to whimper. The heat inside the car was shocking, even though it had been parked with the windows down in the scanty shade of the station poplars.

"Actually I'm considering—," said Sam as he backed out, "I'm considering turning her in for a truck."

"He doesn't mean it," shrieked Sara.

"For the business," Sam continued. "It'd be a lot handier. And you'd get a certain amount of advertising every time you drove down the street, just from the name on the door."

"He's teasing," Sara said. "How am I going to ride around in a vehicle that says *Fresh Vegetables*? Am I supposed to be the squash or the cabbage?"

"Better pipe down, Missus," Sam said, "or you won't have any breath left when we reach home."

After nearly thirty years of teaching in the public schools around the county—ten years in the last school—Sam had suddenly quit and decided to get into the business of selling vegetables, full-time. He had always cultivated a big vegetable garden, and raspberry canes, in the extra lot beside their house, and they had sold their surplus produce to a few people around town. But now, apparently, this was to change into his way of making a living, selling to grocery stores and perhaps eventually putting up a market stall at the front gate.

"You're serious about all this?" said Juliet quietly.

"Darn right I am."

"You're not going to miss teaching?"

"Not on your Nelly-O. I was fed up. I was fed up to the eyeballs."

It was true that after all those years, he had never been offered, in any school, the job of principal. She supposed that was what he was fed up with. He was a remarkable teacher, the one whose antics and energy everyone would remember, his Grade Six unlike any other year in his pupils' lives. Yet he had been passed over, time and again, and probably for that very reason. His methods could be seen to undercut authority. So you could imagine Authority saying that he was not the sort of man to be in charge, he'd do less harm where he was.

He liked outdoor work, he was good at talking to people, he would probably do well, selling vegetables.

But Sara would hate it.

Juliet did not like it either. If there was a side to be on, however, she would have to choose his. She was not going to define herself as a snob.

And the truth was that she saw herself—she saw herself and Sam and Sara, but particularly herself and Sam—as superior in their own way to everybody around them. So what should his peddling vegetables matter?

Sam spoke now in a quieter, conspiratorial voice.

"What's her name?"

He meant the baby's.

"Penelope. We're never going to call her Penny. Penelope."

"No, I mean—I mean her last name."

"Oh. Well, it's Henderson-Porteous I guess. Or Porteous-Henderson. But maybe that's too much of a mouthful, when she's already called Penelope? We knew that but we wanted Penelope. We'll have to settle it somehow."

"So. He's given her his name," Sam said. "Well, that's something. I mean, that's good."

Juliet was surprised for a moment, then not.

"Of course he has," she said. Pretending to be mystified and amused. "She's his."

"Oh yes. Yes. But given the circumstances."

"I forget about the circumstances," she said. "If you mean the fact that we're not married, it's hardly anything to take into account. Where we live, the people we know, it is not a thing anybody thinks about."

"Suppose not," said Sam. "Was he married to the first one?"

Juliet had told them about Eric's wife, whom he had cared for during the eight years that she had lived after her car accident.

"Ann? Yes. Well, I don't really know. But yes. I think so. Yes."

Sara called into the front seat, "Wouldn't it be nice to stop for ice cream?"

"We've got ice cream in the fridge at home," Sam called back. And added quietly, shockingly, to Juliet, "Take her into anyplace for a treat, and she'll put on a show."

The windows were still down, the warm wind blew through the car. It was full summer—a season which never arrived, as far as Juliet could see, on the west coast. The hardwood trees were humped over the far edge of the fields, making blue-black caves of shade, and the crops and the meadows in front of them, under the hard sunlight, were gold and green. Vigorous young wheat and barley and corn and beans—fairly blistering your eyes.

Sara said, "What's this conference in aid of? In the front seat? We can't hear back here for the wind."

Sam said, "Nothing interesting. Just asking Juliet if her fellow's still doing the fishing."

Eric made his living prawn fishing, and had done so for a long time. Once he had been a medical student. That had come to an end because he had performed an abortion, on a friend (not a girl-friend). All had gone well, but somehow the story got out. This was something Juliet had thought of revealing to her broad-minded parents. She had wanted, perhaps, to establish him as an educated man, not just a fisherman. But why should that matter, especially now that Sam was a vegetable man? Also, their broad-mindedness was possibly not so reliable as she had thought.

THERE WAS MORE TO BE SOLD than fresh vegetables and ber-ries. Jam, bottled juice, relish, were turned out in the kitchen. The first morning of Juliet's visit, raspberry-jam making was in prog-ress. Irene was in charge, her blouse wet with steam or sweat, stick-ing to her skin between the shoulder blades. Every so often she flashed a look at the television set, which had been wheeled down the back hall to the kitchen doorway, so that you had to squeeze around it to get into the room. On the screen was a children's morning program, showing a Bullwinkle cartoon. Now and then Irene gave a loud laugh at the cartoon antics, and Juliet laughed a little, to be comradely. Of this Irene took no notice.

Counter space had to be cleared so that Juliet could boil and mash an egg for Penelope's breakfast, and make some coffee and toast for herself. "Is that enough room?" Irene asked her, in a voice that was dubious, as if Juliet was an intruder whose demands could not be foreseen.

Close-up, you could see how many fine black hairs grew on Irene's forearms. Some grew on her cheeks, too, just in front of her ears.

In her sidelong way she watched everything Juliet did, watched her fiddle with the knobs on the stove (not remembering at first which burners they controlled), watched her lifting the egg out of the saucepan and peeling off the shell (which stuck, this time, and came away in little bits rather than in large easy pieces), then watched her choosing the saucer to mash it in.

"You don't want her to drop that on the floor." This was a reference to the china saucer. "Don't you got a plastic dish for her?"

"I'll watch it," Juliet said.

It turned out that Irene was a mother, too. She had a boy three years old and a daughter just under two. Their names were Trevor and Tracy. Their father had been killed last summer in an accident at the chicken barn where he worked. She herself was three years younger than Juliet—twenty-two. The information about the children and the husband came out in answer to Juliet's questions, and the age could be figured from what she said next.

When Juliet said, "Oh, I'm sorry"—speaking about the accident and feeling that she had been rude to pry, and that it was now hypocritical of her to commiserate—Irene said, "Yeah. Right in time for my twenty-first birthday," as if misfortunes were something to accumulate, like charms on a bracelet.

After Penelope had eaten all of the egg that she would accept, Juliet hoisted her onto one hip and carried her upstairs.

Halfway up she realized that she had not washed the saucer.

There was nowhere to leave the baby, who was not yet walking but could crawl very quickly. Certainly she could not be left for even five minutes in the kitchen, with the boiling water in the sterilizer and the hot jam and the chopping knives—it was too much to ask Irene to watch her. And first thing this morning she had again refused to make friends with Sara. So Juliet carried her up the enclosed stairs to the attic—having shut the door behind—and set her there on the steps to play, while she herself looked for the old playpen. Fortunately Penelope was an expert on steps.

The house was a full two stories tall, its rooms high-ceilinged but boxlike—or so they seemed to Juliet now. The roof was steeply pitched, so that you could walk around in the middle of the attic. Juliet used to do that, when she was a child. She walked around telling herself some story she had read, with certain additions or alterations. Dancing—that too—in front of an imaginary audience. The real audience consisted of broken or simply banished furniture, old trunks, an immensely heavy buffalo coat, the purple martin house (a present from long-ago students of Sam's, which had failed to attract any purple martins), the German helmet supposed to have been brought home by Sam's father from the First World War, and an unintentionally comic amateur painting of the *Empress of Ireland* sinking in the Gulf of St. Lawrence, with matchstick figures flying off in all directions.

And there, leaning against the wall, was *I and the Village*. Face out—no attempt had been made to hide it. And no dust on it to speak of, so it had not been there long.

She found the playpen, after a few moments of searching. It was a handsome heavy piece of furniture, with a wooden floor and spindle sides. And the baby carriage. Her parents had kept everything, had hoped for another child. There had been one miscarriage at least. Laughter in their bed, on Sunday mornings, had made Juliet feel as if the house had been invaded by a stealthy, even shameful, disturbance, not favorable to herself.

The baby carriage was of the kind that folded down to become a stroller. This was something Juliet had forgotten about, or hadn't known. Sweating by now, and covered with dust, she got to work to effect this transformation. This sort of job was never easy for her, she never grasped right away the manner in which things were put together, and she might have dragged the whole thing downstairs and gone out to the garden to get Sam to help her, but for the thought of Irene. Irene's flickering pale eyes, indirect but measuring looks, competent hands. Her vigilance, in which there was something that couldn't quite be called contempt. Juliet didn't know what it could be called. An attitude, indifferent but uncompromising, like a cat's.

She managed at last to get the stroller into shape. It was cumbersome, half again as big as the stroller she was used to. And filthy, of course. As she was herself by now, and Penelope, on the steps, even more so. And right beside the baby's hand was something Juliet hadn't even noticed. A nail. The sort of thing you paid no attention to, till you had a baby at the hand-to-mouth stage, and that you had then to be on the lookout for all the time.

And she hadn't been. Everything here distracted her. The heat,

Irene, the things that were familiar and the things that were unfamiliar.

I and the Village.

"OH," SAID SARA. "I hoped you wouldn't notice. Don't take it to heart."

The sunroom was now Sara's bedroom. Bamboo shades had been hung on all the windows, filling the small room—once part of the verandah—with a brownish-yellow light and a uniform heat. Sara, however, was wearing woolly pink pajamas. Yesterday, at the station, with her pencilled eyebrows and raspberry lipstick, her turban and suit, she had looked to Juliet like an elderly Frenchwoman (not that Juliet had seen many elderly Frenchwomen), but now, with her white hair flying out in wisps, her bright eyes anxious under nearly nonexistent brows, she looked more like an oddly aged child. She was sitting up against the pillows with the quilts pulled up to her waist. When Juliet had walked her to the bathroom, earlier, it had been revealed that in spite of the heat she was wearing both socks and slippers in bed.

A straight-backed chair had been placed by her bed, its seat being easier for her to reach than a table. On it were pills and medicines, talcum powder, moisturizing lotion, a half-drunk cup of milky tea, a glass filmed with the traces of some dark tonic, probably iron. On top of the bed were magazines—old copies of *Vogue* and the *Ladies' Home Journal.*

"I'm not," said Juliet.

"We did have it hanging up. It was in the back hall by the dining-room door. Then Daddy took it down."

"Why?"

"He didn't say anything about it to me. He didn't say that he was going to. Then came a day when it was just gone."

"Why would he take it down?"

"Oh. It would be some notion he had, you know."

"What sort of a notion?"

"Oh. I think—you know, I think it probably had to do with Irene. That it would disturb Irene."

"There wasn't anybody naked in it. Not like the Botticelli."

For indeed there was a print of *The Birth of Venus* hanging in

Sam and Sara's living room. It had been the subject of nervous jokes years ago on the occasion when they had the other teachers to supper.

"No. But it was *modern.* I think it made Daddy uncomfortable. Or maybe looking at it with Irene looking at it—that made him uncomfortable. He might be afraid it would make her feel—oh, sort of contemptuous of us. You know—that we were weird. He wouldn't like for Irene to think we were that kind of people."

Juliet said, "The kind of people who would hang that kind of picture? You mean he'd care so much what she thought of our *pictures?*"

"You know Daddy."

"He's not afraid to disagree with people. Wasn't that the trouble in his job?"

"What?" said Sara. "Oh. Yes. He can disagree. But he's careful sometimes. And Irene. Irene is—he's careful of her. She's very valuable to us, Irene."

"Did he think she'd quit her job because she thought we had a weird picture?"

"I would have left it up, dear. I value anything that comes from you. But Daddy . . ."

Juliet said nothing. From the time when she was nine or ten until she was perhaps fourteen, she and Sara had an understanding about Sam. *You know Daddy.*

That was the time of their being women together. Home permanents were tried on Juliet's stubborn fine hair, dressmaking sessions produced the outfits like nobody else's, suppers were peanut-butter-and-tomato-and-mayonnaise sandwiches on the evenings Sam stayed late for a school meeting. Stories were told and retold about Sara's old boyfriends and girlfriends, the jokes they played and the fun they had, in the days when Sara was a schoolteacher too, before her heart got too bad. Stories from the time before that, when she lay in bed with rheumatic fever and had the imaginary friends Rollo and Maxine who solved mysteries, even murders, like the characters in certain children's books. Glimpses of Sam's besotted courtship, disasters with the borrowed car, the time he showed up at Sara's door disguised as a tramp.

Sara and Juliet, making fudge and threading ribbons through

the eyelet trim on their petticoats, the two of them intertwined. And then abruptly, Juliet hadn't wanted any more of it, she had wanted instead to talk to Sam late at night in the kitchen, to ask him about black holes, the Ice Age, God. She hated the way Sara undermined their talk with wide-eyed ingenuous questions, the way Sara always tried somehow to bring the subject back to herself. That was why the talks had to be late at night and there had to be the understanding neither she nor Sam ever spoke about. *Wait till we're rid of Sara.* Just for the time being, of course.

There was a reminder going along with that. *Be nice to Sara. She risked her life to have you, that's worth remembering.*

"Daddy doesn't mind disagreeing with people that are *over* him," Sara said, taking a deep breath. "But you know how he is with people that are *under* him. He'll do anything to make sure they don't feel he's any different from them, he just has to put himself down on their level—"

Juliet did know, of course. She knew the way Sam talked to the boy at the gas pumps, the way he joked in the hardware store. But she said nothing.

"He has to suck up to them," said Sara with a sudden change of tone, a wavering edge of viciousness, a weak chuckle.

JULIET CLEANED UP THE STROLLER, and Penelope, and herself, and set off on a walk into town. She had the excuse that she needed a certain brand of mild disinfectant soap with which to wash the diapers—if she used ordinary soap the baby would get a rash. But she had other reasons, irresistible though embarrassing.

This was the way she had walked to school for years of her life. Even when she was going to college, and came home on a visit, she was still the same—a girl going to school. Would she never be done going to school? Somebody asked Sam that at a time when she had just won the Intercollegiate Latin Translation Prize, and he had said, " 'Fraid not." He told this story on himself. God forbid that he should mention prizes. Leave Sara to do that—though Sara might have forgotten just what the prize was for.

And here she was, redeemed. Like any other young woman, pushing her baby. Concerned about the diaper soap. And this wasn't just her baby. Her love child. She sometimes spoke of

Penelope that way, just to Eric. He took it as a joke, she said it as a joke, because of course they lived together and had done so for some time, and they intended to go on together. The fact that they were not married meant nothing to him, so far as she knew, and she often forgot about it, herself. But occasionally—and now, especially, here at home, it was the fact of her unmarried state that gave her some flush of accomplishment, a silly surge of bliss.

"SO—YOU WENT UPSTREET TODAY," Sam said. (Had he always said *upstreet*? Sara and Juliet said *uptown*.) "See anybody you knew?"

"I had to go to the drugstore," Juliet said. "So I was talking to Charlie Little."

This conversation took place in the kitchen, after eleven o'clock at night. Juliet had decided that this was the best time to make up Penelope's bottles for tomorrow.

"Little Charlie?" said Sam—who had always had this other habit she hadn't remembered, the habit of continuing to call people by their school nicknames. "Did he admire the offspring?"

"Of course."

"And well he might."

Sam was sitting at the table, drinking rye and smoking a cigarette. His drinking whisky was new. Because Sara's father had been a drunk—not a down-and-out drunk, he had continued to practice as a veterinarian, but enough of a terror around the house to make his daughter horrified by drinking—Sam had never used to so much as drink a beer, at least to Juliet's knowledge, at home.

Juliet had gone into the drugstore because that was the only place to buy the diaper soap. She hadn't expected to see Charlie, though it was his family's store. The last she had heard of him, he was going to be an engineer. She had mentioned that to him, today, maybe tactlessly, but he had been easy and jovial when he told her that it hadn't worked out. He had put on weight around the middle, and his hair had thinned, had lost some of its wave and glisten. He had greeted Juliet with enthusiasm, with flattery for herself as well as her baby, and this had confused her, so that she had felt her face and neck hot, slightly perspiring, all the time he talked to her. In high school he would have had no time for her—except for

a decent greeting, since his manners were always affable, democratic. He took out the most desirable girls in the school, and was
now, as he told her, married to one of them. Janey Peel. They had
two children, one of them about Penelope's age, one older. That
was the reason, he said, with a candor that seemed to owe something to Juliet's own situation—that was the reason he hadn't gone
on to become an engineer.

So he knew how to win a smile and a gurgle from Penelope, and
he chatted with Juliet as a fellow parent, somebody now on the
same level. She felt idiotically flattered and pleased. But there was
more to his attention than that—the quick glance at her unadorned
left hand, the joke about his own marriage. And something else.
He appraised her, covertly, perhaps he saw her now as a woman
displaying the fruits of a boldly sexual life. Juliet, of all people. The
gawk, the scholar.

"Does she look like you?" he had asked, when he squatted down
to peer at Penelope.

"More like her father," said Juliet casually, but with a flood of
pride, the sweat now pearling on her upper lip.

"Does she?" said Charlie, and straightened up, speaking confidentially. "I'll tell you one thing, though. I thought it was a
shame—"

JULIET SAID TO SAM, "He told me he thought it was a shame
what happened with you."

"He did, did he? What did you say to that?"

"I didn't know what to say. I didn't know what he meant. But I
didn't want him to know that."

"No."

She sat down at the table. "I'd like a drink but I don't like
whisky."

"So you drink now, too?"

"Wine. We make our own wine. Everybody in the Bay does."

He told her a joke then, the sort of joke that he would never have
told her before. It involved a couple going to a motel, and it ended
up with the line "So it's like what I always tell the girls at Sunday
school—you don't have to drink and smoke to have a good time."

She laughed but felt her face go hot, as with Charlie.

"Why did you quit your job?" she said. "Were you let go because of me?"

"Come on now." Sam laughed. "Don't think you're so important. I wasn't let go. I wasn't fired."

"All right then. You quit."

"I quit."

"Did it have anything at all to do with me?"

"I quit because I got goddamn sick of my neck always in that noose. I was on the point of quitting for years."

"It had nothing to do with me?"

"All right," Sam said. "I got into an argument. There were things said."

"What things?"

"You don't need to know.

"And don't worry," he said after a moment. "They didn't fire me. They couldn't have fired me. There are rules. It's like I told you—I was ready to go anyway."

"But you don't realize," said Juliet. "You don't *realize*. You don't realize just how *stupid* this is and what a disgusting place this is to live in, where people say that kind of thing, and how if I told people I know this, they wouldn't believe it. It would seem like a joke."

"Well. Unfortunately your mother and I don't live where you live. Here is where we live. Does that fellow of yours think it's a joke too? I don't want to talk any more about this tonight, I'm going to bed. I'm going to look in on Mother and then I'm going to bed."

"The passenger train—," said Juliet with continued energy, even scorn. "It does still stop here. Doesn't it? You didn't want me getting off here. *Did you?*"

On his way out of the room, her father did not answer.

LIGHT FROM THE LAST STREETLIGHT in town now fell across Juliet's bed. The big soft maple tree had been cut down, replaced by a patch of Sam's rhubarb. Last night she had left the curtains closed to shade the bed, but tonight she felt that she needed the outside air. So she had to switch the pillow down to the foot of the bed, along with Penelope, who had slept like an angel with the full light in her face.

She wished she had drunk a little of the whisky. She lay stiff with frustration and anger, composing in her head a letter to Eric. *I don't know what I'm doing here, I should never have come here, I can't wait to go home.*

Home.

WHEN IT WAS BARELY LIGHT IN THE MORNING, she woke to the noise of a vacuum cleaner. Then a voice—Sam's—interrupted this noise, and she must have fallen asleep again. When she woke up later, she thought it must have been a dream. Otherwise Penelope would have woken up, and she hadn't.

The kitchen was cooler this morning, no longer full of the smell of simmering fruit. Irene was fixing little caps of gingham cloth, and labels, onto all the jars.

"I thought I heard you vacuuming," said Juliet, dredging up cheerfulness. "I must have dreamed it. It was only about five o'clock in the morning."

Irene did not answer for a moment. She was writing on a label. She wrote with great concentration, her lips caught between her teeth.

"That was her," she said when she had finished. "She woke your dad up and he had to go and make her quit."

This seemed unlikely. Yesterday Sara had left her bed only to go to the bathroom.

"He told me," said Irene. "She wakes up in the middle of the night and thinks she's going to do something and then he has to get up and make her quit."

"She must have a spurt of energy then," said Juliet.

"Yeah." Irene was getting to work on another label. When that was done, she faced Juliet.

"Wants to wake your dad up and get attention, that's it. Him dead tired and he's got to get out of bed and tend to her."

Juliet turned away. Not wanting to set Penelope down—as if the child wasn't safe here—she juggled her on one hip while she fished the egg out with a spoon, tapped and shelled and mashed it with one hand.

While she fed Penelope she was afraid to speak, lest the tone of her voice alarm the baby and set her wailing. Something communicated itself to Irene, however. She said in a more subdued voice—but with an undertone of defiance—"That's just the way they get. When they're sick like that, they can't help it. They can't think about nobody but themselves."

SARA'S EYES WERE CLOSED, but she opened them immediately. "Oh, my dear ones," she said, as if laughing at herself. "My Juliet. My Penelope."

Penelope seemed to be getting used to her. At least she did not cry, this morning, or turn her face away.

"Here," said Sara, reaching for one of her magazines. "Set her down and let her work at this."

Penelope looked dubious for a moment, then grabbed a page and tore it vigorously.

"There you go," said Sara. "All babies love to tear up magazines. I remember."

On the bedside chair there was a bowl of Cream of Wheat, barely touched.

"You didn't eat your breakfast?" Juliet said. "Is that not what you wanted?"

Sara looked at the bowl as if serious consideration was called for, but couldn't be managed.

"I don't remember. No, I guess I didn't want it." She had a little fit of giggling and gasping. "Who knows? Crossed my mind—she could be poisoning me.

"I'm just kidding," she said when she recovered. "But she's very fierce. Irene. We mustn't underestimate—Irene. Did you see the hairs on her arms?"

"Like cats' hairs," said Juliet.

"Like skunks'."

"We must hope none of them get into the jam."

"Don't make me—laugh any more—"

Penelope became so absorbed in tearing up magazines that in a while Juliet was able to leave her in Sara's room and carry the Cream of Wheat out to the kitchen. Without saying anything, she began to make an eggnog. Irene was in and out, carrying boxes of jam jars to the car. On the back steps, Sam was hosing off the earth that clung to the newly dug potatoes. He had begun to sing—too softly at first for his words to be heard. Then, as Irene came up the steps, more loudly.

> *"Irene, good ni-i-ight,*
> *Irene, good night,*
> *Good night, Irene, good night, Irene,*
> *I'll see you in my dreams."*

Irene, in the kitchen, swung around and yelled, "Don't sing that song about me."

"What song about you?" said Sam, with feigned amazement. "Who's singing a song about you?"

"You were. You just were."

"Oh—that song. That song about Irene? The girl in the song? By golly—I forgot that was your name too."

He started up again, but humming, stealthily. Irene stood listening, flushed, with her chest going up and down, waiting to pounce if she should hear a word.

"Don't you sing about me. If it's got my name in it, it's about me."

Suddenly Sam burst out in full force.

> *"Last Saturday night I got married,*
> *Me and my wife settled down—"*

"Stop it. You stop it," cried Irene, wide-eyed, inflamed. "If you don't stop I'll go out there and squirt the hose on you."

SAM WAS DELIVERING JAM, that afternoon, to various grocery stores and a few gift shops which had placed orders. He invited Juliet to come along. He had gone to the hardware store and bought a brand-new baby's car seat for Penelope.

"That's one thing we don't have in the attic," he said. "When you were little, I don't know if they had them. Anyway, it wouldn't have mattered. We didn't have a car."

"It's very spiffy," said Juliet. "I hope it didn't cost a fortune."

"A mere bagatelle," said Sam, bowing her into the car.

Irene was in the field picking more raspberries. These would be for pies. Sam tooted the horn twice and waved as they set off, and Irene decided to respond, raising one arm as if batting away a fly.

"That's a dandy girl," Sam said. "I don't know how we would have survived without her. But I imagine she seems pretty rough to you."

"I hardly know her."

"No. She's scared stiff of you."

"Surely not." And trying to think of something appreciative or at least neutral to say about Irene, Juliet asked how her husband had been killed at the chicken barn.

"I don't know if he was a criminal type or just immature. Anyway, he got in with some goons who were planning a sideline in stolen chickens and of course they managed to set off the alarm and the farmer came out with a gun and whether he meant to shoot him or not he did—"

"My God."

"So Irene and her in-laws went to court but the fellow got off. Well, he would. It must have been pretty hard on her, though. Even if it doesn't seem that the husband was much of a prize."

Juliet said that of course it must have been, and asked him if Irene was somebody he had taught at school.

"No no no. She hardly got to school, as far as I can make out."

He said that her family had lived up north, somewhere near Huntsville. Yes. Somewhere near there. One day they all went into town. Father, mother, kids. And the father told them he had things to do and he would meet them in a while. He told them where. When. And they walked around with no money to spend, until it was time. And he just never showed up.

"Never intended to show up. Ditched them. So they had to go on welfare. Lived in some shack out in the country, where it was cheap. Irene's older sister, the one who was the mainstay, more than the mother, I gather—she died of a burst appendix. No way of getting her into town, snowstorm on and they didn't have a phone. Irene didn't want to go back to school then, because her sister had sort of protected her from the way the other kids would act towards them. She may seem thick-skinned now but I guess she wasn't always. Maybe even now it's more of a masquerade."

And now, he said, now Irene's mother was looking after the little boy and the little girl, but guess what, after all these years the father had shown up and was trying to get the mother to go back to him, and if that should happen Irene didn't know what she'd do, since she didn't want her kids near him.

"They're cute kids, too. The little girl has some problem with a cleft palate and she's already had one operation but she'll need another later on. She'll be all right. But that's just one more thing."

One more thing.

What was the matter with Juliet? She felt no real sympathy. She felt herself rebelling, deep down, against this wretched litany. It was too much. When the cleft palate appeared in the story what she had really wanted to do was complain. *Too much.*

She knew she was wrong, but the feeling would not budge. She was afraid to say anything more, lest out of her mouth she betray her hard heart. She was afraid she would say to Sam, "Just what is so wonderful about all this misery, does it make her a saint?" Or she might say, most unforgivably, "I hope you don't mean to get us mixed up with people like that."

"I'm telling you," Sam said, "at the time she came to help us out I was at wits' end. Last fall, your mother was a downright catastrophe. And not exactly that she was letting everything go. No. Better if she had let everything go. Better if she'd done nothing. What she did, she'd start one job up and then she could not get on with it. Over and over. Not that this was anything absolutely new. I mean, I always had to pick up after her and look after her and help her do the housework. Me and you both—remember? She'd always been this sweet pretty girl with a bad heart and she was used to being waited on. Once in a while over the years it did occur to me she could have tried harder.

"But it got so bad," he said. "It got so I'd come home to the washing machine in the middle of the kitchen floor and wet clothes slopping all over the place. And some baking mess she'd started on and given up on, stuff charred to a crisp in the oven. I was scared she'd set herself on fire. Set the house on fire. I'd tell her and tell her, stay in bed. But she wouldn't and then she'd be all in this mess, crying. I tried a couple of girls coming in and they just couldn't handle her. So then—Irene.

"Irene," he said with a robust sigh. "I bless the day. I tell you. Bless the day."

But like all good things, he said, this must come to an end. Irene was getting married. To a forty- or fifty-year-old widower. Farmer. He was supposed to have money and for her sake Sam guessed he hoped it was true. Because the man did not have much else to recommend him.

"By Jesus he doesn't. As far as I can see he's only got one tooth in his head. Bad sign, in my opinion. Too proud or stingy to get choppers. Think of it—a grand-looking girl like her."

"When is the event?"

"In the fall sometime. In the fall."

PENELOPE HAD BEEN SLEEPING all this time—she had gone to sleep in her car seat almost as soon as they started to move. The front windows were down and Juliet could smell the hay, which was freshly cut and baled—nobody made hay coils anymore. Some elm trees were still standing, marvels now, in their isolation.

They stopped in a village built all along one street in a narrow valley. Bedrock stuck out of the valley walls—the only place for many miles around where such massive rocks were to be seen. Juliet remembered coming here when there was a special park which you paid to enter. In the park there was a fountain, a teahouse where they served strawberry shortcake and ice cream—and surely other things which she could not remember. Caves in the rock were named after each of the Seven Dwarfs. Sam and Sara had sat on the ground by the fountain eating ice cream while she had rushed ahead to explore the caves. (Which were nothing much, really—quite shallow.) She had wanted them to come with her but Sam had said, "You know your mother can't climb."

"You run," Sara had said. "Come back and tell us all about it." She was dressed up. A black taffeta skirt that spread in a circle around her on the grass. Those were called ballerina skirts.

It must have been a special day.

Juliet asked Sam about this when he came out of the store. At first he could not remember. Then he did. A gyp joint, he said. He didn't know when it had disappeared.

Juliet could see no trace anywhere along the street of a fountain or a teahouse.

"A bringer of peace and order," Sam said, and it took a moment for her to recognize that he was still talking about Irene. "She'll turn her hand to anything. Cut the grass and hoe the garden. Whatever she's doing she gives it her best and she behaves as if it's a privilege to do it. That's what never ceases to amaze me."

What could the carefree occasion have been? A birthday, a wedding anniversary?

Sam spoke insistently, even solemnly, over the noise of the car's struggle up the hill.

"She restored my faith in women."

SAM CHARGED INTO EVERY STORE after telling Juliet that he wouldn't be a minute, and came back to the car quite a while later explaining that he had not been able to get away. People wanted to talk, people had been saving up jokes to tell him. A few followed him out to see his daughter and her baby.

"So that's the girl who talks Latin," one woman said.

"Getting a bit rusty nowadays," Sam said. "Nowadays she has her hands full."

"I bet," the woman said, craning to get a look at Penelope. "But aren't they a blessing? Oh, the wee ones."

Juliet had thought she might talk to Sam about the thesis she was planning to return to—though at present that was just a dream. Such subjects used to come up naturally between them. Not with Sara. Sara would say, "Now, you must tell me what you're doing in your studies," and Juliet would sum things up, and Sara might ask her how she kept all those Greek names straight. But Sam had known what she was talking about. At college she had mentioned how her father had explained to her what *thaumaturgy* meant, when she ran across the word at the age of twelve or thirteen. She was asked if her father was a scholar.

"Sure," she said. "He teaches Grade Six."

Now she had a feeling that he would subtly try to undermine her. Or maybe not so subtly. He might use the word *airy-fairy*. Or claim to have forgotten things she could not believe he had forgotten.

But maybe he had. Rooms in his mind closed up, the windows blackened—what was in there judged by him to be too useless, too discreditable, to meet the light of day.

Juliet spoke out more harshly than she intended.

"Does she want to get married? Irene?"

This question startled Sam, coming as it did in that tone and after a considerable silence.

"I don't know," he said.

And after a moment, "I don't see how she could."

"Ask her," Juliet said. "You must want to, the way you feel about her."

They drove for a mile or two before he spoke. It was clear she had given offense.

"I don't know what you're talking about," he said.

"HAPPY, GRUMPY, DOPEY, SLEEPY, SNEEZY," Sara said.

"Doc," said Juliet.

"Doc. *Doc.* Happy, Sneezy, *Doc,* Grumpy, *Bashful,* Sneezy—No. Sneezy, Bashful, Doc, Grumpy—*Sleepy,* Happy, Doc, Bashful—"

Having counted on her fingers, Sara said, "Wasn't that eight?"

"We went there more than once," she said. "We used to call it the Shrine of Strawberry Shortcake—oh, how I'd like to go again."

"Well, there's nothing there," Juliet said. "I couldn't even see where it was."

"I'm sure I could have. Why didn't I go with you? A summer drive. What strength does it take to ride in a car? Daddy's always saying I haven't the strength."

"You came to meet me."

"Yes I did," said Sara. "But he didn't want me to. I had to throw a fit."

She reached around to pull up the pillows behind her head, but she could not manage it, so Juliet did it for her.

"Drat," said Sara. "What a useless piece of goods I am. I think I could handle a bath, though. What if company comes?"

Juliet asked if she was expecting anybody.

"No. But what if?"

So Juliet took her into the bathroom and Penelope crawled after them. Then when the water was ready and her grandmother hoisted in, Penelope decided that the bath must be for her as well. Juliet undressed her, and the baby and the old woman were bathed together. Though Sara, naked, did not look like an old woman as much as an old girl—a girl, say, who had suffered some exotic, wasting, desiccating disease.

Penelope accepted her presence without alarm, but kept a firm hold on her own duck-shaped yellow soap.

It was in the bath that Sara finally brought herself to ask, circumspectly, about Eric.

"I'm sure he is a nice man," she said.

"Sometimes," said Juliet casually.

"He was so good to his first wife."

"Only wife," Juliet corrected her. "So far."

"But I'm sure now you have this baby—you're happy, I mean. I'm sure you're happy."

"As happy as is consistent with living in sin," Juliet said, surprising her mother by wringing out a dripping washcloth over her soaped head.

"That's what I mean," said Sara after ducking and covering her face, with a joyful shriek. Then, "Juliet?"

"Yes?"

"You know I don't mean it if I ever say mean things about Daddy. I know he loves me. He's just unhappy."

JULIET DREAMED she was a child again and in this house, though the arrangement of the rooms was somewhat different. She looked out the window of one of the unfamiliar rooms, and saw an arc of water sparkling in the air. This water came from the hose. Her father, with his back to her, was watering the garden. A figure moved in and out among the raspberry canes and was revealed, after a while, to be Irene—though a more childish Irene, supple and merry. She was dodging the water sprinkled from the hose. Hiding, reappearing, mostly successful but always caught again for an instant before she ran away. The game was supposed to be lighthearted, but Juliet, behind the window, watched it with disgust. Her father always kept his back to her, yet she believed—she somehow *saw*—that he held the hose low, in front of his body, and that it was only the nozzle of it that he turned back and forth.

The dream was suffused with a sticky horror. Not the kind of horror that jostles its shapes outside your skin, but the kind that curls through the narrowest passages of your blood.

When she woke that feeling was still with her. She found the dream shameful. Obvious, banal. A dirty indulgence of her own.

THERE WAS A KNOCK on the front door in the middle of the afternoon. Nobody used the front door—Juliet found it a bit stiff to open.

The man who stood there wore a well-pressed yellow shirt with short sleeves, and tan pants. He was perhaps a few years older than she was, tall but rather frail-looking, slightly hollow-chested, but vigorous in his greeting, relentless in his smiling.

"I've come to see the lady of the house," he said.

Juliet left him standing there and went into the sunroom.

"There's a man at the door," she said. "He might be selling something. Should I get rid of him?"

Sara was pushing herself up: "No, no," she said breathlessly. "Tidy me a bit, can you? I heard his voice. It's Don. It's my friend Don."

Don had already entered the house and was heard outside the sunroom door.

"No fuss, Sara. It's only me. Are you decent?"

Sara, with a wild and happy look, reached for the hairbrush she could not manage, then gave up and ran her fingers through her hair. Her voice rang out gaily. "I'm as decent as I'll ever be, I'm afraid. Come in here."

The man appeared, hurried up to her, and she lifted her arms to him. "You smell of summer," she said. "What is it?" She fingered his shirt. "Ironing. Ironed cotton. My, that's nice."

"I did it myself," he said. "Sally's over at the church messing about with the flowers. Not a bad job, eh?"

"Lovely," said Sara. "But you almost didn't get in. Juliet thought you were a salesman. Juliet's my daughter. My dear daughter. I told you, didn't I? I told you she was coming. Don is my minister, Juliet. My friend and minister."

Don straightened up, grasped Juliet's hand.

"Good you're here—I'm very glad to meet you. And you weren't so far wrong, actually. I am a sort of salesman."

Juliet smiled politely at the ministerial joke.

"What church are you the minister of?"

The question made Sara laugh. "Oh dear—that gives the show away, doesn't it?"

"I'm from Trinity," said Don, with his unfazed smile. "And as for giving the show away—it's no news to me that Sara and Sam were not involved with any of the churches in the community. I just started dropping in anyway, because your mother is such a charming lady."

Juliet could not remember whether it was the Anglican or United Church that was called Trinity.

"Would you get Don a reasonable sort of chair, dear?" said Sara. "Here he is bending over me like a stork. And some sort of refreshment, Don? Would you like an eggnog? Juliet makes me the most delicious eggnogs. No. No, that's probably too heavy. You've just come in from the heat of the day. Tea? That's hot too. Ginger ale? Some kind of juice? What juice do we have, Juliet?"

Don said, "I don't need anything but a glass of water. That would be welcome."

"No tea? Really?" Sara was quite out of breath. "But I think I'd like some. You could drink half a cup, surely. Juliet?"

IN THE KITCHEN, BY HERSELF—Irene could be seen in the garden, today she was hoeing around the beans—Juliet wondered if the tea was a ruse to get her out of the room for a few private words. A few private words, perhaps even a few words of prayer? The notion sickened her.

Sam and Sara had never belonged to any church, though Sam had told someone, early in their life here, that they were Druids. Word had gone around that they belonged to a church not represented in town, and that information had moved them up a notch from having no religion at all. Juliet herself had gone to Sunday school for a while at the Anglican Church, though that was mostly because she had an Anglican friend. Sam, at school, had never rebelled at having to read the Bible and say the Lord's Prayer every morning, any more than he objected to "God Save the Queen."

"There's times for sticking your neck out and times not to," he had said. "You satisfy them this way, maybe you can get away with telling the kids a few facts about evolution."

Sara had at one time been interested in the Baha'i faith, but Juliet believed that this interest had waned.

She made enough tea for the three of them and found some digestive biscuits in the cupboard—also the brass tray which Sara had usually taken out for fancy occasions.

Don accepted a cup, and gulped down the ice water which she had remembered to bring him, but shook his head at the cookies.

"Not for me, thanks."

He seemed to say this with special emphasis. As if godliness forbade him.

He asked Juliet where she lived, what was the nature of the weather on the west coast, what work her husband did.

"He's a prawn fisherman, but he's actually not my husband," said Juliet pleasantly.

Don nodded. Ah, yes.

"Rough seas out there?"

"Sometimes."

"Whale Bay. I've never heard of it but now I'll remember it. What church do you go to in Whale Bay?"

"We don't go. We don't go to church."

"Is there not a church of your sort handy?"

Smiling, Juliet shook her head.

"There *is* no church of our sort. We don't believe in God."

Don's cup made a little clatter as he set it down in its saucer. He said he was sorry to hear that.

"Truly sorry to hear that. How long have you been of this opinion?"

"I don't know. Ever since I gave it any serious thought."

"And your mother's told me you have a child. You have a little girl, don't you?"

Juliet said yes, she had.

"And she has never been christened? You intend to bring her up a heathen?"

Juliet said that she expected Penelope would make up her own mind about that, someday.

"But we intend to bring her up without religion. Yes."

"That is sad," said Don quietly. "For yourselves, it's sad. You and your—whatever you call him—you've decided to reject God's grace. Well. You are adults. But to reject it for your child—it's like denying her nourishment."

Juliet felt her composure cracking. "But we don't *believe*," she said. "We don't believe in God's grace. It's not like denying her nourishment, it's refusing to bring her up on lies."

"Lies. What millions of people all over the world believe in, you call lies. Don't you think that's a little presumptuous of you, calling God a lie?"

"Millions of people don't believe it, they just go to church," said Juliet, her voice heating. "They just don't think. If there is a God, then God gave me a mind, and didn't he intend me to use it?

"Also," she said, trying to hold herself steady. "Also, millions of people believe something different. They believe in Buddha, for instance. So how does millions of people believing in anything make it true?"

"Christ is alive," said Don readily. "Buddha isn't."

"That's just something to say. What does it mean? I don't see any proof of either one being alive, as far as that goes."

"*You* don't. But others do. Do you know that Henry Ford—Henry Ford the second, who has everything anybody in life could desire—nevertheless he gets down on his knees and prays to God every night of his life?"

"Henry Ford?" cried Juliet. "Henry Ford? What does anything *Henry Ford* does matter to me?"

The argument was taking the course that arguments of this sort are bound to take. The minister's voice, which had started out more sorrowful than angry—though always indicating ironclad conviction—was taking on a shrill and scolding tone, while Juliet, who had begun, as she thought, in reasonable resistance—calm, shrewd, rather maddeningly polite—was now in a cold and biting rage. Both of them cast around for arguments and refutations that would be more insulting than useful.

Meanwhile Sara nibbled on a digestive biscuit, not looking up at them. Now and then she shivered, as if their words struck her, but they were beyond noticing.

What did bring their display to an end was the loud wailing of

Penelope, who had wakened wet and had complained softly for a while, then complained more vigorously, and finally given way to fury. Sara heard her first, and tried to attract their attention.

"Penelope," she said faintly, then, with more effort, "Juliet. Penelope." Juliet and the minister both looked at her distractedly, and then the minister said, with a sudden drop in his voice, "Your baby."

Juliet hurried from the room. She was shaking when she picked Penelope up, she came close to stabbing her when she was pinning on the dry diaper. Penelope stopped crying, not because she was comforted but because she was alarmed by this rough attention. Her wide wet eyes, her astonished stare, broke into Juliet's preoccupation, and she tried to settle herself down, talking as gently as she could and then picking her child up, walking with her up and down the upstairs hall. Penelope was not immediately reassured, but after a few minutes the tension began to leave her body.

Juliet felt the same thing happening to her, and when she thought that a certain amount of control and quiet had returned to both of them, she carried Penelope downstairs.

The minister had come out of Sara's room and was waiting for her. In a voice that might have been contrite, but seemed in fact frightened, he said, "That's a nice baby."

Juliet said, "Thank you."

She thought that now they might properly say good-bye, but something was holding him. He continued to look at her, he did not move away. He put his hand out as if to catch hold of her shoulder, then dropped it.

"Do you know if you have—," he said, then shook his head slightly. The *have* had come out sounding like *hab*.

"Jooze," he said, and slapped his hand against his throat. He waved in the direction of the kitchen.

Juliet's first thought was that he must be drunk. His head was wagging slightly back and forth, his eyes seemed to be filmed over. Had he come here drunk, had he brought something in his pocket? Then she remembered. A girl, a pupil at the school where she had once taught for half a year. This girl, a diabetic, would suffer a kind of seizure, become thick-tongued, distraught, staggering, if she had gone too long without food.

Shifting Penelope to her hip, she took hold of his arm and steadied him along towards the kitchen. Juice. That was what they had given the girl, that was what he was talking about.

"Just a minute, just a minute, you'll be all right," she said. He held himself upright, hands pressed down on the counter, head lowered.

There was no orange juice—she remembered giving Penelope the last of it that morning, thinking she must get more. But there was a bottle of grape soda, which Sam and Irene liked to drink when they came in from work in the garden.

"Here," she said. Managing with one hand, as she was used to doing, she poured out a glassful. "Here." And as he drank she said, "I'm sorry there's no juice. But it's the sugar, isn't it? You have to get some sugar?"

He drank it down, he said, "Yeah. Sugar. Thanks." Already his voice was clearing. She remembered this too, about the girl at the school—how quick and apparently miraculous the recovery. But before he was quite recovered, or quite himself, while he was still holding his head at a slant, he met her eyes. Not on purpose, it seemed, just by chance. The look in his eyes was not grateful, or forgiving—it was not really personal, it was just the raw look of an astounded animal, hanging on to whatever it could find.

And within a few seconds the eyes, the face, became the face of the man, the minister, who set down his glass and without another word fled out of the house.

SARA WAS EITHER ASLEEP or pretending to be, when Juliet went to pick up the tea tray. Her sleeping state, her dozing state, and her waking state had now such delicate and shifting boundaries that it was hard to identify them. At any rate, she spoke, she said in little more than a whisper, "Juliet?"

Juliet paused in the doorway.

"You must think Don is—rather a simpleton," Sara said. "But he isn't well. He's a diabetic. It's serious."

Juliet said, "Yes."

"He needs his faith."

"Foxhole argument," said Juliet, but quietly, and perhaps Sara did not hear, for she went on talking.

"My faith isn't so simple," said Sara, her voice all shaky (and seeming to Juliet, at this moment, strategically pathetic). "I can't describe it. But it's—all I can say—it's *something*. It's a—wonderful—*something*. When it gets really bad for me—when it gets so bad I—you know what I think then? I think, all right. I think— Soon. *Soon I'll see Juliet.*"

Dreaded (Dearest) Eric,

Where to begin? I am fine and Penelope is fine. Considering. She walks confidently now around Sara's bed but is still leery of striking out with no support. The summer heat is amazing, compared with the west coast. Even when it rains. It's a good thing it does rain because Sam is going full-tilt at the market garden business. The other day I rode around with him in the ancient vehicle delivering fresh raspberries and raspberry jam (made by a sort of junior Ilse Koch person who inhabits our kitchen) and newly dug first potatoes of the season. He is quite gung-ho. Sara stays in bed and dozes or looks at outdated fashion magazines. A minister came to visit her and he and I got into a big stupid row about the existence of God or some such hot topic. The visit is going okay though . . .

This was a letter that Juliet found years later. Eric must have saved it by accident—it had no particular importance in their lives.

SHE HAD GONE BACK to the house of her childhood once more, for Sara's funeral, some months after that letter was written. Irene was no longer around, and Juliet had no memory of asking or being told where she was. Most probably she had married. As Sam did again, in a couple of years. He married a fellow teacher, a good-natured, handsome, competent woman. They lived in her house—Sam tore down the house where he and Sara had lived, and extended the garden. When his wife retired, they bought a trailer and began to go on long winter trips. They visited Juliet twice at Whale Bay. Eric took them out in his boat. He and Sam got along well. As Sam said, like a house afire.

When she read the letter, Juliet winced, as anybody does on discovering the preserved and disconcerting voice of some past fabricated self. She wondered at the sprightly cover-up, contrasting with the pain of her memories. Then she thought that some shift must have taken place, at that time, which she had not remembered. Some shift concerning where home was. Not at Whale Bay with Eric but back where it had been before, all her life before.

Because it's what happens at home that you try to protect, as best you can, for as long as you can.

But she had not protected Sara. When Sara had said, *soon I'll see Juliet,* Juliet had found no reply. Could it not have been managed? Why should it have been so difficult? Just to say *Yes.* To Sara it would have meant so much—to herself, surely, so little. But she had turned away, she had carried the tray to the kitchen, and there she washed and dried the cups and also the glass that had held grape soda. She had put everything away.

Passion

~

NOT TOO LONG AGO, Grace went looking for the Traverses' summer house in the Ottawa Valley. She had not been in that part of the country for many years, and of course there had been changes. Highway 7 now avoided towns that it used to go right through, and it went straight in places where, as she remembered, there used to be curves. And this part of the Canadian Shield has many small lakes, which the usual sort of map has no room to identify. Even when she had located Little Sabot Lake, or thought she had, there seemed to be too many roads leading into it from the county road, and then, when she had chosen one of those roads, too many paved roads crossing it, all with names that she did not recall. In fact there had not been any street names when she had been here over forty years ago. And there was no pavement. There was just the one dirt road running towards the lake, then the one dirt road running rather haphazardly along the lake's edge.

Now there was a village. Or a suburb, perhaps you could call it, because she did not see any Post Office or even the most unpromising convenience store. The settlement lay four or five streets deep along the lake, with small houses strung close together on small lots. Some of them were undoubtedly summer places—the windows already boarded up, as was always done for the winter season. But many others showed all the signs of year-round habitation—habitation, in many cases, by people who filled the yards with plastic gym sets and outdoor grills and training bikes and motorcycles and picnic tables, where some of them sat having lunch or beer on this September day which was still warm. And by other people, not so visible—they were students maybe, or old hippies living alone—who put up flags or sheets of tinfoil for curtains. Small, mostly decent, cheap houses, some fixed to withstand the winter, and some not.

Grace would have decided to turn back if she had not seen the octagonal house, with the fretwork along the roof, and the doors in every other wall. The Woodses' house. She had always remembered it as having eight doors, but it seemed there were only four. She had never been inside to see how, or if, the space was divided into rooms. She didn't think any of the Travers family had ever been inside, either. The house was surrounded by great hedges, in the old days, and by the sparkling poplar trees that were always rustled by a wind along the shore. Mr. and Mrs. Woods were old—as Grace was now—and had not seemed to be visited by any friends or children. Their quaint original house had now a forlorn, a mistaken, look. Neighbors with their ghetto blasters and their sometimes dismembered vehicles, their toys and washing, were bunched up against either side of it.

It was the same with the Travers house when she found it, a quarter of a mile or so along this road. The road went past it now, instead of ending there, and the houses on either side were only a few feet away from the wraparound deep verandah.

It had been the first house that Grace had ever seen built in this way—one story high, the main roof continuing without a break out over that verandah, on all sides. Later she had seen many like it, in Australia. A style that made you think of hot summers.

You used to be able to run from the verandah across the dusty end of the driveway, across a sandy trampled patch of weeds and wild strawberries, also the Traverses' property, and then jump—no, actually, wade—into the lake. Now you would hardly be able to see the lake, because of the substantial house—one of the few regular suburban houses here, with a two-car garage—that had been built across that very route.

What was Grace really looking for when she had undertaken this expedition? Maybe the worst thing would have been to get just what she might have thought she was after. Sheltering roof, screened windows, the lake in front, the stand of maple and cedar and balm of Gilead trees behind. Perfect preservation, the past intact, when nothing of the kind could be said of herself. To find something so diminished, still existing but made irrelevant—as the Travers house now seemed to be, with its added dormer windows, its startling blue paint—might be less hurtful in the long run.

And what if you find it gone altogether? You make a fuss. If anybody has come along to listen to you, you bewail the loss. But mightn't a feeling of relief pass over you, of old confusions or obligations wiped away?

MR. TRAVERS had built the house—that is, he had it built, as a surprise wedding present for Mrs. Travers. When Grace first saw it, it would have been perhaps thirty years old. Mrs. Travers' children were widely spaced—Gretchen around twenty-eight or twenty-nine, already married and a mother herself, and Maury twenty-one, going into his last year at college. And then there was Neil, in his midthirties. But Neil was not a Travers. He was Neil Borrow. Mrs. Travers had been married before, to a man who had died. She had earned her living, and supported her child, as a teacher of Business English at a secretarial school. Mr. Travers, when he referred to this time in her life before he met her, spoke of it as a time of hardship almost like penal servitude, something hardly to be made up for by a whole lifetime of comfort, which he would happily provide.

Mrs. Travers herself didn't speak of it this way at all. She had lived with Neil in a big old house broken up into apartments, not far from the railway tracks in the town of Pembroke, and many of the stories she told at the dinner table were about events there, about her fellow tenants, and the French-Canadian landlord, whose harsh French and tangled English she imitated. The stories might have had titles, like the stories of Thurber's that Grace had read in *The Anthology of American Humor,* found unaccountably on the library shelf at the back of her Grade Ten classroom. (Also on that shelf was *The Last of the Barons,* and *Two Years Before the Mast.*)

"The Night Old Mrs. Cromarty Got Out on the Roof." "How the Postman Courted Miss Flowers." "The Dog Who Ate Sardines."

Mr. Travers never told stories and had little to say at dinner, but if he came upon you looking, say, at the fieldstone fireplace, he might say, "Are you interested in rocks?" and tell you where each of them had come from, and how he had searched and searched for the particular pink granite, because Mrs. Travers had once exclaimed over a rock like that, glimpsed in a road cut. Or he might show you such not really unusual features as he himself had added to the house design—the corner cupboard shelves swinging outwards in the kitchen, the storage space under the window seats. He was a tall stooped man with a soft voice and thin hair slicked over his scalp. He wore bathing shoes when he went into the water, and though he did not look fat in his usual clothes, he displayed then a pancake fold of white flesh slopping over the top of his bathing trunks.

GRACE WORKED THAT SUMMER at the hotel at Bailey's Falls, north of Little Sabot Lake. Early in the season the Travers family had come to dinner there. She had not noticed them—they were not at one of her tables and it was a busy night. She was setting up a table for a new party when she realized that someone was waiting to speak to her.

It was Maury. He said, "I was wondering if you would like to go out with me sometime?"

Grace barely looked up from shooting out the silverware. She said, "Is this a dare?" Because his voice was high and nervous and he stood there stiffly, as if forcing himself. And it was known that sometimes a party of young men from the cottages would dare one another to ask a waitress out. It wasn't entirely a joke—they really would show up, if accepted, though sometimes they only meant to park, without taking you to a movie or even for coffee. So it was considered rather shameful, rather hard up, for a girl to agree.

"What?" he said painfully, and then Grace did stop and look at him. It seemed to her that she saw the whole of him in that moment, the true Maury. Scared, fierce, innocent, determined.

"Okay," she said quickly. She might have meant, okay, calm down, I know it's not a dare, I know you wouldn't do that. Or, okay, I'll go out with you. She herself hardly knew which. But he took it as agreement, and at once arranged—without lowering his voice, or noticing the looks he was getting from diners around them—that he would pick her up after work on the following night.

He did take her to the movies. They saw *Father of the Bride.* Grace hated it. She hated girls like Elizabeth Taylor in that movie, she hated spoiled rich girls of whom nothing was ever asked but that they wheedle and demand. Maury said that it was only supposed to be a comedy, but she said that was not the point. She could not make clear what the point was. Anybody would think that it was because she worked as a waitress and was too poor to go to college, and that if she wanted anything like that kind of wedding she would have to spend years saving up to pay for it herself. (Maury did think this, and was stricken with respect for her, almost with reverence.)

She could not explain or quite understand that it wasn't altogether jealousy she felt, it was rage. And not because she couldn't shop like that or dress like that. It was because that was what girls were supposed to be like. That was what men—people, everybody—thought they should be like. Beautiful, treasured, spoiled, selfish, pea-brained. That was what a girl should be, to be fallen in love with. Then she would become a mother and she'd be all mushily devoted to her babies. Not selfish anymore, but just as pea-brained. Forever.

She was fuming about this while sitting beside a boy who had fallen in love with her because he had believed—instantly—in the integrity and uniqueness of her mind and soul, and had seen her poverty as a romantic gloss on that. (He would have known she was poor not just because of the job she was working at but because of her strong Ottawa Valley accent, of which she was as yet unaware.)

He honored her feelings about the movie. Indeed, now that he had listened to her angry struggles to explain, he struggled to tell her something in turn. He said that he saw now that it was not anything so simple, so *feminine,* as jealousy. He saw that. It was that she would not stand for frivolity, was not content to be like most girls. She was special.

Grace always remembered what she was wearing on that night. A dark-blue ballerina skirt, a white blouse, through whose eyelet frills you could see the tops of her breasts, a wide rose-colored elasticized belt. There was a discrepancy, no doubt, between the way she presented herself and the way she wanted to be judged. But nothing about her was dainty or pert or polished in the style of the time. A bit ragged round the edges, in fact, giving herself gypsy airs, with the very cheapest silver-painted bangles, and the long, wild-looking curly dark hair that she had to put into a snood when she waited on tables.

Special.

He had told his mother about her and his mother had said, "You must bring this Grace of yours to dinner."

IT WAS ALL NEW TO HER, all immediately delightful. In fact she fell in love with Mrs. Travers, rather as Maury had fallen in love with her. It was not in her nature, of course, to be so openly dumbfounded, so worshipful, as he was.

GRACE HAD BEEN BROUGHT UP by her aunt and uncle, really her great-aunt and great-uncle. Her mother had died when she was three years old, and her father had moved to Saskatchewan, where he had another family. Her stand-in parents were kind, even proud of her, though bewildered, but they were not given to conversation. The uncle made his living caning chairs, and he had taught Grace how to cane, so that she could help him, and eventually take over as his eyesight failed. But then she had got the job at Bailey's Falls for the summer, and though it was hard for him—for her aunt as well—to let her go, they believed she needed a taste of life before she settled down.

She was twenty years old, and had just finished high school. She should have finished a year ago, but she had made an odd choice. In the very small town where she lived—it was not far from Mrs. Travers' Pembroke—there was nevertheless a high school, which offered five grades, to prepare you for the government exams and what was then called senior matriculation. It was never necessary to study all the subjects offered, and at the end of her first year—what should have been her final year, Grade Thirteen—Grace tried examinations in History and Botany and Zoology and English and Latin and French, receiving unnecessarily high marks. But there she was in September, back again, proposing to study Physics and Chemistry, Trigonometry, Geometry, and Algebra, though these subjects were considered particularly hard for girls. When she had finished that year, she would have covered all Grade Thirteen subjects except Greek and Italian and Spanish and German, which were not taught by any teacher in her school. She did creditably well in all three branches of mathematics and in the sciences, though her results were nothing like so spectacular as the year before. She had even thought, then, of teaching herself Greek and Spanish and

Italian and German so that she could try those exams the next year. But the principal of the school had a talk with her, telling her this was getting her nowhere since she was not going to be able to go to college, and anyway no college course required such a full plate. Why was she doing it? Did she have any plans?

No, said Grace, she just wanted to learn everything you could learn for free. Before she started her career of caning.

It was the principal who knew the manager of the inn, and said he would put in a word for her if she wanted to try for a summer waitressing job. He too mentioned getting a taste of life.

So even the man in charge of all learning in that place did not believe that learning had to do with life. And anybody Grace told about what she had done—she told it to explain why she was late leaving high school—had said something like *you must have been crazy.*

Except for Mrs. Travers, who had been sent to business college instead of a real college because she was told she had to be useful, and who now wished like anything—she said—that she had crammed her mind instead, or first, with what was useless.

"Though you do have to earn a living," she said. "Caning chairs seems like a useful sort of thing to do anyway. We'll have to see."

See what? Grace didn't want to think ahead at all. She wanted life to continue just as it was now. By trading shifts with another girl, she had managed to get Sundays off, from breakfast on. This meant that she always worked late on Saturdays. In effect, it meant that she had traded time with Maury for time with Maury's family. She and Maury could never see a movie now, never have a real date. But he would pick her up when her work was finished, around eleven o'clock, and they would go for a drive, stop for ice cream or a hamburger—Maury was scrupulous about not taking her into a bar, because she was not yet twenty-one—then end up parking somewhere.

Grace's memories of these parking sessions—which might last till one or two in the morning—proved to be much hazier than her memories of sitting at the Traverses' round dining table or—when everybody finally got up and moved, with coffee or fresh drinks—sitting on the tawny leather sofa, the rockers, the cushioned wicker chairs, at the other end of the room. (There was no fuss about doing the dishes and cleaning up the kitchen—a woman Mrs. Travers called "my friend the able Mrs. Abel" would come in the morning.)

Maury always dragged cushions onto the rug and sat there. Gretchen, who never dressed for dinner in anything but jeans or army pants, usually sat cross-legged in a wide chair. Both she and Maury were big and broad-shouldered, with something of their mother's good looks—her wavy caramel-colored hair, and warm hazel eyes. Even, in Maury's case, a dimple. *Cute,* the other waitresses called Maury. They whistled softly. *Hubba hubba.* Mrs. Travers, however, was barely five feet tall, and under her bright muumuus she seemed not fat but sturdily plump, like a child who hasn't stretched up yet. And the shine, the intentness, of her eyes, the gaiety always ready to break out, had not or could not be imitated or inherited. No more than the rough red, almost a rash, on her cheeks. That was probably the result of going out in any weather without taking thought of her complexion, and like her figure, like her muumuus, it showed her independence.

There were sometimes guests, besides family, on these Sunday evenings. A couple, maybe a single person as well, usually close to Mr. and Mrs. Travers' age, and usually resembling them in the way the women would be eager and witty and the men quieter, slower, tolerant. People told amusing stories, in which the joke was often on themselves. (Grace has been an engaging talker for so long now that she sometimes gets sick of herself, and it's hard for her to remember how novel these dinner conversations once seemed to her. Where she came from, most of the lively conversation took the form of dirty jokes, which of course her aunt and uncle did not go in for. On the rare occasions when they had company, there was praise of and apology for the food, discussion of the weather, and a fervent wish for the meal to be finished as soon as possible.)

After dinner at the Traverses', if the evening was cool enough, Mr. Travers lit a fire. They played what Mrs. Travers called "idiotic word games," at which, in fact, people had to be fairly clever, even if they thought up silly definitions. And here was where somebody who had been rather quiet at dinner might begin to shine. Mock arguments could be built up around claims of great absurdity. Gretchen's husband Wat did this, and so after a bit did Grace, to

Mrs. Travers' and Maury's delight (Maury calling out, to every-one's amusement but Grace's own, "See? I told you. She's smart"). And it was Mrs. Travers herself who led the way in this making up of words with outrageous defenses, insuring that the play should not become too serious or any player too anxious.

The only time there was a problem of anyone's being unhappy with a game was when Mavis, who was married to Mrs. Travers' son Neil, came to dinner. Mavis and her two children were staying not far away, at her parents' place down the lake. That night there was only family, and Grace, as Mavis and Neil had been expected to bring their small children. But Mavis came by herself—Neil was a doctor, and it turned out that he was busy in Ottawa that week-end. Mrs. Travers was disappointed but she rallied, calling out in cheerful dismay, "But the children aren't in Ottawa, surely?"

"Unfortunately not," said Mavis. "But they're not being particu-larly charming. I'm sure they'd shriek all through dinner. The baby's got prickly heat and God knows what's the matter with Mikey."

She was a slim suntanned woman in a purple dress, with a matching wide purple band holding back her dark hair. Hand-some, but with little pouches of boredom or disapproval hiding the corners of her mouth. She left most of her dinner untouched on her plate, explaining that she had an allergy to curry.

"Oh, Mavis. What a shame," said Mrs. Travers. "Is this new?"

"Oh no. I've had it for ages but I used to be polite about it. Then I got sick of throwing up half the night."

"If you'd only told me— What can we get you?"

"Don't worry about it, I'm fine. I don't have any appetite any-way, what with the heat and the joys of motherhood."

She lit a cigarette.

Afterwards, in the game, she got into an argument with Wat over a definition he used, and when the dictionary proved it acceptable she said, "Oh, I'm sorry. I guess I'm just outclassed by you people." And when it came time for everybody to hand in their own word on a slip of paper for the next round, she smiled and shook her head.

"I don't have one."

"Oh, Mavis," said Mrs. Travers. And Mr. Travers said, "Come on, Mavis. Any old word will do."

"But I don't have any old word. I'm so sorry. I just feel stupid tonight. The rest of you just play around me."

Which they did, everybody pretending nothing was wrong, while Mavis smoked and continued to smile her determined sweetly hurt unhappy smile. In a little while she got up and said she was awfully tired, and she couldn't leave her children on their grandparents' hands any longer, she'd had a lovely and instructive visit, and she must now go home.

"I have to give you an Oxford dictionary next Christmas," she said to nobody in particular as she went out with a bitter tinkle of a laugh.

The Traverses' dictionary that Wat had used was an American one.

When she was gone none of them looked at each other. Mrs. Travers said, "Gretchen, do you have the strength to make us all a pot of coffee?" And Gretchen went off to the kitchen, muttering, "What fun. Jesus wept."

"Well. Her life is trying," said Mrs. Travers. "With the two little ones."

DURING THE WEEK Grace got a break, for one day, between clearing breakfast and setting up dinner, and when Mrs. Travers found out about this she started driving up to Bailey's Falls to bring her down to the lake for those free hours. Maury would be at work then—he was working for the summer with the road gang repairing Highway 7—and Wat would be in his office in Ottawa and Gretchen would be swimming with the children or rowing with them on the lake. Usually Mrs. Travers herself would announce that she had shopping to do, or preparations to make for supper, or letters to write, and she would leave Grace on her own in the big, cool, shaded living-dining room, with its permanently dented leather sofa and crowded bookshelves.

"Read anything that takes your fancy," Mrs. Travers said. "Or curl up and go to sleep if that's what you'd like. It's a hard job, you must be tired. I'll make sure you're back on time."

Grace never slept. She read. She barely moved, and below her shorts her bare legs became sweaty and stuck to the leather. Perhaps it was because of the intense pleasure of reading. Quite often she saw nothing of Mrs. Travers until it was time for her to be driven back to work.

Mrs. Travers would not start any sort of conversation until enough time had passed for Grace's thoughts to have got loose from whatever book she had been in. Then she might mention having read it herself, and say what she had thought of it—but always in a way that was both thoughtful and lighthearted. For instance she said, about *Anna Karenina,* "I don't know how many times I've read it, but I know that first I identified with Kitty, and then it was Anna—oh, it was awful, with Anna, and now, you know, the last time I found myself sympathizing all the time with Dolly. Dolly when she goes to the country, you know, with all those children, and she has to figure out how to do the washing, there's the problem about the washtubs—I suppose that's just how your sympathies change as you get older. Passion gets pushed behind the washtubs. Don't pay any attention to me, anyway. You don't, do you?"

"I don't know if I pay much attention to anybody." Grace was surprised at herself and wondered if she sounded conceited or juvenile. "But I like listening to you talk."

Mrs. Travers laughed. "I like listening to myself."

SOMEHOW, AROUND THIS TIME, Maury had begun to talk about their being married. This would not happen for quite a while—not until after he was qualified and working as an engineer—but he spoke of it as of something that she as well as he must be taking for granted. *When we are married,* he would say, and instead of questioning or contradicting him, Grace would listen curiously.

When they were married they would have a place on Little Sabot Lake. Not too close to his parents, not too far away. It would be just a summer place, of course. The rest of the time they would live wherever his work as an engineer should take them. That might be anywhere—Peru, Iraq, the Northwest Territories. Grace was delighted by the idea of such travels—rather more than she was delighted by the idea of what he spoke of, with a severe pride, as *our own home.* None of this seemed at all real to her, but then, the idea of helping her uncle, of taking on the life of a chair caner, in the town and the very house where she had grown up, had never seemed real either.

Maury kept asking her what she had told her aunt and uncle about him, when she was going to take him home to meet them. Even his easy use of that word—*home*—seemed slightly off kilter to her, though surely it was one she herself had used. It seemed more fitting to say *my aunt and uncle's house.*

In fact she had said nothing in her brief weekly letters, except to mention that she was "going out with a boy who works around here for the summer." She might have given the impression that he worked at the hotel.

It wasn't as if she had never thought of getting married. That possibility—half a certainty—had been in her thoughts, along with the life of caning chairs. In spite of the fact that nobody had ever courted her, she had thought that it would happen, someday, and in exactly this way, with the man making up his mind immediately. He would see her—perhaps he would have brought a chair to be fixed—and seeing her, he would fall in love. He would be handsome, like Maury. Passionate, like Maury. Pleasurable physical intimacies would follow.

This was the thing that had not happened. In Maury's car, or out on the grass under the stars, she was willing. And Maury was ready, but not willing. He felt it his responsibility to protect her. And the ease with which she offered herself threw him off balance. He sensed, perhaps, that it was cold. A deliberate offering which he could not understand and which did not fit in at all with his notions of her. She herself did not understand how cold she was—she believed that her show of eagerness must be leading to the pleasures she knew about, in solitude and imagining, and she felt it was up to Maury to take over. Which he would not do.

These sieges left them both disturbed and slightly angry or ashamed, so that they could not stop kissing, clinging, using fond words, to make it up to each other as they said good night. It was a relief to Grace to be alone, to get into bed in the dormitory and blot the last couple of hours out of her mind. And she thought it must be a relief to Maury to be driving down the highway by himself, rearranging his impressions of his Grace so that he could stay wholeheartedly in love with her.

.   .   .

MOST OF THE WAITRESSES left after Labour Day to go back to school or college. But the hotel was staying open till Thanksgiving with a reduced staff—Grace among them. There was talk, this year, about opening again in early December for a winter season, or at least a Christmas season, but nobody amongst the kitchen or dining-room staff seemed to know if this would really happen. Grace wrote to her aunt and uncle as if the Christmas season was a certainty. In fact she did not mention any closing at all, unless possibly after New Year's. So they should not expect her.

Why did she do this? It was not as if she had any other plans. She had told Maury that she thought she should spend this one year helping her uncle, maybe trying to find somebody else to learn caning, while he, Maury, was taking his final year at college. She had even promised to have him visit at Christmas so that he could meet her family. And he had said that Christmas would be a good time to make their engagement formal. He was saving from his summer wages to buy her a diamond ring.

She too had been saving her wages. So she would be able to take the bus to Kingston, to visit him during his school term.

She spoke of this, promised it, so easily. But did she believe, or even wish, that it would happen?

"Maury is a sterling character," said Mrs. Travers. "Well, you can see that for yourself. He will be a dear uncomplicated man, like his father. Not like his brother. His brother Neil is very bright. I don't mean that Maury isn't, you certainly don't get to be an engineer without a brain or two in your head, but Neil is—he's deep." She laughed at herself. "*Deep unfathomable caves of ocean bear*—what am I talking about? A long time Neil and I didn't have anybody but each other. So I think he's special. I don't mean he can't be fun. But sometimes people who are the most fun can be melancholy, can't they? You wonder about them. But what's the use of worrying about your grown-up children? With Neil I worry a bit, with Maury only a tiny little bit. And Gretchen I don't worry about at all. Because women always have got something, haven't they, to keep them going? That men haven't got."

.   .   .

THE HOUSE ON THE LAKE was never closed up till Thanksgiving. Gretchen and the children had to go back to Ottawa, of course, because of school. And Maury, whose job was finished, had to go to Kingston. Mr. Travers would come out only on weekends. But usually, Mrs. Travers had told Grace, she stayed on, sometimes with guests, sometimes by herself.

Then her plans were changed. She went back to Ottawa with Mr. Travers in September. This happened unexpectedly—the weekend dinner was cancelled.

Maury said that she got into trouble, now and then, with her nerves. "She has to have a rest," he said. "She has to go into the hospital for a couple of weeks or so and they get her stabilized. She always comes out fine."

Grace said that his mother was the last person she would have expected to have such troubles.

"What brings it on?"

"I don't think they know," Maury said.

But after a moment he said, "Well. It could be her husband. I mean, her first husband. Neil's father. What happened with him, et cetera."

What had happened was that Neil's father had killed himself.

"He was unstable, I guess.

"But it maybe isn't that," he continued. "It could be other stuff. Problems women have around her age. It's okay though—they can get her straightened around easy now, with drugs. They've got terrific drugs. Not to worry about it."

BY THANKSGIVING, as Maury had predicted, Mrs. Travers was out of the hospital and feeling well. Thanksgiving dinner was taking place at the lake as usual. And it was being held on Sunday—that was also as usual, to allow for packing up and closing the house on Monday. And it was fortunate for Grace, because Sunday had remained her day off.

The whole family would be there. No guests—unless you counted Grace. Neil and Mavis and their children would be staying at Mavis' parents' place, and having dinner there on Monday, but they would be spending Sunday at the Traverses'.

By the time Maury brought Grace down to the lake on Sunday

morning, the turkey was already in the oven. Because of the children, dinner would be early, around five o'clock. The pies were on the kitchen counter—pumpkin, apple, wild blueberry. Gretchen was in charge of the kitchen—as coordinated a cook as she was an athlete. Mrs. Travers sat at the kitchen table, drinking coffee and working at a jigsaw puzzle with Gretchen's younger daughter, Dana.

"Ah, Grace," she said, jumping up for an embrace—the first time she had ever done this—and with a clumsy motion of her hand scattering the jigsaw pieces.

Dana wailed, *"Grandma,"* and her older sister, Janey, who had been watching critically, scooped up the pieces.

"We can put them back together," she said. "Grandma didn't mean to."

"Where do you keep the cranberry sauce?" said Gretchen.

"In the cupboard," said Mrs. Travers, still squeezing Grace's arms and ignoring the destroyed puzzle.

"Where in the cupboard?"

"Oh. Cranberry sauce," Mrs. Travers said. "Well—I make it. First I put the cranberries in a little water. Then I keep it on low heat—no, I think I soak them first—"

"Well, I haven't got time for all that," Gretchen said. "You mean you don't have any canned?"

"I guess not. I must not have, because I make it."

"I'll have to send somebody to get some."

"Maybe you could ask Mrs. Woods?"

"No. I've hardly even spoken to her. I haven't got the nerve. Somebody'll have to go to the store."

"Dear—it's Thanksgiving," said Mrs. Travers gently. "Nowhere will be open."

"That place down the highway, it's always open." Gretchen raised her voice. "Where's Wat?"

"He's out in the rowboat," called Mavis from the back bedroom. She made it sound like a warning, because she was trying to get her baby to sleep. "He took Mikey out in the boat."

Mavis had driven over in her own car with Mikey and the baby. Neil was coming later—he had some phone calls to make.

And Mr. Travers had gone golfing.

"It's just that I need somebody to go to the store," Gretchen said.

She waited, but no offer came from the bedroom. She raised her eyebrows at Grace.

"You can't drive, can you?"

Grace said no.

Mrs. Travers looked around to see where her chair was, and sat down, with a grateful sigh.

"Well," said Gretchen. "Maury can drive. Where's Maury?"

Maury was in the front bedroom looking for his swimming trunks, though everybody had told him that the water would be too cold for swimming. He said the store would not be open.

"It will be," said Gretchen. "They sell gas. And if it isn't there's that one just coming into Perth, you know, with the ice-cream cones—"

Maury wanted Grace to come with him, but the two little girls, Janey and Dana, were pulling her to come with them to see the swing their grandfather had put up under the Norway maple at the side of the house.

Going down the steps, she felt the strap of one of her sandals break. She took both shoes off and walked without difficulty on the sandy soil, the flat-pressed plantain, and the many curled leaves that had already fallen.

First she pushed the children in the swing, then they pushed her. It was when she jumped off, barefoot, that one leg crumpled and she let out a yelp of pain, not knowing what had happened.

It was her foot, not her leg. The pain had shot up from the sole of her left foot, which had been cut by the sharp edge of a clamshell.

"Dana brought those shells," Janey said. "She was going to make a house for her snail."

"He got away," said Dana.

Gretchen and Mrs. Travers and even Mavis had come hurrying out of the house, thinking the cry came from one of the children.

"She's got a bloody foot," said Dana. "There's blood all over the ground."

Janey said, "She cut it on a shell. Dana left those shells here, she was going to build a house for Ivan. Ivan her snail."

Then there was a basin brought out, water to wash the cut, a towel, and everyone was asking how much it hurt.

"Not too bad," said Grace, limping to the steps, with both little girls competing to hold her up and generally getting in her way.

"Oh, that's nasty," Gretchen said. "But why weren't you wearing your shoes?"

"Broke her strap," said Dana and Janey together, as a wine-colored convertible, making very little sound, swerved neatly round in the parking space.

"Now, that is what I call opportune," said Mrs. Travers. "Here's the very man we need. The doctor."

This was Neil, the first time Grace had ever seen him. He was tall, spare, quick-moving.

"Your bag," cried Mrs. Travers gaily. "We've already got a case for you."

"Nice piece of junk you've got there," said Gretchen. "New?"

Neil said, "Piece of folly."

"Now the baby's wakened." Mavis gave a sigh of unspecific accusation and she went back into the house.

Janey said severely, "You can't do anything without that baby waking up."

"*You* better be quiet," said Gretchen.

"Don't tell me you haven't got it with you," said Mrs. Travers. But Neil swung a doctor's bag out of the backseat, and she said, "Oh, yes you have, that's good, you never know."

"You the patient?" Neil said to Dana. "What's the matter? Swallow a toad?"

"It's her," said Dana with dignity. "It's *Grace*."

"I see. She swallowed the toad."

"She *cut her foot*. It's bleeding and bleeding."

"On a clamshell," said Janey.

Now Neil said "Move over" to his nieces, and sat on the step below Grace, and carefully lifted the foot and said, "Give me that cloth or whatever," then carefully blotted away the blood to get a look at the cut. Now that he was so close to her, Grace noticed a smell she had learned to identify this summer working at the inn—the smell of liquor edged with mint.

"It sure is," he said. "It's bleeding and bleeding. That's a good thing, clean it out. Hurts?"

Grace said, "Some."

He looked searchingly, though briefly, into her face. Perhaps wondering if she had caught the smell, and what she thought about it.

"I bet. See that flap? We have to get under there and make sure it's clean, then I'll put a stitch or two in it. I've got some stuff I can rub on so that won't hurt as bad as you might think." He looked up at Gretchen. "Hey. Let's get the audience out of the way here."

He had not spoken a word, as yet, to his mother, who now repeated that it was such a good thing that he had come along just when he did.

"Boy Scout," he said. "Always at the ready."

His hands didn't feel drunk, and his eyes didn't look it. Neither did he look like the jolly uncle he had impersonated when he talked to the children, or the purveyor of reassuring patter he had chosen to be with Grace. He had a high pale forehead, a crest of tight curly gray-black hair, bright gray eyes, a wide thin-lipped mouth that seemed to curl in on some vigorous impatience, or appetite, or pain.

When the cut had been bandaged, out on the steps—Gretchen having gone back to the kitchen and made the children come with her, but Mrs. Travers remaining, watching intently, with her lips pressed together as if promising that she would not make any interruptions—Neil said that he thought it would be a good idea to run Grace into town, to the hospital.

"For an anti-tetanus shot."

"It doesn't feel too bad," said Grace.

Neil said, "That's not the point."

"I agree," said Mrs. Travers. "Tetanus—that's terrible."

"We shouldn't be long," he said. "Here. Grace? Grace, I'll get you to the car." He held her under one arm. She had strapped on the one sandal, and managed to get her toes into the other so that she could drag it along. The bandage was very neat and tight.

"I'll just run in," he said, when she was sitting in the car. "Make my apologies."

To Gretchen? To Mavis.

Mrs. Travers came down from the verandah, wearing the look of hazy enthusiasm that seemed natural to her, and indeed irrepressible, on this day. She put her hand on the car door.

"This is good," she said. "This is very good. Grace, you are a godsend. You'll try to keep him away from drinking today, won't you? You'll know how to do it."

Grace heard these words, but gave them hardly any thought. She was too dismayed by the change in Mrs. Travers, by what looked like an increase in bulk, a stiffness in all her movements, a random and rather frantic air of benevolence, a weepy gladness leaking out of her eyes. And a faint crust showing at the corners of her mouth, like sugar.

THE HOSPITAL was in Carleton Place, three miles away. There was a highway overpass above the railway tracks, and they took this at such speed that Grace had the impression that at its crest the car had lifted off the pavement, they were flying. There was hardly any traffic about, she was not frightened, and anyway there was nothing she could do.

NEIL KNEW THE NURSE who was on duty in Emergency, and after he had filled out a form and let her take a passing look at Grace's foot ("Nice job," she said without interest), he was able to go ahead and give the tetanus shot himself. ("It won't hurt now, but it could later.") Just as he finished, the nurse came back into the cubicle and said, "There's a guy in the waiting room to take her home."

She said to Grace, "He says he's your fiancé."

"Tell him she's not ready yet," Neil said. "No. Tell him we've already gone."

"I said you were in here."

"But when you came back," said Neil, "we were gone."

"He said you were his brother. Won't he see your car in the lot?"

"I parked out back. I parked in the doctors' lot."

"Pret-ty tric-ky," said the nurse, over her shoulder.

And Neil said to Grace, "You didn't want to go home yet, did you?"

"No," said Grace, as if she'd seen the word written in front of her, on the wall. As if she was having her eyes tested.

Once more she was helped to the car, sandal flopping from the toe strap, and settled on the creamy upholstery. They took a back street out of the lot, an unfamiliar way out of the town. She knew they wouldn't see Maury. She did not have to think of him. Still less of Mavis.

Describing this passage, this change in her life, later on, Grace might say—she did say—that it was as if a gate had clanged shut behind her. But at the time there was no clang—acquiescence simply rippled through her, the rights of those left behind were smoothly cancelled.

Her memory of this day remained clear and detailed, though there was a variation in the parts of it she dwelt on.

And even in some of those details she must have been wrong.

FIRST THEY DROVE WEST on Highway 7. In Grace's recollection, there is not another car on the highway, and their speed approaches the flight on the highway overpass. This cannot have been true—there must have been people on the road, people on their way home that Sunday morning, on their way to spend Thanksgiving with their families. On their way to church or coming home from church. Neil must have slowed down when driving through villages or the edges of towns, and for the many curves on the old highway. She was not used to driving in a convertible with the top down, wind in her eyes, wind taking charge of her hair. That gave her the illusion of constant speed, perfect flight—not frantic but miraculous, serene.

And though Maury and Mavis and the rest of the family were wiped from her mind, some scrap of Mrs. Travers did remain, hovering, delivering in a whisper and with a strange, shamed giggle, her last message.

You'll know how to do it.

Grace and Neil did not talk, of course. As she remembers it, you would have had to scream to be heard. And what she remembers is, to tell the truth, hardly distinguishable from her idea, her fantasies at that time, of what sex should be like. The fortuitous meeting, the muted but powerful signals, the nearly silent flight in which she herself would figure more or less as a captive. An airy surrender, flesh nothing now but a stream of desire.

They stopped, finally, at Kaladar, and went into the hotel—the old hotel which is still there. Taking her hand, kneading his fingers between hers, slowing his pace to match her uneven steps.

Neil led her into the bar. She recognized it as a bar, though she had never been in one before. (Bailey's Falls Inn did not yet have a license—drinking was done in people's rooms, or in a rather ramshackle so-called nightclub across the road.) This was just as she would have expected—an airless darkened big room, with the chairs and tables put back in a careless way after a hasty cleanup, a smell of Lysol not erasing the smell of beer, whisky, cigars, pipes, men.

There was nobody there—perhaps it wasn't open till afternoon. But might it not now be afternoon? Her idea of time seemed faulty.

Now a man came in from another room, and spoke to Neil. He said, "Hello there, Doc," and went behind the bar.

Grace believed that it would be like this—everywhere they went, there would be somebody Neil knew already.

"You know it's Sunday," the man said in a raised, stern, almost shouting voice, as if he wanted to be heard out in the parking lot. "I can't sell you anything in here on a Sunday. And I can't sell anything to her, ever. She shouldn't even be in here. You understand that?"

"Oh yes, sir. Yes indeed, sir," said Neil. "I heartily agree, sir."

While both men were talking, the man behind the bar had taken a bottle of whisky from a hidden shelf and poured some into a glass and shoved it to Neil across the counter.

"You thirsty?" he said to Grace. He was already opening a Coke. He gave it to her without a glass.

Neil put a bill on the counter and the man shoved it away.

"I told you," he said. "Can't sell."

"What about the Coke?" said Neil.

"Can't sell."

The man put the bottle away, Neil drank what was in the glass very quickly. "You're a good man," he said. "Spirit of the law."

"Take the Coke along with you. Sooner she's out of here the happier I'll be."

"You bet," Neil said. "She's a good girl. My sister-in-law. Future sister-in-law. So I understand."

"Is that the truth?"

They didn't go back to Highway 7. Instead they took the road north, which was not paved, but wide enough and decently graded.

The drink seemed to have had the opposite effect to what drinks were supposed to have on Neil's driving. He had slowed down to the seemly, even cautious, rate this road required.

"You don't mind?" he said.

Grace said, "Mind what?"

"Being dragged into any old place."

"No."

"I need your company. How's your foot?"

"It's fine."

"It must hurt some."

"Not really. It's okay."

He picked up the hand that was not holding the Coke bottle, pressed the palm of it to his mouth, gave it a lick, and let it drop.

"Did you think I was abducting you for fell purposes?"

"No," lied Grace, thinking how like his mother that word was. *Fell.*

"There was a time when you would have been right," he said, just as if she had answered yes. "But not today. I don't think so. You're safe as a church today."

The changed tone of his voice, which had become intimate, frank, and quiet, and the memory of his lips pressed to, then his tongue flicked across, her skin, affected Grace to such an extent that she was hearing the words, but not the sense, of what he was telling her. She could feel a hundred, hundreds of flicks of his tongue, a dance of supplication, all over her skin. But she thought to say, "Churches aren't always safe."

"True. True."

"And I'm not your sister-in-law."

"Future. Didn't I say future?"

"I'm not that either."

"Oh. Well. I guess I'm not surprised. No. Not surprised."

Then his voice changed again, became businesslike.

"I'm looking for a turnoff up here, to the right. There's a road I ought to recognize. Do you know this country at all?"

"Not around here, no."

"Don't know Flower Station? Oompah, Poland? Snow Road?"

She had not heard of them.

"There's somebody I want to see."

A turn was made, to the right, with some dubious mutterings on his part. There were no signs. This road was narrower and rougher, with a one-lane plank-floored bridge. The trees of the hardwood forest laced their branches overhead. The leaves were late to turn this year because of the strangely warm weather, so these branches were still green, except for the odd one here and there that flashed out like a banner. There was a feeling of sanctuary. For miles Neil and Grace were quiet, and there was still no break in the trees, no end to the forest. But then Neil broke the peace.

He said, "Can you drive?" and when Grace said no, he said, "I think you should learn."

He meant, right then. He stopped the car, got out and came around to her side, and she had to move behind the wheel.

"No better place than this."

"What if something comes?"

"Nothing will. We can manage if it does. That's why I picked a straight stretch. And don't worry, you do all the work with your right foot."

They were at the beginning of a long tunnel under the trees, the ground splashed with sunlight. He did not bother explaining anything about how cars ran—he simply showed her where to put her foot, and made her practice shifting the gears, then said, "Now go, and do what I tell you."

The first leap of the car terrified her. She ground the gears, and she thought he would put an end to the lesson immediately, but he laughed. He said, "Whoa, easy. Easy. Keep going," and she did. He did not comment on her steering, or the way the steering made her forget about the accelerator, except to say, "Keep going, keep going, keep on the road, don't let the engine die."

"When can I stop?" she said.

"Not till I tell you how."

He made her keep driving until they came out of the tunnel, and then instructed her about the brake. As soon as she had stopped she opened the door so that they could trade sides, but he said, "No. This is just a breather. Soon you'll be getting to like it." And when they started again she began to see that he might be right. Her momentary surge of confidence almost took them into the ditch. Still, he laughed when he had to grab the wheel, and the lesson continued.

He did not let her stop until they had driven for what seemed miles, and even gone—slowly—around several curves. Then he said they had better switch, because he could not get a feeling of direction unless he was driving.

He asked how she felt now, and though she was shaking all over, she said, "Okay."

He rubbed her arm from shoulder to elbow and said, "What a liar." But he did not touch her, beyond that, did not let any part of her feel his mouth again.

He must have got the feeling of direction back some miles on when they came to a crossroads, for he turned left, and the trees thinned out and they climbed a rough road up a long hill, and after a few miles they came to a village, or at least a roadside collection of buildings. A church and a store, neither of them open to serve their original purposes, but probably lived in, to judge by vehicles around them and the sorry-looking curtains in the windows. A couple of houses in the same state and behind one of them a barn that had fallen in on itself, with old dark hay bulging out between its cracked beams like swollen innards.

Neil exclaimed in celebration at the sight of this place, but did not stop there.

"What a relief," he said. "What—a—relief. Now I know. Thank you."

"Me?"

"For letting me teach you to drive. It calmed me down."

"Calmed you down?" said Grace. "Really?"

"True as I live." Neil was smiling, but did not look at her. He was busy looking from side to side across the fields that lay along the road after it had passed through the village. He was talking as if to himself.

"This is it. Got to be it. Now we know."

And so on, till he turned onto a lane that didn't go straight but wound around through a field, avoiding rocks and patches of juniper. At the end of the lane was a house in no better shape than the houses in the village.

"Now, this place," he said, "this place I am not going to take you in. I won't be five minutes."

HE WAS longer than that.

She sat in the car, in the house's shade. The door to the house was open, just the screen door closed. The screen had mended patches in it, newer wire woven in with the old. Nobody came to look at her, not even a dog. And now that the car had stopped, the day filled up with an unnatural silence. Unnatural because you would expect such a hot afternoon to be full of the buzzing and humming and chirping of insects in the grass, in the juniper bushes. Even if you couldn't see them anywhere, their noise would seem to rise out of everything growing on the earth, as far as the horizon. But it was too late in the year, maybe too late even to hear geese honking as they flew south. At any rate, she didn't hear any.

It seemed they were up on top of the world here, or on one of the tops. The field fell away on all sides, the trees around being only partly visible because they grew on lower ground.

Who did he know here, who lived in this house? A woman? It didn't seem possible that the sort of woman he would want could live in a place like this, but there was no end to the strangeness Grace could encounter today. No end to it.

Once this had been a brick house, but someone had begun to take the brick walls down. Plain wooden walls had been bared, underneath, and the bricks that had covered them were roughly piled in the yard, maybe waiting to be sold. The bricks left on this wall of the house formed a diagonal line, stairsteps, and Grace, with nothing to do, leaned back, pushed her seat back, in order to count them. She did this both foolishly and seriously, the way you could pull petals off a flower, but not with any words so blatant as *He loves me, he loves me not.*

Lucky. Not. Lucky. Not. That was all she dared.

She found that it was hard to keep track of bricks arranged in this zigzag fashion, especially since the line flattened out above the door.

She knew. What else could this be? A bootlegger's place. She thought of the bootlegger at home—a raddled, skinny old man, morose and suspicious. He sat on his front step with a shotgun on Halloween night. And he painted numbers on the sticks of firewood stacked by his door so he'd know if any were stolen. She thought of him—or this one—dozing in the heat in his dirty but tidy room (she knew it would be that way by the mended patches in the screen). Getting up from his creaky cot or couch, with the stained quilt on it that some woman relative of his, some woman now dead, had made long ago.

Not that she had ever been inside a bootlegger's house, but the partitions were thin, at home, between some threadbare ways of living that were respectable, and some that were not. She knew how things were.

How strange that she'd thought of marrying Maury. A kind of treachery it would be. A treachery to herself. But not a treachery to be riding with Neil, because he knew some of the same things she did. And she knew more and more, all the time, about him.

And now in the doorway it seemed that she could see her uncle, stooped and baffled, looking out at her, as if she had been away for years and years. As if she had promised to go home and then she had forgotten about it, and in all this time he should have died but he hadn't.

She struggled to speak to him, but he was lost. She was waking up, moving. She was in the car with Neil, on the road again. She had been asleep with her mouth open and she was thirsty. He turned to her for a moment, and she noticed, even with the wind that they made blowing round them, a fresh smell of whisky.

It was true.

"You awake? You were fast asleep when I came out of there," he said. "Sorry—I had to be sociable for a while. How's your bladder?"

That was a problem she had been thinking about, in fact, when they were stopped at the house. She had seen a toilet back there, beyond the house, but had felt shy about getting out and walking to it.

He said, "This looks like a possible place," and stopped the car. She got out and walked in amongst some blooming goldenrod and Queen Anne's lace and wild aster, to squat down. He stood in such flowers on the other side of the road, with his back to her. When she got back into the car she saw the bottle on the floor beside her feet. More than a third of its contents seemed already to be gone.

He saw her looking.

"Oh, don't worry," he said. "I just poured some in here." He held up a flask. "Easier when I'm driving."

On the floor there was also another Coca-Cola. He told her to look in the glove compartment and find the bottle opener.

"It's cold," she said in surprise.

"Icebox. They cut ice off the lakes in the winter and store it in sawdust. He keeps it under the house."

"I thought I saw my uncle in the doorway of that house," she said. "But I was dreaming."

"You could tell me about your uncle. Tell me about where you live. Your job. Anything. I just like to hear you talk."

There was a new strength in his voice, and a change in his face, but it wasn't any manic glow of drunkenness. It was just as if he'd been sick—not terribly sick, just down, under the weather—and was now wanting to assure you he was better. He capped the flask and laid it down and reached for her hand. He held it lightly, a comrade's clasp.

"He's quite old," said Grace. "He's really my great-uncle. He's a caner—that means he canes chairs. I can't explain that to you, but I could show you if we had a chair to cane—"

"I don't see one."

She laughed, and said, "It's boring, really."

"Tell me about what interests you, then. What interests you?"

She said, "You do."

"Oh. What interests you about me?" His hand slid away.

"What you're doing now," said Grace determinedly. "Why."

"You mean drinking? Why I'm drinking?" The cap came off the flask again. "Why don't you ask me?"

"Because I know what you'd say."

"What's that? What would I say?"

"You'd say, what else is there to do? Or something like that."

"That's true," he said. "That's about what I'd say. Well, then you'd try to tell me why I was wrong."

"No," said Grace. "No. I wouldn't."

When she'd said that, she felt cold. She had thought she was serious, but now she saw that she'd been trying to impress him with these answers, trying to show herself as worldly as he was, and in the middle of that she had come on this rock-bottom truth. This lack of hope—genuine, reasonable, and everlasting.

Neil said, "You wouldn't? No. You wouldn't. That's a relief. You are a relief, Grace."

In a while, he said, "You know—I'm sleepy. Soon as we find a good spot I'm going to pull over and go to sleep. Just for a little while. You don't mind that?"

"No. I think you should."

"You'll watch over me?"

"Yes."

"Good."

The spot he found was in a little town called Fortune. There was a park on the outskirts, beside a river, and a gravelled space for cars. He settled the seat back, and at once fell asleep. Evening had come on as it did now, around suppertime, proving that this wasn't a summer day after all. A short while ago people had been having a Thanksgiving picnic here—there was still some smoke rising from the outdoor fireplace, and a smell of hamburgers in the air. The smell did not make Grace hungry, exactly—it made her remember being hungry in other circumstances.

He went to sleep immediately, and she got out. Some dust had settled on her with all the stopping and starting of her driving lesson. She washed her arms and hands and her face as well as she could at an outdoor tap. Then, favoring her cut foot, she walked slowly to the edge of the river, saw how shallow it was, with reeds breaking the surface. A sign there warned that profanity, obscenity, or vulgar language was forbidden in this place and would be punished.

She tried the swings, which faced west. Pumping herself high, she looked into the clear sky—faint green, fading gold, a fierce pink rim at the horizon. Already the air was getting cold.

She'd thought it was touch. Mouths, tongues, skin, bodies, banging bone on bone. Inflammation. Passion. But that wasn't what had been meant for them at all. That was child's play, compared to how she knew him, how far she'd seen into him, now.

What she had seen was final. As if she was at the edge of a flat dark body of water that stretched on and on. Cold, level water. Looking out at such dark, cold, level water, and knowing it was all there was.

It wasn't the drinking that was responsible. The same thing was waiting, no matter what, and all the time. Drinking, needing to drink—that was just some sort of distraction, like everything else.

She went back to the car and tried to wake him up. He stirred but wouldn't waken. So she walked around again to keep warm, and to practice the easiest way with her foot—she understood now that she would be working again, serving breakfast, in the morning.

She tried once more, talking to him urgently. He answered with various promises and mutters, and once more he fell asleep. By the time it was really dark she had given up. Now with the cold of night settled in some other facts became clear to her. That they could not remain here, that they were still in the world after all. That she had to get back to Bailey's Falls.

With some difficulty she got him over into the passenger seat. If that did not wake him, it was clear nothing could. She took a while to figure out how the headlights went on, and then she began to move the car, jerkily, slowly, back onto the road.

She had no idea of directions, and there was not a soul on the street to ask. She just kept driving to the other side of the town, and there, most blessedly, there was a sign pointing the way to Bailey's Falls, among other places. Only nine miles.

She drove along the two-lane highway at never more than thirty miles an hour. There was little traffic. Once or twice a car passed her, honking, and the few she met honked also. In one case it was probably because she was going so slowly, and in the other, because she did not know how to dim the lights. Never mind. She couldn't stop to get her courage up again in the middle of the road. She could just keep going, as he had said. Keep going.

At first she did not recognize Bailey's Falls, coming upon it in this unfamiliar way. When she did, she became more frightened than she had been in all the nine miles. It was one thing to drive in unknown territory, another to turn in at the inn gates.

He was awake when she got stopped in the parking lot. He didn't show any surprise at where they were, or at what she had done. In fact, he told her, the honking had wakened him, miles back, but he had pretended to be still asleep, because the important thing was not to startle her. He hadn't been worried, though. He knew she would make it.

She asked if he was awake enough to drive now.

"Wide-awake. Bright as a dollar."

He told her to slip her foot out of its sandal, and he felt and pressed it here and there before saying, "Nice. No heat. No swelling. Your arm hurt? Maybe it won't." He walked her to the door, and thanked her for her company. She was still amazed to be safely back. She hardly realized it was time to say good-bye.

As a matter of fact she does not know to this day if those words were spoken, or if he only caught her, wound his arms around her, held her so tightly, with such continual, changing pressures that it seemed more than two arms were needed, that she was surrounded by him, his body strong and light, demanding and renouncing all at once, as if he was telling her she was wrong to give up on him, everything was possible, but then again that she was not wrong, he meant to stamp himself on her and go.

EARLY IN THE MORNING, the manager knocked on the dormitory door, calling for Grace.

"Somebody on the phone," he said. "Don't bother, they just wanted to know if you were here. I said I'd go and check. Okay now."

It would be Maury, she thought. One of them, anyway. But probably Maury. Now she'd have to deal with Maury.

When she went down to serve breakfast—wearing her canvas shoes—she heard about the accident. A car had gone into a bridge abutment halfway down the road to Little Sabot Lake. It had been rammed right in, it was totally smashed and burned up. There were no other cars involved, and apparently no passengers. The driver would have to be identified by dental records. Or probably had been, by this time.

"One hell of a way," the manager said. "Better to go and cut your throat."

"It could've been an accident," said the cook, who had an optimistic nature. "Could've just fell asleep."

"Yeah. Sure."

Her arm hurt now as if it had taken a wicked blow. She couldn't balance her tray but had to carry it in front of her, using both hands.

SHE DID NOT have to deal with Maury face-to-face. He wrote her a letter.

Just say he made you do it. Just say you didn't want to go.

She wrote back five words. *I did want to go.* She was going to add *I'm sorry,* but stopped herself.

MR. TRAVERS came to the inn to see her. He was polite and businesslike, firm, cool, not unkind. She saw him now in circumstances that let him come into his own. A man who could take charge, who could tidy things up. He said that it was very sad, they were all very sad, but that alcoholism was a terrible thing. When Mrs. Travers was a little better he was going to take her on a trip, a vacation, somewhere warm.

Then he said that he had to be going, many things to do. As he shook her hand good-bye he put an envelope into it.

"We both hope you'll make good use of this," he said.

The cheque was for one thousand dollars. Immediately she thought of sending it back or tearing it up, and sometimes even now she thinks that would have been a grand thing to do. But in the end, of course, she was not able to do it. In those days, it was enough money to insure her a start in life.

The View from Castle Rock

∾

THE FIRST TIME Andrew was ever in Edinburgh he was ten years old. With his father and some other men he climbed a slippery black street. It was raining, the city smell of smoke filled the air, and the half-doors were open, showing the firelit insides of taverns which he hoped they might enter, because he was wet through. They did not, they were bound somewhere else. Earlier on the same afternoon they had been in some such place, but it was not much more than an alcove, a hole in the wall, with planks on which bottles and glasses were set and coins laid down. He had been continually getting squeezed out of that shelter into the street and into the puddle that caught the drip from the ledge over the entryway. To keep that from happening, he had butted in low down between the cloaks and sheepskins, wedged himself amongst the drinking men and under their arms.

He was surprised at the number of people his father seemed to know in the city of Edinburgh. You would think the people in the drinking place would be strangers to him, but it was evidently not so. Amongst the arguing and excited queer-sounding voices his father's voice rose the loudest. *America*, he said, and slapped his hand on the plank for attention, the very way he would do at home. Andrew had heard that word spoken in that same tone long before he knew it was a land across the ocean. It was spoken as a challenge and an irrefutable truth but sometimes—when his father was not there—it was spoken as a taunt or a joke. His older brothers might ask each other, "Are ye awa to America?" when one of them put on his plaid to go out and do some chore such as penning the sheep. Or, "Why don't ye be off to America?" when they had got into an argument, and one of them wanted to make the other out to be a fool.

The cadences of his father's voice, in the talk that succeeded that word, were so familiar, and Andrew's eyes so bleary with the smoke, that in no time he had fallen asleep on his feet. He wakened when several pushed together out of the place and his father with them. Some one of them said, "Is this your lad here or is it some tinker squeezed in to pick our pockets?" and his father laughed and took Andrew's hand and they began their climb. One man stumbled and another man knocked into him and swore. A couple of women swiped their baskets at the party with great scorn, and made some remarks in their unfamiliar speech, of which Andrew could only make out the words "daecent bodies" and "public foot-paths."

Then his father and the friends stepped aside into a much broader street, which in fact was a courtyard, paved with large blocks of stone. His father turned and paid attention to Andrew at this point.

"Do you know where you are, lad? You're in the castle yard, and this is Edinburgh Castle that has stood for ten thousand years and will stand for ten thousand more. Terrible deeds were done here. These stones have run with blood. Do you know that?" He raised his head so that they all listened to what he was telling.

"It was King Jamie asked the young Douglases to have supper with him and when they were fair sitten down he says, oh, we won't bother with their supper, take them out in the yard and chop off their heads. And so they did. Here in the yard where we stand.

"But that King Jamie died a leper," he went on with a sigh, then a groan, making them all be still to consider this fate.

Then he shook his head.

"Ah, no, it wasn't him. It was King Robert the Bruce that died a leper. He died a king but he died a leper."

Andrew could see nothing but enormous stone walls, barred gates, a redcoat soldier marching up and down. His father did not give him much time, anyway, but shoved him ahead and through an archway, saying, "Watch your heads here, lads, they was wee little men in those days. Wee little men. So is Boney the Frenchman, there's a lot of fight in your wee little men."

They were climbing uneven stone steps, some as high as Andrew's knees—he had to crawl occasionally—inside what as far as he could make out was a roofless tower. His father called out, "Are ye all with me then, are ye all in for the climb?" and some straggling voices answered him. Andrew got the impression that there was not such a crowd following as there had been on the street.

They climbed far up in the roundabout stairway and at last came out on a bare rock, a shelf, from which the land fell steeply away. The rain had ceased for the present.

"Ah, there," said Andrew's father. "Now where's all the ones was tramping on our heels to get here?"

One of the men just reaching the top step said, "There's two-three of them took off to have a look at the Meg."

"Engines of war," said Andrew's father. "All they have eyes for is engines of war. Take care they don't go and blow themselves up."

"Haven't the heart for the stairs, more like," said another man who was panting. And the first one said cheerfully, "Scairt to get all the way up here, scairt they're bound to fall off."

A third man—and that was the lot—came staggering across the shelf as if he had in mind to do that very thing.

"Where is it then?" he hollered. "Are we up on Arthur's seat?"

"Ye are not," said Andrew's father. "Look beyond you."

The sun was out now, shining on the stone heap of houses and streets below them, and the churches whose spires did not reach to this height, and some little trees and fields, then a wide silvery stretch of water. And beyond that a pale green and grayish-blue land, part in sunlight and part in shadow, a land as light as mist, sucked into the sky.

"So did I not tell you?" Andrew's father said. "America. It is only a little bit of it, though, only the shore. There is where every man is sitting in the midst of his own properties, and even the beggars is riding around in carriages."

"Well the sea does not look so wide as I thought," said the man who had stopped staggering. "It does not look as if it would take you weeks to cross it."

"It is the effect of the height we're on," said the man who stood beside Andrew's father. "The height we're on is making the width of it the less."

"It's a fortunate day for the view," said Andrew's father. "Many a day you could climb up here and see nothing but the fog."

He turned and addressed Andrew.

"So there you are my lad and you have looked over at America," he said. "God grant you one day you will see it closer up and for yourself."

ANDREW HAS BEEN to the Castle one time since, with a group of the lads from Ettrick, who all wanted to see the great cannon, Mons Meg. But nothing seemed to be in the same place then and he could not find the route they had taken to climb up to the rock. He saw a couple of places blocked off with boards that could have been it. But he did not even try to peer through them—he had no wish to tell the others what he was looking for. Even when he was ten years old he had known that the men with his father were drunk. If he did not understand that his father was drunk—due to his father's sure-footedness and sense of purpose, his commanding behavior—he did certainly understand that something was not as it should be. He knew he was not looking at America, though it was some years before he was well enough acquainted with maps to know that he had been looking at Fife.

Still, he did not know if those men met in the tavern had been mocking his father, or if it was his father playing one of his tricks on them.

OLD JAMES THE FATHER. Andrew. Walter. Their sister Mary. Andrew's wife Agnes, and Agnes and Andrew's son James, under two years old.

In the harbor of Leith, on the 4th of June, 1818, they set foot on board a ship for the first time in their lives.

Old James makes this fact known to the ship's officer who is checking off the names.

"The first time, serra, in all my long life. We are men of the Ettrick. It is a landlocked part of the world."

The officer says a word which is unintelligible to them but plain in meaning. Move along. He has run a line through their names. They move along or are pushed along, Young James riding on Mary's hip.

"What is this?" says Old James, regarding the crowd of people on deck. "Where are we to sleep? Where have all these rabble come from? Look at the faces on them, are they the blackamoors?"

"Black Highlanders, more like," says his son Walter. This is a joke, muttered so his father cannot hear—Highlanders being one of the sorts the old man despises.

"There are too many people," his father continues. "The ship will sink."

"No," says Walter, speaking up now. "Ships do not often sink because of too many people. That's what the fellow was there for, to count the people."

Barely on board the vessel and this seventeen-year-old whelp has taken on knowing airs, he has taken to contradicting his father. Fatigue, astonishment, and the weight of the greatcoat he is wearing prevent Old James from cuffing him.

All the business of life aboard ship has already been explained to the family. In fact it has been explained by the old man himself. He was the one who knew all about provisions, accommodations, and the kind of people you would find on board. All Scotsmen and all decent folk. No Highlanders, no Irish.

But now he cries out that it is like the swarm of bees in the carcass of the lion.

"An evil lot, an evil lot. Oh, that ever we left our native land!"

"We have not left yet," says Andrew. "We are still looking at Leith. We would do best to go below and find ourselves a place."

More lamentation. The bunks are narrow, bare planks with horsehair pallets both hard and prickly.

"Better than nothing," says Andrew.

"Oh, that it was ever put in my head to bring us here, onto this floating sepulchre."

Will nobody shut him up? thinks Agnes. This is the way he will go on and on, like a preacher or a lunatic, when the fit takes him. She cannot abide it. She is in more agony herself than he is ever likely to know.

"Well, are we going to settle here or are we not?" she says.

Some people have hung up their plaids or shawls to make a half-private space for their families. She goes ahead and takes off her outer wrappings to do the same.

The child is turning somersaults in her belly. Her face is hot as a coal and her legs throb and the swollen flesh in between them—the lips the child must soon part to get out—is a scalding sack of pain. Her mother would have known what to do about that, she would have known which leaves to mash to make a soothing poultice.

At the thought of her mother such misery overcomes her that she wants to kick somebody.

Andrew folds up his plaid to make a comfortable seat for his father. The old man seats himself, groaning, and puts his hands up to his face, so that his speaking has a hollow sound.

"I will see no more. I will not harken to their screeching voices or their satanic tongues. I will not swallow a mouth of meat nor meal until I see the shores of America."

All the more for the rest of us, Agnes feels like saying.

Why does Andrew not speak plainly to his father, reminding him of whose idea it was, who was the one who harangued and borrowed and begged to get them just where they are now? Andrew will not do it, Walter will only joke, and as for Mary she can hardly get her voice out of her throat in her father's presence.

Agnes comes from a large Hawick family of weavers, who work in the mills now but worked for generations at home. And working there they learned all the arts of cutting each other down to size, of squabbling and surviving in close quarters. She is still surprised by the rigid manners, the deference and silences in her husband's family. She thought from the beginning that they were a queer sort of people and she thinks so still. They are as poor as her own folk, but they have such a great notion of themselves. And what have they got to back this up? The old man has been a wonder in the tavern for years, and their cousin is a raggedy lying poet who had to flit to Nithsdale when nobody would trust him to tend sheep in Ettrick. They were all brought up by three witchey-women of aunts who were so scared of men that they would run and hide in the sheep pen if anybody but their own family was coming along the road.

As if it wasn't the men that should be running from them.

Walter has come back from carrying their heavier possessions down to a lower depth of the ship.

"You never saw such a mountain of boxes and trunks and sacks of meal and potatoes," he says excitedly. "A person has to climb over them to get to the water pipe. Nobody can help but spill their water on the way back and the sacks will be wet through and the stuff will be rotted."

"They should not have brought all that," says Andrew. "Did they not undertake to feed us when we paid our way?"

"Aye," says the old man. "But will it be fit for us to eat?"

"So a good thing I brought my cakes," says Walter, who is still in the mood to make a joke of anything. He taps his foot on the snug metal box filled with oat cakes that his aunts gave him as a particular present because he was the youngest and they still thought of him as the motherless one.

"You'll see how merry you'll be if we're starving," says Agnes. Walter is a pest to her, almost as much as the old man. She knows there is probably no chance of them starving, because Andrew is looking impatient, but not anxious. It takes a good deal, of course, to make Andrew anxious. He is apparently not anxious about her, since he thought first to make a comfortable seat for his father.

MARY HAS TAKEN YOUNG JAMES back up to the deck. She could tell that he was alarmed down there in the half-dark. He does not have to whimper or complain—she knows his feelings by the way he digs his little knees into her.

The sails are furled tight. "Look up there, look up there," Mary says, and points to a sailor who is busy high up in the rigging. The boy on her hip makes his sound for bird. "Sailor-peep, sailor-peep," she says. She says the right word for *sailor* but his word for *bird*. She and he communicate in a half-and-half language—half her teaching and half his invention. She believes that he is one of the cleverest children ever born into the world. Being the eldest of her family, and the only girl, she has tended all of her brothers, and been proud of them all at one time, but she has never known a child like this. Nobody else has any idea of how original and independent and clever he is. Men have no interest in children so young, and Agnes his mother has no patience with him.

"Talk like folk," Agnes says to him, and if he doesn't, she may give him a clout. "What are you?" she says. "Are you a folk or an elfit?"

Mary fears Agnes's temper, but in a way she doesn't blame

her. She thinks that women like Agnes—men's women, mother women—lead an appalling life. First with what the men do to them—even so good a man as Andrew—and then what the children do, coming out. She will never forget her own mother, who lay in bed out of her mind with a fever, not knowing any of them, till she died, three days after Walter was born. She had screamed at the black pot hanging over the fire, thinking it was full of devils.

Her brothers call Mary *Poor Mary*, and indeed the meagreness and timidity of many of the women in their family has caused that word to be attached to the names they were given at their christening—names that were themselves altered to something less substantial and graceful. Isabel became Poor Tibbie; Margaret, Poor Maggie; Jane, Poor Jennie. People in Ettrick said it was a fact that the looks and the height went to the men.

Mary is under five feet tall and has a little tight face with a lump of protruding chin, and a skin that is subject to fiery eruptions that take a long time to fade. When she is spoken to her mouth twitches as if the words were all mixed up with her spittle and her crooked little teeth, and the response she manages is a dribble of speech so faint and scrambled that it is hard for people not to think her dim-witted. She has great difficulty in looking anybody in the face—even the members of her own family. It is only when she gets the boy hitched onto the narrow shelf of her hip that she is capable of some coherent and decisive speech—and then it is mostly to him.

Somebody is saying something to her now. It is a person almost as small as herself—a little brown man, a sailor, with gray whiskers and not a tooth in his head. He is looking straight at her and then at Young James and back to her again—right in the middle of the pushing or loitering, bewildered or inquisitive crowd. At first she thinks it is a foreign language he is speaking, but then she makes out the word *cu*. She finds herself answering with the same word, and he laughs and waves his arms, pointing to somewhere farther back on the ship, then pointing at James and laughing again. Something she should take James to see. She has to say, "Aye. Aye," to stop him gabbling, and then to step off in that direction so that he won't be disappointed.

She wonders what part of the country or the world he could have come from, then realizes that this is the first time in her life that she has ever spoken to a stranger. And except for the difficulty of understanding what he was saying, she has managed it more easily than when having to speak to a neighbor in the Ettrick, or to her father.

She hears the bawling of the cow before she can see it. The press of people increases around her and James, forms a wall in front of her and squeezes her from behind. Then she hears the bawling in the sky and looking up sees the brown beast dangling in the air, all caged in ropes and kicking and roaring frantically. It is held by a hook on a crane, which now hauls it out of sight. People around her are hooting and clapping hands. Some child's voice cries out in the language she understands, wanting to know if the cow will be dropped into the sea. A man's voice tells him no, she will go along with them on the ship.

"Will they milk her then?"

"Aye. Keep still. They'll milk her," says the man reprovingly. And another man's voice climbs boisterously over his.

"They'll milk her till they take the hammer to her, and then ye'll have the blood pudding for yer dinner."

Now follow the hens swung through the air in crates, all squawking and fluttering in their confinement and pecking each other when they can, so that some feathers escape and float down through the air. And after them a pig trussed up like the cow, squealing with a human note in its distress and shitting wildly in midair, so that howls of both outrage and delight rise below, depending on whether they come from those who are hit or those who see others hit.

James is laughing too, he recognizes shite, and cries out his own word for it, which is *gruggin*.

Someday he may remember this. *I saw a cow and a pig fly through the air.* Then he may wonder if it was a dream. And nobody will be there—she will certainly not be there—to tell that it was not a dream, it happened on this ship. He will know that he was once on a ship because he will have been told that, but it's possible that he will never see a ship like this again in all his waking life. She has no idea where they will go when they reach the other shore, but imagines it will be some place inland, among the hills, some place like the Ettrick.

She does not think she will live long, wherever they go. She coughs in the summer as well as the winter and when she coughs her chest aches. She suffers from sties, and cramps in the stomach, and her bleeding comes rarely but may last a month when it does come. She hopes, though, that she will not die while James is still of a size to ride on her hip or still in need of her, which he will be for a while yet. She knows that the time will come when he will turn away as her brothers did, when he will become ashamed of the connection with her. That is what she tells herself will happen, but like anybody in love she cannot believe it.

ON A TRIP TO PEEBLES before they left home, Walter bought himself a book to write in, but for several days he has found too much to pay attention to, and too little space or quiet on the deck, even to open it. He has a vial of ink, as well, held in a leather pouch and strapped to his chest under his shirt. That was the trick used by their cousin, Jamie Hogg the poet, when he was out in the wilds of Nithsdale, watching the sheep. When a rhyme came on Jamie he would pull a wad of paper out of his breeks' pocket and uncork the ink which the heat of his heart had kept from freezing and write it all down, no matter where he was or in what weather.

Or so he said. And Walter had thought to put this method to the test. But it might have been an easier matter amongst sheep than amongst people. Also the wind can surely blow harder over the sea even than it could blow in Nithsdale. And it is essential of course for him to get out of the sight of his own family. Andrew might mock him mildly but Agnes would do it boldly, incensed as she could be by the thought of anybody doing anything she would not want to do. Mary, of course, would never say a word, but the boy on her hip that she idolized and spoiled would be all for grabbing and destroying both pen and paper. And there was no knowing what interference might come from their father.

Now after some investigating around the deck he has found a favorable spot. The cover of his book is hard, he has no need of a table. And the ink warmed on his chest flows as willingly as blood.

We came on board on the 4th day of June and lay the 5th, 6th, 7th, and 8th in the Leith roads getting the ship to our place where we could set sail which was on the 9th. We passed the corner of Fifeshire all well nothing occurring worth mentioning till this day the 13th in the morning when we were awakened by a cry, John O'Groats house. We could see it plain and had a fine sail across the Pentland Firth having both wind and tide in our favour and it was in no way dangerous as we had heard tell. Their was a child had died, the name of Ormiston and its body was thrown overboard sewed up in a piece of canvas with a large lump of coal at its feet . . .

He pauses in his writing to think of the weighted sack falling down through the water. Darker and darker grows the water with the surface high overhead gleaming faintly like the night sky. Would the piece of coal do its job, would the sack fall straight down to the very bottom of the sea? Or would the current of the sea be strong enough to keep lifting it up and letting it fall, pushing it sideways, taking it as far as Greenland or south to the tropical waters full of rank weeds, the Sargasso Sea? Or some ferocious fish might come along and rip the sack and make a meal of the body before it had even left the upper waters and the region of light.

He has seen drawings of fish as big as horses, fish with horns as well, and scores of teeth each like a skinner's knife. Also some that are smooth and smiling, and wickedly teasing, having the breasts of women but not the other parts which the sight of the breasts conducts a man's thoughts to. All this in a book of stories and engravings that he got out of the Peebles Subscription Library.

These thoughts do not distress him. He always sets himself to think clearly and if possible to picture accurately the most disagreeable or shocking things, so as to reduce their power over him. As he pictures it now, the child is being eaten. Not swallowed whole as in the case of Jonah but chewed into bits as he himself would chew a tasty chunk from a boiled sheep. But there is the matter of a soul. The soul leaves the body at the moment of death. But from which part of the body does it leave, what has been its particular bodily location? The best guess seems to be that it emerges with the last breath, having been hidden somewhere in the chest around the place of the heart and the lungs. Though Walter has heard a joke they used to tell about an old fellow in the Ettrick, to the effect that he was so dirty that when he died his soul came out his arsehole, and was heard to do so, with a mighty explosion.

This is the sort of information that preachers might be expected to give you—not mentioning anything like an arsehole of course but explaining something of the soul's proper location and exit. But they shy away from it. Also they cannot explain—or he has never heard one explain—how the souls maintain themselves outside of bodies until the Day of Judgment and how on that day each one finds and recognizes the body that is its own and reunites with it, though it be not so much as a skeleton at that time. *Though it be dust.* There must be some who have studied enough to know how all this is accomplished. But there are also some—he has learned this recently—who have studied and read and thought till they have come to the conclusion that there are no souls at all. No one cares to speak about these people either, and indeed the thought of them is terrible. How can they live with the fear—indeed, the certainty—of Hell before them?

There was the man like that who came from by Berwick, Fat Davey he was called, because he was so fat the table had to be cut away so he could sit down to his meal. And when he died in Edinburgh, where he was some sort of scholar, the people stood in the street outside his house waiting to see if the Devil would come to claim him. A sermon had been preached on that in Ettrick, which claimed as far as Walter could understand it that the Devil did not go in for displays of that sort and only superstitious and vulgar and Popish sort of people would expect him to, but that his embrace was nevertheless far more horrible and the torments that accompanied it more subtle than any such minds could imagine.

ON THE THIRD DAY aboard ship Old James got up and started to walk around. Now he is walking all the time. He stops and speaks to anybody who seems ready to listen. He tells his name, and says that he comes from Ettrick, from the valley and forest of Ettrick, where the old Kings of Scotland used to hunt.

"And on the field at Flodden," he says, "after the battle of Flodden, they said you could walk up and down among the corpses and pick out the men from the Ettrick, because they were the tallest and the strongest and the finest-looking men on the ground. I have five sons and they are all good strong lads but only two of them are with me. One of my sons is in Nova Scotia, he is the one with my own name and the last I heard of him he was in a place called Economy, but we have not had any word of him since, and I do not know whether he is alive or dead. My eldest son went off to work in the Highlands, and the son that is next to the youngest took it into his head to go off there too, and I will never see either of them again. Five sons and by the mercy of God all grew to be men, but it was not the Lord's will that I should keep them with me. Their mother died after the last of them was born. She took a fever and she never got up from her bed after she bore him. A man's life is full of sorrow. I have a daughter as well, the oldest of them all, but she is nearly a dwarf. Her mother was chased by a ram when she was carrying her. I have three old sisters all the same, all dwarfs."

His voice rises over all the hubbub of shipboard life and his sons make tracks in some other direction in dread embarrassment, whenever they hear it.

On the afternoon of the 14th a wind came from the North and the ship began to shake as if every board that was in it would fly loose from every other. The buckets overflowed from the people that were sick and vomiting and there was the contents of them slipping all over the deck. All people were ordered below but many of them crumpled up against the rail and did not care if they were washed over. None of our family was sick however and now the wind has dropped and the sun has come out and those who did not care if they died in the filth a little while ago have got up and dragged themselves to be washed where the sailors are splashing buckets of water over the decks. The women are busy too washing and rinsing and wringing out all the foul clothing. It is the worst misery and the suddenest recovery I have seen ever in my life . . .

A young girl ten or twelve years old stands watching Walter write. She is wearing a fancy dress and bonnet and has light-brown curly hair. Not so much a pretty face as a pert one.

"Are you from one of the cabins?" she says.

Walter says, "No. I am not."

"I knew you were not. There are only four of them and one is for my father and me and one is for the captain and one is for his mother and she never comes out and one is for the two ladies. You are not supposed to be on this part of the deck unless you are from one of the cabins."

"Well, I did not know that," Walter says, but does not bestir himself to move away.

"I have seen you before writing in your book."

"I haven't seen you."

"No. You were writing, so you didn't notice."

"Well," says Walter. "I'm finished with it now anyway."

"I haven't told anybody about you," she says carelessly, as if that was a matter of choice, and she might well change her mind.

AND ON THAT SAME DAY but an hour or so on, there comes a great cry from the port side that there is a last sight of Scotland. Walter and Andrew go over to see that, and Mary with Young James on her hip and many others. Old James and Agnes do not go—she because she objects now to moving herself anywhere, and he on account of perversity. His sons have urged him to go but he has said, "It is nothing to me. I have seen the last of the Ettrick so I have seen the last of Scotland already."

It turns out that the cry to say farewell has been premature—a gray rim of land will remain in place for hours yet. Many will grow tired of looking at it—it is just land, like any other—but some will stay at the rail until the last rag of it fades, with the daylight.

"You should go and say farewell to your native land and the last farewell to your mother and father for you will not be seeing them again," says Old James to Agnes. "And there is worse yet you will have to endure. Aye, but there is. You have the curse of Eve." He says this with the mealy relish of a preacher and Agnes calls him an old shite-bag under her breath, but she has hardly the energy even to scowl.

Old shite-bag. You and your native land.

WALTER WRITES at last a single sentence.

And this night in the year 1818 we lost sight of Scotland.

The words seem majestic to him. He is filled with a sense of grandeur, solemnity, and personal importance.

16th was a very windy day with the wind coming out of the S.W. the sea was running very high and the ship got her gib-boom broken on account of the violence of the wind. And this day our sister Agnes was taken into the cabin.

Sister, he has written, as if she was all the same to him as poor Mary, but that is hardly the case. Agnes is a tall well-built girl with thick dark hair and dark eyes. The flush on one of her cheeks slides into a splotch of pale brown as big as a handprint. It is a birthmark, which people say is a pity, because without it she would be handsome. Walter can hardly bear looking at it, but this is not because it is ugly. It is because he longs to touch it, to stroke it with the tips of his fingers. It looks not like ordinary skin but like the velvet on a deer. His feelings about her are so troubling that he can only speak unpleasantly to her if he speaks at all. And she pays him back with a good seasoning of contempt.

AGNES THINKS that she is in the water and the waves are heaving her up and slamming her down again. Every time the waves slap her down it is worse than the time before and she sinks farther and deeper, with the moment of relief passing before she can grab it, for the wave is already gathering its power to hit her again.

Then sometimes she knows she is in a bed, a strange bed and strangely soft, but it is all the worse for that because when she sinks down there is no resistance, no hard place where the pain has to stop. And here or on the water people keep rushing back and forth in front of her. They are all seen sideways and all transparent, talking very fast so she can't make them out, and maliciously taking no heed of her. She sees Andrew in the midst of them, and two or three of his brothers. Some of the girls she knows are there too—the friends she used to lark around with in Hawick. And they do not give a glance or a poor penny for the plight she is in now.

She shouts at them to take themselves off but not one of them pays any attention and she sees more of them coming right through the wall. She never knew before that she had so many enemies. They are grinding her and pretending they don't even know it. Their movement is grinding her to death.

Her mother bends over her and says in a drawling, cold, lackadaisical voice, "You are not trying, my girl. You must try harder." Her mother is all dressed up and talking fine, like some Edinburgh lady.

Evil stuff is poured into her mouth. She tries to spit it out, knowing it is poison.

I will just get up and get out of this, she thinks. She starts trying to pull herself loose from her body, as if it were a heap of rags all on fire.

A man's voice is heard, giving some order.

"Hold her," he says and she is split and stretched wide open to the world and the fire.

"Ah—ah—ahh," the man's voice says, panting as if he has been running in a race.

Then a cow that is so heavy, bawling heavy with milk, rears up and sits down on Agnes's stomach.

"Now. Now," says the man's voice, and he groans at the end of his strength as he tries to heave it off.

The fools. The fools, ever to have let it in.

She was not better till the 18th when she was delivered of a daughter. We having a surgeon on board nothing happened. Nothing occurred till the 22nd this was the roughest day we had till then experienced. The gib-boom was broken a second time. Nothing worth mentioning happened Agnes was mending in an ordinary way till the 29th we saw a great shoal of porpoises and the 30th (yesterday) was a very rough sea with the wind blowing from the west we went rather backwards than forwards . . .

"In the Ettrick there is what they call the highest house in Scotland," James says, "and the house that my grandfather lived in was a higher one than that. The name of the place is Phauhope, they call it Phaup, my grandfather was Will O'Phaup and fifty years ago you would have heard of him if you came from any place south of the Forth and north of the Debatable Lands."

Unless a person stops up his ears, what is to be done but listen? thinks Walter. There are people who curse to see the old man coming but there do seem to be others who are glad of any distraction.

He is telling about Will and his races, and the wagers on him, and other foolishness more than Walter can bear.

"And he married a woman named Bessie Scott and one of his sons was named Robert and that same Robert was my father. My father. And I am standing here in front of you.

"In but one leap Will could clear the river Ettrick, and the place is marked."

FOR THE FIRST TWO OR THREE DAYS Young James has refused to be unfastened from Mary's hip. He has been bold enough, but only if he can stay there. At night he has slept in her cloak, curled up beside her, and she has wakened aching along her left side because she lay stiffly all night not to disturb him. Then in the space of one morning he is down and running about and kicking at her if she tries to hoist him up.

Everything on the ship is calling out for his attention. Even at night he tries to climb over her and run away in the dark. So she gets up aching not only from her stiff position but from lack of sleep altogether. One night she drops off and the child gets loose but most fortunately stumbles against his father's body in his bid for escape. Henceforth Andrew insists that he be tied down every night. He howls of course, and Andrew shakes him and cuffs him and then he sobs himself to sleep. Mary lies by him softly explaining how this is necessary so that he should not fall off the ship into the ocean, but he regards her at these times as his enemy and if she puts a hand to stroke his face he tries to bite it with his baby teeth. Every night he goes to sleep in a rage, but in the morning when she unties him, still half-asleep and full of his infant sweetness, he clings to her drowsily and she is suffused with love.

The truth is that she loves even his howls and his rages and his kicks and his bites. She loves his dirty and his curdled smells as well as his fresh ones. As his drowsiness leaves him his clear blue eyes, looking into hers, fill with a marvellous intelligence and an imperious will, which seem to her to come straight from Heaven. (Though her religion has always taught her that self-will comes from the opposite direction.) She loved her brothers too when they were sweet and wild and had to be kept from falling into the burn, but surely not as passionately as she loves James.

Then one day he is gone. She is in the line for the wash water and she turns around and he is not beside her. She has just been speaking a few words to the woman ahead of her, answering a question about Agnes and the infant, she has just told its name—Isabel—and in that moment he has got away. When she was saying the name, Isabel, she felt a surprising longing to hold that new, exquisitely light bundle, and as she abandons her place in line and chases about for sight of James it seems to her that he must have felt her disloyalty and vanished to punish her.

Everything in an instant is overturned. The nature of the world is altered. She runs back and forth, crying out James's name. She runs up to strangers, to sailors who laugh at her as she begs them, "Have you seen a little boy, have you seen a little boy this high, he has blue eyes?"

"I seen a fifty or sixty of them like that in the last five minutes," a man says to her. A woman trying to be kind says that he will turn up, Mary should not worry herself, he will be playing with some of the other children. Some women even look about as if they would help her to search, but of course they cannot, they have their own responsibilities.

This is what Mary plainly sees, in those moments of anguish— that the world which has turned into a horror for her is still the same ordinary world for all these other people and will remain so even if James has truly vanished, even if he has crawled through the ship's railings—she has noticed, all over, the places where this could be possible—and is swallowed in the ocean.

The most brutal and unthinkable of all events, to her, could seem to most others like a sad but not extraordinary misadventure. It would not be unthinkable to them.

Or to God. For in fact when God makes some rare and remarkably beautiful human child, is He not particularly tempted to take His creature back, as if the world did not deserve it?

But she is praying to Him, all the time. At first she only called on the Lord's name. But as her search grows more specific and in some ways more bizarre—she is ducking under clotheslines that people have contrived for privacy, she thinks nothing of interrupting folk at any business, she flings up the lids of their boxes and roots in their bedclothes, not even hearing them when they curse her—her prayers also become more complicated and audacious. She seeks for something to offer, something that could be the price of James's being restored to her. But what does she have? Nothing of her own—not health or prospects or anybody's regard. There is no piece of luck or even a hope she can offer to give up. What she has is James.

And how can she offer James for James?

This is what is knocking around in her head.

But what about her love of James? Her extreme and perhaps idolatrous, perhaps wicked love of another creature. She will give up that, she will give it up gladly, if only he isn't gone, if only he can be found. If only he isn't dead.

SHE RECALLS ALL THIS, an hour or two after somebody has noticed the boy peeping out from under an empty bucket, listening to the hubbub. And she retracted her vow at once. She grabbed him in her arms and held him hard against her and took deep groaning breaths, while he struggled to get free.

Her understanding of God is shallow and unstable and the truth is that except in a time of terror such as she has just experienced, she does not really care. She has always felt that God or even the idea of Him was more distant from her than from other people. Also she does not fear His punishments after death as she should and she does not even know why. There is a stubborn indifference in her mind that nobody knows about. In fact, everybody may think that she clings secretly to religion because so little else is available to her. They are quite wrong, and now she has James back she gives no thanks but thinks what a fool she was and how she could not give up her love of him any more than stop her heart beating.

. . .

AFTER THAT, Andrew insists that James be tied not only by night but to the post of the bunk or to their own clothesline on the deck, by day. Mary wishes him to be tethered to her but Andrew says a boy like that would kick her to pieces. Andrew has trounced him for the trick he played, but the look in James's eyes says that his tricks are not finished.

THAT CLIMB IN EDINBURGH, that sighting across the water, was a thing Andrew did not even mention to his own brothers— America being already a sore enough matter. The oldest brother, Robert, went off to the Highlands as soon as he was grown, leaving home without a farewell on an evening when his father was at Tibbie Shiel's. He made it plain that he was doing this in order not to have to join any expedition that their father might have in mind. Then the brother James perversely set out for America on his own, saying that at least if he did that, he could save himself hearing any more about it. And finally Will, younger than Andrew but always the most contrary and the most bitterly set against the father, Will too had run away, to join Robert. That left only Walt, who was still childish enough to be thinking of adventures—he had grown up bragging about how he was going to fight the French, so maybe now he thought he'd fight the Indians.

And then there was Andrew himself, who ever since that day on the rock has felt about his father a deep bewildered sense of responsibility, much like sorrow.

But then, Andrew feels a responsibility for everybody in his family. For his often ill-tempered young wife, whom he has again brought into a state of peril, for the brothers far away and the brother at his side, for his pitiable sister and his heedless child. This is his burden—it never occurs to him to call it love.

AGNES KEEPS ASKING FOR SALT, till they begin to fear that she will fuss herself into a fever. The two women looking after her are cabin passengers, Edinburgh ladies, who took on the job out of charity.

"You be still now," they tell her. "You have no idea what a fortunate lassie you are that we had Mr. Suter on board."

They tell her that the baby was turned the wrong way inside her, and they were all afraid that Mr. Suter would have to cut her, and that might be the end of her. But he had managed to get it turned so that he could wrestle it out.

"I need salt for my milk," says Agnes, who is not going to let them put her in her place with their reproaches and Edinburgh speech. They are idiots anyway. She has to tell them how you must put a little salt in the baby's first milk, just place a few grains on your finger and squeeze a drop or two of milk onto it and let the child swallow that before you put it to the breast. Without this precaution there is a good chance that it will grow up half-witted.

"Is she even a Christian?" says the one of them to the other.

"I am as much as you," Agnes says. But to her own surprise and shame she starts to weep aloud, and the baby howls along with her, out of sympathy or out of hunger. And still she refuses to feed it.

Mr. Suter comes in to see how she is. He asks what all the grief is about, and they tell him the trouble.

"A newborn baby to get salt on its stomach—where did she get the idea?"

He says, "Give her the salt." And he stays to see her squeeze the milk on her salty finger, lay the finger to the infant's lips, and follow it with her nipple.

He asks her what the reason is and she tells him.

"And does it work every time?"

She tells him—a little surprised that he is as stupid as they are, though kinder—that it works without fail.

"So where you come from they all have their wits about them? And are all the girls strong and good-looking like you?"

She says that she would not know about that.

Sometimes visiting young men, educated and from the town, used to hang around her and her friends, complimenting them and trying to work up a conversation, and she always thought any girl was a fool who allowed it, even if the man was handsome. Mr. Suter is far from handsome—he is too thin, and his face is badly pocked, so that at first she took him for an old fellow. But he has a kind voice, and if he is teasing her a little there could be no harm in it. No man would have the nature left to deal with a woman after looking at them spread wide, their raw parts open to the air.

"Are you sore?" he says, and she believes there is a shadow on his damaged cheeks, a slight blush rising. She says that she is no worse than she has to be, and he nods, picks up her wrist, and bows over it, strongly pressing her pulse.

"Lively as a racehorse," he says, with his hands still above her, as if he did not know where to drop them next. Then he decides to push back her hair and press his fingers to her temples, as well as behind her ears.

She will recall this touch, this curious, gentle, tingling pressure, with an addled mixture of scorn and longing, for many years to come.

"Good," he says. "No touch of a fever."

He watches, for a moment, the child sucking.

"All's well with you now," he says, with a sigh. "You have a fine daughter and she can say all her life that she was born at sea."

ANDREW ARRIVES LATER and stands at the foot of the bed. He has never looked on her in such a bed as this (a regular bed even though bolted to the wall). He is red with shame in front of the ladies, who have brought in the basin to wash her.

"That's it, is it?" he says, with a nod—not a glance—at the bundle beside her.

She laughs in a vexed way and asks, what did he think it was? That is all it takes to knock him off his unsteady perch, puncture his pretense of being at ease. Now he stiffens up, even redder, doused with fire. It isn't just what she has said, it is the whole scene, the smell of the infant and milk and blood, most of all the basin, the cloths, the women standing by, with their proper looks that can seem to a man both admonishing and full of derision.

He can't think of another word to say, so she has to tell him, with rough mercy, to get on his way, there's work to do here.

Some of the girls used to say that when you finally gave in and lay down with a man—even granting he was not the man of your first choice—it gave you a helpless but calm and even sweet feeling. Agnes does not recall that she felt that with Andrew. All she felt was that he was an honest lad and the one that she needed in her circumstances, and that it would never occur to him to run off and leave her.

WALTER HAS CONTINUED to go to the same private place to write in his book and nobody has caught him there. Except the girl, of course. But things are even now with her. One day he arrived at the place and she was there before him, skipping with a red-tasselled rope. When she saw him she stopped, out of breath. And no sooner did she catch her breath but she began to cough, so that it was several minutes before she could speak. She sank down against the pile of canvas that concealed the spot, flushed and her eyes full of bright tears from the coughing. He simply stood and watched her, alarmed at this fit but not knowing what to do.

"Do you want me to fetch one of the ladies?"

He is on speaking terms with the Edinburgh women now, on account of Agnes. They take a kind interest in the mother and baby and Mary and Young James, and think that the old father is comical. They are also amused by Andrew and Walter, who seem to them so bashful. Walter is actually not so tongue-tied as Andrew is, but this business of humans giving birth (though he is used to it with sheep) fills him with dismay or outright disgust. Agnes has lost a great part of her sullen allure because of it. (As happened before, when she gave birth to Young James. But then, gradually, her offending powers returned. He thinks that unlikely to happen again. He has seen more of the world now, and on board this ship he has seen more of women.)

The coughing girl is shaking her curly head violently.

"I don't want them," she says, when she can gasp the words out. "I have never told anybody you come here. So you mustn't tell anybody about me."

"Well you are here by rights."

She shakes her head again and gestures for him to wait till she can speak more easily.

"I mean that you saw me skipping. My father hid my skipping rope but I found where he hid it—but he doesn't know that."

"It isn't the Sabbath," Walter says reasonably. "So what is wrong with you skipping?"

"How do I know?" she says, regaining her saucy tone. "Perhaps

he thinks I am too old for it. Will you swear not to tell anyone?"
She holds up her forefingers to make a cross. The gesture is innocent, he knows, but nevertheless he is shocked, knowing how some
people might look at it.

But he says that he is willing to swear.

"I swear too," she says. "I won't tell anyone you come here."

After saying this quite solemnly, she makes a face.

"Though I was not going to tell about you anyway."

What a queer self-important little thing she is. She speaks only
of her father, so he thinks it must be she has no brothers or sisters
and—like himself—no mother. That condition has probably made
her both spoiled and lonely.

FOLLOWING THIS SWEARING, the girl—her name is Nettie—
becomes a frequent visitor when Walter intends to write in his
book. She always says that she does not want to disturb him but
after keeping ostentatiously quiet for about five minutes she will
interrupt him with some question about his life or bit of information about hers. It is true that she is motherless and an only child
and she has never even been to school. She talks most about her
pets—those dead and those living at her house in Edinburgh—
and a woman named Miss Anderson who used to travel with
her and teach her. It seems she was glad to see the back of this
woman, and surely Miss Anderson would be glad to depart, after
all the tricks that were played on her—the live frog in her boot and
the woolen but lifelike mouse in her bed. Also Nettie's stomping
on books that were not in favor and her pretense of being struck
deaf and dumb when she got sick of reciting her spelling exercises.

She has been back and forth to America three times. Her father
is a wine merchant whose business takes him to Montreal.

She wants to know all about how Walter and his people live. Her
questions are by country standards quite impertinent. But Walter
does not really mind—in his own family he has never been in a
position that allowed him to instruct or teach or tease anybody
younger than himself, and in a way it gives him pleasure.

It is certainly true, though, that in his own world, nobody would
ever have got away with being so pert and forward and inquisitive
as this Nettie. What does Walter's family have for supper when

they are at home, how do they sleep? Are there animals kept in the house? Do the sheep have names, and what are the sheepdogs' names, and can you make pets of them? Why not? What is the arrangement of the scholars in the schoolroom, what do they write on, are the teachers cruel? What do some of his words mean that she does not understand, and do all the people where he is talk like him?

"Oh, aye," says Walter. "Even His Majesty the Duke does. The Duke of Buccleugh."

She laughs and freely pounds her little fist on his shoulder.

"Now you are teasing me. I know it. I know that dukes are not called Your Majesty. They are not."

One day she arrives with paper and drawing pencils. She says she has brought them to keep her busy so she will not be a nuisance to him. She says that she will teach him to draw if he wants to learn. But his attempts make her laugh, and he deliberately does worse and worse, till she laughs so hard she has one of her coughing fits. (These don't bother him so much anymore because he has seen how she always manages to survive them.) Then she says she will do some drawings in the back of his notebook, so that he will have them to remember the voyage. She does a drawing of the sails up above and of a hen that has escaped its cage somehow and is trying to travel like a seabird over the water. She sketches from memory her dog that died. Pirate. At first she claims his name was Walter but relents and admits later that she was not telling the truth. And she makes a picture of the icebergs she has seen, higher than houses, on one of her past voyages with her father. The setting sun shone through these icebergs and made them look—she says—like castles of gold. Rose-colored and gold.

"I wish I had my paint box. Then I could show you. But I do not know where it is packed. And my painting is not very good anyway, I am better at drawing."

Everything that she has drawn, including the icebergs, has a look that is both guileless and mocking, peculiarly expressive of herself.

"THE OTHER DAY I was telling you about that Will O'Phaup that was my grandfather but there was more to him than I told you. I did not tell you that he was the last man in Scotland to speak to the fairies. It is certain that I have never heard of any other, in his time or later."

Walter has been trapped into hearing this story—which he has, of course, heard often before, though not by his father's telling. He is sitting around a corner where some sailors are mending the torn sails. They talk among themselves from time to time—in English, maybe, but not any English that Walt can well make out—and occasionally they seem to listen to a bit of what Old James is telling. By the sounds that are made throughout the story Walter can guess that the out-of-sight audience is made up mostly of women.

But there is one tall well-dressed man—a cabin passenger, certainly—who has paused to listen within Walter's view. There is a figure close to this man's other side, and at one moment in the tale this figure peeps around to look at Walter and he sees that it is Nettie. She seems about to laugh but she puts a finger to her lips as if warning herself—and Walter—to keep silent.

The man must of course be her father. The two of them stand there listening quietly till the tale is over.

Then the man turns and speaks directly, in a familiar yet courteous way, to Walter.

"There is no telling what happened to the fellow's sheep. I hope the fairies did not get them."

Walter is alarmed, not knowing what to say. But Nettie looks at him with calming reassurance and the slightest smile, then drops her eyes and waits beside her father as a demure little miss should.

"Are you writing down what you can make of this?" the man asks, nodding at Walter's notebook.

"I am writing a journal of the voyage," Walter says stiffly.

"Now that is interesting. That is an interesting fact because I too am keeping a journal of this voyage. I wonder if we find the same things worth writing of."

"I only write what happens," Walter says, wanting to make clear that this is a job for him and not any idle pleasure. Still he feels that some further justification is called for. "I am writing to keep track of every day so that at the end of the voyage I can send a letter home."

The man's voice is smoother and his manner gentler than any

address Walter is used to. He wonders if he is being made sport of in some way. Or if Nettie's father is the sort of person who strikes up an acquaintance with you in the hope of getting hold of your money for some worthless investment.

Not that Walter's looks or dress would mark him out as any likely prospect.

"So you do not describe what you see? Only what—as you say—is *happening*?"

Walter is about to say no, and then yes. For he has just thought, if he writes that there is a rough wind, is that not describing? You do not know where you are with this kind of person.

"You are not writing about what we have just heard?"

"No."

"It might be worth it. There are people who go around now prying into every part of Scotland and writing down whatever these old country folk have to say. They think that the old songs and stories are disappearing and that they are worth recording. I don't know about that, it isn't my business. But I would not be surprised if the people who have written it all down will find that it was worth their trouble—I mean to say, there will be money in it."

Nettie speaks up unexpectedly.

"Oh, hush, Father. The old fellow is going to start again."

This is not what any daughter would say to her father in Walter's experience, but the man seems ready to laugh, looking down at her fondly.

"Just one more thing I have to ask," he says. "What do you think of this about the fairies?"

"I think it is all nonsense," says Walter.

"He *has* started again," says Nettie crossly.

And indeed, Old James's voice has been going this little while, breaking in determinedly and reproachfully on those of his audience who might have thought it was time for their own conversations.

". . . and still another time, but in the long days in the summer, out on the hills late in the day but before it was well dark . . ."

The tall man nods but looks as if he had something still to inquire of Walter. Nettie reaches up and claps her hand over his mouth.

"And I will tell you and swear my life upon it that Will could not tell a lie, him that in his young days went to church to the preacher Thomas Boston, and Thomas Boston put the fear of the Lord like a knife into every man and woman, till their dying day. No, never. He would not lie."

"SO THAT WAS ALL NONSENSE?" says the tall man quietly, when he is sure that the story has ended. "Well I am inclined to agree. You have a modern turn of mind?"

Walter says yes, he has, and he speaks more stoutly than he did before. He has heard these stories his father is spouting, and others like them, for the whole of his life, but the odd thing is that until they came on board this ship he never heard them from his father. The father he has known up till a short while ago would, he is certain, have had no use for them.

"This is a terrible place we live in," his father used to say. "The people is all full of nonsense and bad habits and even our sheep's wool is so coarse you cannot sell it. The roads are so bad a horse cannot go more than four miles in an hour. And for ploughing here they use the spade or the old Scotch plough though there has been a better plough in other places for fifty years. Oh, aye, aye, they say when you ask them, oh aye but it's too steep hereabouts, the land is too heavy.

"To be born in the Ettrick is to be born in a backward place," he would say. "Where the people is all believing in old stories and seeing ghosts and I tell you it is a curse to be born in the Ettrick."

And very likely that would lead him on to the subject of America, where all the blessings of modern invention were put to eager use and the people could never stop improving the world around them.

But harken at him now.

"I don't believe those were fairies," Nettie says.

"So do you think they were his neighbors all the time?" says her father. "Do you think they were playing a trick on him?"

Never has Walter heard a father speak to a child so indulgently. And fond as he has grown of Nettie he cannot approve of it. It can only make her believe that there are no opinions on the face of the earth that are more worthy of being listened to than hers.

"No I do not," she says.

"What then?" says her father.

"I think they were dead people."

"What do you know about dead people?" her father asks her, finally speaking with some sternness. "Dead people won't rise up till the Day of Judgment. I don't care to hear you making light about things of that sort."

"I was not making light," says Nettie carelessly.

The sailors are scrambling loose from their sails and pointing at the sky, far to the west. They must see there something that excites them. Walter makes bold to ask, "Are they English? I cannot tell what they say."

"Some of them are English, but from parts that sound foreign to us. Some are Portuguese. I cannot make them out either but I think that they are saying they see the rotches. They all have very keen eyes."

Walter believes that he too has very keen eyes, but it takes him a moment or two before he can see these birds, the ones that must be called rotches. Flocks and flocks of seabirds flashing and rising overhead, mere bright speckles on the air.

"You must make sure to mention those in your journal," Nettie's father says. "I have seen them when I made this voyage before. They feed on fish and here is the great place for them. Soon you'll see the fishermen as well. But the rotches filling the sky are the very first sign that we must be on the Grand Banks of Newfoundland.

"You must come up and talk to us on the deck above," he says, in bidding good-bye to Walter. "I have business to think about and I am not much company for my daughter. She is forbidden to run around because she is not quite recovered from the cold she had in the winter but she is fond of sitting and talking."

"I don't believe it is the rule for me to go there," says Walter, in some confusion.

"No, no, that is no matter. My girl is lonely. She likes to read and draw but she likes company too. She could show you how to draw, if you like. That would add to your journal."

If Walter flushes it is not noticed. Nettie remains quite composed.

· · ·

SO THEY SIT OUT IN THE OPEN and draw and write. Or she reads aloud to him from her favorite book, which is *The Scottish Chiefs*. He already knows much about what happens in the story—who does not know about William Wallace?—but she reads smoothly and at just the proper speed and makes some things solemn and others terrifying and something else comical, so that he is as much in thrall to the book as she is herself. Even though, as she says, she has read it twelve times already.

He understands a little better now why she has all those questions to ask him. He and his folk remind her of some people in her book. Such people as there were out on the hills and valleys in the olden times. What would she think if she knew that the *old fellow,* the old tale-spinner spouting all over the boat and penning people up to listen as if they were the sheep and he was the sheepdog—if she knew that he was Walter's father?

She would be delighted, probably, more curious about Walter's family than ever. She would not look down on them, except in a way she could not help or know about.

We came on the fishing banks of Newfoundland on the 12th of July and on the 19th we saw land and it was a joyful sight to us. It was a part of Newfoundland. We sailed between Newfoundland and St. Paul's Island and having a fair wind both the 18th and the 19th we found ourselves in the river on the morning of the 20th and within sight of the mainland of North America. We were awakened at about 1 o'clock in the morning and I think every passenger was out of bed at 4 o'clock gazing at the land, it being wholly covered with wood and quite a new sight to us. It was a part of Nova Scotia and a beautiful hilly country. We saw several whales this day such creatures as I never saw in my life.

This is the day of wonders. The land is covered with trees like a head with hair and behind the ship the sun rises tipping the top trees with light. The sky is clear and shining as a china plate and the water just playfully ruffled with wind. Every wisp of fog has gone and the air is full of the resinous smell of the trees. Seabirds are flashing above the sails all golden like creatures of Heaven, but the sailors raise a few shots to keep them from the rigging.

Mary holds Young James up so that he may always remember this first sight of the continent that will forever be his home. She tells him the name of this land—Nova Scotia.

"It means New Scotland," she says.

Agnes hears her. "Then why doesn't it say so?"

Mary says, "It's Latin, I think."

Agnes snorts with impatience. The baby has been waked up early by all the hubbub and celebration, and now she is miserable, wanting to be on the breast all the time, wailing whenever Agnes tries to take her off. Young James, observing all this closely, makes an attempt to get on the other breast, and Agnes bats him off so hard that he staggers.

"Suckie-laddie," Agnes calls him. He yelps a bit, then crawls around behind her and pinches the baby's toes.

Another whack.

"You're a rotten egg, you are," his mother says. "Somebody's been spoiling you till you think you're the Laird's arse."

Agnes's roused voice always makes Mary feel as if she is about to catch a blow herself.

Old James is sitting with them on the deck, but pays no attention to this domestic unrest.

"Will you come and look at the country, Father?" says Mary uncertainly. "You can have a better view from the rail."

"I can see it well enough," Old James says. Nothing in his voice suggests that the revelations around them are pleasing to him.

"Ettrick was covered with trees in the old days," he says. "The monks had it first and after that it was the royal forest. It was the King's forest. Beech trees, oak trees, rowan trees."

"As many trees as this?" says Mary, made bolder than usual by the novel splendors of the day.

"Better trees. Older. It was famous all over Scotland. The Royal Forest of Ettrick."

"And Nova Scotia is where our brother James is," Mary continues.

"He may be or he may not. It would be easy to die here and nobody know you were dead. Wild animals could have eaten him."

"Come near this baby again and I'll skin you alive," says Agnes to Young James who is circling her and the baby, pretending that they hold no interest for him.

Agnes is thinking it would serve him right, the fellow who never even took his leave of her. But she has to hope he will show up sometime and see her married to his brother. So that he will wonder. Also he will understand that in the end he did not get the better of her.

Mary wonders how her father can talk in that way, about how wild animals could have eaten his own son. Is that how the sorrows of the years take hold on you, to turn your heart of flesh to a heart of stone, as it says in the old song? And if it is so, how carelessly and disdainfully might he talk about her, who never meant to him a fraction of what the boys did?

SOMEBODY HAS BROUGHT A FIDDLE onto the deck and is tuning up to play. People who have been hanging on to the rail and pointing out to each other what any one of them could see on their own—likewise repeating the name that by now everyone knows, Nova Scotia—are distracted by these sounds and begin to call for dancing. They call out the names of the reels and dances they want the fiddler to play. Space is cleared and couples line up in some sort of order and after a lot of uneasy fiddle-scraping and impatient shouts of encouragement, the music comes through and gathers its authority and the dancing begins.

Dancing, at seven o'clock in the morning.

Andrew comes up from below, bearing their supply of water. He stands and watches for a little, then surprises Mary by asking, would she dance?

"Who will look after the boy?" says Agnes immediately. "I am not going to get up and chase him." She is fond of dancing, but is prevented now, not only by the nursing baby but by the soreness of the parts of her body that were so battered in the birth.

Mary is already refusing, saying she cannot go, but Andrew says, "We will put him on the tether."

"No, no," says Mary. "I've no need to dance." She believes that Andrew has taken pity on her, remembering how she used to be left on the sidelines in school games and at the dancing, though she can actually run and dance perfectly well. Andrew is the only one of her brothers capable of such consideration, but she would almost rather he behaved like the others, and left her ignored as she has always been. Pity does gall her.

Young James begins to complain loudly, having recognized the word *tether.*

"You be still," says his father. "Be still or I'll clout you."

Then Old James surprises them all by turning his attention to his grandson.

"You. Young lad. You sit by me."

"Oh, he will not sit," says Mary. "He will run off and then you cannot chase him, Father. I will stay."

"He will sit," says Old James.

"Well, settle it," says Agnes to Mary. "Go or stay."

Young James looks from one to the other, cautiously snuffling.

"Does he not know even the simplest word?" says his grandfather. "Sit. Lad. Here."

"He knows all kinds of words," says Mary. "He knows the name of the gib-boom."

Young James repeats, "Gib-boom."

"Hold your tongue and sit down," says Old James. Young James lowers himself, reluctantly, to the spot indicated.

"Now go," says Old James to Mary. And all in confusion, on the verge of tears, she is led away.

"What a suckie-laddie she's made of him," says Agnes, not exactly to her father-in-law but into the air. She speaks almost indifferently, teasing the baby's cheek with her nipple.

PEOPLE ARE DANCING, not just in the figure of the reel but quite outside of it, all over the deck. They are grabbing anyone at all and twirling around. They are even grabbing some of the sailors if they can get hold of them. Men dance with women, men dance with men, women dance with women, children dance with each other or all alone and without any idea of the steps, getting in the way—but everybody is in everybody's way already and it is no matter. Some children dance in one spot, whirling around with their arms in the air till they get so dizzy they fall down. Two seconds later they are on their feet, recovered, and ready to begin the same thing all over again.

Mary has caught hands with Andrew, and is swung around by him, then passed on to others, who bend to her and fling her undersized body about. She has lost sight of Young James and cannot know if he has remained with his grandfather. She dances down at the level of the children, though she is less bold and carefree. In the thick of so many bodies she is helpless, she cannot pause—she has to stamp and wheel to the music or be knocked down.

"NOW YOU LISTEN AND I WILL TELL YOU," says Old James. "This old man, Will O'Phaup, my grandfather—he was my grandfather as I am yours—Will O'Phaup was sitting outside his house in the evening, resting himself, it was mild summer weather. All alone, he was.

"And there was three little lads hardly bigger than you are yourself, they came around the corner of Will's house. They told him good evening. *Good evening to you, Will O'Phaup,* they says.

"*Well good evening to you, lads, what can I do for you?*

"*Can you give us a bed for the night or a place to lay down,* they says. And *Aye,* he says, *Aye, I'm thinking three bits of lads like yourselves should not be so hard to find the room for.* And he goes into the house with them following and they says, *And by the by could you give us the key, too, the big silver key that you had of us?* Well, Will looks around, and he looks for the key, till he thinks to himself, what key was that? And turns around to ask them. *What key was that?* For he knew he never had such a thing in his life. Big key or silver key, he never had it. *What key are you talking to me about?* And turns himself round and they are not there. Goes out of the house, all round the house, looks to the road. No trace of them. Looks to the hills. No trace.

"Then Will knew it. They was no lads at all. Ah, no. They was no lads at all."

Young James has not made any sound. At his back is the thick and noisy wall of dancers, to the side his mother, with the small clawing beast that bites into her body. And in front of him is the old man with his rumbling voice, insistent but remote, and his

blast of bitter breath, his sense of grievance and importance absolute as the child's own. His nature hungry, crafty, and oppressive.
It is Young James's first conscious encounter with someone as perfectly self-centered as himself.

He is barely able to focus his intelligence, to show himself not
quite defeated.

"Key," he says. "Key?"

AGNES, WATCHING THE DANCING, catches sight of Andrew,
red in the face and heavy on his feet, linked arm to arm with various jovial women. They are doing the "Strip the Willow" now.
There is not one girl whose looks or dancing gives Agnes any worries. Andrew never gives her any worries anyway. She sees Mary
tossed around, with even a flush of color in her cheeks—though
she is too shy, and too short, to look anybody in the face. She sees
the nearly toothless witch of a woman who birthed a child a week
after her own, dancing with her hollow-cheeked man. No sore
parts for her. She must have dropped the child as slick as if it was
a rat, then given it over to one or the other of her weedy-looking
daughters to mind.

She sees Mr. Suter, the surgeon, out of breath, pulling away from
a woman who would grab him, ducking through the dance and
coming to greet her.

She wishes he would not. Now he will see who her father-in-law
is, he may have to listen to the old fool's gabble. He will get a look
at their drab, and now not even clean, country clothes. He will see
her for what she is.

"So here you are," he says. "Here you are with your treasure."

That is not a word that Agnes has ever heard used to refer to a
child. It seems as if he is talking to her in the way he might talk to a
person of his own acquaintance, some sort of a lady, not as a doctor
talks to a patient. Such behavior embarrasses her and she does not
know how to answer.

"Your baby is well?" he says, taking a more down-to-earth
tack. He is still catching his breath from the dancing, and his face,
though not flushed, is covered with a fine sweat.

"Aye."

"And you yourself? You have your strength again?"

She shrugs very slightly, so as not to shake the child off the nipple.

"You have a fine color, anyway, that is a good sign."

She thinks that he sighs as he says this, and wonders if that may be because his own color, seen in the morning light, is sickly as whey.

He asks then if she will permit him to sit and talk to her for a few moments, and once more she is confused by his formality, but says he may do as he likes.

Her father-in-law gives the surgeon—and her as well—a despising glance, but Mr. Suter does not notice it, perhaps does not even understand that the old man, and the fair-haired boy who sits straight-backed and facing this old man, have anything to do with her.

"The dancing is very lively," he says. "And you are not given a chance to decide who you would dance with. You get pulled about by all and sundry." And then he asks, "What will you do in Canada West?"

It seems to her the silliest question. She shakes her head—what can she say? She will wash and sew and cook and almost certainly suckle more children. Where that will be does not much matter. It will be in a house, and not a fine one.

She knows now that this man likes her, and in what way. She remembers his fingers on her skin. What harm can happen, though, to a woman with a baby at her breast?

She feels stirred to show him a bit of friendliness.

"What will you do?" she says.

He smiles and says that he supposes he will go on doing what he has been trained to do, and that the people in America—so he has heard—are in need of doctors and surgeons just like other people in the world.

"But I do not intend to get walled up in some city. I'd like to get as far as the Mississippi River, at least. Everything beyond the Mississippi used to belong to France, you know, but now it belongs to America and it is wide open, anybody can go there, except that you may run into the Indians. I would not mind that either. Where there is fighting with the Indians, there'll be all the more need for a surgeon."

She does not know anything about this Mississippi River, but she knows that he does not look like a fighting man himself—he does not look as if he could stand up in a quarrel with the brawling lads of Hawick, let alone red Indians.

Two dancers swing so close to them as to put a wind into their faces. It is a young girl, a child really, whose skirts fly out—and who should she be dancing with but Agnes's brother-in-law, Walter. Walter makes some sort of silly bow to Agnes and the surgeon and his father, and the girl pushes him and turns him around and he laughs at her. She is all dressed up like a young lady, with bows in her hair. Her face is lit with enjoyment, her cheeks are glowing like lanterns, and she treats Walter with great familiarity, as if she had got hold of a large toy.

"That lad is your friend?" says Mr. Suter.

"No. He is my husband's brother."

The girl is laughing quite helplessly, as she and Walter—through her heedlessness—have almost knocked down another couple in the dance. She is not able to stand up for laughing, and Walter has to support her. Then it appears that she is not laughing but in a fit of coughing and every time the fit seems ready to stop she laughs and gets it started again. Walter is holding her against himself, half-carrying her to the rail.

"There is one lass that will never have a child to her breast," says Mr. Suter, his eyes flitting to the sucking child before resting again on the girl. "I doubt if she will live long enough to see much of America. Does she not have anyone to look after her? She should not have been allowed to dance."

He stands up so that he can keep the girl in view as Walter holds her by the rail.

"There, she has got stopped," he says. "No hemorrhaging. At least not this time."

Agnes does not pay attention to most people, but she can sense things about any man who is interested in her, and she can see now that he takes a satisfaction in the verdict he has passed on this young girl. And she understands that this must be because of some condition of his own—that he must be thinking that he is not so badly off, by comparison.

There is a cry at the rail, nothing to do with the girl and Walter.

Another cry, and many people break off dancing, hurrying to look at the water. Mr. Suter rises and goes a few steps in that direction, following the crowd, then turns back.

"A whale," he says. "They are saying there is a whale to be seen off the side."

"You stay here," cries Agnes in an angry voice, and he turns to her in surprise. But he sees that her words are meant for Young James, who is on his feet.

"This is your lad then?" says Mr. Suter as if he has made a remarkable discovery. "May I carry him over to have a look?"

AND THAT IS HOW MARY—happening to raise her face in the crush of passengers—beholds Young James, much amazed, being carried across the deck in the arms of a hurrying stranger, a pale and determined though slyly courteous-looking dark-haired man who is surely a foreigner. A child-stealer, or child-murderer, heading for the rail.

She gives so wild a shriek that anybody would think she was in the Devil's clutches herself, and people make way for her as they would do for a mad dog.

"Stop thief, stop thief," she is crying. "Take the boy from him. Catch him. James. James. Jump down!"

She flings herself forward and grabs the child's ankles, yanking him so that he howls in fear and outrage. The man bearing him nearly topples over but doesn't give him up. He holds on and pushes at Mary with his foot.

"Take her arms," he shouts, to those around them. He is short of breath. "She is in a fit."

Andrew has pushed his way in, among people who are still dancing and people who have stopped to watch the drama. He manages somehow to get hold of Mary and Young James and to make clear that the one is his son and the other his sister and that it is not a question of fits. Young James throws himself from his father to Mary and then begins kicking to be let down.

All is shortly explained with courtesies and apologies from Mr. Suter—through which Young James, quite recovered to himself, cries out over and over again that he must see the whale. He insists upon this just as if he knew perfectly well what a whale was.

Andrew tells him what will happen if he does not stop his racket.
"I had just stopped for a few minutes' talk with your wife, to ask
her if she was well," the surgeon says. "I did not take time to bid her
good-bye, so you must do it for me."

THERE ARE WHALES for Young James to see all day and for
everybody to see who can be bothered. People grow tired of looking at them.

"Is there anybody but a fine type of rascal would sit down to
talk with a woman that had her bosoms bared," says Old James,
addressing the sky.

Then he quotes from the Bible regarding whales.

*"There go the ships and there is that leviathan whom thou hast
made to play therein. That crooked serpent, the dragon that is in the
sea."*

But he will not stir himself to go and have a look.

Mary remains unconvinced by the surgeon's story. Of course
he would have to say to Agnes that he was taking the child to look
at the whale. But that does not make it the truth. Whenever the
picture of that devilish man carrying Young James flashes through
her mind, and she feels in her chest the power of her own cry, she
is astonished and happy. It is still her own belief that she has saved
him.

NETTIE'S FATHER'S NAME IS MR. CARBERT. Sometimes he
sits and listens to Nettie read or talks to Walter. The day after all
the celebration and the dancing, when many people are in a bad
humor from exhaustion and some from drinking whiskey, and
hardly anybody looks at the shore, he seeks Walter out to talk to
him.

"Nettie is so taken with you," he says, "that she has got the idea
that you must come along with us to Montreal."

He gives an apologetic laugh, and Walter laughs too.

"Then she must think that Montreal is in Canada West," says
Walter.

"No, no. I am not making a joke. I looked out for you to talk to
you on purpose when she was not with us. You are a fine compan-
ion for her and it makes her happy to be with you. And I can see

you are an intelligent lad and a prudent one and one who would do well in my business."

"I am with my father and my brother," says Walter, so startled that his voice has a youthful yelp in it. "We are going to get land."

"Well then. You are not the only son your father has. There may not be enough good land for all of you. And you may not always want to be a farmer."

Walter says to himself, that is true.

"My daughter now, how old do you think she is?"

Walter cannot think. He shakes his head.

"She is fourteen, nearly fifteen," Nettie's father says. "You would not think so, would you? But it does not matter, that is not what I am talking about. Not about you and Nettie, anything in years to come. You understand that? There is no question of years to come. But I would like for you to come with us and let her be the child that she is and make her happy now with your company. Then I would naturally want to repay you, and there would also be work for you and if all went well you could count on advancement."

Both of them at this point notice that Nettie is coming towards them. She sticks out her tongue at Walter, so quickly that her father apparently does not notice.

"No more now. Think about it and pick your time to tell me," says her father. "But sooner rather than later would be best."

We were becalmed the 21st and 22nd but we had rather more wind the 23rd but in the afternoon were all alarmed by a squall of wind accompanied by thunder and lightening which was very terrible and we had one of our mainsails that had just been mended torn to rags again with the wind. The squall lasted about 8 or 10 minutes and the 24th we had a fair wind which set us a good way up the River, where it became more strait so that we saw land on both sides of the River. But we becalmed again till the 31st when we had a breeze only two hours . . .

Walter has not taken long to make up his mind. He knows enough to thank Mr. Carbert, but says that he has not thought of working in a city, or any indoor job. He means to work with his family until they are set up with some sort of house and land to farm and then when they do not need his help so much he thinks of being a trader to the Indians, a sort of explorer. Or a miner for gold.

"As you will," says Mr. Carbert. They walk several steps together, side by side. "I must say I had thought you were rather more serious than that. Fortunately I said nothing to Nettie."

But Nettie has not been fooled as to the subject of their talks together. She pesters her father until he has to let her know how things have gone and then she seeks out Walter.

"I will not talk to you anymore from now on," she says, in a more grown-up voice than he has ever heard from her. "It is not because I am angry but just because if I go on talking to you I will have to think all the time about how soon I'll be saying good-bye to you. But if I stop now I will have already said good-bye so it will all be over sooner."

She spends the time that is left walking sedately with her father in her finest clothes.

Walter feels sorry to see her—in these lady's cloaks and bonnets she seems lost, she looks more of a child than ever, and her show of haughtiness is touching—but there is so much for him to pay attention to that he seldom thinks of her when she is out of sight.

Years will pass before she will reappear in his mind. But when she does, he will find that she is a source of happiness, available to him till the day he dies. Sometimes he will even entertain himself with thoughts of what might have happened, had he taken up the offer. Most secretly, he will imagine a radiant recovery, Nettie's acquiring a tall and maidenly body, their life together. Such foolish thoughts as a man may have in secret.

Several boats from the land came alongside of us with fish, rum, live sheep, tobacco, etc. which they sold very high to the passengers. The 1st of August we had a slight breeze and on the morning of the 2nd we passed by the Isle of Orleans and about six in the morning we were in sight of Quebec in as good health I think as when we left Scotland. We are to sail for Montreal tomorrow in a steamboat . . .

My brother Walter in the former part of this letter has written a large journal which I intend to sum up in a small ledger.

We have had a very prosperous voyage being wonderfully preserved in health. Out of three hundred passengers only 3 died,
two of which being unhealthy when they left their native land
and the other a child born in the ship. Our family has been as
healthy on board as in their ordinary state in Scotland. We can
say nothing yet about the state of the country. There is a great
number of people landing here but wages is good. I can neither
advise nor discourage people from coming. The land is very
extensive and very thin-peopled. I think we have seen as much
land as might serve all the people in Britain uncultivated and
covered with wood. We will write you again as soon as settled.

When Andrew has added this paragraph, Old James is persuaded to add his signature to those of his two sons before this
letter is sealed and posted to Scotland, from Quebec. He will write
nothing else, saying, "What does it matter to me? It cannot be my
home. It can be nothing to me but the land where I will die."

"It will be that for all of us," says Andrew. "But when the time
comes we will think of it more as a home."

"Time will not be given to me to do that."

"Are you not well, Father?"

"I am well and I am not."

Young James is now paying occasional attention to the old man,
sometimes stopping in front of him and looking straight into his
face and saying one word to him, with a sturdy insistence, as if that
could not help but lead to a conversation.

He chooses the same word every time. *Key.*

"He bothers me," Old James says. "I don't like the boldness of
him. He will go on and on and not remember a thing of Scotland
where he was born or the ship he travelled on, he will get to talking
another language the way they do when they go to England, only
it will be worse than theirs. He looks at me with the kind of a look
that says he knows that me and my times is all over with."

"He will remember plenty of things," says Mary. Since the
dancing on deck and the incident of Mr. Suter she has grown more
forthright within the family.

"And he doesn't mean his look to be bold," she says. "It is just
that he is interested in everything. He understands what you say,

far more than you think. He takes everything in and he thinks about it. He may grow up to be a preacher."

Although she has such a stiff and distant regard for her religion, that is still the most distinguished thing that she can imagine a man to be.

Her eyes fill with tears of enthusiasm, but the rest of them look down at the child with sensible reservations.

Young James stands in the midst of them—bright-eyed, fair, and straight. Slightly preening, somewhat wary, unnaturally solemn, as if he has indeed felt descend on him the burden of the future.

The adults too feel the astonishment of the moment, as if they have been borne for these past six weeks not on a ship but on one great wave, which has landed them with a mighty thump among such clamor of the French tongue and cries of gulls and clanging of Papist church bells, altogether an infidel commotion.

Mary thinks that she could snatch up Young James and run away into some part of the strange city of Quebec and find work as a sewing-woman (talk on the boat has made her aware that such work is in demand) and bring him up all by herself as if she was his mother.

Andrew thinks of what it would be like to be here as a free man, without wife or father or sister or children, without a single burden on your back, what could you do then? He tells himself it is no use to think about it.

Agnes has heard women on the boat say that the officers you see in the street here are surely the best-looking men you can meet anywhere in the world, and she thinks now that this is surely true. A girl would have to watch herself with them. She has heard also that the men anyplace over here are ten or twenty times more numerous than the women. That must mean you can get what you want out of them. Marriage. Marriage to a man with enough money to let you ride in a carriage and buy paints to cover any birthmark on your face and send presents to your mother. If you were not married already and dragged down with two children.

Walter reflects that his brother is strong and Agnes is strong—she can help him on the land while Mary cares for the children. Whoever said that he should be a farmer? When they get to Montreal he will go and attach himself to the Hudson's Bay Company and they will send him to the frontier where he will find riches as well as adventure.

OLD JAMES has sensed defection, and begins to lament openly. "How shall we sing the Lord's song in a strange land?"

BUT HE RECOVERED HIMSELF. Here he is, a year or so later, in the New World, in the new town of York which is just about to have its name changed to Toronto. He is writing to his eldest son Robert.

> . . . the people here speaks very good English there is many of
> our Scots words they cannot understand what we are saying
> and they live far more independent then King George . . .
> There is a Road goes Straight North from York for fifty miles
> and the farm Houses almost all Two Stories High. Some will
> have as good as 12 Cows and four or five horses for they pay no
> Taxes just a perfect trifell and ride in their Gigs or chire like
> Lords . . . there is no Presbetarian minister in this town as yet
> but there is a large English Chapel and Methodist Chapel . . .
> the English minister reads all that he Says unless it be for his
> Clark Craying always at the end of every Period Good Lord
> Deliver us and the Methodist prays as Loud as Ever He Can
> and the people is all doun on there knees Craying Amen so
> you can Scarce Hear what the Priest is Saying and I have
> Seen some of them Jumping up as if they would have gone to
> Heaven Soul and Body but there Body was a filthy Clog to
> them for they always fell down again altho craying O Jesus O
> Jesus as He had been there to pull them up threw the Loft . . .
> Now Robert I do not advise you to Come Hear so you may
> take your own will when you did not come along with us I
> do not Expect Ever to See you again . . . May the good will of
> Him that Dwelt in the Bush rest up on you . . . if I had thought
> that you would have deserted us I would not have comed
> hear it was my ame to get you all Near me made me Come to
> America but mans thoughts are Vanity for have Scattered you
> far wider but I Can not help it now . . . I shall say no more but
> wish that the God of Jacob be your god and may be your gide

*for Ever and Ever is the sincer prayer of your Loving Father till
Death . . .*

There is more—the whole letter passed on by Hogg's connivance and printed in *Blackwoods Magazine,* where I can look it up
today.

And some considerable time after that, he writes another letter,
addressed to the Editor of *The Colonial Advocate,* and published
in that newspaper. By this time the family is settled in Esquesing
Township, in Canada West.

*. . . The Scots Bodys that lives heare is all doing Tolerably well
for the things of this world but I am afraid that few of them
thinks about what will Come of thear Soul when Death there
Days doth End for they have found a thing they call Whiskey
and a great mony of them dabbales and drinks at it till they
make themselves worse than a ox or an ass . . . Now sir I could
tell you bit of Stories but I am afraid you will put me in your
Calonial Advocate I do not Like to be put in prent I once wrote
a bit of a letter to my Son Robert in Scotland and my friend
James Hogg the Poet put it in Blackwoods Magazine and had
me all through North America before I knew my letter was
gone Home . . . Hogg poor man has spent most of his life in
conning Lies and if I read the Bible right I think it says that all
Liares is to have there pairt in the Lake that Burns with Fire
and Brimstone but I supose they find it a Loquarative trade for
I belive that Hogg and Walter Scott has got more money for
Lieing than old Boston and the Erskins got for all the Sermons
ever they Wrote . . .*

And I am surely one of the liars the old man talks about, in what
I have written about the voyage. Except for Walter's journal, and
the letters, the story is full of my invention.

The sighting of Fife from Castle Rock is related by Hogg, so it
must be true.

THOSE TRAVELLERS LIE BURIED—all but one of them—in
the graveyard of Boston Church, in Esquesing, in Halton County,

almost within sight, and well within sound, of Highway 401 north of Milton, which at that spot may be the busiest road in Canada.

The church—built on what was once the farm of Andrew Laidlaw—is of course named for Thomas Boston. It is built of blackened limestone blocks. The front wall rises higher than the rest of·the building—rather in the style of the false fronts on old-fashioned main streets—and it has an archway on top of it, rather than a tower—for the church bell.

Old James is here. In fact he is here twice, or at least his name is, along with the name of his wife, born Helen Scott, and buried in Ettrick in the year 1800. Their names appear on the same stone that bears the names of Andrew and Agnes. But surprisingly, the same names are written on another stone that looks older than others in the graveyard—a darkened, blotchy slab such as you are more apt to see in the churchyards of the British Isles. Anyone trying to fig-ure this out might wonder if they carried it across the ocean, with the mother's name on it, waiting for the father's to be added—if it was perhaps an awkward burden, wrapped in sacking and tied with stout cord, borne by Walter down into the hold of the ship.

But why would someone have taken the trouble to have the names also added to those on the newer column above Andrew and Agnes's grave?

It looks as if the death and burial of such a father was a matter worth recording twice over.

Nearby, close to the graves of her father and her brother Andrew and her sister-in-law Agnes, is the grave of Little Mary, married after all and buried beside Robert Murray, her husband. Women were scarce and so were prized in the new country. She and Robert did not have any children together, but after Mary's early death he married another woman and by her he had four sons who lie here, dead at the ages of two, and three, and four, and thirteen. The second wife is there too. Her stone says *Mother*. Mary's says *Wife*.

And here is the brother James who was not lost to them, who made his way from Nova Scotia to join them, first in York and then in Esquesing, farming with Andrew. He brought a wife with him, or found her in the community. Perhaps she helped with Agnes's babies before she started having her own. For Agnes had a great number of pregnancies, and raised many children. In a letter written to his brothers Robert and William in Scotland, telling of the death of their father, in 1829 (a cancer, not much pain until near the end, though *it eat away a great part of his cheek and jaw*), Andrew mentions that his wife has been feeling poorly for the past three years. This may be a roundabout way of saying that during those years she bore her sixth, seventh, and eighth child. She must have recovered her health, for she lived into her eighties.

ANDREW GAVE THE LAND that the church is built on. Or possibly sold it. It is hard to measure devoutness against business sense. He seems to have prospered, though he spread himself less than Walter. Walter married an American girl from Montgomery County in New York State. Eighteen when she married him, thirty-three when she died after the birth of her ninth child. Walter did not marry again, but farmed successfully, educated his sons, speculated in land, and wrote letters to the government complaining about his taxes, also objecting to the township's participation in a proposed railway—the interest being squandered, he says, for the benefit of capitalists in Britain.

Nevertheless it is a fact that he and Andrew supported the British governor, Sir Francis Bond Head, who was surely representing those capitalists, against the rebellion led by their fellow Scot, William Lyon Mackenzie, in 1837. They wrote to the governor a letter of assiduous flattery, in the grand servile style of their times. Some of their descendants might wish this not to be true, but there is not much to be done about the politics of our relatives, living or dead.

And Walter was able to take a trip back to Scotland, where he had himself photographed wearing a plaid and holding on to a bouquet of thistles.

On the stone commemorating Andrew and Agnes (and Old James and Helen) there appears also the name of their daughter Isabel, who like her mother Agnes died an old woman. She has a married name, but there is no further sign of her husband.

Born at Sea.

And here also is the name of Andrew and Agnes's firstborn child, Isabel's elder brother. His dates as well.

Young James was dead within a month of the family's landing at Quebec. His name is here but surely he cannot be. They had not taken up their land when he died, they had not even seen this place. He may have been buried somewhere along the way from Montreal to York or in that hectic new town itself. Perhaps in a raw temporary burying ground now paved over, perhaps without a stone in a churchyard where other bodies would someday be laid on top of his. Dead of some mishap in the busy streets of York, or of a fever, or dysentery—of any of the ailments, the accidents, that were the common destroyers of little children in his time.

Working for a Living

~

WHEN MY FATHER WAS TWELVE YEARS OLD and had gone as far as he could go at the country school, he went into town to write a set of exams. Their proper name was the Entrance Examinations, but they were known collectively as the Entrance. The Entrance meant, literally, the entrance to high school, but it also meant, in an undefined way, the entrance to the world. The world of professions such as medicine or law or engineering or teaching. Country boys did enter that world in the years before the First World War, more easily than they did a generation later. It was a time of prosperity in Huron County and expansion in the country. It was 1913 and the country was not yet fifty years old.

My father passed the Entrance with high honors and went on to the Continuation School in the town of Blyth. Continuation Schools offered four years of high school, without the final year called Upper School, or Fifth Form—you would have to go to a larger town for that. It looked as if he was on his way.

During his first week at Continuation School my father heard the teacher read a poem.

> *Liza Grayman Ollie Minus.*
> *We can make Eliza blind.*
> *Andy Parting, Lee Beehinus.*
> *Foo Prince in the Sansa Time.*

He used to recite this to us as a joke, but the fact was, he did not hear it as a joke. Around the same time, he went into the stationery store and asked for Signs Snow Paper.

Signs Snow Paper.
Science notepaper.

Soon he was surprised to see the poem written on the blackboard.

> Lives of Great Men all remind us,
> We can make our lives sublime.
> And, departing, leave behind us
> Footprints on the Sands of Time.

He had not hoped for such reasonable clarification, would not
have dreamed of asking for it. He had been quite willing to give
the people at the school the right to have a strange language or
logic. He did not ask for them to make sense on his terms. He had a
streak of pride which might look like humility, making him scared
and touchy, ready to bow out. I know that very well. He made a
mystery there, a hostile structure of rules and secrets, far beyond
anything that really existed. He felt nearby the fierce breath of ridicule, he overestimated the competition, and the family caution,
the country wisdom, came to him then: stay out of it.

In those days people in town did generally look upon the people from the country as more apt to be slow-witted, tongue-tied,
uncivilized, than themselves, and somewhat more docile in spite
of their strength. And farmers saw people who lived in towns as
having an easy life and being unlikely to survive in situations calling for fortitude, self-reliance, hard work. They believed this in
spite of the fact that the hours men worked at factory jobs or in
stores were long and the wages low, in spite of the fact that many
houses in town had no running water or flush toilets or electricity.
But the people in town had Saturday or Wednesday afternoons and
the whole of Sundays off and that was enough to make them soft.
The farmers had not one holiday in their lives. Not even the Scots
Presbyterians; cows don't recognize the Sabbath.

The country people when they came into town to shop or to
go to church often seemed stiff and shy and the town people did
not realize that this could actually be seen as a superior behavior.
I'm-not-going-to-let-any-of-them-make-a-fool-out-of-me behavior.
Money would not make much difference. Farmers might maintain
their proud and wary reserve in the presence of citizens whom they
could buy and sell.

My father would say later that he had gone to Continuation School too young to know what he was doing, and that he should have stayed there, he should have made something out of himself. But he said this almost as a matter of form, not as if he cared very much. And it wasn't as if he had run off home at the first indication that there were things he didn't understand. He was never very clear about how long he had stayed. Three years and part of the fourth? Two years and part of the third? And he didn't quit suddenly—it was not a matter of going to school one day and staying away the next and never showing up again. He just began to spend more and more time in the bush and less and less time at school, so that his parents decided there was not much point in thinking about sending him to a larger town to do his Fifth Form, not much hope of university or the professions. They could have afforded that—though not easily—but it was evidently not what he wanted. And it could not be seen as a great disappointment. He was their only son, the only child. The farm would be his.

There was no more wild country in Huron County then than there is now. Perhaps there was less. The farms had been cleared in the period between 1830 and 1860, when the Huron Tract was being opened up, and they were cleared thoroughly. Many creeks had been dredged—the progressive thing to do was to straighten them out and make them run like tame canals between the fields. The early farmers hated the very sight of a tree and admired the look of open land. And the masculine approach to the land was managerial, dictatorial. Only women were allowed to care about landscape and not to think always of its subjugation and productivity. My grandmother, for example, was famous for having saved a line of silver maples along the lane. These trees grew beside a crop field and they were getting big and old—their roots interfered with the ploughing and they shaded too much of the crop. My grandfather and my father went out one morning and made ready to cut the first of them down. But my grandmother saw what they were doing from the kitchen window and she flew out in her apron and harangued and upbraided them so that they finally had to take up the axes and the crosscut saw and leave the scene. The trees stayed and spoiled the crop at the edge of the field until the terrible winter of 1935 finished them off.

But at the back of the farms the farmers were compelled by law to leave a woodlot. They could cut trees there both for their own use and to sell. Wood of course had been their first crop—rock elm went for ships' timbers and white pine for the ships' masts, until hardly any rock elm or white pine remained. Now there was protection decreed for the poplar and ash and maple and oak and beech, the cedar and hemlock that were left.

Through the woodlot—called the bush—at the back of my grandfather's farm ran the Blyth Creek, dredged a long time ago when the farm was first cleared. The earth dredged out then made a high, hummocky bank on which thick clumps of cedars grew. This was where my father started trapping. He eased himself out of school and into the life of a fur-trapper. He could follow the Blyth Creek for many miles in either direction, to its rising in Grey Township or to the place where it flows into the Maitland River which flows into Lake Huron. In some places—most particularly in the village of Blyth—the creek became public for a while, but for much of its length it ran through the backs of farms, with the bush on either side, so that it was possible to follow it and be hardly aware of the farms, the cleared land, the straight-laid roads and fences—it was possible to imagine that you were out in the forest as it was a hundred years ago, and for hundreds of years before that.

My father had read a lot of books by this time, books he found at home and in the Blyth Library and in the Sunday School Library. He had read books by Fenimore Cooper and he had absorbed the myths or half-myths about wilderness that most of the country boys around him knew nothing about, since few of them were readers. Most boys whose imaginations were lit up by the same notions as his would live in cities. If they were rich enough they would travel north every summer with their families, they would go on canoe trips and later on fishing and hunting trips. If their families were truly rich they would navigate the rivers of the Far North with Indian guides. People eager for this experience of the wilderness would drive right through our part of the country without noticing there was one bit of wilderness there.

But farm boys from Huron County, knowing hardly anything about this big deep country of the Precambrian Shield and the wild rivers, nevertheless were drawn—some of them were, for a time—drawn to the strips of bush along the creeks, where they fished and hunted and built rafts and set traps. Even if they hadn't read a word about that sort of life they might make their forays into it. But they soon gave it up to enter upon the real, heavy work of their lives, as farmers.

And one of the differences between farmers then and now was that in those days nobody expected recreation to play any regular part in the farming life.

My father, being a farm boy with that extra, inspired or romantic perception (he would not have cared for those words), with a Fenimore Cooper–cultivated hunger, did not turn aside from these juvenile pursuits at the age of eighteen or nineteen or twenty. Instead of giving up the bush, he took to it more steadily and seriously. He began to be talked about and thought about more as a trapper than as a young farmer. And as a solitary and slightly odd young man, though not a person who was in any way feared or disliked. He was edging away from the life of a farmer, just as he had edged away earlier from the idea of getting an education and becoming a professional man. He was edging towards a life he probably could not clearly visualize, since he would know what he didn't want so much better than what he wanted.

A life in the bush, away from the towns, on the edge of the farms—how could it be managed?

Even here, where men and women mostly took whatever was cut out for them, some men had managed it. Even in this tamed country there were a few hermits, a few men who had inherited farms and didn't keep them up, or who were just squatters come from God knows where. They fished and hunted and travelled around, were gone and came back, were gone and never came back—not like the farmers who whenever they left their own localities went in buggies or sleighs or more often now by car, bound on definite errands to certain destinations.

He was making money from his trapline. Some skins could bring him as much as a fortnight's work on a threshing gang. So at home they could not complain. He paid board, and he still helped his father when it was necessary. He and his father never talked. They could work all morning cutting wood in the bush, and never say a word, except when they had to, speak about the work. His father was not interested in the bush except as a woodlot. It was to him just like a field of oats, with the difference that the crop was firewood.

His mother was more curious. She walked back to the bush on Sunday afternoons. She was a tall upright woman with a stately figure, but she still had a tomboy's stride. She would bunch up her skirts and expertly swing her legs over a fence. She was knowledgeable about wildflowers and berries and she could tell you the name of any bird from its song.

He showed her the snares where he caught fish. That made her uneasy, because the fish could be caught in the snares on a Sunday, just as on any other day. She was very strict about all Presbyterian rules and observances, and this strictness had a peculiar history. She had not been brought up as a Presbyterian at all, but had led a carefree childhood and girlhood as a member of the Anglican Church, also known as the Church of England. There were not many Anglicans in that part of the country and they were sometimes thought of as next thing to Papists—but also as next door to freethinkers. Their religion often seemed to outsiders to be all a matter of bows and responses, with short sermons, easy interpretations, worldly ministers, much pomp and frivolity. A religion to the liking of her father, who had been a convivial Irishman, a storyteller, a drinker. But when my grandmother married she had wrapped herself up in her husband's Presbyterianism, becoming fiercer than many who were brought up in it. She was a born Anglican who took on the Presbyterian righteousness-competition just as she was a born tomboy who took on the farm-housewife competition, with her whole heart. People might have wondered, did she do this for love?

My father and those who knew her well did not think so. She and my grandfather were mismatched, though they didn't fight. He thoughtful, silent; she spirited, sociable. No, not for love but for pride's sake she did what she did. Not to be outdone or criticized in any way. And not to have anybody say that she regretted a decision that she had made, or wanted anything that she couldn't have.

She stayed friends with her son in spite of the Sunday fish, which she wouldn't cook. She took an interest in the animal skins he showed her, and heard how much he got for them. She washed his smelly clothes, whose smell was as much from the fish bait he carried as from the pelts and guts. She could be exasperated but tolerant with him as if he was a much younger son. And perhaps he did seem younger to her, with his traps and treks along the creek, and his unsociability. He never went after girls, and gradually lost touch with his childhood friends who were doing so. She did not mind. His behavior might have helped her to bear a disappointment that he had not gone on in school, he was not going to become a doctor or a minister. Maybe she could pretend that he might still do that, the old plans—her plans for him—being not forgotten but just postponed. At least he was not just turning into a silent farmer, a copy of his father.

As for my grandfather, he passed no opinion, did not say whether he approved or disapproved. He maintained his air of discipline and privacy. He was a man born in Morris, settled in to be a farmer, a Grit and a Presbyterian. Born to be against the English Church and the Family Compact and Bishop Strachan and saloons; to be for universal suffrage (but not for women), free schools, responsible government, the Lord's Day Alliance. To live by hard routines, and refusals.

My grandfather diverged a little—he learned to play the fiddle, he married the tall temperamental Irish girl with eyes of two colors. That done, he withdrew, and for the rest of his life was diligent, orderly, and quiet. He too was a reader. In the winter he managed to get all his work done—and well done—and then he would read. He never talked about what he read, but the whole community knew about it. And respected him for it. That is an odd thing—there was a woman too who read, she got books from the library all the time, and nobody respected her in the least. The talk was always about how the dust grew under her beds and her husband ate a cold dinner. Perhaps it was because she read novels, stories, and the books my grandfather read were heavy. Heavy books, as everybody remembered, but their titles are not remembered. They came from the library, which at that time contained Blackstone, Macauley, Carlyle, Locke, Hume's *History of England*. What about *An Enquiry Concerning Human Understanding*? What about Voltaire? Karl Marx? It's possible.

Now—if the woman with the dustballs under the beds had read the heavy books, would she have been forgiven? I don't believe so. It was women who judged her, and women judged women more harshly than they did men. Also, it must be remembered that my grandfather got his work done first—his woodpiles were orderly and his stable shipshape. In no point of behavior did his reading affect his life.

Another thing said of my grandfather was that he prospered. But prosperity was not pursued, or understood, in those days, quite in the way it is now. I remember my grandmother saying, "When we needed something done—when your father went into Blyth to school and needed books and new clothes and so on—I would say to your grandfather, well we better raise another calf or something to get a bit extra." So it would seem that if they knew what to do to get that bit extra, they could have had it all along.

That is, in their ordinary life they were not always making as much money as they could have made. They were not stretching themselves to the limit. They did not see life in those terms. Nor did they see it in terms of saving at least a part of their energies for good times, as some of their Irish neighbors did.

How, then? I believe they saw it mostly as ritual. Seasonal and inflexible, very much like housework. To try to make more money, for an increase in status or so that life could become easier, might have seemed unbecoming.

A change in outlook from that of the man who went to Illinois. Maybe a lingering influence from that setback, on his more timid or thoughtful descendants.

This must have been the life my father saw waiting for him—a life that my grandmother, in spite of her own submission to it, was not altogether sorry to see him avoid.

There is one contradiction here. When you write about real people you are always up against contradictions. My grandfather owned the first car on the Eighth Line of Morris. It was a Gray-Dorrit. And my father in his teens had a crystal set, something that all boys wanted. Of course, he may have paid for it himself.

He may have paid for it with his trapping money.

The animals my father trapped were muskrats, mink, marten,

now and then a bobcat. Otter, weasels, foxes. Muskrats he trapped in the spring because their fur stays prime until about the end of April. All the others were at their best from the end of October on into winter. The white weasel does not attain its purity until around the tenth of December. He went out on snowshoes. He built up deadfalls, with a figure 4 trigger, set so the boards and branches fell onto the muskrat or mink. He nailed weasel traps to trees. He nailed boards together to make a square box trap working on the same principle as a deadfall—something less conspicuous to other trappers. The steel traps for muskrats were staked so the animal would drown, often at the end of a sloping cedar rail. Patience and foresight and guile were necessary. For the vegetarians he set out tasty bits of apple and parsnip; for the meat-eaters, such as mink, there was delectable fish bait mixed by himself and ripened in a jar in the ground. A similar meat mix for foxes was buried in June or July and dug up in the fall; they sought it out to roll upon, revelling in the pungency of decay.

Foxes interested him more and more. He followed them away from the creeks to the little rough sandy hills that are found sometimes between bush and pasture—they love the sandy hills at night. He learned to boil his traps in water and soft maple bark to kill the smell of metal. Such traps were set out in the open with a sifting of sand over them.

How do you kill a trapped fox? You don't want to shoot him, because of the wound left in the pelt and the blood smell spoiling the trap.

You stun him with the blow of a long, strong stick, and then put your foot on his heart.

Foxes in the wild are usually red. But occasionally a black fox will occur among them as a spontaneous mutation. He had never caught one. But he knew that some of these had been caught elsewhere and bred selectively to increase the show of white hairs along the back and tail. Then they were called silver foxes. Silver-fox farming was just beginning in Canada.

In 1925 my father bought a pair, a male silver fox and a female, and built a pen for them beside the barn. At first they must have seemed just another kind of animal being raised on the farm, something more bizarre than the chickens or the pigs or even the banty rooster, something rare and showy as peacocks, interesting for visitors. When my father bought them and built the pen for them it might even have been taken as a sign that he meant to stay, to be a slightly different farmer from most, but still a farmer.

The first litter was born, and he built more pens. He took a snapshot of his mother holding the three little pups. She looks apprehensive but sporting. Two of the pups were males and one female. He killed the males in the fall when their fur was prime and sold the pelts for an impressive price. The trapline began to seem less important than these animals raised in captivity.

A young woman came to visit. A cousin on the Irish side—a schoolteacher, lively and persistent and good-looking, a few years older than he. She was immediately interested in the foxes, and not, as his mother thought, pretending to be interested in order to entice him. (Between his mother and the visitor there was an almost instant antipathy, though they were cousins.) She came from a much poorer home, a poorer farm, than this one, and she had become a schoolteacher by her own desperate efforts. The only reason she had stopped there was that schoolteaching was the best thing for women that she had come across so far. She was a hardworking popular teacher, but some gifts that she knew she had were not being used. These gifts had something to do with taking chances, making money. They were gifts as out of place in my father's house as they had been in her own, looked at askance in both places, although they were the very gifts (less often mentioned than the hard work, the perseverance) that had built the country. She looked at the foxes and she did not see any romantic connection to the wilderness; she saw a new industry, the possibility of riches. She had a little money saved to buy a place where all this could get started in earnest. She became my mother.

WHEN I THINK OF MY PARENTS in the time before they became my parents, after they had made their decision but before their marriage had made it—in those days—irrevocable, they seem not only touching and helpless, marvellously deceived, but more attractive than at any later time. It is as if nothing was thwarted then and life still bloomed with possibilities, as if they enjoyed all sorts of power before they bent themselves towards each other. That can't be true, of course—they must have been anxious already—my mother must certainly have been anxious about being in her late twenties and unmarried. They must have known failure already, they may have turned to each other with reservations rather than the luxuriant optimism that I imagine. But I do imagine it, as we must all like to do, so we won't think that we were born out of affection that was always stingy, or an undertaking that was always half-hearted. I think that when they came and picked out the place where they would live for the rest of their lives, on the Maitland River just west of Wingham in Turnberry Township in the County of Huron, they were travelling in a car that ran well on dry roads on a bright spring day, and that they themselves were kind and handsome and healthy and trusting their luck.

NOT VERY LONG AGO I was driving with my husband on the back roads of Grey County, which is to the north and east of Huron County. We passed a country store standing empty at a crossroads. It had old-fashioned store windows, with long narrow panes. Out in front there was a stand for gas pumps which weren't there anymore. Close beside it was a mound of sumac trees and strangling vines, into which all kinds of junk had been thrown. The sumacs jogged my memory and I looked back at the store. It seemed to me that I had been here once, and that the scene was connected with some disappointment or dismay. I knew that I had never driven this way before in my adult life and I did not think I could have come here as a child. It was too far from home. Most of our drives out of town were to my grandparents' house in Blyth—they had retired there after they sold the farm. And once a summer we drove to the lake at Goderich. But even as I was saying this to my husband I remembered the disappointment. Ice cream. Then I remembered everything—the trip my father and I had made to Muskoka in 1941, when my mother was already there, selling furs at the Pine Tree Hotel north of Gravenhurst.

My father had stopped for gas at a country store and he had bought me an ice-cream cone. It was an out-of-the-way place and the ice cream must have been sitting in its tub for a long time. It had probably been partly melted at one stage, then refrozen. It had splinters of ice in it, pure ice, and its flavor was dismally altered. Even the cone was soft and stale.

"But why would he go this way to Muskoka?" my husband said. "Wouldn't he go along No. 9 and then go up on Highway 11?"

He was right. I wondered whether I could have been mistaken. It could have been another store at another crossroads where we bought the gas and the ice cream.

As we drove west, heading over the long hills for Bruce County and Highway 21, after sunset and before dark, I talked about what any long car trip—that is, any car trip over ten miles long—used to be like for our family, how arduous and uncertain. I described to my husband—whose family, more realistic than ours, considered themselves too poor to own a car—how the car's noises and movements, the jolting and rattling, the straining of the engine and the groan of the gears, made the crowning of hills and the covering of miles an effort that everybody in the car seemed to share. Would a tire go flat, would the radiator boil over, would there be a breakdown? The use of that word—*breakdown*—made it sound as if the car was frail and skittish, with a mysterious, almost human vulnerability.

Of course it wouldn't be like that if you had a newer car, or if you could afford to keep it in good repair, I said.

And it came to me why we would have been driving to Muskoka along back roads. I was not mistaken after all. My father must have been wary of taking the car through any sizable town or on a main highway. There were too many things wrong with it. It should not have been on the road at all. There were times when he could not afford to take it to the garage and this must have been one of them. He did what he could to fix it himself, to keep it running. Sometimes a neighbor helped him. I remember my father's saying, "The man's a mechanical genius," which makes me suspect that he was no mechanical genius himself.

Now I knew why such a feeling of risk and trepidation was mixed up with my memory of the unpaved, sometimes ungravelled roads—some were ridged in such a way that my father called them washboard roads—and the one-lane plank bridges. As things came back to me I could recall my father's telling me that he had only enough money to get to the hotel where my mother was, and that if she didn't have any money he didn't know what he was going to do. He didn't tell me this at the time, of course. He bought me the ice-cream cone, he told me to push on the dashboard when we were going up the hills, and I did so, though it was a ritual now, a joke, my faith having long ago evaporated. He seemed to be enjoying himself.

He told me about the circumstances of the trip years later, after my mother was dead, when he was remembering some times that they had gone through together.

THE FURS THAT MY MOTHER WAS SELLING to American tourists (we always spoke of American tourists, as if acknowledging that they were the only kind who could be of any use to us) were not raw furs, but tanned and dressed. Some skins were cut and sewn together in strips, to make capes; others were left whole and were made into what were called scarves. A fox scarf was one whole skin, a mink scarf was two or three skins. The head of the animal was left on and was given bright golden-brown glass eyes, also an artificial jaw. Fasteners were sewn on the paws. I believe that in the case of the mink the pelts were attached tail to mouth. The fox scarf was fastened paw to paw, and the fox cape sometimes had the fox's head sewn on out of place entirely, in the middle of the back, as a decoration.

Thirty years later these furs would have found their way into second-hand clothing stores and might be bought and worn as a joke. Of all the moldering and grotesque fashions of the past, this wearing of animal skins that were undisguised animal skins would seem the most amazing and barbaric.

My mother sold the fox scarves for twenty-five, thirty-five, forty, fifty dollars, depending on the number of white hairs, the "silver," in the pelt. Capes cost fifty, seventy-five, maybe a hundred dollars. My father had started raising mink as well as foxes during the late 1930s, but she did not have many mink scarves for sale and I do not remember what she charged for them. Perhaps we had been able to dispose of them to the furriers in Montreal without taking a loss.

THE COLONY OF FOX PENS took up a good deal of the territory on our farm. It stretched from behind the barn to the high bank overlooking the river flats. The first pens my father had made had roofs and walls of fine wire on a framework of cedar poles. They had earth floors. The pens built later on had raised wire floors. All the pens were set side by side on intersecting "streets" so that they made a town, and around the town was a high guard fence. Inside each pen was a kennel—a large wooden box with ventilation holes and a sloping roof or lid that could be lifted up. And there was a wooden ramp along one side of the pen, for the foxes' exercise. Because the building had been done at different times and not all planned out in the beginning, there were all the differences there are in a real town—there were wide streets and narrow streets, some spacious earth-floored old-fashioned pens and some smaller wire-floored modern pens that seemed less agreeably proportioned even if more sanitary. There were two long apartment buildings called the Sheds. The New Sheds had a covered walkway between two facing rows of pens with slanting wooden roofs and high wire floors. The Old Sheds was just a short row of attached pens rather primitively patched together. The New Sheds was a hellishly noisy place full of adolescents due to be pelted—most of them—before they were a year old. The Old Sheds was a slum and contained disappointing breeders who would not be kept another year, and the occasional cripple, and even, for a time, a red female fox who was well-disposed to humans and by way of being a pet. Either because of that, or her color, all the other foxes shunned her, and her name—for they all had names—was Old Maid. How she came to be there I don't know. A sport in a litter? A wild fox who tunnelled the wrong way under the guard fence?

When the hay was cut in our field some of it was spread on top of the pens to give the foxes shelter from the sun and keep their fur from turning brown. They looked very scruffy anyway, in the summertime—old fur falling out and new fur just coming in. By November they were resplendent, the tips of their tails snowy and their back fur deep and black, with its silver overlay. They were ready to be killed—unless they were to carry on as breeders. Their skins would be stretched, cleaned, sent off to be tanned, and then to the auctions.

Up to this time everything was in my father's control, barring some disease, or the chanciness of breeding. Everything was of his making—the pens, the kennels where the foxes could hide and have their young, the water dishes—made from tins—that tipped from the outside and were filled twice a day with fresh water, the tank that was trundled down the streets, carrying water from the pump, the feed trough in the barn where meal and water and ground horse meat were mixed, the killing box where the animal's trapped head met the blast of chloroform. Then, once the pelts were dried and cleaned and peeled off the stretch boards, nothing was within his control anymore. The pelts were laid flat in shipping boxes and sent off to Montreal and there was nothing to do but wait and see how they were graded and sold at the fur auctions. The whole year's income, the money to pay the feed bill, the money to pay the bank, the money he had to pay on the loan he had from his mother after she was widowed, had to come out of that. In some years the price of the furs was fairly good, in some years not too bad, in other years terrible. Though nobody could have seen it at the time, the truth was that he had got into the business just a little too late, and without enough capital to get going in a big way during the first years when the profits were high. Before he was fairly started the Depression arrived. The effect on his business was erratic, not steadily bad, as you might think. In some years he was slightly better off than he might have been on the farm, but there were more bad years than good. Things did not pick up much with the beginning of the war—in fact, the prices in 1940 were among the worst ever. During the Depression bad prices were not so hard to take—he could look around and see that nearly everybody was in the same boat—but now, with the war jobs opening up and the country getting prosperous again, it was very hard to have worked as he had and come up with next to nothing.

He said to my mother that he was thinking of joining the Army. He was thinking of pelting and selling all his stock, and going into the Army as a tradesman. He was not too old for that, and he had skills which would make him useful. He could be a carpenter—think of all the building he had done around his place. Or he could be a butcher—think of all the old horses he had slaughtered and cut up for the foxes.

My mother had another idea. She suggested that they keep out all the best skins, not sending them to the auctions but having them tanned and dressed—that is, made into scarves and capes, provided with eyes and claws—and then take them out and sell them. People were getting some money now. There were women around who had the money and the inclination to get dressed up. And there were tourists. We were off the beaten track for tourists, but she had heard about them, how the hotel resorts of Muskoka were full of them. They came up from Detroit and Chicago with money to spend on bone china from England, Shetland sweaters, Hudson's Bay blankets. So why not silver-fox furs?

When it comes to changes, to invasions and upheavals, there are two kinds of people. If a highway is built through their front yard, some people will be affronted, they will mourn the loss of privacy, of peony bushes and lilacs and a dimension of themselves. The other sort will see an opportunity—they will put up a hot-dog stand, get a fast-food franchise, open a motel. My mother was the second sort of person. The very idea of the tourists with their American money flocking to the northern woods filled her with vitality.

In the summer, then, the summer of 1941, she went off to Muskoka with her trunkload of furs. My father's mother arrived to take over our house. She was still an upright and handsome woman and she entered my mother's domain magnificent with foreboding. She hated what my mother was doing. Peddling. She said that when she thought of American tourists all she hoped was that none of them ever came near her. For one day she and my mother were together in the house and during that time my grandmother withdrew into a harsh and unforthcoming version of herself. My mother was too steamed up to notice. But after my grandmother had been in charge on her own for a day she thawed out. She decided to forgive my father his marriage, for the time being, also his exotic enterprise and its failure, and my father decided to forgive her the humiliating fact that he owed her money. She baked bread and pies, and did well by the garden vegetables, the new-laid eggs and the rich milk and cream from the Jersey cow. (Though we had no money we were never badly fed.) She scoured the inside of the cupboards and scraped away the black on the bottom of the saucepans, which we had believed to be permanent. She ferreted out many items in need of mending. In the evenings she carried pails of water to the flower border and the tomato plants. Then my father came up from his work in the barn and the fox pens and we all sat out on yard chairs, under the heavy trees.

Our nine-acre farm—no farm at all as my grandmother saw things—had an unusual location. To the east was the town, the church towers and the tower of the Town Hall visible when the leaves were off the trees, and on the mile or so of road between us and the main street there was a gradual thickening of houses, a turning of dirt paths into sidewalks, an appearance of a lone streetlight, so that you might say we were at the town's farthest edges, though beyond its legal municipal boundaries. But to the west there was only one farmhouse to be seen, and that one far away, at the top of a hill almost at the midpoint in the western horizon. We always referred to this as Roly Grain's house, but who Roly Grain might be, or what road led to his house, I had never asked or imagined. It was all too far away, across, first, a wide field planted in corn or oats, then the woods and the river flats sloping down to the great hidden curve of the river, and the pattern of overlapping bare or wooded hills beyond. It was very seldom that you could see a stretch of country so empty, so seductive to the imagination, in our thickly populated farmland.

When we sat looking out at this view my father rolled and smoked a cigarette, and he and my grandmother talked about the old days on the farm, their old neighbors, and funny things—that is, both strange and comical things—that had happened. My mother's absence brought a sort of peace—not only between them, but for all of us. Some alert and striving note was removed. An edge of ambition, self-regard, perhaps discontent, was absent. At the time, I did not know exactly what it was that was missing. I did not know either what a deprivation, rather than a relief, it would be for me, if that was gone for good.

My younger brother and sister pestered my grandmother to let them look into her window. My grandmother's eyes were a hazel color, but in one of them she had a large spot, taking up at least a third of the iris, and the color of this spot was blue. So people said that her eyes were of two different colors, though this was not quite the truth. We called the blue spot her window. She would pretend to be cross at being asked to show it, she would duck her head and

beat off whoever was trying to look in, or she would screw her
eyes shut, opening the plain hazel one a crack to see if she was still
being watched. She was always caught out in the end and gave in
to sitting still with eyes wide open, being looked into. The blue was
clear, without a speck of any other color in it, a blue made brighter
by the brownish-yellow at its edges, as the summer sky is by the
puffs of clouds.

IT WAS EVENING by the time my father turned into the hotel
driveway. We drove between the stone gateposts and there it was
ahead of us—a long stone building with gables and a white verandah. Hanging pots overflowing with flowers. We missed the turn
into the parking lot and followed the semicircular drive, which
brought us in front of the verandah, driving past the people who
sat there on swings and rockers, with nothing to do but look at us,
as my father said.

Nothing to do but gawk.

We spotted the inconspicuous sign and found our way to a
gravel lot next to the tennis court. We got out of the car. It was
covered with dust and looked like a raffish interloper amongst the
other cars there.

We had travelled the whole way with the windows down and
a hot wind blowing in on us, tangling and drying my hair. My
father saw that there was something wrong with me and asked me
if I had a comb. I got back into the car and looked for one, finding
it at last wedged down against the back of the seat. It was dirty,
and some teeth were missing. I tried, and he tried, and finally he
said, "Maybe if you just shoved it back behind your ears." Then
he combed his own hair, frowning as he bent to look in the car
mirror. We walked across the lot, with my father wondering out
loud whether we should try the front or the back door. He seemed
to think I might have some useful opinion about this—something
he had never thought in any circumstances before. I said that we
should try the front, because I wanted to get another look at the lily
pond in the semicircle of lawn bounded by the drive. There was a
statue of a bare-shouldered girl in a tunic draped closely against
her breasts, with a jug on her shoulder—one of the most elegant
things I had ever seen in my life.

"Run the gauntlet," my father said softly, and we went up the steps and crossed the verandah in front of people pretending not to look at us. We entered the lobby, where it was so dark that little lights were turned on, in frosted globes, high up on the dark shiny wood of the walls. To one side was the dining room, visible through glass doors. It was all cleaned up after supper, each table covered with a white cloth. On the other side, with the doors open, was a long rustic room with a huge stone fireplace at the end of it, and the skin of a bear stretched on the floor.

"Look at that," said my father. "She must be here somewhere."

What he had noticed in the corner of the lobby was a waist-high display case, and behind its glass was a silver-fox cape beautifully spread on what looked like a piece of white velvet. A sign set on top said, *Silver Fox, the Canadian Luxury,* in a flowing script done with white and silvery paint on a black board.

"Here somewhere," my father repeated. We peered into the room with the fireplace. A woman writing at a desk looked up and said, in an agreeable but somehow distant voice, "I think that if you ring the bell somebody will come."

It seemed strange to me to be addressed by a person you had never seen before.

We backed out and crossed to the doors of the dining room. Across the acre of white tables with their laid-out silverware and turned-down glasses and bunches of flowers and napkins peaked like wigwams, we saw two figures, ladies, seated at a table near the kitchen door, finishing a late supper or having evening tea. My father turned the doorknob and they looked up. One of them rose and came towards us, between the tables.

The moment in which I did not realize that this was my mother was not long, but there was a moment. I saw a woman in an unfamiliar dress, a cream-colored dress with a pattern of little red flowers. The skirt was pleated and swishing, the material crisp, glowing as the tablecloths did in the dark-panelled room. The woman wearing it looked brisk and elegant, her dark hair parted in the middle and pinned up in a neat coronet of braids. And even when I knew this was my mother, when she had put her arms around me and kissed me, spilling out an unaccustomed fragrance and showing none of her usual hurry and regrets, none of her usual dissatisfaction with my appearance, or my nature, I felt that she was somehow still a stranger. She had crossed effortlessly, it seemed, into the world of the hotel, where my father and I stood out like tramps or scarecrows—it was as if she had always been living there. I felt first amazed, then betrayed, then excited and hopeful, my thoughts running on to advantages to be gained for myself, in this new situation.

The woman my mother had been talking to turned out to be the dining-room hostess—a tanned, tired-looking woman with dark-red lipstick and nail polish, who was subsequently revealed to have many troubles which she had confided to my mother. She was immediately friendly. I broke into the adult conversation to tell about the ice splinters and the bad taste of the ice cream, and she went out to the kitchen and brought me a large helping of vanilla ice cream covered with chocolate sauce and bearing a cherry on top.

"Is that a sundae?" I said. It looked like the sundaes I had seen in advertisements, but since it would be the first I had ever tasted I wanted to be sure of its name.

"I believe it is," she said. "A sundae."

Nobody reproved me, in fact my parents laughed, and then the woman brought fresh tea and some sort of sandwich for my father.

"Now I'll leave you to your chat," she said, and went away and left us three alone in that hushed and splendid room. My parents talked, but I paid little attention to their conversation. I interrupted from time to time to tell my mother something about the trip or about what had been happening at home. I showed her where a bee had stung me, on my leg. Neither of them told me to be quiet—they answered me with cheerfulness and patience. My mother said that we would all sleep tonight in her cabin. She had one of the little cabins behind the hotel. She said we would eat breakfast here in the morning.

She said that when I had finished I should run out and look at the lily pond.

That must have been a happy conversation. Relieved, on my father's side—triumphant, on my mother's. She had done very well, she had sold almost everything she had brought with her, the venture was a success. Vindication for her, salvation for us all.

My father must have been thinking of what had to be done first, whether to get the car fixed in a garage up here or chance it once more on the back roads and take it to the garage at home, where he knew the people. Which bills should be paid at once, and which should be paid in part. And my mother must have been looking further into the future, thinking of how she could expand, which other hotels she could try this in, how many more capes and scarves they should get made up next year, and whether this could develop into a year-round business.

She couldn't have foreseen how soon the Americans were going to get into the war, and how that was going to keep them at home, how gas rationing was going to curtail the resort business. She couldn't foresee the attack on her own body, the destruction gathering within.

She would talk for years afterwards about what she had achieved in that summer. How she had known the right way to go about it, never pushing too hard, showing the furs as if it was a great pleasure to her and not a matter of money. A sale would seem to be the last thing on her mind. It was necessary to show the people who ran the hotel that she would not cheapen the impression they wanted to make, that she was anything but a huckster. A lady, rather, whose offerings added a unique distinction. She had to become a friend of the management and the employees as well as the guests.

And that was no chore for her. She had the true instinct for mixing friendship and business considerations, the instinct that all good salespersons have. She never had to calculate her advantage and coldly act upon it. Everything she did she did naturally and felt a real warmth of heart where her interests lay. She who had always had difficulty with her mother-in-law and her husband's family, who was thought stuck-up by our neighbors, and somewhat pushy by the town women at the church, had found a world of strangers in which she was at once at home.

FOR ALL THIS, as I grew older, I came to feel something like revulsion. I despised the whole idea of putting yourself to use in that way, making yourself dependent on the response of others, employing flattery so adroitly and naturally that you did not even recognize it as flattery. And all for money. I thought such behavior shameful, as of course my grandmother did. I took it for granted that my father felt the same way though he did not show it. I believed—or thought I believed—in working hard and being proud, not caring about being poor and indeed having a subtle contempt for those who led easeful lives.

I did, then, regret the loss of the foxes. Not of the business, but of the animals themselves, with their beautiful tails and angry golden eyes. As I grew older, and more and more aloof from country ways, country necessities, I began for the first time to question their captivity, to feel regret for their killing, their conversion into money. (I never got so far as feeling anything like this for the mink, who seemed to me mean and rat-like, deserving of their fate.) I knew this feeling to be a luxury, and when I mentioned it to my father, in later years, I spoke of it lightly. In the same spirit he said that he believed there was some religion in India that held with all animals getting into Heaven. Think, he said, if that were true—what a pack of snarling foxes he would meet there, not to mention all the other fur-bearers he had trapped, and the mink, and a herd of thundering horses he had butchered for their meat.

Then he said, not so lightly, "You get into things, you know. You sort of don't realize what you're getting into."

It was in those later years, after my mother was dead, that he spoke of my mother's salesmanship and how she had saved the day. He spoke of how he didn't know what he was going to do, at the end of that trip, if it turned out that she hadn't made any money.

"But she had," he said. "She had it." And the tone in which he said this convinced me that he had never shared those reservations of my grandmother's and mine. Or that he'd resolutely put away such shame, if he'd ever had it.

A shame that has come full circle, finally being shameful in itself to me.

ON A SPRING EVENING IN 1949—the last spring, in fact the last whole season, that I was to live at home—I was riding my bicycle to the Foundry, to deliver a message to my father. I seldom rode my bicycle anymore. For a while, maybe all through the fifties, it was considered eccentric for any girl to be riding a bicycle after she was old enough, say, to wear a brassiere. But to get to the Foundry I could travel on back roads, I didn't have to go through town.

My father had started working in the Foundry in 1947. It had become apparent the year before that not just our fox farm but the whole fur-farming industry was going downhill very fast. Perhaps the mink would have tided us over if we had gone more heavily into mink, or if we had not owed so much money still, to the feed company, to my grandmother, to the bank. As it was, mink could not save us. My father had made the mistake many fox farmers made just at that time. It was believed that a new paler kind of fox, called a platinum, was going to save the day, and with borrowed money my father had bought two male breeders, one an almost snowy-white Norwegian platinum and one called a pearl platinum, a lovely bluish-gray. People were sick of silver foxes, but surely with these beauties the market would revive.

Of course there is always the chance, with a new male, of how well he will perform, and how many of the offspring will have their father's color. I think there was trouble on both fronts, though my mother would not allow questions or household talk about these matters. I think one of the males had a standoffish nature and another sired mostly dark litters. It did not matter much, because the fashion went against long-haired furs altogether.

When my father went looking for a job it was necessary to find a night job, because he had to spend all day going out of business. He had to pelt all the animals and sell the pelts for whatever he could get and he had to tear down the guard fence, the Old Sheds and the New Sheds, and all the pens. I suppose he did not have to do that immediately, but he must have wanted all traces of the enterprise destroyed.

He got a job as night watchman at the Foundry, covering the hours from five in the afternoon till ten o'clock in the evening. There was not so much money in being a night watchman, but the good fortune in it was that he was able to do another job at that time as well. This extra job was called shaking down floors. He was never finished with it when his watchman's shift was over, and sometimes he got home after midnight.

The message I was taking to my father was not an important message, but it was important in our family life. It was simply a reminder that he must not forget to call in at my grandmother's house on his way home from work, no matter how late he was. My grandmother had moved to our town, with her sister, so that she could be useful to us. She baked pies and muffins and mended our clothes and darned my father's and my brother's socks. My father was supposed to go around by her house in town after work, to pick up these things, and have a cup of tea with her, but often he forgot. She would sit up knitting, dozing under the light, listening to the radio, until the Canadian radio stations went off at midnight and she would find herself picking up distant news reports, American jazz. She would wait and wait and my father wouldn't come. This had happened last night, so tonight at suppertime she had phoned and asked with painful tact, "Was it tonight or last night your father was supposed to come?"

"I don't know," I said.

I always felt that something had not been done right, or not done at all, when I heard my grandmother's voice. I felt that our family had failed her. She was still energetic, she looked after her house and yard, she could still carry armchairs upstairs, and she had my great-aunt's company, but she needed something more—more gratitude, more compliance, than she ever got.

"Well, I sat up for him last night, but he didn't come."

"He must be coming tonight then." I did not want to spend time talking to her because I was preparing for my Grade Thirteen exams on which my whole future would depend. (Even now, on cool bright spring evenings, with the leaves just out on the trees, I can feel the stirring of expectation connected with this momentous old event, my ambition roused and quivering like a fresh blade to meet it.)

I told my mother what the call was about and she said, "Oh, you'd better ride up and remind your father, or there'll be trouble."

Whenever she had to deal with the problem of my grandmother's touchiness my mother brightened up, as if she had got back some competence or importance in our family. She had Parkinson's disease. It had been overtaking her for some time with erratic symptoms but had recently been diagnosed and pronounced incurable. Its progress took up more and more of her attention. She could no longer walk or eat or talk normally—her body was stiffening out of her control. But she had a long time yet to live.

When she said something like this about the situation with my grandmother—when she said anything that showed an awareness of other people, or even of the work around the house, I felt my heart soften towards her. But when she finished up with a reference to herself, as she did this time (*and that will upset me*), I hardened again, angry at her for her abdication, sick of her self-absorption, which seemed so flagrant, so improper in a mother.

I had never been to the Foundry in the two years my father had worked there, and I did not know where to find him. Girls of my age did not hang around men's workplaces. If they did that, if they went for long walks by themselves along the railway track or the river, or if they bicycled alone on the country roads (I did these last two things) they were sometimes said to be *asking for it*.

I did not have much interest in my father's work at the Foundry, anyway. I had never expected the fox farm to make us rich, but at least it made us unique and independent. When I thought of my father working in the Foundry I felt that he had suffered a great defeat. My mother felt the same way. Your father is too *fine* for that, she would say. But instead of agreeing with her I would argue, intimating that she did not like being an ordinary workingman's wife and that she was a snob.

The thing that most upset my mother was receiving the Foundry's Christmas basket of fruit, nuts, and candy. She could not bear to be on the receiving, not the distributing, end of that sort of thing, and the first time it happened we had to put the basket in the car and drive down the road to a family she had picked out as suitable recipients. By the next Christmas her authority had weakened and I broke into the basket, declaring that we needed treats as much as anybody. She wiped away tears at my hard tone, and I ate the chocolate, which was old and brittle and turning gray.

I could not see any light in the Foundry buildings. The windows were painted blue on the inside—perhaps a light would not get through. The office was an old brick house at the end of the long main building, and there I saw a light through the venetian blinds, and I thought that the manager or one of the office staff must be working late. If I knocked they would tell me where my father was.

But when I looked through the little window in the door I saw that it was my father in there. He was alone, and he was scrubbing the floor.

I had not known that scrubbing the office floor every night was one of the watchman's duties. (This does not mean that my father had deliberately kept quiet about it—I might not have been listening.) I was surprised, because I had never seen him doing any work of this sort before. Housework. Now that my mother was sick, such work was my responsibility. He would never have had time. Besides that, there was men's work and there was women's work. I believed this, and so did everybody else I knew.

My father's scrubbing apparatus was unlike anything anybody would have at home. He had two buckets on a stand, on rollers, with attachments on either side to hold various mops and brushes. His scrubbing was vigorous and efficient—it had no resigned and ritualistic, feminine sort of rhythm. He seemed to be in a good humor.

He had to come and unlock the door to let me in.

His face changed when he saw it was me.

"No trouble at home, is there?"

I said no, and he relaxed. "I thought you were Tom."

Tom was the factory manager. All the men called him by his first name.

"Well then. You come up to see if I'm doing this right?"

I gave him the message, and he shook his head.

"I know. I forgot."

I sat on a corner of the desk, swinging my legs up out of his way. He said he was nearly finished here, and that if I wanted to wait he would show me around the Foundry. I said I would wait.

When I say that he was in a good humor here, I don't mean that his humor around home was bad, that he was sullen and irritable there. But he showed a cheerfulness now that at home might have seemed inappropriate. It seemed, in fact, as if there was a weight off him here.

When he had finished the floor to his satisfaction he hooked the mop to the side and rolled the apparatus down a slanting passageway that connected the office with the main building. He opened a door that had a sign on it.

Caretaker.

"My domain."

He emptied the water from the buckets into an iron tub, rinsed and emptied them again, swished the tub clean. There on a shelf above the tub among the tools and rubber hose and fuses and spare windowpanes was his lunch bucket, which I packed every day when I got home from school. I filled the thermos with strong black tea and put in a bran muffin with butter and jam and a piece of pie if we had any and three thick sandwiches of fried meat and ketchup. The meat was cottage roll ends or baloney, the cheapest meat you could buy.

He led the way into the main building. The lights burning there were like streetlights—that is, they cast their light at the intersections of the passageways, but didn't light up the whole inside of the building, which was so large and high that I had the sense of being in a forest with thick dark trees, or in a town with tall, even buildings. My father switched on some more lights and things shrank a bit. You could now see the brick walls, blackened on the inside, and the windows not only painted over but covered with black wire mesh. What lined the passageways were stacks of bins, one on top of the other higher than my head, and elaborate, uniform metal trays.

We came on an open area with a great heap of metal lumps on the floor, all disfigured with what looked like warts or barnacles.

"Castings," my father said. "They haven't been cleaned yet. They put them in a contraption called a wheelabrator and it blasts shot at them, takes all the bumps off."

Then a pile of black dust, or fine black sand.

"That looks like coal dust but you know what they call it? Green sand."

"*Green* sand?"

"Use it for molding. It's sand with a bonding agent in it, like clay. Or sometimes it's linseed oil. Are you any way interested in all this?"

I said yes, partly for pride's sake. I didn't want to seem like a stupid girl. And I was interested, but not so much in the particular explanations my father began to provide me with, as in the general effects—the gloom, the fine dust in the air, the idea of there being places like this all over the country, in every town and city. Places with their windows painted over. You passed them in a car or on the train and never gave a thought to what was going on inside. Something that took up the whole of people's lives. A never-ending over-and-over attention-consuming, life-consuming process.

"Like a tomb in here," my father said, as if he had picked up some of my thoughts.

But he meant something different.

"Compared to the daytime. The racket then, you can't imagine it. They try to get them to wear earplugs, but they won't do it."

"Why not?"

"I don't know. Too independent. They won't wear the fire aprons either. See here. Here's what they call the cupola."

This was an immense black pipe which did have a cupola on top. He showed me where they made the fire, and the ladles used to carry the molten metal and pour it into the molds. He showed me chunks of metal that were like grotesque stubby limbs, and told me that those were the shapes of the hollows in the castings. The air in the hollows, that is, made solid. He told me these things with a prolonged satisfaction in his voice, as if what he revealed gave him reliable pleasure.

We turned a corner and came on two men working, stripped to their pants and undershirts.

"Now here's a couple of good hardworking fellows," my father said. "You know Ferg? You know Geordie?"

I did know them, or at least I knew who they were. Geordie Hall delivered bread, but had to work in the Foundry at night to make extra money, because he had so many children. There was a joke that his wife made him work to keep him away from her. Ferg was a younger man you saw around town. He couldn't get girls because he had a wen on his face.

"She's seeing how us working fellows live," my father said, with a note of humorous apology. Apologizing to them for me, for me to them—light apologies all round. This was his style.

Working carefully together, using long, strong hooks, the two men lifted a heavy casting out of a box of sand.

"That's plenty hot," my father said. "It was cast today. Now they have to work the sand around and get it ready for the next casting. Then do another. It's piecework, you know. Paid by the casting."

We moved away.

"Two of them been together for a while," he said. "They always work together. I do the same job by myself. Heaviest job they've got around here. It took me a while to get used to it, but it doesn't bother me now."

Much that I saw that night was soon to disappear. The cupola, the hand-lifted ladles, the killing dust. (It was truly killing—around town, on the porches of small neat houses, there were always a few yellow-faced, stoical men set out to take the air. Everybody knew and accepted that they were dying of *the foundry disease,* the dust in their lungs.) Many particular skills and dangers were going to go. Many everyday risks, along with much foolhardy pride, and random ingenuity and improvisation. The processes I saw were probably closer to those of the Middle Ages than to those of today.

And I imagine that the special character of the men who worked in the Foundry was going to change, as the processes of the work changed. They would become not so different from the men who worked in the factories, or at other jobs. Up until the time I'm talking about they had seemed stronger and rougher than those other workers; they had more pride and were perhaps more given to self-dramatization than men whose jobs were not so dirty or dangerous. They were too proud to ask for any protection from the hazards they had to undergo, and in fact, as my father had said, they disdained what protection was offered. They were said to be too proud to bother about a union.

Instead, they stole from the Foundry.

"Tell you a story about Geordie," my father said, as we walked along. He was "doing a round" now, and had to punch clocks in various parts of the building. Then he would get down to shaking out his own floors. "Geordie likes to take a bit of lumber and whatnot home with him. A few crates or whatever. Anything he thinks might come in handy to fix the house or build a back shed. So the other night he had a load of stuff, and he went out after dark and put it in the back of his car so it'd be there when he went off work. And he didn't know it, but Tom was in the office and just happened to be standing by the window and watching him. Tom hadn't brought the car, his wife had the car, she'd gone somewhere, and Tom had just walked over to do a little work or pick up something he forgot. Well, he saw what Geordie was up to and he waited around till he saw him coming off work and then he stepped out and said, hey. He said, hey, wonder if you could give me a lift home. The wife's got the car, he said. So they got in Geordie's car with the other fellows standing around spluttering and Geordie sweating buckets, and Tom never said a word. Sat there whistling while Geordie's trying to get the key in the ignition. He let Geordie drive him home and never said a word. Never turned and looked in the back. Never intended to. Just let him sweat. And told it all over the place next day."

It would be easy to make too much of this story and to suppose that between management and workers there was an easy familiarity, tolerance, even an appreciation of each other's dilemmas. And there was some of that, but it didn't mean there wasn't also plenty of rancor and callousness and of course deceit. But jokes were important. The men who worked in the evenings would gather in my father's little room, the caretaker's room, in most weather—but outside the main door when the evenings were hot—and smoke and talk while they took their unauthorized break. They would tell about jokes that had been played recently and in years past. They talked about jokes played by and upon people now long dead. Sometimes they talked seriously as well. They argued about whether there were ghosts, and talked about who claimed to have seen one. They discussed money—who had it, who'd lost it, who'd expected it and not got it, and where people kept it. My father told me about these talks years later.

One night somebody asked, when is the best time in a man's life?

Some said, it's when you are a kid and can fool around all the time and go down to the river in the summer and play hockey on the road in the winter and that's all you think about, fooling around and having a good time.

Or when you're a young fellow going out and haven't got any responsibilities.

Or when you're first married if you're fond of your wife and a bit later, too, when the children are just little and running around and haven't shown any bad characteristics yet.

My father spoke up and said, "Now. I think maybe now."

They asked him why.

He said because you weren't old yet, with one thing or another collapsing on you, but old enough that you could see that a lot of things you might have wanted out of life you would never get. It was hard to explain how you could be happy in such a situation, but sometimes he thought you were.

When he was telling me about this he said, "I think it was the company I enjoyed. Up till then I'd been so much on my own. They weren't maybe the cream of the crop, but those were some of the best fellows I ever met."

He also told me that one night not long after he had started working at the Foundry he came off work around midnight and found that there was a great snowstorm in progress. The roads were full and the snow blowing so hard and fast that the snowplows would not get out till morning. He had to leave the car where it was—even if he got it shovelled out he couldn't tackle the roads. He started to walk home. It was a distance of about two miles. The walking was heavy, in the freshly drifted snow, and the wind was coming against him from the west. He had done several floors that night, and he was just getting used to the work. He wore a heavy overcoat, an Army greatcoat, which one of our neighbors had given him, having no use for it when he got home from the war. My father did not often wear it either. Usually he wore a windbreaker. He must have put it on that night because the temperature had dropped even below the usual winter cold, and there was no heater in the car.

He felt dragged down, pushing against the storm, and about a quarter of a mile from home he found that he wasn't moving. He was standing in the middle of a drift and he could not move his legs. He could hardly stand against the wind. He was worn out. He thought perhaps his heart was giving out. He thought of his death.

He would die leaving a sick crippled wife who could not even take care of herself, an old mother full of disappointment, a younger daughter whose health had always been delicate, an older girl who was strong and bright enough but who often seemed to

be self-centered and mysteriously incompetent, a son who promised to be clever and reliable but who was still only a little boy. He
would die in debt, and before he had even finished pulling down
the pens. They would stand there—drooping wire on the cedar
poles that he had cut in Austins swamp in the summer of 1927—to
show the ruin of his enterprise.

"Was that all you thought about?" I said when he told me this.

"Wasn't that enough?" he said, and went on to tell me how he
pulled one leg out of the snow, and then the other: he got out of
that drift and then there were no more drifts quite so deep, and
before long he was in the shelter of the windbreak of pine trees that
he himself had planted the year that I was born. He got home.

But I had meant, didn't he think of himself, of the boy who had
trapped along the Blyth Creek, and who went into the store and
asked for Signs Snow Paper, didn't he struggle for his own self? I
meant, was his life now something only other people had a use for?

MY FATHER ALWAYS SAID he didn't really grow up till he went
to work in the Foundry. He never wanted to talk about the fox farm
or the fur business, until he was old and could talk easily about
almost anything. But my mother, walled in by increasing paralysis,
was always eager to recall the Pine Tree Hotel, the friends and the
money she had made there.

AND MY FATHER, as it turned out, had another occupation waiting for him. I'm not talking about his raising turkeys, which came
after the work at the Foundry and lasted till he was seventy or over,
and which may have done damage to his heart, since he would
find himself wrestling and hauling around fifty- and sixty-pound
birds. It was after giving up such work that he took up writing. He
began to write reminiscences and to turn some of them into stories, which were published in an excellent though short-lived local
magazine. And not long before his death he completed a novel
about pioneer life, called *The Macgregors*.

He told me that writing it had surprised him. He was surprised
that he could do such a thing, and surprised that doing it could
make him so happy. Just as if there was a future in it for him.

Here is part of a piece called "Grandfathers," part of what my father wrote about his own grandfather Thomas Laidlaw, the same Thomas who had come to Morris at the age of seventeen and been appointed to do the cooking in the shanty.

He was a frail white-haired old man, with thin longish hair and a pale skin. Too pale, because he was anemic. He took Vita-Ore, a much-advertised patent medicine. It must have helped, because he lived into his eighties ... When I first became aware of him he had retired to the village and leased the farm to my father. He would visit the farm, or me, as I thought, and I would visit him. We would go for walks. There was a sense of security. He talked much more easily than Dad but I don't recall that we conversed at any length. He explained things much as if he were discovering them himself at the same time. Perhaps he was in a way looking at the world from a child's viewpoint.

He never spoke harshly, he never said, "Get down off that fence," or "Mind that puddle." He preferred to let nature take its course so I could learn that way. The freedom of action inspired a certain amount of caution. There was no undue sympathy when one did get hurt.

We took slow staid walks because he couldn't go very fast. We gathered stones with fossils of weird creatures of another age, for this was gravelly country in which such stones might be found. We each had a collection. I inherited his when he died and kept both assortments for many years. They were a link with him with which I was very reluctant to part.

We walked along the nearby railway tracks to the huge embankment carrying the tracks over another railway and a big creek. There was a giant stone and cement arch over these. One could look down hundreds of feet to the railway below. I was back there lately. The embankment has shrunk strangely; the railway no longer runs along it. The C.P.R. is still down there but not nearly so far down and the creek is much smaller ...

We went to the planing mill nearby and watched the saws whirling and whining. These were the days of all sorts of gingerbread woodwork used for ornamenting the eaves of houses, the verandahs, or any place that could be decorated. There were all sorts of discarded pieces with interesting designs, which one could take home.

In the evening we went to the station, the old Grand Trunk, or the Butter and Eggs, as it was known in London. One could put an ear to the track and hear the rumble of the train, far away. Then a distant whistle, and the air became tense with anticipation. The whistles became closer and louder and finally the train burst into view. The earth shook, the heavens all but opened, and the huge monster slid screaming with tortured brakes to a stop . . .

Here we got the evening daily paper. There were two London papers, the *Free Press* and the *'Tiser* (*Advertiser*). The *'Tiser* was Grit and the *Free Press* was Tory.

There was no compromise about this. Either you were right or you were wrong. Grandfather was a good Grit of the old George Brown school and took the *'Tiser,* so I also have become a Grit and have remained one up to now . . . And so in this best of all systems were governments chosen according to the number of little Grits or little Tories who got old enough to vote . . .

The conductor grasped the handhold by the steps. He shouted, "Bort!" and waved his hand. The steam shot down in jets, the wheels clanked and groaned and moved forward, faster and faster, past the weigh scales, past the stockyards, over the arches, and grew smaller and smaller like a receding galaxy until the train disappeared into the unknown world to the north . . .

Once there was a visitor, my namesake from Toronto, a cousin of Grandfather. The great man was reputed to be a millionaire, but he was disappointing, not at all impressive, only a slightly smoother and more polished version of Grandfather. The two old men sat under the maples in front of our house and talked. Probably they talked of the past as old men will. I kept discreetly in the background. Grandpa didn't say outright but delicately hinted that children were to be seen and not heard.

Sometimes they talked in the broad Scots of the district from which they came. It was not the Scots of the burring R's which we hear from the singers and comedians but was rather soft and plaintive, with a lilt like Welsh or Swedish.

That is where I feel it best to leave them—my father a little boy, not venturing too close, and the old men sitting through a summer afternoon on wooden chairs placed under one of the great benevolent elm trees that used to shelter my grandparents' farmhouse. There they spoke the dialect of their childhood—discarded as they became men—which none of their descendants could understand.

Hired Girl

~

MRS. MONTJOY was showing me how to put the pots and pans away. I had put some of them in the wrong places.

Above all things, she said, she hated a higgledy-piggledy cupboard.

"You waste more time," she said. "You waste more time looking for something because it wasn't where it was last time."

"That's the way it was with our hired girls at home," I said. "The first few days they were there they were always putting things away where we couldn't find them.

"We called our maids hired girls," I added. "That was what we called them, at home."

"Did you?" she said. A moment of silence passed. "And the colander on that hook there."

Why did I have to say what I had said? Why was it necessary to mention that we had hired girls at home?

Anybody could see why. To put myself somewhere near her level. As if that was possible. As if anything I had to say about myself or the house I came from could interest or impress her.

IT WAS TRUE, though, about the hired girls. In my early life there was a procession of them. There was Olive, a soft drowsy girl who didn't like me because I called her Olive Oyl. Even after I was made to apologize she didn't like me. Maybe she didn't like any of us much because she was a Bible Christian, which made her mistrustful and reserved. She used to sing as she washed the dishes and I dried. *There is a Balm in Gilead* . . . If I tried to sing with her she stopped.

Then came Jeanie, whom I liked, because she was pretty and she did my hair up in pin curls at night when she did her own. She kept a list of the boys she went out with and made peculiar signs after their names: x x x o o * *. She did not last long.

Neither did Dorothy, who hung the clothes on the line in an eccentric way—pinned up by the collar, or by one sleeve or one leg—and swept the dirt into a corner and propped the broom up to hide it.

And when I was around ten years old hired girls became a thing of the past. I don't know if it was because we became poorer or because I was considered old enough to be a steady help. Both things were true.

Now I was seventeen and able to be hired out myself, though only as summer help because I had one more year to go at high school. My sister was twelve, so she could take over at home.

MRS. MONTJOY had picked me up at the railway station in Pointe au Baril, and transported me in an outboard-motor boat to the island. It was the woman in the Pointe au Baril store who had recommended me for the job. She was an old friend of my mother's—they had taught school together. Mrs. Montjoy had asked her if she knew of a country girl, used to doing housework, who would be available for the summer, and the woman had thought that it would be the very thing for me. I thought so too—I was eager to see more of the world.

Mrs. Montjoy wore khaki shorts and a tucked-in shirt. Her short, sun-bleached hair was pushed behind her ears. She leapt aboard the boat like a boy and gave a fierce tug to the motor, and we were flung out on the choppy evening waters of Georgian Bay. For thirty or forty minutes we dodged around rocky and wooded islands with their lone cottages and boats bobbing beside the docks. Pine trees jutted out at odd angles, just as they do in the paintings.

I held on to the sides of the boat and shivered in my flimsy dress.

"Feeling a tad sick?" said Mrs. Montjoy, with the briefest possible smile. It was like the signal for a smile, when the occasion did not warrant the real thing. She had large white teeth in a long tanned face, and her natural expression seemed to be one of impatience barely held in check. She probably knew that what I was feeling was fear, not sickness, and she threw out this question so that I—and she—need not be embarrassed.

Here was a difference, already, from the world I was used to. In that world, fear was commonplace, at least for females. You could be afraid of snakes, thunderstorms, deep water, heights, the dark, the bull, and the lonely road through the swamp, and nobody thought any the worse of you. In Mrs. Montjoy's world, however, fear was shameful and always something to be conquered.

The island that was our destination had a name—Nausicaa. The name was written on a board at the end of the dock. I said it aloud, trying to show that I was at ease and quietly appreciative, and Mrs. Montjoy said with slight surprise, "Oh, yes. That was the name it already had when Daddy bought it. It's for some character in Shakespeare."

I opened up my mouth to say no, no, not Shakespeare, and to tell her that Nausicaa was the girl on the beach, playing ball with her friends, surprised by Ulysses when he woke up from his nap. I had learned by this time that most of the people I lived amongst did not welcome this kind of information, and I would probably have kept quiet even if the teacher had asked us in school, but I believed that people out in the world—the real world—would be different. Just in time I recognized the briskness of Mrs. Montjoy's tone when she said "some character in Shakespeare"—the suggestion that Nausicaa, and Shakespeare, as well as any observations of mine, were things she could reasonably do without.

The dress I was wearing for my arrival was one I had made myself, out of pink and white striped cotton. The material had been cheap, the reason being that it was not really meant for a dress but for a blouse or a nightgown, and the style I had chosen—the full-skirted, tight-waisted style of those days—was a mistake. When I walked, the cloth bunched up between my legs, and I kept having to yank it loose. Today was the first day the dress had been worn, and I still thought that the trouble might be temporary—with a firm enough yank the material might be made to hang properly. But I found when I took off my belt that the day's heat and my hot ride on the train had created a worse problem. The belt was wide and elasticized, and of a burgundy color, which had run. The waistline of the dress was circled with strawberry dye.

I made this discovery when I was getting undressed in the loft of the boathouse, which I was to share with Mrs. Montjoy's ten-year-old daughter, Mary Anne.

"What happened to your dress?" Mary Anne said. "Do you sweat a lot? That's too bad."

I said that it was an old dress anyway and that I hadn't wanted to wear anything good on the train.

Mary Anne was fair-haired and freckled, with a long face like her mother's. But she didn't have her mother's look of quick judgments marshalled at the surface, ready to leap out at you. Her expression was benign and serious, and she wore heavy glasses even when sitting up in bed. She was to tell me soon that she had had an operation to get her eyes straightened, but even so her eyesight was poor.

"I've got Daddy's eyes," she said. "I'm intelligent like him too so it's too bad I'm not a boy."

Another difference. Where I came from, it was generally held to be more suspect for boys to be smart than for girls to be, though not particularly advantageous for one or the other. Girls could go on to be teachers, and that was all right—though quite often they became old maids—but for boys to continue with school usually meant they were sissies.

All night long you could hear the water slapping against the boards of the boathouse. Morning came early. I wondered whether I was far enough north of home for the sun to actually be rising sooner. I got up and looked out. Through the front window, I saw the silky water, dark underneath but flashing back from its surface the light of the sky. The rocky shores of this little cove, the moored sailboats, the open channel beyond, the mound of another island or two, shores and channels beyond that. I thought that I would never, on my own, be able to find my way back to the mainland.

I did not yet understand that maids didn't have to find their way anywhere. They stayed put, where the work was. It was the people who made the work who could come and go.

The back window looked out on a gray rock that was like a slanting wall, with shelves and crevices on it where little pine and cedar trees and blueberry bushes had got a foothold. Down at the foot of this wall was a path—which I would take later on—through the woods, to Mrs. Montjoy's house. Here everything was still damp and almost dark, though if you craned you could see bits of the sky whitening through the trees on top of the rock. Nearly all of the trees were strict-looking, fragrant evergreens, with heavy boughs that didn't allow much growth underneath—no riot of grapevine and brambles and saplings such as I was used to in the hardwood forest. I had noticed that when I looked out from the train on the day before—how what we called the bush turned into the more authentic-looking *forest*, which had eliminated all lavishness and confusion and seasonal change. It seemed to me that this real forest belonged to rich people—it was their proper though sombre playground—and to Indians, who served the rich people as guides and exotic dependents, living out of sight and out of mind, somewhere that the train didn't go.

Nevertheless, on this morning I was really looking out, eagerly, as if this was a place where I would live and everything would become familiar to me. And everything did become familiar, at least in the places where my work was and where I was supposed to go. But a barrier was up. Perhaps *barrier* is too strong a word—there was not a warning so much as something like a shimmer in the air, an indolent reminder. *Not for you.* It wasn't a thing that had to be said. Or put on a sign.

Not for you. And though I felt it, I would not quite admit to myself that such a barrier was there. I would not admit that I ever felt humbled or lonely, or that I was a real servant. But I stopped thinking about leaving the path, exploring among the trees. If anybody saw me I would have to explain what I was doing, and *they*—Mrs. Montjoy—would not like it.

And to tell the truth, this wasn't so different from the way things were at home, where taking any impractical notice of the out-of-doors, or mooning around about Nature—even using that word, *Nature*—could get you laughed at.

MARY ANNE LIKED TO TALK when we were lying on our cots at night. She told me that her favorite book was *Kon-Tiki* and that she did not believe in God or Heaven.

"My sister is dead," she said. "And I don't believe she is floating around somewhere in a white nightie. She is just dead, she is just nothing.

"My sister was pretty," she said. "Compared to me she was, anyway. Mother wasn't ever pretty and Daddy is really ugly. Aunt Margaret used to be pretty but now she's fat, and Nana used to be pretty but now she's old. My friend Helen is pretty but my friend Susan isn't. You're pretty, but it doesn't count because you're the maid. Does it hurt your feelings for me to say that?"

I said no.

"I'm only the maid when I'm here."

It wasn't that I was the only servant on the island. The other servants were a married couple, Henry and Corrie. They did not feel diminished by their jobs—they were grateful for them. They had come to Canada from Holland a few years before and had been hired by Mr. and Mrs. Foley, who were Mrs. Montjoy's parents. It was Mr. and Mrs. Foley who owned the island, and lived in the large white bungalow, with its awnings and verandas, that crowned the highest point of land. Henry cut the grass and looked after the tennis court and repainted the lawn chairs and helped Mr. Foley with the boats and the clearing of paths and the repairs to the dock. Corrie did the housework and cooked the meals and looked after Mrs. Foley.

Mrs. Foley spent every sunny morning sitting outside on a deck chair, with her feet stretched out to get the sun and an awning attached to the chair protecting her head. Corrie came out and shifted her around as the sun moved, and took her to the bathroom, and brought her cups of tea and glasses of iced coffee. I was witness to this when I went up to the Foleys' house from the Montjoys' house on some errand, or to put something into or remove something from the freezer. Home freezers were still rather a novelty and a luxury at this time, and there wasn't one in the Montjoys' cottage.

"You are not going to suck the ice cubes," I heard Corrie say to Mrs. Foley. Apparently Mrs. Foley paid no attention and proceeded to suck an ice cube, and Corrie said, "Bad. No. Spit out. Spit right out in Corrie's hand. Bad. You didn't do what Corrie say."

Catching up to me on the way into the house, she said, "I tell them she could choke to death. But Mr. Foley always say, give her the ice cubes, she wants a drink like everybody else. So I tell her and tell her. Do not suck ice cubes. But she won't do what I say."

Sometimes I was sent up to help Corrie polish the furniture or buff the floors. She was very exacting. She never just wiped the kitchen counters—she scoured them. Every move she made had the energy and concentration of somebody rowing a boat against the current and every word she said was flung out as if into a high wind of opposition. When she wrung out a cleaning rag she might have been wringing the neck of a chicken. I thought it might be interesting if I could get her to talk about the war, but all she would say was that everybody was very hungry and they saved the potato skins to make soup.

"No good," she said. "No good to talk about that."

She preferred the future. She and Henry were saving their money to go into business. They meant to start up a nursing home. "Lots of people like her," said Corrie, throwing her head back as she worked to indicate Mrs. Foley out on the lawn. "Soon more and more. Because they give them the medicine, that makes them not die so soon. Who will be taking care?"

One day Mrs. Foley called out to me as I crossed the lawn.

"Now, where are you off to in such a hurry?" she said. "Come and sit down by me and have a little rest."

Her white hair was tucked up under a floppy straw hat, and when she leaned forward the sun came though the holes in the straw, sprinkling the pink and pale-brown patches of her face with pimples of light. Her eyes were a color so nearly extinct I couldn't make it out and her shape was curious—a narrow flat chest and a swollen stomach under layers of loose, pale clothing. The skin of the legs she stuck out into the sunlight was shiny and discolored and covered with faint cracks.

"Pardon my not having put my stockings on," she said. "I'm afraid I'm feeling rather lazy today. But aren't you the remarkable girl. Coming all that way by yourself. Did Henry help you carry the groceries up from the dock?"

Mrs. Montjoy waved to us. She was on her way to the tennis court, to give Mary Anne her lesson. Every morning she gave Mary Anne a lesson, and at lunch they discussed what Mary Anne had done wrong.

"There's that woman who comes to play tennis," Mrs. Foley said of her daughter. "She comes every day, so I suppose it's all right. She may as well use it if she hasn't a court of her own."

Mrs. Montjoy said to me later, "Did Mrs. Foley ask you to come over and sit on the grass?"

I said yes. "She thought I was somebody who'd brought the groceries."

"I believe there was a grocery girl who used to run a boat. There hasn't been any grocery delivery in years. Mrs. Foley does get her wires crossed now and then."

"She said you were a woman who came to play tennis."

"Did she really?" Mrs. Montjoy said.

THE WORK THAT I HAD TO DO here was not hard for me. I knew how to bake, and iron, and clean an oven. Nobody tracked barnyard mud into this kitchen and there were no heavy men's work clothes to wrestle through the wringer. There was just the business of putting everything perfectly in place and doing quite a bit of polishing. Polish the rims of the burners of the stove after every use, polish the taps, polish the glass door to the deck till the glass disappears and people are in danger of smashing their faces against it.

The Montjoys' house was modern, with a flat roof and a deck extending over the water and a great many windows, which Mrs. Montjoy would have liked to see become as invisible as the glass door.

"But I have to be realistic," she said. "I know if you did that you'd hardly have time for anything else." She was not by any means a slave driver. Her tone with me was firm and slightly irritable, but that was the way it was with everybody. She was always on the lookout for inattention or incompetence, which she detested. *Sloppy* was a favorite word of condemnation. Others were *wishy-washy* and *unnecessary*. A lot of things that people did were unnecessary, and some of these were also wishy-washy. Other people might have used the words *arty* or *intellectual* or *permissive*. Mrs. Montjoy swept all those distinctions out of the way.

I ate my meals alone, between serving whoever was eating on the deck or in the dining room. I had almost made a horrible mistake about that. When Mrs. Montjoy caught me heading out to the deck with three plates—held in a show-off waitress-style—for the first lunch, she said, "Three plates there? Oh, yes, two out on the deck and yours in here. Right?"

I read as I ate. I had found a stack of old magazines—*Life* and *Look* and *Time* and *Collier's*—at the back of the broom closet. I could tell that Mrs. Montjoy did not like the idea of my sitting reading these magazines as I ate my lunch, but I did not quite know why. Was it because it was bad manners to eat as you read, or because I had not asked permission? More likely she saw my interest in things that had nothing to do with my work as a subtle kind of impudence. Unnecessary.

All she said was, "Those old magazines must be dreadfully dusty."

I said that I always wiped them off.

Sometimes there was a guest for lunch, a woman friend who had come over from one of the nearby islands. I heard Mrs. Montjoy say, ". . . have to keep your girls happy or they'll be off to the hotel, off to the port. They can get jobs there so easily. It's not the way it used to be."

The other woman said, "That's so true."

"So you just make allowances," said Mrs. Montjoy. "You do the best with them you can." It took me a moment to realize who they were talking about. Me. "Girls" meant girls like me. I wondered, then, how I was being kept happy. By being taken along on the occasional alarming boat ride when Mrs. Montjoy went to get supplies? By being allowed to wear shorts and a blouse, or even a halter, instead of a uniform with a white collar and cuffs?

And what hotel was this? What port?

"WHAT ARE YOU BEST AT?" Mary Anne said. "What sports?"

After a moment's consideration, I said, "Volleyball." We had to play volleyball at school. I wasn't very good at it, but it was my best sport because it was the only one.

"Oh, I don't mean team sports," said Mary Anne. "I mean, what are you *best* at. Such as tennis. Or swimming or riding or what? My really best thing is riding, because that doesn't depend so much on your eyesight. Aunt Margaret's best used to be tennis and Nana's used to be tennis too, and Grandad's was always sailing, and Daddy's is swimming I guess and Uncle Stewart's is golf and sailing and Mother's is golf and swimming and sailing and tennis and everything, but maybe tennis a little bit the best of all. If my sister Jane hadn't died I don't know what hers would have been, but it might have been swimming because she could swim already and she was only three."

I had never been on a tennis court and the idea of going out in a sailboat or getting up on a horse terrified me. I could swim, but not very well. Golf to me was something that silly-looking men did in cartoons. The adults I knew never played any games that involved physical action. They sat down and rested when they were not working, which wasn't often. Though on winter evenings they might play cards. Euchre. Lost Heir. Not the kind of cards Mrs. Montjoy ever played.

"Everybody I know works too hard to do any sports," I said. "We don't even have a tennis court in our town and there isn't any golf course either." (Actually we had once had both these things, but there hadn't been the money to keep them up during the Depression and they had not been restored since.) "Nobody I know has a sailboat."

I did not mention that my town did have a hockey rink and a baseball park.

"Really?" said Mary Anne thoughtfully. "What do they do then?"

"*Work.* And they never have any money, all of their lives."

Then I told her that most people I knew had never seen a flush toilet unless it was in a public building and that sometimes old people (that is, people too old to work) had to stay in bed all winter in order to keep warm. Children walked barefoot until the frost came in order to save on shoe leather, and died of stomach aches that were really appendicitis because their parents had no money for a doctor. Sometimes people had eaten dandelion leaves, nothing else, for supper.

Not one of these statements—even the one about dandelion leaves—was completely a lie. I had heard of such things. The one about flush toilets perhaps came closest to the truth, but it applied to country people, not town people, and most of those it applied to would be of a generation before mine. But as I talked to Mary Anne all the isolated incidents and bizarre stories I had heard spread out in my mind, so that I could almost believe that I myself had walked with bare blue feet on cold mud—I who had benefited from cod liver oil and inoculations and been bundled up for school within an inch of my life, and had gone to bed hungry only because I refused to eat such things as junket or bread pudding or fried liver. And this false impression I was giving seemed justified, as if my exaggerations or near lies were substitutes for something I could not make clear.

How to make clear, for instance, the difference between the Montjoys' kitchen and our kitchen at home. You could not do that simply by mentioning the perfectly fresh and shining floor surfaces of one and the worn-out linoleum of the other, or the fact of soft water being pumped from a cistern into the sink contrasted with hot and cold water coming out of taps. You would have to say that you had in one case a kitchen that followed with absolute correctness a current notion of what a kitchen ought to be, and in the other a kitchen that changed occasionally with use and improvisation, but in many ways never changed at all, and belonged entirely to one family and to the years and decades of that family's life. And when I thought of that kitchen, with the combination wood and electric stove that I polished with waxed-paper bread wrappers, the dark old spice tins with their rusty rims kept from year to year in the cupboards, the barn clothes hanging by the door, it seemed as if I had to protect it from contempt—as if I had to protect a whole precious and intimate though hardly pleasant way of life from contempt. Contempt was what I imagined to be always waiting, swinging along on live wires, just under the skin and just behind the perceptions of people like the Montjoys.

"That isn't fair," said Mary Anne. "That's awful. I didn't know people could eat dandelion leaves." But then she brightened. "Why don't they go and catch some fish?"

"People who don't need the fish have come and caught them all already. Rich people. For fun."

Of course some of the people at home did catch fish when they had time, though others, including me, found the fish from our river too bony. But I thought that would keep Mary Anne quiet, especially since I knew that Mr. Montjoy went on fishing trips with his friends.

She could not stop mulling over the problem. "Couldn't they go to the Salvation Army?"

"They're too proud."

"Well I feel sorry for them," she said. "I feel really sorry for them, but I think that's stupid. What about the little babies and the children? They ought to think about them. Are the children too proud too?"

"Everybody's proud."

WHEN MR. MONTJOY CAME to the island on weekends, there was always a great deal of noise and activity. Some of that was because there were visitors who came by boat to swim and have drinks and watch sailing races. But a lot of it was generated by Mr. Montjoy himself. He had a loud blustery voice and a thick body with a skin that would never take a tan. Every weekend he turned red from the sun, and during the week the burned skin peeled away and left him pink and muddy with freckles, ready to be burned again. When he took off his glasses you could see that one eye was quick and squinty and the other boldly blue but helpless-looking, as if caught in a trap.

His blustering was often about things that he had misplaced, or dropped, or bumped into. "Where the hell is the—?" he would say, or "You didn't happen to see the—?" So it seemed that he had also misplaced, or failed to grasp in the first place, even the name of the thing he was looking for. To console himself he might grab up a handful of peanuts or pretzels or whatever was nearby, and eat handful after handful until they were all gone. Then he would stare at the empty bowl as if that too astounded him.

One morning I heard him say, "Now where in hell is that—?" He was crashing around out on the deck.

"Your book?" said Mrs. Montjoy, in a tone of bright control. She was having her midmorning coffee.

"I thought I had it out here," he said. "I was reading it."

"The Book-of-the-Month one?" she said. "I think you left it in the living room."

She was right. I was vacuuming the living room, and a few moments before I had picked up a book pushed partway under the sofa. Its title was *Seven Gothic Tales*. The title made me want to open it, and even as I overheard the Montjoys' conversation I was reading, holding the book open in one hand and guiding the vacuum cleaner with the other. They couldn't see me from the deck.

"Nay, I speak from my heart," said Mira. "I have been trying for a long time to understand God. Now I have made friends with him. To love him truly you must love change, and you must love a joke, these being the true inclinations of his own heart."

"There it is," said Mr. Montjoy, who for a wonder had come into the room without his usual bumping and banging—or none at least that I had heard. "Good girl, you found my book. Now I remember. Last night I was reading it on the sofa."

"It was on the floor," I said. "I just picked it up."

He must have seen me reading it. He said, "It's a queer kind of book, but sometimes you want to read a book that isn't like all the others."

"I couldn't make heads or tails of it," said Mrs. Montjoy, coming in with the coffee tray. "We'll have to get out of the way here and let her get on with the vacuuming."

Mr. Montjoy went back to the mainland, and to the city, that evening. He was a bank director. That did not mean, apparently, that he worked in a bank. The day after he had gone I looked everywhere. I looked under the chairs and behind the curtains, in case he might have left that book behind. But I could not find it.

"I ALWAYS THOUGHT it would be nice to live up here all the year round, the way you people do," said Mrs. Foley. She must have cast me again as the girl who brought the groceries. Some days she said, "I know who you are now. You're the new girl helping the Dutch woman in the kitchen. But I'm sorry, I just can't recall your name." And other days she let me walk by without giving any greeting or showing the least interest.

"We used to come up here in the winter," she said. "The bay would be frozen over and there would be a road across the ice. We used to go snowshoeing. Now that's something people don't do anymore. Do they? Snowshoeing?"

She didn't wait for me to answer. She leaned towards me. "Can you tell me something?" she said with embarrassment, speaking almost in a whisper. "Can you tell me where Jane is? I haven't seen her running around here for the longest time."

I said that I didn't know. She smiled as if I was teasing her, and reached out a hand to touch my face. I had been stooping down to listen to her, but now I straightened up, and her hand grazed my chest instead. It was a hot day and I was wearing my halter, so it happened that she touched my skin. Her hand was light and dry as a wood shaving, but the nail scraped me.

"I'm sure it's all right," she said.

After that I simply waved if she spoke to me and hurried on my way.

ON A SATURDAY AFTERNOON towards the end of August, the Montjoys gave a cocktail party. The party was given in honor of the friends they had staying with them that weekend—Mr. and Mrs. Hammond. A good many small silver forks and spoons had to be polished in preparation for this event, so Mrs. Montjoy decided that all the silver might as well be done at the same time. I did the polishing and she stood beside me, inspecting it.

On the day of the party, people arrived in motorboats and sailboats. Some of them went swimming, then sat around on the rocks in their bathing suits, or lay on the dock in the sun. Others came up to the house immediately and started drinking and talking in the living room or out on the deck. Some children had come with their parents, and older children by themselves, in their own boats. They were not children of Mary Anne's age—Mary Anne had been taken to stay with her friend Susan, on another island. There were a few very young ones, who came supplied with folding cribs and playpens, but most were around the same age as I was. Girls and boys fifteen or sixteen years old. They spent most of the afternoon in the water, shouting and diving and having races to the raft.

Mrs. Montjoy and I had been busy all morning, making all the different things to eat, which we now arranged on platters and offered to people. Making them had been fiddly and exasperating work. Stuffing various mixtures into mushroom caps and sticking one tiny slice of something on top of a tiny slice of something else on top of a precise fragment of toast or bread. All the shapes had to be perfect—perfect triangles, perfect rounds and squares, perfect diamonds.

Mrs. Hammond came into the kitchen several times and admired what we were doing.

"How marvellous everything looks," she said. "You notice I'm not offering to help. I'm a perfect mutt at this kind of thing."

I liked the way she said that. *I'm a perfect mutt.* I admired her husky voice, its weary good-humored tone, and the way she seemed to suggest that tiny geometrical bits of food were not so necessary, might even be a trifle silly. I wished I could be her, in a sleek black bathing suit with a tan like dark toast, shoulder-length smooth dark hair, orchid-colored lipstick.

Not that she looked happy. But her air of sullenness and complaint seemed glamorous to me, her hints of cloudy drama enviable. She and her husband were an altogether different type of rich people from Mr. and Mrs. Montjoy. They were more like the people I had read about in magazine stories and in books like *The Hucksters*—people who drank a lot and had love affairs and went to psychiatrists.

Her name was Carol and her husband's name was Ivan. I thought of them already by their first names—something I had never been tempted to do with the Montjoys.

Mrs. Montjoy had asked me to put on a dress, so I wore the pink and white striped cotton, with the smudged material at its waist tucked under the elasticized belt. Nearly everybody else was in shorts and bathing suits. I passed among them, offering food. I was not sure how to do this. Sometimes people were laughing or talking with such vigor that they didn't notice me, and I was afraid that their gestures would send the food bits flying. So I said, "Excuse me—would you like one of these?" in a raised voice that sounded very determined or even reproving. Then they looked at me with startled amusement, and I had the feeling that my interruption had become another joke.

"Enough passing for now," said Mrs. Montjoy. She gathered up some glasses and told me to wash them. "People never keep track of their own," she said. "It's easier just to wash them and bring in clean ones. And it's time to get the meatballs out of the fridge and heat them up. Could you do that? Watch the oven—it won't take long."

While I was busy in the kitchen I heard Mrs. Hammond calling, "Ivan! Ivan!" She was roaming through the back rooms of the
house. But Mr. Hammond had come in through the kitchen door
that led to the woods. He stood there and did not answer her. He
came over to the counter and poured gin into his glass.

"Oh, Ivan, there you are," said Mrs. Hammond, coming in from
the living room.

"Here I am," said Mr. Hammond.

"Me, too," she said. She shoved her glass along the counter.

He didn't pick it up. He pushed the gin towards her and spoke to
me. "Are you having fun, Minnie?"

Mrs. Hammond gave a yelp of laughter. "Minnie? Where did
you get the idea her name was Minnie?"

"Minnie," said Mr. Hammond. Ivan. He spoke in an artificial,
dreamy voice. "Are you having fun, Minnie?"

"Oh yes," I said, in a voice that I meant to make as artificial as
his. I was busy lifting the tiny Swedish meatballs from the oven and
I wanted the Hammonds out of my way in case I dropped some.
They would think that a big joke and probably report on me to
Mrs. Montjoy, who would make me throw the dropped meatballs
out and be annoyed at the waste. If I was alone when it happened I
could just scoop them up off the floor.

Mr. Hammond said, "Good."

"I swam around the point," Mrs. Hammond said. "I'm working
up to swimming around the entire island."

"Congratulations," Mr. Hammond said, in the same way that he
had said "Good."

I wished that I hadn't sounded so chirpy and silly. I wished that
I had matched his deeply skeptical and sophisticated tone.

"Well then," said Mrs. Hammond. Carol. "I'll leave you to it."

I had begun to spear the meatballs with toothpicks and arrange
them on a platter. Ivan said, "Care for some help?" and tried to do
the same, but his toothpicks missed and sent meatballs skittering
onto the counter.

"Well," he said, but he seemed to lose track of his thoughts, so
he turned away and took another drink. "Well, Minnie."

I knew something about him. I knew that the Hammonds were
here for a special holiday because Mr. Hammond had lost his job.

Mary Anne had told me this. "He's very depressed about it," she had said. "They won't be poor, though. Aunt Carol is rich."

He did not seem depressed to me. He seemed impatient—chiefly with Mrs. Hammond—but on the whole rather pleased with himself. He was tall and thin, he had dark hair combed straight back from his forehead, and his mustache was an ironic line above his upper lip. When he talked to me he leaned forward, as I had seen him doing earlier, when he talked to women in the living room. I had thought then that the word for him was *courtly*.

"Where do you go swimming, Minnie? Do you go swimming?"

"Yes," I said. "Down by the boathouse." I decided that his calling me Minnie was a special joke between us.

"Is that a good place?"

"Yes." It was, for me, because I liked being close to the dock. I had never, till this summer, swum in water that was over my head.

"Do you ever go in without your bathing suit on?"

I said, "No."

"You should try it."

Mrs. Montjoy came through the living-room doorway, asking if the meatballs were ready.

"This is certainly a hungry crowd," she said. "It's the swimming does it. How are you getting on, Ivan? Carol was just looking for you."

"She was here," said Mr. Hammond.

Mrs. Montjoy dropped parsley here and there among the meatballs. "Now," she said to me. "I think you've done about all you need to here. I think I can manage now. Why don't you just make yourself a sandwich and run along down to the boathouse?"

I said I wasn't hungry. Mr. Hammond had helped himself to more gin and ice cubes and had gone into the living room.

"Well. You'd better take something," Mrs. Montjoy said. "You'll be hungry later."

She meant that I was not to come back.

On my way to the boathouse I met a couple of the guests—girls of my own age, barefoot and in their wet bathing suits, breathlessly laughing. They had probably swum partway round the island and climbed out of the water at the boathouse. Now they were sneaking back to surprise somebody. They stepped aside politely, not to drip water on me, but did not stop laughing. Making way for my body without a glance at my face.

They were the sort of girls who would have squealed and made a fuss over me, if I had been a dog or a cat.

THE NOISE OF THE PARTY continued to rise. I lay down on my cot without taking off my dress. I had been on the go since early morning and I was tired. But I could not relax. After a while I got up and changed into my bathing suit and went down to swim. I climbed down the ladder into the water cautiously as I always did—I thought that I would go straight to the bottom and never come up if I jumped—and swam around in the shadows. The water washing my limbs made me think of what Mr. Hammond had said and I worked the straps of my bathing suit down, finally pulling out one arm after the other so that my breasts could float free. I swam that way, with the water sweetly dividing at my nipples . . .

I thought it was not impossible that Mr. Hammond might come looking for me. I thought of him touching me. (I could not figure out exactly how he would get into the water—I did not care to think of him stripping off his clothes. Perhaps he would squat down on the deck and I would swim over to him.) His fingers stroking my bare skin like ribbons of light. The thought of being touched and desired by a man that old—forty, forty-five?—was in some way repulsive, but I knew I would get pleasure from it, rather as you might get pleasure from being caressed by an amorous tame crocodile. Mr. Hammond's—Ivan's—skin might be smooth, but age and knowledge and corruptness would be on him like invisible warts and scales.

I dared to lift myself partly out of the water, holding with one hand to the dock. I bobbed up and down and rose into the air like a mermaid. Gleaming, with nobody to see.

Now I heard steps. I heard somebody coming. I sank down into the water and held still.

For a moment I believed that it was Mr. Hammond, and that I had actually entered the world of secret signals, abrupt and wordless forays of desire. I did not cover myself but shrank against the dock, in a paralyzed moment of horror and submission.

The boathouse light was switched on, and I turned around

noiselessly in the water and saw that it was old Mr. Foley, still in his party outfit of white trousers and yachting cap and blazer. He had stayed for a couple of drinks and explained to everybody that Mrs. Foley was not up to the strain of seeing so many people but sent her best wishes to all.

He was moving things around on the tool shelf. Soon he either found what he wanted or put back what he had intended to put back, and he switched off the light and left. He never knew that I was there.

I pulled up my bathing suit and got out of the water and went up the stairs. My body seemed such a weight to me that I was out of breath when I got to the top.

The sound of the cocktail party went on and on. I had to do something to hold my own against it, so I started to write a letter to Dawna, who was my best friend at that time. I described the cocktail party in lurid terms—people vomited over the deck railing and a woman passed out, falling down on the sofa in such a way that part of her dress slid off and exposed a purple-nippled old breast (I called it a bezoom). I spoke of Mr. Hammond as a letch, though I added that he was very good-looking. I said that he had fondled me in the kitchen while my hands were busy with the meatballs and that later he had followed me to the boathouse and grabbed me on the stairs. But I had kicked him where he wouldn't forget and he had retreated. *Scurried away,* I said.

"So hold your breath for the next installment," I wrote. "Entitled, 'Sordid Adventures of a Kitchen Maid.' Or 'Ravaged on the Rocks of Georgian Bay.'"

When I saw that I had written "ravaged" instead of "ravished," I thought I could let it go, because Dawna would never know the difference. But I realized that the part about Mr. Hammond was overdone, even for that sort of letter, and then the whole thing filled me with shame and a sense of my own failure and loneliness. I crumpled it up. There had not been any point in writing this letter except to assure myself that I had some contact with the world and that exciting things—sexual things—happened to me. And I hadn't. They didn't.

"MRS. FOLEY ASKED ME where Jane was," I had said, when Mrs. Montjoy and I were doing the silver—or when she was keeping an eye on me doing the silver. "Was Jane one of the other girls who worked here in the summer?"

I thought for a moment that she might not answer, but she did.

"Jane was my other daughter," she said. "She was Mary Anne's sister. She died."

I said, "Oh. I didn't know." I said, "Oh. I'm sorry.

"Did she die of polio?" I said, because I did not have the sense, or you might say the decency, not to go on. And in those days children still died of polio, every summer.

"No," said Mrs. Montjoy. "She was killed when my husband moved the dresser in our bedroom. He was looking for something he thought he might have dropped behind it. He didn't realize she was in the way. One of the casters caught on the rug and the whole thing toppled over on her."

I knew every bit of this, of course. Mary Anne had already told me. She had told me even before Mrs. Foley asked me where Jane was and clawed at my breast.

"How awful," I said.

"Well. It was just one of those things."

My deception made me feel queasy. I dropped a fork on the floor. Mrs. Montjoy picked it up.

"Remember to wash this again."

How strange that I did not question my right to pry, to barge in and bring this to the surface. Part of the reason must have been that in the society I came from, things like that were never buried for good, but ritualistically resurrected, and that such horrors were like a badge people wore—or, mostly, that women wore—throughout their lives.

Also it may have been because I would never quite give up when it came to demanding intimacy, or at least some kind of equality, even with a person I did not like.

Cruelty was a thing I could not recognize in myself. I thought I was blameless here, and in any dealings with this family. All because of being young, and poor, and knowing about Nausicaa.

I did not have the grace or fortitude to be a servant.

. . .

ON MY LAST SUNDAY I was alone in the boathouse, packing up my things in the suitcase I had brought—the same suitcase that had gone with my mother and father on their wedding trip and the only one we had in the house. When I pulled it out from under my cot and opened it up, it smelled of home—of the closet at the end of the upstairs hall where it usually sat, close to the mothballed winter coats and the rubber sheet once used on children's beds. But when you got it out at home it always smelled faintly of trains and coal fires and cities—of travel.

I heard steps on the path, a stumbling step into the boathouse, a rapping on the wall. It was Mr. Montjoy.

"Are you up there? Are you up there?"

His voice was boisterous, jovial, as I had heard it before when he had been drinking. As of course he had been drinking—for once again there were people visiting, celebrating the end of summer. I came to the top of the stairs. He had a hand against the wall to steady himself—a boat had gone by out in the channel and sent its waves into the boathouse.

"See here," said Mr. Montjoy, looking up at me with frowning concentration. "See here—I thought I might as well bring this down and give it to you while I thought of it.

"This book," he said.

He was holding *Seven Gothic Tales*.

"Because I saw you were looking in it that day," he said. "It seemed to me you were interested. So now I finished it and I thought I might as well pass it along to you. It occurred to me to pass it along to you. I thought, maybe you might enjoy it."

I said, "Thank you."

"I'm probably not going to read it again though I thought it was very interesting. Very unusual."

"Thank you very much."

"That's all right. I thought you might enjoy it."

"Yes," I said.

"Well then. I hope you will."

"Thank you."

"Well then," he said. "Good-bye."

I said, "Thank you. Good-bye."

Why were we saying good-bye when we were certain to see each other again before we left the island, and before I got on the train? It might have meant that this incident, of his giving me the book, was to be closed, and I was not to reveal or refer to it. Which I didn't. Or it might have been just that he was drunk and did not realize that he would see me later. Drunk or not, I see him now as pure of motive, leaning against the boathouse wall. A person who could think me worthy of this gift. Of this book.

At the moment, though, I didn't feel particularly pleased, or grateful, in spite of my repeated thank-yous. I was too startled, and in some way embarrassed. The thought of having a little corner of myself come to light, and be truly understood, stirred up alarm, just as much as being taken no notice of stirred up resentment. And Mr. Montjoy was probably the person who interested me least, whose regard meant the least to me, of all the people I had met that summer.

He left the boathouse and I heard him stumping along the path, back to his wife and his guests. I pushed the suitcase aside and sat down on the cot. I opened the book just anywhere, as I had done the first time, and began to read.

The walls of the room had once been painted crimson, but with time the colour had faded into a richness of hues, like a glassful of dying red roses . . . Some potpourri was being burned on the tall stove, on the sides of which Neptune, with a trident, steered his team of horses through high waves . . .

I forgot Mr. Montjoy almost immediately. In hardly any time at all I came to believe that this gift had always belonged to me.

Home

~

I COME HOME as I have done several times in the past year, travelling on three buses. The first bus is large, air-conditioned, fast, and comfortable. People on it pay little attention to each other. They look out at the highway traffic, which the bus negotiates with superior ease. We travel west then north from the city, and after fifty miles or so reach a large, prosperous market-and-manufacturing town. Here with those passengers who are going in my direction, I switch to a smaller bus. It is already fairly full of people whose journey home starts in this town—farmers too old to drive anymore, and farmers' wives of all ages; nursing students and agricultural college students going home for the weekend; children being transferred between parents and grandparents. This is an area with a heavy population of German and Dutch settlers, and some of the older people are speaking in one or another of those languages. On this leg of the trip you may see the bus stop to deliver a basket or a parcel to somebody waiting at a farm gate.

THE THIRTY-MILE TRIP to the town where the last change is made takes as long as, or longer than, the fifty-mile lap from the city. By the time we reach that town the large good-humored descendants of Germans, and the more recent Dutch, have all got off, the evening has grown darker and chillier and the farms less tended and rolling. I walk across the road with one or two survivors from the first bus, two or three from the second—here we smile at each other, acknowledging a comradeship or even a similarity that would not have been apparent to us in the places we started from. We climb onto the small bus waiting in front of a gas station. No bus depot here.

This is an old school bus, with very uncomfortable seats which cannot be adjusted in any way, and windows cut by horizontal metal frames. That makes it necessary to slump down or to sit up very straight and crane your neck, in order to get an unobstructed view. I find this irritating, because the countryside here is what I most want to see—the reddening fall woods and the dry fields of stubble and the cows crowding the barn porches. Such unremarkable scenes, in this part of the country, are what I have always thought would be the last thing I would care to see in my life.

And it does strike me that this might turn out to be true, and sooner than I had expected, as the bus is driven at what seems a reckless speed, bouncing and swerving, over the remaining twenty miles of roughly paved road.

This is great country for accidents. Boys too young to have a license will come to grief driving at ninety miles an hour over gravel roads with blind hills. Celebrating drivers will roar through villages late at night without their lights on, and most grown males seem to have survived at least one smashed telephone pole and one roll in the ditch.

MY FATHER AND STEPMOTHER may tell me of these casualties when I get home. My father simply speaks of a terrible accident. My stepmother takes it further. Decapitation, a steering-wheel stove into the chest, the bottle somebody was drinking from pulping the face.

"Idiots," I say shortly. It's not just that I have no sympathy with the gravel-runners, the blind drunks. It's that I think this conversation, my stepmother's expansion and relish, may be embarrassing my father. Later I'll understand that this probably isn't so.

"That's the very word for them," says my stepmother. "Idiots. They have nobody but themself to blame."

I sit with my father and my stepmother—whose name is Irlma—at the kitchen table, drinking whiskey. Their dog Buster lies at Irlma's feet. My father pours rye into three juice glasses until they are about three-quarters full, then fills them up with water. While my mother was alive there was never a bottle of liquor in this house, or even a bottle of beer or wine. She had made my father promise, before they were married, that he would never take a drink. This was not because she had suffered from men's drinking in her own home—it was just the promise that many self-respecting women required before they would bestow themselves on a man in those days.

The wooden kitchen table that we always ate from, and the chairs we sat on, have been taken to the barn. The chairs did not match. They were very old, and a couple of them were supposed to have come from what was called the chair factory—it was probably just a workshop—at Sunshine, a village that had passed out of existence by the end of the nineteenth century. My father is ready to sell them for next to nothing, or give them away, if anybody wants them. He can never understand an admiration for what he calls old junk, and thinks that people who profess it are being pretentious. He and Irlma have bought a new table with a plastic surface that looks something like wood and will not mark, and four chairs with plastic-covered cushions that have a pattern of yellow flowers and are, to tell the truth, much more comfortable than the old wooden chairs to sit on.

Now that I am living only a hundred miles away I come home every couple of months or so. Before this, for a long time, I lived more than a thousand miles away and would go for years without seeing this house. I thought of it then as a place I might never see again and I was greatly moved by the memory of it. I would walk through its rooms in my mind. All those rooms are small, and as is usual in old farmhouses, they are not designed to take advantage of the out-of-doors but, if possible, to ignore it. People may not have wanted to spend their time of rest or shelter looking out at the fields they had to work in, or at the snowdrifts they had to shovel their way through in order to feed their stock. People who openly admired nature—or who even went so far as to use that word, *Nature*—were often taken to be slightly soft in the head.

In my mind, when I was far away, I would also see the kitchen ceiling, made of narrow, smoke-stained, tongue-in-groove boards, and the frame of the kitchen window gnawed by some dog that had been locked in before my time. The wallpaper was palely splotched by a leaking chimney, and the linoleum was repainted by my mother every spring, as long as she was able. She painted it a dark color—brown or green or navy—then, using a sponge, she made a design on it, with bright speckles of yellow or red.

That ceiling is hidden now behind squares of white tiles, and a new metal window frame has replaced the gnawed wooden one. The window glass is new as well, and doesn't contribute any odd whorls or waves to what there is to see through it. And what there is to see, anyway, is not the bush of golden glow that was seldom cut back and that covered both bottom panes, or the orchard with the scabby apple trees and the two pear trees that never bore much fruit, being too far north. There is now only a long, gray, window-less turkey barn and a turkey yard, for which my father sold off a strip of land.

The front rooms have been repapered—a white paper with a cheerful but formal red embossed design—and wall-to-wall moss-green carpeting has been put down. And because my father and Irlma both grew up and lived through part of their adult lives in houses lit by coal-oil lamps, there is light everywhere—ceiling lights and plug-in lights, long blazing tubes and hundred-watt bulbs.

Even the outside of the house, the red brick whose crumbling mortar was particularly penetrable by an east wind, is going to be covered up with white metal siding. My father is thinking of putting it on himself. So it seems that this peculiar house—the kitchen part of it built in the 1860s—can be dissolved, in a way, and lost, inside an ordinary comfortable house of the present time.

I do not lament this loss as I would once have done. I do say that the red brick has a beautiful, soft color, and that I've heard of people (*city* people) paying a big price for just such old bricks, but I say this mostly because I think my father expects it. I am now a city person in his eyes, and when was I ever practical? (This is not accounted such a fault as it used to be, because I have made my way, against expectations, among people who are probably as impractical as myself.) And he is pleased to explain again about the east wind and the cost of fuel and the difficulty of repairs. I know that he speaks the truth, and I know that the house being lost was not a fine or handsome one in any way. A poor man's house, always, with the stairs going up between walls, and bedrooms opening out of one another. A house where people have lived close to the bone for over a hundred years. So if my father and Irlma wish to be comfortable combining their old-age pensions, which make them richer than they've ever been in their lives, if they wish to be (they use this word without quotation marks, quite simply and positively) *modern,* who am I to complain about the loss of some rosy bricks, a crumbling wall?

But it's also true that in a way my father wants some objections, some foolishness from me. And I feel obliged to hide from him the fact that the house does not mean as much to me as it once did, and that it really does not matter to me now how he changes it.

"I know how you love this place," he says to me, apologetically yet with satisfaction. And I don't tell him that I am not sure now whether I love any place, and that it seems to me it was myself that I loved here—some self that I have finished with, and none too soon.

I don't go into the front room now, to rummage in the piano bench for old photographs and sheet music. I don't go looking for my old high-school texts, my Latin poetry, *Maria Chapdelaine.* Or for the best sellers of some year in the 1940s when my mother belonged to the Book-of-the-Month Club—a great year for novels about the wives of Henry the Eighth, and for three-name women writers, and understanding books about the Soviet Union. I don't open the "classics" bound in limp imitation leather, bought by my mother before she was married, just to see her maiden name written in graceful, conventional schoolteacher's handwriting on the marbled endpaper, after the publisher's pledge: *Everyman, I will go with thee, and be thy guide, in thy most need to go by thy side.*

Reminders of my mother in this house are not so easy to locate, although she dominated it for so long with what seemed to us her embarrassing ambitions, and then with her just as embarrassing though justified complaints. The disease she had was so little known then, and so bizarre in its effects, that it did seem to be just the sort of thing she might have contrived, out of perversity and her true need for attention, for bigger dimensions in her life. Attention that her family came to give her out of necessity, not quite grudgingly, but so routinely that it seemed—it sometimes was—cold, impatient, untender. Never enough for her, never enough.

The books that used to lie under beds and on tables all over the house have been corralled by Irlma, chased and squeezed into this front-room bookcase, glass doors shut upon them. My father, loyal to his wife, reports that he hardly reads at all anymore, he has too much to do. (Though he does like to look at the *Historical Atlas* that I sent him.) Irlma doesn't care for the sight of people reading because it is not sociable and at the end of it all what has been accomplished? She thinks people are better off playing cards, or making things. Men can do woodworking, women can quilt and hook rugs or crochet or do embroidery. There is always plenty to do.

Contrarily, Irlma honors the writing that my father has taken up in his old age. "His writing is very good excepting when he gets too tired," she has said to me. "Anyway it's better than yours."

It took me a moment to figure out that she was talking about handwriting. That's what "writing" has always meant around here. The other business was or is called "making things up." For her they're joined together somehow and she does not raise objections. Not to any of it.

"It keeps his head working," she says.

Playing cards, she believes, would do the same. But she doesn't always have the time to sit down to that in the middle of the day.

My father talks to me about putting siding on the house. "I need a job like that to get me back to the shape I was in a couple of years ago."

About fifteen months ago he had a serious heart attack.

Irlma sets out coffee mugs, a plate of soda crackers and graham crackers, cheese and butter, bran muffins, baking-powder biscuits, squares of spice cake with boiled icing.

"It's not a lot," she says. "I'm getting lazy in my old age."

I say that will never happen, she'll never get lazy.

"The cake's even a mix, I'm shamed to tell you. Next thing you know it'll be boughten."

"It's good," I say. "Some mixes are really good."

"That's a fact," says Irlma.

HARRY CROFTON—who works part-time at the turkey barn where my father used to work—drops in at dinnertime the next day and after some necessary and expected protests is persuaded to stay. Dinnertime is at noon. We are having round steak pounded and floured and cooked in the oven, mashed potatoes with gravy, boiled parsnips, cabbage salad, biscuits, raisin cookies, crab-apple preserves, pumpkin pie with marshmallow topping. Also bread and butter, various relishes, instant coffee, tea.

Harry passes on the message that Joe Thoms, who lives up the river in a trailer, with no telephone, would be obliged if my father would drop by with a sack of potatoes. He would pay for them, of course. He would come and pick them up if he could, but he can't.

"Bet he can't," says Irlma.

My father covers this taunt by saying to me, "He's next thing to blind, these days."

"Barely find his way to the liquor store," Harry says.

All laugh.

"He could find his way there by his nose," Irlma says. And repeats herself, with relish, as she often does. "Find his way there by his nose!"

Irlma is a stout and rosy woman, with tinted butterscotch curls, brown eyes in which there is still a sparkle, a look of emotional readiness, of being always on the brink of hilarity. Or on the brink of impatience flaring into outrage. She likes to make people laugh, and to laugh herself. At other times she will put her hands on her hips and thrust her head forward and make some harsh statement, as if she hoped to provoke a fight. She connects this behavior with being Irish and with being born on a train.

"I'm Irish, you know. I'm fighting Irish. And I was born on a moving train. I couldn't wait. Kicking Horse Railway, what do you think of that? Born on a kicking horse you know how to stick up for yourself, and that's a fact." Then, whether her listeners reply in kind or shrink back in disconcerted silence, she will throw out a challenging laugh.

She says to Harry, "Joe still got that Peggy-woman living with him?"

I don't know who Peggy is, so I ask.

"Don't you mind Peggy?" Harry says reproachfully. And to Irlma, "You bet he has."

Harry used to work for us when my father had the fox farm and I was a little girl. He gave me licorice whips, out of the fuzzy depths of his pockets, and tried to teach me how to drive the truck and tickled me up to the elastic of my bloomers.

"Peggy Goring?" he says. "Her and her brothers used to live up by the tracks this side of the Canada Packers? Part Indian. Hugh and Bud Goring. Hugh used to work at the creamery?"

"Bud was the caretaker at the Town Hall," my father puts in.

"You mind them now?" says Irlma with a slight sharpness. Forgetting local names and facts can be seen as deliberate, unmannerly.

I say that I do, though I don't, really.

"Hugh went off and he never come back," she says. "So Bud shut the house up. He just lives in the one back room of it. He's got the pension now but he's too cheap to heat the whole house all the same."

"Got a little queer," my father says. "Like the rest of us."

"So Peggy?" says Harry, who knows and always has known every story, rumor, disgrace, and possible paternity within many miles. "Peggy used to be going around with Joe? Years back. But then she took off and got married to somebody else and was living up north. Then after a while Joe took off up there too and he was living with her but they got into some big kind of a fight and he went away out west." He laughs as he has always done, silently, with a great private derision that seems to be held inside him, shuddering through his chest and his shoulders.

"That's the way they did," says Irlma. "That's the way they carried on."

"So then Peggy went out west chasing after him," Harry resumes, "and they ended up living together out there and it seems like he was beating up on her pretty bad so finally she got on the train and come back here. Beat her up so bad before she got on the train they thought they'd have to stop and put her in a hospital."

"I'd like to see that," Irlma says. "I'd like to see a man try that on me."

"Yeah, well," says Harry. "But she must've got some money or she made Bud pay her a share on the house because she bought herself the trailer. Maybe she thought she was going to travel. But Joe showed up again and they moved the trailer out to the river and went and got married. Her other husband must've died."

"Married according to what they say," says Irlma.

"I don't know," says Harry. "They say he still thumps her good when he takes the notion."

"Anybody tried that on me," Irlma says, "I'd let him have it. I'd let him have it in the you-know-where."

"Now now," says my father, in mock consternation.

"Her being part Indian might have something to do with it," Harry says. "They say the Indians thump their women every once in a while and it makes them love 'em better."

I feel obliged to say, "Oh, that's just the way people talk about Indians," and Irlma—immediately sniffing out some high-mindedness or superiority—says that what people say about the Indians has a lot of truth to it, never mind.

"Well, this conversation is way too stimulating for an old chap like me," says my father. "I think I'll go and lie down for a while upstairs."

"HE'S NOT HIMSELF," Irlma says, after we have listened to my father's slow steps on the stairs. "He's been feeling tough two or three days now."

"Has he?" I say, guilty that I haven't noticed. He has seemed to me the way he always seems now when a visit brings Irlma and me together—just a bit shaky and apprehensive, as if he had to be on guard, as if it took some energy explaining and defending us, one to the other.

"He don't feel right," Irlma says. "I can tell."

She turns to Harry, who has put on his outdoor jacket.

"Just tell me something before you go out that door," she says, getting between him and the door to block his way. "Tell me—how much string does it take to tie up a woman?"

Harry pretends to consider. "Big woman or little woman, would that be?"

"Any size woman at all."

"Oh, I couldn't tell you. Couldn't say."

"Two balls and six inches," cries Irlma, and some far gurgles reach us, from Harry's subterranean enjoyment.

"Irlma, you're a Tartar."

"I am so. I'm an old Tartar. I am so."

I GO ALONG IN THE CAR with my father, to take the potatoes to Joe Thoms.

"You aren't feeling well?"

"Not the very best."

"*How* aren't you feeling well?"

"I don't know. Can't sleep. I wouldn't be surprised if I've got the flu."

"Are you going to call the doctor?"

"If I don't get better I'll call him. Call him now I'd just be wasting his time."

Joe Thoms, a man about ten years older than I am, is alarmingly frail and shaky, with long stringy arms, an unshaven, ruined, handsome face, grayed-over eyes. I can't see how he could manage to thump anybody. He gropes to meet us and take the sack of potatoes, urges us inside the smoky trailer.

"I mean to pay you for these here," he says. "Just tell me what they're worth?"

My father says, "Now now."

An enormous woman stands at the stove, stirring something in a pot.

My father says, "Peggy, this is my daughter. Smells good, whatever you got there."

She doesn't respond, and Joe Thoms says, "It's just a rabbit we got give for a present. No use to talk to her, she's got her deaf ear to you. She's deaf and I'm blind. Isn't that the devil? It's just a rabbit but we don't mind rabbit. Rabbit's a clean feeder."

I see now that the woman is not so enormous all over. The upper part of the arm next to us is out of proportion to the rest of her body, swollen like a puffball. The sleeve has been ripped out of her dress, leaving the armhole frayed, threads dangling, and the great swelling of flesh exposed and gleaming in the smoke and shadow of the trailer.

My father says, "It can be pretty good all right, rabbit."

"Sorry not to offer you a shot," Joe says. "But we don't have it in the house. We don't drink no more."

"I'm not feeling up to it either, to tell you the truth."

"Nothing in the house since we joined the Tabernacle. Peggy and me both. You hear we joined up?"

"No, Joe. I didn't hear about that."

"We did. And it's a comfort to us."

"Well."

"I realize now I spent a lot of my life in the wrong way. Peggy, she realizes it too."

My father says, "H'm-h'm."

"I say to myself it's no wonder the Lord struck me blind. He struck me blind but I see His purpose in it. I see the Lord's purpose. We have not had a drop of liquor in the place since the first of July weekend. That was the last time. First of July."

He sticks his face close to my father's.

"You see the Lord's purpose?"

"Oh Joe," says my father with a sigh. "Joe, I think all that's a lot of hogwash."

I am surprised at this, because my father is usually a man of great diplomacy, of kind evasions. He has always spoken to me, almost warningly, about the need to *fit in,* not to rile people.

Joe Thoms is even more surprised than I am.

"You don't mean to say that. You don't mean it. You don't know what you're saying."

"Yes I do."

"Well you should read your Bible. You should see what all it says in the Bible."

My father slaps his hands nervously or impatiently on his knees.

"A person can agree or disagree with the Bible, Joe. The Bible is just a book like any other book."

"It's a sin to say that. The Lord wrote the Bible and He planned and created the world and every one of us here."

More hand slapping. "I don't know about that, Joe. I don't know. Come to planning the world, who says it has to've been planned at all?"

"Well then, who created it?"

"I don't know the answer to that. And I don't care."

I see that my father's face is not as usual, that it is not agreeable (that has been its most constant expression) and not ill-humored either. It is stubborn but not challenging, simply locked into itself in an unyielding weariness. Something has shut down in him, ground to a halt.

HE DRIVES HIMSELF to the hospital. I sit beside him with a washed-out can on my knees, ready to hold it for him if he should have to pull off the road and be sick again. He has been up all night, vomiting often. In between times he sat at the kitchen table looking at the *Historical Atlas*. He who has rarely been out of the province of Ontario knows about rivers in Asia and ancient boundaries in the Middle East. He knows where the deepest trench is in the ocean floor. He knows Alexander's route, and Napoleon's, and that the Khazars had their capital city where the Volga flows into the Caspian Sea.

He said he had a pain across his shoulders, across his back. And what he called his old enemy, his gut pain.

About eight o'clock he went upstairs to try to sleep, and Irlma and I spent the morning talking and smoking in the kitchen, hoping that he was doing that.

Irlma recalled the effect she used to have on men. It started early. A man tried to lure her off when she was watching a parade, only nine years old. And during the early years of her first marriage she found herself walking down a street in Toronto, looking for a place she'd heard about, that sold vacuum-cleaner parts. And a man, a perfect stranger, said to her, "Let me give you a piece of advice, young lady. Don't walk around in the city with a smile like that on your face. People could take that up the wrong way."

"I didn't know how I was smiling. I wasn't meaning any harm. I'd always've rather smiled than frowned. I was never so flabbergasted in my life. *Don't walk around in the city with a smile like that on your face.*" She leans back in her chair, opens her arms helplessly, laughs.

"Hot stuff," she says. "And didn't even know it."

She tells me what my father has said to her. He has said that he wished that she'd always been his wife, and not my mother.

"That's what he said. He said I was the one what would have suited him. Should've got me the first time."

And that's the truth, she says.

WHEN MY FATHER came downstairs he said he felt better, he had slept a little and the pain was gone, or at least he thought it was going. He could try to eat something. Irlma offered a sandwich, scrambled eggs, applesauce, a cup of tea. My father tried the cup of tea, and then he vomited and kept vomiting bile.

But before he would leave for the hospital he had to take me out to the barn and show me where the hay was, how to put it down for the sheep. He and Irlma keep two dozen or so sheep. I don't know why they do this. I don't think they make enough money on the sheep for the work that is created to be worthwhile. Perhaps it is just reassuring to have some animals around. They have Buster of course, but he is not exactly a farm animal. The sheep provide chores, farm work still to be done, the kind of work they have known all their lives.

The sheep are still out to pasture, but the grass they get has lost some of its nourishment—there have been a couple of frosts—so they must have the hay as well.

IN THE CAR I sit beside him holding the can and we follow slowly that old, usual route—Spencer Street, Church Street, Wexford Street, Ladysmith Street—to the hospital. The town, unlike the house, stays very much the same—nobody is renovating or changing it. Nevertheless it has changed for me. I have written about it and used it up. Here are more or less the same banks and hardware and grocery stores and the barbershop and the Town Hall tower, but all their secret, plentiful messages for me have drained away.

Not for my father. He has lived here and nowhere else. He has not escaped things by such use.

TWO SLIGHTLY STRANGE THINGS happen when I take my father into the hospital. They ask me how old he is, and I say immediately, "Fifty-two," which is the age of a man I am in love with. Then I laugh and apologize and run to the bed in the Emergency Ward where he is lying, and ask him if he is seventy-two or seventy-three. He looks at me as if the question bewilders him too. He says, "Beg your pardon?" in a formal way, to gain time, then is able to tell me, seventy-two. He is trembling slightly all over, but his chin is trembling conspicuously, just the way my mother's did. In the short time since he has entered the hospital some abdication has taken place. He knew it would, of course—that is why he held off coming. The nurse comes to take his blood pressure and he tries to roll up his shirtsleeve but is not able—she has to do it for him.

"You can go and sit in the room outside," the nurse says to me. "It's more comfortable there."

The second strange thing: It happens that Dr. Parakulam, my father's own doctor—known locally as the Hin-doo doctor—is the doctor on call in the Emergency Ward. He arrives after a while and I hear my father making an effort to greet him in an affable way. I hear the curtains being pulled shut around the bed. After the examination Dr. Parakulam comes out and speaks to the nurse, who is now busy at the desk in the room where I am waiting.

"All right. Admit him. Upstairs."

He sits down opposite me while the nurse gets on the phone.

"No?" she says on the phone. "Well he wants him up there. No. Okay, I'll tell him."

"They say he'll have to go in Three-C. No beds."

"I don't want him in Chronic," the doctor says—perhaps he speaks to her in a more authoritarian way, or in a more aggrieved tone, than a doctor who had been brought up in this country would use. "I want him in Intensive. I want him upstairs."

"Well maybe you should talk to them then," she says. "Do you want to talk to them?"

She is a tall lean nurse, with some air of a middle-aged tomboy, cheerful and slangy. Her tone with him is less discreet, less correct and deferential, than the tone I would expect a nurse to take with a doctor. Maybe he is not a doctor who wins respect. Or maybe it is just that country and small-town women, who are generally so conservative in opinion, can often be bossy and unintimidated in manner.

Dr. Parakulam picks up the phone.

"I do not want him in Chronic. I want him upstairs. Well can't you— Yes I know. But can't you?— This is a case— I know. But I am saying— Yes. Yes all right. All right. I see."

He puts down the phone and says to the nurse, "Get him down to Three." She takes the phone to arrange it.

"But you want him in Intensive Care," I say, thinking that there must be some way in which my father's needs can prevail.

"Yes. I want him there but there is not anything I can do about it." For the first time the doctor looks directly at me and now it is I who am perhaps his enemy, and not the person on the phone. A short, brown, elegant man he is, with large glossy eyes.

"I did my best," he says. "What more do you think I can do? What is a doctor? A doctor is not anything anymore."

I do not know who he thinks is to blame—the nurses, the hospital, the government—but I am not used to seeing doctors flare up like this and the last thing I want from him is a confession of helplessness. It seems a bad omen for my father.

"I am not blaming you—," I say.

"Well then. Do not blame me."

The nurse has finished talking on the phone. She tells me I will have to go to Admitting and fill out some forms. "You've got his card?" she says. And to the doctor, "They're bringing in somebody that banged up on the Lucknow highway. Far as I can make out it's not too bad."

"All right. All right."

"Just your lucky day."

MY FATHER has been put in a four-bed ward. One bed is empty. In the bed beside him, next to the window, there is an old man who has to lie flat on his back and receive oxygen but is able to make conversation. During the past two years, he says, he has had nine operations. He spent most of the past year in the Veterans Hospital in the city.

"They took out everything they could take out and then they pumped me full of pills and sent me home to die." He says this as if it is a witticism he has delivered successfully many times.

He has a radio, which he has tuned to a rock station. Perhaps it is all he can get. Perhaps he likes it.

Across from my father is the bed of another old man, who has been removed from it and placed in a wheelchair. He has cropped white hair, still thick, and the big head and frail body of a sickly child. He wears a short hospital gown and sits in the wheelchair with his legs apart, revealing a nest of dry brown nuts. There is a tray across the front of his chair, like the tray on a child's high chair. He has been given a washcloth to play with. He rolls up the washcloth and pounds it three times with his fist. Then he unrolls it and rolls it up again, carefully, and pounds it again. He always pounds it three times, once at each end and once in the middle. The procedure continues and the timing does not vary.

"Dave Ellers," my father says in a low voice.

"You know him?"

"Oh sure. Old railroad man."

The old railroad man gives us a quick look, without breaking his routine. "Ha," he says, warningly.

My father says, apparently without irony, "He's gone away downhill."

"Well you are the best-looking man in the room," I say. "Also the best dressed."

He does smile then, weakly and dutifully. They have let him wear the maroon and gray striped pyjamas that Irlma took out of their package for him. A Christmas present.

"Does it feel to you like I've got a bit of a fever?"

I touch his forehead, which is burning.

"Maybe a bit. They'll give you something." I lean close to whisper. "I think you've got a head start in the intellectual stakes, too."

"What?" he says. "Oh." He looks around. "I may not keep it." Even as he says this he gives me the wild helpless look I have learned today to interpret and I snatch the basin from the bedside stand and hold it for him.

As my father retches, the man who has had nine operations turns up the volume on his radio.

>*Sitting on the ceiling*
>*Looking upside down*
>*Watching all the people*
>*Goin' roun' and roun'*

I go home and eat supper with Irlma. I will go back to the hospital after supper. Irlma will go tomorrow. My father has said it would be better if she didn't come tonight.

"Wait till they get me under control," he said. "I don't want her upset."

"Buster's out somewhere," Irlma says. "I can't call him back. And if he won't come to me he won't come to nobody."

Buster is really Irlma's dog. He is the dog she brought with her when she married my father. Part German shepherd, part collie, he is very old, smelly, and generally dispirited. Irlma is right—he doesn't trust anybody but her. At intervals during our meal she gets up and calls from the kitchen door.

"Here Buster. Buster, Buster. Come on home."

"Do you want me to go out and call him?"

"Wouldn't work. He'd just not pay no attention."

It seems to me her voice is weaker and more discouraged when she calls Buster than she allows it to be when she speaks to anybody else. She whistles for him, as strongly as she can, but her whistle, too, lacks vigor.

"I bet you I know where he's gone," she says. "Down to the river."

I am thinking that, whatever she says, I will have to put on my father's rubber boots and go looking for him. Then, at no noise that I can hear, she lifts her head and hurries to the door and calls, "Here Buster old boy. There he is. There he is. Come on in now. Come on Buster. There's the old boy.

"Where you been?" she says, bending and hugging him. "Where you been, you old bugger? I know. I know. You gone and wet yourself in the river."

Buster smells of rot and river weeds. He stretches himself out on the mat between the couch and the television set.

"He's got his bowel trouble again, that's it. That's why he went in the water. It burns him and burns so he goes in the water to relieve it. But he won't get no real relief till he passes it. No he won't," she says, cuddling him in the towel she uses to wipe him. "Poor old fellow."

She explains to me as she has done before that Buster's bowel trouble comes from going poking around the turkey barn and eating whatever he finds there.

"Old dead turkey stuff. With quills in it. He gets them into his system and he can't pass them through the way a younger dog would. He can't manage them. They get all bunched up in his bowels and they block all up in there and he can't pass it out and he's in agony. Just listen to him."

Sure enough Buster is grunting, groaning. He pushes himself to his feet. *Hunh. Hunh.*

"He'll be all night like that, maybe. I don't know. Maybe never get it out at all. That's what I can't help but be scared of. Take him to the vet's I know they won't help him. They'll just tell me he's too old, and they'll want to put him down."

Hunh. Hunh.

"NOBODY EVEN GOEN TO COME to put me to bed," says Mr. Ellers the railroad man. He is in bed, propped up. His voice is harsh and strong but he does not wake my father. My father's eyelids tremble. His false teeth have been taken out so that his mouth sinks down at the corners, his lips have nearly disappeared. On his sleeping face there is a look of the most unalterable disappointment.

"Shut up that racket out there," says Mr. Ellers to the silent hall. "Shut up or I'll fine you a hunderd and eighty dollars."

"Shut up yourself, you old looney," says the man with the radio, and turns it on.

"A hunderd and eighty dollars."

My father opens his eyes, tries to sit up, sinks back, and says to me in a tone of some urgency, "How can we tell that the end product is man?"

Get yo' hans outa my pocket—

"Evolution," my father says. "We might've got the wrong end of the stick about that. Something going on we don't know the first thing about."

I touch his head. Hot as ever.

"What do you think about it?"

"I don't know, Dad."

Because I don't think—I don't think about things like that. I did at one time, but not anymore. Now I think about my work, and about men.

His conversational energy is already running out.

"May be coming—new Dark Ages."

"Do you think so?"

"Irlma's got the jump on you and me."

His voice sounds fond to me, yet rueful. Then he faintly smiles. The word I think he says is . . . *wonder.*

. . .

"BUSTER COME THROUGH," Irlma greets me when I get home. A glow of relief and triumph has spread over her face.

"Oh. That's good."

"Just after you went to the hospital he got down to business. I'll have you a cup of coffee in a minute." She plugs in the kettle. On the table she has set out ham sandwiches, mustard pickles, cheese, biscuits, dark and light honey. It is just a couple of hours since we finished supper.

"He started grunting and pacing and worrying at the mat. He was just crazy with the misery and wasn't nothing I could do. Then about quarter past seven I heard the change. I can tell by the sound he makes when he's got it worked down into a better position where he can make the effort. There's some pie left, we never finished it, would you rather have the pie?"

"No thanks. This is fine."

I pick up a ham sandwich.

"So I open the door and try to persuade him to get outside where he can pass it."

The kettle is whistling. She pours water on my instant coffee.

"Wait a minute, I'll get you some real cream—but too late. Right on the mat there he passed it. A hunk like that." She shows me her fists bunched together. "And *hard*. Oh boy. You should of seen it. Like rock.

"And I was right," she says. "It was chock-full of turkey quills."

I stir the muddy coffee.

"And after that *whoosh*, out with the soft stuff. Bust the dam, you did." She says this to Buster, who has raised his head. "You went and stunk the place up something fierce, you did. But the most of it went on the mat so I took it outside and put the hose on it," she said, turning back to me. "Then I took the soap and the scrub-brush and then I renched it with the hose all over again. Then scrubbed up the floor too and sprayed with Lysol and left the door open. You can't smell it in here now, can you?"

"No."

"I was sure good and happy to see him get relief. Poor old fellow. He'd be the age of ninety-four if he was human."

DURING THE FIRST VISIT I made to my father and Irlma after I left my marriage and came east, I went to sleep in the room that used to be my parents' bedroom. (My father and Irlma now sleep in the bedroom that used to be mine.) I dreamed that I had just entered this room where I was really sleeping, and I found my mother on her knees. She was painting the baseboard yellow. Don't you know, I said, that Irlma is going to paint this room blue and white? Yes I do know, my mother said, but I thought if I hurried up and got it all done she would leave it alone, she wouldn't go to the trouble of covering up fresh paint. But you will have to help me, she said. You will have to help me get it done because I have to do it while she's asleep.

And that was exactly like her, in the old days—she would start something in a big burst of energy, then marshall everybody to help her, because of a sudden onslaught of fatigue and helplessness.

"I'm dead you know," she said in explanation. "So I have to do this while she's asleep."

Irlma's got the jump on you and me.

What did my father mean by that?

That she knows only the things which are useful to her, but she knows those things very well? That she could be depended upon to take what she needs, under almost any circumstances? Being a person who doesn't question her wants, doesn't question that she is right in whatever she feels or says or does.

In describing her to a friend I have said, she's a person who would take the boots off a dead body on the street. And then of course I said, what's wrong with that?

. . . wonder.

She's a wonder.

SOMETHING HAPPENED that I am ashamed of. When Irlma said what she did about my father having wished he'd been with her all the time, about his having preferred her to my mother, I said to her in a cool judicious tone—that educated tone which in itself has power to hurt—that I didn't doubt that he had said that. (Nor do

I. My father and I share a habit—not too praiseworthy—of often saying to people more or less what we think they'd like to hear.) I said that I didn't doubt that he had said it but I did not think it had been tactful of her to tell me. *Tactful*, yes. That was the word I used.

She was amazed that anybody could try to singe her so, when she was happy with herself, flowering. She said that if there was one thing she could not stand it was people who took her up wrong, people who were so touchy. And her eyes filled up with tears. But then my father came downstairs and she forgot her own grievance—at least temporarily, she forgot it—in her anxiety to care for him, to provide him with something he could eat.

In her anxiety? I could say, in her love. Her face utterly softened, pink, tender, suffused with love.

I TALK to Dr. Parakulam on the phone.

"Why do you think he is running this temperature?"

"He has an infection somewhere." *Obviously*, is what he does not say.

"Is he on—well, I suppose he's on antibiotics for that?"

"He is on everything."

A silence.

"Where do you think the infection—"

"I'm having tests done on him today. Blood tests. Another electro-cardiogram."

"Do you think it's his heart?"

"Yes. I think basically it is. That is the main trouble. His heart."

ON MONDAY AFTERNOON, Irlma has gone to the hospital. I was going to take her—she does not drive—but Harry Crofton has shown up in his truck and she has decided to go with him, so that I can stay at home. Both she and my father are nervous about there being *nobody on the place*.

I go out to the barn. I put down a bale of hay and cut the twine around it and separate the hay and spread it.

When I come here I usually stay from Friday night until Sunday night, no longer, and now that I have stayed on into the next week something about my life seems to have slipped out of control. I don't feel so sure that it is just a visit. The buses that run from place to place no longer seem so surely to connect with me.

I am wearing open sandals, cheap water-buffalo sandals. This type of footwear is worn by a lot of women I know and it is seen to indicate a preference for country life, a belief in what is simple and natural. It is not practical when you are doing the sort of job I am doing now. Bits of hay and sheep pellets, which are like big black raisins, get squashed between my toes.

The sheep come crowding at me. Since they were sheared in the summer, their wool has grown back, but it is not yet very long. Right after the shearing they look from a distance surprisingly like goats, and they are not soft and heavy even yet. The big hip bones stand out, the bunting foreheads. I talk to them rather self-consciously, spreading the hay. I give them oats in the long trough.

People I know say that work like this is restorative and has a peculiar dignity, but I was born to it and feel it differently. Time and place can close in on me, it can so easily seem as if I have never got away, that I have stayed here my whole life. As if my life as an adult was some kind of dream that never took hold of me. I see myself not like Harry and Irlma, who have to some extent flourished in this life, or like my father, who has trimmed himself to it, but more like one of those misfits, captives—nearly useless, celibate, rusting—who should have left but didn't, couldn't, and are now unfit for any place. I think of a man who let his cows starve to death one winter after his mother died, not because he was frozen in grief but because he couldn't be bothered going out to the barn to feed them, and there was nobody to tell him he had to. I can believe that, I can imagine it. I can see myself as a middle-aged daughter who did her duty, stayed at home, thinking that someday her chance would come, until she woke up and knew it wouldn't. Now she reads all night and doesn't answer her door, and comes out in a surly trance to spread hay for the sheep.

WHAT HAPPENS as I'm finishing with the sheep is that Irlma's niece Connie drives into the barnyard. She has picked up her younger son from the high school and come to see how we are getting on.

Connie is a widow with two sons and a marginal farm a few miles away. She works as a nurse's aide at the hospital. As well as being Irlma's niece she is a second cousin of mine—it was through her, I think, that my father got better acquainted with Irlma. Her eyes are brown and sparkling, like Irlma's, but they are more thoughtful, less demanding. Her body is capable, her skin dried, her arms hard muscled, her dark hair cropped and graying. There is a fitful charm in her voice and her expression and she still moves like a good dancer. She fixes her lipstick and makes up her eyes before she goes to work and again when work is over, she surfaces full of what you might describe inadequately as high spirits or good humor or human kindness, from a life whose choices have not been plentiful, whose luck has not been in good supply.

She sends her son to shut the gate for me—I should have done that—to keep the sheep from straying into the lower field.

She says that she has been in to see my father at the hospital and that he seems a good deal better today, his fever is down and he ate up his dinner.

"You must be wanting to get back to your own life," she says, as if that was the most natural thing in the world and exactly what she would be wanting herself in my place. She can't know anything about my life of sitting in a room writing and going out sometimes to meet a friend or a lover, but if she did know, she would probably say that I have a right to it.

"The boys and I can run up and do what we have to for Aunt Irlma. One of them can stay with her if she doesn't like to be alone. We can manage for now, anyway. You can phone and see how things develop. You could come up again on the weekend. How about that?"

"Are you sure that would be all right?"

"I don't think this is so dire," she says. "The way it usually is, you have to go through quite a few scares before—you know, before it's curtains. Usually, anyway."

I think that I can get here in a hurry if I have to, I can always rent a car.

"I can get in to see him every day," she says. "Him and I are friends, he'll talk to me. I'll be sure and let you know anything. Any change or anything."

And that seems to be the way we're going to leave it.

I remember something my father once said to me. *She restored my faith in women.*

Faith in women's instinct, their natural instinct, something warm and active and straightforward. Something not mine, I had thought, bridling. But now talking to Connie I could see more of what was meant. Though it wasn't Connie he'd been talking about. It was Irlma.

WHEN I THINK ABOUT ALL THIS LATER, I will recognize that the very corner of the stable where I was standing, to spread the hay, and where the beginning of panic came on me, is the scene of the first clear memory of my life. There is in that corner a flight of steep wooden steps going up to the hayloft, and in the scene I remember I am sitting on the first or second step watching my father milk the black-and-white cow. I know what year it was—the black-and-white cow died of pneumonia in the worst winter of my childhood, which was 1935. Such an expensive loss is not hard to remember.

And since the cow is still alive and I am wearing warm clothes, a woolen coat and leggings, and at milking-time it is already dark—there is a lantern hanging on a nail beside the stall—it is probably the late fall or early winter. Maybe it was still 1934. Just before the brunt of the season hit us.

The lantern hangs on the nail. The black-and-white cow seems remarkably large and definitely marked, at least in comparison with the red cow, or muddy-reddish cow, her survivor, in the next stall. My father sits on the three-legged milking stool, in the cow's shadow. I can recall the rhythm of the two streams of milk going into the pail, but not quite the sound. Something hard and light, like tiny hailstones? Outside the small area of the stable lit by the lantern are the mangers filled with shaggy hay, the water tank where a kitten of mine will drown some years into the future; the cobwebbed windows, the large brutal tools—scythes and axes and rakes—hanging out of my reach. Outside of that, the dark of the country nights when few cars came down our road and there were no outdoor lights.

And the cold which even then must have been gathering, building into the cold of that extraordinary winter which killed all the chestnut trees, and many orchards.

Dimensions

∿

DOREE HAD TO TAKE THREE BUSES—one to Kincardine, where she waited for the one to London, where she waited again for the city bus out to the facility. She started the trip on a Sunday at nine in the morning. Because of the waiting times between buses, it took her till about two in the afternoon to travel the hundred-odd miles. All that sitting, either on the buses or in the depots, was not a thing she should have minded. Her daily work was not of the sitting-down kind.

She was a chambermaid at the Blue Spruce Inn. She scrubbed bathrooms and stripped and made beds and vacuumed rugs and wiped mirrors. She liked the work—it occupied her thoughts to a certain extent and tired her out so that she could sleep at night. She was seldom faced with a really bad mess, though some of the women she worked with could tell stories to make your hair curl. These women were older than she was, and they all thought she should try to work her way up. They told her she should get trained for a job behind the desk while she was still young and decent looking. But she was content to do what she did. She didn't want to have to talk to people.

None of the people she worked with knew what had happened. Or, if they did, they didn't let on. Her picture had been in the paper—they'd used the picture he took of her and the three kids, the new baby, Dimitri, in her arms, and Barbara Ann and Sasha on either side, looking on. Her hair had been long and wavy and brown then, natural in curl and color, as he liked it, and her face bashful and soft—a reflection less of the way she was than of the way he wanted to see her.

Since then, she had cut her hair short and bleached and spiked it, and she had lost a lot of weight. And she went by her second name now: Fleur. Also, the job they had found for her was in a town a good distance away from where she used to live.

This was the third time she had made the trip. The first two times he had refused to see her. If he did that again she would just quit trying. Even if he did see her, she might not come again for a while. She was not going to go overboard. As a matter of fact, she didn't really know what she was going to do.

On the first bus she was not too troubled. Just riding along and looking at the scenery. She had grown up on the coast, where there was such a thing as spring, but here winter jumped almost directly into summer. A month ago there had been snow, and now it was hot enough to go bare armed. Dazzling patches of water lay in the fields, and the sunlight was pouring down through the naked branches.

On the second bus she began to feel jittery, and she couldn't help trying to guess which of the women around her might be bound for the same place. They were women alone, usually dressed with some care, maybe to make themselves look as if they were going to church. The older ones looked like they belonged to strict old-fashioned churches where you had to wear a skirt and stockings and some sort of hat, while the younger ones might have been part of a livelier congregation which accepted pantsuits, bright scarves, earrings, and puffy hairdos.

Doree didn't fit into either category. In the whole year and a half she had been working she had not bought herself a single new piece of clothing. She wore her uniforms at work and her jeans everywhere else. She had got out of the way of wearing makeup because he hadn't allowed it, and now, though she could have, she didn't. Her spikes of corn-colored hair didn't suit her bony bare face, but it didn't matter.

On the third bus she got a seat by the window and tried to keep herself calm by reading the signs—both the advertising and street signs. There was a certain trick she had picked up to keep her mind occupied. She took the letters of whatever words her eyes lit on, and she tried to see how many new words she could make out of them. "Coffee," for instance, would give you "fee," and then "foe," and "off" and "of," and "shop" would provide "hop" and "sop" and

"so" and—wait a minute—"posh." Words were more than plentiful on the way out of the city, as they passed billboards, monster
stores, car lots, even balloons moored on roofs to advertise sales.

DOREE HAD NOT TOLD Mrs. Sands about her last two attempts,
and probably wouldn't tell her about this one either. Mrs. Sands,
whom she saw on Monday afternoons, spoke of moving on, though
she always said that it would take time, that things should not be
hurried. She told Doree that she was doing fine, that she was gradually discovering her own strength.

"I know those words have been done to death," she said. "But
they're still true."

She blushed at what she heard herself say—"death"—but did
not make it worse by apologizing.

When Doree was sixteen—that was seven years ago—she'd
gone to visit her mother in the hospital every day after school. Her
mother was recovering from an operation on her back, which was
said to be serious but not dangerous. Lloyd was an orderly. He and
Doree's mother had in common the fact that they both were old
hippies—though Lloyd was actually a few years the younger—and
whenever he had time he'd come in and chat with her about the
concerts and protest marches they'd both attended, the outrageous
people they'd known, drug trips that had knocked them out, that
sort of thing.

Lloyd was popular with the patients because of his jokes and
his sure, strong touch. He was stocky and broad shouldered and
authoritative enough to be sometimes taken for a doctor. (Not that
he was pleased by that—he held the opinion that a lot of medicine
was a fraud and a lot of doctors were jerks.) He had sensitive reddish skin and light hair and bold eyes.

He kissed Doree in the elevator and told her she was a flower in
the desert. Then he laughed at himself and said, "How original can
you get?"

"You're a poet and don't know it," she said, to be kind.

One night her mother died suddenly, of an embolism. Doree's
mother had a lot of women friends who would have taken Doree
in—and she stayed with one of them for a time—but the new
friend Lloyd was the one Doree preferred. By her next birthday she

was pregnant, then married. Lloyd had never been married before, though he had at least two children whose whereabouts he was not certain of. They would have been grown up by then, anyway. His philosophy of life had changed as he got older—he believed now in marriage, constancy, and no birth control. And he found the Sechelt Peninsula, where he and Doree lived, too full of people these days—old friends, old ways of life, old lovers. Soon he and Doree moved across the country to a town they picked from a name on the map: Mildmay. They didn't live in town; they rented a place in the country. Lloyd got a job in an ice-cream factory. They planted a garden. Lloyd knew a lot about gardening, just as he did about house carpentry, managing a woodstove, and keeping an old car running.

Sasha was born.

"PERFECTLY NATURAL," Mrs. Sands said.

Doree said, "Is it?"

Doree always sat on a straight-backed chair in front of a desk, not on the sofa, which had a flowery pattern and cushions. Mrs. Sands moved her own chair to the side of the desk, so they could talk without any kind of barrier between them.

"I've sort've been expecting you would," she said. "I think it's what I might have done in your place."

Mrs. Sands would not have said that in the beginning. A year ago, even, she'd have been more cautious, knowing how Doree would have revolted, then, at the idea that anybody, any living soul, could be in her place. Now she knew that Doree would just take it as a way, even a humble way, of trying to understand.

Mrs. Sands was not like some of them. She was not brisk, not thin, not pretty. Not too old either. She was about the age that Doree's mother would have been, though she did not look as if she'd ever been a hippie. Her graying hair was cut short and she had a mole riding on one cheekbone. She wore flat shoes and loose pants and flowered tops. Even when they were of a raspberry or turquoise color these tops did not make her look as if she really cared what she put on—it was more as if somebody had told her she needed to smarten herself up and she had obediently gone shopping for something she thought might do that. Her large, kind, impersonal sobriety drained all assaulting cheerfulness, all insult, out of those clothes.

"Well the first two times I never saw him," Doree said. "He wouldn't come out."

"But this time he did? He did come out?"

"Yes, he did. But I wouldn't hardly have known him."

"He'd aged?"

"I guess so. I guess he's lost some weight. And those clothes. Uniforms. I never saw him in anything like that."

"He looked to you like a different person?"

"No." Doree caught at her upper lip, trying to think what the difference was. He'd been so still. She had never seen him so still. He hadn't even seemed to know that he would sit down opposite her. Her first words to him had been "Aren't you going to sit down?" And he had said, "Is it all right?"

"He looked sort of vacant," she said. "I wondered if they had him on drugs?"

"Maybe something to keep him on an even keel. Mind you, I don't know. Did you have a conversation?"

Doree wondered if it could be called that. She had asked him some stupid, ordinary questions. How was he feeling? (Okay.) Did he get enough to eat? (He thought so.) Was there anyplace where he could walk if he wanted to? (Under supervision, yes. He guessed you could call it a place. He guessed you could call it walking.)

She'd said, "You have to get fresh air."

He'd said, "That's true."

She nearly asked him if he had made any friends. The way you ask your kid about school. The way, if your kids went to school, you would ask them.

"Yes, yes," Mrs. Sands said, nudging the ready box of Kleenex forward. Doree didn't need it; her eyes were dry. The trouble was in the bottom of her stomach. The heaves.

Mrs. Sands just waited, knowing enough to keep her hands off.

And, as if he'd detected what she was on the verge of saying, Lloyd had told her that there was a psychiatrist who came and talked to him every so often.

"I tell him he's wasting his time," Lloyd said. "I know as much as he does."

That was the only time he had sounded to Doree anything like himself.

All through the visit her heart had kept thumping. She'd thought she might faint or die. It cost her such an effort to look at him, to get him into her vision as this thin and gray, diffident yet cold, mechanically moving yet uncoordinated man.

She had not said any of this to Mrs. Sands. Mrs. Sands might have asked—tactfully—who she was afraid of. Herself or him?

But she wasn't *afraid*.

WHEN SASHA WAS ONE AND A HALF, Barbara Ann was born, and, when Barbara Ann was two, they had Dimitri. They had named Sasha together, and they made a pact after that that he would name the boys and she would name the girls.

Dimitri was the first one to be colicky. Doree thought that he was maybe not getting enough milk, or that her milk was not rich enough. Or too rich? Not right, anyway. Lloyd had a lady from the La Leche League come and talk to her. Whatever you do, the lady said, you must not put him on a supplementary bottle. That would be the thin edge of the wedge, she said, and pretty soon you would have him rejecting the breast altogether.

Little did she know that Doree had been giving him a supplement already. And it seemed to be true that he preferred that—he fussed more and more at the breast. By three months he was entirely bottle-fed, and then there was no way to keep it from Lloyd. She told him that her milk had dried up, and she'd had to start supplementing. Lloyd squeezed one breast after the other with frantic determination and succeeded in getting a couple of drops of miserable-looking milk out. He called her a liar. They fought. He said that she was a whore like her mother.

All those hippies were whores, he said.

Soon they made up. But whenever Dimitri was fretful, whenever he had a cold, or was afraid of Sasha's pet rabbit, or still hung on to chairs at the age when his brother and sister had been walking unsupported, the failure to breast-feed was recalled.

THE FIRST TIME Doree had gone to Mrs. Sands's office, one of the other women there had given her a pamphlet. On the front of it was a gold cross and words made up of gold and purple letters. "When Your Loss Seems Unbearable . . ." Inside there was a softly colored picture of Jesus and some finer print Doree did not read.

In her chair in front of the desk, still clutching the pamphlet, Doree began to shake. Mrs. Sands had to pry it out of her hand.

"Did somebody give you this?" Mrs. Sands said.

Doree said, "Her," and jerked her head at the closed door.

"You don't want it?"

"When you're down is when they'll try to get at you," Doree said, and then realized this was something her mother had said when some ladies with a similar message came to visit her in the hospital. "They think you'll fall on your knees and then it will be all right."

Mrs. Sands sighed.

"Well," she said, "it's certainly not that simple."

"Not even possible," Doree said.

"Maybe not."

They never spoke of Lloyd in those days. Doree never thought of him if she could help it, and then only as if he were some terrible accident of nature.

"Even if I believed in that stuff," she said, meaning what was in the pamphlet, "it would be only so that . . ." She meant to say that such a belief would be convenient because she could then think of Lloyd burning in hell, or something of that sort, but she was unable to go on, because it was too stupid to talk about. And because of the familiar impediment, that was like a hammer hitting her in the belly.

LLOYD THOUGHT that their children should be educated at home. This was not for religious reasons—going against dinosaurs and cavemen and monkeys and all that—but because he wanted them to be close to their parents and to be introduced to the world carefully and gradually, rather than thrown into it all at once. "I just happen to think they are my kids," he said. "I mean, they are our kids, not the Department of Education's kids."

Doree was not sure that she could handle this, but it turned out that the Department of Education had guidelines, and lesson plans that you could get from your local school. Sasha was a bright boy who practically taught himself to read, and the other two were still too little to learn much yet. In evenings and on weekends Lloyd taught Sasha about geography and the solar system and the hibernation of animals and how a car runs, covering each subject as the questions came up. Pretty soon Sasha was ahead of the school plans, but Doree picked them up anyway and put him through the exercises right on time so that the law would be satisfied.

There was another mother in the district doing homeschooling. Her name was Maggie, and she had a minivan. Lloyd needed his car to get to work, and Doree had not learned to drive, so she was glad when Maggie offered her a ride to the school once a week to turn in the finished exercises and pick up the new ones. Of course they took all the children along. Maggie had two boys. The older one had so many allergies that she had to keep a strict eye on everything he ate—that was why she taught him at home. And then it seemed that she might as well keep the younger one there as well. He wanted to stay with his brother and he had a problem with asthma, anyway.

How grateful Doree was then, comparing her healthy three. Lloyd said it was because she'd had all her children when she was still young, while Maggie had waited until she was on the verge of the menopause. He was exaggerating how old Maggie was, but it was true that she had waited. She was an optometrist. She and her husband had been partners, and they hadn't started their family until she could leave the practice and they had a house in the country.

Maggie's hair was pepper-and-salt, cropped close to her head. She was tall, flat-chested, cheerful, and opinionated. Lloyd called her the Lezzie. Only behind her back, of course. He kidded with her on the phone but mouthed at Doree, "It's the Lezzie." That didn't really bother Doree—he called lots of women Lezzies. But she was afraid that the kidding would seem overly friendly to Maggie, an intrusion, or at least a waste of time.

"You want to speak to the ole lady? Yeah. I got her right here. Workin at the scrub board. Yeah, I'm a real slave driver. She tell you that?"

DOREE AND MAGGIE got into the habit of shopping for groceries together after they'd picked up the papers at the school. Then sometimes they'd get takeout coffees at Tim Hortons and drive the children to Riverside Park. They sat on a bench while Sasha and Maggie's boys raced around or hung from the climbing contraptions, and Barbara Ann pumped on the swing and Dimitri played in the sandbox. Or they sat in the mini, if it was cold. They talked mostly about the children and things they cooked, but somehow Doree found out how Maggie had trekked around Europe before training as an optometrist, and Maggie found out how young Doree had been when she got married. Also about how easily she had become pregnant at first, and how she didn't so easily anymore, and how that made Lloyd suspicious, so that he went through her dresser drawers looking for birth-control pills—thinking she must be taking them on the sly.

"And are you?" Maggie asked.

Doree was shocked. She said she wouldn't dare.

"I mean, I'd think that was awful to do, without telling him. It's just kind of a joke when he goes looking for them."

"Oh," Maggie said.

And one time Maggie said, "Is everything all right with you? I mean in your marriage? You're happy?"

Doree said yes, without hesitation. After that she was more careful about what she said. She saw that there were things that she was used to that another person might not understand. Lloyd had a certain way of looking at things: that was just how he was. Even when she'd first met him, in the hospital, he'd been like that. The head nurse was a starchy sort of person, so he'd call her Mrs. Bitch-out-of-Hell, instead of her name, which was Mrs. Mitchell. He said it so fast that you could barely catch on. He'd thought that she picked favorites, and he wasn't one of them. Now there was someone he detested at the ice-cream factory, somebody he called Suck-Stick Louie. Doree didn't know the man's real name. But at least that proved that it wasn't only women who provoked him.

Doree was pretty sure that these people weren't as bad as Lloyd thought, but it was no use contradicting him. Perhaps men just had to have enemies, the way they had to have their jokes. And sometimes Lloyd did make the enemies into jokes, just as if he was laughing at himself. She was even allowed to laugh with him, as long as she wasn't the one who started the laughing.

She hoped he wouldn't get that way about Maggie. At times she was afraid she saw something of the sort coming. If he prevented her from riding to the school and the grocery store with Maggie it would be a big inconvenience. But worse would be the shame. She would have to make up some stupid lie to explain things. But Maggie would know—at least she would know that Doree was lying, and she would interpret that probably as meaning that Doree was in a worse situation than she really was. Maggie had her own sharp way of looking at things.

Then Doree asked herself why she should care what Maggie might think. Maggie was an outsider, not even somebody Doree felt comfortable with. It was Lloyd said that, and he was right. The truth of things between them, the bond, was not something that anybody else could understand and it was not anybody else's business. If Doree could watch her own loyalty it would be all right.

IT GOT WORSE, GRADUALLY. No direct forbidding, but more criticism. Lloyd coming up with the theory that Maggie's boys' allergies and asthma might be Maggie's fault. The reason was often the mother, he said. He used to see it at the hospital all the time. The overcontrolling, usually overeducated mother.

"Some of the time kids are just born with something," Doree said, unwisely. "You can't say it's the mother every time."

"Oh. Why can't I?"

"I didn't mean *you*. I didn't mean you can't. I mean, couldn't they be born with things?"

"Since when are you such a medical authority?"

"I didn't say I was."

"No. And you're not."

Bad to worse. He wanted to know what they talked about, she and Maggie.

"I don't know. Nothing really."

"That's funny. Two women riding in a car. First I heard of it. Two women talking about nothing. She is out to break us up."

"Who is? *Maggie?*"

"I've got experience of her kind of woman."

"What kind?"

"Her kind."

"Don't be silly."

"Careful. Don't call me silly."

"What would she want to do that for?"

"How am I supposed to know? She just wants to do it. You wait. You'll see. She'll get you over there bawling and whining about what a bastard I am. One of these days."

AND IN FACT it turned out as he had said. At least it would certainly have looked that way, to Lloyd. She did find herself at around ten o'clock one night in Maggie's kitchen, sniffling back her tears and drinking herbal tea. Maggie's husband had said, "What the hell?" when she knocked—she heard him through the door. He hadn't known who she was. She'd said, "I'm really sorry to bother you—" while he stared at her with lifted eyebrows and a tight mouth. And then Maggie had come.

Doree had walked all the way there in the dark, first along the gravel road that she and Lloyd lived on, and then on the highway. She headed for the ditch every time a car came, and that slowed her down considerably. She did take a look at the cars that passed, thinking that one of them might be Lloyd. She didn't want him to find her, not yet, not till he was scared out of his craziness. Other times she had been able to scare him out of it herself, by weeping and howling and even banging her head on the floor, chanting, "It's not true, it's not true, it's not true" over and over. Finally he would back down. He would say, "Okay, okay. I'll believe you. Honey, be quiet. Think of the kids. I'll believe you, honest. Just stop."

But tonight she had pulled herself together just as she was about to start that performance. She had put on her coat and walked out the door, with him calling after her, "Don't do this. I warn you!"

Maggie's husband had gone to bed, not looking any better pleased about things, while Doree kept saying, "I'm sorry. I'm so sorry, barging in on you at this time of night."

"Oh, shut up," Maggie said, kind and businesslike. "Do you want a glass of wine?"

"I don't drink."

"Then you'd better not start now. I'll get you some tea. It's very soothing. Raspberry-chamomile. It's not the kids, is it?"

"No."

Maggie took her coat and handed her a wad of Kleenex for her eyes and nose. "Don't tell me anything yet. We'll soon get you settled down."

Even when she was partly settled down, Doree didn't want to blurt out the whole truth and let Maggie know that she herself was at the heart of the problem. More than that, she didn't want to have to explain Lloyd. No matter how worn out she got with him, he was still the closest person in the world to her, and she felt that everything would collapse if she were to bring herself to tell someone exactly how he was, if she were to be entirely disloyal.

She said that she and Lloyd had got into an old argument and she was so sick and tired of it that all she'd wanted was to get out. But she would get over it, she said. They would.

"Happens to every couple sometime," Maggie said.

The phone rang then, and Maggie answered.

"Yes. She's okay. She just needed to walk something out of her system. Fine. Okay then, I'll deliver her home in the morning. No trouble. Okay. Good night.

"That was him," she said. "I guess you heard."

"How did he sound? Did he sound normal?"

Maggie laughed. "Well, I don't know how he sounds when he's normal, do I? He didn't sound drunk."

"He doesn't drink either. We don't even have coffee in the house."

"Want some toast?"

IN THE MORNING, early, Maggie drove her home. Maggie's husband hadn't left for work yet, and he stayed with the boys.

Maggie was in a hurry to get back, so she just said, "Bye-bye. Phone me if you need to talk," as she turned the minivan around in the yard.

It was a cold morning in early spring, snow still on the ground, but there was Lloyd sitting on the steps without a jacket on.

"Good morning," he said, in a loud, sarcastically polite voice. And she said good morning, in a voice that pretended not to notice his.

He did not move aside to let her up the steps.

"You can't go in there," he said.

She decided to take this lightly.

"Not even if I say please? Please."

He looked at her but did not answer. He smiled with his lips held together.

"Lloyd?" she said. "Lloyd?"

"You better not go in."

"I didn't tell her anything, Lloyd. I'm sorry I walked out. I just needed a breathing space, I guess."

"Better not go in."

"What's the matter with you? Where are the kids?"

He shook his head, as he did when she said something he didn't like to hear. Something mildly rude, like "holy shit."

"*Lloyd*. Where are the kids?"

He shifted just a little, so that she could pass if she liked.

Dimitri still in his crib, lying sideways. Barbara Ann on the floor beside her bed, as if she'd got out or been pulled out. Sasha by the kitchen door—he had tried to get away. He was the only one with bruises on his throat. The pillow had done for the others.

"When I phoned last night?" Lloyd said. "When I phoned, it had already happened.

"You brought it all on yourself," he said.

THE VERDICT WAS that he was insane, he couldn't be tried. He was criminally insane—he had to be put in a secure institution.

Doree had run out of the house and was stumbling around the yard, holding her arms tight across her stomach as if she had been sliced open and was trying to keep herself together. This was the scene that Maggie saw, when she came back. She had had a premonition, and had turned the van around in the road. Her first thought was that Doree had been hit or kicked in the stomach by her husband. She could understand nothing of the noises Doree was making. But Lloyd, who was still sitting on the steps, moved aside courteously for her, without a word, and she went into the house and found what she was now expecting to find. She phoned the police.

For some time Doree kept stuffing whatever she could grab into her mouth. After the dirt and grass it was sheets or towels or her own clothing. As if she were trying to stifle not just the howls that rose up but the scene in her head. She was given a shot of something, regularly, to quiet her down, and this worked. In fact she became very quiet, though not catatonic. She was said to be stabilized. When she got out of the hospital and the social worker brought her to this new place, Mrs. Sands took over, found her somewhere to live, found her a job, established the routine of talking with her once a week. Maggie would have come to see her, but she was the one person Doree could not stand to see. Mrs. Sands said that that feeling was natural—it was the association. She said that Maggie would understand.

Mrs. Sands said that whether or not Doree continued to visit Lloyd was up to her. "I'm not here to approve or disapprove, you know. Did it make you feel good to see him? Or bad?"

"I don't know."

Doree could not explain that it had not really seemed to be him she was seeing. It was almost like seeing a ghost. So pale. Pale loose clothes on him, shoes that didn't make any noise—probably slippers—on his feet. She had the impression that some of his hair had fallen out. His thick and wavy, honey-colored hair. There seemed to be no breadth to his shoulders, no hollow in his collarbone where she used to rest her head.

What he had said, afterwards, to the police—and it was quoted in the newspapers—was "I did it to save them the misery."

What misery?

"The misery of knowing that their mother had walked out on them," he said.

That was burned into Doree's brain, and maybe when she decided to try to see him it had been with the idea of making him take it back. Making him see, and admit, how things had really gone.

"You told me to stop contradicting you or get out of the house. So I got out of the house.

"I only went to Maggie's for one night. I fully intended to come back. I wasn't walking out on anybody."

She remembered perfectly how the argument had started. She had bought a tin of spaghetti that had a very slight dent in it. Because of that it had been on sale, and she had been pleased with her thriftiness. She had thought she was doing something smart.

But she didn't tell him that, once he had begun questioning her about it. For some reason she'd thought it better to pretend she hadn't noticed.

Anybody would notice, he said. We could have all been poisoned. What was the matter with her? Or was that what she had in mind? Was she planning to try it out on the kids or on him?

She told him not to be crazy.

He had said it wasn't him who was crazy. Who but a crazy woman would buy poison for her family?

The children had been watching from the doorway of the front room. That was the last time she'd seen them alive.

So was that what she had been thinking—that she could make him see, finally, who it was who was crazy?

WHEN SHE REALIZED what was in her head, she should have got off the bus. She could have got off even at the gates, with the few other women who plodded up the drive. She could have crossed the road and waited for the bus back to the city. Probably some people did that. They were going to make a visit and then decided not to. People probably did that all the time.

But maybe it was better that she had gone on, and seen him so strange and wasted. Not a person worth blaming for anything. Not a person. He was like a character in a dream.

She had dreams. In one dream she had run out of the house after finding them, and Lloyd had started to laugh in his old easy way, and then she had heard Sasha laughing behind her and it had dawned on her, wonderfully, that they were all playing a joke.

"YOU ASKED ME if it made me feel good or bad when I saw him? Last time you asked me?"

"Yes, I did," Mrs. Sands said.

"I had to think about it."

"Yes."

"I decided it made me feel bad. So I haven't gone again."

It was hard to tell with Mrs. Sands, but the nod she gave seemed to show some satisfaction or approval.

So when Doree decided that she would go again, after all, she thought it was better not to mention it. And since it was hard not to mention whatever happened to her—there being so little, most of the time—she phoned and cancelled her appointment. She said that she was going on a holiday. They were getting into summer, when holidays were the usual thing. With a friend, she said.

"YOU AREN'T WEARING THE JACKET you had on last week."

"That wasn't last week."

"Wasn't it?"

"It was three weeks ago. The weather's hot now. This is lighter, but I don't really need it. You don't need a jacket at all."

He asked about her trip, what buses she'd had to take from Mildmay.

She told him that she wasn't living there anymore. She told him where she lived, and about the three buses.

"That's quite a trek for you. Do you like living in a bigger place?"

"It's easier to get work there."

"So you work?"

She had told him last time about where she lived, the buses, where she worked.

"I clean rooms in a motel," she said. "I told you."

"Yes, yes. I forgot. I'm sorry. Do you ever think of going back to school? Night school?"

She said she did think about it but never seriously enough to do anything. She said she didn't mind the cleaning work.

Then it seemed as if they could not think of anything more to say.

He sighed. He said, "Sorry. Sorry. I guess I'm not used to conversation."

"So what do you do all the time?"

"I guess I read quite a bit. Kind of meditate. Informally."

"Oh."

"I appreciate your coming here. It means a lot to me. But don't think you have to keep it up. I mean, just when you want to. If something comes up, or if you feel like it—what I'm trying to say is, just the fact that you could come at all, that you even came once, that's a bonus for me. Do you get what I mean?"

She said yes, she thought so.

He said that he didn't want to interfere with her life.

"You're not," she said.

"Was that what you were going to say? I thought you were going to say something else."

In fact, she had almost said, What life?

No, she said, not really, nothing else.

"Good."

THREE MORE WEEKS and she got a phone call. It was Mrs. Sands herself on the line, not one of the women in the office.

"Oh, Doree. I thought you might not be back yet. From your holiday. So you are back?"

"Yes," Doree said, trying to think where she could say she had been.

"But you hadn't got around to arranging another appointment?"

"No. Not yet."

"That's okay. I was just checking. You are all right?"

"I'm all right."

"Fine. Fine. You know where I am if you ever need me. Ever just want to have a talk."

"Yes."

"So take care."

She hadn't mentioned Lloyd, hadn't asked if the visits had continued. Well, of course, Doree had said that they weren't going to. But Mrs. Sands was pretty good, usually, about sensing what was going on. Pretty good at holding off, too, when she understood that a question might not get her anywhere. Doree didn't know what she would have said, if asked—whether she would have backtracked and told a lie or come out with the truth. She had gone back, in fact, the very next Sunday after he more or less told her it didn't matter whether she came or not.

He had a cold. He didn't know how he got it.

Maybe he had been coming down with it, he said, the last time he saw her, and that was why he'd been so morose.

"Morose." She seldom had anything to do, nowadays, with anyone who used a word like that, and it sounded strange to her. But he had always had a habit of using such words, and of course at one time they hadn't struck her as they did now.

"Do I seem like a different person to you?" he asked.

"Well, you look different," she said cautiously. "Don't I?"

"You look beautiful," he said sadly.

Something softened in her. But she fought against it.

"Do you feel different?" he asked. "Do you feel like a different person?"

She said she didn't know. "Do you?"

He said, "Altogether."

LATER IN THE WEEK a large envelope was given to her at work. It had been addressed to her care of the motel. It contained several sheets of paper, with writing on both sides. She didn't think at first of its being from him—she somehow had the idea that people in prison were not allowed to write letters. But, of course, he was a different sort of prisoner. He was not a criminal; he was only criminally insane.

There was no date on the document and not even a "Dear Doree." It just started talking to her in such a way that she thought it had to be some sort of religious invitation:

> *People are looking all over for the solution. Their minds are sore (from looking). So many things jostling around and hurting them. You can see in their faces all their bruises and pains. They are troubled. They rush around. They have to shop and go to the laundromat and get their hair cut and earn a living or pick up their welfare checks. The poor ones have to do that and the rich ones have to look hard for the best ways to spend their money. That is work too. They have to build the best houses with gold faucets for their hot and cold water. And their Audis and magical toothbrushes and all possible contraptions and then burglar alarms to proteet against slaughter and all (neigh) neither rich nor poor have any peace in their souls. I was going to write "neighbor" instead of "neither," why was that? I have not got any neighbor here. Where I am at least people have got beyond a lot of confusion. They know what their possessions are and always will be and they don't even have to buy or cook their own food. Or choose it. Choices are eliminated.*
>
> *All we that are here can get is what we can get out of our own minds.*

At the beginning all in my head was purturbation (Sp?).
There was everlasting storm, and I would knock my head
against cement in the hope of getting rid of it. Stopping my
agony and my life. So punishments were meted. I got hosed
down and tied up and drugs introduced in my bloodstream. I
am not complaining either, because I had to learn there is no
profit in that. Nor is it any different from the so-called real
world, in which people drink and carry on and commit crimes
to eliminate their thoughts which are painful. And often they
get hauled off and incarcerated but it is not long enough for
them to come out on the other side. And what is that? It is
either total insanity or peace.

Peace. I arrived at peace and am still sane. I imagine
reading this now you are thinking I am going to say something
about God Jesus or at any rate Buddha as if I had arrived
at a religious conversion. No. I do not close my eyes and
get lifted up by any specific Higher Power. I do not really
know what is meant by any of that. What I do is Know
Myself. Know Thyself is some kind of Commandment from
somewhere, probably the Bible so at least in that I have
followed Christianity. Also, To Thy Own Self Be True—I have
attempted that if it is in the Bible also. It does not say which
parts—the bad or the good—to be true to so it is not intended
as a guide to morality. Also Know Thyself does not relate to
morality as we know it in Behavior. But Behavior is not really
my concern because I have been judged quite correctly as a
person who cannot be trusted to judge how he should behave
and that is the reason I am here.

Back to the Know part of Know Thyself. I can say perfectly
soberly that I know myself and I know the worst I am capable
of and I know that I have done it. I am judged by the World
as a Monster and I have no quarrel with that, even though I
might say in passing that people who rain down bombs or burn
cities or starve and murder hundreds of thousands of people
are not generally considered Monsters but are showered with
medals and honors, only acts against small numbers being
considered shocking and evil. This being not meant as an
excuse but just observation.

What I Know in Myself is my own Evil. That is the secret
of my comfort. I mean I know my Worst. It may be worse than
other people's worst but in fact I do not have to think or worry
about that. No excuses. I am at peace. Am I a Monster? The
World says so and if it is said so then I agree. But then I say,
the World does not have any real meaning for me. I am my
Self and have no chance to be any other Self. I could say that I
was crazy then but what does that mean? Crazy. Sane. I am I.
I could not change my I then and I cannot change it now.

Doree, if you have read this far, there is one special thing
I want to tell you about but cannot write it down. If you ever
think of coming back here then maybe I can tell you. Do not
think I am heartless. It isn't that I wouldn't change things if I
could, but I can't.

I am sending this to your place of work which I remember and
the name of the town so my brain is working fine in some respects.

She thought that they would have to discuss this piece of writing at their next meeting and she read it over several times, but
she could not think of anything to say. What she really wanted
to talk about was whatever he had said was impossible to put in
writing. But when she saw him again he behaved as if he had never
written to her at all. She searched for a topic and told him about a
once-famous folksinger who had stayed at the motel that week. To
her surprise he knew more than she did about the singer's career.
It turned out that he had a television, or at least access to one, and
watched some shows and, of course, the news, regularly. That gave
them a bit more to talk about, until she could not help herself.

"What was the thing you couldn't tell me except in person?"

He said he wished she hadn't asked him. He didn't know if they
were ready to discuss it.

Then she was afraid that it would be something she really could
not handle, something unbearable, such as that he still loved her.
"Love" was a word she could not stand to hear.

"Okay," she said. "Maybe we're not."

Then she said, "Still, you better tell me. If I walked out of here
and was struck down by a car, then I would never know, and you
would never have the chance to tell me again."

"True," he said.

"So what is it?"

"Next time. Next time. Sometimes I can't talk anymore. I want to but I just dry up, talking."

I have been thinking of you Doree ever since you left and regret I disappointed you. When you are sitting opposite me I tend to get more emotional than perhaps I show. It is not my right to go emotional in front of you, since you certainly have the right more than me and you are always very controlled. So I am going to reverse what I said before because I have come to the conclusion I can write to you after all better than I can talk.

Now where do I start.

Heaven exists.

That is one way but not right because I never believed in Heaven and Hell, etc. As far as I was concerned that was always a pile of crap. So it must sound pretty weird of me to bring up the subject now.

I will just say then: I have seen the children.

I have seen and talked to them.

There. What are you thinking at the moment? You are thinking well, now he is really round the bend. Or, it's a dream and he can't distinguish a dream, he doesn't know the difference between a dream and awake. But I want to tell you I do know the difference and what I know is, they exist. I say they exist, not they are alive, because alive means in our particular Dimension, and I am not saying that is where they are. In fact I think they are not. But they do exist and it must be that there is another Dimension or maybe innumerable Dimensions, but what I know is that I have got across to whatever one they are in. Possibly I got hold of this from being so much on my own and having to think and think and with such as I have to think about. So after such suffering and solitude there is a Grace that has seen the way to giving me this reward. Me the very one that deserves it the least to the world's way of thinking.

Well if you have kept reading this far and not torn this to pieces you must want to know something. Such as how they are.

*They are fine. Really happy and smart. They don't seem
to have any memory of anything bad. They are maybe a
little older than they were but that is hard to say. They seem
to understand at different levels. Yes. You can notice with
Dimitri he has learned to talk which he was not able to do.
They are in a room I can partly recognize. It's like our house
but more spacious and nice. I asked them how they were being
looked after and they just laughed at me and said something
like they were able to look after themselves. I think Sasha was
the one who said that. Sometimes they talk separately or at
least I can't separate their voices but their identities are quite
clear and, I must say, joyful.*

*Please don't conclude that I am crazy. That is the fear
that made me not want to tell you about this. I was crazy
at one time but believe me I have shed all my old craziness
like the bear that sheds his coat. Or maybe I should say the
snake that sheds his skin. I know that if I had not done that
I would never have been given this ability to reconnect with
Sasha and Barbara Ann and Dimitri. Now I wish that you
could be granted this chance as well because if it is a matter of
deserving, then you are way ahead of me. It may be harder for
you to do because you live in the world so much more than I do
but at least I can give you this information—the Truth—and
in telling you I have seen them, I hope that it will make your
heart lighter.*

Doree wondered what Mrs. Sands would say or think if she read
this letter. Mrs. Sands would be careful, of course. She would be
careful not to pass an outright verdict of craziness, but she would
carefully, kindly, steer Doree around in that direction.

Or you might say she wouldn't steer—she would just pull the
confusion away so that Doree would have to face what would
seem to have been her own conclusion all along. She would have
to put the whole dangerous nonsense—this was Mrs. Sands
speaking—out of her mind.

That was why Doree was not going anywhere near her.

Doree did think that he was crazy. And in what he had written
there seemed to be some trace of the old bragging. She didn't write

back. Days went by. Weeks. She didn't alter her opinion, but she still held on to what he'd written, like a secret. And from time to time, when she was in the middle of spraying a bathroom mirror or tightening a sheet, a feeling came over her. For almost two years she had not taken any notice of the things that generally made people happy, such as nice weather or flowers in bloom or the smell of a bakery. She still did not have that spontaneous sense of happiness, exactly, but she had a reminder of what it was like. It had nothing to do with the weather or flowers. It was the idea that the children were in what he had called their Dimension that came sneaking up on her in this way, and for the first time brought a light feeling to her, not pain.

In all the time since what had happened, any thought of the children had been something she had to get rid of, pull out immediately like a knife in her throat. She could not think their names, and if she heard a name that sounded like one of theirs she had to pull that out too. Even children's voices, their shrieks and slapping feet as they ran to and from the motel swimming pool, had to be banished by a sort of gate that she could slam down behind her ears. What was different now was that she had a refuge she could go to as soon as such dangers arose anywhere around her.

And who had given it to her? Not Mrs. Sands—that was for sure. Not in all those hours sitting by the desk with the Kleenex discreetly handy.

Lloyd had given it to her. Lloyd, that terrible person, that isolated and insane person.

Insane if you wanted to call it that. But wasn't it possible that what he said was true—that he had come out on the other side? And who was to say that the visions of a person who had done such a thing and made such a journey might not mean something?

This notion wormed its way into her head and stayed there.

Along with the thought that Lloyd, of all people, might be the person she should be with now. What other use could she be in the world—she seemed to be saying this to somebody, probably to Mrs. Sands—what was she here for if not at least to listen to him?

I didn't say "forgive," she said to Mrs. Sands in her head. I would never say that. I would never do it.

But think. Aren't I just as cut off by what happened as he is? Nobody who knew about it would want me around. All I can do is remind people of what nobody can stand to be reminded of.

Disguise wasn't possible, not really. That crown of yellow spikes was pathetic.

SO SHE FOUND HERSELF travelling on the bus again, heading down the highway. She remembered those nights right after her mother had died, when she would sneak out to meet Lloyd, lying to her mother's friend, the woman she was staying with, about where she was going. She remembered the friend's name, her mother's friend's name. Laurie.

Who but Lloyd would remember the children's names now, or the color of their eyes. Mrs. Sands, when she had to mention them, did not even call them children but "your family," putting them in one clump together.

Going to meet Lloyd in those days, lying to Laurie, she had felt no guilt, only a sense of destiny, submission. She had felt that she was put on earth for no reason other than to be with him and to try to understand him.

Well, it wasn't like that now. It was not the same.

She was sitting in the front seat across from the driver. She had a clear view through the windshield. And that was why she was the only passenger on the bus, the only person other than the driver, to see a pickup truck pull out from a side road without even slowing down, to see it rock across the empty Sunday-morning highway in front of them and plunge into the ditch. And to see something even stranger: the driver of the truck flying through the air in a manner that seemed both swift and slow, absurd and graceful. He landed in the gravel at the edge of the pavement.

The other passengers didn't know why the driver had put on the brakes and brought them to a sudden uncomfortable stop. And at first all that Doree thought was, How did he get out? The young man or boy, who must have fallen asleep at the wheel. How did he fly out of the truck and launch himself so elegantly into the air?

"Fellow right in front of us," the driver said to the passengers. He was trying to speak loudly and calmly, but there was a tremor of amazement, something like awe, in his voice. "Just plowed across the road and into the ditch. We'll be on our way again as soon as we can, and in the meantime please don't get out of the bus."

As if she had not heard that, or had some special right to be useful, Doree got out behind him. He did not reprimand her.

"Goddamn asshole," he said as they crossed the road, and there was nothing in his voice now but anger and exasperation. "Goddamn asshole kid, can you believe it?"

The boy was lying on his back, arms and legs flung out, like somebody making an angel in the snow. Only there was gravel around him, not snow. His eyes were not quite closed. He was so young, a boy who had shot up tall before he even needed to shave. Possibly without a driver's license.

The driver was talking on his phone.

"Mile or so south of Bayfield, on Twenty-one, east side of the road."

A trickle of pink foam came out from under the boy's head, near the ear. It did not look like blood at all, but like the stuff you skim off from strawberries when you're making jam.

Doree crouched down beside him. She laid a hand on his chest. It was still. She bent her ear close. Somebody had ironed his shirt recently—it had that smell.

No breathing.

But her fingers on his smooth neck found a pulse.

She remembered something she'd been told. It was Lloyd who had told her, in case one of the children had an accident and he wasn't there. The tongue. The tongue can block the breathing, if it has fallen into the back of the throat. She laid the fingers of one hand on the boy's forehead and two fingers of the other hand under his chin. Press down on the forehead, press up the chin, to clear the airway. A slight but firm tilt.

If he still didn't breathe she would have to breathe into him.

She pinches the nostrils, takes a deep breath, seals his mouth with her lips, and breathes. Two breaths and check. Two breaths and check.

Another male voice, not the driver's. A motorist must have stopped. "You want this blanket under his head?" She shook her head slightly. She had remembered something else, about not moving the victim, so that you do not injure the spinal cord. She enveloped his mouth. She pressed his warm fresh skin. She breathed and waited. She breathed and waited again. And a faint moisture seemed to rise against her face.

The driver said something but she could not look up. Then she felt it for sure. A breath out of the boy's mouth. She spread her hand on the skin of his chest and at first she could not tell if it was rising and falling because of her own trembling.

Yes. Yes.

It was a true breath. The airway was open. He was breathing on his own. He was breathing.

"Just lay it over him," she said to the man with the blanket. "To keep him warm."

"Is he alive?" the driver said, bending over her.

She nodded. Her fingers found the pulse again. The horrible pink stuff had not continued to flow. Maybe it was nothing important. Not from his brain.

"I can't hold the bus for you," the driver said. "We're behind schedule as it is."

The motorist said, "That's okay. I can take over."

Be quiet, be quiet, she wanted to tell them. It seemed to her that silence was necessary, that everything in the world outside the boy's body had to concentrate, help it not to lose track of its duty to breathe.

Shy but steady whiffs now, a sweet obedience in the chest. Keep on, keep on.

"You hear that? This guy says he'll stay and watch out for him," the driver said. "Ambulance is coming as fast as they can."

"Go on," Doree said. "I'll hitch a ride to town with them and catch you on your way back tonight."

He had to bend to hear her. She spoke dismissively, without raising her head, as if she were the one whose breath was precious.

"You sure?" he said.

Sure.

"You don't have to get to London?"

No.

Wood

~

ROY IS AN UPHOLSTERER and refinisher of furniture. He will also take on the job of rebuilding chairs and tables that have lost some rungs or a leg, or are otherwise in a dilapidated condition. There aren't many people doing that kind of work anymore, and he gets more business than he can handle. He doesn't know what to do about it. His excuse for not hiring somebody to help him is that the government will make him go through a lot of red tape, but the real reason may be that he's used to working alone—he's been doing this ever since he got out of the army—and it's hard for him to imagine having somebody else around all the time. If he and his wife, Lea, had had a boy, the boy might have grown up with an interest in the work and joined him in the shop when he was old enough. Or even if they'd had a daughter. Once he'd thought of training his wife's niece Diane. When she was a child she had hung around watching him and after she got married—suddenly, at the age of seventeen—she helped him with some jobs because she and her husband needed the money. But she was pregnant, and the smells of paint stripper, wood stain, linseed oil, polish, and wood smoke made her sick. Or that was what she told Roy. She told his wife the real reason—that her husband didn't think it was the right kind of work for a woman.

So now she has four children and works in the kitchen of an old people's home. Apparently her husband thinks that is all right.

Roy's workshop is in a shed behind the house. It is heated by a woodstove, and getting the fuel for the stove has led him to another interest, which is private but not secret. That is, everybody knows about it but nobody knows how much he thinks about it or how much it means to him.

Wood cutting.

He has a four-wheel-drive truck and a chain saw and an

eight-pound splitting ax. He spends more and more time in the bush, cutting firewood. More than he needs for himself, as it turns out—so he has taken to selling it. Modern houses often have a fireplace in the living room and another in the dining room and a stove in the family room. And they want to have fires all the time—not just when they're having a party or at Christmas.

When he first started going to the bush Lea used to worry about him. She worried about whether he would have an accident out there by himself, but also about whether he was letting the business go slack. She didn't mean that his workmanship might suffer, but his timetable. "You don't want to let people down," she said. "If somebody says they want something for a certain time there's a reason."

She had the idea of his business being an obligation—something he did to help people out. She was embarrassed when he raised his prices—so in fact was he—and went out of her way to tell people what the materials were costing him nowadays.

While she had her job, it was not difficult for him to take off for the bush after she had gone to work and try to be back before she got home. She worked as a receptionist and bookkeeper for one of the dentists in town. It was a good job for her, because she enjoyed talking to people, and good for the dentist because she came from a large and loyal family who would never think of having their teeth tended to by anybody but the man who was her boss.

These relatives of hers, the Boles and the Jetters and the Pooles, used to be around the house a lot, or else Lea wanted to be at one of their houses. It was a clan that didn't always enjoy one another's company but who made sure they got plenty of it. Twenty or thirty would be crammed into one place for Christmas or Thanksgiving, and they could manage a dozen on an ordinary Sunday—watching television, talking, cooking, and eating. Roy likes to watch television and he likes to talk and he likes to eat, but not any two at the same time and certainly not all three. So when they chose to gather in his house on a Sunday, he got into the habit of getting up and going out to the shed and building up a fire of ironwood or applewood—either of those but particularly the apple has a sweet comforting smell. Right out in the open, on the shelf with the stains and oils, he always kept a bottle of rye. He had rye in the house as well, and he was not stingy about offering it to his company, but the drink he poured when he was alone in the shed tasted better, just as the smoke smelled better when there was nobody around to say, Oh, isn't that lovely? He never drank when he was working on the furniture, or going into the bush—just on these Sundays full of visitors.

His going off on his own like that didn't cause trouble. The relatives didn't feel slighted—they had a limited interest in people like Roy who had just married into the family, and not even contributed any children to it, and who were not like themselves. They were large, expansive, talkative. He was short, compact, quiet. His wife was an easygoing woman generally and she liked Roy the way he was, so she didn't reproach or apologize for him.

They both felt that they meant more to each other, somehow, than couples who were overrun with children.

Last winter Lea had been sick with almost steady flu and bronchitis. She thought that she was catching all the germs people brought into the dentist's office. So she quit her job—she said that she was getting a bit tired of it anyway and she wanted more time to do things she had always wanted to do.

But Roy never found out what those things were. Her strength had taken a slump that she could not recover from. And that seemed to bring about a profound change in her personality. Visitors made her nervous—her family more than anybody. She felt too tired for conversation. She didn't want to go out. She kept up the house adequately, but she rested between chores so that simple routines took her all day. She lost most of her interest in television, though she would watch it when Roy turned it on, and she lost also her rounded, jolly figure, becoming thin and shapeless. The warmth, the glow—whatever had made her nice looking—were drained out of her face and her brown eyes.

The doctor gave her some pills but she couldn't tell whether they did her any good or not. One of her sisters took her to a practitioner of holistic medicine, and the consultation cost three hundred dollars. She could not tell if that did her any good either.

Roy misses the wife he was used to, with her jokes and energy. He wants her back, but there's nothing he can do, except be patient with this grave, listless woman who sometimes waves her hand in front of her face as if she is bothered by cobwebs or has got stuck in a nest of brambles. Questioned about her eyesight, however, she claims that it is fine.

She no longer drives her car. She no longer says anything about Roy going to the bush.

She may snap out of it, Diane says. (Diane is about the only person who still comes to the house.) Or she may not.

That is pretty well what the doctor said, in a lot more careful words. He says that the pills he's got her on will keep her from sinking too low. How low is too low, Roy thinks, and when can you tell?

SOMETIMES he finds a bush that the sawmill people have logged out, leaving the tops on the ground. And sometimes he finds one where the forest management people have gone in and girdled the trees they think should come out because they are diseased or crooked or no good for lumber. Ironwood, for instance, is no good for lumber, and neither is hawthorn or blue beech. When he spots a bush like this he gets in touch with the farmer or whoever owns it, and they bargain, and if the payment is agreed on he goes in to get the wood. A lot of this activity happens in the late fall—now, in November, or early December—because that is the time for selling firewood and because it is the best time for getting his truck into the bush. Farmers nowadays don't always have a well-travelled lane going back there, as they did when they cut and hauled wood themselves. Often you have to drive in across the fields, and this is possible only at two times during the year—before the field is plowed and after the crop is off.

After the crop is off is the better time, when the ground is hardened by frost. And this fall the demand for wood is greater than ever, and Roy has been going out two or three times in one week.

Many people recognize trees by their leaves or by their general shape and size, but walking through the leafless deep bush Roy knows them by their bark. Ironwood, that heavy and reliable firewood, has a shaggy brown bark on its stocky trunk, but its limbs are smooth at their tips and decidedly reddish. Cherry is the blackest tree in the bush, and its bark lies in picturesque scales. Most people would be surprised at how high cherry trees grow here—they are nothing like the cherry trees in fruit orchards. Apple trees are more like their orchard representatives—not very tall, bark not so definitely scaled or dark as the cherry's. Ash is a soldierly tree with a corduroy-ribbed trunk. The maple's gray bark has an irregular surface, the shadows creating black streaks, which meet sometimes in rough rectangles, sometimes not. There is a comfortable carelessness about that bark, suitable to the maple tree, which is homely and familiar and what most people think of when they think of a tree.

Beech trees and oaks are another matter—there is something notable and dramatic about them, though neither has as lovely a shape as the big elm trees which are now nearly all gone. Beech has the smooth gray bark, the elephant skin, which is usually chosen for the carving of initials. These carvings widen with the years and decades, from the slim knife groove to the blotches that make the letters at last illegible, wider than they are long.

Beech will grow a hundred feet high in the bush. In the open they spread out and are as wide as high, but in the bush they shoot up, the limbs at the top will take radical turns and can look like stag horns. But this arrogant-looking tree may have a weakness of twisted grain, which can be detected by ripples in the bark. That's a sign that it may break, or go down in a high wind. As for oak trees, they are not so common in this country, not so common as beech but always easy to spot. Just as maple trees always look like the common necessary tree in the backyard, so oak trees always look like trees in storybooks, as if, in all the stories that begin, "Once upon a time in the woods," the woods were full of oak trees. Their dark, shiny, elaborately indented leaves contribute to this look, but they seem just as legendary when the leaves are off and you can see so well the thick corky bark with its gray-black color and intricate surface, and the devilish curling and curving of the branches.

Roy thinks that there is very little danger in going tree cutting alone if you know what you are doing. When you are going to cut down a tree, the first thing is to assess its center of gravity, then cut a seventy-degree wedge, so that the center of gravity is just over it. The side the wedge is on, of course, determines the direction in which the tree will fall. You make a falling cut, from the opposite side, not to connect with the wedge cut but in line with its high point. The idea is to cut through the tree, leaving at the end a hinge of wood which is the very center of the tree's weight and from which it must fall. It is best to make it fall clear of all other branches, but sometimes there is no way this can happen. If a tree is leaning into the branches of other trees, and you can't get a truck into position to haul it out with a chain, you cut the trunk in sections from beneath, till the upper part drops free and falls. When you've dropped a tree and it's resting on its branches, you get the trunk to the ground by cutting through the limb wood until you come to the limbs that are holding it up. These limbs are under pressure—they may be bent like a bow—and the trick is to cut so that the tree will roll away from you and the limbs won't whack you. When it is safely down, you cut the trunk into stove lengths and split the stove lengths with the ax.

Sometimes there's a surprise. Some squirrelly wood blocks can't be split with the ax; they have to be laid on their sides and ripped with a chain saw; the sawdust cut this way, with the grain, is taken away in long shreds. Also, some beech or maple has to be side split, the great round chunk cut along the growth rings on all sides until it is almost square and can be more easily attacked. Sometimes there's dozy wood, in which a fungus has grown between the rings. But in general the toughness of the blocks is as you'd expect—greater in the body wood than in the limb wood, and greater in the broad trunks that have grown up partly in the open than in the tall slim ones that have pushed up in the middle of the bush.

Surprises. But you can be prepared for those. And if you're prepared, there's not the danger. He used to think of explaining all this to his wife. The procedures, the surprises, the identification. But he couldn't think of the way to go about it, so that she'd be interested. Sometimes he wished he had got around to passing on his knowledge to Diane when she was younger. She would never have the time to listen now.

And in a way his thoughts about wood are too private—they are covetous and nearly obsessive. He has never been a greedy man in any other way. But he can lie awake nights thinking of a splendid beech he wants to get at, wondering if it will prove as satisfactory as it looks or has some tricks up its sleeve. He thinks of all the woodlots in the county that he has never even seen, because they lie at the backs of farms, behind private fields. If he is driving along a road that goes through a bush, he swings his head from side to side, afraid of missing something. Even what is worthless for his purposes will interest him. A stand of blue beech, for instance, too delicate, too weedy, to bother with. He sees the dark vertical ribs slanting down the paler trunks—he will remember where these are. He would like to get a map in his mind of every bush he sees, and though he might justify this by citing practical purposes, that wouldn't be the whole truth.

A DAY OR SO after the first snow, he is out in a bush looking at some girdled trees. He has a right to be there—he has already been talking to the farmer, whose name is Suter.

At the edge of this bush there is an illegal dump. People have been throwing their trash in this hidden spot rather than taking it to the township dump, whose open hours may not have suited them, or whose location may not have been so handy. Roy sees something moving there. A dog?

But then the figure straightens up and he sees that it is a man in a filthy coat. In fact it is Percy Marshall, poking around the dump to see what he can find. Sometimes in these places you used to be able to find valuable old crocks or bottles or even a copper boiler, but that is not so likely anymore. And Percy is not a knowledgeable scavenger anyway. He will just be on the lookout for anything he can use—though it is hard to see what that could be in this heap of plastic containers and torn screens and mattresses with the stuffing popped out.

Percy lives alone in one room at the back of an otherwise empty and boarded-up house at a crossroads a few miles from here. He walks the roads, walks along the creeks and through the town, talking to himself, sometimes playing the part of a half-wit vagabond and sometimes presenting himself as a shrewd local character. His life of malnutrition, dirt, and discomfort is his own choice. He has tried the County Home, but he couldn't stand the routine and the company of so many other old people. Long ago he started out with a fairly good farm, but the life of a farmer was too monotonous—so he worked his way down through bootlegging, botched house-breaking, some spells in jail, and in the past decade or so he has worked his way up again, with the help of the old-age pension, to a certain protected status. He has even had his picture and a write-up in the local paper.

The Last of a Breed. Local Free Spirit Shares Stories and Insights.

He climbs out of the dump laboriously, as if he felt obliged to have a little conversation.

"You going to be taking them trees out?"

Roy says, "I might be." He thinks Percy may be after a donation of firewood.

"Then you better hurry up," Percy says.

"Why's that?"

"All of this here is going under contract."

Roy cannot but help gratifying him by asking what contract this might be. Percy is a gossip but not a liar. At least not about the things he is truly interested in, which are deals, inheritances, insurance, house break-ins, money matters of all sorts. It is a mistake to think that people who have never managed to get hold of money aren't busy thinking about it. A surprise, this would be, to people who expect him to be a philosophical tramp, all wrapped up in memories of olden times. Though he can shoot off a little of that too when required.

"Heard about this fellow," Percy says, drawing it out. "When I was in town. I don't know. Seems this fellow runs a sawmill and he's got a contract to the River Inn and he's going to supply them all the wood they want for the winter. Cord a day. That's what they burn. Cord a day."

Roy says, "Where did you hear that?"

"Beer parlor. All right, I go in there now and again. I never have no more than a pint. And these fellows I don't know who they were, but they weren't drunk neither. Talking about where the bush was and it was this one all right. Suter's bush."

Roy had talked to the farmer just last week, and he had thought he had the deal pretty well sewed up, just to do the usual cleanout.

"That's a pile of wood," he says easily.

"It is so."

"If they mean to take it all they'd have to have a license."

"You bet. Unless there's something crooked," said Percy with intense pleasure.

"None of my business. I got all the work I can handle."

"I bet you do. All you can handle."

ALL THE WAY HOME Roy can't keep himself from thinking about this story. He has sold some wood now and then to the River Inn. But now they must have decided to take on one steady supplier, and he is not the one.

He thinks about the problems of getting that much wood out now, when the snow has already started. The only thing you could do would be to pull the logs out into the open field, before the real winter got under way. You'd have to get them out as quickly as possible, make a big pile of them there, saw them, and chop them up later. And to get them out you'd need a bulldozer or at least a big tractor. You'd have to make a road in and pull them out with chains. You'd need a crew—there was no way this could be a one- or two-man operation. It would have to be done on a big scale.

So it wasn't sounding like a part-time enterprise, the kind he carried on himself. It could be a big outfit, somebody from out of the county altogether.

Eliot Suter had not given any hint of this offer when Roy was talking to him. But it is quite possible that an approach was made to him later and he decided to forget the casual sort of arrangement that had been put forward by Roy. Decided to let the bulldozer go in.

During the evening Roy thinks of phoning up and asking what is going on. But then he thinks that if the farmer has indeed changed his mind there is nothing to be done. A spoken agreement is nothing to hold to. The man could just tell him to clear off.

The best thing for Roy to do might be just to act as if he has never heard Percy's story, never heard about any other fellow—just go in and take what trees he can as quickly as he can, before the bulldozer gets there.

Of course there is always a possibility that Percy may have been mistaken about the whole thing. He isn't likely to have made it up just to bother Roy, but he could have got it twisted.

Yet the more Roy thinks about it the more he comes to discount this possibility. He just keeps seeing in his mind the bulldozer and the chained logs, the great log piles out in the field, the men with chain saws. That is the way they do things nowadays. Wholesale.

Part of the reason the story has made such an impact is that he has a dislike for the River Inn, which is a resort hotel on the Peregrine River. It is built on the remains of an old mill not far from the crossroads where Percy Marshall lives. In fact the inn owns the land Percy lives on and the house he lives in. There was a plan to tear the house down, but it turned out that the inn's guests, having nothing much to do, like to walk down the road and take pictures of this derelict building and the old harrow and upturned wagon beside it, and the useless pump, and Percy, when he allows himself to be photographed. Some guests do sketches. They come from as far away as Ottawa and Montreal and no doubt think of themselves as being in the backwoods.

Local people go to the inn for a special lunch or dinner. Lea went once, with the dentist and his wife and the hygienist and her husband. Roy would not go. He said that he didn't want to eat a meal that cost an arm and a leg, even when somebody else was paying. But he is not altogether sure what it is that he has against the inn. He is not exactly opposed to the idea of people spending money in the hope of enjoying themselves, or against the idea of other people making money out of the people who want to spend it. It is true that the antiques at the inn have been restored and reupholstered by craftsmen other than himself—people not from around here at all—but if he had been asked to do them he would probably have refused, saying he had more than enough work to do already. When Lea asked him what he thought was the matter with the inn, the only thing he could think of to say was that when Diane had applied for a job there, as a waitress, they had turned her down, saying that she was overweight.

"Well, she was," said Lea. "She is. She says so herself."

True. But Roy still thinks of those people as snobs. Grabbers and snobs. They are putting up new buildings supposed to be like an old-time store and an old-time opera house, just for show. They burn wood for show. A cord a day. So now some operator with a bulldozer will be levelling the bush as if it was a cornfield. This is just the sort of high-handed scheme you would expect, the kind of pillage you might know they would get up to.

HE TELLS LEA THE STORY he has heard. He still tells her things—it's a habit—but he is so used to her now not paying any real attention that he hardly notices whether there is an answer or not. This time she echoes what he himself has said.

"Never mind. You've got enough to do anyway."

That's what he would have expected, whether she was well or not. Missing the point. But isn't that what wives do—and husbands probably the same—around fifty percent of the time?

THE NEXT MORNING he works on a drop-leaf table for a while. He means to stay in the shed all day and get a couple of past-due jobs finished. Near noon he hears Diane's noisy muffler and looks out the window. She'll be here to take Lea to the reflexologist—she thinks it does Lea good and Lea doesn't object.

But she is heading for the shed, not the house.

"Howdy," she says.

"Howdy."

"Hard at work?"

"Hard as ever," Roy says. "Offer you a job?"

This is their routine.

"I got one. Listen, what I came in here for, I want to ask you a favor. What I want is to borrow the truck. Tomorrow, to take Tiger to the vet. I can't handle him in the car. He's got too big for the car. I hate to have to ask you."

Roy says not to worry about it.

Tiger to the vet, he thinks, that's going to cost them.

"You weren't going to need the truck?" she says. "I mean, you can use the car?"

He has of course been meaning to go out to the bush tomorrow, providing he got his jobs done today. What he'll have to do, he decides now, is get out there this afternoon.

"I'll fill it up with gas for you," Diane says.

So another thing he'll have to do is remember to fill it up himself, to prevent her. He is just about to say, "You know the reason I want to get out there is something's come up that I can't help thinking about—" But she's out the door and going to get Lea.

As soon as they are out of sight and he has things cleaned up, he gets into the truck and drives out to where he was the day before. He thinks about stopping by and questioning Percy further but concludes that it would not be any use. Such a show of interest might just get Percy inventing things. He thinks again about talking to the farmer but decides against it for the same reasons as last night.

He parks the truck on the trail that leads into the bush. This trail soon peters out, and even before it does he has left it. He is walking around looking at the trees, which appear the same as they did yesterday and don't give a sign of being party to any hostile scheme. He has the chain saw and the ax with him, and he feels as if he has to hurry. If anybody else shows up here, if anybody challenges him, he will say that he has permission from the farmer and he knows nothing about any other deal. He will say that furthermore he intends to go on cutting unless the farmer comes and personally tells him to get out. If that really happens, of course he will have to go. But it's not likely it will happen because Suter is a hefty man with a bad hip, so he is not much taken to wandering around his property.

"...no authority...," Roy says, talking to himself like Percy Marshall, "I want to see it on paper."

He's talking to the stranger he's never even seen.

The floor of any bush is usually rougher than the surface of the surrounding land. Roy has always thought that this was caused by trees falling, pulling up the earth with their roots, then just lying there, rotting. Where they had lain and rotted there would be a mound—where their roots had torn out the earth there would be hollows. But he read somewhere—fairly recently, and he wishes he could remember where it was—that the cause was what happened long ago, just after the Ice Age, when ice formed between layers of earth and pushed it up into odd humps, just as it does today in the arctic regions. Where the land has not been cleared and worked the humps remain.

WHAT HAPPENS TO ROY NOW is the most ordinary and yet the most unbelievable thing. It is what might happen to any stupid daydreamer walking in the bush, to any holidayer gawking around at nature, to somebody who thought the bush was a kind of park to stroll in. Somebody who wore light shoes instead of boots and didn't bother to keep an eye on the ground. It has never happened to Roy before in hundreds of times of walking in the bush, it has never once come near to happening.

A light snow has been falling for some time, making the earth and dead leaves slippery. One of his feet skids and twists, and then the other foot plunges through a cover of snowy brush to the ground, which is farther down than he expected. That is, he steps carelessly—is thrown, almost—into the sort of spot where you should always step testingly, carefully, and not at all if you can see a nearby place that is better. Even so, what happens? He doesn't go down hard, it's not as if he has stumbled into a groundhog hole. He is thrown off balance, but he sways reluctantly, almost disbelievingly, then goes down with the skidding foot caught somehow under the other leg. He holds the saw out from himself as he falls, and flings the ax clear. But not clear enough—the ax handle hits him hard, against the knee of his twisted leg. The saw has pulled him over in its direction but at least he hasn't fallen against it.

He has felt himself go down almost in slow motion, thoughtfully and inevitably. He could have broken a rib, but he didn't. And the ax handle could have flown up and hit him in the face, but it didn't. He could have gashed his leg. He thinks of all these possibilities not with immediate relief, but as if he can't be sure yet that they have not happened. Because the way this started—the way he skidded and stepped onto the brush and fell—was so stupid and awkward, so hard to believe, that any preposterous outcome could follow.

He starts to pull himself up. Both knees hurt—one from being hit by the handle and one from coming down hard on the ground. He gets hold of the trunk of a young cherry tree—where he could have bashed his head—and pulls himself up gradually. Tentatively he puts weight on one foot and just touches the ground with the other—the one that skidded and twisted underneath him. In a minute he'll try it. He bends to pick up the saw and nearly buckles again. A pain shoots up from the ground and doesn't stop till it reaches his skull. He forgets the saw, straightens up, not sure where the pain started. That foot—did he put weight on it as he bent over? The pain has drawn back into that ankle. He straightens the leg as much as he can, considering it, then very cautiously tries the foot on the ground, tries his weight. He can't believe the pain. He can't believe that it would continue so, could continue to defeat him. The ankle must be more than twisted—it must be sprained. Could it be broken? In his boot it doesn't look any different from his other, faithful, ankle.

He knows that he will have to bear it. He will have to get used to it to get out of here. And he keeps trying, but he does not make any progress. He can't set his weight on it. It must be broken. A broken ankle—even that is surely a minor injury, the sort of thing old ladies get when they slip on the ice. He has been lucky. A broken ankle, a minor injury. Nevertheless he can't take a step. He can't walk.

What he understands, finally, is that in order to get back to the truck he's going to have to abandon his ax and his chain saw and get down on his hands and knees and crawl. He lets himself down as easily as he can and hauls himself around into the track of his bootprints, which are now filling with snow. He thinks to check the pocket where his keys are, making sure it's zipped. He shakes off his cap and lets it lie—the peak interferes with his vision. Now the snow is falling on his bare head. But it's not so cold. Once he accepts crawling as a method of locomotion it's not bad—that is, it's not impossible, though it's hard on his hands and his good knee. He's careful enough now, dragging himself over the brush and through the saplings, over the hummocky ground. Even if he gets a little bit of a slope to roll himself down, he doesn't dare—he has to guard the bad leg. He's glad he didn't track through any boggy places and he's glad he didn't wait any longer before starting back; the snow is getting heavier and his prints are almost blotted out. Without that track to follow it would be hard to know, at ground level, whether he was going the right way.

The situation, which seemed at first so unreal to him, is getting to seem more natural. Going along on hands and elbows and the one knee, close to the ground, testing a log for rot, then pulling himself over it on his stomach, getting his hands full of rotten leaves and dirt and snow—he can't keep his gloves on, can't get the proper hold and feel of things on the bush floor except with his cold bare scratched hands—he is no longer surprised at himself.

He doesn't think anymore about his ax and his saw back there, though at first he could hardly pull himself away from them. He scarcely thinks back as far as the accident itself. It happened, no matter how. The whole thing no longer seems in the least unbelievable or unnatural.

There is a fairly steep bank to get up, and when he reaches it he takes a breather, relieved to have come this far. He warms his hands inside his jacket, one at a time. For some reason he thinks of Diane in her unbecoming red ski jacket and decides that her life is her life, there is not much use worrying about it. And he thinks of his wife, pretending to laugh at the television. Her quietness. At least she's fed and warm, she isn't some refugee shuffling along the roads. Worse things happen, he thinks. Worse things.

He starts up the bank, digging in his elbows and his sore but serviceable knee where he can. He keeps going; he grits his teeth as if that will keep him from sliding back; he grabs at any exposed root or halfway-sturdy stem that he can see. Sometimes he slides, his hold breaks, but he gets himself stopped and inches upwards again. He never raises his head to judge how far he still has to go. If he pretends the incline goes on forever, it'll be a kind of bonus, a surprise, to get to the top.

It takes a long time. But he pulls himself onto level ground at last, and through the trees ahead and the falling snow he can see the truck. The truck, the old red Mazda, a faithful old friend, miraculously waiting. Being on the level raises his expectations of himself again and he gets onto his knees, going easy, easy on the bad leg, rises shakily onto his good leg, dragging the other, swaying like a drunk. He tries a sort of hop. No good—he'd lose his balance that way. He tries a little weight on the bad leg, just gently, and realizes that the pain could make him black out. He sinks back to the old position and crawls. But instead of crawling through the trees towards the truck he turns at right angles and makes for where he knows the track to be. When he gets there he begins to make better time, crawling over the hard ruts, the mud that has thawed in the daylight but is now starting to freeze again. It's cruel on the knee and his palms but otherwise so much easier than the route he had to take before that he feels almost light-headed. He can see the truck ahead. Looking at him, waiting for him.

He'll be able to drive. So lucky the damage is to the left leg. Now that the worst is over a lot of vexing questions come at him, along with his relief. Who will go and get the saw and the ax for him, how can he explain to anybody just where to find them? How soon will the snow cover them up? When will he be able to walk?

No use. He pushes all that away, raises his head to get another encouraging look at the truck. He stops again to rest and warm his hands. He could put his gloves on now, but why ruin them?

A large bird rises out of the bush to one side of him and he cranes his neck to see what it is. He thinks it's a hawk, but it could be a buzzard. If it's a buzzard will it have its eye on him, thinking it's in luck now, seeing he's hurt?

He waits to see it circle back, so he can tell what it is by the manner of its flight, and its wings.

And while he's doing that, while he's waiting, and taking note of the bird's wings—it is a buzzard—he is also getting a drastically new idea about the story that has preoccupied him for the last twenty-four hours.

THE TRUCK IS MOVING. When did it start? When he was watching the bird? At first just a little movement, a wobble in the ruts—it could almost be a hallucination. But he can hear the engine. It's going. Did somebody just get into it while he was distracted, or was somebody waiting in it all the time? Surely he locked it, and he has the keys with him. He feels his zipped pocket again. Someone stealing the truck in front of his eyes and without the keys. He hollers and waves, from his crouched position—as if that would do any good. But the truck isn't backing into the turnaround to drive out; it's bumping along the track straight at him, and now the person driving it is honking the horn, not in a warning but a greeting way, and slowing down.

He sees who it is.

The only person who has the other set of keys. The only person it could be. Lea.

He struggles to get his weight onto the one leg. She jumps out of the truck and runs to him and supports him.

"I just went down," he tells her, panting. "It was the dumbest damn thing I ever did in my life." Then he thinks to ask how she got here.

"Well, I didn't fly," she says.

She came in the car, she says—she speaks just as if she'd never given up driving at all—she came in the car but she left it back at the road.

"It's way too light for this track," she says. "And I thought I might get stuck. But I wouldn't't've, the mud's froze hard.

"I could see the truck," she says. "So I just walked in and when I got to it I unlocked it and got in and sat there. I figured you'd be coming back soon, seeing it's snowing. But I never figured you'd be doing it on your hands and knees."

The walk, or maybe the cold, has brightened her face and sharpened her voice. She gets down and looks at his ankle, says she thinks it's swollen.

"Could have been worse," he says.

She says this was the one time she hadn't been worried. The one time she wasn't and she should have been. (He doesn't bother telling her that she hasn't shown worry about anything for a matter of months.) She didn't have a single premonition.

"I just came to meet you to tell you," she says, "because I couldn't wait to tell you. This idea I got when the woman was working on me. Then I saw you crawling. And I thought, *Oh my God.*"

What idea?

"Oh that," she says. "Oh—well, I don't know what you'll think. I could tell you later. We gotta get your ankle fixed."

What idea?

Her idea is that the outfit Percy heard about doesn't exist. Percy heard some talk but not about some strangers getting a license to log the bush. What he heard was all about Roy himself.

"Because that old Eliot Suter is all big talk. I know that family, his wife was Annie Poole's sister. He's going round blowing about the deal he got and added on to it quite a bit and first thing what have you? Ends up the River Inn for good measure and a hundred cords a day. Somebody drinking beer and listening in on somebody else drinking beer and there you are. And you have got a kind of a contract—I mean you've got an agreement—"

"It may be stupid all right—" Roy says.

"I knew you'd say that but you think about it—"

"It may be stupid but it's the same idea I had myself about five minutes ago."

And this is so. This is what came to him when he was looking up at the buzzard.

"So there you are," Lea says, with a satisfied laugh. "Everything remotely connected with the inn, it just turns into some big story. Some big-money kind of a story."

That was it, he thinks. He was hearing about himself. All the ruction comes back to himself.

The bulldozer isn't coming, the men with the chain saws are not converging. The ash, the maple, the beech, the ironwood, the cherry, are all safe for him. For the time being, all safe.

Lea is out of breath with the effort of supporting him, but able to say, "Great minds think alike."

This is not the moment to mention the change in her. No more than you'd call your congratulations to somebody up on a ladder.

He has knocked his foot hoisting himself—and partly being hoisted—into the passenger seat of the truck. He groans, and it's a different kind of groan than would come out of him if he was alone. It's not that he means to dramatize the pain, just that he takes this way of describing it to his wife.

Or even offering it to his wife. Because he knows that he isn't feeling quite the way he thought he would if her vitality came back to her. And the noise he makes could be to cover that lack, or excuse it. Of course it's natural that he'd feel a bit cautious, not knowing if this is for good, or just a flash in the pan.

But even if it is for good, even if it's all good there's something more. Some loss fogging up this gain. Some loss he'd be ashamed to admit to, if he had the energy.

The dark and the snow are too thick for him to see beyond the first trees. He's been in there before at this time, when the dark shuts down in early winter. But now he pays attention, he notices something about the bush that he thinks he has missed those other times. How tangled up in itself it is, how dense and secret. It's not a matter of one tree after another, it's all the trees together, aiding and abetting one another and weaving into one thing. A transformation, behind your back.

There's another name for the bush, and this name is stalking around in his mind, in and out of where he can almost grasp it. But not quite. It's a tall word that seems ominous but indifferent.

"I left the ax," he says mechanically. "I left the saw."

"So what if you did. We'll find somebody to go and get them."

"And there's the car too. Are you going to get out and drive that and let me take the truck?"

"Are you insane?"

Her voice is absentminded, because she is in the process of backing the truck into the turnaround. Slowly but not too slowly, bouncing in the ruts but keeping on the track. He is not used to the rearview mirrors from this angle, so he lowers the window and cranes around, getting the snow in his face. This is not just to see how she's doing but to clear to a certain extent the warm wooziness coming on him.

"Easy," he says. "That's it. Easy. Okay now. You're okay. You're okay."

While he is saying this she is saying something about the hospital.

". . . get them to take a look at you. First things first."

To his knowledge, she has never driven the truck before.

It's remarkable the way she manages it.

Forest. That's the word. Not a strange word at all but one he has possibly never used. A formality about it that he would usually back away from.

"The Deserted Forest," he says, as if that put the cap on something.

Child's Play

≈

I SUPPOSE there was talk in our house, afterwards.

How sad, how *awful*. (My mother.)

There should have been supervision. Where were the counsellors? (My father.)

IT IS POSSIBLE that if we ever passed the yellow house my mother said, "Remember? Remember you used to be so scared of her? The poor thing."

My mother had a habit of hanging on to—even treasuring—the foibles of my distant infantile state.

EVERY YEAR, when you're a child, you become a different person. Generally it's in the fall, when you reenter school, take your place in a higher grade, leave behind the muddle and lethargy of the summer vacation. That's when you register the change most sharply. Afterwards you are not sure of the month or year but the changes go on, just the same. For a long while the past drops away from you easily and it would seem automatically, properly. Its scenes don't vanish so much as become irrelevant. And then there's a switchback, what's been all over and done with sprouting up fresh, wanting attention, even wanting you to do something about it, though it's plain there is not on this earth a thing to be done.

MARLENE AND CHARLENE. People thought we must be twins. There was a fashion in those days for naming twins in rhyme. Bonnie and Connie. Ronald and Donald. And then of course we—Charlene and I—had matching hats. Coolie hats, they were called, wide shallow cones of woven straw with some sort of tie or elastic under the chin. They became familiar later on in the century, from television shots of the war in Vietnam. Men on bicycles riding along a street in Saigon would be wearing them, or women walking in the road against the background of a bombed village.

It was possible at that time—I mean the time when Charlene and I were at camp—to say *coolie,* without a thought of offense. Or *darkie,* or to talk about *jewing* a price down. I was in my teens, I think, before I ever related that verb to the noun.

So we had those names and those hats, and at the first roll call the counsellor—the jolly one we liked, Mavis, though we didn't like her as well as the pretty one, Pauline—pointed at us and called out, "Hey. Twins," and went on calling out other names before we had time to deny it.

Even before that we must have noticed the hats and approved of each other. Otherwise one or both of us would have pulled off those brand-new articles, and been ready to shove them under our cots, declaring that our mothers had made us wear them and we hated them, and so on.

I may have approved of Charlene, but I was not sure how to make friends with her. Girls nine or ten years old—that was the general range of this crop, though there were a few a bit older—do not pick friends or pair off as easily as girls do at six or seven. I simply followed some other girls from my town—none of them my particular friends—to one of the cabins where there were some unclaimed cots, and dumped my things on top of the brown blanket. Then I heard a voice behind me say, "Could I please be next to my twin sister?"

It was Charlene, speaking to somebody I didn't know. The dormitory cabin held perhaps two dozen girls. The girl she had spoken to said, "Sure," and moved along.

Charlene had used a special voice. Ingratiating, teasing, self-mocking, and with a seductive merriment in it, like a trill of bells. It was evident right away that she had more confidence than I did. And not simply confidence that the other girl would move, and not say sturdily, "I got here first." (Or—if she was a roughly brought-up sort of girl—and some were, having their way paid by the Lions Club or the church and not by their parents—she might have said, "Go poop your pants, I'm not moving.") No. Charlene had confidence that anybody would *want* to do as she asked, not just agree to do it. With me too she had taken a chance, for could I not have said, "I don't want to be twins," and turned back to sort my things. But of course I didn't. I felt flattered, as she had expected, and I watched her dump out the contents of her suitcase with such an air of celebration that some things fell on the floor.

All I could think of to say was, "You got a tan already."

"I always tan easy," she said.

The first of our differences. We applied ourselves to learning them. She tanned, I freckled. We both had brown hair but hers was darker. Hers was wavy, mine bushy. I was half an inch taller, she had thicker wrists and ankles. Her eyes had more green in them, mine more blue. We did not grow tired of inspecting and tabulating even the moles or notable freckles on our backs, length of our second toes (mine longer than the first toe, hers shorter). Or of recounting all the illnesses or accidents that had befallen us so far, as well as the repairs or removals performed on our bodies. Both of us had had our tonsils out—a usual precaution in those days—and both of us had had measles and whooping cough but not mumps. I had had an eyetooth pulled because it was growing in over my other teeth and she had a thumbnail with an imperfect half-moon, because her thumb had been slammed under a window.

And once we had the peculiarities and history of our bodies in place we went on to the stories—the dramas or near dramas or distinctions—of our families. She was the youngest and the only girl in her family and I was an only child. I had an aunt who had died of polio in high school and she—Charlene—had an older brother who was in the Navy. For it was wartime, and at the campfire sing-song we would choose "There'll Always Be an England" and "Hearts of Oak," and "Rule Britannia," and sometimes "The Maple Leaf Forever." Bombing raids and battles and sinking ships were the constant, though distant, backdrop of our lives. And once in a while there was a near strike, frightening but solemn and exhilarating, as when a boy from our town or our street would be killed, and the house where he had lived, without having any special wreath or black drapery on it, seemed nevertheless to have a special weight inside it, a destiny fulfilled and dragging it down. Though there was nothing special inside it at all, maybe just a car that didn't belong there parked at the curb, showing that some relatives or a minister had come to sit with the bereaved family.

One of the camp counsellors had lost her fiancé in the war and wore his watch—we believed it was his watch—pinned to her blouse. We would like to have felt for her a mournful interest and concern, but she was sharp voiced and bossy, and she even had an unpleasant name. Arva.

The other backdrop of our lives, which was supposed to be emphasized at camp, was religion. But since the United Church of Canada was officially in charge there was not so much harping on that subject as there would have been with the Baptists or the Bible Christians, or so much formal acknowledgment as the Roman Catholics or even the Anglicans would have provided. Most of us had parents who belonged to the United Church (though some of the girls who were having their way paid for them might not have belonged to any church at all), and being used to its hearty secular style, we did not even realize that we were getting off easy with just evening prayers and grace sung at meals and the half-hour special talk—it was called a Chat—after breakfast. Even the Chat was relatively free of references to God or Jesus and was more about honesty and loving-kindness and clean thoughts in our daily lives, and promising never to drink or smoke when we grew up. Nobody had any objection to this sort of thing or tried to get out of attending, because it was what we were used to and because it was pleasant to sit on the beach in the warming sun and a little too cold yet for us to long to jump into the water.

Grown-up women do the same sort of thing that Charlene and I did. Not counting the moles on each other's backs and comparing toe lengths, maybe. But when they meet and feel a particular sympathy with each other they also feel a need to set out the important information, the big events whether public or secret, and then go ahead to fill in all the blanks between. If they feel this warmth and eagerness it is quite impossible for them to bore each other. They will laugh at the very triviality and silliness of what they're telling, or at the revelation of some appalling selfishness, deception, meanness, sheer badness.

There has to be great trust, of course, but that trust can be established at once, in an instant.

I've observed this. It's supposed to have begun in those long periods of sitting around the campfire stirring the manioc porridge or whatever while the men were out in the bush deprived of conversation because it would warn off the wild animals. (I am an anthropologist by training though a rather slack one.) I've observed but never taken part in these female exchanges. Not truly. Sometimes I've pretended because it seemed to be required, but the woman I was supposed to be making friends with always got wind of my pretense and became confused and cautious.

As a rule, I've felt less wary with men. They don't expect such transactions and are seldom really interested.

This intimacy I'm talking about—with women—is not erotic, or pre-erotic. I've experienced that as well, before puberty. Then too there would be confidences, probably lies, maybe leading to games. A certain hot temporary excitement, with or without genital teasing. Followed by ill feeling, denial, disgust.

Charlene did tell me about her brother, but with true repugnance. This was the brother now in the Navy. She went into his room looking for her cat and there he was doing it to his girlfriend. They never knew she saw them.

She said they slapped as he went up and down.

You mean they slapped on the bed, I said.

No, she said. It was his thing slapped when it was going in and out. It was gross. Sickening.

And his bare white bum had pimples on it. Sickening.

I told her about Verna.

UP UNTIL THE TIME I was seven years old my parents had lived in what was called a double house. The word "duplex" was perhaps not in use at that time, and anyway the house was not evenly divided. Verna's grandmother rented the rooms at the back and we rented the rooms at the front. The house was tall and bare and ugly, painted yellow. The town we lived in was too small to have residential divisions that amounted to anything, but I suppose that as far as there were divisions, that house was right on the boundary between decent and fairly dilapidated. I am speaking of the way things were just before the Second World War, at the end of the Depression. (That word, I believe, was unknown to us.)

My father being a teacher had a regular job but little money. The street petered out beyond us between the houses of those who had neither. Verna's grandmother must have had a little money because she spoke contemptuously of people who were On Relief. I believe my mother argued with her, unsuccessfully, that it was Not Their Fault. The two women were not particular friends but they were cordial about clothesline arrangements.

The grandmother's name was Mrs. Home. A man came to see her occasionally. My mother spoke of him as Mrs. Home's friend.

You are not to speak to Mrs. Home's friend.

In fact I was not even allowed to play outside when he came, so there was not much chance of my speaking to him. I don't even remember what he looked like, though I remember his car, which was dark blue, a Ford V-8. I took a special interest in cars, probably because we didn't have one.

Then Verna came.

Mrs. Home spoke of her as her granddaughter and there is no reason to suppose that not to be true, but there was never any sign of a connecting generation. I don't know if Mrs. Home went away and came back with her, or if she was delivered by the friend with the V-8. She appeared in the summer before I was to start school. I can't remember her telling me her name—she was not communicative in the ordinary way and I don't believe I would have asked her. From the very beginning I had an aversion to her unlike anything I had felt up to that time for any other person. I said that I hated her, and my mother said, How can you, what has she ever done to you?

The poor thing.

Children use that word "hate" to mean various things. It may mean that they are frightened. Not that they feel in danger of being attacked—the way I did, for instance, by certain big boys on bicycles who liked to cut in front of you, yelling fearsomely, as you walked on the sidewalk. It is not physical harm that is feared—or that I feared in Verna's case—so much as some spell, or dark intention. It is a feeling you can have when you are very young even about certain house faces, or tree trunks, or very much about moldy cellars or deep closets.

She was a good deal taller than I was and I don't know how

much older—two years, three years? She was skinny, indeed so narrowly built and with such a small head that she made me think of a snake. Fine black hair lay flat on this head, and fell over her forehead. The skin of her face seemed dull to me as the flap of our old canvas tent, and her cheeks puffed out the way the flap of that tent puffed in a wind. Her eyes were always squinting.

But I believe there was nothing remarkably unpleasant about her looks, as other people saw her. Indeed my mother spoke of her as pretty, or almost pretty (as in, *isn't it too bad, she could be pretty*). Nothing to object to either, as far as my mother could see, in her behavior. *She is young for her age.* A roundabout and inadequate way of saying that Verna had not learned to read or write or skip or play ball, and that her voice was hoarse and unmodulated, her words oddly separated, as if they were chunks of language caught in her throat.

Her way of interfering with me, spoiling my solitary games, was that of an older not a younger girl. But of an older girl who had no skill or rights, nothing but a strenuous determination and an inability to understand that she wasn't wanted.

Children of course are monstrously conventional, repelled at once by whatever is off-center, out of whack, unmanageable. And being an only child I had been coddled a good deal (also scolded). I was awkward, precocious, timid, full of my private rituals and aversions. I hated even the celluloid barrette that kept slipping out of Verna's hair, and the peppermints with red or green stripes on them that she kept offering to me. In fact she did more than offer; she would try to catch me and push these candies into my mouth, chuckling all the time in her disconnected way. I dislike peppermint flavoring to this day. And the name Verna—I dislike that. It doesn't sound like spring to me, or like green grass or garlands of flowers or girls in flimsy dresses. It sounds more like a trail of obstinate peppermint, green slime.

I didn't believe my mother really liked Verna either. But because of some hypocrisy in her nature, as I saw it, because of a decision she had made, as it seemed to spite me, she pretended to be sorry for her. She told me to be kind. At first, she said that Verna would not be staying long and at the end of the summer holidays would go back to wherever she had been before. Then, when it became clear that there was nowhere for Verna to go back to, the placating message was that we ourselves would be moving soon. I had only to be kind for a little while longer. (As a matter of fact it was a whole year before we moved.) Finally, out of patience, she said that I was a disappointment to her and that she would never have thought I had so mean a nature.

"How can you blame a person for the way she was born? How is it her fault?"

That made no sense to me. If I had been more skilled at arguing I might have said that I didn't blame Verna, I just did not want her to come near me. But I certainly did blame her. I did not question that it was somehow her fault. And in this, whatever my mother might say, I was in tune to some degree with an unspoken verdict of the time and place I lived in. Even grown-ups smiled in a certain way, there was some irrepressible gratification and taken-for-granted superiority that I could see in the way they mentioned people who were *simple* or *a few bricks short of a load*. And I believed my mother must be really like this, underneath.

I started to school. Verna started to school. She was put into a special class in a special building in a corner of the school grounds. This was actually the original school building in the town, but nobody had any time for local history then, and a few years later it was pulled down. There was a fenced-off corner in which pupils housed in that building spent recess. They went to school a half hour later than we did in the morning and got out a half hour earlier in the afternoon. Nobody was supposed to harass them at recess but since they usually hung on the fence watching whatever went on in the regular school grounds there would be occasions when there was a rush, a whooping and brandishing of sticks, to scare them. I never went near that corner, hardly ever saw Verna. It was at home I still had to deal with her.

First she would stand at the corner of the yellow house, watching me, and I would pretend that I didn't know she was there. Then she would wander into the front yard, taking up a position on the front steps of the part of the house that was mine. If I wanted to go inside to the bathroom or because I was cold, I would have to go so close as to touch her and to risk her touching me.

She could stay in one place longer than anybody I ever knew, staring at just one thing. Usually me.

I had a swing hung from a maple tree, so that I either faced the house or the street. That is, I either had to face her or to know that she was staring at my back, and might come up to give me a push. After a while she would decide to do that. She always pushed me crooked, but that was not the worst thing. The worst was that her fingers had pressed my back. Through my coat, through my other clothing, her fingers like so many cold snouts. Another activity of mine was to build a leaf house. I raked up and carried armloads of leaves fallen from the maple tree that held the swing, and I dumped and arranged these leaves into a house plan. Here was the living room, here was the kitchen, here was a big soft pile for the bed in the bedroom, and so on. I had not invented this occupation—leaf houses of a more expansive sort were laid out in, and even in a way furnished, every recess in the girls' playground at school, until the janitor finally raked up all the leaves and burned them.

At first Verna just watched what I was doing, with her squinty-eyed expression of what seemed to me superior (how could she think herself superior?) puzzlement. Then the time came when she moved closer, lifted an armful of leaves which dripped all over because of her uncertainty or clumsiness. And these came not from the pile of spare leaves but from the very wall of my house. She picked them up and carried them a short distance and let them fall—dumped them—in the middle of one of my tidy rooms.

I yelled at her to stop, but she bent to pick up her scattered load again, and was unable to hang on to them, so she just flung them about and when they were all on the ground began to kick them foolishly here and there. I was still yelling at her to stop, but this had no effect, or else she took it for encouragement. So I lowered my head and ran at her and butted her in the stomach. I was not wearing a cap, so the hairs of my head came in contact with the woolly coat or jacket she had on, and it seemed to me that I had actually touched bristling hairs on the skin of a gross hard belly. I ran hollering with complaint up the steps of the house and when my mother heard the story she further maddened me by saying, "She only wants to play. She doesn't know how to *play*."

By the next fall we were in a new bungalow and I never had to go past the yellow house which reminded me so much of Verna, as if it had positively taken on her narrow slyness, her threatening squint. The yellow paint seemed to be the very color of insult, and the front door, being off center, added a touch of deformity.

The bungalow was only three blocks away from that house, close to the school. But my idea of the town's size and complexity was still such that it seemed I was escaping Verna altogether. I realized that this was not true, not altogether true, when a schoolmate and I came face-to-face with her one day on the main street. We must have been sent on some errand by one of our mothers. I did not look up but I believed I heard a chuckle of greeting or recognition as we passed.

The other girl said a horrifying thing to me.

She said, "I used to think that was your sister."

"What?"

"Well, I knew you lived in the same house so I thought you must be related. Like cousins, anyway. Aren't you? Cousins?"

"*No.*"

THE OLD BUILDING where the Special Classes had been held was condemned, and its pupils were transferred to the Bible Chapel, now rented on weekdays by the town. The Bible Chapel happened to be across the street and around a corner from the bungalow where my mother and father and I now lived. There were a couple of ways that Verna could have walked to school, but the way she chose was past our house. And our house was only a few feet from the sidewalk, so this meant that her shadow could practically fall across our steps. If she wished she could kick pebbles onto our grass, and unless we kept the blinds down she could peer into our hall and front room.

The hours of the Special Classes had been changed to coincide with ordinary school hours, at least in the morning—the Specials still went home earlier in the afternoon. Once they were in the Bible Chapel it must have been felt that there was no need to keep them free of the rest of us on the way to school. This meant, now, that I had a chance of running into Verna on the sidewalk. I would always look in the direction from which she might be coming, and if I saw her I would duck back into the house with the excuse that I had forgotten something, or that one of my shoes was rubbing my heel and needed a plaster, or a ribbon was coming loose in my hair. I would never have been so foolish now as to mention Verna, and hear my mother say, "What's the problem, what are you afraid of, do you think she's going to eat you?"

What was the problem? Contamination, infection? Verna was decently clean and healthy. And it was hardly likely that she was going to attack and pummel me or pull out my hair. But only adults would be so stupid as to believe she had no power. A power, moreover, that was specifically directed at me. I was the one she had her eye on. Or so I believed. As if we had an understanding between us that could not be described and was not to be disposed of. Something that clings, in the way of love, though on my side it felt absolutely like hate.

I suppose I hated her as some people hate snakes or caterpillars or mice or slugs. For no decent reason. Not for any certain harm she could do but for the way she could disturb your innards and make you sick of your life.

WHEN I TOLD CHARLENE about her we had got into the deeper reaches of our conversation—that conversation which seems to have been broken only when we swam or slept. Verna was not so solid an offering, not so vividly repulsive, as Charlene's brother's pumping pimpled bum, and I remember saying that she was awful in a way that I could not describe. But then I did describe her, and my feelings about her, and I must have done not too bad a job because one day towards the end of our two-week stay at camp Charlene came rushing into the dining hall at midday, her face lit up with horror and strange delight.

"She's here. She's here. That girl. That awful girl. Verna. She's *here*."

Lunch was over. We were in the process of tidying up, putting our plates and mugs on the kitchen shelf to be grabbed away and washed by the girls on kitchen duty that day. Then we would line up to go to the Tuck Shop, which opened every day at one o'clock. Charlene had just run back to the dormitory to get some money. Being rich, with a father who was an undertaker, she was rather careless, keeping money in her pillowcase. Except when swimming I always had mine on my person. All of us who could in any way afford to went to the Tuck Shop after lunch, to get something to take away the taste of the desserts we hated but always tried, just to see if they were as disgusting as we expected. Tapioca pudding, mushy baked apples, slimy custard. When I first saw the look on Charlene's face I thought that her money had been stolen. But then I thought that such a calamity would not have made her look so transformed, the shock on her face so joyful.

Verna? How could Verna be here? Some mistake.

This must have been a Friday. Two more days at camp, two more days to go. And it turned out that a contingent of Specials—here too they were called Specials—had been brought in to enjoy with us the final weekend. Not many of them—maybe twenty altogether—and not all from my town but from other towns nearby. In fact as Charlene was trying to get the news through to me a whistle was being blown, and Counsellor Arva had jumped up on a bench to address us.

She said that she knew we would all do our best to make these visitors—these new campers—welcome, and that they had brought their own tents and their own counsellor with them. But they would eat and swim and play games and attend the Morning Chat with the rest of us. She was sure, she said, with that familiar warning or upbraiding note in her voice, that we would all treat this as an opportunity to make new friends.

It took some time to get the tents up and these newcomers and their possessions settled. Some apparently took no interest and wandered off and had to be yelled at and fetched back. Since it was our free time, or rest hour, we got our chocolate bars or licorice whips or sponge toffee from the Tuck Shop and went to lie on our bunks and enjoy them.

Charlene kept saying, "Imagine. Imagine. She's here. I can't believe it. Do you think she followed you?"

"Probably," I said.

"Do you think I can always hide you like that?"

When we were in the Tuck Shop lineup I had ducked my head and made Charlene get between me and the Specials as they were

being herded by. I had taken one peek and recognized Verna from
behind. Her drooping snaky head.

"We should think of some way to disguise you."

From what I had said, Charlene seemed to have got the idea
that Verna had actively harassed me. And I believed that was true,
except that the harassment had been more subtle, more secret,
than I had been able to describe. Now I let Charlene think as she
liked because it was more exciting that way.

Verna did not spot me immediately, because of the elaborate
dodges Charlene and I kept making, and perhaps because she was
rather dazed, as most of the Specials appeared to be, trying to figure out what they were doing here. They were soon taken off to
their own swimming class, at the far end of the beach.

At the supper table they were marched in while we sang.

> *The more we get together, together, together,*
> *The more we get together,*
> *The happier we'll be.*

They were then deliberately separated, and distributed amongst
the rest of us. They all wore name tags. Across from me there was
one named Mary Ellen something, not from my town. But I had
hardly time to be glad of that when I saw Verna at the next table,
taller than those around her but thank God facing the same way I
was so she could not see me during the meal.

She was the tallest of them, and yet not so tall, not so notable a
presence, as I remembered her. The reason was probably that I had
had a growing spurt during the last year, while she had perhaps
stopped her growing altogether.

After the meal, when we stood up and collected our dishes, I
kept my head bowed, I never looked in her direction, and yet I
knew when her eyes rested on me, when she recognized me, when
she smiled her sagging little smile or made that odd chuckle in her
throat.

"She's seen you," said Charlene. "Don't look. Don't look. I'll get
between you and her. Move. Keep moving."

"Is she coming this way?"

"No. She's just standing there. She's just looking at you."

"Smiling?"

"Sort of."

"I can't look at her. I'd be sick."

How much did she persecute me in the remaining day and a half? Charlene and I used that word constantly, though in fact Verna never got near us. *Persecute.* It had an adult, legal sound. We were always on the lookout, as if we were being stalked, or I was. We tried to keep track of Verna's whereabouts, and Charlene reported on her attitude or expression. I did risk looking at her a couple of times, when Charlene had said, "Okay. She won't notice now."

At those times Verna appeared slightly downcast, or sullen, or bewildered, as if, like most of the Specials, she had been set adrift and did not completely understand where she was or what she was doing there. Some of them—though not she—had caused a commotion by wandering away into the pine and cedar and poplar woods on the bluff behind the beach, or along the sandy road that led to the highway. After that a meeting was called, and we were all asked to watch out for our new friends, who were not so familiar with the place as we were. Charlene poked me in the ribs at that. She of course was not aware of any change, any falling away of confidence or even a diminishing of physical size, in this Verna, and she continually reported on her sly and evil expression, her look of menace. And maybe she was right—maybe Verna saw in Charlene, this new friend or bodyguard of mine, this stranger, some sign of how everything was changed and uncertain here, and that made her scowl, though I didn't see it.

"You never told me about her hands," said Charlene.

"What about them?"

"She's got the longest fingers I have ever seen. She could just twist them round your neck and strangle you. She could. Wouldn't it be awful to be in a tent with her at night?"

I said that it would be. Awful.

"But those others in her tent are too idiotic to notice."

There was a change, that last weekend, a whole different feeling in the camp. Nothing drastic. The meals were announced by the dining room gong at the regular times, and the food served did not improve or deteriorate. Rest time arrived, game time and swimming time. The Tuck Shop operated as usual, and we were drawn together as always for the Chat. But there was an air of growing restlessness and inattention. You could detect it even in the counsellors, who might not have the same reprimands or words of encouragement on the tip of their tongues and would look at you for a second as if trying to recall what it was they usually said. And all this seemed to have begun with the arrival of the Specials. Their presence had changed the camp. There had been a real camp before, with all its rules and deprivations and enjoyments set up, inevitable as school or any part of a child's life, and then it had begun to crumple at the edges, to reveal itself as something provisional. Playacting.

Was it because we could look at the Specials and think that if they could be campers, then there was no such thing as real campers? Partly it was that. But it was partly that the time was coming very soon when all this would be over, the routines would be broken up, and we would be fetched by our parents to resume our old lives, and the counsellors would go back to being ordinary people, not even teachers. We were living in a stage set about to be dismantled, and with it all the friendships, enmities, rivalries that had flourished in the last two weeks. Who could believe it had been only two weeks?

Nobody knew how to speak of this, but a lassitude spread amongst us, a bored ill temper, and even the weather reflected this feeling. It was probably not true that every day during the past two weeks had been hot and sunny, but most of us would certainly go away with that impression. And now, on Sunday morning, there was a change. While we were having the Outdoor Devotions (that was what we had on Sundays instead of the Chat) the clouds darkened. There was no change in temperature—if anything, the heat of the day increased—but there was in the air what some people called the smell of a storm. And yet such stillness. The counsellors and even the minister, who drove out on Sundays from the nearest town, looked up occasionally and warily at the sky.

A few drops did fall, but no more. The service came to its end and no storm had broken. The clouds grew somewhat lighter, not so much as to promise sunshine, but enough so that our last swim would not have to be cancelled. After that there would be no lunch; the kitchen had been closed down after breakfast. The shutters on the Tuck Shop would not be opened. Our parents would begin arriving shortly after noon to take us home, and the bus would come for the Specials. Most of our things were already packed, the sheets were stripped, and the rough brown blankets, that always felt clammy, were folded across the foot of each cot.

Even when it was full of us, chattering and changing into our bathing suits, the inside of the dormitory cabin revealed itself as makeshift and gloomy.

It was the same with the beach. There appeared to be less sand than usual, more stones. And what sand there was seemed gray. The water looked as if it might be cold, though in fact it was quite warm. Nevertheless our enthusiasm for swimming had waned and most of us were wading about aimlessly. The swimming counsellors—Pauline and the middle-aged woman in charge of the Specials—had to clap their hands at us.

"Hurry up, what are you waiting for? Last chance this summer."

There were good swimmers among us who usually struck out at once for the raft. And all who were even passably good swimmers—that included Charlene and me—were supposed to swim out to the raft at least once and turn around and swim back in order to prove that we could swim at least a couple of yards in water over our heads. Pauline would usually swim out there right away, and stay in the deeper water to watch out for anybody who got into trouble and also to make sure that everybody who was supposed to do the swim had done it. On this day, however, fewer swimmers than usual seemed to be going out there as they were supposed to, and Pauline herself after her first cries of encouragement or exasperation—required simply to get everybody into the water—was just bobbing around the raft, laughing and teasing with the faithful expert swimmers. Most of us were still paddling around in the shallows, swimming a few feet or yards, then standing on the bottom and splashing one another or turning over and doing the dead man's float, as if swimming was something hardly anybody could be bothered with anymore. The woman in charge of the Specials was standing where the water came barely up to her waist—most of the Specials themselves went no farther than where

the water came up to their knees—and the top part of her flowered, skirted bathing suit had not even got wet. She was bending
over and making little hand splashes at her charges, laughing and
telling them, Isn't this fun.

The water Charlene and I were in was probably up to our chests
and no more. We were in the ranks of the silly swimmers, doing
the dead man's, and flopping about backstroking or breaststrok-
ing, with nobody telling us to stop fooling around. We were trying
to see how long we could keep our eyes open underwater, we were
sneaking up and jumping on one another's backs. All around us
were plenty of others yelling and screeching with laughter as they
did the same things.

During this swim some parents or collectors of campers had
arrived early and let it be known they had no time to waste, so the
campers who belonged to them were being summoned from the
water. This made for some extra calling and confusion.

"Look. Look," said Charlene. Or sputtered, in fact, because I
had pushed her underwater and she had just come up soaked and
spitting.

I looked, and there was Verna making her way towards us,
wearing a pale blue rubber bathing cap, slapping at the water with
her long hands and smiling, as if her rights over me had suddenly
been restored.

I HAVE NOT KEPT UP with Charlene. I don't even remember
how we said good-bye. If we said good-bye. I have a notion that
both sets of parents arrived at around the same time and that we
scrambled into separate cars and gave ourselves over—what else
could we do?—to our old lives. Charlene's parents would certainly
have had a car not so shabby and noisy and unreliable as the one
my parents now owned, but even if that had not been so we would
never have thought of making the two sets of relatives acquainted
with each other. Everybody, and we ourselves, would have been in
a hurry to get off, to leave behind the pockets of uproar about lost
property or who had or had not met their relatives or boarded the
bus.

By chance, years later, I did see Charlene's wedding picture. This
was at a time when wedding pictures were still published in the

newspapers, not just in small towns but in the city papers as well. I saw it in a Toronto paper which I was looking through while I waited for a friend in a café on Bloor Street.

The wedding had taken place in Guelph. The groom was a native of Toronto and a graduate of Osgoode Hall. He was quite tall—or else Charlene had turned out to be quite short. She barely came up to his shoulder, even with her hair done up in the dense, polished helmet-style of the day. The hair made her face seem squashed and insignificant, but I got the impression her eyes were outlined heavily, Cleopatra fashion, her lips pale. This sounds grotesque but it was certainly the look admired at the time. All that reminded me of her child-self was the little humorous bump of her chin.

She—the bride, it said—had graduated from St. Hilda's College in Toronto.

So she must have been here in Toronto, going to St. Hilda's, while I was in the same city, going to University College. We had been walking around perhaps at the same time and on some of the same streets or paths on the campus. And never met. I did not think that she would have seen me and avoided speaking to me. I would not have avoided speaking to her. Of course I would have considered myself a more serious student, once I discovered she was going to St. Hilda's. My friends and I regarded St. Hilda's as a Ladies College.

Now I was a graduate student in anthropology. I had decided never to get married, though I did not rule out having lovers. I wore my hair long and straight—my friends and I were anticipating the style of the hippies. My memories of childhood were much more distant and faded and unimportant than they seem today.

I could have written to Charlene in care of her parents, whose Guelph address was in the paper. But I didn't do so. I would have thought it the height of hypocrisy to congratulate any woman on her marriage.

BUT SHE WROTE TO ME, perhaps fifteen years later. She wrote in care of my publishers.

"My old pal Marlene," she wrote. "How excited and happy I was to see your name in *Maclean's* magazine. And how dazzled I am to think you have written a book. I have not picked it up yet because we had been away on holidays but I mean to do so—and read it too—as soon as I can. I was just going through the magazines that had accumulated in our absence and there I saw the striking picture of you and the interesting review. And I thought that I must write and congratulate you.

"Perhaps you are married but use your maiden name to write under? Perhaps you have a family? Do write and tell me all about yourself. Sadly, I am childless, but I keep busy with volunteer work, gardening, and sailing with Kit (my husband). There always seems to be plenty to do. I am presently serving on the Library Board and will twist their arms if they have not already ordered your book.

"Congratulations again. I must say I was surprised but not entirely because I always suspected you might do something special."

I did not get in touch with her at that time either. There seemed to be no point to it. At first I took no notice of the word "special" right at the end, but it gave me a small jolt when I thought of it later. However, I told myself, and still believe, that she meant nothing by it.

The book that she referred to was one that had grown out of a thesis I had been discouraged from writing. I went ahead and wrote another thesis but went back to the earlier one as a sort of hobby project when I had time. I have collaborated on a couple of books since then, as was duly expected of me, but that book I did on my own is the only one that got me a small flurry of attention in the outside world (and needless to say some disapproval from colleagues). It is out of print now. It was called *Idiots and Idols*—a title I would never get away with today and which even then made my publishers nervous, though it was admitted to be catchy.

What I was trying to explore was the attitude of people in various cultures—one does not dare say the word "primitive" to describe such cultures—the attitude towards people who are mentally or physically unique. The words "deficient," "handicapped," "retarded" being of course also consigned to the dustbin and probably for good reason—not simply because such words may indicate a superior attitude and habitual unkindness but because they are not truly descriptive. Those words push aside a good deal that is remarkable, even awesome—or at any rate peculiarly powerful—in such people. And what was interesting was to discover a certain amount of veneration as well as persecution, and the ascribing—not entirely inaccurately—of quite a range of abilities, seen as sacred, magical, dangerous, or valuable. I did the best I could with historical as well as contemporary research and took into account poetry and fiction and of course religious custom. Naturally I was criticized in my profession for being too literary and for getting all my information out of books, but I could not run around the world then; I had not been able to get a grant.

Of course I could see a connection, a connection that I thought it just possible Charlene might get to see too. It's strange how distant and unimportant that seemed, only a starting point. As anything in childhood appeared to me then. Because of the journey I had made since, the achievement of adulthood. Safety.

"Maiden name," Charlene had written. That was an expression I had not heard for quite a while. It is next door to "maiden lady," which sounds so chaste and sad. And remarkably inappropriate in my case. Even when I looked at Charlene's wedding picture I was not a virgin—though I don't suppose she was either. Not that I have had a swarm of lovers—or would even want to call most of them lovers. Like most women in my age group who have not lived in monogamous marriage, I know the number. Sixteen. I'm sure that for many younger women that total would have been reached before they were out of their twenties or possibly out of their teens. (When I got Charlene's letter, of course, the total would have been less. I cannot—this is true—I cannot be bothered getting that straight now.) Three of them were important and all three of those in the chronological first half-dozen of the count. What I mean by "important" is that with those three—no, only two, the third meaning a great deal more to me than I to him—with those two, then, the time would come when you want to split open, surrender far more than your body, dump your whole life safely into one basket with his.

I kept myself from doing so, but just barely.

So it seems I was not entirely convinced of that safety.

NOT LONG AGO I got another letter. This was forwarded from the college where I taught before I retired. I found it waiting when

I returned from a trip to Patagonia. (I have become a hardy travel-ler.) It was over a month old.

A typed letter—a fact for which the writer immediately apolo-gized.

"My handwriting is lamentable," he wrote, and went on to introduce himself as the husband of "your old childhood buddy, Charlene." He said that he was sorry, very sorry, to send me bad news. Charlene was in Princess Margaret Hospital in Toronto. Her cancer had begun in the lungs and spread to the liver. She had, regrettably, been a lifelong smoker. She had only a short time left to live. She had not spoken of me very often, but when she did, over the years, it was always with delight in my remark-able accomplishments. He knew how much she valued me and now at the end of her life she seemed very keen to see me. She had asked him to get hold of me. It may be that childhood memories mean the most, he said. Childhood affections. Strength like no other.

Well, she is probably dead by now, I thought.

But if she was—this is how I worked things out—if she was, I would run no risk in going to the hospital and inquiring. Then my conscience or whatever you wanted to call it would be clear. I could write him a note saying that unfortunately I had been away, but had come as soon as I could.

No. Better not a note. He might show up in my life, thanking me. The word "buddy" made me uncomfortable. So in a different way did "remarkable accomplishments."

PRINCESS MARGARET HOSPITAL is only a few blocks away from my apartment building. On a sunny spring day I walked over there. I don't know why I didn't just phone. Perhaps I wanted to think I'd made as much effort as I could.

At the main desk I discovered that Charlene was still alive. When asked if I wanted to see her I could hardly say no.

I went up in the elevator still thinking that I might be able to turn away before I found the nurses' station on her floor. Or that I might make a simple U-turn, taking the next elevator down. The receptionist at the main desk downstairs would never notice my leaving. As a matter of fact she would not have noticed my leaving the moment she had turned her attention to the next person in line, and even if she had noticed, what would it have mattered?

I would have been ashamed, I suppose. Not ashamed at my lack of feeling so much as my lack of fortitude.

I stopped at the nurses' station and was given the number of the room.

It was a private room, quite a small room, with no impressive apparatus or flowers or balloons. At first I could not see Charlene. A nurse was bending over the bed in which there seemed to be a mound of bedclothes but no visible person. The enlarged liver, I thought, and wished I had run while I could.

The nurse straightened up, turned, and smiled at me. She was a plump brown woman who spoke in a soft beguiling voice that might have meant she came from the West Indies.

"You are the Marlin," she said.

Something in the word seemed to delight her.

"She was so wanting for you to come. You can come closer."

I obeyed, and looked down at a bloated body and a sharp ruined face, a chicken's neck for which the hospital gown was a mile too wide. A frizz of hair—still brown—about a quarter of an inch long on her scalp. No sign of Charlene.

I had seen the faces of dying people before. The faces of my mother and father, even the face of the man I had been afraid to love. I was not surprised.

"She is sleeping now," said the nurse. "She was so hoping you would come."

"She's not unconscious?"

"No. But she sleeps."

Yes, I saw it now, there was a sign of Charlene. What was it? Maybe a twitch, that confident playful tucking away of a corner of her mouth.

The nurse was speaking to me in her soft happy voice. "I don't know if she would recognize you," she said. "But she hoped you would come. There is something for you."

"Will she wake up?"

A shrug. "We have to give her injections often for the pain."

She was opening the bedside table.

"Here. This. She told me to give it to you if it was too late for her. She did not want her husband to give it. Now you are here, she would be glad."

A sealed envelope with my name on it, printed in shaky capital letters.

"Not her husband," the nurse said, with a twinkle, then a broadening smile. Did she scent something illicit, a women's secret, an old love?

"Come back tomorrow," she said. "Who knows? I will tell her if it is possible."

I read the note as soon as I got down to the lobby. Charlene had managed to write in an almost normal script, not wildly as in the sprawling letters on the envelope. Of course she might have written the note first and put it in the envelope, then sealed the envelope and put it by, thinking she would get to hand it to me herself. Only later would she see a need to put my name on it.

Marlene. I am writing this in case I get too far gone to speak.
Please do what I ask you. Please go to Guelph and go to
the cathedral and ask for Father Hofstrader. Our Lady of
Perpetual Help Cathedral. It is so big you don't need the name.
Father Hofstrader. He will know what to do. This I cannot ask
C. and do not want him ever to know. Father H. knows and I
have asked him and he says it is possible to help me. Marlene
please do this bless you. Nothing about you.

C. That must be her husband. He doesn't know. Of course he doesn't.

Father Hofstrader.

Nothing about me.

I was free to crumple this up and throw it away once I got out into the street. And so I did, I threw the envelope away and let the wind sweep it into the gutter on University Avenue. Then I realized the note was not in the envelope; it was still in my pocket.

I would never go to the hospital again. And I would never go to Guelph.

Kit was her husband's name. Now I remembered. They went sailing. Christopher. Kit. Christopher. C.

When I got back to my apartment building I found myself taking the elevator down to the garage, not up to my apartment. Dressed just as I was I got into my car and drove out onto the street, and began to head towards the Gardiner Expressway.

The Gardiner Expressway, Highway 427, Highway 401. It was rush hour now, a bad time to get out of the city. I hate this sort of driving, I don't do it often enough to be confident. There was under half a tank of gas, and what was more, I had to go to the bathroom. Around Milton, I thought, I could pull off the highway and fill up on gas and use the toilet and reconsider. At present I could do nothing but what I was doing, heading north, then heading west.

I didn't get off. I passed the Mississauga exit, and the Milton exit. I saw a highway sign telling me how many kilometers to Guelph, and I translated that roughly into miles in my head, as I always have to do, and I figured the gas would hold out. The excuse I made to myself for not stopping was that the sun would be getting lower and more troublesome, now that we were leaving the haze that lies over the city even on the finest day.

At the first stop after I took the Guelph turnoff I got out and walked to the ladies' washroom with stiff trembling legs. Afterwards I filled the tank with gas and asked, when I paid, for directions to the cathedral. The directions were not very clear but I was told that it was on a big hill and I could find it from anywhere in the heart of town.

Of course that was not true, though I could see it from almost anywhere. A collection of delicate spires rising from four fine towers. A beautiful building where I had expected only a grand one. It was grand too, of course, a grand dominating cathedral for such a relatively small city (though someone told me later it was not actually a cathedral).

Could that have been where Charlene was married?

No. Of course not. She had been sent to a United Church camp, and there were no Catholic girls at that camp, though there was quite a variety of Protestants. And then there was the business about C. not knowing.

She might have converted secretly. Since.

I found my way in time to the cathedral parking lot, and sat there wondering what I should do. I was wearing slacks and a jacket. My idea of what was required in a Catholic church—a Catholic cathedral—was so antiquated that I was not even sure if my outfit would be all right. I tried to recall visits to great churches in Europe. Something about the arms being covered? Headscarves, skirts?

What a bright high silence there was up on this hill. April, not a leaf out yet on the trees, but the sun after all was still well up in the sky. There was one low bank of snow gray as the paving in the church lot.

The jacket I had on was too light for evening wear, or maybe it was colder here, the wind stronger, than in Toronto.

The building might well be locked at this time, locked and empty.

The grand front doors appeared to be so. I did not even bother to climb the steps to try them, because I decided to follow a couple of old women—old like me—who had just come up the long flight from the street and who bypassed those steps entirely, heading around to an easier entrance at the side of the building.

There were more people inside, maybe two or three dozen people, but there wasn't a sense that they were gathered for a service. They were scattered here and there in the pews, some kneeling and some chatting. The women ahead of me dipped their hands in a marble font without looking at what they were doing and said hello—hardly lowering their voices—to a man who was setting out baskets on a table.

"It looks a lot warmer out than it is," said one of them, and the man said the wind would bite your nose off.

I recognized the confessionals. Like separate small cottages or large playhouses in a Gothic style, with a lot of dark wooden carving, dark brown curtains. Elsewhere all was glowing, dazzling. The high curved ceiling most celestially blue, the lower curves of the ceiling—those that joined the upright walls—decorated with holy images on gold-painted medallions. Stained-glass windows hit by the sun at this time of day were turned into columns of jewels. I made my way discreetly down one aisle, trying to get a look at the altar, but the chancel being in the western wall was too bright for me to look into. Above the windows, though, I saw that there were painted angels. Flocks of angels, all fresh and gauzy and pure as light.

It was a most insistent place but nobody seemed to be over-whelmed by all the insistence. The chatting ladies kept chatting softly but not in whispers. And other people after some businesslike nodding and crossing knelt down and went about their routines.

As I ought to be going about mine. I looked around for a priest but there was not one in sight. Priests as well as other people must have a working day. They must drive home and go into their living rooms or offices or dens and turn on the television and loosen their collars. Fetch a drink and wonder if they were going to get anything decent for supper. When they did come into the church they would come officially. In their vestments, ready to perform' some ceremony. Mass?

Or to hear confessions. But then you would never know when they were there. Didn't they enter and leave their grilled stalls by a private door?

I would have to ask somebody. The man who had distributed the baskets seemed to be here for reasons that were not purely private, though he was apparently not an usher. Nobody needed an usher. People chose where they wanted to sit—or kneel—and sometimes decided to get up and choose another spot, perhaps being bothered by the glare of the jewel-inflaming sun. When I spoke to him I whispered, out of old habit in a church—and he had to ask me to speak again. Puzzled or embarrassed, he nodded in a wobbly way towards one of the confessionals. I had to become very specific and convincing.

"No, no. I just want to talk to a priest. I've been sent to talk to a priest. A priest called Father Hofstrader."

The basket man disappeared down the more distant side aisle and came back in a little while with a briskly moving stout young priest in ordinary black costume.

He motioned me into a room I had not noticed—not a room, actually, we went through an archway, not a doorway—at the back of the church.

"Give us a chance to talk, in here," he said, and pulled out a chair for me.

"Father Hofstrader—"

"Oh no, I must tell you, I am not Father Hofstrader. Father Hof-strader is not here. He is on vacation."

For a moment I did not know how to proceed.

"I will do my best to help you."

"There is a woman," I said, "a woman who is dying in Princess Margaret Hospital in Toronto—".

"Yes, yes. We know of Princess Margaret Hospital."

"She asks me—I have a note from her here—she wants to see Father Hofstrader."

"Is she a member of this parish?"

"I don't know. I don't know if she is a Catholic or not. She is from here. From Guelph. She is a friend I have not seen for a long time."

"When did you talk with her?"

I had to explain that I hadn't talked with her, she had been asleep, but she had left the note for me.

"But you don't know if she is a Catholic?"

He had a cracked sore at the corner of his mouth. It must have been painful for him to talk.

"I think she is, but her husband isn't and he doesn't know she is. She doesn't want him to know."

I said this in the hope of making things clearer, even though I didn't know for sure if it was true. I had an idea that this priest might shortly lose interest altogether. "Father Hofstrader must have known all this," I said.

"You didn't speak with her?"

I said that she had been under medication but that this was not the case all the time and I was sure she would have periods of lucidity. This too I stressed because I thought it necessary.

"If she wishes to make a confession, you know, there are priests available at Princess Margaret's."

I could not think of what else to say. I got out the note, smoothed the paper, and handed it to him. I saw that the handwriting was not as good as I had thought. It was legible only in comparison with the letters on the envelope.

He made a troubled face.

"Who is this C.?"

"Her husband." I was worried that he might ask for the husband's name, to get in touch with him, but instead he asked for Charlene's. This woman's name, he said.

"Charlene Sullivan." It was a wonder that I even remembered the surname. And I was reassured for a moment, because it was a name that sounded Catholic. Of course that meant that it was the husband who could be Catholic. But the priest might conclude that the husband had lapsed, and that would surely make Charlene's secrecy more understandable, her message more urgent.

"Why does she need Father Hofstrader?"

"I think perhaps it's something special."

"All confessions are special."

He made a move to get up, but I stayed where I was. He sat down again.

"Father Hofstrader is on vacation but he is not out of town. I could phone and ask him about this. If you insist."

"Yes. Please."

"I do not like to bother him. He has not been well."

I said that if he was not well enough to drive himself to Toronto I could drive him.

"We can take care of his transportation if necessary."

He looked around and did not see what he wanted, unclipped a pen from his pocket, and then decided that the blank side of the note would do to write on.

"If you'll just make sure I've got the name. Charlotte—"

"Charlene."

WAS I NOT TEMPTED, during all this palaver? Not once? You'd think that I might break open, be wise to break open, glimpsing that vast though tricky forgiveness. But no. It's not for me. What's done is done. Flocks of angels, tears of blood, notwithstanding.

I SAT IN THE CAR without thinking to turn the motor on, though it was freezing cold by now. I didn't know what to do next. That is, I knew what I could do. Find my way to the highway and join the bright everlasting flow of cars towards Toronto. Or find a place to stay overnight, if I did not think I had the strength to drive. Most places would provide you with a toothbrush, or direct you to a machine where you could get one. I knew what was necessary and possible but it was beyond my strength, for the moment, to do it.

· · ·

THE MOTORBOATS on the lake were supposed to stay a good distance out from the shore. And especially from our camping area, so that the waves they raised would not disturb our swimming. But on that last morning, that Sunday morning, a couple of them started a race and circled close in—not as close as the raft, of course, but close enough to raise waves. The raft was tossed around and Pauline's voice was lifted in a cry of reproach and dismay. The boats made far too much noise for their drivers to hear her, and anyway they had set a big wave rolling towards the shore, causing most of us in the shallows either to jump with it or be tumbled off our feet.

Charlene and I both lost our footing. We had our backs to the raft, because we were watching Verna come towards us. We were standing in water about up to our armpits, and we seemed to be lifted and tossed at the same moment that we heard Pauline's cry. We may have cried out as many others did, first in fear and then in delight as we regained our footing and that wave washed on ahead of us. The waves that followed proved to be not as strong, so that we could hold ourselves against them.

At the moment we tumbled, Verna had pitched towards us. When we came up, with our faces streaming, arms flailing, she was spread out under the surface of the water. There was a tumult of screaming and shouting all around, and this increased as the lesser waves arrived and people who had somehow missed the first attack pretended to be knocked over by the second. Verna's head did not break the surface, though now she was not inert, but turning in a leisurely way, light as a jellyfish in the water. Charlene and I had our hands on her, on her rubber cap.

This could have been an accident. As if we, in trying to get our balance, grabbed on to this nearby large rubbery object, hardly realizing what it was or what we were doing. I have thought it all out. I think we would have been forgiven. Young children. Terrified.

Yes, yes. Hardly knew what they were doing.

Is this in any way true? It is true in the sense that we did not decide anything, in the beginning. We did not look at each other and decide to do what we subsequently and consciously did. Consciously, because our eyes did meet as the head of Verna tried to rise up to the surface of the water. Her head was determined to rise, like a dumpling in a stew. The rest of her was making misguided feeble movements down in the water, but the head knew what it should do.

We might have lost our grip on the rubber head, the rubber cap, were it not for the raised pattern that made it less slippery. I can recall the color perfectly, the pale insipid blue, but I never deciphered the pattern—a fish, a mermaid, a flower—whose ridges pushed into my palms.

Charlene and I kept our eyes on each other, rather than looking down at what our hands were doing. Her eyes were wide and gleeful, as I suppose mine were too. I don't think we felt wicked, triumphing in our wickedness. More as if we were doing just what was—amazingly—demanded of us, as if this was the absolute high point, the culmination, in our lives, of our being ourselves.

We had gone too far to turn back, you might say. We had no choice. But I swear that choice had not occurred, did not occur, to us.

The whole business probably took no more than two minutes. Three? Or a minute and a half?

It seems too much to say that the discouraging clouds cleared up just at that time, but at some point—perhaps at the trespass of the motorboats, or when Pauline screamed, or when the first wave hit, or when the rubber object under our palms ceased to have a will of its own—the sun burst out, and more parents popped up on the beach, and there were calls to all of us to stop horsing around and come out of the water. Swimming was over. Over for the summer, for those who lived out of reach of the lake or municipal swimming pools. Private pools were only in the movie magazines.

As I've said, my memory fails when it comes to parting from Charlene, getting into my parents' car. Because it didn't matter. At that age, things ended. You expected things to end.

I am sure we never said anything as banal, as insulting or unnecessary, as *Don't tell.*

I can imagine the unease starting, but not spreading quite so fast as it might have if there had not been competing dramas. A child has lost a sandal, one of the youngest children is screaming that she got sand in her eye from the waves. Almost certainly a child is throwing up, because of the excitement in the water or the excitement of families arriving or the too-swift consumption of contraband candy.

And soon but not right away the anxiety running through this, that someone is missing.

"Who?"

"One of the Specials."

"Oh drat. Wouldn't you know."

The woman in charge of the Specials running around, still in her flowered bathing suit, with the custard flesh wobbling on her thick arms and legs. Her voice wild and weepy.

Somebody go check in the woods, run up the trail, call her name.

"What is her name?"

"*Verna.*"

"Wait."

"What?"

"Is that not something out there in the water?"

BUT I believe we were gone by then.

Too Much Happiness

~

Many persons who have not studied mathematics
confuse it with arithmetic and consider it a dry
and arid science. Actually, however, this science
requires great fantasy.

—SOPHIA KOVALEVSKY

I

ON THE FIRST DAY OF JANUARY, in the year 1891, a small
woman and a large man are walking in the Old Cemetery, in
Genoa. Both of them are around forty years old. The woman has a
childishly large head, with a thicket of dark curls, and her expression is eager, faintly pleading. Her face has begun to look worn.
The man is immense. He weighs 285 pounds, distributed over a
large frame, and being Russian, he is often referred to as a bear,
also as a Cossack. At present he is crouching over tombstones and
writing in his notebook, collecting inscriptions and puzzling over
abbreviations not immediately clear to him, though he speaks
Russian, French, English, Italian, and has an understanding of
classical and medieval Latin. His knowledge is as expansive as
his physique, and though his speciality is governmental law, he is
capable of lecturing on the growth of contemporary political insti-
tutions in America, the peculiarities of society in Russia and the
West, and the laws and practices of ancient empires. But he is not a
pedant. He is witty and popular, at ease on various levels, and able
to live a most comfortable life, due to his properties near Kharkov.
He has, however, been forbidden to hold an academic post in Russia, because of being a Liberal.

His name suits him. Maksim. Maksim Maksimovich Kovalevsky.

The woman with him is also a Kovalevsky. She was married to a distant cousin of his, but is now a widow.

She speaks to him teasingly.

"You know that one of us will die," she says. "One of us will die this year."

Only half listening, he asks her, Why is that?

"Because we have gone walking in a graveyard on the first day of the New Year."

"Indeed."

"There are still a few things you don't know," she says in her pert but anxious way. "I knew that before I was eight years old."

"Girls spend more time with kitchen maids and boys in the stables—I suppose that is why."

"Boys in the stables do not hear about death?"

"Not so much. Concentration is on other things."

There is snow that day but it is soft. They leave melted, black footprints where they've walked.

SHE MET HIM for the first time in 1888. He had come to Stockholm to advise on the foundation of a school of social sciences. Their shared nationality, going so far as a shared family name, would have thrown them together even if there was no particular attraction. She would have had a responsibility to entertain and generally take care of a fellow Liberal, unwelcome at home.

But that turned out to be no duty at all. They flew at each other as if they had indeed been long-lost relatives. A torrent of jokes and questions followed, an immediate understanding, a rich gabble of Russian, as if the languages of Western Europe had been flimsy formal cages in which they had been too long confined, or paltry substitutes for true human speech. Their behavior, as well, soon overflowed the proprieties of Stockholm. He stayed late at her apartment. She went alone to lunch with him at his hotel. When he hurt his leg in a mishap on the ice, she helped him with the soaking and dressing and, what was more, she told people about it. She was so sure of herself then, and especially sure of him. She wrote a description of him to a friend, borrowing from De Musset.

> *He is very joyful, and at the same*
> *time very gloomy—*
> *Disagreeable neighbor, excellent*
> *comrade—*
> *Extremely light-minded, and yet*
> *very affected—*
> *Indignantly naïve, nevertheless very*
> *blasé—*
> *Terribly sincere, and at the same*
> *time very sly.*

And at the end she wrote, "A real Russian, he is, into the bargain." Fat Maksim, she called him then.

"I have never been so tempted to write romances, as when with Fat Maksim."

And "He takes up too much room, on the divan and in one's mind. It is simply impossible for me, in his presence, to think of anything but him."

This was at the very time when she should have been working day and night, preparing her submission for the Bordin Prize. "I am neglecting not only my Functions but my Elliptic Integrals and my Rigid Body," she joked to her fellow mathematician, Mittag-Leffler, who persuaded Maksim that it was time to go and deliver lectures in Uppsala for a while. She tore herself from thoughts of him, from daydreams, back to the movement of rigid bodies and the solution of the so-called mermaid problem by the use of theta functions with two independent variables. She worked desperately but happily, because he was still in the back of her mind. When he returned she was worn out but triumphant. Two triumphs—her paper ready for its last polishing and anonymous submission; her lover growling but cheerful, eagerly returned from his banishment and giving every indication, as she thought, that he intended to make her the woman of his life.

THE BORDIN PRIZE was what spoiled them. So Sophia believed. She herself was taken in by it at first, dazzled by all the chandeliers and champagne. The compliments quite dizzying, the marvelling and the hand kissing spread thick on top of certain inconvenient but immutable facts. The fact that they would never grant her a job worthy of her gift, that she would be lucky indeed to find herself teaching in a provincial girls' high school. While she was basking Maksim decamped. Never a word about the real reason, of course—just the papers he had to write, his need for the peace and quiet of Beaulieu.

HE HAD FELT HIMSELF IGNORED. A man who was not used to being ignored, who had probably never been in any salon, at any reception, since he was a grown man, where that had been the case. And it wasn't so much the case in Paris either. It wasn't that he was invisible there, in Sophia's limelight, as that he was the usual. A man of solid worth and negotiable reputation, with a certain bulk of frame and intellect, together with a lightness of wit, an adroit masculine charm. While she was an utter novelty, a delightful freak, the woman of mathematical gifts and female timidity, quite charming, yet with a mind most unconventionally furnished, under her curls.

He wrote his cold and sulky apologies from Beaulieu, refusing her offer to visit once her flurry was over. He had a lady staying with him, he said, whom he could not possibly present to her. This lady was in distress and needed his attention at the moment. Sophia should make her way back to Sweden, he said; she should be happy where her friends were waiting for her. Her students would have need of her and so would her little daughter. (A jab there, a suggestion familiar to her, of faulty motherhood?)

And at the end of his letter one terrible sentence.

"If I loved you I would have written differently."

THE END OF EVERYTHING. Back from Paris with her prize and her freaky glittery fame, back to her friends who suddenly meant no more than a snap of her fingers to her. Back to the students who meant something more, but only when she stood before them transformed into her mathematical self, which was oddly still accessible. And back to her supposedly neglected but devastatingly merry little Fufu.

Everything in Stockholm reminded her.

She sat in the same room, with the furniture brought at such foolish expense across the Baltic Sea. The same divan in front of her that had recently, gallantly, supported his bulk. And hers in addition when he skillfully gathered her into his arms. In spite of his size he was never clumsy in lovemaking.

This same red damask, on which distinguished and undistinguished guests had sat in her old lost home. Maybe Fyodor Dostoyevsky had sat there in his lamentable nervous state, dazzled by Sophia's sister Aniuta. And certainly Sophia herself as her mother's unsatisfactory child, displeasing as usual.

The same old cabinet brought also from her home at Palibino, with the portraits of her grandparents set into it, painted on porcelain.

The Shubert grandparents. No comfort there. He in uniform, she in a ball gown, displaying absurd self-satisfaction. They had got what they wanted, Sophia supposed, and had only contempt for those not so conniving or so lucky.

"Did you know I'm part German?" she had said to Maksim.

"Of course. How else could you be such a prodigy of industry? And have your head filled with mythical numbers?"

If I loved you.

Fufu brought her jam on a plate, asked her to play a child's card game.

"Leave me alone. Can't you leave me alone?"

Later she wiped the tears out of her eyes and begged the child's pardon.

BUT SOPHIA WAS, after all, not one to mope forever. She swallowed her pride and gathered her resources, wrote lighthearted letters which by their easy mention of frivolous pleasures—her skating, her horseback riding—and by their attention to Russian and French politics might be enough to put him at his ease, and perhaps even enough to make him feel that his warning had been brutal and unnecessary. She managed to pry out another invitation, and was off to Beaulieu as soon as her lectures were over, in the summer.

Pleasant times. Also misunderstandings, as she called them.

(She changed this, in time, to "conversations.") Chilly spells, breakups, near breakups, sudden geniality. A bumpy trip around Europe, presenting themselves, openly and scandalously, as lovers.

She sometimes wondered whether he had other women. She herself toyed with the idea of marrying a German who paid court to her. But the German was far too punctilious, and she suspected him of wanting a hausfrau. Also, she was not in love with him. Her blood ran cooler and cooler as he spoke the scrupulous German words of love.

Maksim, once he had heard of this honorable courtship, said that she had better marry himself. Provided, he said, that she could be comfortable with what he had to offer. He pretended to be talking about money, when he said this. To be comfortable with his wealth was of course a joke. To be comfortable with a tepid, courteous offering of feeling, ruling out the disappointments and scenes which had mostly originated with her—that was another matter altogether.

She took refuge in teasing, letting him think she believed him not to be in earnest, and no more was decided. But when she was back in Stockholm she thought herself a fool. And so she had written to Julia, before she went south at Christmas, that she did not know whether she was going to happiness or sorrow. She meant that she would declare herself in earnest and find out if he was. She had prepared herself for the most humiliating disappointment.

She had been spared that. Maksim was after all a gentleman and he kept to his word. They would be married in the spring. That decided, they became more comfortable with each other than since the very beginning. Sophia behaved well, with no sulks or outbursts. He expected some decorum, but not the decorum of the hausfrau. He would never object, as a Swedish husband might, to her cigarettes and endless tea drinking and political outbursts. And she was not displeased to see that when his gout bothered him he could be as unreasonable, as irritating and self-pitying, as herself. They were countryfellows, after all. And she was guiltily bored with the reasonable Swedes who had been the only people in Europe willing to hire a female mathematician for their new university. Their city was too clean and tidy, their habits too regular, their parties too polite. Once they decided that some course was correct they just went ahead and followed it, with none of those exhilarating and probably dangerous nights of argument that would go on forever in Petersburg or Paris.

Maksim would not interfere with her real work, which was research, not teaching. He would be glad she had something to absorb her, though she suspected that he found mathematics not trivial, but somehow beside the point. How could a professor of law and sociology think otherwise?

THE WEATHER IS WARMER at Nice, a few days later, when he takes her to board her train.

"How can I go, how can I leave this soft air?"

"Ah, but your desk and your differential equations will be waiting. In the spring you won't be able to tear yourself away."

"Do you think not?"

She must not think—she must not think that is a roundabout way of saying he wished they would not marry in the spring.

She has already written to Julia, saying it is to be happiness after all. Happiness after all. Happiness.

ON THE STATION PLATFORM a black cat obliquely crosses their path. She detests cats, particularly black ones. But she says nothing and contains her shudder. And as if to reward her for this self-control he announces that he will ride with her as far as Cannes, if she is agreeable. She can barely answer, she feels such gratitude. Also a disastrous pressure of tears. Weeping in public is something he finds despicable. (He does not think he should have to put up with it in private either.)

She manages to reabsorb her tears, and when they reach Cannes, he folds her into his capacious well-cut garments with their smell of manliness—some mixture of fur-bearing animals and expensive tobacco. He kisses her with decorum but with a small flick of his tongue along her lips, a reminder of private appetites.

She has not, of course, reminded him that her work was on the Theory of *Partial* Differential Equations, and that it was completed some time ago. She spends the first hour or so of her solitary journey as she usually spends some time after a parting from him—balancing signs of affection against those of impatience, and indifference against a certain qualified passion.

"Always remember that when a man goes out of the room, he leaves everything in it behind," her friend Marie Mendelson has told her. "When a woman goes out she carries everything that happened in the room along with her."

At least she has time now to discover that she has a sore throat. If he has caught it she hopes he won't suspect her. Being a bachelor in robust health he regards any slight contagion as an insult, bad ventilation or tainted breath as personal attacks. In certain ways he is really quite spoiled.

Spoiled and envious, actually. A while ago he wrote to her that certain writings of his own had begun to be attributed to her, because of the accident of the names. He had received a letter from a literary agent in Paris, starting off by addressing him as Dear Madam.

Alas he had forgotten, he said, that she was a novelist as well as a mathematician. What a disappointment for the Parisian that he was neither. Merely a scholar, and a man.

Indeed a great joke.

II

SHE FALLS ASLEEP before the lamps are lit in the train. Her last waking thoughts—unpleasant thoughts—are of Victor Jaclard, her dead sister's husband, whom she plans to see in Paris. It is really her young nephew, Urey, her sister's child, that she is anxious to see, but the boy lives with his father. She always sees Urey in her mind as he was at about the age of five or six, angelically blond, trusting and sweet natured, but not in temperament so much like his mother, Aniuta.

She finds herself in a confused dream of Aniuta, but of an Aniuta long before Urey and Jaclard were on the scene. Aniuta unmarried, golden haired, beautiful, and bad tempered, back at the family estate of Palibino, where she is decorating her tower room with Orthodox icons and complaining that these are not the proper religious artifacts for medieval Europe. She has been reading a novel by Bulwer-Lytton and has draped herself in veils, the better to impersonate Edith Swan-neck, the mistress of Harold of Hastings. She plans to write her own novel about Edith, and has already written a few pages describing the scene where the heroine must identify her butchered lover's body by certain marks known only to herself.

Having somehow arrived on this train she reads these pages to Sophia who cannot bring herself to explain to her how things have changed and what has come about since those days in the tower room.

When she wakes Sophia thinks how all that was true—Aniuta's obsession with medieval and particularly English history—and how one day that vanished, veils and all, as if none of it had ever been, and instead a serious and contemporary Aniuta was writing about a young girl who at her parents' urging and for conventional reasons rejects a young scholar who dies. After his death she realizes that she loves him, so has no choice but to follow him in death.

She secretly submitted this story to a magazine edited by Fyodor Dostoyevsky, and it was printed.

Her father was outraged.

"Now you sell your stories, how soon before you will sell yourself?"

In this turmoil Fyodor himself appeared on the scene, behaving badly at a party but mollifying Aniuta's mother by a private call, and ending up by proposing marriage. Her father's being so decidedly against this did almost persuade Aniuta to accept, to elope. But she had after all a fondness for her own limelight, and perhaps a premonition of how that might have to be sacrificed, with Fyodor, so she refused him. He put her into his novel *The Idiot* as Aglia, and married a young stenographer.

Sophia dozes again, slips into another dream in which she and Aniuta are both young but not so young as when at Palibino, and they are together in Paris, and Aniuta's lover Jaclard—not yet her husband—has supplanted Harold of Hastings and Fyodor the novelist as her hero, and Jaclard is a genuine hero, though bad mannered (he glories in his peasant background) and, from the first, unfaithful. He is fighting somewhere outside of Paris, and Aniuta is afraid he will be killed, because he is so brave. Now in Sophia's dream Aniuta has gone looking for him, but the streets where she wanders weeping and calling his name are in Petersburg, not Paris, and Sophia is left behind in a huge Parisian hospital full of dead soldiers and bloodied citizens, and one of the dead is her own husband, Vladimir. She runs away from all these casualties, she is looking for Maksim, who is safe from the fighting in the Hotel Splendide. Maksim will get her out of this.

She wakes. It's raining outside and dark, and she is not alone in the compartment. An untidy-looking young woman sits next to the door, holding a drawing portfolio. Sophia is afraid she might have cried out in her dream, but she probably didn't, because the girl is sleeping undisturbed.

Suppose this girl had been awake and Sophia had said to her, "Forgive me, I was dreaming of 1871. I was there, in Paris, my sister was in love with a Communard. He was captured and he might have been shot or sent to New Caledonia but we were able to get him away. My husband did it. My husband Vladimir who was not a Communard at all but only wanted to look at the fossils in the Jardin des Plantes."

The girl would have been bored. She might have been polite but would still have conveyed the feeling that all this, in her opinion, might have happened before the banishment of Adam and Eve. She was probably not even French. French girls who could afford to travel second class did not usually travel alone. American?

It was strangely true that Vladimir had been able to spend some of those days in the Jardin des Plantes. And untrue that he had been killed. In the midst of the turmoil he was laying the foundations of his only real career, as a paleontologist. And true too that Aniuta took Sophia along to a hospital from which all the professional nurses had been fired. They were considered counterrevolutionary, and were to be replaced by the wives and comrades from the Commune. The common women cursed the replacements because they did not even know how to make bandages, and the wounded died, but most of them might have died anyway. There was disease as well as the wounds of battle to be dealt with. The common people were said to be eating dogs and rats.

Jaclard and his revolutionaries fought for ten weeks. After the defeat he was imprisoned at Versailles, in an underground cell. Several men had been shot because they were mistaken for him. Or so it was reported.

By that time Aniuta and Sophia's father, the General, had arrived from Russia. Aniuta had been taken off to Heidelberg, where she collapsed in bed. Sophia went back to Berlin and her study of mathematics, but Vladimir remained, abandoning his tertiary mammifers to connive with the General to get Jaclard free. This was managed by bribery and daring. Jaclard was to be transferred under guard of one soldier to a jail in Paris, and taken along a certain street where there would be a crowd of people, because of an exhibition. Vladimir would snatch him away while the guard looked aside, as he was being paid to do. And still under Vladimir's guidance Jaclard would be hustled through the crowd to a room where a civilian suit of clothes was waiting, then taken to the railway station and supplied with Vladimir's own passport, so that he could escape to Switzerland.

All this was accomplished.

Jaclard did not bother to mail back the passport until Aniuta joined him, and then she returned it. No money was ever repaid.

SOPHIA SENT NOTES from her hotel in Paris to Marie Mendelson and Jules Poincaré. Marie's maid responded that her mistress was in Poland. Sophia sent a further note to say that she might ask her friend's assistance, come spring, in "selecting whatever costume would suit that event which the world might consider the most important in a woman's life." In brackets she added that she herself and the fashionable world were "still on fairly confused terms."

Poincaré arrived at an exceptionally early hour of the morning, complaining at once about the behavior of the mathematician Weierstrass, Sophia's old mentor, who had been one of the judges for the king of Sweden's recent mathematical prize. Poincaré had indeed been awarded the prize, but Weierstrass had seen fit to announce that there were possible errors in his—Poincaré's—work which he, Weierstrass, had not been given time to investigate. He had sent a letter submitting his annotated queries to the king of Sweden—as if such a personage would know what he was talking about. And he had made some statement about Poincaré being valued in future more for the negative than the positive aspects of his work.

Sophia soothed him, telling him she was on her way to see Weierstrass and would take the matter up with him. She pretended not to have heard anything about it, though she had actually written a teasing letter to her old teacher.

"I am sure the king has had much of his royal sleep disturbed since your information arrived. Just think of how you have upset the royal mind hitherto so happily ignorant of mathematics. Take care you don't make him repent of his generosity . . ."

"And after all," she said to Jules, "after all you do have the prize and will have it forever."

Jules agreed, adding that his own name would shine when Weierstrass would be forgotten.

Every one of us will be forgotten, Sophia thought but did not say, because of the tender sensibilities of men—particularly of a young man—on this point.

She said good-bye to him at noon and went to see Jaclard and Urey. They lived in a poor part of the city. She had to cross a courtyard where laundry was hung—the rain had stopped but the day was still dark—and mount a long, somewhat slippery outdoor staircase. Jaclard called out that the door was unbolted, and she entered to find him sitting on an overturned box, blacking a pair of boots. He did not stand up to greet her, and when she started to remove her cloak he said, "Better not. The stove isn't lit till evening." He motioned her to the only armchair, which was tattered and greasy. This was worse than she had expected. Urey was not here, had not waited to see her.

There were two things she had wanted to find out about Urey. Was he getting more like Aniuta and the Russian side of his family? And was he getting any taller? At fifteen, last year in Odessa, he had not looked more than twelve.

Soon she discovered that things had taken a turn that made such concerns less important.

"Urey?" she said.

"He's out."

"He's at school?"

"He may be. I know little about him. And the more I do know the less I care."

She thought to soothe him and take up the matter later. She inquired about his—Jaclard's—health, and he said his lungs were bad. He said he had never got over the winter of '71, the starvation and the nights in the open. Sophia did not remember that the fighters had starved—it was their duty to eat, so that they could fight—but she said agreeably that she had just been thinking about those times, on the train. She had been thinking, she said, about Vladimir and the rescue that was like something out of a comic opera.

It was no comedy, he said, and no opera. But he grew animated, talking about it. He spoke of the men shot because they were taken for him, and of the desperate fighting between the twentieth and the thirtieth of May. When he was captured at last, the time of summary executions was over, but he still expected to die after their farcical trial. How he had managed to escape God only knew. Not that he believed in God, he added, as he did every time.

Every time. And every time he told the story, Vladimir's part—and the General's money's part—grew smaller. No mention of the passport either. It was Jaclard's own bravery, his own agility, that counted. But he did seem to be better disposed to his audience, as he talked.

His name was still remembered. His story still was told.

And more stories followed, also familiar. He rose and fetched a strongbox from under the bed. Here was the precious paper, the paper that had ordered him out of Russia, when he was in Petersburg with Aniuta some time after the days of the Commune. He must read it all.

"Gracious sir, Konstantin Petrovich, I hasten to bring to your attention that the Frenchman Jaclard, a member of the former Commune, when living in Paris was in constant contact with representatives of the Polish Revolutionary Proletariat Party, the Jew Karl Mendelson, and thanks to the Russian connection through his wife was involved in the transfer of Mendelson's letters to Warsaw. He is a friend of many outstanding French radicals. From Petersburg Jaclard sent most false and harmful news into Paris about Russian political affairs and after the first of March and the attempt against the czar this information passed all bounds of patience. That is why at my insistence the minister decided to send him beyond the borders of our empire."

Delight had come back to him as he read, and Sophia remembered how he used to tease and caper, and how she, and even Vladimir, felt somehow honored to be noticed by him, even if it was only as an audience.

"Ah, too bad," he said. "Too bad the information is not complete. He never mentions that I was chosen by the Marxists of the International in Lyon to represent them in Paris."

At this moment Urey came in. His father went on talking.

"That was secret, of course. Officially they put me on the Lyon Committee for Public Safety." He was walking back and forth now, in joyful rampaging earnest. "It was in Lyon that we heard that Napoleon le Neveu had been captured. Painted like a whore."

Urey nodded to his aunt, removed his jacket—evidently he did not feel the cold—and sat down on the box to take up his father's task with the boots.

Yes. He did look like Aniuta. But it was the Aniuta of later days to whom he bore a resemblance. The tired sullen droop to the eyelids, the skeptical—in him scornful—curl to the full lips. There was not a sign of the golden-haired girl with her hunger for danger, for righteous glory, her bursts of wild invective. Of that creature Urey would have no memory, only of a sick woman, shapeless, asthmatic, cancerous, declaring herself eager for death.

Jaclard had loved her at first, perhaps, as much as he could love anybody. He noted her love for him. In his naïve or perhaps simply braggartly letter to her father, explaining his decision to marry her, he had written that it seemed unfair to desert a woman who had so much attachment to himself. He had never given up other women, not even at the beginning of the liaison when Aniuta was delirious with her discovery of him. And certainly not throughout the marriage. Sophia supposed that he might still be attractive to women, though his beard was untidy and gray and when he talked he sometimes got so excited that his words came in a splutter. A hero worn out by his struggle, one who had sacrificed his youth—that was how he might present himself, not without effect. And it was true, in a way. He was physically brave, he had ideals, he was born a peasant and knew what it was to be despised.

And she too, just now, had been despising him.

The room was shabby, but when you looked at it closely you saw that it had been cleaned as well as possible. A few cooking pots hung from nails on the wall. The cold stove had been polished, and so had the bottoms of those pots. It occurred to her that there might be a woman with him, even now.

He was talking about Clemenceau, saying they were on good terms. He was ready now to brag about a friendship with a man she would have expected him to accuse of being in the pay of the British Foreign Office (though she herself believed this false).

She deflected him by praising the apartment's tidiness.

He looked around, surprised at the change of subject, then slowly smiled, and with a new vindictiveness.

"There is a person I am married to, she takes care of my welfare. A French lady, I am glad to say, she is not so garrulous and lazy as the Russians. She is educated, she was a governess but was dismissed for her political sympathies. I am afraid I cannot introduce you to her. She is poor but decent and she still values her reputation."

"Ah," said Sophia, rising. "I meant to tell you that I too am marrying again. A Russian gentleman."

"I had heard that you went about with Maksim Maksimovich. I did not hear anything about a marriage."

Sophia was trembling from sitting so long in the cold. She spoke to Urey, as cheerfully as she could.

"Will you walk with your old aunt to the station? I have not had a chance to talk to you."

"I hope I have not offended you," said Jaclard quite poisonously. "I always believe in speaking the truth."

"Not at all."

Urey put on his jacket, which she now saw was too big for him. It had probably been bought in a rag market. He had grown, but he was no taller than Sophia herself. He might not have had the right food at an important time in his life. His mother had been tall, and Jaclard was tall still.

Though he had not seemed eager to accompany her, Urey began

to talk before they had reached the bottom of the stairs. And he had picked up her bag immediately, without being asked.

"He is too stingy to even light a fire for you. There is firewood in the box, she brought some up this morning. She is as ugly as a sewer rat, that's why he didn't want you to meet her."

"You shouldn't talk that way about women."

"Why not, if they want to be equal?"

"I suppose I should say 'about people.' But I don't want to talk about her or your father. I want to talk about you. How are you doing with your studies?"

"I hate them."

"You cannot hate all of them."

"Why can't I? It isn't at all difficult to hate all of them."

"Can you speak Russian to me?"

"It's a barbaric language. Why can't you speak better French? He says your accent is barbaric. He says my mother's accent was barbaric too. Russians are barbaric."

"Does he say that too?"

"I make up my own mind."

They walked for a time in silence.

"It's a bit dreary in Paris this time of year," Sophia said. "Do you remember what a good time we had that summer at Sèvres? We talked about all kinds of things. Fufu remembers you still and talks about you. She remembers how much you wanted to come and live with us."

"That was childish. I didn't think realistically at that time."

"So have you now? Have you thought of a lifework for yourself?"

"Yes."

Because of a taunting satisfaction in his voice she did not ask what this might be. He told her anyway.

"I'm going to be an omnibus boy and call out the stations. I got a job doing that when I ran away at Christmastime, but he came and got me back. When I am one year older he won't be able to do that."

"Perhaps you would not always be happy calling out the stations."

"Why not? It's very useful. It's always necessary. Being a mathematician isn't necessary, as I see it."

She kept silent.

"I could not respect myself," he said. "Being a professor of mathematics."

They were climbing to the station platform.

"Just getting prizes and a lot of money for things nobody understands or cares about and that are no use to anybody."

"Thank you for carrying my bag."

She handed him some money, though not so much as she had intended. He took it with an unpleasant grin, as if to say, You thought I'd be too proud, didn't you? Then he thanked her, hurriedly, as if this was against his will.

She watched him go and thought it was quite likely she would never see him again. Aniuta's child. And how like Aniuta he was, after all. Aniuta disrupting almost every family meal at Palibino with her lofty tirades. Aniuta pacing the garden paths, full of scorn for her present life and faith in her destiny which would take her into some entirely new and just and ruthless world.

Urey might change his course; there was no telling. He might even come to have some fondness for his aunt Sophia, though probably not till he was as old as she was now, and she long dead.

III

SOPHIA WAS HALF AN HOUR EARLY for her train. She wanted some tea, and lozenges for her throat, but she could not face the waiting in line or the speaking French. No matter how well you can manage when you are in good health, it does not take much of a droop of spirits or a premonition of sickness to send you back to the shelter of your nursery language. She sat on a bench and let her head drop. She could sleep for a moment.

More than a moment. Fifteen minutes had passed by the station clock. There was a crowd gathered now, a great deal of bustle around her, baggage carts on the move.

As she hurried towards her train she saw a man wearing a fur hat like Maksim's. A big man, in a dark overcoat. She could not see his face. He was moving away from her. But his wide shoulders, his courteous but determined manner of making way for himself, strongly reminded her of Maksim.

A cart piled high with freight passed between them, and the man was gone.

Of course it could not be Maksim. What could he be doing in Paris? What train or appointment could he be hurrying towards? Her heart had begun to beat unpleasantly as she climbed aboard her train and found her seat by a window. It stood to reason that there should have been other women in Maksim's life. There had been, for instance, the woman he could not introduce Sophia to, when he refused to invite her to Beaulieu. But she believed that he was not a man for tawdry complications. Much less for jealous fits, for female tears and scoldings. He had pointed out on that earlier occasion that she had no rights, no hold on him.

Which surely meant that he would consider she had some hold now, and would have felt it beneath his dignity to deceive her.

And when she thought she saw him she had just wakened out of an unnatural unhealthy sleep. She had been hallucinating.

The train got itself together with the usual groans and clatter and slowly passed beyond the station roof.

How she used to love Paris. Not the Paris of the Commune where she had been under Aniuta's excited and sometimes incomprehensible orders, but the Paris she had visited later, in the fullness of her adult life, with introductions to mathematicians and political thinkers. In Paris, she had proclaimed, there is no such thing as boredom or snobbishness or deception.

THEN THEY HAD GIVEN HER the Bordin Prize, they had kissed her hand and presented her with speeches and flowers in the most elegant lavishly lit rooms. But they had closed their doors when it came to giving her a job. They would no more think of that than of employing a learned chimpanzee. The wives of the great scientists preferred not to meet her, or invite her into their homes.

Wives were the watchers on the barricade, the invisible implacable army. Husbands shrugged sadly at their prohibitions but gave them their due. Men whose brains were blowing old notions apart were still in thrall to women whose heads were full of nothing but the necessity of tight corsets, calling cards, and conversations that filled your throat with a kind of perfumed fog.

She must stop this litany of resentment. The wives of Stockholm invited her into their houses, to the most important parties and intimate dinners. They praised her and showed her off. They welcomed her child. She might have been an oddity there, but she was an oddity that they approved of. Something like a multilingual parrot or those prodigies who could tell you without hesitation or apparent reflection that a certain date in the fourteenth century fell on a Tuesday.

No, that was not fair. They had respect for what she did, and many of them believed that more women should do such things and someday they would. So why was she a little bored by them, longing for late nights and extravagant talk. Why did it bother her that they dressed either like parsons' wives or like Gypsies?

She was in a shocking mood, and that was on account of Jaclard and Urey and the respectable woman she could not be introduced to. And her sore throat and slight shivers, surely a full-fledged cold coming on her.

At any rate she would soon be a wife herself, and the wife of a rich and clever and accomplished man into the bargain.

THE TEA WAGON HAS COME. That will help her throat, though she wishes it was Russian tea. Rain started soon after they left Paris, and now that rain has turned to snow. She prefers snow to rain, white fields to land dark and sodden, as every Russian does. And where there is snow most people recognize the fact of winter and take more than halfhearted measures to keep their houses warm. She thinks of the Weierstrass house, where she will sleep tonight. The professor and his sisters would not hear of a hotel.

Their house is always comfortable, with its dark rugs and heavy fringed curtains and deep armchairs. Life there follows a ritual—it is dedicated to study, particularly to the study of mathematics. Shy, generally ill-dressed male students pass through the sitting room to the study, one after the other. The professor's two unmarried sisters greet them kindly as they pass, but scarcely expect a reply. They are busy with their knitting or their mending or rug hooking. They know that their brother has a wonderful brain, that he is a great man, but they know also that he must have a dose of prunes every day, because of his sedentary occupation, that he cannot wear even the finest wool next to his skin, because it gives him a rash, that his feelings are hurt when a colleague has failed to give credit to him in a published article (though he pretends to take no notice, both in conversation and in his writing, praising punctiliously the very person who has slighted him).

Those sisters—Clara and Elisa—had been startled the first day Sophia entered their sitting room on her way to the study. The servant who admitted her had not been trained to be selective, because those in the house lived such a retired life, also because the students who came were often shabby and unmannerly, so that the standards of most respectable houses did not apply. Even so, there had been some hesitation in the maid's voice before she admitted this small woman whose face was mostly hidden by a dark bonnet and who moved in a frightened way, like a shy mendicant. The sisters could get no idea of her real age but concluded—after she was admitted to the study—that she might be some student's mother, come to haggle or beg about the fees.

"My goodness," said Clara, whose speculations were the more lively, "my goodness, we thought, what have we here, is it a Charlotte Corday?"

This was all told to Sophia later, when she had become their friend. And Elisa added drily, "Fortunately our brother was not in his bath. And we could not get up to protect him because we were all wrapped up in those endless mufflers."

They had been knitting mufflers for the soldiers at the front. It was 1870, before Sophia and Vladimir took what they meant to be their study trip to Paris. So deep they were then in other dimensions, past centuries, so scant their attention to the world they lived in, that they had scarcely heard of a contemporary war.

Weierstrass had no more idea than his sisters of Sophia's age or mission. He told her afterwards that he had thought her some misguided governess who wanted to use his name, claiming mathematics among her credentials. He was thinking he must scold the maid, and his sisters, for letting her break in on him. But he was a courteous and kindly man, so instead of sending her away at once, he explained that he took only advanced students, with recognized degrees, and that he had at the moment as many of those as he could handle. Then, as she remained standing—and trembling—in front of him, with that ridiculous hat shading her face and her hands clutching her shawl, he remembered the method, or trick, he had used once or twice before, to discourage an inadequate student.

"What I am able to do in your case," he said, "is to set you a series of problems, and ask you to solve them and bring them back to me one week from today. If they are done to my satisfaction, we will talk again."

A week from that day he had forgotten all about her. He had expected, of course, never to see her again. When she came into his study he did not recognize her, perhaps because she had cast off the cloak that had disguised her slender figure. She must have felt bolder, or perhaps the weather had changed. He had not remembered the hat—his sisters had—but he had not much of an eye for female accessories. But when she pulled the papers out of her bag and set them down on his desk, he remembered, and sighed, and put on his spectacles.

Great was his surprise—he told her this too at a later time—to see that every one of the problems had been solved, and sometimes in an entirely original way. But he suspected her still, thinking now that she must be presenting the work of someone else, perhaps a brother or lover who was in hiding for political reasons.

"Sit down," he said. "And now explain to me each of these solutions, every step taken."

She began to talk, leaning forward, and the floppy hat fell over her eyes, so she pulled it off and let it lie on the floor. Her curls were revealed, her bright eyes, her youth, and her shivering excitement.

"Yes," he said. "Yes. Yes. Yes." He spoke with ponderous consideration, hiding as well as he could his astonishment, especially at the solutions whose method diverged most brilliantly from his own.

She was a shock to him in many ways. She was so slight and young and eager. He felt that he must soothe her, hold her carefully, letting her learn how to manage the fireworks in her own brain.

All his life—he had difficulty saying this, as he admitted, being always wary of too much enthusiasm—all his life he had been waiting for such a student to come into this room. A student who would challenge him completely, who was not only capable of following the strivings of his own mind but perhaps of flying beyond them. He had to be careful about saying what he really believed—that there must be something like intuition in a first-rate mathematician's mind, some lightning flare to uncover what has been there all along. Rigorous, meticulous, one must be, but so must the great poet.

When he finally brought himself to say all this to Sophia, he also said that there were those who would bridle at the very word, "poet," in connection with mathematical science. And others, he said, who would leap at the notion all too readily, to defend a muddle and laxity in their own thinking.

AS SHE HAD EXPECTED, there was deeper and deeper snow outside the train windows as they travelled east. This was a second-class train, quite spartan in comparison with the train she had taken from Cannes. There was no dining car, but cold buns—some filled with various spicy sausages—were available from the tea wagon. She bought a cheese-filled bun half the size of a boot and thought she would never finish it, but in time she did. Then she got out her little volume of Heine, to assist in bringing the German language to the surface of her mind.

Every time she lifted her eyes to the window it seemed that the snow fell more thickly, and sometimes the train slowed, almost stopping. They would be lucky at this rate to reach Berlin by midnight. She wished that she had not let herself be talked out of going to a hotel, instead of to the house on Potsdam Street.

"It will do poor Karl so much good just to have you for one night under the same roof. He still thinks of you as the little girl on our doorstep, even though he gives great credit to your achievements and takes pride in your great success."

IT WAS IN FACT after midnight when she rang the bell. Clara came, in her wrapper, having sent the servant to bed. Her brother—she said this in a half whisper—had been wakened by the noise of the cab and Elisa had gone to settle him down and to assure him that he would see Sophia in the morning.

The word "settle" sounded ominous to Sophia. The sisters' letters had mentioned nothing but a certain fatigue. And Weierstrass's own letters had held no personal news, being full of Poincaré and his—Weierstrass's—duty to mathematics in making matters clear to the king of Sweden.

Now hearing the old woman's voice take that little pious or fearful drop as she mentioned her brother, now smelling the once-familiar and reassuring but tonight faintly stale and dreary odors of that house, Sophia felt that teasing was not perhaps so much in order as it used to be, that she herself had brought not only the cold fresh air, but some bustle of success, an edge of energy, of which she had been quite unaware, and which might be a little daunting and disturbing. She who used to be welcomed with hugs and robust pleasure (one of the surprises about the sisters was how jolly they could be yet how conventional) was still hugged, but with tears standing in faded eyes, with old arms trembling.

But there was warm water in the jug in her room, there was bread and butter on her night table.

As she undressed she could hear faintly agitated whispering out in the upper hall. It might have been about their brother's state or about herself or about the absence of a cover on the bread and butter, which maybe had not been noticed until Clara ushered her into her room.

WHEN SHE WORKED with Weierstrass, Sophia had lived in a small dark apartment, most of the time with her friend Julia, who was studying chemistry. They did not go to concerts or plays—they had limited funds and were absorbed by their work. Julia did go out to a private laboratory where she had obtained privileges hard for a woman to get. Sophia spent day after day at her writing table, not rising from her chair sometimes till the lamp had to be lit. Then she would stretch and walk, quickly, quickly, from one end of the apartment to the other—a short enough distance—sometimes breaking into a run and talking aloud, bursting into nonsense, so that anybody who did not know her as well as Julia did would wonder if she was sane.

Weierstrass's thoughts, and now hers, were concerned with elliptic and Abelian functions, and the theory of analytic functions based on their representation as an infinite series. The theory named for him contended that every bounded infinite sequence of real numbers has a convergent subsequence. In this she followed him and later challenged him and even for a time jumped ahead of him, so that they progressed from being teacher and pupil to being fellow mathematicians, she being often the catalyst to his investigations. But this relationship took time to develop, and at the Sunday suppers—to which she was invited readily because he had given up his Sunday afternoons to her—she was like a young relation, an eager protégée.

When Julia came she was invited as well, and the two girls were fed roast meat and creamed potatoes and light delectable puddings that upset all the ideas that they had about German cooking. After the meal they sat by the fire and heard Elisa read aloud. She read with great spirit and expression from the stories of the Swiss writer Conrad Ferdinand Meyer. Literature was the weekly treat, after all the knitting and mending.

At Christmas there was a tree for Sophia and Julia, though the Weierstrasses themselves had not bothered about one for years. There were bonbons wrapped in glittery paper, and fruitcake and roast apples. As they said, for the children.

But there came before long a disturbing surprise.

THE SURPRISE WAS that Sophia, who seemed the very image of a shy and inexperienced young girl, should have a husband. In the first few weeks of her lessons, before Julia arrived, she had been picked up at their door, on Sunday nights, by a young man who was not introduced to the Weierstrass family and was taken to be a servant. He was tall and unattractive, with a thin red beard, a large nose, untidy clothes. In fact, if the Weierstrasses had been more worldly, they would have realized that no self-respecting noble family—which they knew Sophia's to be—would have such an unkempt servant, and that therefore he must be a friend.

Then Julia came, and the young man disappeared.

It was some time later that Sophia released the information that he was named Vladimir Kovalevsky and that she was married to him. He was studying in Vienna and Paris though he already had a law degree and had been trying to make his way in Russia as a publisher of textbooks. He was several years older than Sophia.

Almost as surprising as this news was the fact that Sophia gave it out to Weierstrass and not to the sisters. In the household they were the ones who had some dealings with life—if only in the lives of their servants and the reading of fairly up-to-date fiction. But Sophia had not been a favorite with her mother or her governess. Her negotiations with the General had not always been successful but she respected him and thought that perhaps he respected her. So it was to the man of the house that she turned with an important confidence.

She realized that Weierstrass must have been embarrassed—not when she was talking to him but when he had to tell his sisters. For there was more to it than the fact that Sophia was married. She was well and legally married, but it was a White Marriage—a thing he had never heard of, nor the sisters either. Husband and wife not only did not live in the same place, they did not live together at all. They did not marry for the universally accepted reasons but were bound by their secret vow never to live in that way, never to—

"Consummate?" Perhaps it would be Clara who said this. Briskly, even impatiently, to get the moment over with.

Yes. And young people—young women—who wanted to study abroad were compelled to go through with this deception because no Russian woman who was unmarried could leave the country without her parents' consent. Julia's parents were enlightened enough to let her go, but not Sophia's.

What a barbarous law.

Yes. Russian. But some young women found their way around this with the help of young men who were very idealistic and sympathetic. Perhaps they were anarchists as well. Who knows?

It was Sophia's older sister who had located one of these young men, and she and a friend of hers set up a meeting with him. Their reasons were perhaps political, rather than intellectual. God knows why they took Sophia along—she had no passion for politics and did not think herself ready for any such venture. But the young man looked over the two older girls—the sister named Aniuta however businesslike could not disguise her beauty—and he said no. No, I do not wish to go through with this contract with either of you estimable young ladies, but I would agree to do so with your younger sister.

"Possibly he thought the older ones would be troublesome"—it

might be Elisa who said this, with her experience of novels—
"particularly the beauty. He fell in love with our little Sophia."

Love is not supposed to enter into it, Clara may have reminded
her.

Sophia accepts the proposal. Vladimir calls upon the General, to ask the hand of his younger daughter in marriage. The
General is polite, aware the young man comes from a good family, though he has not so far made much of a mark in the world.
But Sophia is too young, he says. Does she even know of these
intentions?

Yes, said Sophia, and she was in love with him.

The General said that they could not act on their feelings immediately but must spend some time, some very considerable time,
getting to know each other at Palibino. (They were at present in
Petersburg.)

Things were at a standstill. Vladimir would never make a good
impression. He did not try hard enough to disguise his radical
views and he dressed badly, as if on purpose. The General was confident that the more Sophia saw of this suitor, the less she would
want to marry him.

Sophia, however, was making plans of her own.

There came a day on which her parents were giving an important dinner party. They had invited a diplomat, professors, military
comrades of the General's from the School of Artillery. Amidst all
the bustle Sophia was able to slip away.

She went out alone into the streets of Petersburg, where she had
never walked before without a servant or a sister. She went to Vladimir's lodgings in a part of the city where poor students lived. The
door was opened to her at once, and as soon as she was inside she
sat down and wrote a letter to her father.

"My dear father, I have gone to Vladimir and will remain here. I
beg you that you will no longer oppose our marriage."

All were seated at the table before Sophia's absence was noticed.
A servant found her room empty. Aniuta was asked about her sister
and flushed as she answered that she knew nothing. To hide her
face she dropped her napkin.

The General was handed a note. He excused himself and left
the room. Sophia and Vladimir were soon to hear his angry foot-

steps outside their door. He told his compromised daughter and the man for whom she was willing to forfeit her reputation to come with him at once. They rode home, all three without a word, and at the dinner table he said, "Allow me to introduce to you my future son-in-law, Vladimir Kovalevsky."

So it was done. Sophia was overjoyed, not indeed to be marrying Vladimir but to be pleasing Aniuta by striking a blow for the emancipation of Russian women. There was a conventional and splendid wedding in Palibino, and the bride and groom went off to live under one roof in Petersburg.

And once their way was clear they went abroad and did not continue to live under one roof anymore. Heidelberg, then Berlin for Sophia, Munich for Vladimir. He visited Heidelberg when he could, but after Aniuta and her friend Zhanna arrived there, and Julia—all four women theoretically under his protection—there was not enough room for him any longer.

Weierstrass did not reveal to the women that he had been in correspondence with the General's wife. He had written to her when Sophia returned from Switzerland (really from Paris) looking so worn and frail that he was concerned for her health. The mother had replied, informing him that it was Paris, in these most dangerous times, that was responsible for her daughter's state. But she seemed less upset by the political upheaval her daughters had lived through than by the revelations that one of them, while unmarried, lived openly with a man, and the other, properly wed, did not truly live with her husband at all. So he was made rather against his will to be the mother's confidant even before he was the daughter's. And indeed he told Sophia nothing about this until her mother was dead.

But when he did tell her at last, he told her also that Clara and Elisa had asked immediately what was to be done.

This seemed to be the way of women, he had said, to assume that something should be done.

He had replied, quite severely, "Nothing."

IN THE MORNING Sophia took a clean though crumpled frock out of her bag—she had never learned how to pack tidily—fixed her curly hair as well as she could to hide some little patches of gray, and came downstairs to the sounds of a household already astir. Her place was the only one still set in the dining room. Elisa brought in the coffee and the first German breakfast that Sophia had ever eaten in this house—cold sliced meat and cheese and thickly buttered bread. She said that Clara was upstairs preparing their brother for his meeting with Sophia.

"At first we had the barber come in," she said. "But then Clara learned to do it quite well. She turned out to be the one who has the skills of a nurse, it is fortunate one of us has them."

Even before she said this Sophia had sensed that they were short of money. The damask and net curtains had a dingy look, the silver knife and fork she used had not recently been polished. Through the open door to the sitting room a rough-looking young girl, their present servant, was visible cleaning out the grate and raising clouds of dust. Elisa looked her way, as if to ask her to shut the door, then got up and did it herself. She came back to the table with a flushed, downcast face, and Sophia asked hastily, if rather impolitely, what was the illness of Herr Weierstrass?

"It is a weakness of his heart for one thing, and the pneumonia he had in the autumn that he cannot seem to get over. Also he has a growth in the generative organs," said Elisa, lowering her voice but speaking frankly as German women did.

Clara appeared in the doorway.

"He is waiting for you now."

Sophia climbed the stairs thinking not of the professor but of these two women who had made him the center of their lives. Knitting mufflers, mending the linen, making the puddings and preserves that could never be trusted to a servant. Honoring the Roman Catholic Church as their brother did—a cold undiverting religion in Sophia's opinion—and all without a moment of mutiny as far as you could see, or any flicker of dissatisfaction.

I would go mad, she thought.

Even to be a professor, she thought, I would go mad. Students have mediocre minds, generally speaking. Only the most obvious, regular patterns can be impressed on them.

She would not have dared admit this to herself before she had Maksim.

She entered the bedroom smiling at her luck, her coming freedom, her soon-to-be husband.

"Ah, here you are at last," said Weierstrass, speaking somewhat weakly and laboriously. "The naughty child, we thought she had deserted us. Are you on your way to Paris again, off to amuse yourself?"

"I am on my way back from Paris," said Sophia. "I am going back to Stockholm. Paris was not at all amusing, it was dreary as can be." She gave him her hands to kiss, one after the other.

"Is your Aniuta ill, then?"

"She is dead, *mein liebe* professor."

"She died in prison?"

"No, no. That was long ago. She was not in prison that time. Her husband was. She died of pneumonia, but she had been suffering in many ways for a long time."

"Oh, pneumonia, I have had it too. Still, that was sad for you."

"My heart will never heal. But I have something good to tell you, something happy. I am to be married in the spring."

"Are you divorcing the geologist? I do not wonder, you should have done that long ago. Still, a divorce is always unpleasant."

"He is dead too. And he was a paleontologist. It is a new study, very interesting. They learn things from fossils."

"Yes. I remember now. I have heard of the study. He died young then. I did not wish him to stand in your way, but truly I did not wish him dead. Was he ill long?"

"You might say that he was. You surely remember how I left him and you recommended me to Mittag-Leffler?"

"In Stockholm. Yes? You left him. Well. It had to be done."

"Yes. But it is over now and I am going to marry a man of the same name but not closely related and a different sort of man entirely."

"A Russian, then? Does he read fossils also?"

"Not at all. He is a professor of law. He is very energetic and very good-humored except when he is very gloomy. I will bring him to meet you and you shall see."

"We will be pleased to entertain him," said Weierstrass sadly. "It will put an end to your work."

"Not at all, not at all. He does not wish it. But I will not teach anymore, I will be free. And I will live in a delightful climate in the south of France and I shall be healthy there all the time and do all the more work."

"We shall see."

"*Mein Liebe,*" she said. "I order you, order you to be happy for me."

"I must seem very old," he said. "And I have led a sedate life. I have not as many sides to my nature as you have. It was such a surprise to me that you would write novels."

"You did not like the idea."

"You are wrong. I did like your recollections. Very pleasant to read."

"That book is not really a novel. You would not like the one I have written now. Sometimes I don't even like it myself. It is all about a girl who is more interested in politics than in love. Never mind, you will not have to read it. The Russian censors will not let it be published and the world outside will not want it because it is so Russian."

"I am not generally fond of novels."

"They are for women?"

"Truly I sometimes forget that you are a woman. I think of you as—as a—"

"As a what?"

"As a gift to me and to me alone."

Sophia bent and kissed his white forehead. She held back her tears till she had said good-bye to his sisters and left the house.

I will never see him again, she thought.

She thought of his face as white as the fresh starched pillows that Clara must have placed behind his head just that morning. Perhaps she had already taken them away, letting him slump down into the softer shabbier ones beneath. Perhaps he had fallen asleep at once, tired out from their exchange. He would have thought that they were meeting for the last time and he would have known that the thought was in her mind as well, but he would not know—this was her shame, her secret—how lightened, how free, she felt now, in spite of her tears, freer with every step away from that house.

Was his life, she thought, so much more satisfactory to contemplate than his sisters'?

His name would last awhile, in textbooks. And among mathematicians. Not so long as it might have done if he had been more zealous about establishing his reputation, keeping himself to the fore in his select and striving circle. He cared more for the work than for his name, when so many of his colleagues cared equally for both.

SHE SHOULD NOT have mentioned her writing. Frivolity to him. She had written the recollections of her life at Palibino in a glow of love for everything lost, things once despaired of as well as things once treasured. She had written it far from home when that home and her sister were gone. And *Nihilist Girl* came out of pain for her country, a burst of patriotism and perhaps a feeling that she had not been paying enough attention, with her mathematics and the tumults of her life.

Pain for her country, yes. But in some sense she had written that story in tribute to Aniuta. It was the story of a young woman who gives up the prospect of any normal life in order to marry a political prisoner exiled to Siberia. In this way she ensured that his life, his punishment, should be somewhat alleviated—southern instead of northern Siberia—as was the rule for men accompanied by their wives. The story would be praised by those banished Russians who might manage to read it in manuscript. A book had only to be refused publication in Russia to engender such praises among political exiles, as Sophia well knew. *The Raevsky Sisters*—the recollections—pleased her more, though the censor had passed it, and some critics dismissed it as nostalgia.

IV

SHE HAD FAILED WEIERSTRASS once before. She failed him when she had achieved her early success. It was true, though he never mentioned it. She had turned her back on him and on mathematics altogether; she had not even answered his letters. She went home to Palibino in the summer of 1874, with her degree won, stored in a velvet case, and then put away in a trunk, to be forgotten for months—years—at a time.

The smell of the hay fields and the pine woods, the golden hot summer days, and the long bright evenings of northern Russia intoxicated her. There were picnics and amateur plays, balls, birthdays, the welcome of old friends, and the presence of Aniuta, happy with her year-old son. Vladimir was there as well, and in the easy summer atmosphere, with the warmth and wine and long merry suppers, the dances and the singing, it was natural to give in to him, to establish him after all this time as not just her husband but her lover.

This was not done because she had fallen in love with him. She had been grateful to him, and had convinced herself that such a feeling as love did not exist in real life. It would make them both happier, she thought, to agree with what he wanted, and for a while it did.

In the autumn they went to Petersburg, and the life of important amusement continued. Dinners, plays, receptions, and all the papers and periodicals to read, both frivolous and serious. Weierstrass begged Sophia, by letter, not to desert the world of mathematics. He saw to it that her dissertation was published in *Crelle's Journal* for mathematicians. She barely looked at it. He asked her to spend a week—just a week—polishing up her work on the rings of Saturn, so that it too might be published. She could not be bothered. She was too busy, wrapped up in more or less constant celebration. A celebration of name days and court honors and new operas and ballets, but really, it seemed to be, a celebration of life itself.

She was learning, quite late, what many people around her appeared to have known since childhood—that life can be perfectly satisfying without major achievements. It could be brimful of occupations which did not weary you to the bone. Acquiring what you needed for a comfortably furnished life, and then to take on a social and public life of entertainment, would keep you from even being bored or idle, and would make you feel at the end of the day that you had done exactly what pleased everybody. There need be no agonizing.

Except in the matter of how to get money.

Vladimir revived his publishing business. They borrowed where they could. Both of Sophia's parents died before long, and her inheritance was invested in public baths attached to a greenhouse, a bakery, and a steam laundry. They had grand projects. But the weather in Petersburg happened to have turned colder than usual, and people were not tempted even by steam baths. The builders and other people cheated them, the market became unstable, and instead of managing to make a reliable foundation for their lives they went deeper and deeper into debt.

And behaving like other married couples had the usual expensive result. Sophia had a baby girl. The infant was given her mother's name but they called her Fufu. Fufu had a nurse and a wet nurse and her own suite of rooms. The family employed also a cook and a maid. Vladimir bought fashionable new clothes for Sophia and wonderful presents for his daughter. He had his degree from Jena and he had managed to become a subprofessor in Petersburg, but this was not enough. The publishing business was more or less in ruins.

Then the czar was assassinated and the political climate became disturbing and Vladimir entered a period of such deep melancholy that he could not work or think.

Weierstrass had heard of the death of Sophia's parents, and to allay her grief a little, as he said, he sent her information on his own new and excellent system of integrals. But instead of being drawn back to mathematics she took to writing theater reviews and popular science pieces for the papers. That was using a talent more marketable and not so disturbing to other people or so exhausting to herself, as mathematics.

The Kovalevsky family moved to Moscow, hoping that their luck would change.

Vladimir recovered, but he did not feel able to go back to teaching. He found a new opportunity for speculation, being offered a job in a company that produced naphtha from a petroleum spring. The company was owned by the brothers Ragozin, who had a refinery and a modern castle on the Volga. The job was contingent on Vladimir's investing a sum of money, which he managed to borrow.

But this time Sophia sensed trouble ahead. The Ragozins did not like her and she did not like them. Vladimir was now more and more in their power. These are the new men, he said, they have no nonsense in them. He became aloof, he took on rough and superior airs. Name me one truly important woman, he said. One who has made any real difference in the world, except by seducing and murdering men. They are congenitally backwards and self-centered and if they get hold of any idea, any decent idea to devote themselves to, they become hysterical and ruin it with their self-importance.

That is the Ragozins talking, said Sophia.

Now she picked up her correspondence with Weierstrass. She left Fufu with her old friend Julia and set out for Germany. She wrote to Vladimir's brother Alexander that Vladimir had bitten at the Ragozins' bait so readily that it was really as if he were tempting fate to send him another blow. Nevertheless she wrote to her husband offering to come back. He did not reply favorably.

They met once more, in Paris. She was living there cheaply while Weierstrass tried to get her a job. She was again submerged in mathematical problems and so were the people she knew. Vladimir had become suspicious of the Ragozins but he had involved himself to the point where he could not pull out. Yet he talked of going to the United States. And did go, but came back.

In the fall of 1882 he wrote to his brother that he realized now that he was a completely worthless person. In November he reported the bankruptcy of the Ragozins. He was afraid that they might try to implicate him in certain criminal procedures. At Christmas he saw Fufu, who was now in Odessa with his brother's family. He was happy that she remembered him, and that she was healthy and clever. After that he prepared farewell letters for Julia, his brother, certain other friends, but not Sophia. Also a letter for the court explaining some actions of his in the Ragozin matter.

He delayed a while longer. It was not until April that he tied a bag over his head and inhaled chloroform.

Sophia, in Paris, refused food and wouldn't come out of her room. She concentrated all her thought on the refusal of food, so she would not have to feel what she was feeling.

She was force-fed, at last, and fell asleep. When she woke she was deeply ashamed of this performance. She asked for a pencil and paper, that she might continue working on a problem.

THERE WAS NO MONEY LEFT. Weierstrass wrote and asked her to live with him as another sister. But he continued to pull strings wherever he could and was successful, finally, with his past student and friend Mittag-Leffler, in Sweden. The new University of Stockholm agreed to be the first university in Europe to take on a female mathematics professor.

At Odessa Sophia collected her daughter, taking her to live for the present with Julia. She was furious with the Ragozins. She wrote to Vladimir's brother calling them "subtle, poisonous villains." She persuaded the magistrate hearing the case to proclaim that all the evidence showed Vladimir to have been gullible but honest.

Then she took a train once more from Moscow to Petersburg to travel to her new and much publicized—and no doubt deplored—job in Sweden. She made the trip from Petersburg by sea. The boat rode into an overwhelming sunset. No more foolishness, she thought. I am now going to make a proper life.

She had not then met Maksim. Or won the Bordin Prize.

V

SHE LEFT BERLIN in the early afternoon, shortly after having said that last sad but relieved good-bye to Weierstrass. The train was old and slow, but clean and well heated, as you would expect any German train to be.

About halfway in the journey the man across from her opened up his newspaper, offering her any section she might like to read.

She thanked him, and refused.

He nodded towards the window, at the fine driving snow.

"Ah well," he said. "What can one expect?"

"What indeed," said Sophia.

"You are going beyond Rostock?"

He might have noted an accent that was not German. She did not mind his speaking to her or coming to such a conclusion about her. He was a good deal younger than she, decently dressed, slightly deferential. She had a feeling that he was someone she had met or seen before. But this did happen when you were travelling.

"To Copenhagen," she said. "And then to Stockholm. For me the snow will only get thicker."

"I will be leaving you at Rostock," he said, perhaps to reassure her that she was not letting herself in for a long conversation. "Are you satisfied with Stockholm?"

"I detest Stockholm at this time of year. I hate it."

She was surprised at herself. But he smiled delightedly and began to speak in Russian.

"Excuse me," he said. "I was right. Now it is I who speak like a foreigner to you. But I studied in Russia at one time. In Petersburg."

"You recognized my accent as Russian?"

"Not surely. Until you said what you did about Stockholm."

"Do all Russians hate Stockholm?"

"No. No. But they say they hate. They hate. They love."

"I should not have said it. The Swedes have been very good to me. They teach you things—"

At this point he shook his head, laughing.

"Really," she said. "They have taught me to skate—"

"Assuredly. You did not learn to skate in Russia?"

"They are not so—so insistent about teaching you things as the Swedes are."

"Nor on Bornholm," he said. "I live now on Bornholm. The Danes are not so—insistent, that is the word. But of course on Bornholm we are not even Danes. We say we are not."

He was a doctor, on the island of Bornholm. She wondered if it would be entirely out of line to ask him to look at her throat, which was now very sore. She decided that it would be.

He said that he had a long and probably a rough ferry ride ahead of him, after they had crossed the Danish border.

People on Bornholm did not think of themselves as Danes, he said, because they thought of themselves as Vikings taken over by the Hanseatic League in the sixteenth century. They had a fierce history, they took captives. Had she ever heard of the wicked Earl of Bothwell? Some people say he died on Bornholm, though the people of Zealand say he died there.

"He murdered the husband of the queen of Scotland and married her himself. But he died in chains. He died insane."

"Mary Queen of Scots," she said. "So I have heard." And indeed she had, for the Scottish queen had been one of Aniuta's early heroines.

"Oh, forgive me. I am chattering."

"Forgive you?" said Sophia. "What have I to forgive you for?"

He flushed. He said, "I know who you are."

He had not known in the beginning, he said. But when she spoke in Russian, he was sure.

"You are the female professor. I have read about you in a journal. There was a photograph as well, but you looked much older in it than you do. I am sorry to intrude on you but I could not help myself."

"I looked quite stern in the photograph because I think people will not trust me if I smile," said Sophia. "Is it not something the same for physicians?"

"It may be. I am not accustomed to being photographed."

Now there was a slight constraint between them; it was up to her to put him at ease. It had been better before he told her. She returned to the subject of Bornholm. It was bold and rugged, he said, not gentle and rolling like Denmark. People came there for the scenery and the clear air. If she should ever wish to come he would be honored to show her around.

"There is the most rare blue rock there," he said. "It is called blue marble. It is broken up and polished for ladies to wear around the neck. If you would ever like to have one—"

He was talking foolishly because there was something he wanted to say but couldn't. She could see that.

They were approaching Rostock. He was becoming more and more agitated. She was afraid he would ask her to sign her name on a piece of paper or a book he had with him. It was very seldom that anybody did that, but it always made her feel sad; there was no telling why.

"Please listen to me," he said. "Something I must say to you. It is not supposed to be spoken of. Please. On your way to Sweden, please do not go to Copenhagen. Do not look frightened, I am completely in my right mind."

"I am not frightened," she said. Though she was, a little.

"You must go the other way, by the Danish Islands. Change your ticket in the station."

"May I ask why? Is there a spell on Copenhagen?"

She was suddenly sure he was going to tell her about a plot, a bomb.

So he was an anarchist?

"There is smallpox in Copenhagen. There is an epidemic. Many people have left the city, but the authorities are trying to keep it quiet. They are afraid of a panic or that some people will burn down the government buildings. The problem is the Finns. People say the Finns brought it. They don't want the people to rise up against the Finnish refugees. Or against the government for letting them in."

The train stopped and Sophia stood up, checking her bags.

"Promise me. Do not leave me here without promising me."

"Very well," said Sophia. "I promise."

"You will be taking the ferry to Gedser. I would go with you to change the ticket but I must go on to Rutgen."

"I promise."

Was it Vladimir he reminded her of? Vladimir in the early days. Not his features, but his beseeching care for her. His constant humble and stubborn and beseeching care.

He held out his hand and she gave him hers to shake, but that was not his only intention. He placed in her palm a small tablet, saying, "This will give you a little rest if you find the journey tedious."

I will have to talk to some responsible person about this epidemic of smallpox, she decided.

BUT THAT SHE DID NOT DO. The man who changed her ticket was annoyed at having to do anything so complicated and would be even angrier if she changed her mind. He seemed at first to answer to no language except Danish, as spoken by her fellow passengers, but when he finished the transaction with her he said in German that the trip would take a good deal longer now, did she understand that? Then she realized that they were still in Germany and he might know nothing about Copenhagen—what had she been thinking of?

He added gloomily that it was snowing on the islands.

The small German ferry to Gedser was well heated, though you had to sit on wooden slat seats. She was about to swallow the tablet, thinking that seats like these might be what he meant when he spoke of the journey being tedious. Then she decided to save it, in case of seasickness.

The local train she got into had regular though threadbare second-class seats. It was chilly, however, with a smoky almost useless stove at one end of the car.

This conductor was friendlier than the ticket master, and not in so much of a hurry. Understanding that they really were in Danish territory, she asked him in Swedish—which she thought might be closer than German to Danish—whether it was true that there was sickness in Copenhagen. He replied that no, the train she was on did not go to Copenhagen.

The words "train" and "Copenhagen" seemed to be all he knew of Swedish.

In this train there were of course no compartments, only the two coaches with their wooden benches. Some of the passengers had brought their own cushions and their blankets and cloaks to wrap around themselves. They did not look at Sophia, much less try to speak to her. What use would it be if they did? She would not be able to understand or reply.

No tea wagon either. Packages wrapped in oiled paper were being opened, cold sandwiches taken out. Thick slices of bread, sharp-smelling cheese, slabs of cold cooked bacon, somewhere a herring. One woman took a fork out from a pocket in the folds of her clothing and ate pickled cabbage from a jar. That made Sophia think of home, of Russia.

But these are not Russian peasants. None of them are drunk, or garrulous, or laughing. They are stiff as boards. Even the fat that blankets the bones of some of them is stiff fat, self-respecting, Lutheran fat. She knows nothing about them.

But what does she really know about Russian peasants, the peasants at Palibino, when it comes to that? They were always putting on a show for their betters.

Except perhaps the one time, the Sunday when all the serfs and their owners had to go to church to hear the Proclamation read. Afterwards Sophia's mother was completely broken in spirit and moaned and cried, "Now what will become of us? What will become of my poor children?" The General took her into his study to comfort her. Aniuta sat down to read one of her books, and their little brother Feodor played with his blocks. Sophia wandered about, making her way to the kitchen where house serfs and even many field serfs were eating pancakes and celebrating—but in a rather dignified way, as if it was a saint's day. An old man whose only job was to sweep the yard laughed and called her Little Missus. "Here's the Little Missus come to wish us well." Then some cheered for her. How nice they were, she thought, though she understood that the cheering was some kind of joke.

Soon the governess appeared with a face like a black cloud and took her away.

Afterwards things went on pretty much as usual.

Jaclard had told Aniuta she could never be a true revolutionary, she was only good for getting money out of her criminal parents. As for Sophia and Vladimir (Vladimir who had snatched him away from the police), they were preening parasites, soaking up their worthless studies.

THE SMELL OF THE CABBAGE and the herring is making her slightly sick.

At some farther point the train stops and they are all told to get out. At least that is what she assumes, from the conductor's bark and the heaving up of reluctant but obedient bodies. They find themselves in knee-deep snow, with no town or platform in sight and smooth white hills around them, looming up through what is now lightly falling snow. Ahead of the train men are shovelling away the snow that has collected in a railway cut. Sophia moves around to keep her feet from freezing in their light boots, sufficient for city streets but not here. The other passengers stand still, and pass no comment on the state of affairs.

After half an hour, or perhaps only fifteen minutes, the track is clear and the passengers clamber back onto the train. It must be a mystery to all of them, as to Sophia, why they had to get out in the first place, instead of waiting in their seats, but of course nobody complains. On and on they go, through the dark, and there is something other than snow driving against the windows. A scratching malevolent sound. Sleet.

Then the dim lamps of a village, and some passengers are getting up, methodically bundling themselves and collecting their bags and packages and clambering down from the train, disappearing. The journey resumes, but in a short time everybody is ordered off again. Not because of snowdrifts this time. They are herded onto a boat, another small ferry, which takes them out onto black water. Sophia's throat is so sore now that she is sure she could not speak if she had to.

She has no idea how long this crossing is. When they dock everybody has to enter a three-sided shed, where there is little shelter and no benches. A train arrives after a wait she cannot measure. And when this train comes, what gratitude Sophia feels, though it is no warmer and has the same wooden benches as the first train. One's appreciation of meager comforts, it seems, depends on what misery one has gone through before getting them. And is not that, she wants to say to somebody, a dreary homily?

In a while they stop in a larger town where there is a station buffet. She is too tired to get off and make her way to it as some passengers do, coming back with steaming cups of coffee. The woman who ate the cabbage is, however, carrying two cups, and it turns out that one is for Sophia. Sophia smiles and does her best to express gratitude. The woman nods as if this fuss is unnecessary, even unseemly. But she keeps standing there till Sophia takes out the Danish coins she received from the ticket agent. Now the woman, grunting, picks out two of them with her damp mittened fingers. The cost of the coffee, very likely. For the thought, and for carrying it, no charge. This is the way of things. Without a word the woman then returns to her seat.

Some new passengers have got on. A woman with a child about four years old, one side of its face bandaged and one arm in a sling. An accident, a visit to a country hospital. A hole in the bandage shows a sad dark eye. The child puts its good cheek down in its mother's lap and she spreads part of her shawl over its body. She does this in a way that is not particularly tender or concerned, but somewhat automatic. Something bad has happened, more care has been added on to her, that is all. And the children waiting at home, and perhaps one in her belly.

How terrible it is, Sophia thinks. How terrible is the lot of women. And what might this woman say if Sophia told her about the new struggles, women's battle for votes and places at the universities? She might say, But that is not as God wills. And if Sophia urged her to get rid of this God and sharpen her mind, would she not look at her—Sophia—with a certain stubborn pity, and exhaustion, and say, How then, without God, are we to get through this life?

They cross the black water again, this time on a long bridge, and stop in another village where the woman and child get off. Sophia has lost interest, does not look to see if there is somebody waiting for them, she is trying to see the clock outside the station, lit up by the train. She expects the time to be near midnight, but it is just past ten o'clock.

She is thinking of Maksim. Would Maksim ever in his life board such a train as this? She imagines her head lying comfortably on his broad shoulder—though the truth is he would not care for that, in public. His coat of rich expensive cloth, its smell of money and comfort. Good things he believes he has a right to expect and a duty to maintain, even though he is a Liberal unwelcome in his own country. That marvellous assurance he has, that her father had, you can feel it when you are a little girl snuggled up in their arms and you want it all your life. More delightful of course if they love you, but comforting even if it is only a kind of ancient noble pact that they have made, a bond that has been signed, necessarily even if not enthusiastically, for your protection.

They would be displeased to have anybody call them docile, yet in a way they are. They submit themselves to manly behavior. They submit themselves to manly behavior with all its risks and cruelties, its complicated burdens and deliberate frauds. Its rules, which in some cases you benefited from, as a woman, and then some that you didn't.

Now she had an image of him—Maksim, not sheltering her at all but striding through the station in Paris as befitted a man who had a private life.

His commanding headgear, his courtly assurance.

That had not happened. It was not Maksim. Assuredly it was not.

.   .   .

VLADIMIR HAD NOT BEEN A COWARD—look how he had res-
cued Jaclard—but he did not have the manly certainties. That was
why he could grant her some equality those others couldn't and
why he could never grant her that enveloping warmth and safety.
Then near the end when he came under the Ragozin influence
and changed his tune—desperate as he was and thinking that he
might save himself by aping others—he turned to treating her in
an unconvincing, even ridiculous, lordly style. He had given her
then an excuse for despising him, but maybe she had despised him
all along. Whether he worshipped or insulted her it was impossible
for her to love him.

As Aniuta loved Jaclard. Jaclard was selfish and cruel and
unfaithful and even while she hated him she was in love with him.

What ugly and irksome thoughts could surface, if you didn't
keep a lid on them.

When she closed her eyes she thought she saw him—
Vladimir—sitting on the bench across from her, but it is not Vladimir, it is the doctor from Bornholm, it is only her memory of the
doctor from Bornholm, insistent and alarmed, pushing himself in
that queer humble way into her life.

THERE CAME A TIME—surely it was near midnight—when they
had to leave this train for good. They had reached the border of
Denmark. Helsingor. The land border, at least—she supposed the
true border was somewhere out in the Kattegat.

And there was the last ferry, waiting for them, looking large and
pleasant, with its many bright lights. And here came a porter to
carry her bags on board, and thank her for her Danish coins and
hasten away. Then she showed her ticket to the officer on board
and he spoke to her in Swedish. He assured her that they would
make connections on the other side with the train for Stockholm.
She would not have to spend the rest of the night in a waiting room.

"I feel as if I have come back to civilization," she said to him. He
looked at her with slight misgiving. Her voice was a croak, though
the coffee had helped her throat. It is just because he is a Swede,
she thought. It is not necessary to smile or pass remarks among the
Swedes. Civility can be maintained without that.

The crossing was a little rough, but she was not seasick. She remembered the tablet but she did not need it. And the boat must have been heated, because some people had taken off the upper layer of their winter clothing. But she still shivered. Perhaps it was necessary to shiver, she had collected so much cold in her body in her journey through Denmark. It had been stored inside her, the cold, and now she could shiver it out.

THE TRAIN FOR STOCKHOLM was waiting, as promised, in the busy port of Helsingborg, so much livelier and larger than its similarly named cousin across the water. The Swedes might not smile at you, but the information they gave out would be correct. A porter reached for her bags and held them while she searched in her purse for some coins. She took a generous number out and put them in his hand, thinking they were Danish; she would not need them anymore.

They were Danish. He gave them back to her, saying in Swedish, "These will not do."

"They are all I have," she cried, realizing two things. Her throat felt better and indeed she had no Swedish money.

He put down her bags and walked away.

French money, German money, Danish money. She had forgotten Swedish.

The train was getting up steam, the passengers boarding, while she still stood there in her quandary. She could not carry her bags. But if she could not, they would be left behind.

She grasped the various straps and started to run. She ran lurching and panting with a pain in her chest and around under her arms and the bags bumping against her legs. There were steps to climb. If she stopped for a breath she would be too late. She climbed. With tears of self-pity filling her eyes she beseeched the train not to move.

And it did not. Not till the conductor, leaning out to fasten the door, caught her arm, then somehow managed to catch her bags and pulled all aboard.

Once saved, she began to cough. She was trying to cough something out of her chest. The pain, out of her chest. The pain and tightness out of her throat. But she had to follow the conductor to her compartment, and she was laughing with triumph in between spells of coughing. The conductor looked into a compartment where there were already some people sitting, then took her along to one that was empty.

"YOU WERE RIGHT. To put me where I cannot. Be a nuisance," she said, beaming. "I didn't have money. Swedish money. All other kinds but Swedish. I had to run. I never thought I could—"

He told her to sit down and save her breath. He went away and came back soon with a glass of water. As she drank she thought of the tablet that had been given her, and took it with the last gulp of water. The coughing subsided.

"You must not do that again," he said. "Your chest is heaving. Up and down."

Swedes were very frank, as well as being reserved and punctual.

"Wait," she said.

For there was something else to be established, almost as if the train could not get her to the right place otherwise.

"Wait a moment. Did you hear about—? Did you hear there is smallpox? In Copenhagen?"

"I shouldn't think so," he said. He gave a severe though courteous nod and left her.

"Thank you. Thank you," she called after him.

SOPHIA HAS NEVER BEEN DRUNK in her life. Any medicine she has taken, that might addle her brain, has put her to sleep before any such disturbance could happen. So she has nothing with which to compare the extraordinary feeling—the change of perception—which is rippling through her now. At first it might have been just relief, a grand though silly sense of being favored, because she had managed to carry her bags and run up the steps and reach her train. And then she had survived the fit of coughing and the squeezing of her heart and been able somehow to disregard her throat.

BUT THERE IS MORE, as if her heart could go on expanding, regaining its normal condition, and continuing after that to grow lighter and fresher and puff things almost humorously out of her way. Even the epidemic in Copenhagen could now become something like a plague in a ballad, part of an old story. As her own life could be, its bumps and sorrows turning into illusions. Events and ideas now taking on a new shape, seen through sheets of clear intelligence, a transforming glass.

THERE WAS ONE EXPERIENCE that this reminded her of. That was her first stumbling on trigonometry, when she was twelve years old. Professor Tyrtov, a neighbor at Palibino, had dropped off the new text he had written. He thought it might interest her father the General, with his knowledge of artillery. She came upon it in the study and opened it by chance at the chapter on optics. She began to read it and to study the diagrams and she was convinced that shortly she would be able to understand it. She had never heard of sines or cosines, but by substituting the chord of an arc for the sine, and by the lucky chance that in small angles these almost coincide, she was able to break into this new and delightful language.

She was not very surprised then, though intensely happy.

Such discoveries would happen. Mathematics was a natural gift, like the northern lights. It was not mixed up with anything else in the world, not with papers, prizes, colleagues, and diplomas.

The conductor woke her a little while before the train reached Stockholm. She said, "What day is this?"

"It is Friday."

"Good. Good, I will be able to give my lecture."

"Take care of your health, madam."

AT TWO O'CLOCK she was behind her lectern, and she lectured ably and coherently, without any pain or coughing. The delicate hum that had been travelling through her body, as on a wire, did not affect her voice. And her throat seemed to have healed itself. When she was finished she went home and changed her dress and took a cab to the reception she had been invited to, at the Guldens' house. She was in good spirits, talking brightly about her impressions of Italy and the south of France, though not about her trip back to Sweden. Then she left the room without excusing herself and went outside. She was too full of glowing and exceptional ideas to speak to people any longer.

Darkness already, snow falling, without any wind, the streetlamps enlarged like Christmas globes. She looked around for a cab but did not see one. An omnibus was passing and she waved it down. The driver informed her that this was not a scheduled stop.

"But you stopped," she said without concern.

She did not know the streets of Stockholm at all well, so it was some time later that she realized she had been travelling into the wrong part of town. She laughed as she explained this to the driver, and he let her off to walk home through the snow in her party dress and her light cloak and slippers. The pavements were wonderfully silent and white. She had to walk about a mile, but was pleased to discover that she knew the way, after all. Her feet were soaked but she was not cold. She thought this was because of the lack of wind, and the enchantment in her mind and body that she had never been aware of before, but could certainly count on from now on. It might be quite unoriginal to say so, but the city was like a city in a fairy tale.

THE NEXT DAY she stayed in bed, and sent a note to her colleague Mittag-Leffler asking him to get her his doctor, as she had none. He came himself as well, and during a long visit she talked to him with great excitement about a new mathematical work she was planning. It was more ambitious, more important, more beautiful, than anything that had occurred to her up until this time.

The doctor thought that the problem was with her kidneys, and left her some medicine.

"I forgot to ask him," Sophia said when he had gone.

"Ask him what?" said Mittag-Leffler.

"Is there plague? In Copenhagen?"

"You're dreaming," said Mittag-Leffler gently. "Who told you that?"

"A blind man," she said. Then she said, "No, I meant kind. Kind man." She waved her hands about, as if trying to make some shape that would fit better than words. "My Swedish," she said.

"Wait to speak until you are better."

She smiled and then looked sad. She said with emphasis, "My husband."

"Your betrothed? Ah, he is not your husband yet. I am teasing you. Would you like him to come?"

But she shook her head. She said, "Not him. Bothwell.

"No. No. No," she said rapidly. "The other."

"You must rest."

TERESA GULDEN and her daughter Elsa had come, also Ellen Key. They were to take turns nursing her. After Mittag-Lettler had gone she slept awhile. When she woke she was talkative again but did not mention a husband. She talked about her novel, and about the book of recollections of her youth at Palibino. She said she could do something much better now and started to describe her idea for a new story. She became confused and laughed because she was not doing this more clearly. There was a movement back and forth, she said, there was a pulse in life. Her hope was that in this piece of writing she would discover what went on. Something underlying. Invented, but not.

What could she mean by this? She laughed.

She was overflowing with ideas, she said, of a whole new breadth and importance and yet so natural and self-evident that she couldn't help laughing.

SHE WAS WORSE on Sunday. She could barely speak, but insisted on seeing Fufu in the costume that she was going to wear to a children's party.

It was a Gypsy costume, and Fufu danced in it, around her mother's bed.

ON MONDAY Sophia asked Teresa Gulden to look after Fufu.

That evening she felt better, and a nurse came in to give Teresa and Ellen a rest.

In the early hours of the morning Sophia woke. Teresa and Ellen were wakened from sleep and they roused Fufu that the child might see her mother alive one more time. Sophia could speak just a little. Teresa thought she heard her say, "Too much happiness."

SHE DIED AROUND FOUR O'CLOCK. The autopsy would show her lungs completely ravaged by pneumonia and her heart displaying trouble which went back several years. Her brain, as everybody expected, was large.

. . .

THE DOCTOR from Bornholm read of her death in the newspaper, without surprise. He had occasional presentiments, disturbing to one in his profession, and not necessarily reliable. He had thought that avoiding Copenhagen might preserve her. He wondered if she had taken the drug he had given her, and if it had brought her solace, as it did, when necessary, to him.

SOPHIA KOVALEVSKY was buried in what was then called the New Cemetery, in Stockholm, at three o'clock in the afternoon of a still cold day when the breath of mourners and onlookers hung in clouds on the frosty air.

A WREATH OF LAUREL came from Weierstrass. He had said to his sisters that he knew he would never see her again.

He lived for six more years.

MAKSIM CAME from Beaulieu, summoned by Mittag-Leffler's telegram before her death. He arrived in time to speak at the funeral, in French, referring to Sophia rather as if she had been a professor of his acquaintance, and thanking the Swedish nation on behalf of the Russian nation for giving her a chance to earn her living (to use her knowledge in a worthy manner, he said) as a mathematician.

MAKSIM DID NOT MARRY. He was allowed after some time to return to his homeland, to lecture in Petersburg. He founded the Party for Democratic Reform in Russia, taking a stand for constitutional monarchy. The czarists found him much too liberal. Lenin, however, denounced him as a reactionary.

FUFU PRACTICED MEDICINE in the Soviet Union, dying there in the mid-fifties of the twentieth century. She had no interest in mathematics, so she said.

SOPHIA'S NAME has been given to a crater on the moon.

To Reach Japan

~

ONCE PETER had brought her suitcase on board the train he seemed eager to get himself out of the way. But not to leave. He explained to her that he was just uneasy that the train should start to move. Out on the platform looking up at their window, he stood waving. Smiling, waving. The smile for Katy was wide open, sunny, without a doubt in the world, as if he believed that she would continue to be a marvel to him, and he to her, forever. The smile for his wife seemed hopeful and trusting, with some sort of determination about it. Something that could not easily be put into words and indeed might never be. If Greta had mentioned such a thing he would have said, Don't be ridiculous. And she would have agreed with him, thinking that it was unnatural for people who saw each other daily, constantly, to have to go through explanations of any kind.

When Peter was a baby, his mother had carried him across some mountains whose name Greta kept forgetting, in order to get out of Soviet Czechoslovakia into Western Europe. There were other people of course. Peter's father had intended to be with them but he had been sent to a sanatorium just before the date for the secret departure. He was to follow them when he could, but he died instead.

"I've read stories like that," Greta said, when Peter first told her about this. She explained how in the stories the baby would start to cry and invariably had to be smothered or strangled so that the noise did not endanger the whole illegal party.

Peter said he had never heard such a story and would not say what his mother would have done in such circumstances.

What she did do was get to British Columbia where she improved her English and got a job teaching what was then called Business Practice to high school students. She brought up Peter on her own and sent him to college, and now he was an engineer. When she came to their apartment, and later to their house, she always sat in the front room, never coming into the kitchen unless Greta invited her. That was her way. She carried not noticing to an extreme. Not noticing, not intruding, not suggesting, though in every single household skill or art she left her daughter-in-law far behind.

Also, she got rid of the apartment where Peter had been brought up and moved into a smaller one with no bedroom, just room for a foldout couch. So Peter can't go home to Mother? Greta teased her, but she seemed startled. Jokes pained her. Maybe it was a problem of language. But English was her usual language now and indeed the only language Peter knew. He had learned Business Practice—though not from his mother—when Greta was learning *Paradise Lost*. She avoided anything useful like the plague. It seemed he did the opposite.

With the glass between them, and Katy never allowing the waving to slow down, they indulged in looks of comic or indeed insane goodwill. She thought how nice-looking he was, and how he seemed to be so unaware of it. He wore a brush cut, in the style of the time—particularly if you were anything like an engineer—and his light-colored skin was never flushed like hers, never blotchy from the sun, but evenly tanned whatever the season.

His opinions were something like his complexion. When they went to see a movie, he never wanted to talk about it afterwards. He would say that it was good, or pretty good, or okay. He didn't see the point in going further. He watched television, he read a book in somewhat the same way. He had patience with such things. The people who put them together were probably doing the best they could. Greta used to argue, rashly asking whether he would say the same thing about a bridge. The people who did it did their best but their best was not good enough so it fell down.

Instead of arguing, he just laughed.

It was not the same thing, he said.

No?

No.

Greta should have realized that this attitude—hands off, tolerant—was a blessing for her, because she was a poet, and there were things in her poems that were in no way cheerful or easy to explain.

(Peter's mother and the people he worked with—those who knew about it—still said poetess. She had trained him not to. Otherwise, no training necessary. The relatives she had left behind in her life, and the people she knew now in her role as a housewife and mother, did not have to be trained because they knew nothing about this peculiarity.)

It would become hard to explain, later on in her life, just what was okay in that time and what was not. You might say, well, feminism was not. But then you would have to explain that feminism was not even a word people used. Then you would get all tied up saying that having any serious idea, let alone ambition, or maybe even reading a real book, could be seen as suspect, having something to do with your child's getting pneumonia, and a political remark at an office party might have cost your husband his promotion. It would not have mattered which political party either. It was a woman's shooting off her mouth that did it.

People would laugh and say, Oh surely you are joking and you would have to say, Well, but not that much. Then she would say, one thing, though, was that if you were writing poetry it was somewhat safer to be a woman than a man. That was where the word poetess came in handy, like a web of spun sugar. Peter would not have felt that way, she said, but remember he had been born in Europe. He would have understood, though, how the men he worked with were supposed to feel about such things.

THAT SUMMER Peter was going to spend a month or maybe longer in charge of a job that was being done at Lund, far up, in fact as far as you could go north, on the mainland. There was no accommodation for Katy and Greta.

But Greta had kept in touch with a girl she used to work with in the Vancouver library, who was married now and living in Toronto. She and her husband were going to spend a month in Europe that summer—he was a teacher—and she had written Greta wondering if Greta and her family would do them a favor—she was very polite—by occupying the house in Toronto for part of that time, not letting it stand empty. And Greta had written back telling her about Peter's job but taking up the offer for Katy and herself.

That was why they were now waving and waving from the platform and from the train.

THERE WAS A MAGAZINE THEN, called *The Echo Answers,* published irregularly in Toronto. Greta had found it in the library and sent them some poems. Two of the poems had been published, and the result was that when the editor of the magazine came to Vancouver, last fall, she had been invited to a party, with other writers, to meet him. The party was at the house of a writer whose name had been familiar to her, it seemed, for her whole life. It was held in the late afternoon, when Peter was still at work, so she hired a sitter and set off on the North Vancouver bus across Lions Gate Bridge and through Stanley Park. Then she had to wait in front of the Hudson's Bay for a long ride out to the university campus, which was where the writer lived. Let off at the bus's last turning, she found the street and walked along peering at house numbers. She was wearing high heels which slowed her down considerably. Also her most sophisticated black dress, zipped up at the back and skimming the waist and always a little too tight at the hips. It made her look somewhat ridiculous, she thought, as she stumbled slightly, along the curving streets with no sidewalks, the only person about in the waning afternoon. Modern houses, picture windows, as in any up-and-coming suburb, not at all the kind of neighborhood she had expected. She was beginning to wonder if she had got the street wrong, and was not unhappy to think that. She could go back to the bus stop where there was a bench. She could slip off her shoes and settle down for the long solitary ride home.

But when she saw the cars parked, saw the number, it was too late to turn around. Noise seeped out around the closed door and she had to ring the bell twice.

She was greeted by a woman who seemed to have been expecting somebody else. Greeted was the wrong word—the woman opened the door and Greta said that this must be where they were having the party.

"What does it look like?" the woman said, and leaned on the

doorframe. The way was barred till she—Greta—said, "May I come in?" and then there was a movement that seemed to cause considerable pain. She didn't ask Greta to follow her but Greta did anyway.

Nobody spoke to her or noticed her but in a short time a teenage girl thrust out a tray on which there were glasses of what looked like pink lemonade. Greta took one, and drank it down at a thirsty gulp, then took another. She thanked the girl, and tried to start a conversation about the long hot walk, but the girl was not interested and turned away, doing her job.

Greta moved on. She kept smiling. Nobody looked at her with any recognition or pleasure and why should they? People's eyes slid round her and then they went on with their conversations. They laughed. Everybody but Greta was equipped with friends, jokes, half-secrets, everybody appeared to have found somebody to welcome them. Except for the teenagers who kept sullenly relentlessly passing their pink drinks.

She didn't give up, though. The drink was helping her and she resolved to have another as soon as the tray came around. She watched for a conversational group that seemed to have a hole in it, where she might insert herself. She seemed to have found one when she heard the names of movies mentioned. European movies, such as were beginning to be shown in Vancouver at that time. She heard the name of one that she and Peter had gone to see. *The Four Hundred Blows.* "Oh, I saw that." She said this loudly and enthusiastically, and they all looked at her and one, a spokesperson evidently, said, *"Really?"*

Greta was drunk, of course. Pimm's No. 1 and pink grapefruit juice downed in a hurry. She didn't take this snub to heart as she might have done in a normal way. Just drifted on, knowing she had somehow lost her bearings but getting a feeling that there was a giddy atmosphere of permission in the room, and it didn't matter about not making friends, she could just wander around and pass her own judgments.

There was a knot of people in an archway who were important. She saw among them the host, the writer whose name and face she had known for such a long time. His conversation was loud and hectic and there seemed to be danger around him and a couple of other men, as if they would as soon fire off an insult as look at you. Their wives, she came to believe, made up the circle she had tried to crash into.

The woman who had answered the door was not one of either group, being a writer herself. Greta saw her turn when her name was called. It was the name of a contributor to the magazine in which she herself had been published. On these grounds, might it not be possible to go up and introduce herself? An equal, in spite of the coolness at the door?

But now the woman had her head lolling on the shoulder of the man who had called her name, and they would not welcome an interruption.

This reflection made Greta sit down, and since there were no chairs she sat on the floor. She had a thought. She thought that when she went with Peter to an engineers' party, the atmosphere was pleasant though the talk was boring. That was because everybody had their importance fixed and settled at least for the time being. Here nobody was safe. Judgment might be passed behind backs, even on the known and published. An air of cleverness or nerves obtained, no matter who you were.

And here she had been desperate for anybody to throw her any old bone of conversation at all.

When she got her theory of the unpleasantness worked out she felt relieved and didn't much care if anybody talked to her or not. She took her shoes off and the relief was immense. She sat with her back against a wall and her legs stuck out on one of the lesser of the party's thoroughfares. She didn't want to risk spilling her drink on the rug so she finished it in a hurry.

A man stood over her. He said, "How did you get here?"

She pitied his dull clumping feet. She pitied anybody who had to stand up.

She said that she had been invited.

"Yes. But did you come in your car?"

"I walked." But that was not enough, and in a while she managed to offer up the rest of it.

"I came on a bus, then I walked."

One of the men who had been in the special circle was now

behind the man in the shoes. He said, "Excellent idea." He actually seemed ready to talk to her.

The first man didn't care for this one so much. He had retrieved Greta's shoes, but she refused them, explaining that they hurt too much.

"Carry them. Or I will. Can you get up?"

She looked for the more important man to help her, but he wasn't there. Now she remembered what he'd written. A play about Doukhobors that had caused a big row because the Doukhobors were going to have to be naked. Of course they weren't real Doukhobors, they were actors. And they were not allowed to be naked after all.

She tried explaining this to the man who helped her up, but he was plainly not interested. She asked what he wrote. He said he was not that kind of writer, he was a journalist. Visiting in this house with his son and daughter, grandchildren of the hosts. They—the children—had been passing out the drinks.

"Lethal," he said, referring to the drinks. "Criminal."

Now they were outside. She walked in her stocking feet across the grass, barely avoiding a puddle.

"Somebody has thrown up there," she told her escort.

"Indeed," he said, and settled her into a car. The outside air had altered her mood, from an unsettled elation to something within reach of embarrassment, even shame.

"North Vancouver," he said. She must have told him that. "Okay? We'll proceed. The Lions Gate."

She hoped he wouldn't ask what she was doing at the party. If she had to say she was a poet, her present situation, her overindulgence, would be taken as drearily typical. It wasn't dark out, but it was evening. They seemed to be headed in the right direction, along some water then over a bridge. The Burrard Street bridge. Then more traffic, she kept opening her eyes to trees passing by, then shutting them again without meaning to. She knew when the car stopped that it was too soon for them to be home. That is, at her home.

Those great leafy trees above them. You could not see any stars. But some shine on the water, between wherever they were and the city lights.

"Just sit and consider," he said.

She was enraptured by the word.

"Consider."

"How you're going to walk into the house, for instance. Can you manage dignified? Don't overdo it. Nonchalant? I presume you have a husband."

"I will have to thank you first for driving me home," she said. "So you will have to tell me your name."

He said that he had already told her that. Possibly twice. But once again, okay. Harris Bennett. Bennett. He was the son-in-law of the people who had given the party. Those were his children, passing out the drinks. He and they were visiting from Toronto. Was she satisfied?

"Do they have a mother?"

"Indeed they do. But she is in a hospital."

"I'm sorry."

"No need. It's quite a nice hospital. It's for mental problems. Or you might say emotional problems."

She hurried on to tell him that her husband was named Peter and that he was an engineer and that they had a daughter named Katy.

"Well that's very nice," he said, and started to back out.

On Lions Gate Bridge he said, "Excuse me for sounding how I did. I was thinking whether I would or wouldn't kiss you and I decided I wouldn't."

She thought he was saying that there was something about her that didn't quite measure up to being kissed. The mortification was like being slapped clean back into sobriety.

"Now when we get over the bridge do we go right on Marine Drive?" he continued. "I'll rely on you to tell me."

DURING THE COMING FALL and winter and spring there was hardly a day when she didn't think of him. It was like having the very same dream the minute you fell asleep. She would lean her head against the back pillow of the sofa, thinking that she lay in his arms. You would not think that she'd remember his face but it would spring up in detail, the face of a creased and rather tired-looking, satirical, indoor sort of man. Nor was his body lacking, it was presented as reasonably worn but competent, and uniquely desirable.

She nearly wept with longing. Yet all this fantasy disappeared, went into hibernation when Peter came home. Daily affections sprang to the fore then, reliable as ever.

The dream was in fact a lot like the Vancouver weather—a dismal sort of longing, a rainy dreamy sadness, a weight that shifted round the heart.

So what about the rejection of kissing, that might seem an ungallant blow?

She simply cancelled it out. Forgot about it entirely.

And what about her poetry? Not a line, not a word. Not a hint that she had ever cared for it.

Of course she gave these fits houseroom mostly when Katy was napping. Sometimes she spoke his name out loud, she embraced idiocy. This followed by a scorching shame in which she despised herself. Idiocy indeed. Idiot.

Then a jolt came, the prospect then certainty of the job at Lund, the offer of the house in Toronto. A clear break in the weather, an access of boldness.

SHE FOUND HERSELF writing a letter. It didn't begin in any conventional way. No Dear Harris. No Remember me.

> *Writing this letter is like putting a note*
> *in a bottle—*
> *And hoping*
> *It will reach Japan.*

Nearest thing to a poem in some time.

She had no idea of an address. She was bold and foolish enough to phone the people who had given the party. But when the woman answered her mouth went dry and felt as big as a tundra and she had to hang up. Then she carted Katy over to the public library and found a Toronto phone book. There were lots of Bennetts but not a single Harris or H. Bennett.

She had a shocking idea then, to look in the obituaries. She couldn't stop herself. She waited till the man reading the library copy was finished. She did not see the Toronto paper usually because you had to go over the bridge to get it, and Peter always brought home the *Vancouver Sun*. Rustling through its pages finally she found his name at the top of a column. So he was not dead. A newspaper columnist. Naturally he would not want to be bothered with people calling him by name, at home.

He wrote about politics. His writing seemed intelligent but she did not care anything about it.

She sent her letter to him there, at the newspaper. She could not be sure that he opened his own mail and she thought that putting Private on the envelope was asking for trouble, so she wrote only the day of her arrival and the time of the train, after the bit about the bottle. No name. She thought that whoever opened the envelope might think of an elderly relative given to whimsical turns of phrase. Nothing to implicate him, even supposing such peculiar mail did get sent home and his wife opened it, being now out of the hospital.

KATY HAD EVIDENTLY not understood that Peter's being outside on the platform meant that he would not be travelling with them. When they began to move and he didn't, and when with gathering speed they left him altogether behind, she took the desertion hard. But she settled down in a while, telling Greta that he would be there in the morning.

When that time came Greta was apprehensive, but Katy made no mention at all of the absence. Greta asked her if she was hungry and she said yes, then explained to her mother—as Greta had explained to her before they ever got on the train—that they now had to take off their pajamas and look for their breakfast in another room.

"What do you want for breakfast?"

"Crisp peas." That meant Rice Krispies.

"We'll see if they have them."

They did.

"Now will we go and find Daddy?"

THERE WAS A PLAY AREA for children but it was quite small. A boy and a girl—a brother and sister, by the looks of their matching bunny-rabbit outfits—had taken it over. Their game consisted of running small vehicles at each other then deflecting them at the last moment. CRASH BANG CRASH.

"This is Katy," Greta said. "I'm her mom. What are your names?" The crashing took on more vehemence but they didn't look up. "Daddy isn't here," said Katy.

Greta decided that they had better go back and get Katy's Christopher Robin book and take it up to the dome car and read it. They wouldn't be likely to bother anybody because breakfast wasn't over and the important mountain scenery hadn't started.

The problem was that once she finished Christopher Robin, Katy wanted it started again, immediately. During the first reading she had been quiet, but now she began chiming in with ends of lines. Next time she chanted word for word though still not ready to try it by herself. Greta could imagine this being an annoyance to people once the dome car filled up. Children Katy's age had no problem with monotony. In fact they embraced it, diving into it and wrapping the familiar words round their tongues as if they were a candy that could last forever.

A boy and a girl came up the stairs and sat down across from Greta and Katy. They said good morning with considerable cheer and Greta responded. Katy rather disapproved of her acknowledging them and continued to recite softly with her eyes on the book.

From across the aisle came the boy's voice, almost as quiet as hers:

> *They're changing guard at Buckingham*
> *Palace—*
> *Christopher Robin went down with*
> *Alice.*

After he finished that one he started another. "'I do not like them, Sam-I-am.'"

Greta laughed but Katy didn't. Greta could see that she was a bit scandalized. She understood silly words coming out of a book but not coming out of somebody's mouth without a book.

"Sorry," said the boy to Greta. "We're preschoolers. That's our literature." He leaned across and spoke seriously and softly to Katy.

"That's a nice book, isn't it?"

"He means we work with preschoolers," the girl said to Greta. "Sometimes we do get confused though."

The boy went on talking to Katy.

"I maybe could guess your name now. What is it? Is it Rufus? Is it Rover?"

Katy bit her lips but then could not resist a severe reply.

"I'm not a dog," she said.

"No. I shouldn't have been so stupid. I'm a boy and my name's Greg. This girl's name is Laurie."

"He was teasing you," said Laurie. "Should I give him a swat?"

Katy considered this, then said, "No."

"'Alice is marrying one of the guard,'" Greg continued, "'A soldier's life is terrible hard, says Alice.'"

Katy chimed in softly on the second Alice.

Laurie told Greta that they had been going around to kindergartens, doing skits. This was called reading readiness work. They were actors, really. She was going to get off at Jasper, where she had a summer job waitressing and doing some comic bits. Not reading readiness exactly. Adult entertainment, was what it was called.

"Christ," she said. She laughed. "Take what you can get."

Greg was loose, and stopping off in Saskatoon. His family was there.

They were both quite beautiful, Greta thought. Tall, limber, almost unnaturally lean, he with crinkly dark hair, she black-haired and sleek as a Madonna. When she mentioned their similarity a bit later on, they said they had sometimes taken advantage of it, when it came to living arrangements. It made things no end easier, but they had to remember to ask for two beds and make sure both got mussed up overnight.

AND NOW, THEY TOLD HER, now they didn't need to worry. Nothing to be scandalized about. They were breaking up, after three years together. They had been chaste for months, at least with each other.

"Now no more Buckingham Palace," said Greg to Katy. "I have to do my exercises."

Greta thought this meant that he had to go downstairs or at

least into the aisle for some calisthenics, but instead he and Laurie threw their heads back, stretched their throats, and began to warble and caw and do strange singsongs. Katy was delighted, taking all this as an offering, a show for her benefit. She behaved as a proper audience, too—quite still until it ended, then breaking out in laughter.

Some people who had meant to come up the stairs had stopped at the bottom, less charmed than Katy and not knowing what to make of things.

"Sorry," said Greg, with no explanation but a note of intimate friendliness. He held out a hand to Katy.

"Let's see if there's a playroom."

Laurie and Greta followed them. Greta was hoping that he wasn't one of those adults who make friends with children mostly to test their own charms, then grow bored and grumpy when they realize how tireless a child's affections can be.

By lunchtime or sooner, she knew that she didn't need to worry. What had happened wasn't that Katy's attentions were wearing Greg out, but that various other children had joined the competition and he was giving no sign of being worn out at all.

He didn't set up a competition. He managed things so that he turned the attention first drawn to himself into the children's awareness of each other, and then into games that were lively or even wild, but not bad-tempered. Tantrums didn't occur. Spoils vanished. There simply was not time—so much more interesting stuff was going on. It was a miracle, how much ease with wildness was managed in such a small space. And the energy expended promised naps in the afternoon.

"He's remarkable," Greta said to Laurie.

"He's mostly just there," Laurie said. "He doesn't save himself up. You know? A lot of actors do. Actors in particular. Dead offstage."

Greta thought, That's what I do. I save myself up, most of the time. Careful with Katy, careful with Peter.

In the decade that they had already entered but that she at least had not taken much notice of, there was going to be a lot of attention paid to this sort of thing. Being there was to mean something it didn't use to mean. Going with the flow. Giving. Some people were giving, other people were not very giving. Barriers between the inside and outside of your head were to be trampled down. Authenticity required it. Things like Greta's poems, things that did not flow right out, were suspect, even scorned. Of course she went right on doing as she did, fussing and probing, secretly tough as nails on the counterculture. But at the moment, her child surrendered to Greg, and to whatever he did; she was entirely grateful.

In the afternoon, as Greta had predicted, the children went to sleep. Their mothers too in some cases. Others played cards. Greg and Greta waved to Laurie when she got off at Jasper. She blew kisses from the platform. An older man appeared, took her suitcase, kissed her fondly, looked towards the train and waved to Greg. Greg waved to him.

"Her present squeeze," he said.

More waves as the train got going, then he and Greta took Katy back to the compartment, where she fell asleep between them, asleep in the very middle of a jump. They opened the compartment curtain to get more air, now that there was no danger of the child's falling out.

"Awesome to have a child," Greg said. That was another word new at the time, or at least new to Greta.

"It happens," she said.

"You're so calm. Next you'll say, 'That's life.' "

"I will not," Greta said, and outstared him till he shook his head and laughed.

He told her that he had got into acting by way of his religion. His family belonged to some Christian sect Greta had never heard of. This sect was not numerous but very rich, or at least some of them were. They had built a church with a theater in it in a town on the prairie. That was where he started to act before he was ten years old. They did parables from the Bible but also present day, about the awful things that happened to people who didn't believe what they did. His family was very proud of him and of course so he was of himself. He wouldn't dream of telling them all that went on when the rich converts came to renew their vows and get revitalized in their holiness. Anyway he really liked getting all the approval and he liked the acting.

Till one day he just got the idea that he could do the acting and not go through all that church stuff. He tried to be polite about it, but they said it was the Devil getting hold. He said ha-ha I know who it was getting hold.

Bye-bye.

"I don't want you to think it was all bad. I still believe in praying and everything. But I never could tell my family what went on. Anything halfway true would just kill them. Don't you know people like that?"

She told him that when she and Peter first moved to Vancouver her grandmother, who lived in Ontario, had got in touch with a minister of a church there. He came to call and she, Greta, was very snooty to him. He said he would pray for her, and she as good as said, don't bother. Her grandmother was dying at the time. Greta felt ashamed and mad about being ashamed whenever she thought about it.

Peter didn't understand all that. His mother never went to church though one reason she had carried him through the mountains was presumably so they could be Catholics. He said Catholics probably had an advantage, you could hedge your bets right until you were dying.

This was the first time she had thought of Peter in a while.

The fact was that she and Greg were drinking while all this anguished but also somewhat comforting talk went on. He had produced a bottle of ouzo. She was fairly cautious with it, as she had been with any alcohol she'd had since the writers' party, but some effect was there. Enough that they began to stroke each other's hands and then to engage in some kissing and fondling. All of which had to go on beside the body of the sleeping child.

"We better stop this," Greta said. "Otherwise it will become deplorable."

"It isn't us," said Greg. "It's some other people."

"Tell them to stop, then. Do you know their names?"

"Wait a minute. Reg. Reg and Dorothy."

Greta said, "Cut that out, Reg. What about my innocent child?"

"We could go to my berth. It's not far along."

"I haven't got any—"

"I have."

"Not on you?"

"Certainly not. What kind of a beast do you think I am?"

So they arranged whatever clothing had been disarranged, slipped out of the compartment, carefully fastened every button of the berth where Katy was sleeping, and with a certain fancy nonchalance made their way from Greta's car to his. This was hardly necessary—they met no one. The people who were not in the dome car taking pictures of the everlasting mountains were in the bar car, or dozing.

In Greg's untidy quarters they took up where they had left off. There was no room for two people to lie down properly but they managed to roll over each other. At first no end of stifled laughter, then the great shocks of pleasure, with no place to look but into each other's wide eyes. Biting each other to hold in some ferocious noise.

"Nice," said Greg. "All right."

"I've got to get back."

"So soon?"

"Katy might wake up and I'm not there."

"Okay. Okay. I should get ready for Saskatoon anyway. What if we'd got there just in the middle of it? Hello Mom. Hello Daddy. Excuse me just a minute here while I—Wa—hoo!"

She got herself decent and left him. Actually she didn't much care who met her. She was weak, shocked, but buoyant, like some gladiator—she actually thought this out and smiled at it—after a session in the arena.

Anyway, she didn't meet a soul.

The bottom fastener of the curtain was undone. She was sure she remembered fastening it. Though even with it open Katy could hardly get out and surely wouldn't try. One time when Greta had left for a minute to go to the toilet, she had explained thoroughly that Katy must never try to follow, and Katy had said, "I wouldn't," as if even to suggest that was treating her like a baby.

Greta took hold of the curtains to open them all the way, and when she had done so she saw that Katy was not there.

She went crazy. She yanked up the pillow, as if a child of Katy's size could have managed to cover herself with it. She pounded her hands on the blanket as if Katy could have been hiding underneath it. She got control of herself and tried to think where the train had

stopped, or whether it had been stopped, during the time she had
been with Greg. While it was stopped, if it had been stopped, could
a kidnapper have got on the train and somehow made off with
Katy?

She stood in the aisle, trying to think what she had to do to stop
the train.

Then she thought, she made herself think, that nothing like that
could have happened. Don't be ridiculous. Katy must have wakened and found her not there and gone looking for her. All by herself, she had gone looking.

Right around here, she must be right around here. The doors at
either end of the coach were far too heavy for her to open.

Greta could barely move. Her whole body, her mind, emptied.
This could not have happened. Go back, go back, to before she
went with Greg. Stop there. Stop.

Across the aisle was a seat unoccupied for the time being. A
woman's sweater and some magazine left to claim it. Farther along,
a seat with the fasteners all done up, as hers—theirs—had been.
She pulled them apart with one grab. The old man who was sleeping there turned over on his back but never woke up. There was no
way he could be hiding anybody.

What idiocy.

A new fear then. Supposing Katy had made her way to one or
other end of the car and had actually managed to get a door open.
Or followed a person who had opened it ahead of her. Between the
cars there was a short walkway where you were actually walking
over the place where the cars joined up. There you could feel the
train's motion in a sudden and alarming way. A heavy door behind
you and another in front, and on either side of the walkway clanging metal plates. These covered the steps that were let down when
the train was stopped.

You always hurried through these passages, where the banging
and swaying reminded you how things were put together in a way
that seemed not so inevitable after all. Almost casual, yet in too
much of a hurry, that banging and swaying.

The door at the end was heavy even for Greta. Or she was
drained by her fear. She pushed mightily with her shoulder.

And there, between the cars, on one of those continually noisy sheets of metal—there sat Katy. Eyes wide open and mouth slightly open, amazed and alone. Not crying at all, but when she saw her mother she started.

Greta grabbed her and hoisted her onto her hip and stumbled back against the door that she had just opened.

All of the cars had names, to commemorate battles or explorations or illustrious Canadians. The name of their car was Connaught. She would never forget that.

Katy was not hurt at all. Her clothes hadn't caught as they might have on the shifting sharp edges of the metal plates.

"I went to look for you," she said.

When? Just a moment ago, or right after Greta had left her?

Surely not. Somebody would have spotted her there, picked her up, sounded an alarm.

The day was sunny but not really warm. Her face and hands were quite cold.

"I thought you were on the stairs," she said.

Greta covered her with the blanket in their berth, and it was then that she herself began to shake, as if she had a fever. She felt sick, and actually tasted vomit in her throat. Katy said, "Don't push me," and squirmed away.

"You smell a bad smell," she said.

Greta took her arms away and lay on her back.

This was so terrible, her thoughts of what might have happened so terrible. The child was still stiff with protest, keeping away from her.

Someone would have found Katy, surely. Some decent person, not an evil person, would have spotted her there and carried her to where it was safe. Greta would have heard the dismaying announcement, news that a child had been found alone on the train. A child who gave her name as Katy. She would have rushed from where she was at the moment, having got herself as decent as she could, she would have rushed to claim her child and lied, saying that she had just gone to the ladies' room. She would have been frightened, but she would have been spared the picture she had now, of Katy sitting in that noisy space, helpless between the cars. Not crying, not complaining, as if she was just to sit there forever and there was to be no explanation offered to her, no hope.

Her eyes had been oddly without expression and her mouth just hanging open, in the moment before the fact of rescue struck her and she could begin to cry. Only then could she retrieve her world, her right to suffer and complain.

Now she said she wasn't sleepy, she wanted to get up. She asked where Greg was. Greta said that he was having a nap, he was tired.

She and Greta went to the dome car, to spend the rest of the afternoon. They had it mostly to themselves. The people taking pictures must have worn themselves out on the Rocky Mountains. And as Greg had commented, the prairies left them flat.

The train stopped for a short time in Saskatoon and several people got off. Greg was among them. Greta saw him greeted by a couple who must have been his parents. Also by a woman in a wheelchair, probably a grandmother, and then by several younger people who were hanging about, cheerful and embarrassed. None of them looked like members of a sect, or like people who were strict and disagreeable in any way.

But how could you spot that for sure in anybody?

Greg turned from them and scanned the windows of the train. She waved from the dome car and he caught sight of her and waved back.

"There's Greg," she said to Katy. "See down there. He's waving. Can you wave back?"

But Katy found it too difficult to look for him. Or else she did not try. She turned away with a proper and slightly offended air, and Greg, after one last antic wave, turned too. Greta wondered if the child could be punishing him for desertion, refusing to miss or even acknowledge him.

All right, if this is the way it's going to be, forget it.

"Greg waved to you," Greta said, as the train pulled away.

"I know."

WHILE KATY SLEPT beside her in the bunk that night Greta wrote a letter to Peter. A long letter that she intended to be funny, about all the different sorts of people to be found on the train. The preference most of them had for seeing through their camera, rather than looking at the real thing, and so on. Katy's generally agreeable behavior. Nothing about the loss, of course, or the scare.

She posted the letter when the prairies were far behind and the black spruce went on forever, and they were stopped for some reason in the little lost town of Hornepayne.

All of her waking time for these hundreds of miles had been devoted to Katy. She knew that such devotion on her part had never shown itself before. It was true that she had cared for the child, dressed her, fed her, talked to her, during those hours when they were together and Peter was at work. But Greta had other things to do around the house then, and her attention had been spasmodic, her tenderness often tactical.

And not just because of the housework. Other thoughts had crowded the child out. Even before the useless, exhausting, idiotic preoccupation with the man in Toronto, there was the other work, the work of poetry that it seemed she had been doing in her head for most of her life. That struck her now as another traitorous business—to Katy, to Peter, to life. And now, because of the picture in her head of Katy alone, Katy sitting there amid the metal clatter between the cars—that was something else she, Katy's mother, was going to have to give up.

A sin. She had given her attention elsewhere. Determined, foraging attention to something other than the child. A sin.

THEY ARRIVED IN TORONTO in the middle of the morning. The day was dark. There was summer thunder and lightning. Katy had never seen such commotion on the west coast, but Greta told her there was nothing to be afraid of and it seemed she wasn't. Or of the still greater, electrically lit darkness they encountered in the tunnel where the train stopped.

She said, "Night."

Greta said, No, no, they just had to walk to the end of the tunnel, now that they were off the train. Then up some steps, or maybe there would be an escalator, and then they would be in a big building and then outside, where they would get a taxi. A taxi was a car, that was all, and it would take them to their house. Their new house, where they would live for a while. They would live there for a while and then they would go back to Daddy.

They walked up a ramp, and there was an escalator. Katy halted, so Greta did too, till people got by them. Then Greta picked Katy up and set her on her hip, and managed the suitcase with the other arm, stooping and bumping it on the moving steps. At the top she put the child down and they were able to hold hands again, in the bright lofty light of Union Station.

There the people who had been walking in front of them began to peel off, to be claimed by those who were waiting, and who called out their names, or who simply walked up and took hold of their suitcases.

As someone now took hold of theirs. Took hold of it, took hold of Greta, and kissed her for the first time, in a determined and celebratory way.

Harris.

First a shock, then a tumbling in Greta's insides, an immense settling.

She was trying to hang on to Katy but at this moment the child pulled away and got her hand free.

She didn't try to escape. She just stood waiting for whatever had to come next.

Amundsen

~

ON THE BENCH outside the station I sat and waited. The station had been open when the train arrived but now it was locked. Another woman sat at the end of the bench, holding between her knees a string bag full of parcels wrapped in oiled paper. Meat—raw meat. You could smell it.

Across the tracks was the electric train, empty, waiting.

No other passengers showed up and after a while the stationmaster stuck his head out and called, "San." At first I thought he was calling a man's name, Sam. And another man wearing some kind of official outfit did come around the end of the building. He crossed the tracks and boarded the electric car. The woman with the parcels stood up and followed him, so I did the same. There was a burst of shouting from across the street and the doors of a dark-shingled flat-roofed building opened, letting loose several men who were jamming caps on their heads and banging lunch buckets against their thighs. By the noise they were making you would think the car was going to run away from them at any minute. But when they settled on board nothing happened. The car sat while they counted each other and said who was missing and told the driver he couldn't go yet. Then somebody remembered that it was the missing man's day off. The car started, though you couldn't tell if the driver had been listening to any of this, or cared.

All the men got off at a sawmill in the bush—it would not have been more than a ten-minute walk—and shortly after that the lake came into view, covered with snow. A long white wooden building in front of it. The woman readjusted her meat packages and stood up and I followed. The driver again called "San," and the doors opened. A couple of women were waiting to get on. They greeted the woman with the meat and she said it was a raw day.

All avoided looking at me as I climbed down behind the meat woman.

There was no one to wait for at this end, apparently. The doors banged together and the train started back.

Then there was silence, the air like ice. Brittle-looking birch trees with black marks on their white bark, and some kind of small untidy evergreens rolled up like sleepy bears. The frozen lake not level but mounded along the shore, as if the waves had turned to ice in the act of falling. And the building beyond with its deliberate rows of windows, and its glassed-in porches at either end. Everything austere and northerly, black-and-white under the high dome of clouds.

But the birch bark not white after all as you got closer. Grayish yellow, grayish blue, gray.

So still, so immense an enchantment.

"Where you heading?" the meat woman called to me. "Visiting hours over at three."

"I'm not a visitor," I said. "I'm the teacher."

"Well they won't let you in the front door anyway," said the woman with some satisfaction. "You better head along with me. Didn't you bring a suitcase?"

"The stationmaster said he'd bring it later."

"The way you were just standing there looked like you were lost."

I said that I had stopped because it was so beautiful.

"Some might think so. Less they were too sick or too busy."

Nothing more was said until we entered the kitchen at one end of the building. Already I was in need of its warmth. I did not get a chance to look around me because attention was drawn to my boots.

"You better get those off before they track the floor."

I wrestled off the boots—there was no chair to sit down on—and set them on the mat where the woman had put hers.

"Pick them up and bring them with you, I don't know where they'll be putting you. You better keep your coat on, too, there's no heating in the cloakroom."

No heat, no light, except what came through a little window I could not reach. It was like being punished at school. Sent-to-the-cloakroom. Yes. The same smell of winter clothing that never really dried out, of boots soaked through to dirty socks, unwashed feet.

I climbed up on a bench but still could not see out. On the shelf where caps and scarves were thrown I found a bag with some figs and dates in it. Somebody must have stolen them and stashed them here to take home. All of a sudden I was hungry. Nothing to eat since morning, except for a dry cheese sandwich on the Ontario Northland. I considered the ethics of stealing from a thief. But the figs would catch in my teeth, to betray me.

I got myself down just in time. Somebody was entering the cloakroom. Not any of the kitchen help but a schoolgirl in a bulky winter coat, with a scarf over her hair. She came in with a rush—books thrown on the bench so they scattered on the floor, scarf snatched so her hair sprung out in a bush and at the same time, it seemed, boots kicked loose one after the other and sent skittering across the cloakroom floor. Nobody had got hold of her, apparently, to make her take them off at the kitchen door.

"Hey, I wasn't trying to hit you," the girl said. "It's so dark in here after outside you don't know what you're doing. Aren't you freezing? Are you waiting for somebody to get off work?"

"I'm waiting to see Dr. Fox."

"Well you won't have to wait long, I just rode from town with him. You're not sick, are you? If you're sick you can't come here, you have to see him in town."

"I'm the teacher."

"Are you? Are you from Toronto?"

"Yes."

There was a certain pause, perhaps of respect.

But no. An examination of my coat.

"That's really nice. What's that fur on the collar?"

"Persian lamb. Actually it's imitation."

"Could have fooled me. I don't know what they put you in here for, it'll freeze your butt off. Excuse me. You want to see the doctor, I can show you. I know where everything is, I've lived here practically since I was born. My mother runs the kitchen. My name is Mary. What's yours?"

"Vivi. Vivien."

"If you are a teacher shouldn't it be Miss? Miss what?"

"Miss Hyde."

"Tan your hide," she said. "Sorry, I just thought that up. I'd like if you could be my teacher but I have to go to school in town. It's the stupid rules. Because I have not got TB."

She was leading me while she talked, through the door at the far end of the cloakroom, then along a regular hospital corridor. Waxed linoleum. Dull green paint, an antiseptic smell.

"Now you're here maybe I'll get Reddy to let me switch."

"Who is Reddy?"

"Reddy Fox. It's out of a book. Me and Anabel just started calling him that."

"Who is Anabel?"

"Nobody now. She's dead."

"Oh, I'm sorry."

"Not your fault. It happens around here. I'm in high school this year. Anabel never really got to go to school at all. When I was just in public school Reddy got the town teacher to let me stay home a lot, so I could keep her company."

She stopped at a half-opened door and whistled.

"Hey. I brought the teacher."

A man's voice said, "Okay Mary. Enough out of you for one day."

"Okay. I heard you."

She sauntered away and left me facing a spare man of ordinary height, whose reddish fair hair was cut very short and glistened in the artificial light from the hallway.

"You've met Mary," he said. "She has a lot to say for herself. She won't be in your class so you won't have to undergo that every day. People either take to her or they don't."

He struck me as between ten and fifteen years older than myself and at first he talked to me just in the way an older man would do. A preoccupied future employer. He asked about my trip, about the arrangements for my suitcase. He wanted to know how I would like living up here in the woods, after Toronto, whether I would be bored.

Not in the least, I said, and added that it was beautiful.

"It's like—it's like being inside a Russian novel."

He looked at me attentively for the first time.

"Is it really? Which Russian novel?"

His eyes were a light, bright grayish blue. One eyebrow had risen, like a little peaked cap.

It was not that I hadn't read Russian novels. I had read some all through and some partway. But because of that eyebrow, and his amused but confrontational expression, I could not remember any title except *War and Peace*. I did not want to say that because it was what anybody would remember.

"*War and Peace*."

"Well, it's only the Peace we've got here, I'd say. But if it was the War you were hankering after I suppose you would have joined one of those women's outfits and got yourself overseas."

I was angry and humiliated because I had not really been showing off. Or not only showing off. I had wanted to say what a wonderful effect this scenery had on me.

He was evidently the sort of person who posed questions that were traps for you to fall into.

"I guess I was really expecting some sort of old lady teacher come out of the woodwork," he said, in some slight apology. "As if everybody of reasonable age and qualifications would have got back into the system these days. You didn't study to be a teacher, did you? Just what were you planning to do once you got your B.A.?"

"Work on my M.A.," I said shortly.

"So what changed your mind?"

"I thought I should earn some money."

"Sensible idea. Though I'm afraid you won't earn much here. Sorry to pry. I just wanted to make sure you were not going to run off and leave us in the lurch. Not planning to get married, are you?"

"No."

"All right. All right. You're off the hook now. Didn't discourage you, did I?"

I had turned my head away.

"No."

"Go down the hall to Matron's office and she'll tell you all you need to know. You'll eat your meals with the nurses. She'll let you know where you sleep. Just try not to get a cold. I don't suppose you have any experience with tuberculosis?"

"Well I've read—"

"I know. I know. You've read *The Magic Mountain*." Another trap sprung, and he seemed restored. "Things have moved on a bit from that, I hope. Here, I've got some things I've written out about the kids here and what I was thinking you might try to do with them. Sometimes I'd rather express myself in writing. Matron will give you the lowdown."

I HAD NOT BEEN THERE a week before all the events of the first day seemed unique and unlikely. The kitchen, the kitchen cloak-room where the workers kept their clothes and concealed their thefts, were rooms I hadn't seen again and probably wouldn't see. The doctor's office was similarly out of bounds, Matron's room being the proper place for all inquiries, complaints, and ordinary rearrangements. Matron herself was short and stout, pink-faced, with rimless glasses and heavy breathing. Whatever you asked for seemed to astonish her, and cause difficulties, but eventually it was seen to or provided. Sometimes she ate in the nurses' dining room, where she was served a special junket, and cast a pall. Mostly she kept to her own quarters.

Besides Matron there were three registered nurses, not one of them within thirty years of my age. They had come out of retirement to serve, doing their wartime duty. Then there were the nurse's aides, who were my age or even younger, mostly married or engaged or working on being engaged, generally to men in the forces. They talked all the time if Matron and the nurses weren't there. They didn't have the least interest in me. They didn't want to know what Toronto was like, though some of them knew people who had gone there on their honeymoons, and they did not care how my teaching was going or what I had done before I came to work at the San. It wasn't that they were rude—they passed me the butter (it was called butter but it was really orange-streaked margarine, colored in the kitchen as was the only legal way in those days) and they warned me off the shepherd's pie which they said had groundhog in it. It was just that whatever happened in places they didn't know or to people they didn't know or in times they didn't know had to be discounted. It got in their way and under their skin. They turned off the radio news every chance they got and tried to get music.

"Dance with a dolly with a hole in her stockin' . . ."

Both nurses and aides disliked the CBC which I had been brought up to believe was bringing culture to the hinterlands. Yet they were in awe of Dr. Fox partly because he had read so many books.

They also said that there was nobody like him to tear a strip off you if he felt like it.

I couldn't figure out if they felt there was a connection between reading a lot of books and tearing a strip off.

Usual notions of pedagogy out of place here. Some of these children will reenter the world or system and some will not. Better not a lot of stress. That is testing memorizing classifying nonsense.

Disregard whole grade business entirely. Those who need to can catch up later on or do without. Actually very simple skills, set of facts, etc., necessary for Going into the World. What about Superior Children so-called? Disgusting term. If they are smart in questionable academic way they can easily catch up.

Forget rivers of South America, likewise Magna Carta.

Drawing Music Stories preferred.

Games Okay but watch for overexcitement or too much competitiveness.

Challenge to keep between stress and boredom. Boredom curse of hospitalization.

If Matron can't supply what you need sometimes Janitor will have it stashed away somewhere.

Bon Voyage.

THE NUMBERS OF CHILDREN who showed up varied. Fifteen, or down to half a dozen. Mornings only, from nine o'clock till noon, including rest times. Children were kept away if their temperature had risen or if they were undergoing tests. When they were present they were quiet and tractable but not particularly interested. They had caught on right away that this was a pretend school where they were free of all requirements to learn anything, just as they were free of times-tables and memory work. This freedom didn't make them uppity, it didn't make them bored in any troublesome way, just docile and dreamy. They sang rounds softly.

They played X's and O's. There was a shadow of defeat over the improvised classroom.

I decided to take the doctor at his word. Or some of his words, such as the ones about boredom being the enemy.

In the janitor's cubbyhole I had seen a world globe. I asked to have it brought out. I started on simple geography. The oceans, the continents, the climates. Why not the winds and the currents? The countries and the cities? The Tropic of Cancer and the Tropic of Capricorn? Why not, after all, the rivers of South America?

Some children had learned such things before, but they had nearly forgotten. The world beyond the lake and the forest had dropped away. I thought they cheered up, as if making friends again, with whatever they used to know. I didn't dump everything on them at once, of course. And I had to go easy with the ones who had never learned such things in their lives because of getting sick too soon.

But that was all right. It could be a game. I separated them into teams, got them calling out answers while I darted here and there with the pointer. I was careful not to let the excitement go on too long. But one day the doctor walked in, fresh from morning surgery, and I was caught. I could not stop things cold, but I tried to dampen the competition. He sat down, looking somewhat tired and withdrawn. He made no objection. After a few moments he began to join in the game, calling out quite ridiculous answers, names not just mistaken but imaginary. Then gradually he let his voice die down. Down, down, first to a mumble, then to a whisper, then till nothing could be heard at all. Nothing. In this way, with this absurdity, he took control of the room. The whole class took to mouthing, in order to imitate him. Their eyes were fixed on his lips.

Suddenly he let out a low growl that had them all laughing.

"Why the deuce is everybody looking at me? Is that what your teacher teaches you? To stare at people who aren't bothering anybody?"

Most laughed, but some couldn't stop watching him even for that. They were hungry for further antics.

"Go on. Go off and misbehave yourselves somewhere else."

He apologized to me for breaking up the class. I began to explain to him my reasons for making this more like real school.

"Though I do agree with you about stress—" I said earnestly. "I agree with what you said in your instructions. I just thought—"

"What instructions? Oh, that was just some bits and pieces that went through my head. I never meant them to be set in stone."

"I mean as long as they are not too sick—"

"I'm sure you're right, I don't suppose it matters."

"Otherwise they seemed sort of listless."

"There's not any need to make a song and dance about it," he said, and walked away.

Then turned to make a barely halfhearted apology.

"We can have a talk about it some other time."

That time, I thought, would never come. He evidently thought me a bother and a fool.

I discovered at lunch, from the aides, that somebody had not survived an operation that morning. So my anger did not turn out to be justified, and for that reason I had to feel more of a fool.

EVERY AFTERNOON WAS FREE. My pupils went down for long naps and I sometimes felt like doing the same. My room was cold—every part of the building seemed cold, far colder than the apartment on Avenue Road, even though my grandparents kept the radiators turned low there, to be patriotic. And the covers were thin—surely people with tuberculosis needed something cozier.

I of course did not have tuberculosis. Maybe they skimped on provisions for people like me.

I was drowsy but couldn't sleep. Overhead there was the rumble of bed-carts being wheeled to the open porches for the icy afternoon exposure.

The building, the trees, the lake, could never again be the same to me as they were on that first day, when I was caught by their mystery and authority. On that day I had believed myself invisible. Now it seemed as if that was never true.

There's the teacher. What's she up to?

She's looking at the lake.

What for?

Nothing better to do.

Some people are lucky.

ONCE IN A WHILE I skipped lunch, even though it was part of my salary. I went into Amundsen, where I ate in a coffee shop. The coffee was Postum and the best bet for a sandwich was tinned salmon, if they had any. The chicken salad had to be looked over well for bits of skin and gristle. Nevertheless I felt more at ease there, as if nobody would know who I was.

About that I was probably mistaken.

The coffee shop didn't have a ladies' room, so you had to go next door to the hotel, then past the open door of the beer parlor, always dark and noisy and letting out a smell of beer and whiskey, a blast of cigarette and cigar smoke fit to knock you down. Nevertheless I felt easy enough there. The loggers, the men from the sawmill, would never yelp at you the way the soldiers and the airmen in Toronto did. They were deep down in a world of men, bawling out their own stories, not here to look for women. Possibly more eager in fact to get away from that company now or forever.

The doctor had an office on the main street. Just a small one-story building so he must live elsewhere. I had picked up from the aides that there was no wife. On the only side street I found the house that might possibly belong to him—a stucco-covered house with a dormer window over the front door, books stacked on the sill of that window. There was a bleak but orderly look to the place, a suggestion of minimal but precise comfort, that a lone man—a regulated lone man—might contrive.

The school at the end of that only residential street was two stories high. The downstairs served students up to grade eight, the upstairs to grade twelve. One afternoon I spotted Mary there, taking part in a snowball fight. It seemed to be girls against boys. When she saw me, Mary cried out loudly, "Hey, Teach," and gave the balls in both hands a random toss, then sauntered across the street. "See you tomorrow," she called over her shoulder, more or less as a warning that nobody was to follow.

"You on your way home?" she said. "Me too. I used to ride with Reddy, but he's got too late leaving. What do you do, take the tram?"

I said yes, and Mary said, "Oh I can show you the other way and you can save your money. The bush road."

She took me up a narrow but passable track looking down on the town, then running through the woods and past the sawmill.

"This is the way Reddy goes," she said. "It's higher up but shorter when you turn down at the San."

We passed the sawmill, and beneath us, some ugly cuts in the woods and a few shacks, apparently inhabited because they had woodpiles and clotheslines and rising smoke. From one of them a big wolfish dog ran out with a great display of barking and snarling.

"You shut your face," yelled Mary. In no time she had packed and flung a snowball which caught the animal between the eyes. It whirled around and she had another snowball ready to catch it in the rump. A woman in an apron came out and yelled, "You could of killed him."

"Good riddance to bad rubbish."

"I'll get my old man after you."

"That'll be the day. Your old man can't hit a shithouse."

The dog followed at a distance, with some insincere threatening.

"I can take care of any dog, don't worry," Mary said. "I bet I could take care of a bear if we ran into one."

"Don't bears tend to hibernate at this time of year?"

I had been quite scared by the dog but affected carelessness.

"Yeah, but you never know. One came out early and it got into the garbage down at the San. My mom turned around and there it was. Reddy got his gun and shot it.

"Reddy used to take me and Anabel out on the sled, and sometimes other kids too and he had a special whistle that scared off bears. It was pitched too high for the ears of humans."

"Really. Did you see it?"

"It wasn't that kind. I meant one he could do with his mouth."

I thought of the performance in the classroom.

"I don't know, maybe that was just to keep Anabel from getting scared he said that. She couldn't ride, he had to pull her on a toboggan. I'd go right behind her and sometimes I'd jump on the toboggan and he'd say what's the matter with this thing, it weighs a ton. Then he'd try to turn around quick and catch me, but he never did. And he'd ask Anabel what makes it so heavy what did you have to eat for breakfast, but she never told. If there was other kids I wouldn't do it. It was best when just me and Anabel went. She was the best friend I ever will have."

"What about those girls at the school? Aren't they friends?"

"I just hang around with them when there's nobody else. They're nothing.

"Anabel and me had our birthdays in the same month. June. Our eleventh birthday Reddy took us down the lake in a boat. He taught us swimming. Well, me. He always had to hold Anabel though, she couldn't really learn. Once he went swimming way out by himself and we filled his shoes up with sand. And then our twelfth birthday we couldn't go anywhere like that, but we went to his house and had a cake. She couldn't eat even a little piece of it, so he took us in his car and we threw pieces out the window and fed the seagulls. They were fighting and screaming like mad. We were laughing ourselves crazy and he had to stop and hold Anabel so she wouldn't have a hemorrhage.

"And after that," she said, "after that I wasn't allowed to see her anymore. My mom never wanted me anyway to hang around with kids that had TB. But Reddy talked her into it, he said he'd stop it when he had to. So he did and I got mad. But she wouldn't have been any fun anymore she was too sick. I'd show you her grave but there isn't anything to mark it yet. Reddy and me are going to make something when he gets time. If we'd've gone straight along on the road instead of turning down where we did we would have come to her graveyard. It's just for people that don't have anybody to come and take them home."

By this time we were down on level ground approaching the San.

She said, "Oh I almost forgot," and brought out a fistful of tickets.

"For Valentine's Day. We're putting on this play at the school and it's called *Pinafore*. I got all these to sell and you can be my first sale. I'm in it."

I WAS RIGHT about the house in Amundsen being where the doctor lived. He took me there for supper. The invitation seemed to come rather on the spur of the moment when he met me in the hall. Perhaps he had an uneasy memory of saying we would get together to talk about teaching ideas.

The evening he proposed was the one for which I had bought a ticket for *Pinafore*. I told him that and he said, "Well I did too. It doesn't mean we have to show up."

"I sort of feel as if I'd promised her."

"Well. Now you can sort of unpromise her. It will be dreadful, believe me."

I did as he told me, though I did not see Mary, to tell her. I was waiting where he had instructed me to be, on the open porch outside the front door. I was wearing my best dress of dark green crepe with the little pearl buttons and the real lace collar, and had rammed my feet into suede high-heeled shoes inside my snow boots. I waited past the time mentioned—worried, first, that Matron would come out of her office and spot me, and second, that he would have forgotten all about it.

But then he came along, buttoning up his overcoat, and apologized.

"Always a few bits and bobs to clear up," he said, and led me under the bright stars around the building to his car. "Are you steady?" he said, and when I said yes—though I wondered about the suede shoes—he did not offer his arm.

His car was old and shabby as most cars were in those days. It didn't have a heater. When he said we were going to his house I was relieved. I could not see how we would manage with the crowd at the hotel and I had hoped not to make do with the sandwiches at the café.

In the house, he told me not to take off my coat until the place was warmed up a bit. He got busy at once making a fire in the woodstove.

"I'm your janitor and your cook and your server," he said. "It'll soon be comfortable here and the meal won't take me long. Don't offer to help, I prefer to work alone. Where would you like to wait? If you want to you could look over the books in the front room. It shouldn't be too unbearable in there with your coat on. The house is heated with stoves throughout and I don't heat up a room if it isn't in use. The light switch is just inside the door. You don't mind if I listen to the news? It's a habit I've got into."

I went into the front room, feeling as if I had more or less been ordered to, leaving the kitchen door open. He came and closed it, saying, "Just until we get a bit of warmth in the kitchen," and went back to the somberly dramatic, almost religious voice of the CBC, giving out the news of this last year of the war. I had not been able to hear that voice since I left my grandparents' apartment and I rather wished that I could have stayed in the kitchen. But there were quantities of books to look at. Not just on bookshelves but on tables and chairs and windowsills and piled on the floor. After I had examined several of them I concluded that he favored buying books in batches and probably belonged to several book clubs. The Harvard Classics. The Histories of Will and Ariel Durant—the very same that could be found on my grandfather's shelves. Fiction and poetry seemed in short supply, though there were a few surprising children's classics.

Books on the American Civil War, the South African War, the Napoleonic Wars, the Peloponnesian Wars, the campaigns of Julius Caesar. *Explorations of the Amazon and the Arctic. Shackleton Caught in the Ice. Franklin's Doom, The Donner Party, The Lost Tribes: Buried Cities of Central Africa, Newton and Alchemy, Secrets of the Hindu Kush.* Books suggesting someone anxious to know, to possess great scattered lumps of knowledge. Perhaps not someone whose tastes were firm and exacting.

So when he had asked me, "Which Russian novel?" it was possible that he had not had so firm a platform as I had thought.

When he called "Ready," and I opened the door, I was armed with this new skepticism.

I said, "Who do you agree with, Naphta or Settembrini?"

"I beg your pardon?"

"In *The Magic Mountain.* Do you like Naphta best or Settembrini?"

"To be honest, I've always thought they were a pair of windbags. You?"

"Settembrini is more humane but Naphta is more interesting."

"They tell you that in school?"

"I never read it in school," I said coolly.

He gave me a quick look, the eyebrow raised.

"Pardon me. If there's anything in there that interests you, feel free. Feel free to come down here and read in your time off. There's an electric heater I could set up, since I imagine you are not experienced with woodstoves. Shall we think about that? I can rustle you up an extra key."

"Thank you."

Pork chops for supper, mashed potatoes, canned peas. Dessert was an apple pie from the bakery, which would have been better if he had thought to heat it up.

He asked me about my life in Toronto, my university courses, my grandparents. He said that he supposed I had been brought up on the straight and narrow.

"My grandfather is a liberal clergyman sort of in the Paul Tillich mode."

"And you? Liberal little Christian granddaughter?"

"No."

"*Touché*. Do you think I'm rude?"

"That depends. If you are interviewing me as an employer, no."

"So I'll go on. Do you have a boyfriend?"

"Yes."

"In the forces I suppose."

I said, In the Navy. That struck me as a good choice, accounting for my never knowing where he was and not getting regular letters. I could manage that he did not get shore leave.

The doctor got up and fetched the tea.

"What sort of boat is he on?"

"Corvette." Another good choice. After a while I could have him torpedoed, as was always happening to corvettes.

"Brave fellow. Milk or sugar in your tea?"

"Neither one thanks."

"That's good because I haven't got any. You know it shows when you're lying, you get hot in the face."

If I hadn't got hot before I did then. My flush rose from my feet up and sweat trickled down under my arms. I hoped the dress would not be ruined.

"I always go hot when I drink tea."

"Oh I see."

Things could not get any worse so I resolved to face him down. I changed the subject on him, asking about how he operated on people. Did he remove lungs, as I had heard?

He could have answered that with more teasing, more superiority—possibly his notion of flirtation—and I believed that if he had done so I would have put on my coat and walked out into the cold. And perhaps he knew that. He began to talk about thoracoplasty, and explain that it was, however, not so easy on the patient as collapsing and deflating a lung. Which interestingly enough even Hippocrates had known about. Of course removal of the lobe had also become popular recently.

"But don't you lose some?" I said.

He must have thought it was time to joke again.

"But of course. Running off and hiding in the bush, we don't know where they get to— Jumping in the lake— Or did you mean don't they die? There's cases of things not working. Yes."

But great things were coming, he said. The surgery he went in for was going to become as obsolete as bloodletting. A new drug was on the way. Streptomycin. Already used in trial. Some problems, naturally there would be problems. Toxicity of the nervous system. But there would be a way found to deal with that.

"Put the sawbones like me out of business."

He washed the dishes, I dried. He put a dish towel round my waist to protect my dress. When the ends were efficiently tied he laid his hand against my upper back. Such firm pressure, fingers separated—he might almost have been taking stock of my body in a professional way. When I went to bed that night I could still feel that pressure. I felt it develop its intensity from the little finger to the hard thumb. I enjoyed it. That was more important really than the kiss placed on my forehead later, the moment before I got out of his car. A dry-lipped kiss, brief and formal, set upon me with hasty authority.

THE KEY TO HIS HOUSE showed up on the floor of my room, slipped under the door when I wasn't there. But after all I couldn't use it. If anybody else had made me this offer I would have jumped at the chance. Especially if it included a heater. But in this case his past and future presence would be drawing all ordinary comfort out of the situation and replacing it with a pleasure that was tight and nerve-racking rather than expansive. I would not be able to stop shivering even when it wasn't cold, and I doubted whether I could have read a word.

I THOUGHT THAT MARY would probably appear, to scold me for missing *Pinafore*. I thought of saying that I had not been well.

I'd had a cold. But then I remembered that colds in this place were a serious business, involving masks and disinfectant, banishment. And soon I understood that there was no hope of hiding my visit to the doctor's house, in any case. It was a secret from nobody, not even, surely, from the nurses who said nothing, either because they were too lofty and discreet or because such carryings-on had ceased to interest them. But the aides teased me.

"Enjoy your supper the other night?"

Their tone was friendly, they seemed to approve. It looked as if my particular oddity had joined up with the doctor's familiar and respected oddity, and that was all to the good. My stock had risen. Now, whatever else I was, I at least might turn out to be a woman with a man.

Mary did not put in an appearance all week.

"NEXT SATURDAY," were the words that had been said, just before he administered the kiss. So I waited again on the front porch and this time he was not late. We drove to the house and I went into the front room while he got the fire going. There I noticed the dusty electric heater.

"Didn't take me up on my offer," he said. "Did you think I didn't mean it? I always mean what I say."

I said that I hadn't wanted to come into town for fear of meeting Mary.

"Because of missing her concert."

"That's if you're going to arrange your life to suit Mary," he said.

The menu was much the same as before. Pork chops, mashed potatoes, corn niblets instead of peas. This time he let me help in the kitchen, even asking me to set the table.

"You may as well learn where things are. It's all fairly logical, I believe."

This meant that I could watch him working at the stove. His easy concentration, economical movements, setting up in me a procession of sparks and chills.

We had just begun the meal when there was a knock at the door. He got up and drew the bolt and in burst Mary.

She was carrying a cardboard box which she set on the

table. Then she threw off her coat and displayed herself in a red-and-yellow costume.

"Happy late Valentine's Day," she said. "You never came to see me in the concert so I brought the concert to you. And I brought you a present in the box."

Her excellent balance allowed her to stand on one foot while she kicked off first one boot, then the other. She pushed them out of her way and began to prance around the table, singing at the same time in a plaintive but vigorous young voice.

> *I'm called Little Buttercup,*
> *Poor Little Buttercup,*
> *Though I can never tell why.*
> *But still I'm called Buttercup*
> *Poor Little Buttercup*
> *Dear Little Buttercup I—*

The doctor had got up even before she began to sing. He was standing at the stove, busy scraping at the frying pan that had held the pork chops.

I applauded. I said, "What a gorgeous costume."

It was indeed. Red skirt, bright yellow petticoat, fluttering white apron, embroidered bodice.

"My mom made it."

"Even the embroidery?"

"Sure. She stayed up till four o'clock to get it done the night before."

There was further whirling and stomping to show it off. The dishes tinkled on the shelves. I applauded some more. Both of us wanted only one thing. We wanted the doctor to turn around and stop ignoring us. For him to say, even grudgingly, one polite word.

"And lookit what else," Mary said. "For a Valentine." She tore open the cardboard box and there were Valentine cookies, all cut in heart shapes and plastered with thick red icing.

"How splendid," I said, and Mary resumed her prancing.

> *I am the Captain of the* Pinafore.
> *And a right good captain, too!*

> *You're very, very good, and be it*
> *understood,*
> *I command a right good crew.*

The doctor turned at last and she saluted him.
"All right," he said. "That's enough."
She ignored him.

> *Then give three cheers, and one cheer*
> *more*
> *For the hardy captain of the*
> Pinafore—

"I said, that's enough."
" 'For the gallant captain of the *Pinafore*—' "
"Mary. We are eating supper. And you are not invited. Do you understand that? Not invited."
She was quiet at last. But only for a moment.
"Well pooh on you then. You're not very nice."
"And you could just as well do without any of those cookies. You could quit eating cookies altogether. You're on the way to getting as plump as a young pig."
Mary's face was swollen as if she would start to cry but instead she said, "Look who's talking. You got one eye crooked to the other."
"That's enough."
"Well you have."
The doctor picked up her boots and set them down in front of her.
"Put these on."
She did so, with her eyes full of tears and her nose running. She snuffled mightily. He brought her coat and did not help her as she flailed her way into it and found the buttons.
"That's right. Now—how did you get here?"
She refused to answer.
"Walked, did you? Where's your mother?"
"Euchre."
"Well I can drive you home. So you won't get any chance to fling yourself in a snowbank and freeze to death out of self-pity."

I did not say a word. Mary did not look at me once. The moment was too full of shock for good-byes.

When I heard the car start I began clearing the table. We had not got to dessert, which was apple pie again. Perhaps he did not know of any other kind, or perhaps it was all the bakery made.

I picked up one of the heart-shaped cookies and ate it. The icing was horribly sweet. No berry or cherry flavor, just sugar and red food coloring. I ate another and another.

I knew that I should have said good-bye at least. I should have said thank you. But it wouldn't have mattered. I told myself it wouldn't have mattered. The show had not been for me. Or perhaps only a small part of it had been for me.

He had been brutal. It shocked me, that he had been so brutal. To one so much in need. But he had done it for me, in a way. So that his time with me should not be taken away. This thought flattered me and I was ashamed that it flattered me. I did not know what I would say to him when he got back.

He did not want me to say anything. He took me to bed. Had this been in the cards all along, or was it almost as much of a surprise to him as it was to me? My state of virginity at least did not appear to be a surprise—he provided a towel as well as a condom—and he persisted, going as easily as he could. My passion could have been the surprise to us both. Imagination, as it turned out, might be as good a preparation as experience.

"I do intend to marry you," he said.

Before he took me home he tossed all the cookies, all those red hearts, out in the snow to feed the winter birds.

SO IT WAS SETTLED. Our sudden engagement—he was a little wary of the word—was a private settled fact. I was not to write a word to my grandparents. The wedding would take place whenever he could get a couple of consecutive days off. A bare-bones wedding, he said. I was to understand that the idea of a ceremony, carried on in the presence of others, whose ideas he did not respect, and who would inflict on us all that snickering and simpering, was more than he was prepared to put up with.

Nor was he in favor of diamond rings. I told him that I had never wanted one, which was true, because I had never thought about it. He said that was good, he had known that I was not that idiotic conventional sort of girl.

It was better to stop having supper together, not just because of the talk but because it was hard to get enough meat for two people on one ration card. My card was not available, having been handed over to the kitchen authorities—to Mary's mother—as soon as I began to eat at the San.

Better not to call attention.

OF COURSE everybody suspected something. The elderly nurses turned cordial and even Matron gave me a pained smile. I did preen in a modest way, almost without meaning to. I took to folding myself in, with a velvet stillness, eyes rather cast down. It did not quite occur to me that these older women were watching to see what turn this intimacy might take and that they were ready to turn righteous if the doctor should decide to drop me.

It was the aides who were wholeheartedly on my side, and teased that they saw wedding bells in my tea leaves.

The month of March was grim and busy behind the hospital doors. It was always the worst month for trouble to strike, the aides said. For some reason people took it into their heads to die then, after making it through the attacks of winter. If a child did not show up for class I would not know if there had been a major turn for the worse or just a bedding-down with a suspicion of a cold. I had got hold of a moveable blackboard and had written the children's names all around the edges of it. Now I never even had to wipe off the names of the children whose absences were to be prolonged. Other children did it for me, without a mention. They understood the etiquette which I had still to learn.

Time was found, however, for the doctor to make some arrangements. He slipped a note under the door of my room, saying to be ready by the first week of April. Unless there was some real crisis, he could manage a couple of days then.

WE ARE GOING to Huntsville.

Going to Huntsville—our code for getting married.

We have begun the day that I am sure I will remember all my life. I have my green crepe dry-cleaned and rolled up carefully in my overnight bag. My grandmother once taught me the trick of tight rolling, so much better than folding to prevent wrinkles. I suppose I will have to change my clothes in a ladies' toilet somewhere. I am watching to see if there are any early wildflowers along the road, that I could pick to make a bouquet. Would he agree to my having a bouquet? But it's too early even for marsh marigolds. Along the empty curving road nothing is to be seen but skinny black spruce trees and islands of spreading juniper and bogs. And in the road cuts a chaotic jumble of the rocks that have become familiar to me here—bloodstained iron and slanting shelves of granite.

The car radio is on and playing triumphal music, because the Allies are getting closer and closer to Berlin. The doctor—Alister—says that they are delaying to let the Russians in first. He says they'll be sorry.

Now that we are away from Amundsen I find that I can call him Alister. This is the longest drive we have ever taken together and I am aroused by his male unawareness of me—which I know now can quickly shift to its opposite—and by his casual skill as a driver. I find it exciting that he is a surgeon though I would never admit that. Right now I believe I could lie down for him in any bog or mucky hole, or feel my spine crushed against any roadside rock, should he require an upright encounter. I know too that I must keep these feelings to myself.

I turn my mind to the future. Once we get to Huntsville I expect that we will find a minister and stand side by side in a living room which will have some of the modest gentility of my grandparents' apartment, of the living rooms I have known all my life. I recall times when my grandfather would be sought out for wedding purposes even after his retirement. My grandmother would rub a little rouge on her cheeks and take out the dark blue lace jacket that she kept for being a witness on such occasions.

But I discover there are other ways to get married, and another aversion of my bridegroom's that I hadn't grasped. He won't have anything to do with a minister. In the Town Hall in Huntsville we fill out forms that swear to our single state and make an appointment to be married by a justice of the peace later in the day.

Time for lunch. Alister stops outside a restaurant that could be a first cousin to the coffee shop in Amundsen.

"This'll do?"

But on looking into my face he does change his mind.

"No?" he says. "Okay."

We end up eating lunch in the chilly front room of one of the genteel houses that advertise chicken dinners. The plates are icy cold, there are no other diners, there is no radio music but only the clink of our cutlery as we try to separate parts of the stringy chicken. I am sure he is thinking that we might have done better in the restaurant he suggested in the first place.

Nonetheless I have the courage to ask about the ladies' room, and there, in cold air even more discouraging than that of the front room, I shake out my green dress and put it on, repaint my mouth and fix my hair.

When I come out Alister stands up to greet me and smiles and squeezes my hand and says I look pretty.

We walk stiffly back to the car, holding hands. He opens the car door for me, goes around and gets in, settles himself and turns the key in the ignition, then turns it off.

The car is parked in front of a hardware store. Shovels for snow removal are on sale at half price. There is still a sign in the window that says skates can be sharpened inside.

Across the street there is a wooden house painted an oily yellow. Its front steps have become unsafe and two boards forming an X have been nailed across them.

The truck parked in front of Alister's car is a prewar model, with a runningboard and a fringe of rust on its fenders. A man in overalls comes out of the hardware store and gets into it. After some engine complaint, then some rattling and bouncing in place, it is driven away. Now a delivery truck with the store's name on it tries to park in the space left vacant. There is not quite enough room. The driver gets out and comes and raps on Alister's window. Alister is surprised—if he had not been talking so earnestly he would have noticed the problem. He rolls down the window and the man asks if we are parked there because we intend to buy something in the store. If not, could we please move along?

"Just leaving," says Alister, the man sitting beside me who was going to marry me but now is not going to marry me. "We were just leaving."

We. He has said we. For a moment I cling to that word. Then I think it's the last time. The last time I'll be included in his we.

· It's not the "we" that matters, that is not what tells me the truth. It's his male-to-male tone to the driver, his calm and reasonable apology. I could wish now to go back to what he was saying before, when he did not even notice the van trying to park. What he was saying then had been terrible but his tight grip on the wheel, his grip and his abstraction and his voice had pain in them. No matter what he said and meant, he spoke out of the same deep place then, that he spoke from when he was in bed with me. But it is not so now, after he has spoken to another man. He rolls up the window and gives his attention to the car, to backing it out of its tight spot and moving it so as not to come in contact with the van.

And a moment later I would be glad even to go back to that time, when he craned his head to see behind him. Better that than driving—as he is driving now—down the main street of Huntsville, as if there is no more to be said or managed.

I can't do it, he has said.

He has said that he can't go through with this.

He can't explain it.

Only that it's a mistake.

I think that I will never be able to look at curly S's like those on the Skates Sharpened sign, without hearing his voice. Or at rough boards knocked into an X like those across the steps of the yellow house opposite the store.

"I'm going to drive you to the station now. I'll buy your ticket to Toronto. I'm pretty sure there's a train to Toronto late in the afternoon. I'll think up some very plausible story and I'll get somebody to pack up your things. You'll need to give me your Toronto address, I don't think I've kept it. Oh, and I'll write you a reference. You've done a good job. You wouldn't have finished out a term anyway—I hadn't told you yet but the children are going to be moved. All kinds of big changes going on."

A new tone in his voice, almost jaunty. A knockabout tone of relief. He is trying to hold that in, not let relief out till I am gone.

I watch the streets. It's something like being driven to the place of execution. Not yet. A little while yet. Not yet do I hear his voice for the last time. Not yet.

He doesn't have to ask the way. I wonder out loud if he has put girls on the train before.

"Don't be like that," he says.

Every turn is like a shearing-off of what's left of my life.

There is a train to Toronto at five o'clock. He has told me to wait in the car while he goes in to check. He comes out with the ticket in his hand and what I think is a lighter step. He must have realized this because as he approaches the car he becomes more sedate.

"It's nice and warm in the station. There's a special ladies' waiting room."

He has opened the car door for me.

"Or would you rather I waited and saw you off? Maybe there's a place where we can get a decent piece of pie. That was a horrible dinner."

This makes me stir myself. I get out and walk ahead of him into the station. He points out the ladies' waiting room. He raises his eyebrow at me and tries to make a final joke.

"Maybe someday you'll count this one of the luckiest days of your life."

I CHOOSE A BENCH in the ladies' waiting room that has a view of the station's front doors. That is to be able to see him if he comes back. He will tell me that this is all a joke. Or a test, as in some medieval drama.

Or perhaps he has had a change of mind. Driving down the highway seeing the pale spring sunlight on the rocks that we so lately looked at together. Struck by a realization of his folly he turns in the middle of the road and comes speeding back.

It is an hour at least before the Toronto train comes into the station, but it seems hardly any time at all. And even now fantasies are running through my mind. I board the train as if there are chains on my ankles. I press my face to the window to look along the platform as the whistle blows for our departure. Even now it might not be too late for me to jump from the train. Jump free and run through the station to the street where he would just have parked the car and is running up the steps thinking not too late, pray not too late.

Myself running to meet him, not too late.

And what is the commotion, shouting, hollering, not one but a gaggle of latecomers pounding between the seats. High school girls in athletic outfits, hooting at the trouble they have caused. The conductor displeased and hurrying them along as they scramble for their seats.

One of them, and perhaps the loudest, is Mary.

I turn my head and do not look at them again.

But here she is, crying out my name and wanting to know where I have been.

To visit with a friend, I tell her.

She plunks herself down beside me and tells me that they have been playing basketball against Huntsville. It was a riot. They lost.

"We lost, didn't we?" she calls out in apparent delight, and the others groan and giggle. She mentions the score which is indeed quite shameful.

"You're all dressed up," she says. But she doesn't much care, she seems to take my explanation without real interest.

She barely notices when I say that I am going on to Toronto to visit my grandparents. Except to remark that they must be really old. Not a word about Alister. Not even a bad word. She would not have forgotten. Just tidied up the scene and put it away in a closet with her former selves. Or maybe she really is a person who can deal recklessly with humiliation.

I am grateful to her now, even if I was not able to feel such a thing at the time. Left all to myself, what might I have done when we got to Amundsen? What jumping up and leaving the train and running to his house and demanding to know why, why. What shame on me forever. As it was, the stop there gave the team barely time to get themselves collected and to rap on the windows alerting the people who had come to pick them up, while being warned by the conductor that if they don't get a move on they will be riding to Toronto.

FOR YEARS I thought I might run into him. I lived, and still live, in Toronto. It seemed to me that everybody ended up in Toronto at least for a little while. Of course that hardly means that you will get to see that person, provided that you should in any way want to.

It finally happened. Crossing a crowded street where you could not even slow down. Going in opposite directions. Staring, at the same time, a bare shock on our time-damaged faces.

He called out, "How are you?" and I answered, "Fine." Then added for good measure, "Happy."

At the moment this was only generally true. I was having some kind of dragged-out row with my husband, about our paying a debt run up by one of his children. I had gone that afternoon to a show at an art gallery, to get myself into a more comfortable frame of mind.

He called back to me once more:

"Good for you."

It still seemed as if we could make our way out of that crowd, that in a moment we would be together. But just as certain that we would carry on in the way we were going. And so we did. No breathless cry, no hand on my shoulder when I reached the sidewalk. Just that flash, that I had seen in an instant, when one of his eyes opened wider. It was the left eye, always the left, as I remembered. And it always looked so strange, alert and wondering, as if some whole impossibility had occurred to him, one that almost made him laugh.

For me, I was feeling something the same as when I left Amundsen, the train carrying me still dazed and full of disbelief.

Nothing changes really about love.

Train

THIS IS A SLOW TRAIN ANYWAY, and it has slowed some more
for the curve. Jackson is the only passenger left, the next stop, Clover, being about twenty miles ahead. And after that Ripley, and
Kincardine and the lake. He is in luck and it's not to be wasted.
Already he has taken his ticket stub out of its overhead notch.

He heaves his bag, and sees it land just nicely, in between the
rails. No choice now—the train's not going to get any slower.

He takes his chance. A young man in good shape, agile as he'll
ever be. But the leap, the landing, disappoints him. He's stiffer
than he'd thought, the stillness pitches him forward, his palms
come down hard on the gravel between the ties, he's scraped the
skin. Nerves.

The train is out of sight, he hears it putting on a bit of speed,
clear of the curve. He spits on his hurting hands, getting the gravel
out. Then picks up his bag and starts walking back in the direction
he has just covered on the train. If he followed the train he would
show up at Clover station well after dark. He'd still be able to complain that he'd fallen asleep and wakened all mixed up, thinking
he'd slept through his stop when he hadn't. Jumped off all confused, then had to walk.

He would have been believed. Coming home from so far away,
home from the war, he could have got mixed up in his head. It's not
too late, he would be where he was supposed to be before midnight.

But all the time he's thinking this, he's walking in the opposite
direction.

He doesn't know many names of trees. Maples, that everybody
knows. Pines. Not much else. He'd thought that where he jumped
was in some woods, but it wasn't. The trees are just along the track,
thick on the embankment, but he can see the flash of fields behind

them. Fields green or rusty or yellow. Pasture, crops, stubble. He knows just that much. It's still August.

And once the noise of the train has been swallowed up he realizes there isn't the perfect quiet around that he would have expected. Plenty of disturbance here and there, a shaking of the dry August leaves that wasn't wind, the racket of some unseen birds chastising him.

Jumping off the train was supposed to be a cancellation. You roused your body, readied your knees, to enter a different block of air. You looked forward to emptiness. And instead, what did you get? An immediate flock of new surroundings, asking for your attention in a way they never did when you were sitting on the train and just looking out the window. What are you doing here? Where are you going? A sense of being watched by things you didn't know about. Of being a disturbance. Life around coming to some conclusions about you from vantage points you couldn't see.

People he'd met in the last few years seemed to think that if you weren't from a city, you were from the country. And that was not true. There were distinctions you could miss unless you lived there, between country and town. Jackson himself was the son of a plumber. He had never been in a stable in his life or herded cows or stooked grain. Or found himself as now stumping along a railway track that seemed to have reverted from its normal purpose of carrying people and freight to become a province of wild apple trees and thorny berry bushes and trailing grapevines and crows—he knew that bird at least—scolding from perches you could not see. And right now a garter snake slithering between the rails, perfectly confident he won't be quick enough to tramp on and murder it. He does know enough to figure that it's harmless, but the confidence riles him.

THE LITTLE JERSEY, whose name was Margaret Rose, could usually be counted on to show up at the stable door for milking twice a day, morning and evening. Belle didn't often have to call her. But this morning she was too interested in something down by the dip of the pasture field, or in the trees that hid the railway tracks on the other side of the fence. She heard Belle's whistle and then her call, and started out reluctantly. But then decided to go back for another look.

Belle set the pail and stool down and started tramping through the morning-wet grass.

"So-boss. So-boss."

She was half coaxing, half scolding.

Something moved in the trees. A man's voice called out that it was all right.

Well of course it was all right. Did he think she was afraid of him? Better for him to be afraid of the cow with the horns still on.

Climbing over the rail fence, he waved in what he might have considered a reassuring way.

That was too much for Margaret Rose, she had to put on a display. Jump one way, then the other. Toss of the wicked little horns. Nothing much, but Jerseys can always surprise you in an unpleasant way, with their speed and spurts of temper. Belle called out, to scold her and to reassure him.

"She won't hurt you. Just don't move. It's her nerves."

Now she noticed the bag he had hold of. That was what had caused the trouble. She had thought he was just out walking the tracks, but he was going somewhere.

"She's upset with your bag. If you could just lay it down for a moment. I have to get her back towards the barn to milk her."

He did as she asked, and then stood watching, not wanting to move an inch.

She got Margaret Rose headed back to where the pail was, and the stool, on this side of the barn.

"You can pick it up now," she called. And spoke companionably as he got nearer. "As long as you don't wave it around at her. You're a soldier, aren't you? If you wait till I get her milked I can get you some breakfast. That's a stupid name when you have to holler at her. Margaret Rose."

She was a short sturdy woman with straight hair, gray mixed in with what was fair, and childish bangs.

"I'm the one responsible for it," she said, as she got herself settled. "I'm a royalist. Or I used to be. I have porridge made, on the back of the stove. It won't take me long to milk. If you wouldn't mind going round the barn and waiting where she can't see you. It's too bad I can't offer you an egg. We used to keep hens but the foxes kept getting them and we just got fed up."

We. We used to keep hens. That meant she had a man around somewhere.

"Porridge is good. I'll be glad to pay you."

"No need. Just get out of the way for a bit. She's got herself too interested to let her milk down."

He took himself off, around the barn. It was in bad shape. He peered between the boards to see what kind of a car she had, but all he could make out in there was an old buggy and some other wrecks of machinery.

The place showed some sort of tidiness, but not exactly industry. On the house, white paint all peeling and going gray. A window with boards nailed across it, where there must have been broken glass. The dilapidated henhouse where she had mentioned the foxes getting the hens. Shingles in a pile.

If there was a man on the place he must have been an invalid, or else paralyzed with laziness.

There was a road running by. A small fenced field in front of the house, a dirt road. And in the field a dappled peaceable-looking horse. A cow he could see reasons for keeping, but a horse? Even before the war people on farms were getting rid of them, tractors were the coming thing. And she hadn't looked like the sort to trot round on horseback just for the fun of it.

Then it struck him. The buggy in the barn. It was no relic, it was all she had.

For a while now he'd been hearing a peculiar sound. The road rose up a hill, and from over that hill came a clip-clop, clip-clop. Along with the clip-clop some little tinkle or whistling.

Now then. Over the hill came a box on wheels, being pulled by two quite small horses. Smaller than the one in the field but no end livelier. And in the box sat a half dozen or so little men. All dressed in black, with proper black hats on their heads.

The sound was coming from them. It was singing. Discreet high-pitched little voices, as sweet as could be. They never looked at him as they went by.

That chilled him. The buggy in the barn and the horse in the field were nothing in comparison.

He was still standing there looking one way and another when he heard her call, "All finished." She was standing by the house.

"This is where to go in and out," she said of the back door. "The front is stuck since last winter, it just refuses to open, you'd think it was still frozen."

They walked on planks laid over an uneven dirt floor, in a darkness provided by the boarded-up window. It was as chilly there as it had been in the hollow where he'd slept. He had wakened again and again, trying to scrunch himself into a position where he could stay warm. The woman didn't shiver here—she gave off a smell of healthy exertion and what was likely the cow's hide.

She poured the fresh milk into a basin and covered it with a piece of cheesecloth she kept by, then led him into the main part of the house. The windows there had no curtains, so the light was coming in. Also the woodstove had been in use. There was a sink with a hand pump, a table with oilcloth on it worn in some places to shreds, and a couch covered with a patchy old quilt.

Also a pillow that had shed some feathers.

So far, not so bad, though old and shabby. There was a use for everything that you could see. But raise your eyes and up there on shelves was pile on pile of newspapers or magazines or just some kind of papers, up to the ceiling.

He had to ask her, Was she not afraid of fire? A woodstove for instance.

"Oh, I'm always here. I mean, I sleep here. There isn't anyplace else I can keep the drafts out. I'm watchful. I haven't had a chimney fire even. A couple of times it got too hot and I just threw some baking powder on it. Nothing to it.

"My mother had to be here anyway," she said. "There was noplace else for her to be comfortable. I had her cot in here. I kept an eye on everything. I did think of moving all the papers into the front room but it's really too damp in there, they would all be ruined."

Then she said she should have explained. "My mother's dead. She died in May. Just when the weather got decent. She lived to hear about the end of the war on the radio. She understood perfectly. She lost her speech a long time ago but she could understand. I got so used to her not speaking that sometimes I think she's here but of course she's not."

Jackson felt it was up to him to say he was sorry.

"Oh well. It was coming. Just lucky it wasn't in the winter."

She served him oatmeal porridge and poured tea.

"Not too strong? The tea?"

Mouth full, he shook his head.

"I never economize on tea. If it comes to that, why not drink hot water? We did run out when the weather got so bad last winter. The hydro gave out and the radio gave out and the tea gave out. I had a rope round the back door to hang on to when I went out to milk. I was going to let Margaret Rose into the back kitchen but I figured she'd get too upset with the storm and I couldn't hold her. Anyway, she survived. We all survived."

Finding a space in the conversation, he asked, were there any dwarfs in the neighborhood?

"Not that I've noticed."

"In a cart?"

"Oh. Were they singing? It must have been the little Mennonite boys. They drive their cart to church and they sing all the way. The girls have to go in the buggy with the parents but they let the boys ride in the cart."

"They looked like they never saw me."

"They wouldn't. I used to say to Mother that we lived on the right road because we were just like the Mennonites. The horse and buggy and we drink our milk unpasteurized. The only thing is, neither one of us can sing.

"When Mother died they brought so much food I was eating it for weeks. They must have thought there'd be a wake or something. I'm lucky to have them. But then I say to myself they are lucky too. Because they are supposed to practice charity and here I am practically on their doorstep and an occasion for charity if you ever saw one."

He offered to pay her when he'd finished but she batted her hand at his money.

But there was one thing, she said. If before he went he could manage to fix the horse trough.

What this involved was actually making a new horse trough, and in order to do that he had to hunt around for any materials and tools he could find. It took him all day, and she served him pancakes and Mennonite maple syrup for supper. She said that if he'd only come a week later she might have fed him fresh jam. She picked the wild berries growing along the railway track.

They sat on kitchen chairs outside the back door until after the sun went down. She was telling him something about how she came to be here, and he was listening but not paying full attention because he was looking around and thinking how this place was on its last legs but not absolutely hopeless, if somebody wanted to settle down and fix things up. A certain investment of money was needed, but a greater investment of time and energy. It could be a challenge. He could almost bring himself to regret that he was moving on.

Another reason that he didn't pay full attention to what Belle—her name was Belle—kept telling him was that she was talking about her life which he couldn't very well imagine.

Her father—she called him her daddy—had bought this place just for the summers, she said, and then he decided that they might as well live here all the year round. He could work anywhere, because he made his living with a column for the *Toronto Evening Telegram*. The mailman took what was written and it was sent off on the train. He wrote about all sorts of things that happened. He even put Belle in, referring to her as Pussycat. And mentioning Belle's mother occasionally but calling her Princess Casamassima, out of a book whose name, she said, meant nothing anymore. Her mother might have been the reason they stayed year-round. She had caught the terrible flu of 1918 in which so many people died, and when she came out of it she was strange. Not really mute, because she could make words, but had lost many of them. Or they had lost her. She had to learn all over again to feed herself and go to the bathroom. Besides the words she had to learn to keep her clothes on in the hot weather. So you wouldn't want her just wandering around and being a laughingstock on some city street.

Belle was away at a school in the winters. The name of the school was Bishop Strachan and she was surprised that he had never heard of it. She spelled it out. It was in Toronto and it was full of rich girls but also had girls like herself who got special money from relations or wills to go there. It taught her to be rather snooty, she said. And it didn't give her any idea of what she would do for a living.

But that was all settled for her by the accident. Walking along the railway track, as he often liked to do on a summer evening, her father was hit by a train. She and her mother had both gone to bed before it happened and Belle thought it must be a farm animal loose on the tracks, but her mother was moaning dreadfully and seemed to know first thing.

Sometimes a girl she had been friends with at school would write to ask her what on earth she could find to do up there, but little did they know. There was milking and cooking and taking care of her mother and she had the hens at that time as well. She learned how to cut up potatoes so each part has an eye, and plant them and dig them up the next summer. She had not learned to drive and when the war came she sold her daddy's car. The Mennonites let her have a horse that was not good for farm work anymore, and one of them taught her how to harness and drive it.

One of the old friends, called Robin, came up to visit her and thought the way she was living was a hoot. She wanted her to go back to Toronto, but what about her mother? Her mother was a lot quieter now and kept her clothes on, also enjoyed listening to the radio, the opera on Saturday afternoons. Of course she could do that in Toronto, but Belle didn't like to uproot her. Robin said it was herself she was talking about, scared of uproot. She—Robin—went away and joined whatever they called the women's army.

THE FIRST THING he had to do was to make some rooms other than the kitchen fit to sleep in, come the cold weather. He had some mice to get rid of and even some rats, now coming in from the cooling weather. He asked her why she'd never invested in a cat and heard a piece of her peculiar logic. She said it would always be killing things and dragging them for her to look at, which she didn't want to do. He kept a sharp ear open for the snap of the traps, and got rid of them before she knew what had happened. Then he lectured about the papers filling up the kitchen, the firetrap problem, and she agreed to move them if the front room could be got free of damp. That became his main job. He invested in a heater and repaired the walls, and convinced her to spend the better part of a month climbing up and getting the papers, rereading and reorganizing them and fitting them onto the shelves he had made.

She told him then that the papers contained her father's book. Sometimes she called it a novel. He did not think to ask anything about it, but one day she told him it was about two people named Matilda and Stephen. A historical novel.

"You remember your history?"

He had finished five years of high school with respectable marks and a very good showing in trigonometry and geography but did not remember much history. In his final year, anyway, all you could think about was that you were going to the war.

He said, "Not altogether."

"You'd remember altogether if you went to Bishop Strachan. You'd have had it rammed down your throat. English history, anyway."

She said that Stephen had been a hero. A man of honor, far too good for his times. He was that rare person who wasn't all out for himself or looking to break his word the moment it was convenient to do so. Consequently and finally he was not a success.

. And then Matilda. She was a straight descendant of William the Conqueror and as cruel and haughty as you might expect. Though there might be people stupid enough to defend her because she was a woman.

"If he could have finished it would have been a very fine novel."

Jackson of course knew that books existed because people sat down and wrote them. They didn't just appear out of the blue. But why, was the question. There were books already in existence, plenty of them. Two of which he had to read at school. *A Tale of Two Cities* and *Huckleberry Finn,* each of them with language that wore you down though in different ways. And that was understandable. They were written in the past.

What puzzled him, though he didn't intend to let on, was why anybody would want to sit down and do another one, in the present. Now.

A tragedy, said Belle briskly, and Jackson didn't know if it was her father she was talking about or the people in the book that had not got finished.

Anyway, now that this room was livable his mind was on the roof. No use to fix up a room and have the state of the roof render it unlivable again in a year or two. He had managed to patch it so that it would do her a couple of more winters, but he could not guarantee more than that. And he still planned to be on his way by Christmas.

THE MENNONITE FAMILIES on the next farm ran to older girls, and the younger boys he had seen were not strong enough yet to take on heavier chores. Jackson had been able to hire himself out to them, during the fall harvest. He had been brought in to eat with the others and to his surprise found that the girls behaved giddily as they served him, they were not at all mute as he had expected. The mothers kept an eye on them, he noticed, and the fathers kept an eye on him. He was pleased to know that he could satisfy both sets of parents. They could see that nothing was stirring with him. All safe.

And of course with Belle not a thing had to be spoken of. She was—he had found this out—sixteen years older than he was. To mention it, even to joke about it, would spoil everything. She was a certain kind of woman, he a certain kind of man.

THE TOWN where they shopped, when they needed to, was called Oriole. It was in the opposite direction from the town where he had grown up. He tied up the horse in the United Church shed there, since there were of course no hitching posts left on the main street. At first he was leery of the hardware store and the barbershop. But soon he understood something about small towns which he should have realized just from growing up in one. They did not have much to do with each other, unless it was for games run off in the ballpark or the hockey arena, where all was a fervent made-up sort of hostility. When they needed to shop for something their own stores could not supply they went to a city. The same when they wanted to consult a doctor other than the ones their own town could offer. He didn't run into anybody familiar, and nobody showed a curiosity about him, though they might look twice at the horse. In the winter months, not even that, because the back roads were not plowed and people taking their milk to the creamery or eggs to the grocery had to make do with horses, just as he and Belle did.

Belle always stopped to see what movie was on though she had no intention of going to see any of them. Her knowledge of movies and movie stars was intensive but came from some years back, something like Matilda and Stephen. For instance she could tell you who Clark Gable was married to in real life before he became Rhett Butler.

Soon Jackson was going to get his hair cut when he needed to and buying his tobacco when he had run out. He smoked now like a farmer, rolling his own and never lighting up indoors.

Secondhand cars didn't become available for a while, but when they did, with the new models finally on the scene, and farmers who'd made money in the war ready to turn in the old ones, he had a talk with Belle. The horse Freckles was God knows how old and stubborn on any sort of hill.

He found that the car dealer had been taking notice of him, though not counting on a visit.

"I always thought you and your sister was Mennonites but ones that wore a different kind of outfit," the dealer said.

That shook Jackson up a little but at least it was better than husband and wife. It made him realize how he must have aged and changed over the years, and how the person who had jumped off the train, that skinny nerve-racked soldier, would not be so recognizable in the man he was now. Whereas Belle, so far as he could see, was stopped at some point in life where she remained a grown-up child. And her talk reinforced this impression, jumping back and forth, into the past and out again, so that it seemed she made no difference between their last trip to town and the last movie she had seen with her mother and father, or the comical occasion when Margaret Rose—now dead—had tipped her horns at a worried Jackson.

IT WAS THE SECOND CAR that they had owned, a used one of course, that took them to Toronto in the summer of 1962. This was a trip they had not anticipated and it came at an awkward time for Jackson. For one thing, he was building a new horse barn for the Mennonites, who were busy with the crops, and for another, he had his own harvest of vegetables coming on that he had sold to the grocery store in Oriole. But Belle had a lump that she had finally been persuaded to pay attention to, and she was booked now for an operation in Toronto.

What a change, Belle kept saying. Are you so sure we are still in Canada?

This was before they got past Kitchener. Once they got on the new highway she was truly alarmed, imploring him to find a side road or else turn around and go home. He found himself speaking sharply at that—the traffic was surprising him too. She stayed quiet all the way after that, and he had no way of knowing whether she had her eyes closed because she had given up or because she was praying. He had never known her to pray.

Even this morning she had tried to get him to change his mind about going. She said the lump was getting smaller, not larger. Since the health insurance for everybody had come in, she said, nobody did anything but run to the doctor, and make their lives into one long drama of hospitals and operations, which did nothing but prolong the period of being a nuisance at the end of life.

She calmed down and cheered up once they got to their turn-off and were actually in the city. They found themselves on Avenue Road, and in spite of exclamations about how everything had changed, she seemed to be able on every block to recognize something she knew. There was the apartment building where one of the teachers from Bishop Strachan had lived. In its basement there was a shop where you could buy milk and cigarettes and the newspaper. Wouldn't it be strange, she said, if you could go in there and still find the *Telegram,* where there would be not only her father's name but his smudgy picture, taken when he still had all his hair?

Then a little cry, and down a side street she had seen the very church—she could swear it was the very church—in which her parents had been married. They had taken her there to show her, though it wasn't a church they had gone to. They did not go to any church, far from it. It was sort of a joke. Her father said they had been married in the basement but her mother said the vestry.

Her mother could talk readily then, she was like anybody else.

Perhaps there was a law at the time, to make you get married in a church or it wasn't legal.

At Eglinton she saw the subway sign.

"Just think, I have never been on a subway train."

She said this with some sort of mixed pain and pride.

"Imagine remaining so ignorant."

At the hospital they were ready for her. She continued to be lively, telling them about her horrors in the traffic and about the changes, wondering if there was still such a show put on at Christmas by Eaton's store. And did anybody still read the *Telegram*?

"You should have driven in through Chinatown," one of the nurses said. "Now that's something."

"I'll look forward to seeing it on my way home." She laughed, and said, "If I get to go home."

"Now don't be silly."

Another nurse was talking to Jackson about where he'd parked the car, and telling him where to move it so he wouldn't get a ticket. Also making sure that he knew about the accommodations for out-of-town relations, much cheaper than you'd have to pay at a hotel.

Belle would be put to bed now, they said. A doctor would come to have a look at her, and Jackson could come back later to say good night. He might find her a little dopey by that time.

She overheard, and said that she was dopey all the time so he wouldn't be surprised, and there was a little merriment all round.

The nurse took him to sign something before he left. He hesitated where it asked what relation. Then he wrote "Friend."

WHEN HE CAME BACK in the evening he did see a change, though he would not have described Belle then as dopey. They had put her into some kind of green cloth sack that left her neck and most of her arms quite bare. He had seldom seen her so bare, or noticed the raw-looking cords that stretched between her collarbone and chin.

She was angry that her mouth was dry.

"They won't let me have anything but the meanest little sip of water."

She wanted him to go and get her a Coke, something that she never had drunk in her life as far as he knew.

"There's a machine down the hall—there must be. I see people going by with a bottle in their hands and it makes me so thirsty."

He said he couldn't go against orders.

Tears came into her eyes and she turned pettishly away.

"I want to go home."

"Soon you will."

"You could help me find my clothes."

"No I couldn't."

"If you won't I'll do it myself. I'll get to the train station myself."

"There isn't any passenger train that goes up our way anymore."

Abruptly then, she seemed to give up on her plans for escape. In a few moments she started to recall the house and all the improvements that they—or mostly he—had made on it. The white paint shining on the outside, and even the back kitchen whitewashed and furnished with a plank floor. The roof reshingled and the windows restored to their plain old style, and most of all glories, the plumbing that was such a joy in the wintertime.

"If you hadn't shown up I'd have soon been living in absolute squalor."

He didn't voice his opinion that she already had been.

"When I come out of this I am going to make a will," she said. "All yours. You won't have wasted your labors."

He had of course thought about this, and you would have expected that the prospects of ownership would have brought a sober satisfaction to him, though he would have expressed a truthful and companionable hope that nothing would happen too soon. But not now. It seemed to have little to do with him, to be quite far away.

She returned to her fret.

"Oh, I wish I was there and not here."

"You'll feel a lot better when you wake up after the operation."

Though from everything that he had heard that was a whopping lie.

Suddenly he felt so tired.

HE HAD SPOKEN closer to the truth than he could have guessed. Two days after the lump's removal Belle was sitting up in a different room, eager to greet him and not at all disturbed by the moans coming from a woman behind the curtain in the next bed. That was more or less what she—Belle—had sounded like yesterday, when he never got her to open her eyes or notice him at all.

"Don't pay any attention to her," said Belle. "She's completely out of it. Probably doesn't feel a thing. She'll come round tomorrow bright as a dollar. Or else she won't."

A somewhat satisfied, institutional authority was showing, a veteran's callousness. She was sitting up in bed and swallowing some kind of bright orange drink through a conveniently bent straw. She looked a lot younger than the woman he had brought to the hospital such a short time before.

SHE WANTED TO KNOW if he was getting enough sleep, if he'd found someplace where he liked to eat, if the weather had been not too warm for walking, if he had found time to visit the Royal Ontario Museum, as she thought she had advised.

But she could not concentrate on his replies. She seemed to be in a state of amazement. Controlled amazement.

"Oh, I do have to tell you," she said, breaking right into his explanation of why he had not got to the museum. "Oh, don't look so alarmed. You'll make me laugh with that face on, it'll hurt my stitches. Why on earth should I be thinking of laughing anyway? It's a dreadfully sad thing really, it's a tragedy. You know about my father, what I've told you about my father—"

The thing he noticed was that she said father instead of Daddy.

"My father and my mother—"

She seemed to have to search around and get started again.

"The house was in better shape than when you first got to see it. Well, it would be. We used that room at the top of the stairs for our bathroom. Of course we had to carry the water up and down. Only later, when you came, I was using the downstairs. With the shelves in it, you know, that had been a pantry?"

How could she not remember that he was the one who had taken out the shelves and put in the bathroom?

"Oh well, what does it matter?" she said, as if she followed his thoughts. "So I had heated the water and I carried it upstairs to have my sponge bath. And I took off my clothes. Well, I would. There was a big mirror over the sink, you see it had a sink like a real bathroom, only you had to pull out the plug and let the water back into the pail when you were finished. The toilet was elsewhere. You get the picture. So I proceeded to wash myself and I was bare naked, naturally. It must have been around nine o'clock at night so there was plenty of light. It was summer, did I say? That little room facing the west?"

"Then I heard steps and of course it was Daddy. My father. He must have been finished putting Mother to bed. I heard the steps coming up the stairs and I did notice they sounded heavy. Somewhat not like usual. Very deliberate. Or maybe that was just my impression afterwards. You are apt to dramatize things afterwards. The steps stopped right outside the bathroom door and if I thought anything I thought, Oh, he must be tired. I didn't have any bolt across the door because of course there wasn't one. You just assumed somebody was in there if the door was closed.

"So he was standing outside the door and I didn't think anything of it and then he opened the door and he just stood and looked at me. And I have to say what I mean. Looking at all of me, not just my face. My face looking into the mirror and him looking at me in the mirror and also what was behind me and I couldn't see. It wasn't in any sense a normal look.

"I'll tell you what I thought. I thought, He's walking in his sleep. I didn't know what to do, because you are not supposed to startle anybody that is sleepwalking.

"But then he said, 'Excuse me,' and I knew he was not asleep. But he spoke in a funny kind of voice, I mean it was a strange voice, very much as if he was disgusted with me. Or mad at me, I didn't know. Then he left the door open and just went away down the hall. I dried myself and got into my nightgown and went to bed and went to sleep right away. When I got up in the morning there was the water I hadn't drained, and I didn't want to go near it, but I did.

"But everything seemed normal and he was up already typing away. He just yelled good morning and then he asked me how to spell some word. The way he often did, because I was a better speller. So I gave it to him and then I said he should learn how to spell if he was going to be a writer, he was hopeless. But sometime later in the day when I was washing some dishes he came up right behind me and I froze. He just said, 'Belle, I'm sorry.' And I thought, Oh, I wish he had not said that. It scared me. I knew it was true he was sorry but he was putting it out in the open in a way I could not ignore. I just said, 'That's okay,' but I couldn't make myself say it in an easy voice or as if it really was okay.

"I couldn't. I had to let him know he had changed us. I went to throw out the dishwater and then I went back to whatever else I was doing and not another word. Later I got Mother up from her nap and I had supper ready and I called him but he didn't come. I said to Mother that he must have gone for a walk. He often did when he got stuck in his writing. I helped Mother cut up her food, but I couldn't help thinking about disgusting things. Primarily about noises I heard sometimes coming from their room, and I muffled myself so I wouldn't hear. Now I wondered about Mother sitting there eating her supper, and I wondered what she thought of it or understood of it at all.

"I didn't know where he could have gone. I got Mother ready for bed though that was his job. Then I heard the train coming and all at once the commotion and the screeching which was the train brakes and I must have known what had happened though I don't know exactly when I knew.

"I told you before. I told you he got run over by the train.

"But I'm telling you this. And I am not telling you just to be harrowing. At first I couldn't stand it and for the longest time I was actually making myself think that he was walking along the tracks with his mind on his work and never heard the train. That was the story all right. I was not going to think it was about me or even what it primarily was about.

"Sex.

"Now I see. Now I have got a real understanding of it and it was nobody's fault. It was the fault of human sex in a tragic situation. Me growing up there and Mother the way she was and Daddy, naturally, the way he would be. Not my fault nor his fault.

"There should be acknowledgment, that's all I mean, places where people can go if they are in a situation. And not be all ashamed and guilty about it. If you think I mean brothels, you are right. If you think prostitutes, right again. Do you understand?"

Jackson, looking over her head, said yes.

"I feel so released. It's not that I don't feel the tragedy, but I have got outside the tragedy, is what I mean. It is just the mistakes of humanity. You mustn't think because I'm smiling that I don't have compassion. I have serious compassion. But I have to say I am relieved. I have to say I somehow feel happy. You are not embarrassed by listening to all this?"

"No."

"You realize I am in an abnormal state. I know I am. Everything so clear. I am so grateful for it."

The woman on the next bed had not let up on her rhythmical groaning, all through this. Jackson felt as if that refrain had entered into his head.

He heard the nurse's squishy shoes in the hall and hoped that they would enter this room. They did.

The nurse said that she had come to give a sleepy-time pill. He was afraid that he would be required to kiss Belle good night. He had noticed that a lot of kissing went on in the hospital. He was glad that when he stood up there was no mention of it.

"See you tomorrow."

HE WOKE UP EARLY, and decided to take a walk before breakfast. He had slept all right but told himself he ought to take a break from the hospital air. It wasn't that he was worried so much by the change in Belle. He thought that it was possible or even probable that she would get back to normal, either today or in a couple of more days. She might not even remember the story she had told him. Which would be a blessing.

The sun was well up, as you could expect at this time of year, and the buses and streetcars were already pretty full. He walked south for a bit, then turned west onto Dundas Street, and after a while found himself in the Chinatown he had heard about. Loads of recognizable and many not so recognizable vegetables were being trundled into shops, and small skinned apparently edible animals were already hanging up for sale. The streets were full of illegally parked trucks and noisy, desperate-sounding snatches of the Chinese language. Chinese. All the high-pitched clamor sounded like they had a war going on, but probably to them it was just everyday. Nevertheless he felt like getting out of the way, and he went into a restaurant run by Chinese but advertising an ordinary breakfast of eggs and bacon. When he came out of there he intended to turn around and retrace his steps.

But instead he found himself heading south again. He had got onto a residential street lined with tall and fairly narrow brick houses. They must have been built before people in the area felt any need for driveways or possibly before they even had cars. Before there were such things as cars. He walked until he saw a sign for Queen Street, which he had heard of. He turned west again and after a few blocks he came to an obstacle. In front of a doughnut shop he ran into a small crowd of people.

They were stopped by an ambulance, backed right up on the sidewalk so you could not get by. Some of them were complaining about the delay and asking loudly if it was even legal to park an ambulance on the sidewalk and others were looking peaceful enough while they chatted about what the trouble might be. Death was mentioned, some of the onlookers speaking of various candidates and others saying that was the only legal excuse for the vehicle being where it was.

The man who was finally carried out, bound to the stretcher, was surely not dead or they'd have had his face covered. He was unconscious however and his skin the gray of cement. He was not being carried out through the doughnut shop, as some had jokingly predicted—that was some sort of dig at the quality of the doughnuts—but through the main door of the building. It was a decent enough brick apartment building five stories high, a Laundromat as well as the doughnut shop on its main floor. The name carved over its main door suggested pride as well as some foolishness in its past.

Bonnie Dundee.

A man not in ambulance uniform came out last. He stood there looking with exasperation at the crowd that was now thinking of breaking up. The only thing to wait for now was the grand wail of the ambulance as it found its way onto the street and tore away.

Jackson was one of those who didn't bother to walk away. He wouldn't have said he was curious about any of this, more that he was just waiting for the inevitable turn he had been expecting, to take him back to where he'd come from. The man who had come out of the building walked over and asked if he was in a hurry.

No. Not specially.

This man was the owner of the building. The man taken away in the ambulance was the caretaker and superintendent.

"I've got to get to the hospital and see what's the trouble with him. Right as rain yesterday. Never complained. Nobody close that

I can call on, so far as I know. The worst, I can't find the keys. Not on him and not where he usually keeps them. So I got to go home and get my spares and I just wondered, could you keep a watch on things meanwhile? I got to go home and I got to go to the hospital too. I could ask some of the tenants but I'd just rather not, if you know what I mean. I don't want them bugging me what's the matter when I don't know any better than they do."

He asked again if Jackson was sure he would not mind, and Jackson said no, fine.

"Just keep an eye for anybody going in, out, ask to see their keys. Tell them it's an emergency, won't be long."

He was leaving, then turned around.

"You might as well sit down."

There was a chair Jackson had not noticed. Folded and pushed out of the way so the ambulance could park. It was just one of those canvas chairs but comfortable enough and sturdy. Jackson set it down with thanks in a spot where it would not interfere with passersby or apartment dwellers. No notice was taken of him. He had been about to mention the hospital and the fact that he himself had to get back there before too long. But the man had been in a hurry, and he already had enough on his mind, and he had made the point that he would be as quick as he could.

Jackson realized, once he got sitting down, just how long he'd been on his feet walking here or there.

The man had told him to get a coffee or something to eat from the doughnut shop if he felt the need.

"Just tell them my name."

But that name Jackson did not even know.

When the owner came back he apologized for being late. The fact was that the man who had been taken away in the ambulance had died. Arrangements had to be made. A new set of keys had become necessary. Here they were. There'd be some sort of funeral involving those in the building who had been around a long time. Notice in the paper might bring in a few more. A troublesome spell, till this was sorted out.

It would solve the problem. If Jackson could. Temporarily. It only had to be temporarily.

Jackson heard himself say, Yes, all right with him.

If he wanted to take a little time, that could be managed. He heard this man—his new boss—say so. Right after the funeral and some disposal of goods. A few days he could have then, to get his affairs together and do the proper moving-in.

That would not be necessary, Jackson said. His affairs were together and his possessions were on his back.

Naturally this roused a little suspicion. Jackson was not surprised a couple of days later to hear that his new employer had made a visit to the police. But all was well, apparently. He had emerged as just one of those loners who may have got themselves in too deep some way or another but have not been guilty of breaking any law.

It looked as if there was nobody looking for him anyway.

AS A RULE, Jackson liked to have older people in the building. And as a rule, single people. Not what you would call zombies. People with interests. You might sometimes say talent. The sort of talent that had been noticed once, made some kind of a living once, though not enough to hang on to all through a life. An announcer whose voice had been familiar on the radio years ago during the war but whose vocal cords were shot to pieces now. Most people probably believed he was dead. But here he was in his bachelor suite, keeping up with the news and subscribing to *The Globe and Mail* which he passed on to Jackson in case there was anything of interest to him in it.

Once, there was.

Marjorie Isabella Treece, daughter of Willard Treece, longtime columnist for the *Toronto Evening Telegram,* and his wife, Helena (née Abbott) Treece, lifelong friend of Robin (née Shillingham) Ford, has passed away after a courageous battle with cancer. Oriole paper please copy. July 18, 1965.

No mention of where she had been living. Probably in Toronto, with Robin so much in the picture. She had lasted maybe longer than you might have expected and might even have been in reasonable comfort and spirits, till of course near the end. She had shown a certain gift for adapting to circumstances. More, perhaps, than he possessed himself.

Not that he spent his time picturing the rooms he'd shared with her or the work he'd done on her place. He didn't have to—such things were often recalled in dreams, and his feeling then was more of exasperation than of longing, as if he had to get to work right away on something that had not been finished.

In the Bonnie Dundee, the tenants were generally uneasy about anything that might be called improvements, thinking that these might cause a raise in their rent. He talked them around, with respectful manners and good fiscal sense. The place improved and became one with a waiting list. The owner complained that it was getting to be a haven for loonies. But Jackson said they were generally tidier than average and old enough not to misbehave. There was a woman who had once played in the Toronto Symphony and an inventor who had missed out so far with his inventions but was hopeful, and a Hungarian refugee actor whose accent was against him but who still had a commercial running somewhere in the world. They were all well behaved and somehow scared up the money to go to the Epicure Restaurant and tell their stories through the afternoon. Also they had a few friends who were truly famous and might show up in a blue moon for a visit. And not to be sneezed at was the fact that the Bonnie Dundee had an in-house preacher on shaky terms with his church, whatever it was, but always able to officiate when called upon.

People did get in the habit of staying until his final offices were necessary, but it was better than skipping and running.

An exception was the young couple named Candace and Quincy, who never settled their rent and skipped out in the middle of the night. The owner happened to have been in charge when they came looking for a room, and he excused himself for his bad choice by saying that a fresh face was needed around the place. Candace's face, not the boyfriend's. The boyfriend was a jerk.

ON A HOT SUMMER DAY Jackson had the double back doors, the delivery doors, open, to let in what air he could while he worked at varnishing a table. It was a pretty table he'd got for nothing because its polish was all worn away. He thought it would look nice in the entryway, to put the mail on.

He was able to be out of the office because the owner was in there checking some rents.

There was a light touch on the front doorbell. Jackson was ready to haul himself up, cleaning his brush, because he thought the owner in the midst of figures might not care to be disturbed. But it was all right, he heard the door being opened, a woman's voice. A voice on the edge of exhaustion, yet able to maintain something of its charm, its absolute assurance that whatever it said would win over anybody who came within listening range.

She would probably have got that from her father the preacher. Jackson was thinking this before the whole impact hit him.

This was the last address she had, she said, for her daughter. She was looking for her daughter. Candace, her daughter. Who might have been travelling with a friend. She, the mother, had come here from British Columbia. From Kelowna where she and the girl's father lived.

Ileane. Jackson knew her voice without a doubt. That woman was Ileane.

He heard her ask if it was possible for her to sit down. Then the owner pulling out his—Jackson's—chair.

Toronto so much hotter than she had expected, though she knew Ontario, had grown up there.

She wondered if she could possibly ask for a glass of water.

She must have put her head down in her hands as her voice grew muffled. The owner came out into the hall and dropped some change into the machine to get a 7UP. He might have thought that more ladylike than a Coke.

Around the corner he saw Jackson listening, and he made a gesture that he—Jackson—should take over, being perhaps more used to distraught tenants. But Jackson shook his head violently.

No.

She did not stay distraught long.

She begged the owner's pardon and he said the heat could play those tricks today.

Now about Candace. They had left within the month, it could be three weeks ago. No forwarding address.

"In such cases there usually isn't."

She got the hint.

"Oh of course I can settle—"

There was some muttering and rustling while this was done.

Then, "I don't suppose you could let me see where they were living—"

"The tenant isn't in now. But even if he was I don't think he'd agree to it."

"Of course. That's silly."

"Was there anything you were particularly interested in?"

"Oh no. No. You've been kind. I've taken your time."

She had got up now, and they were moving. Out of the office, down the couple of steps to the front door. Then the door was opened and street noises swallowed up her further farewells if there were any.

However she had been disappointed, she would get herself through it with a good grace.

Jackson came out of hiding as the owner returned to the office.

"Surprise," was all the owner said. "We got our money."

He was a man who was basically incurious, at least about personal matters. A thing which Jackson valued in him.

Of course Jackson would like to have seen her. Now that she was gone he almost regretted his chance. He would never stoop so low as to ask the owner was her hair still dark, black almost, her body tall and slim and with very little bosom to it. He hadn't got much of an impression of the daughter. Her hair was blond but very likely dyed. No more than twenty years old though it was sometimes hard to tell nowadays. Very much under the thumb of the boyfriend. Run away from home, run away from your bills, break your parents' hearts, all for a sulky piece of business like the boyfriend.

Where was Kelowna? In the west somewhere. Alberta, British Columbia. A long way to come looking. Of course that mother was a persistent woman. An optimist. Probably that was true of her still. She had married. Unless the girl was born out of wedlock and that struck him as very unlikely. She'd be sure, sure of herself the next time, she wouldn't be one for tragedy. The girl wouldn't be, either. She'd come home when she'd had enough. She might bring along a baby but that was all the style nowadays.

SHORTLY BEFORE CHRISTMAS in the year 1940 there had been an uproar in the high school. It had even reached the third floor where the clamor of typewriters and adding machines usually kept all the downstairs noises at bay. The oldest girls in the school were up there—girls who last year had been learning Latin and biology and European history and were now learning to type.

One of these was Ileane Bishop, who oddly enough was a minister's daughter, although there were no bishops in her father's United Church. Ileane had arrived with her family when she was in grade nine and for five years, due to the custom of alphabetical seating, she had sat behind Jackson Adams. By that time Jackson's phenomenal shyness and silence had been accepted by everybody else in the class, but it was new to her, and during the next five years, by not acknowledging it she had produced a thaw. She borrowed erasers and pen nibs and geometry tools from him, not so much to break the ice as because she was naturally scatterbrained. They exchanged answers to problems and marked each other's tests. When they met on the street they said hello, and to her his hello was actually more than a mumble—it had two syllables and an emphasis to it. Nothing much was presumed beyond that, except that they had certain jokes. Ileane was not a shy girl but she was clever and aloof and not particularly popular, and that might have suited him.

From her position on the stairs, when everybody came out to watch the ruckus, Ileane was surprised to see that one of the two boys causing it was Jackson. The other was Billy Watts. Boys who only a year ago had sat hunched over books and shuffled dutifully between one classroom and another were now transformed. In army uniforms they looked twice the size they had been, and their boots made a powerful racket as they galloped around. They were shouting out that school was cancelled for the day, because everybody had to join the war. They were distributing cigarettes everywhere, tossing them on the floor where they could be picked up by boys who didn't even shave.

Careless warriors, whooping invaders. Drunk up to their eyeballs.

"I'm no piker," was what they were yelling.

The principal was trying to order them out. But because this was still early in the war and there was as yet some awe and special respect concerning the boys who had signed up, he was not able to show the ruthlessness he would have called upon a year later.

"Now now," he said.

"I'm no piker," Billy Watts told him.

Jackson had his mouth open probably to say the same, but at that moment his eyes met the eyes of Ileane Bishop and a certain piece of knowledge passed between them.

Ileane Bishop understood that Jackson was truly drunk but that the effect of this was to enable him to play drunk, therefore the drunkenness displayed could be managed. (Billy Watts was just drunk, through and through.) With this understanding Ileane walked down the stairs, smiling, and accepted a cigarette which she held unlit between her fingers. She linked arms with both heroes and marched them out of the school.

Once outside they lit up their cigarettes.

There was a conflict of opinion about this later, in Ileane's father's congregation. Some said Ileane had not actually smoked hers, just pretended, to pacify the boys, while others said she certainly had. Smoked. Their minister's daughter. Smoked.

Billy did put his arms around Ileane and tried to kiss her, but he stumbled and sat down on the school steps and crowed like a rooster.

Within two years he would be dead.

Meanwhile he had to be got home, and Jackson pulled him so that they could get his arms over their shoulders and drag him along. Fortunately his house was not far from the school. They left him there, passed out on the steps. Then they entered into a conversation.

Jackson did not want to go home. Why not? Because his stepmother was there, he said. He hated his stepmother. Why? No reason.

Ileane knew that his mother had died in a car accident when he was very small—this was sometimes mentioned to account for his shyness. She thought that the drink was probably making him exaggerate, but she didn't try to make him talk about it any further.

"Okay," she said. "You can stay at my place."

It just happened that Ileane's mother was away, looking after Ileane's sick grandmother. Ileane was at the time keeping house in a haphazard style for her father and her two younger brothers. This was unfortunate in some opinions. Not that her mother would have made a fuss, but she would have wanted to know the ins and outs, and who was this boy? At the very least she would have made Ileane go to school as usual.

A soldier and a girl, suddenly so close. Where there had been nothing all this time but logarithms and declensions.

Ileane's father didn't pay attention to them. He was more interested in the war than some of his parishioners thought a minister should be, and this made him proud to have a soldier in the house. Also he was unhappy not to be able to send his daughter to college. He had to save up to send her brothers there someday, they would have to earn a living. That made him go easy on Ileane whatever she did.

Jackson and Ileane didn't go to the movies. They didn't go to the dance hall. They went for walks, in any weather and often after dark. Sometimes they went into the restaurant and drank coffee, but did not try to be friendly to anybody. What was the matter with them, were they falling in love? When they were walking they might brush hands, and he made himself get used to that. Then when she changed the accidental to the deliberate, he found that he could get used to that also, overcoming a slight dismay.

He grew calmer, and was even prepared for kissing.

ILEANE WENT BY HERSELF to Jackson's house to collect his bag. His stepmother showed her bright false teeth and tried to look as if she was ready for some fun.

She asked what they were up to.

"You better watch that stuff," she said.

She had a reputation for being a loudmouth. A dirty mouth, actually.

"Ask him if he remembers I used to wash his bottom," she said.

Ileane, reporting this, said that she herself had been especially courteous, even snooty, because she could not stand the woman.

But Jackson went red, cornered and desperate, the way he used to when asked a question in school.

"I shouldn't even have mentioned her," Ileane said. "You get in the habit of caricaturing people, living in a parsonage."

He said it was okay.

That time turned out to be Jackson's last leave. They wrote to

each other. Ileane wrote about finishing her typing and short-
hand and getting a job in the office of the Town Clerk. She was
determinedly satirical about everything, more than she had been
in school. Maybe she thought that someone at war needed joking.
And she insisted on being in the know. When hurry-up marriages
had to be arranged through the clerk's office, she would refer to the
Virgin Bride.

And when she mentioned some minister visiting the parsonage
and sleeping in the spare room, she said she wondered if the mattress would induce Peculiar Dreams.

He wrote about the crowds on the *Île de France* and the ducking
around to avoid U-boats. When he got to England he bought a
bicycle and he told her about places he had biked around to see, if
they were not out of bounds.

These letters though more prosaic than hers were always signed
"With Love." When D-day did come there was what she called an
agonizing silence but she understood the reason for it, and when he
wrote again all was well, though details were not permitted.

In this letter he spoke as she had been doing, about marriage.

And at last VE-day and the voyage home. There were showers of
summer stars, he said, all overhead.

Ileane had learned to sew. She was making a new summer dress
in honor of his homecoming, a dress of lime-green rayon silk with
a full skirt and cap sleeves, worn with a narrow belt of gold imitation leather. She meant to wind a ribbon of the same green material around the crown of her summer hat.

"All this is being described to you so you will notice me and
know it's me and not go running off with some other beautiful
woman who happens to be at the train station."

He mailed his letter to her from Halifax, telling her that he
would be on the evening train on Saturday. He said that he remembered her very well and there was no danger of getting her mixed
up with another woman even if the train station happened to be
swarming with them that evening.

ON THEIR LAST EVENING before he left, they had sat up late in
the parsonage kitchen where there was the picture of King George
VI you saw everywhere that year. And the words beneath it.

And I said to the man who stood at the gate of the year,
"Give me a light that I may tread safely into the unknown."
And he replied, "Go out into the darkness and put your
hand into the hand of God. That shall be to you better than
light and safer than a known way."

Then they went upstairs very quietly and he went to bed in the
spare room. Her coming to him must have been by mutual agreement but perhaps he had not quite understood what for.

It was a disaster. But by the way she behaved, she might not even
have known that. The more disaster, the more frantically she carried on. There was no way he could stop her trying, or explain. Was
it possible a girl could know so little? They parted finally as if all
had gone well. And the next morning said good-bye in the presence of her father and brothers. In a short while the letters began.

He got drunk and tried once more, in Southampton. But the
woman said, "That's enough, sonny boy, you're down and out."

A thing he didn't like was women or girls dressing up. Gloves,
hats, swishy skirts, all some demand and bother about it. But how
could she know that? Lime green. He wasn't sure he knew the color.
It sounded like acid.

Then it came to him quite easily, that a person could just not
be there.

Would she tell herself or tell anybody else, that she must have
mistaken the date? He could make himself believe that she would
find some lie, surely. She was resourceful, after all.

NOW THAT SHE IS GONE out onto the street, Jackson does feel
a wish to see her. He could never ask the owner what she looked
like, whether her hair was dark or gray, and she herself still skinny
or gone stout. Her voice even in distress had been marvellously
unchanged. Drawing all importance to itself, to its musical levels,
and at the same time setting up its so-sorries.

She had come a long way, but she was a persistent woman. You
could say so.

And the daughter would come back. Too spoiled to stay away.
Any daughter of Ileane's would be spoiled, arranging the world
and the truth to suit herself, as if nothing could foil her for long.

If she had seen him, would she have known him? He thought so. No matter what the changes. And she'd have forgiven him, yes, right on the spot. To keep up her notion of herself, always.

The next day whatever ease he had felt about Ileane passing from his life was gone. She knew this place, she might come back. She might settle herself in for a while, walking up and down these streets, trying to find where the trail was warm. Humbly but not really humbly making inquiries of people, in that pleading but spoiled voice. It was possible he would run into her right outside this door. Surprised only for a moment, as if she had always expected him. Holding out the possibilities of life, the way she thought she could.

Things could be locked up, it only took some determination. When he was as young as six or seven he had locked up his stepmother's fooling, what she called her fooling or her teasing. He had run out into the street after dark and she got him in but she saw there'd be some real running away if she didn't stop so she stopped. And said that he was no fun because she could never say that anybody hated her.

HE SPENT THREE MORE NIGHTS in the building called Bonnie Dundee. He wrote an account for the owner of every apartment and when upkeep was due and what it would consist of. He said that he had been called away, without indicating why or where to. He emptied his bank account and packed the few things belonging to him. In the evening, late in the evening, he got on the train.

He slept off and on during the night and in one of those snatches he saw the little Mennonite boys go by in their cart. He heard their small voices singing.

In the morning he got off in Kapuskasing. He could smell the mills, and was encouraged by the cooler air. Work there, sure to be work in a lumbering town.

The Eye

~

WHEN I WAS FIVE YEARS OLD my parents all of a sudden produced a baby boy, which my mother said was what I had always wanted. Where she got this idea I did not know. She did quite a bit of elaborating on it, all fictitious but hard to counter.

Then a year later a baby girl appeared, and there was another fuss but more subdued than with the first one.

Up until the time of the first baby I had not been aware of ever feeling different from the way my mother said I felt. And up until that time the whole house was full of my mother, of her footsteps her voice her powdery yet ominous smell that inhabited all the rooms even when she wasn't in them.

Why do I say ominous? I didn't feel frightened. It wasn't that my mother actually told me what I was to feel about things. She was an authority on that without having to question a thing. Not just in the case of a baby brother but in the matter of Red River cereal which was good for me and so I must be fond of it. And in my interpretation of the picture that hung at the foot of my bed, showing Jesus suffering the little children to come unto him. Suffering meant something different in those days, but that was not what we concentrated on. My mother pointed out the little girl half hiding round a corner because she wanted to come to Jesus but was too shy. That was me, my mother said, and I supposed it was though I wouldn't have figured it out without her telling me and I rather wished it wasn't so.

The thing I really felt miserable about was Alice in Wonderland huge and trapped in the rabbit hole, but I laughed because my mother seemed delighted.

It was with my brother's coming, though, and the endless carryings-on about how he was some sort of present for me, that I began to accept how largely my mother's notions about me might differ from my own.

I suppose all this was making me ready for Sadie when she came to work for us. My mother had shrunk to whatever territory she had with the babies. With her not around so much, I could think about what was true and what wasn't. I knew enough not to speak about this to anybody.

The most unusual thing about Sadie—though it was not a thing stressed in our house—was that she was a celebrity. Our town had a radio station where she played her guitar and sang the opening welcome song which was her own composition.

"Hello, hello, hello, everybody—"

And half an hour later it was, "Good-bye, good-bye, good-bye, everybody." In between she sang songs that were requested, as well as some she picked out herself. The more sophisticated people in town tended to joke about her songs and about the whole station which was said to be the smallest one in Canada. Those people listened to a Toronto station that broadcast popular songs of the day—three little fishes and a momma fishy too—and Jim Hunter hollering out the desperate war news. But people on the farms liked the local station and the kind of songs Sadie sang. Her voice was strong and sad and she sang about loneliness and grief.

> Leanin' on the old top rail,
> in a big corral.
> Lookin' down the twilight trail
> For my long lost pal—

Most of the farms in our part of the country had been cleared and settled around a hundred and fifty years ago, and you could look out from almost any farmhouse and see another farmhouse only a few fields away. Yet the songs the farmers wanted were all about lone cowhands, the lure and disappointment of far-off places, the bitter crimes that led to criminals dying with their mothers' names on their lips, or God's.

This was what Sadie sang with such sorrow in a full-throated alto, but in her job with us she was full of energy and confidence, happy to talk and mostly to talk about herself. There was usually nobody to talk to but me. Her jobs and my mother's kept them divided most of the time and somehow I don't think they would have enjoyed talking together anyway. My mother was a serious person as I have indicated, one who used to teach school before she taught me. She maybe would have liked Sadie to be somebody she could help, teaching her not to say "youse." But Sadie did not give much indication that she wanted the help anybody could offer, or to speak in any way that was different from how she had always spoken.

After dinner, which was the noon meal, Sadie and I were alone in the kitchen. My mother took time off for a nap and if she was lucky the babies napped too. When she got up she put on a different sort of dress as if she expected a leisurely afternoon, even though there would certainly be more diapers to change and also some of that unseemly business that I tried never to catch sight of, when the littlest one guzzled at a breast.

My father took a nap too—maybe fifteen minutes on the porch with the *Saturday Evening Post* over his face, before he went back to the barn.

Sadie heated water on the stove and washed the dishes with me helping and the blinds down to keep out the heat. When we were finished she mopped the floor and I dried it, by a method I had invented—skating around and around it on rags. Then we took down the coils of sticky yellow flypaper that had been put up after breakfast and were already heavy with dead or buzzing nearly dead black flies, and hung up the fresh coils which would be full of newly dead ones by suppertime. All this while Sadie was telling me about her life.

I didn't make easy judgments about ages then. People were either children or grown-ups and I thought her a grown-up. Maybe she was sixteen, maybe eighteen or twenty. Whatever her age, she announced more than once that she was not in any hurry to get married.

She went to dances every weekend but she went by herself. By herself and for herself, she said.

She told me about the dance halls. There was one in town, off the main street, where the curling rink was in the winter. You paid a dime for a dance, then went up and danced on a platform with people gawking all around, not that she cared. She always liked to pay her own dime, not to be beholden. But sometimes a fellow got to her first. He asked if she wanted to dance and the first thing she said was, Can you? Can you dance? she asked him bluntly. Then he would look at her funny and say yes, meaning why else would he be here? And it would turn out usually that what he meant by dance was shuffling around on two feet with his sweaty big meats of hands grabbing at her. Sometimes she just broke off and left him stranded, danced by herself—which was what she liked to do anyway. She finished up the dance that had been paid for, and if the money-taker objected and tried to make her pay for two when it was only one, she told him that was enough out of him. They could all laugh at her dancing by herself if they liked.

The other dance hall was just out of town on the highway. You paid at the door there and it wasn't for one dance but the whole night. The place was called the Royal-T. She paid her own way there too. There was generally a better class of dancer, but she did try to get an idea of how they managed before she let them take her out on the floor. They were usually town fellows while the ones at the other place were country. Better on their feet—the town ones—but it was not always the feet you had to look out for. It was where they wanted to get hold of you. Sometimes she had to read them the riot act and tell them what she would do to them if they didn't quit it. She let them know she'd come there to dance and paid her own way to do it. Furthermore she knew where to jab them. That would straighten them out. Sometimes they were good dancers and she got to enjoy herself. Then when they played the last dance she bolted for home.

She wasn't like some, she said. She didn't mean to get caught.

Caught. When she said that, I saw a big wire net coming down, some evil little creatures wrapping it around and around you and choking you so you could never get out. Sadie must have seen something like this on my face because she said not to be scared.

"There's nothing in this world to be scared of, just look out for yourself."

"YOU AND SADIE TALK TOGETHER A LOT," my mother said.

I knew something was coming that I should watch for but I didn't know what.

"You like her, don't you?"

I said yes.

"Well of course you do. I do too."

I hoped that was going to be all and for a moment I thought it was.

Then, "You and I don't get so much time now we have the babies. They don't give us much time, do they?

"But we do love them, don't we?"

Quickly I said yes.

She said, "Truly?"

She wasn't going to stop till I said truly, so I said it.

MY MOTHER WANTED SOMETHING very badly. Was it nice friends? Women who played bridge and had husbands who went to work in suits with vests? Not quite, and no hope of that anyway. Was it me as I used to be, with my sausage curls that I didn't mind standing still for, and my expert Sunday School recitations? No time for her to manage that anymore. And something in me was turning traitorous, though she didn't know why, and I didn't know why either. I hadn't made any town friends at Sunday School. Instead, I worshipped Sadie. I heard my mother say that to my father. "She worships Sadie."

My father said Sadie was a godsend. What did that mean? He sounded cheerful. Maybe it meant he wasn't going to take anybody's side.

"I wish we had proper sidewalks for her," my mother said. "Maybe if we had proper sidewalks she could learn to roller-skate and make friends."

I did wish for roller skates. But now without any idea why, I knew that I was never going to admit it.

Then my mother said something about it being better when school started. Something about me being better or something concerning Sadie that would be better. I didn't want to hear.

Sadie was teaching me some of her songs and I knew I wasn't very good at singing. I hoped that wasn't what had to get better or else stop. I truly did not want it to stop.

My father didn't have much to say. I was my mother's business, except for later on when I got really mouthy and had to be punished. He was waiting for my brother to get older and be his. A boy would not be so complicated.

And sure enough my brother wasn't. He would grow up to be just fine.

NOW SCHOOL HAS STARTED. It started some weeks ago, before the leaves turned red and yellow. Now they were mostly gone. I am not wearing my school coat but my good coat, the one with the dark velvet cuffs and collar. My mother is wearing the coat she wears to church, and a turban covers most of her hair.

My mother is driving to whatever place it is that we are going to. She doesn't drive often, and her driving is always more stately and yet uncertain than my father's. She peeps her horn at any curve.

"Now," she says, but it takes a little while for her to get the car into place.

"Here we are then." Her voice seems meant to be encouraging. She touches my hand to give me a chance to hold hers, but I pretend not to notice and she takes her hand away.

The house has no driveway or even a sidewalk. It's decent but quite plain. My mother has raised her gloved hand to knock but it turns out we don't have to. The door is opened for us. My mother has just started to say something encouraging to me—something like, It will go more quickly than you think—but she doesn't get finished. The tone in which she spoke to me had been somewhat stern but slightly comforting. It changes when the door is opened into something more subdued, softened as if she was bowing her head.

The door has been opened to let some people go out, not just to let us go in. One of the women going out calls back over her shoulder in a voice that does not try to be soft at all.

"It's her that she worked for, and that little girl."

Then a woman who is rather dressed up comes and speaks to my mother and helps her off with her coat. That done, my mother takes my coat off and says to the woman that I was especially fond of Sadie. She hopes it was all right to bring me.

"Oh the dear little thing," the woman says and my mother touches me lightly to get me to say hello.

"Sadie loved children," the woman said. "She did indeed."

I notice that there are two other children there. Boys. I know them from school, one being in the first grade with me, and the other one older. They are peering out from what is likely the kitchen. The younger one is stuffing a whole cookie into his mouth in a comical way and the other, older, one is making a disgusted face. Not at the cookie stuffer, but at me. They hate me of course. Boys either ignored you if they met you somewhere that wasn't school (they ignored you there too) or they made these faces and called you horrid names. If I had to go near one I would stiffen and wonder what to do. Of course it was different if there were adults around. These boys stayed quiet but I was slightly miserable until somebody yanked the two of them into the kitchen. Then I became aware of my mother's especially gentle and sympathetic voice, more ladylike even than the voice of the spokeswoman she was talking to, and I thought maybe the face was meant for her. Sometimes people imitated her voice when she called for me at school.

The woman she was talking to and who seemed to be in charge was leading us to a part of the room where a man and a woman sat on a sofa, looking as if they did not quite understand why they were here. My mother bent over and spoke to them very respectfully and pointed me out to them.

"She did so love Sadie," she said. I knew that I was supposed to say something then but before I could the woman sitting there let out a howl. She did not look at any of us and the sound she made seemed like a sound you might make if some animal was biting or gnawing at you. She slapped away at her arms as if to get rid of whatever it was, but it did not go away. She looked at my mother as if my mother was the person who should do something about this.

The old man told her to hush.

"She's taking it very hard," said the woman who was guiding us. "She doesn't know what she's doing." She bent down lower and said, "Now, now. You'll scare the little girl."

"Scare the little girl," the old man said obediently.

By the time he finished saying that, the woman was not making the noise anymore and was patting her scratched arms as if she didn't know what had happened to them.

My mother said, "Poor woman."

"An only child too," said the conducting woman. To me she said, "Don't you worry."

I was worried but not about the yelling.

I knew Sadie was somewhere and I did not want to see her. My mother had not actually said that I would have to see her but she had not said that I wouldn't have to, either.

Sadie had been killed when walking home from the Royal-T dance hall. A car had hit her just on that little bit of gravel road between the parking space belonging to the dance hall and the beginning of the proper town sidewalk. She would have been hurrying along just the way she always did, and was no doubt thinking cars could see her, or that she had as much right as they did, and perhaps the car behind her swerved or perhaps she was not quite where she thought she was. She was hit from behind. The car that hit her was getting out of the way of the car that was behind it, and that second car was looking to make the first turn onto a town street. There had been some drinking at the dance hall, though you could not buy liquor there. And there was always some honking and yelling and whipping around too fast when the dancing was over. Sadie scurrying along without even a flashlight would behave as if it was everybody's business to get out of her way.

"A girl without a boyfriend going to dances on foot," said the woman who was still being friends with my mother. She spoke quite softly and my mother murmured something regretful.

It was asking for trouble, the friendly woman said still more softly.

I had heard talk at home that I did not understand. My mother wanted something done that might have had to do with Sadie and the car that hit her, but my father said to leave it alone. We've got no business in town, he said. I did not even try to figure this out because I was trying not to think about Sadie at all, let alone about her being dead. When I had realized that we were going into Sadie's house I longed not to go, but didn't see any way to get out of it except by behaving with enormous indignity.

Now after the old woman's outburst it seemed to me we might turn around and go home. I would never have to admit the truth, which was that I was in fact desperately scared of any dead body.

Just as I thought this might be possible, I heard my mother and the woman she seemed now to be conniving with speak of what was worse than anything.

Seeing Sadie.

Yes, my mother was saying. Of course, we must see Sadie.

Dead Sadie.

I had kept my eyes pretty well cast down, seeing mostly just those boys who were hardly taller than I was, and the old people who were sitting down. But now my mother was taking me by the hand in another direction.

There had been a coffin in the room all the time but I had thought it was something else. Because of my lack of experience I didn't know exactly what such a thing looked like. A shelf to put flowers on, this object we were approaching might have been, or a closed piano.

Perhaps the people being around it had somehow disguised its real size and shape and purpose. But now these people were making way respectfully and my mother spoke in a new very quiet voice.

"Come now," she said to me. Her gentleness sounded hateful to me, triumphant.

She bent to look into my face, and this, I was sure, was to prevent me from doing what had just occurred to me—keeping my eyes squeezed shut. Then she took her gaze away from me but kept my hand tightly held in hers. I did manage to lower my lids as soon as she took her eyes off me, but I did not shut them quite lest I stumble or somebody push me right where I didn't want to be. I was able to see just a blur of the stiff flowers and the sheen of polished wood.

Then I heard my mother sniffling and felt her pulling away. There was a click of her purse being opened. She had to get her hand in there, so her hold on me weakened and I was able to get myself free of her. She was weeping. It was attention to her tears and sniffles that had set me loose.

I looked straight into the coffin and saw Sadie.

The accident had spared her neck and face but I didn't see all of that at once. I just got the general impression that there was nothing about her as bad as I had been afraid of. I shut my eyes quickly but found myself unable to keep from looking again. First at the little yellow cushion that was under her neck and that also managed to cover her throat and chin and the one cheek I could easily see. The trick was in seeing a bit of her quickly, then going back to the cushion, and the next time managing a little bit more that you were not afraid of. And then it was Sadie, all of her or at least all I could reasonably see on the side that was available.

Something moved. I saw it, her eyelid on my side moved. It was not opening or halfway opening or anything like that, but lifting just such a tiny bit as would make it possible, if you were her, if you were inside her, to be able to see out through the lashes. Just to distinguish maybe what was light outside and what was dark.

I was not surprised then and not in the least scared. Instantly, this sight fell into everything I knew about Sadie and somehow, as well, into whatever special experience was owing to myself. And I did not dream of calling anybody else's attention to what was there, because it was not meant for them, it was completely for me.

My mother had taken my hand again and said that we were ready to go. There were some more exchanges, but before any time had passed, as it seemed to me, we found ourselves outside.

My mother said, "Good for you." She squeezed my hand and said, "Now then. It's over." She had to stop and speak to somebody else who was on the way to the house, and then we got into the car and began to drive home. I had an idea that she would like me to say something, or maybe even tell her something, but I didn't do it.

There was never any other appearance of that sort and in fact Sadie faded rather quickly from my mind, what with the shock of school, where I learned somehow to manage with an odd mixture of being dead scared and showing off. As a matter of fact some of her importance had faded in that first week in September when she said she had to stay home now to look after her father and mother, so she wouldn't be working for us anymore.

And then my mother had found out she was working in the creamery.

Yet for a long time when I did think of her, I never questioned what I believed had been shown to me. Long, long afterwards, when I was not at all interested in any unnatural display, I still had it in my mind that such a thing had happened. I just believed it easily, the way you might believe and in fact remember that you once had another set of teeth, now vanished but real in spite of that. Until one day, one day when I may even have been in my teens, I knew with a dim sort of hole in my insides that now I didn't believe it anymore.

Dear Life

❧

I LIVED WHEN I WAS YOUNG at the end of a long road, or a road that seemed long to me. Back behind me, as I walked home from primary school, and then from high school, was the real town with its activity and its sidewalks and its streetlights for after dark. Marking the end of town were two bridges over the Maitland River: one narrow iron bridge, where cars sometimes got into trouble over which one should pull off and wait for the other, and a wooden walkway which occasionally had a plank missing, so that you could look right down into the bright, hurrying water. I liked that, but somebody always came and replaced the plank eventually.

Then there was a slight hollow, a couple of rickety houses that got flooded every spring, but that people—different people—always came and lived in anyway. And then another bridge, over the mill race, which was narrow but deep enough to drown you. After that, the road divided, one part of it going south up a hill and over the river again to become a genuine highway, and the other jogging around the old fairgrounds to turn west.

That westward road was mine.

There was also a road heading north, which had a brief but real sidewalk and several houses close together, as if they were in town. One of them had a sign in the window that said "Salada Tea," evidence that groceries had once been for sale there. Then there was a school, which I had attended for two years of my life and wished never to see again. After those years, my mother had made my father buy an old shed in town so that he would be paying town taxes and I could go to the town school. As it turned out, she hadn't needed to do that, because in the year, in the very month, that I started school in town, war was declared with Germany and, as if by magic, the old school, the school where bullies had taken away my lunch and threatened to beat me up and where nobody seemed to learn anything in the midst of the uproar, had quieted down. Soon it had only one room and one teacher, who probably did not even lock the doors at recess. It appeared that the same boys who'd always asked me rhetorically and alarmingly if I wanted to fuck were just as eager to get jobs as their older brothers were to go into the Army.

I don't know if the school toilets had improved by then or not, but they had been the worst thing. It was not as if we didn't resort to an outhouse at home, but it was clean and even had a linoleum floor. At that school, for reasons of contempt or whatever, nobody seemed to bother to aim for the hole. In many ways it wasn't easy for me in town, either, because everybody else had been together since grade one, and there were many things that I hadn't learned yet, but it was a comfort to see my new school's unsoiled seats and to hear the noble urban sound of its flush toilets.

During my time at the first school, I did make one friend. A girl whom I'll call Diane arrived partway through my second year. She was about my age, and she lived in one of those houses with a sidewalk. She asked me one day if I could do the Highland fling, and when I said no she offered to teach me. With this in mind, we went to her place after school. Her mother had died and she had come to live with her grandparents. To dance the Highland fling, she told me, you needed clicking shoes, which she had and, of course, I didn't, but our feet were nearly the same size, so we could trade while she tried to teach me. Eventually we got thirsty and her grandmother gave us a drink of water, but it was horrid water from a dug well, just like at school. I explained about the superior water we got from a drilled well at home, and the grandmother said, without taking any sort of offense, that she wished they had that, too.

But then, too soon, my mother was outside, having gone to the school and discovered my whereabouts. She honked the car horn to summon me and didn't even respond to the grandmother's friendly wave. My mother did not drive often, and when she did there was a nervous solemnity to the occasion. On the way home, I was told that I was never to enter that house again. (This proved not to be a difficulty, because Diane stopped appearing at school a few days later—she had been sent away somewhere.) I told my mother that Diane's mother was dead and she said yes, she knew. I told her about the Highland fling, and she said that I might learn it properly sometime, but not in that house.

I did not find out then—and I don't know when I did find out—that Diane's mother had been a prostitute and had died of some ailment it seemed that prostitutes caught. She'd wanted to be buried at home, and the minister of our own church had done the service. There had been controversy over the text he had used. Some people thought he should have left it out, but my mother believed that he had done the right thing.

The wages of sin is death.

My mother told me this a long time later, or what seemed a long time later, when I was at the stage of hating a good many things she said, and particularly when she used that voice of shuddering, even thrilled, conviction.

I kept running into the grandmother now and again. She always had a little smile for me. She said it was wonderful how I kept going to school, and she reported on Diane, who also continued at school for a notable time, wherever she was—though not for as long as I did. According to her grandmother, she then got a job in a restaurant in Toronto, where she wore an outfit with sequins on it. I was old enough at that point, and mean enough, to assume that it was probably a place where you also took the sequin outfit off.

Diane's grandmother wasn't the only one who thought I was taking a long time at school. Along my road, there were a number of houses set farther apart than they would have been in town but that still didn't have much in the way of property around them. One of them, on a small hill, belonged to Waitey Streets, a one-armed veteran of the First World War. He kept some sheep and had a wife I saw only once in all those years, when she was filling the drinking pail at the pump. Waitey liked to joke about the long time I had been at school and how it was a pity that I could never pass my exams and be done with it. And I joked back, pretending that was true. I was not sure what he really believed. This was the way you knew people on the road, and they knew you. You'd say hello, and they'd say hello and something about the weather, and if they had a car and you were walking, they would give you a ride. It wasn't like the real country, where people usually knew the insides of one another's houses and everybody had more or less the same way of making a living.

I wasn't taking longer to finish high school than anybody else who went through the full five grades would do. But few students did that. Nobody expected in those days that the same number of people who entered high school in grade nine would come out, all stuffed with knowledge and proper grammar, at the end of grade thirteen. People got part-time jobs and gradually those turned into full-time jobs. Girls got married and had babies, in that order or the other. In grade thirteen, with only about a quarter of the original class left, there was a sense of scholarship, of serious achievement, or perhaps just a special kind of serene impracticality that hung on, no matter what happened to you later.

I felt as if I were a lifetime away from most of the people I had known in grade nine, let alone in that first school.

IN A CORNER of our dining room was something that always surprised me a little when I got out the Electrolux to clean the floor. I knew what it was—a very new looking golf bag, with the golf clubs and balls inside. I just wondered what it was doing in our house. I knew hardly anything about the game, but I had my ideas about the type of people who played it. They were not people who wore overalls, as my father did, though he put on better work pants when he went downtown. I could, to some extent, imagine my mother getting into the sporty kind of clothes you would have to wear, tying a scarf around her fine, blowing hair. But not actually trying to hit a ball into a hole. The frivolity of such an act was surely beyond her.

She must have thought differently at one time. She must have thought that she and my father were going to transform themselves into a different sort of people, people who enjoyed a degree of leisure. Golf. Dinner parties. Perhaps she had convinced herself that certain boundaries were not there. She had managed to get herself off a farm on the bare Canadian Shield—a farm much more hopeless than the one my father came from—and she had become a schoolteacher, who spoke in such a way that her own relatives were not easy around her. She might have got the idea that after such striving she would be welcomed anywhere.

My father had other ideas. It wasn't that he thought that town people or any people were actually better than he was. But he believed perhaps that was what they were thinking. And he preferred never to give them a chance to show it.

It seemed that, in the matter of golf, it was my father who had won.

It wasn't as if he'd been content to live the way his parents had expected him to live, taking over their decent farm. When he and my mother left their communities behind and bought this plot of land at the end of a road near a town they didn't know, their idea was almost certainly to become prosperous by raising silver foxes and, later on, mink. As a boy, my father had found himself happier following a trapline than helping on the farm or going to high school—and richer, too, than he had ever been before—and this idea had come upon him and he had taken it up, as he thought, for a lifetime. He put what money he had collected into it, and my mother contributed her teacher's savings. He built all the pens and shelters in which the animals would live, and put up the wire walls that would contain their captive lives. The plot of land, twelve acres large, was the right size, with a hayfield and enough pasture for our own cow and whatever old horses were waiting to be fed to the foxes. The pasture ran right down to the river and had twelve elm trees shading it.

There was quite a lot of killing going on, now that I think of it. The old horses had to be turned into meat and the fur-bearing animals culled every fall to leave just the breeders. But I was used to this and could easily ignore it all, constructing for myself a scene that was purified to resemble something out of the books I liked, such as *Anne of Green Gables* or *Pat of Silver Bush*. I had the help of the elm trees, which hung over the pasture, and the shining river, and the surprise of a spring that came out of the bank above the pasture, providing water for the doomed horses and the cow and also for me, out of a tin mug I brought there. Fresh manure was always around, but I ignored it, as Anne must have done at Green Gables.

In those days, I had to help my father sometimes, because my brother wasn't old enough yet. I pumped fresh water, and I walked up and down the rows of pens, cleaning out the animals' drinking tins and refilling them. I enjoyed this. The importance of the work, the frequent solitude were just what I liked. Later on, I had to stay in the house to help my mother, and I was full of resentment and quarrelsome remarks. "Talking back," it was called. I hurt her feelings, she said, and the outcome was that she would go to the barn to tell on me, to my father. Then he'd have to interrupt his work to give me a beating with his belt. (This was not an uncommon punishment at the time.) Afterwards, I'd lie weeping in bed and make plans to run away. But that phase also passed, and in my teens I became manageable, even jolly, noted for my funny recountings of things that I had heard about in town or that had happened at school.

Our house was of a decent size. We didn't know exactly when it had been built but it had to be less than a century old, because 1858 was the year the first settler had stopped at a place called Bodmin—which had now disappeared—built himself a raft, and come down the river to clear trees from the land that later became a whole village. That early village soon had a sawmill and a hotel and three churches and a school, the same school that was my first, and so dreaded by me. Then a bridge was built across the river, and it began to dawn on people how much more convenient it would be to live over on the other side, on higher ground, and the original settlement dwindled away to the disreputable, and then just peculiar, half-village that I have spoken of.

Our house would not have been one of the very first houses in that early settlement, because it was covered with brick, and they were all just wood, but it had probably gone up not long afterwards. It turned its back on the village; it faced west across slightly downsloping fields to the hidden curve where the river made what was called the Big Bend. Beyond the river was a patch of dark evergreen trees, probably cedar but too far away to tell. And even farther away, on another hillside, was another house, quite small at that distance, facing ours, that we would never visit or know and that was to me like a dwarf's house in a story. But we knew the name of the man who lived there, or had lived there at one time, for he might have died by now. Roly Grain, his name was, and he does not have any further part in what I'm writing now, in spite of his troll's name, because this is not a story, only life.

MY MOTHER had two miscarriages before she had me, so when I was born, in 1931, there must have been some satisfaction. But the times were getting less and less promising. The truth was that my father had got into the fur business just a little too late. The success he'd hoped for would have been more likely back in the mid-twenties, when furs were newly popular and people had money. But he had not got started then. Still, we survived, right up to and through the war, and even at the end of the war there must have been an encouraging flurry, because that was the summer my father fixed up the house, adding a layer of brown paint over the traditional redbrick. There was some problem with the way the bricks and boards were fitted; they did not keep out the cold as well as they were supposed to. It was thought that the coat of paint would help, though I can't recall that it ever did. Also, we got a bathroom, and the unused dumbwaiter became kitchen cupboards, and the big dining room with the open stairway changed into a regular room with enclosed stairs. That change comforted me in some unexamined way, because my father's beatings of me had taken place in the old room, with me wanting to die for the misery and shame of it all. Now the difference in the setting made it hard even to imagine such a thing happening. I was in high school and doing better every year, as activities like hemstitching and writing with a straight pen were left behind, and social studies became history and you could learn Latin.

After the optimism of that season of redecoration, however, our business dried up again, and this time it never came back. My father pelted all the foxes, then the mink, and got what shockingly little money he could for them, then he worked by day pulling down the sheds where that enterprise had been born and had died, before heading off to take the five o'clock watch in the foundry. He would not come home until around midnight.

As soon as I got home from school, I went to work making my father's lunch. I fried two slices of cottage roll and put lots of ketchup on them. I filled his thermos with strong black tea. I put in a bran muffin with jam on it, or perhaps a heavy piece of homemade pie. Sometimes on Saturdays I made a pie, and sometimes my mother did, though her baking was getting to be unreliable.

Something had come upon us that was even more unexpected and would become more devastating than the loss of income, though we didn't know it yet. It was the early onset of Parkinson's disease, which showed up when my mother was in her forties.

At first, it was not too bad. Her eyes only rarely turned up into her head in a wandering way, and the soft down from an oversupply of saliva was just visible around her lips. She could get dressed in the mornings with some help, and she was able to do occasional chores around the house. She held on to some strength in herself for a surprisingly long time.

You would think that this was just too much. The business gone, my mother's health going. It wouldn't do in fiction. But the strange thing is that I don't remember that time as unhappy. There wasn't a particularly despairing mood around the house. Maybe it was not understood then that my mother wouldn't get any better, only worse. As for my father, he had his strength and would have it for a long time yet. He liked the men he worked with at the foundry, who were, for the most part, men like himself, who'd had some sort of downturn or extra burden added to their lives. He liked the challenging work he did in addition to being the early-night watchman. That work involved pouring molten metal into molds. The foundry made old-fashioned stoves that were sold all over the world. It was a dangerous job, but it was up to you to look out, as my father said. And there was decent pay—a novelty for him.

I believe he was glad to get away, even to do this hard and risky work. To get out of the house and into the company of other men who had their own problems but made the best of things.

Once he was gone, I'd start on supper. I could make things that I thought were exotic, like spaghetti or omelettes, as long as they were cheap. And after the dishes were done—my sister had to dry them, and my brother had to be nagged into throwing the dishwater out over the dark field (I could do that myself but liked giving orders)—I sat down with my feet in the warming oven, which had lost its door, and read the big novels I borrowed from the town library: *Independent People*, which was about life in Iceland, harder than ours by far, but with a hopeless grandeur to it, or *Remembrance of Things Past*, which was about nothing I could understand at all but was not on that account to be given up on, or *The Magic Mountain,* about tuberculosis and containing a great argument between what on one side seemed to be a genial and progressive notion of life and, on the other, a dark and somehow thrilling despair. I never did homework in this precious time, but when exams came I buckled down and stayed up almost all night, cramming my head with whatever I was supposed to know. I had a prodigious short-term memory, and that worked quite well for what was required.

Against several odds, I believed myself a lucky person.

Sometimes my mother and I talked, mostly about her younger days. I seldom objected now to her way of looking at things.

Several times, she told me a story that had to do with the house that now belonged to the war veteran named Waitey Streets—the man who marvelled at the length of time it was taking me to get through school. The story was not about him but about someone who had lived in that house long before he did, a crazy old woman named Mrs. Netterfield. Mrs. Netterfield had had her groceries delivered, as we all did, after ordering them over the phone. One day, my mother said, the grocer forgot to put in her butter, or she forgot to order it, and when the delivery boy was opening the back of the truck she noticed the mistake and became upset. And she was prepared, in a way. She had her hatchet with her and she raised it as if to punish the grocery boy—though, of course, it wasn't his fault—and he ran up to the driver's seat and pulled off without even closing the back doors.

Some things about this story were puzzling, though I didn't think about them at the time and neither did my mother. How could the old woman have been sure already that the butter was missing in the load of groceries? And why would she have come equipped with a hatchet before she knew there was any fault to find? Did she carry it with her at all times, in case of provocations in general?

Mrs. Netterfield was said to have been quite a lady when she was younger.

There was another story about Mrs. Netterfield that had more interest because it featured me and took place around our house.

It was a beautiful day in the fall. I had been set out to sleep in my baby carriage on the little patch of new lawn. My father was away for the afternoon—perhaps helping out his father on the old farm, as he sometimes did—and my mother was doing some clothes-washing at the sink. For a first baby there was a celebratory load of knitwear, ribbons, things to be washed carefully by hand, in soft water. There was no window in front of my mother as she washed and wrung things out at the sink. To get a look outside, you had to cross the room to the north window. That gave you a view of the driveway, which led from the mailbox to the house.

Why did my mother decide to leave her washing and wringing out in order to look at the driveway? She was not expecting any company. My father wasn't late. Possibly she had asked him to get something at the grocery store, something she needed for whatever she was making for supper, and she was wondering if he would be home in time for her to make it. She was a fairly fancy cook in those days—more so, in fact, than her mother-in-law and the other women in my father's family thought necessary. When you looked at the cost, as they would say.

Or it may have had nothing to do with supper but have involved a clothes pattern he was picking up, or a piece of material for a new dress she wanted to make for herself.

She never said afterwards why she had done it.

Misgivings about my mother's cooking were not the only problem with my father's family. There must have been some discussion about her clothes, too. I think of how she used to wear an afternoon dress, even if she was only washing things at the sink. She took a half-hour nap after the noon meal and always put on a different dress when she got up. When I looked at photographs later on, I thought that the fashions of the time had not been becoming to her, or to anybody. The dresses were shapeless, and bobbed hair did not suit my mother's full, soft face. But this would not have been the objection of my father's female relatives who lived close enough to keep tabs on her. Her fault was that she did not look like what she was. She did not look as if she had been brought up on a farm, or as if she intended to remain on one.

SHE DID NOT SEE my father's car coming down the lane. Instead, she saw the old woman, Mrs. Netterfield. Mrs. Netterfield must have walked over from her own house. The same house where, much later on, I would see the one-armed man who teased me, and just the one time his bob-haired wife, at the pump. The house from which, long before I knew anything about her, the crazy woman had pursued the delivery boy with a hatchet, on account of butter.

My mother must have seen Mrs. Netterfield at various times before she saw her walking down our lane. Maybe they had never spoken. It's possible, though, that they had. My mother might have made a point of it, even if my father had told her that it was not necessary. It might even lead to trouble was what he probably would have said. My mother had sympathy for people who were like Mrs. Netterfield, as long as they were decent.

But now she was not thinking of friendliness or decency. Now she was running out the kitchen door to grab me out of my baby carriage. She left the carriage and the covers where they were and ran back into the house, attempting to lock the kitchen door behind her. The front door she did not need to worry about—it was always locked.

But there was a problem with the kitchen door. As far as I know, it never had a proper lock. There was just a custom, at night, of pushing one of the kitchen chairs against that door, and tilting it with the chair back under the doorknob in such a way that anybody pushing it to get in would have made a dreadful clatter. A fairly haphazard way of maintaining safety, it seems to me, and not in keeping, either, with the fact that my father had a revolver in the house, in a desk drawer. Also, as was natural in the house of a man who regularly had to shoot horses, there was a rifle and a couple of shotguns. Unloaded, of course.

Did my mother think of any weapon, once she had got the doorknob wedged in place? Had she ever picked up a gun, or loaded one, in her life?

Did it cross her mind that the old woman might just be paying a neighborly visit? I don't think so. There must have been a difference in the walk, a determination in the approach of a woman who was not a visitor coming down the lane, not making a friendly approach down our road.

It is possible that my mother prayed, but never mentioned it.

She knew that there was an investigation of the blankets in the carriage, because, just before she pulled down the kitchen-door blind, she saw one of those blankets being flung out to land on the ground. After that, she did not try to get the blind down on any other window, but stayed with me in her arms in a corner where she could not be seen.

No decent knock on the door. But no pushing at the chair, either. No banging or rattling. My mother in the hiding place by the dumbwaiter, hoping against hope that the quiet meant the woman had changed her mind and gone home.

Not so. She was walking around the house, taking her time, and stopping at every downstairs window. The storm windows, of course, were not on now, in summer. She could press her face against every pane of glass. The blinds were all up as high as they could go, because of the fine day. The woman was not very tall, but she did not have to stretch to see inside.

How did my mother know this? It was not as if she was running around with me in her arms, hiding behind one piece of furniture after another, peering out, distraught with terror, to meet with the staring eyes and maybe a wild grin.

She stayed by the dumbwaiter. What else could she do?

There was the cellar, of course. The windows were too small for anybody to get through them. But there was no inside hook on the cellar door. And it would have been more horrible, somehow, to be trapped down there in the dark, if the woman did finally push her way into the house and came down the cellar steps.

There were also the rooms upstairs, but to get there my mother would have had to cross the big main room—that room where the beatings would take place in the future, but which lost its malevolence after the stairs were closed in.

I don't know when my mother first told me this story, but it seems to me that that was where the earlier versions stopped—with Mrs. Netterfield pressing her face and hands against the glass while my mother hid. But in later versions there was an end to just looking. Impatience or anger took hold and then the rattling and the banging came. No mention of yelling. The old woman may not have had the breath to do it. Or perhaps she forgot what it was she'd come for, once her strength ran out.

Anyway, she gave up; that was all she did. After she had made her tour of all the windows and doors, she went away. My mother finally got the nerve to look around in the silence and concluded that Mrs. Netterfield had gone somewhere else.

She did not, however, take the chair away from the doorknob until my father came home.

I don't mean to imply that my mother spoke of this often. It was not part of the repertoire that I got to know and, for the most part, found interesting. Her struggle to get to high school. The school where she taught, in Alberta, and where the children arrived on horseback. The friends she had at normal school, the innocent tricks that were played.

I could always make out what she was saying, though often, after her voice got thick, other people couldn't. I was her interpreter, and sometimes I was full of misery when I had to repeat elaborate phrases or what she thought were jokes, and I could see that the nice people who stopped to talk were dying to get away.

The visitation of old Mrs. Netterfield, as she called it, was not something I was ever required to talk about. But I must have known about it for a long time. I remember asking her at some point if she knew what had become of the woman afterwards.

"They took her away," she said. "Oh, I think so. She wasn't left to die alone."

AFTER I WAS MARRIED and had moved to Vancouver, I still got the weekly paper that was published in the town where I grew up. I think somebody, maybe my father and his second wife, made sure that I had a subscription. Often I barely looked at it, but one time, when I did, I saw the name Netterfield. It was not the name of someone who was living in the town at present but had apparently been the maiden name of a woman in Portland, Oregon, who had written a letter to the paper. This woman, like me, still had a subscription to her hometown paper, and she had written a poem about her childhood there.

> I know a grassy hillside
> Above a river clear
> A place of peace and pleasure
> A memory very dear—

There were several verses, and as I read I began to understand that she was talking about the same river flats that I had thought belonged to me.

"The lines I am enclosing were written from memories of that old hillside," she said. "If they are worthy of a little space in your time-honored paper, I thank you."

> *The sun upon the river*
> *With ceaseless sparkles play*
> *And over on the other bank*
> *Are blossoms wild and gay—*

That was our bank. My bank. Another verse was about a stand of maples, but there I believe she was remembering it wrong—they were elms, which had all died of Dutch elm disease by now.

The rest of the letter made things clearer. The woman said that her father—his name had been Netterfield—had bought a piece of land from the government in 1883, in what was later called the Lower Town. The land ran down to the Maitland River.

> *Across the Iris-bordered stream*
> *The shade of maples spread*
> *And, on the river's watery field,*
> *White geese, in flocks are fed*

She had left out, just as I would have done, the way the spring got muddied up and soiled all around by horses' hooves. And of course left out the manure.

In fact, I had once made up some poems myself, of a very similar nature, though they were lost now, and maybe had never been written down. Verses that commended Nature, then were a bit hard to wind up. I would have composed them right around the time that I was being so intolerant of my mother, and my father was whaling the unkindness out of me. Or beating the tar out of me, as people would cheerfully say back then.

This woman said that she was born in 1876. She had spent her youth, until she was married, in her father's house. It was where the town ended and the open land began, and it had a sunset view.

Our house.

IS IT POSSIBLE that my mother never knew this, never knew that our house was where the Netterfield family had lived and that the old woman was looking in the windows of what had been her own home?

It is possible. In my old age, I have become interested enough to bother with records and the tedious business of looking things up, and I have found that several different families owned that house between the time that the Netterfields sold it and the time that my parents moved in. You might wonder why it had been disposed of when that woman still had years to live. Had she been left a widow, short of money? Who knows? And who was it who came and took her away, as my mother said? Perhaps it was her daughter, the same woman who wrote poems and lived in Oregon. Perhaps that daughter, grown and distant, was the one she was looking for in the baby carriage. Just after my mother had grabbed me up, as she said, for dear life.

The daughter lived not so far away from me for a while in my adult life. I could have written to her, maybe visited. If I had not been so busy with my own young family and my own invariably unsatisfactory writing. But the person I would really have liked to talk to then was my mother, who was no longer available.

I DID NOT GO HOME for my mother's last illness or for her funeral. I had two small children and nobody in Vancouver to leave them with. We could barely have afforded the trip, and my husband had a contempt for formal behavior, but why blame it on him? I felt the same. We say of some things that they can't be forgiven, or that we will never forgive ourselves. But we do—we do it all the time.

Bibliographic Note

~

The stories in this volume appear in roughly chronological sequence of their book publication. We also used the date of the first book publication in the dates of the subtitle, so that the two volumes of selected stories cover Alice Munro's entire years of publishing books. The stories are listed here in the same order as they appear in the book, with the place and year of first publication following.

"The Love of a Good Woman," *The New Yorker*, December 1996

"Jakarta," *Saturday Night* (Toronto, Canada), February 1998

"The Children Stay," *The New Yorker*, December 1997

"My Mother's Dream," *The Love of a Good Woman*, November 1998

"Hateship, Friendship, Courtship, Loveship, Marriage," *Hateship, Friendship, Courtship, Loveship, Marriage*, November 2001

"Family Furnishings," *The New Yorker*, July 2001

"Nettles," *The New Yorker*, February 2000

"The Bear Came Over the Mountain," *The New Yorker*, December 1999 and January 2000

"Runaway," *The New Yorker*, August 2003

"Soon," *The New Yorker*, June 2004

"Passion," *The New Yorker*, March 2004

"The View from Castle Rock," *The New Yorker*, August 2005

"Working for a Living," *Grand Street* 1, no. 1 (1981)

"Hired Girl," *The New Yorker*, April 1994

"Home," *New Canadian Short Stories: 74*, eds. David Helwig and Joan Harcourt, 1974

"Dimensions," *The New Yorker*, June 2006

"Wood," *The New Yorker*, November 1980. The revised version was also published in the *New Haven Review* in 2009.

"Child's Play," *Harper's Magazine*, February 2007
"Too Much Happiness," *Harper's Magazine*, August 2009
"To Reach Japan," *Narrative*, Winter 2012
"Amundsen," *The New Yorker*, August 2012
"Train," *Harper's Magazine*, April 2012
"The Eye," *Dear Life*, November 2012
"Dear Life," *The New Yorker*, September 2011